THIS WAS OUR PACT

RYAN ANDREWS

First Second
New York

For Ai

First Second

Copyright © 2019 by Ryan Andrews

Published by First Second
First Second is an imprint of Roaring Brook Press,
a division of Holtzbrinck Publishing Holdings Limited Partnership
175 Fifth Avenue, New York, NY 10010

Don't miss your next favorite book from First Second!
For the latest updates go to firstsecondnewsletter.com and sign up for our enewsletter.

Library of Congress Control Number: 2018944916

Paperback ISBN: 978-1-62672-053-4
Hardcover ISBN: 978-1-250-19695-8

Our books may be purchased in bulk for promotional, educational, or business use.
Please contact your local bookseller or the Macmillan Corporate and Premium Sales Department
at (800) 221-7945 ext. 5442 or by e-mail at MacmillanSpecialMarkets@macmillan.com.

First edition, 2019
Edited by Calista Brill, Carol Burrell, and Steve Behling
Book design by Andrew Arnold, Molly Johanson, and Chris Dickey

Drawn with Mitsubishi Uni series pencils on Arches hot pressed watercolor paper.
Colored digitally in Photoshop.

Printed in China by 1010 Printing International Limited, North Point, Hong Kong

Paperback: 10 9 8 7 6 5 4 3 2 1
Hardcover: 10 9 8 7 6 5 4 3 2 1

BY ART
WE LIVE

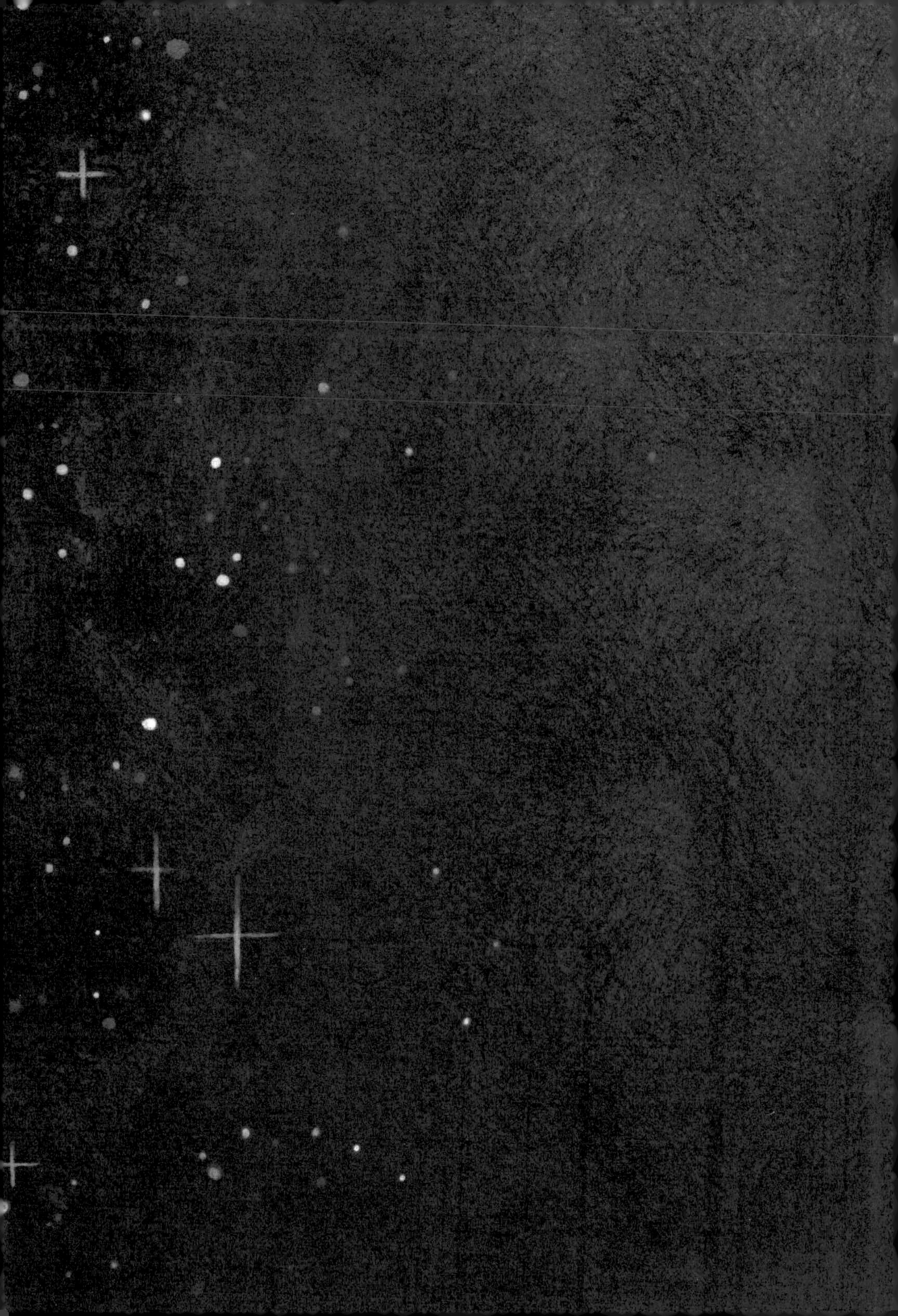

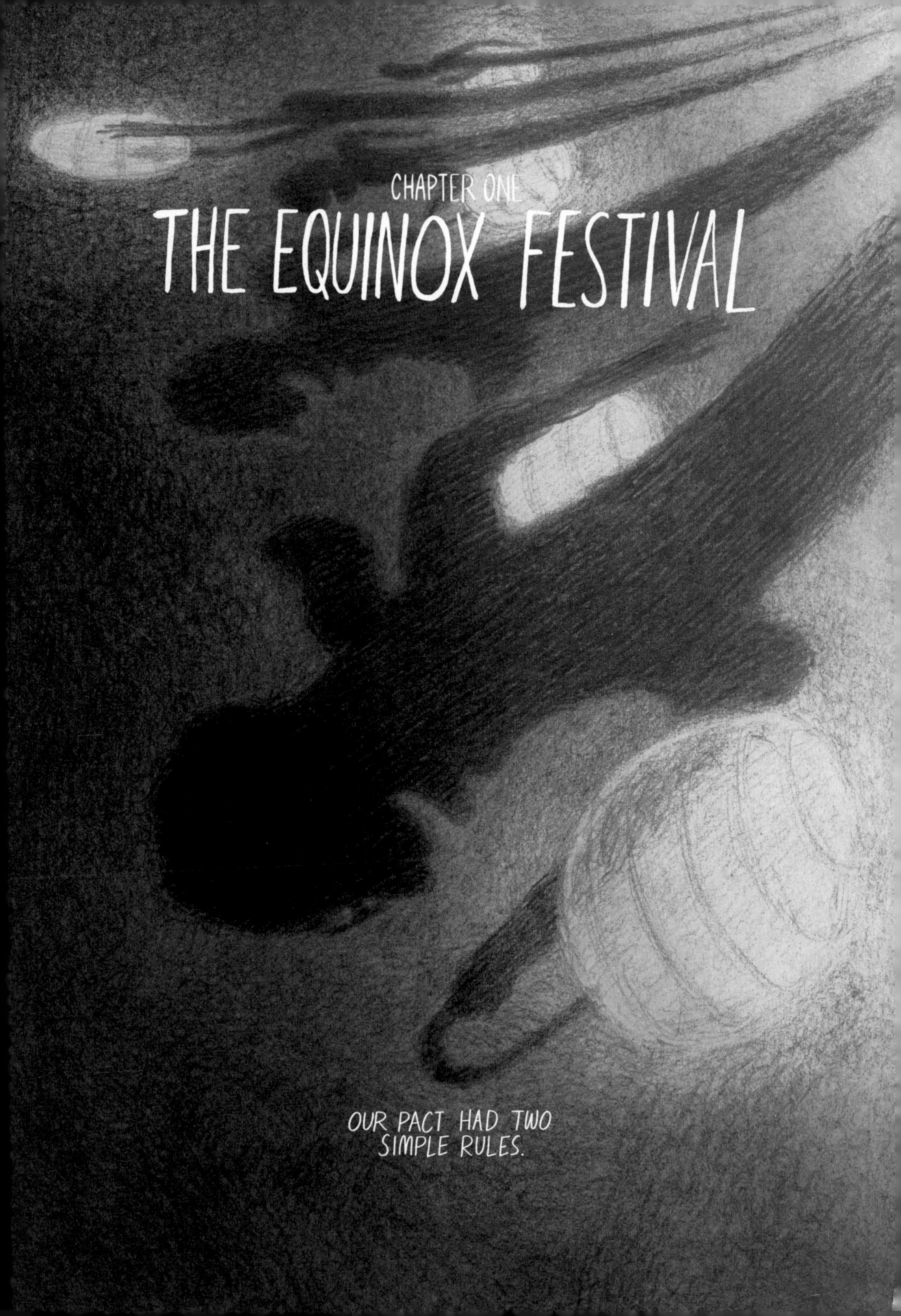
CHAPTER ONE
THE EQUINOX FESTIVAL
OUR PACT HAD TWO SIMPLE RULES.

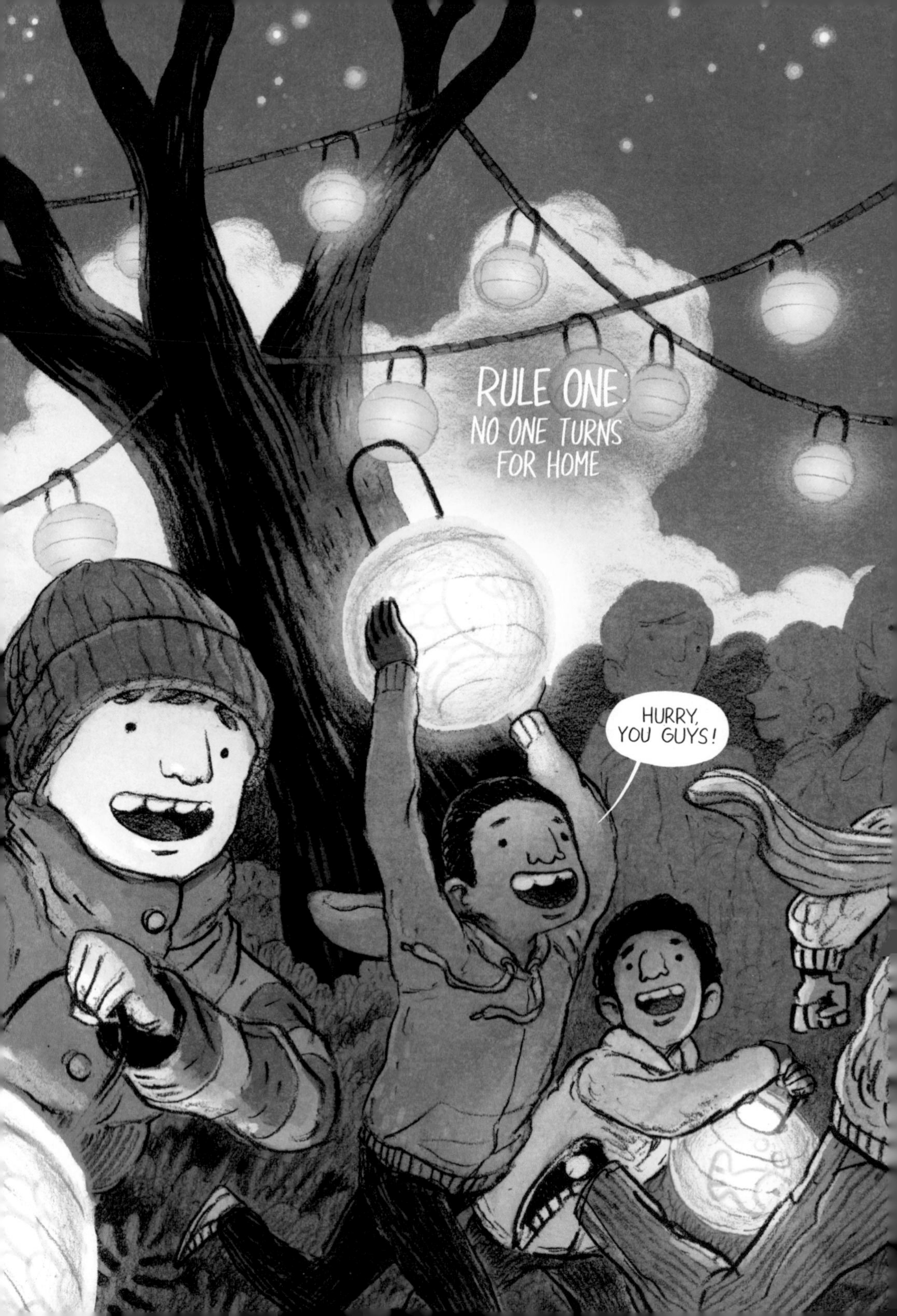
RULE ONE:
NO ONE TURNS FOR HOME
HURRY, YOU GUYS!

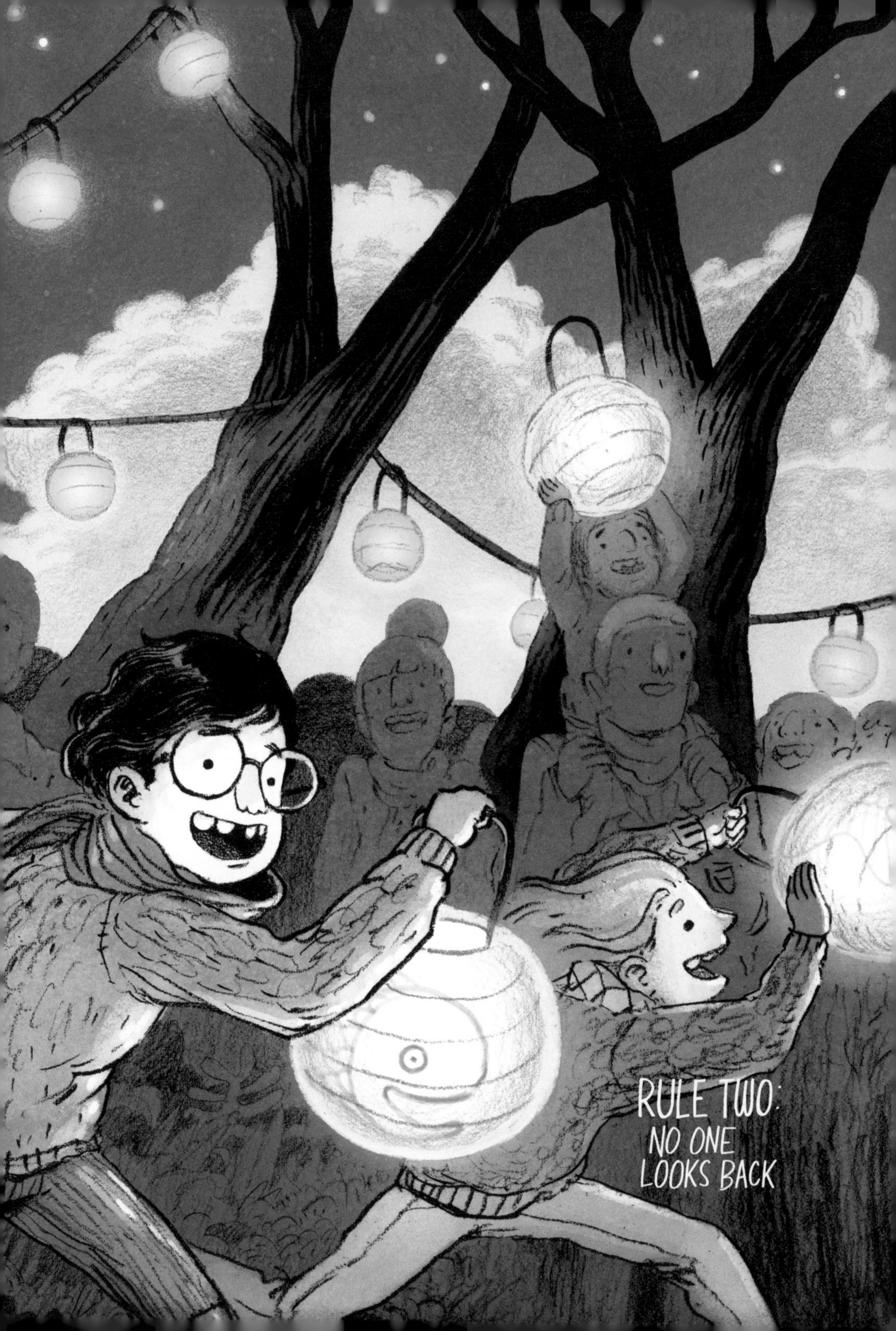
RULE TWO:
NO ONE
LOOKS BACK

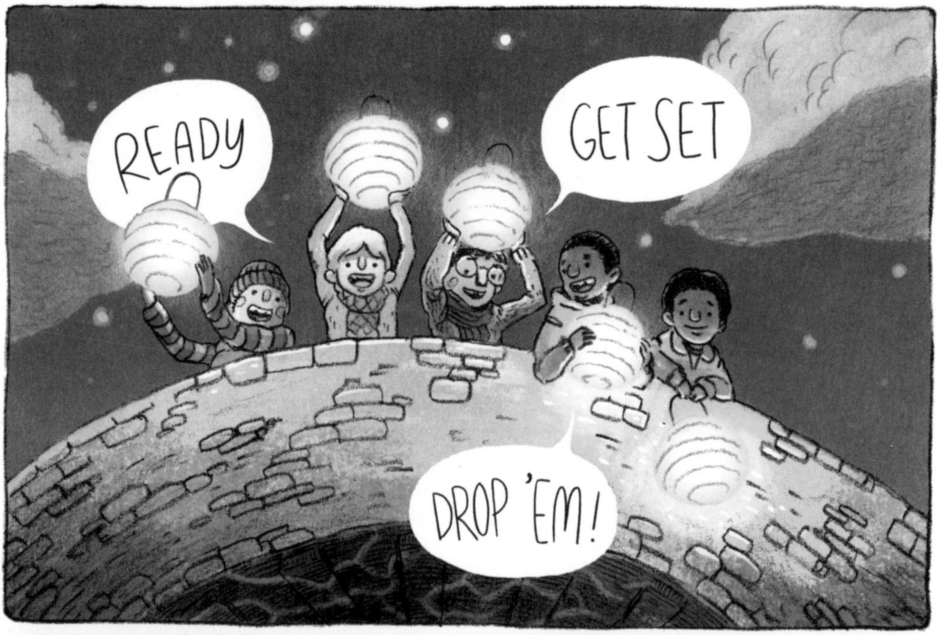
READY
GET SET
DROP 'EM!

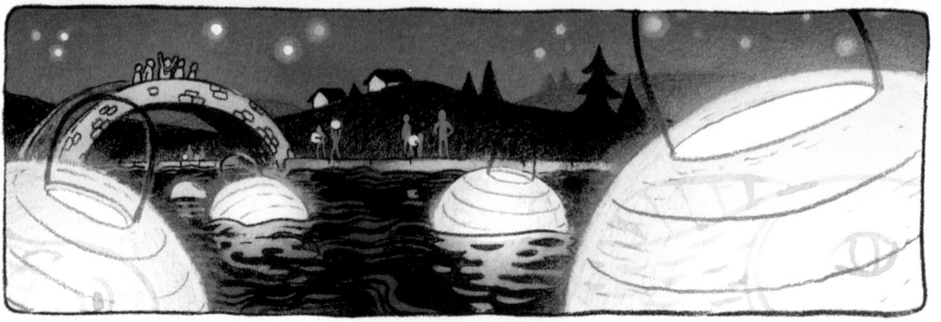

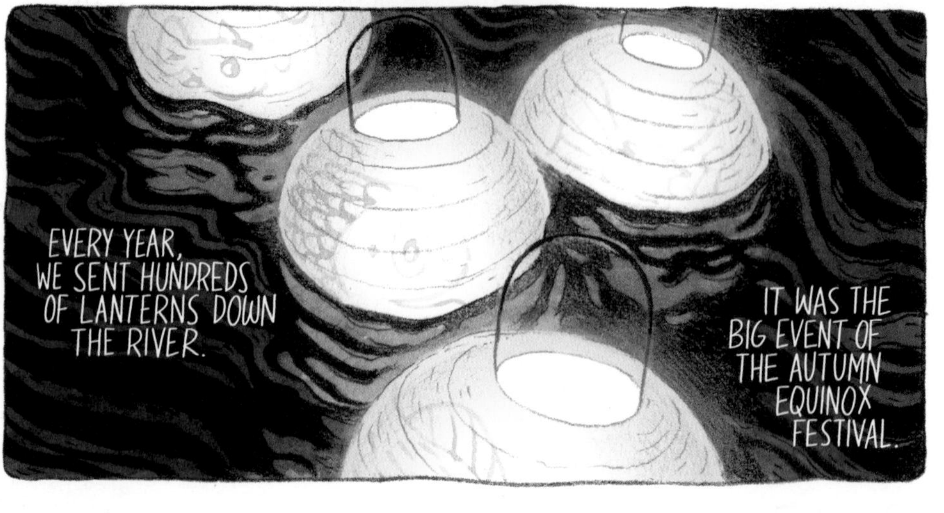
EVERY YEAR, WE SENT HUNDREDS OF LANTERNS DOWN THE RIVER.
IT WAS THE BIG EVENT OF THE AUTUMN EQUINOX FESTIVAL.

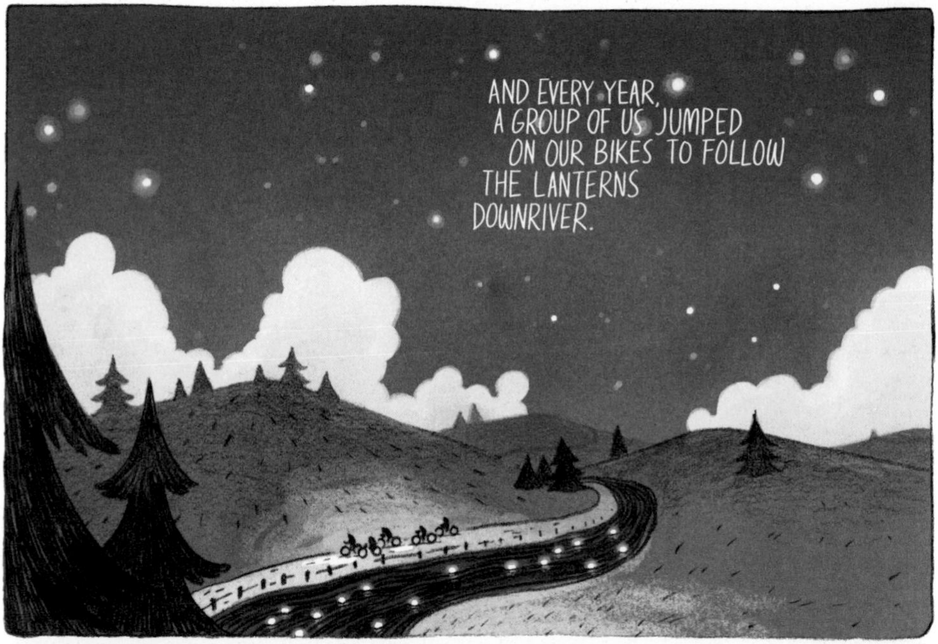
AND EVERY YEAR, A GROUP OF US JUMPED ON OUR BIKES TO FOLLOW THE LANTERNS DOWNRIVER.

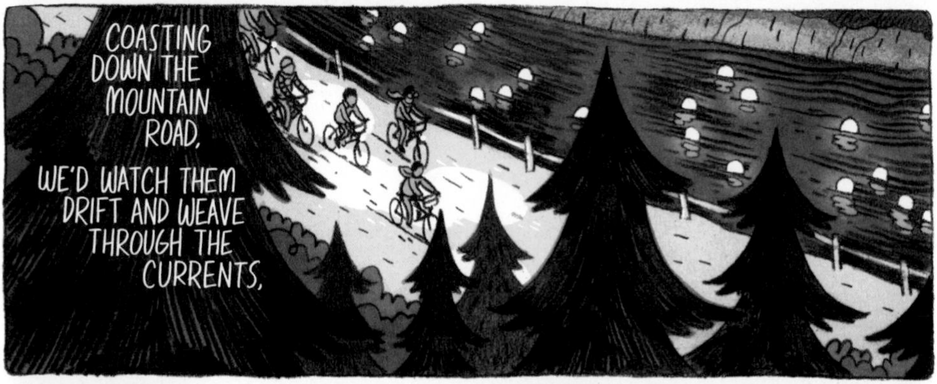
COASTING DOWN THE MOUNTAIN ROAD,
WE'D WATCH THEM DRIFT AND WEAVE THROUGH THE CURRENTS,

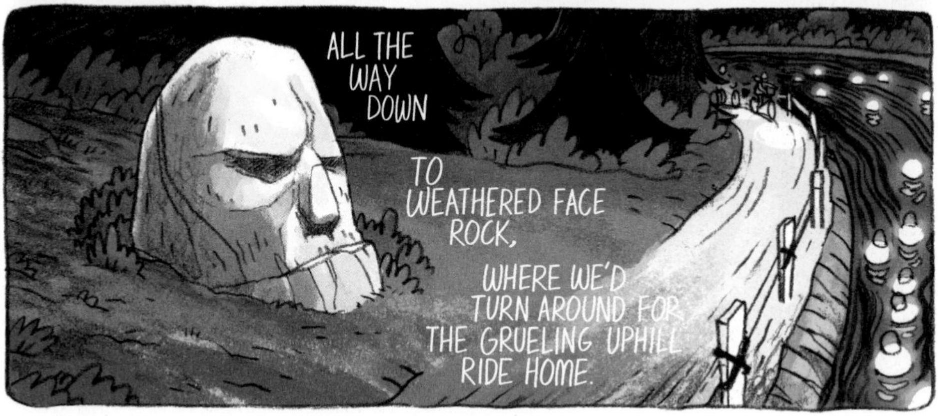
ALL THE WAY DOWN
TO WEATHERED FACE ROCK,
WHERE WE'D TURN AROUND FOR THE GRUELING UPHILL RIDE HOME.

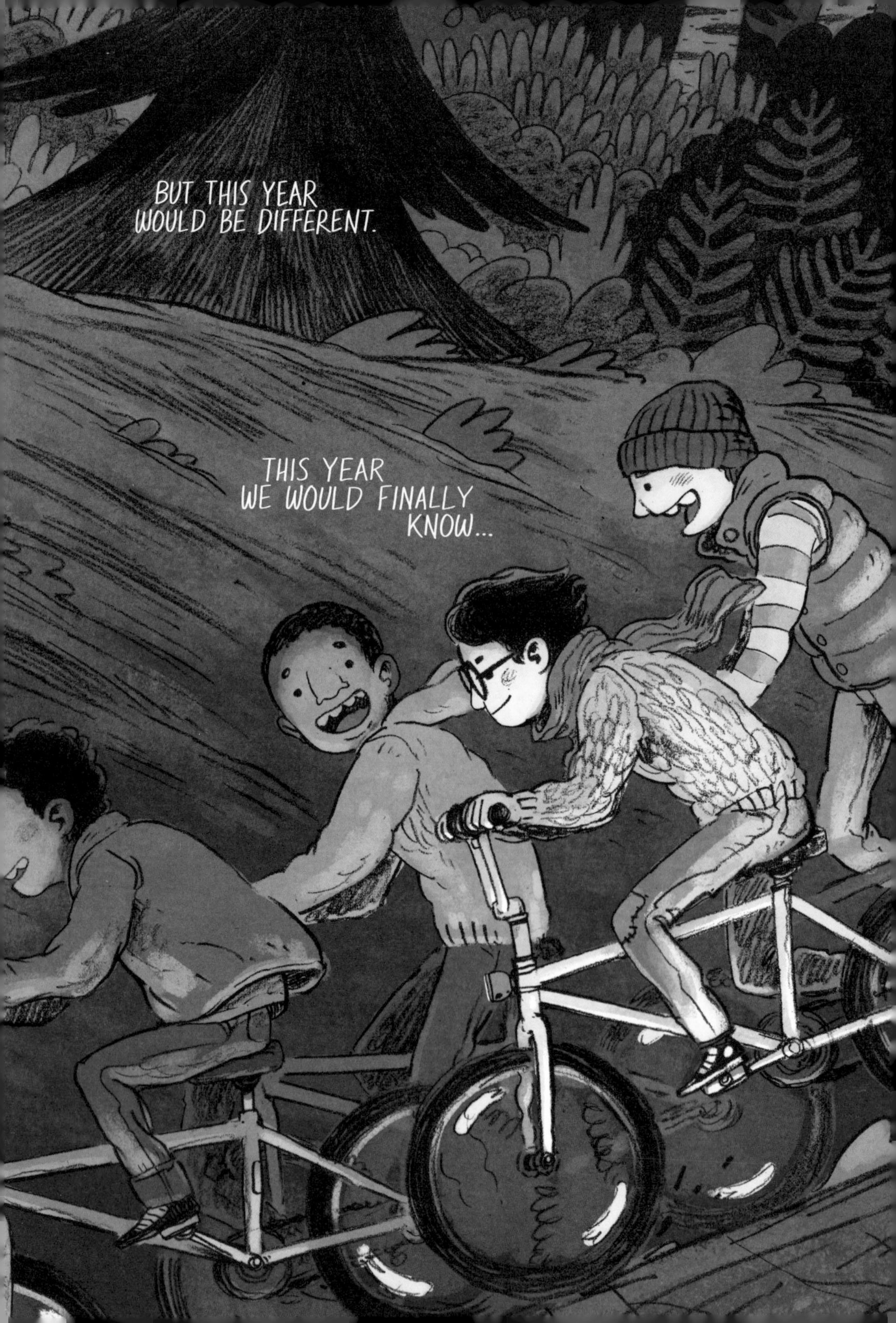
BUT THIS YEAR WOULD BE DIFFERENT.
THIS YEAR WE WOULD FINALLY KNOW...

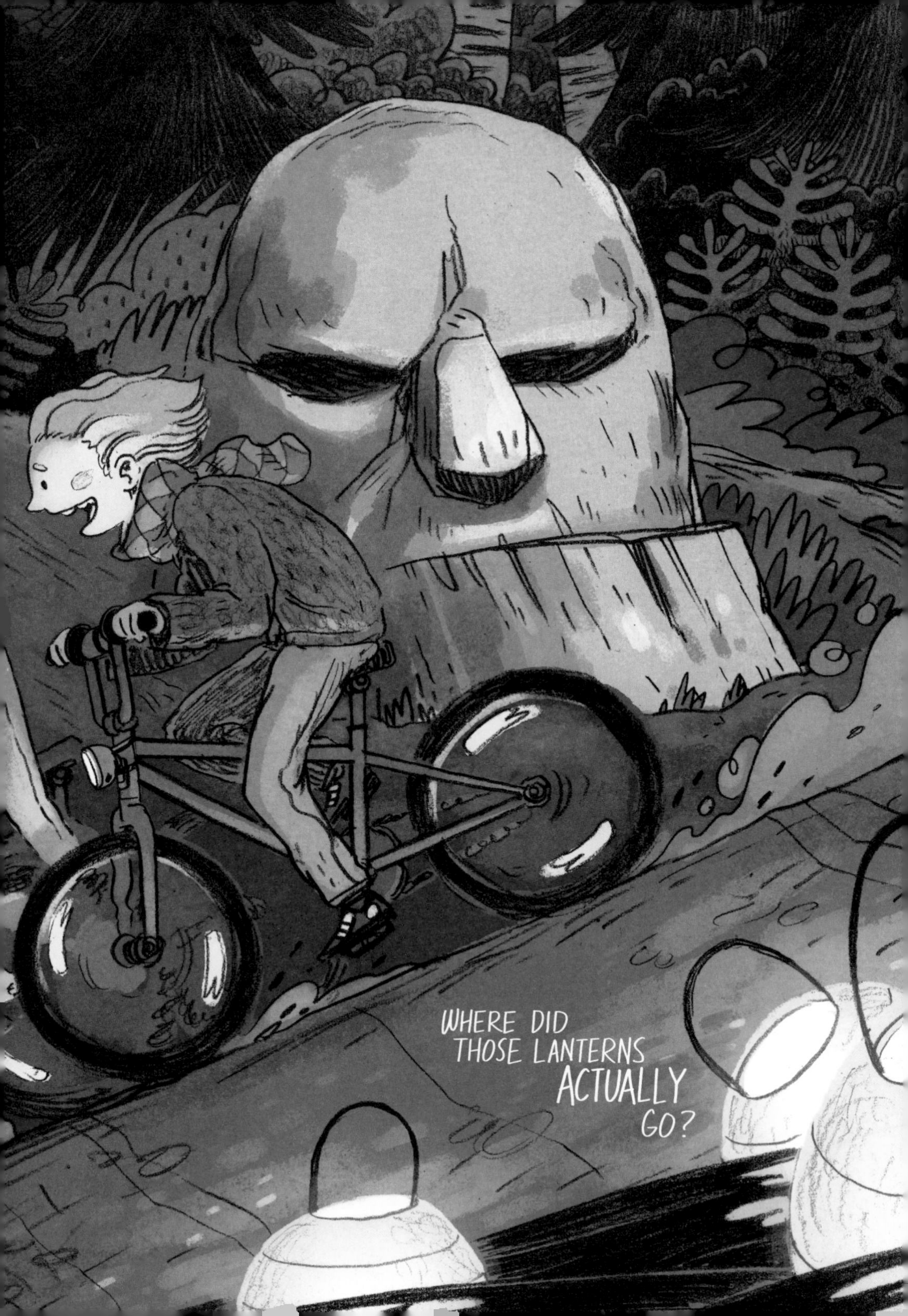
WHERE DID THOSE LANTERNS ACTUALLY GO?

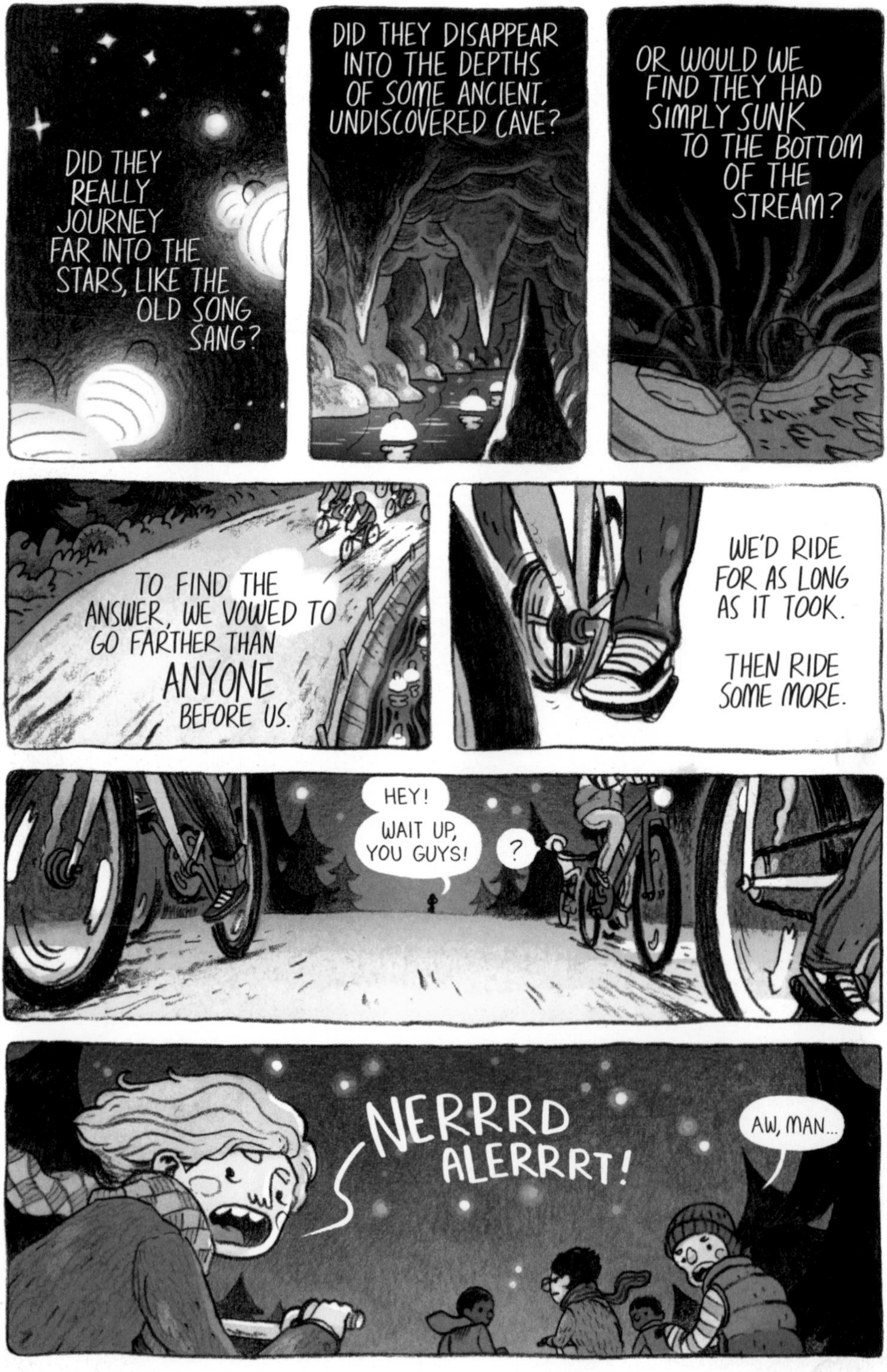
DID THEY REALLY JOURNEY FAR INTO THE STARS, LIKE THE OLD SONG SANG?
DID THEY DISAPPEAR INTO THE DEPTHS OF SOME ANCIENT, UNDISCOVERED CAVE?
OR WOULD WE FIND THEY HAD SIMPLY SUNK TO THE BOTTOM OF THE STREAM?
TO FIND THE ANSWER, WE VOWED TO GO FARTHER THAN ANYONE BEFORE US.
WE'D RIDE FOR AS LONG AS IT TOOK.
THEN RIDE SOME MORE.
HEY!
WAIT UP, YOU GUYS!
?
NERRRD ALERRRT!
AW, MAN...

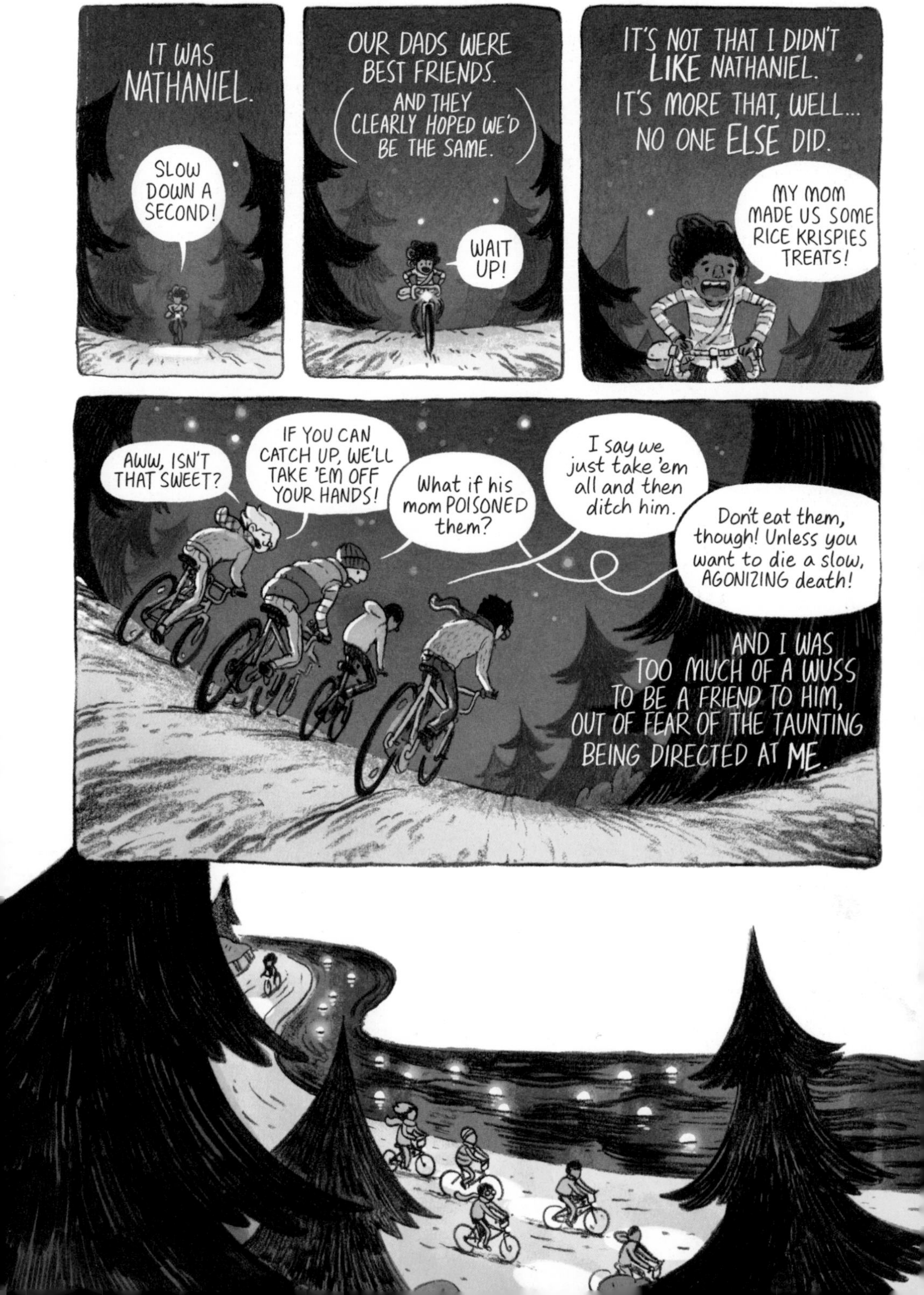

IT WAS NATHANIEL.
SLOW DOWN A SECOND!
OUR DADS WERE BEST FRIENDS.
(AND THEY CLEARLY HOPED WE'D BE THE SAME.)
WAIT UP!
IT'S NOT THAT I DIDN'T LIKE NATHANIEL. IT'S MORE THAT, WELL... NO ONE ELSE DID.
MY MOM MADE US SOME RICE KRISPIES TREATS!
AWW, ISN'T THAT SWEET?
IF YOU CAN CATCH UP, WE'LL TAKE 'EM OFF YOUR HANDS!
What if his mom POISONED them?
I say we just take 'em all and then ditch him.
Don't eat them, though! Unless you want to die a slow, AGONIZING death!
AND I WAS TOO MUCH OF A WUSS TO BE A FRIEND TO HIM, OUT OF FEAR OF THE TAUNTING BEING DIRECTED AT ME.

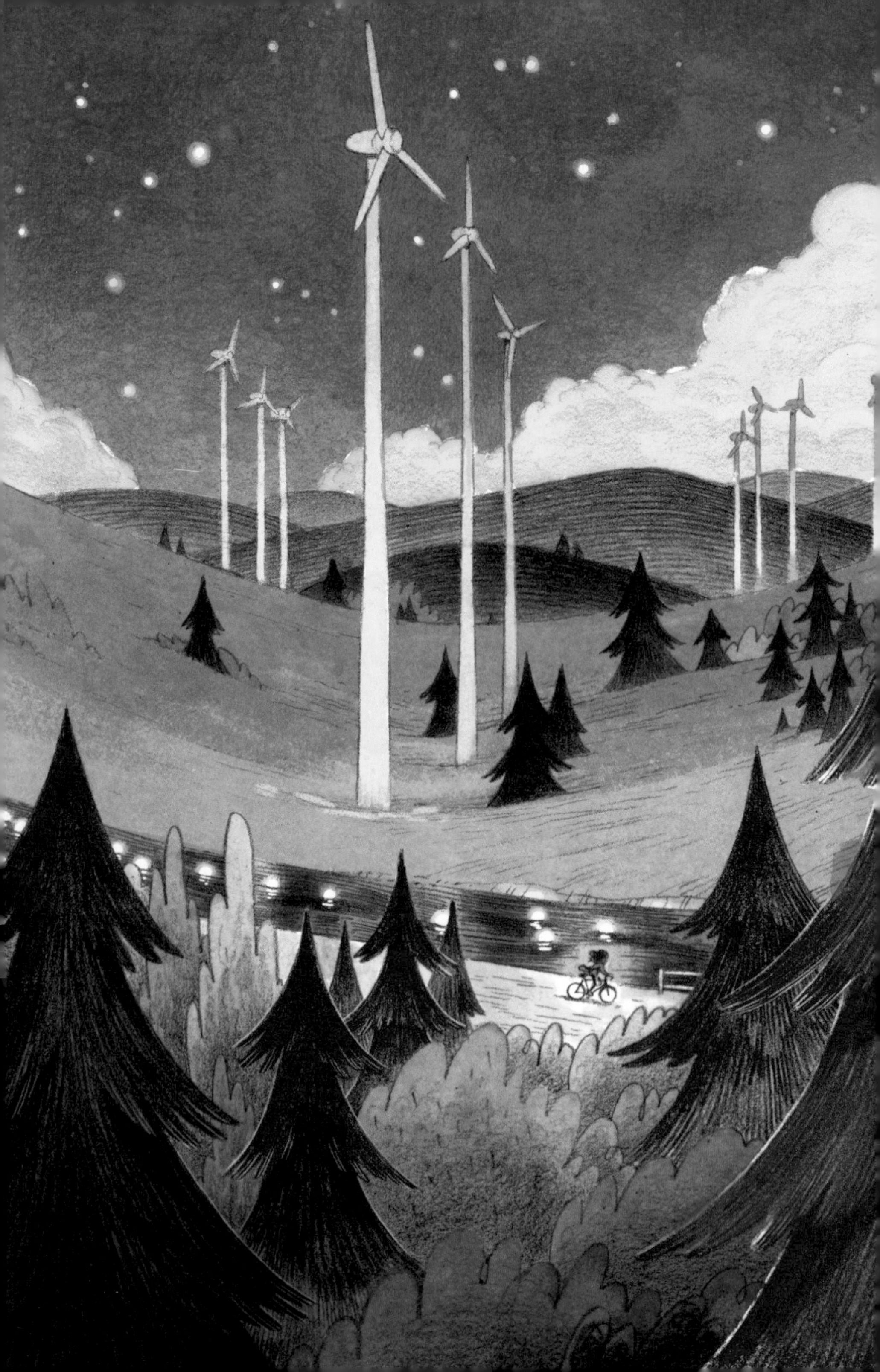

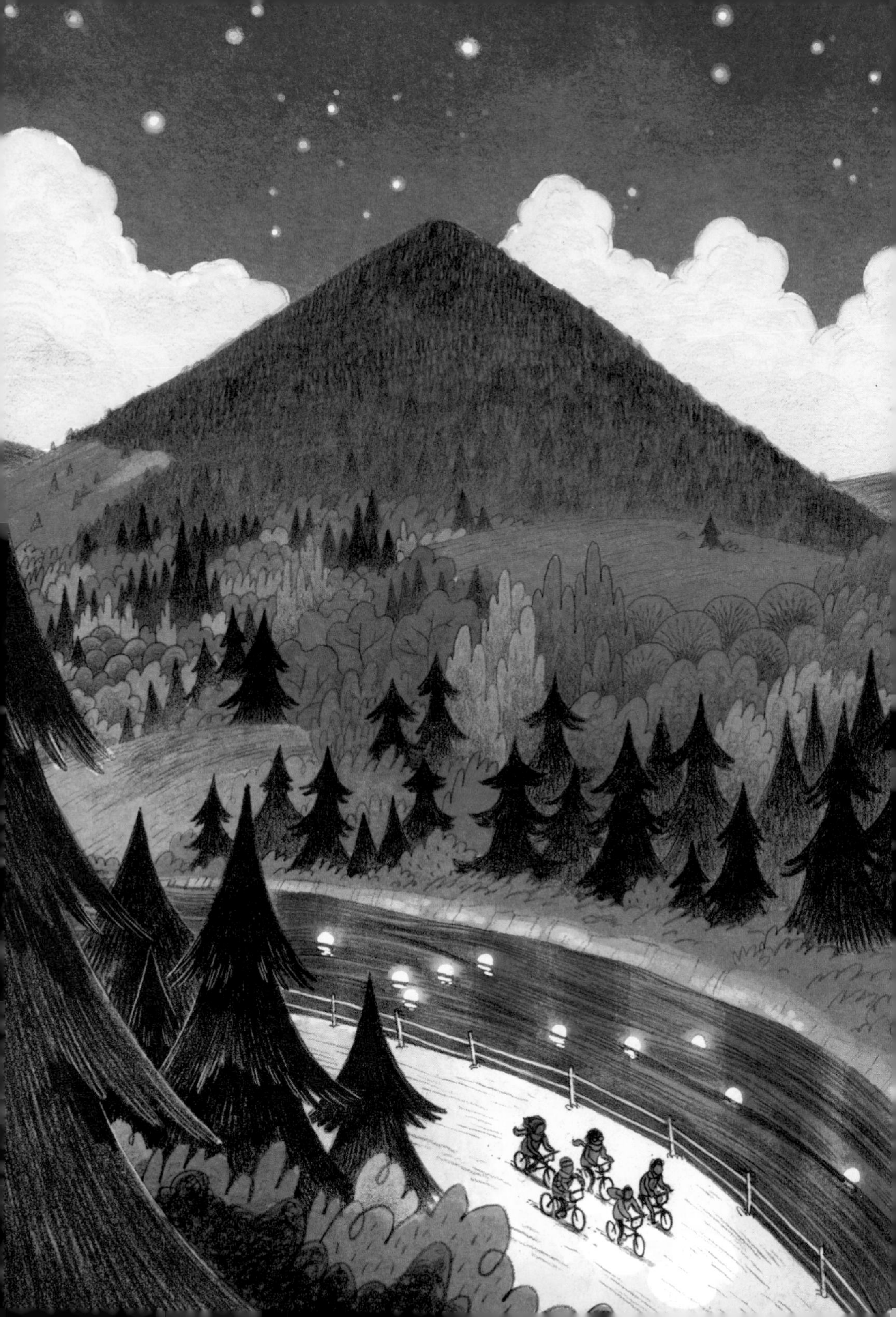

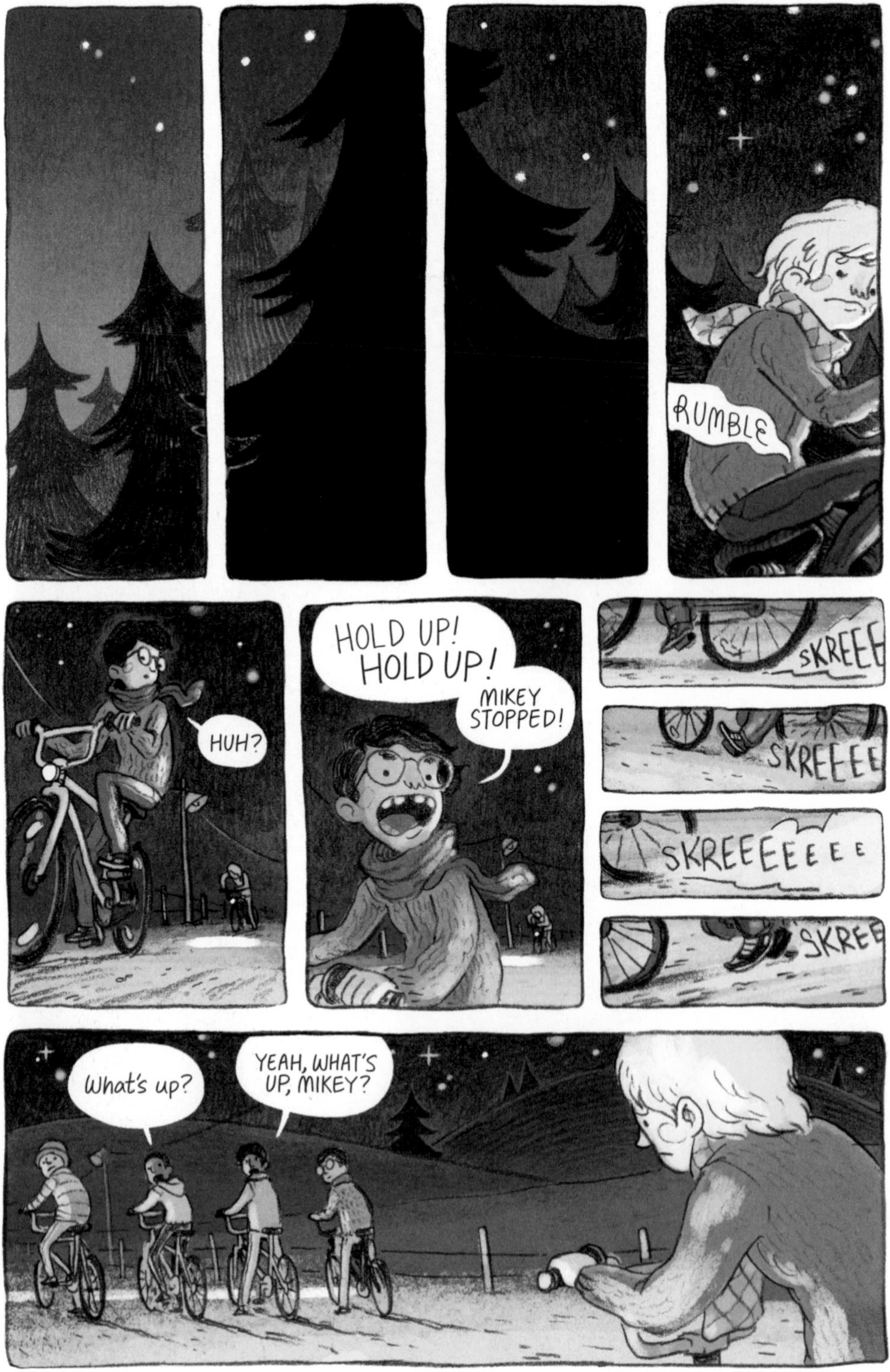
RUMBLE
HUH?
HOLD UP! HOLD UP!
MIKEY STOPPED!
SKREEE
SKREEEEE
SKREEEEEEEE
SKREE
What's up?
YEAH, WHAT'S UP, MIKEY?

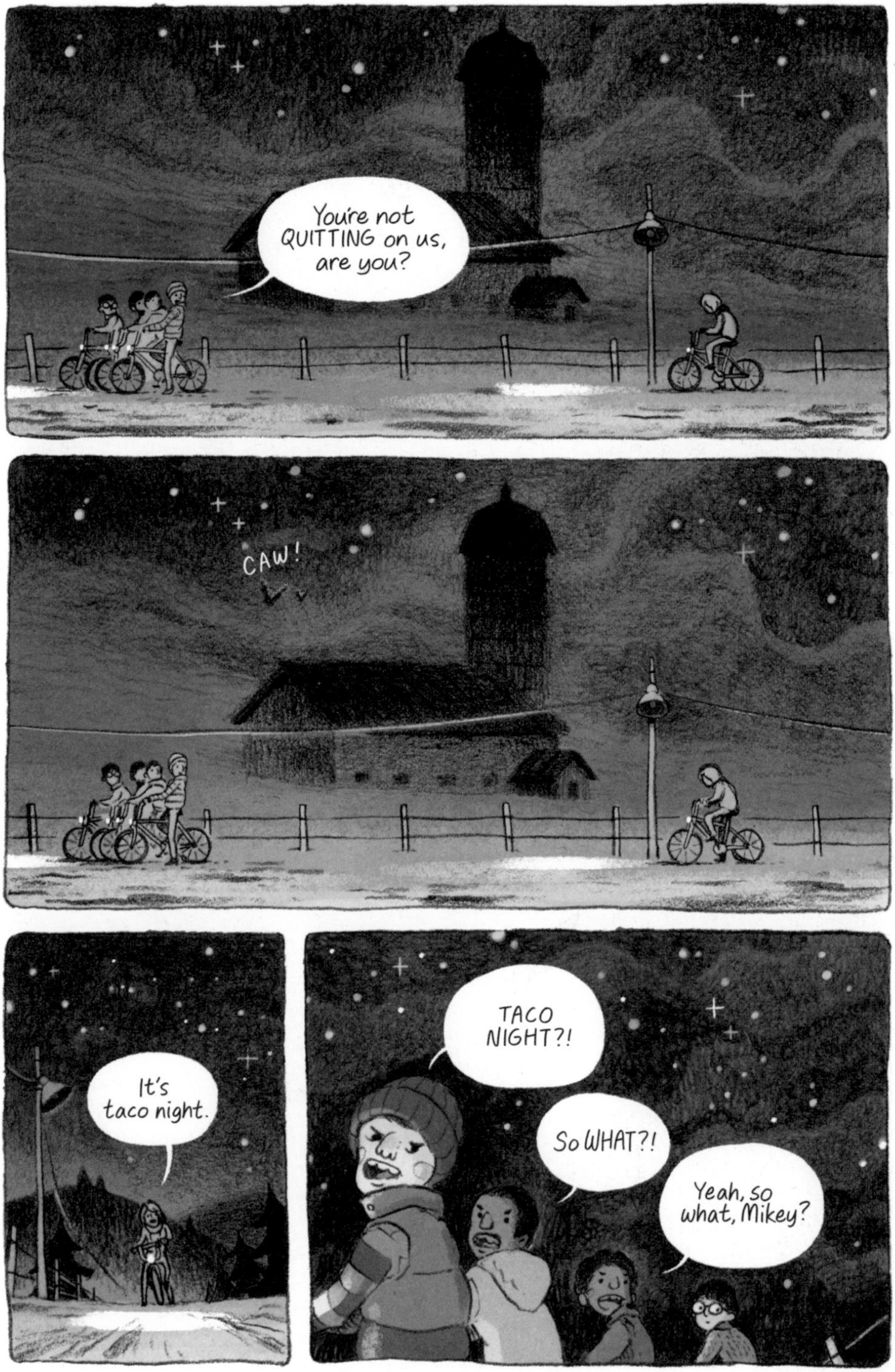
You're not QUITTING on us, are you?
CAW!
It's taco night.
TACO NIGHT?!
So WHAT?!
Yeah, so what, Mikey?

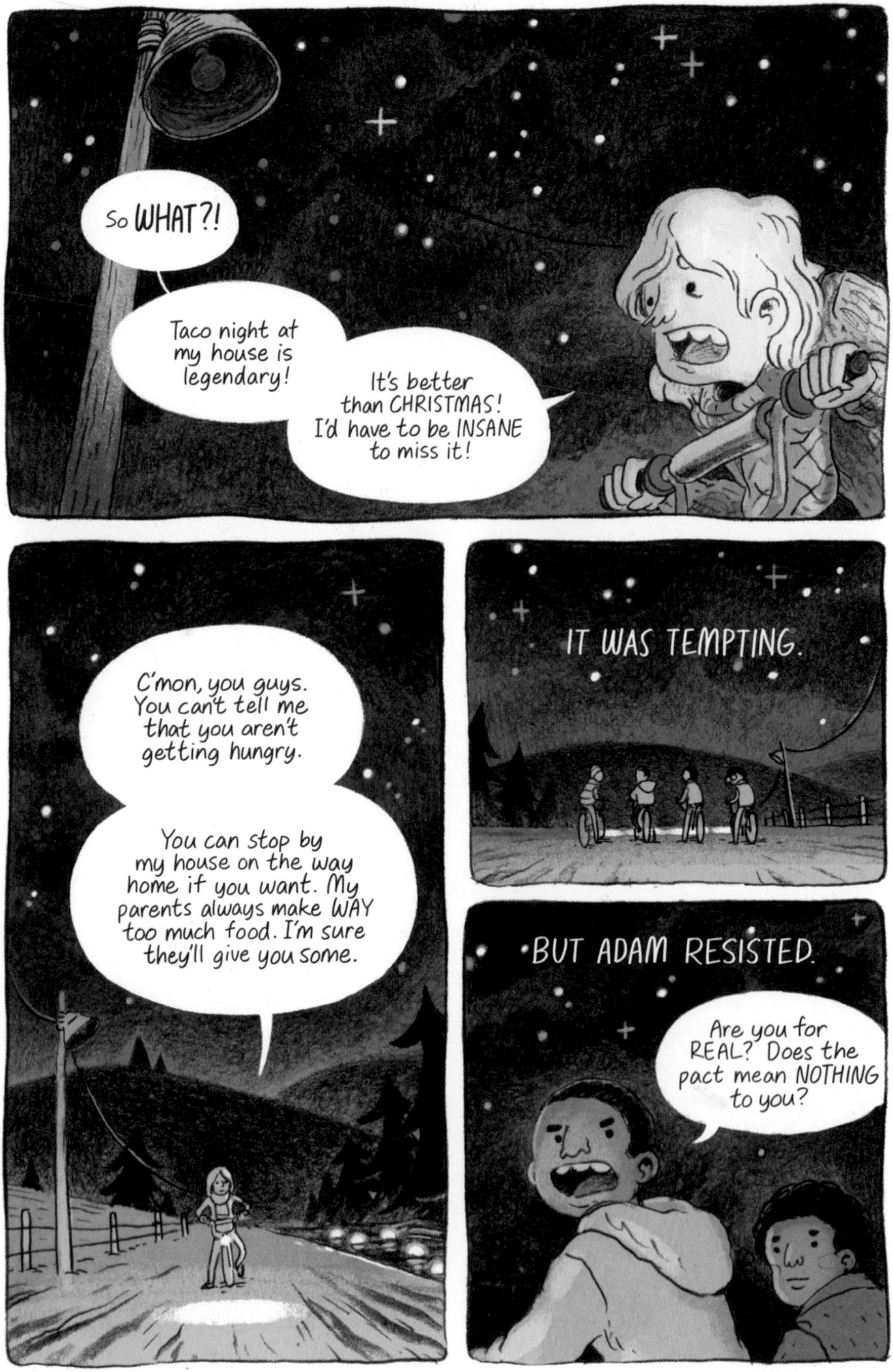
So WHAT?!
Taco night at my house is legendary!
It's better than CHRISTMAS! I'd have to be INSANE to miss it!
C'mon, you guys. You can't tell me that you aren't getting hungry.
You can stop by my house on the way home if you want. My parents always make WAY too much food. I'm sure they'll give you some.
IT WAS TEMPTING.
BUT ADAM RESISTED.
Are you for REAL? Does the pact mean NOTHING to you?

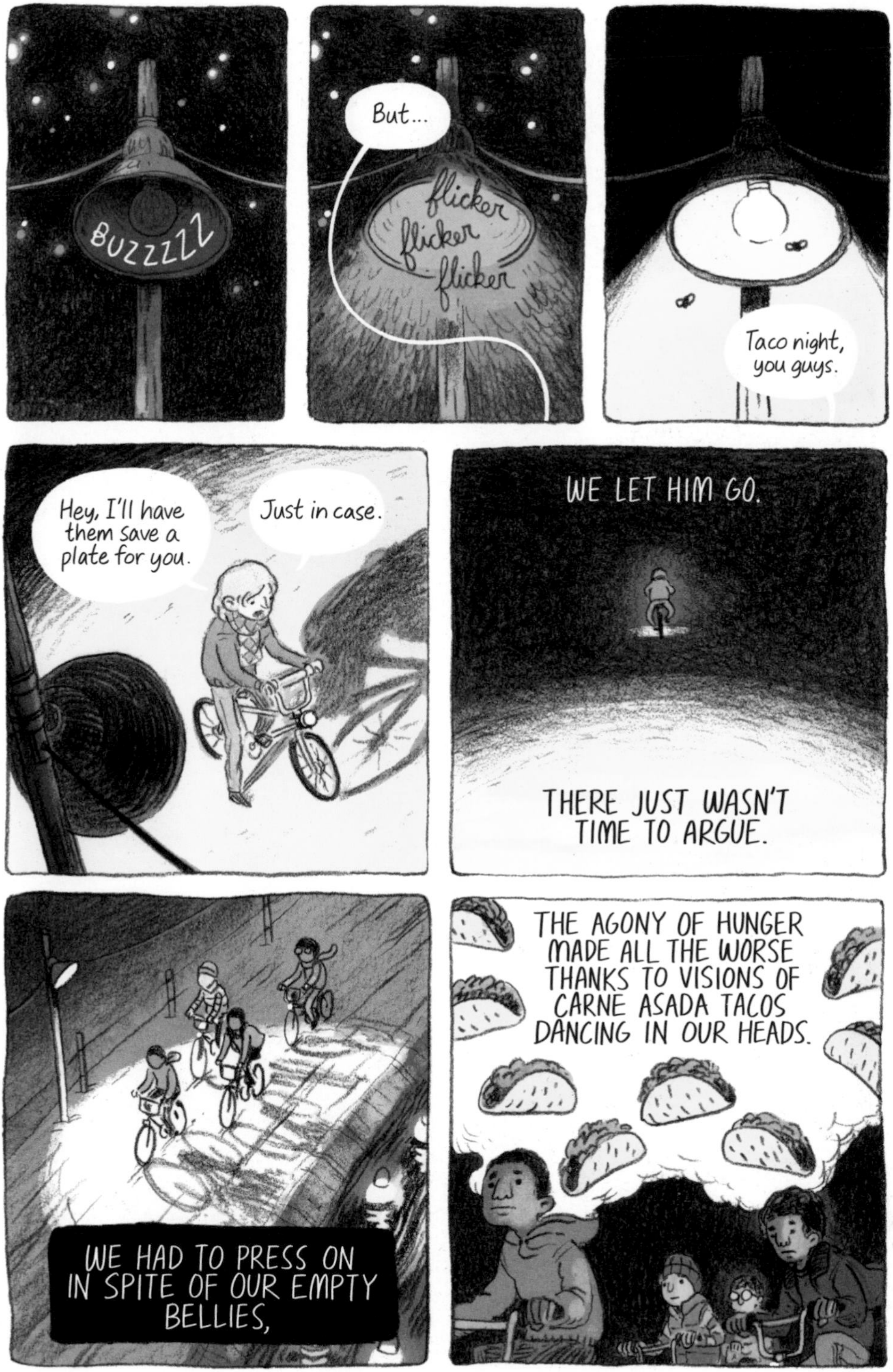
BUZZZZZ
But...
flicker flicker flicker
Taco night, you guys.
Hey, I'll have them save a plate for you.
Just in case.
WE LET HIM GO.
THERE JUST WASN'T TIME TO ARGUE.
WE HAD TO PRESS ON IN SPITE OF OUR EMPTY BELLIES,
THE AGONY OF HUNGER MADE ALL THE WORSE THANKS TO VISIONS OF CARNE ASADA TACOS DANCING IN OUR HEADS.

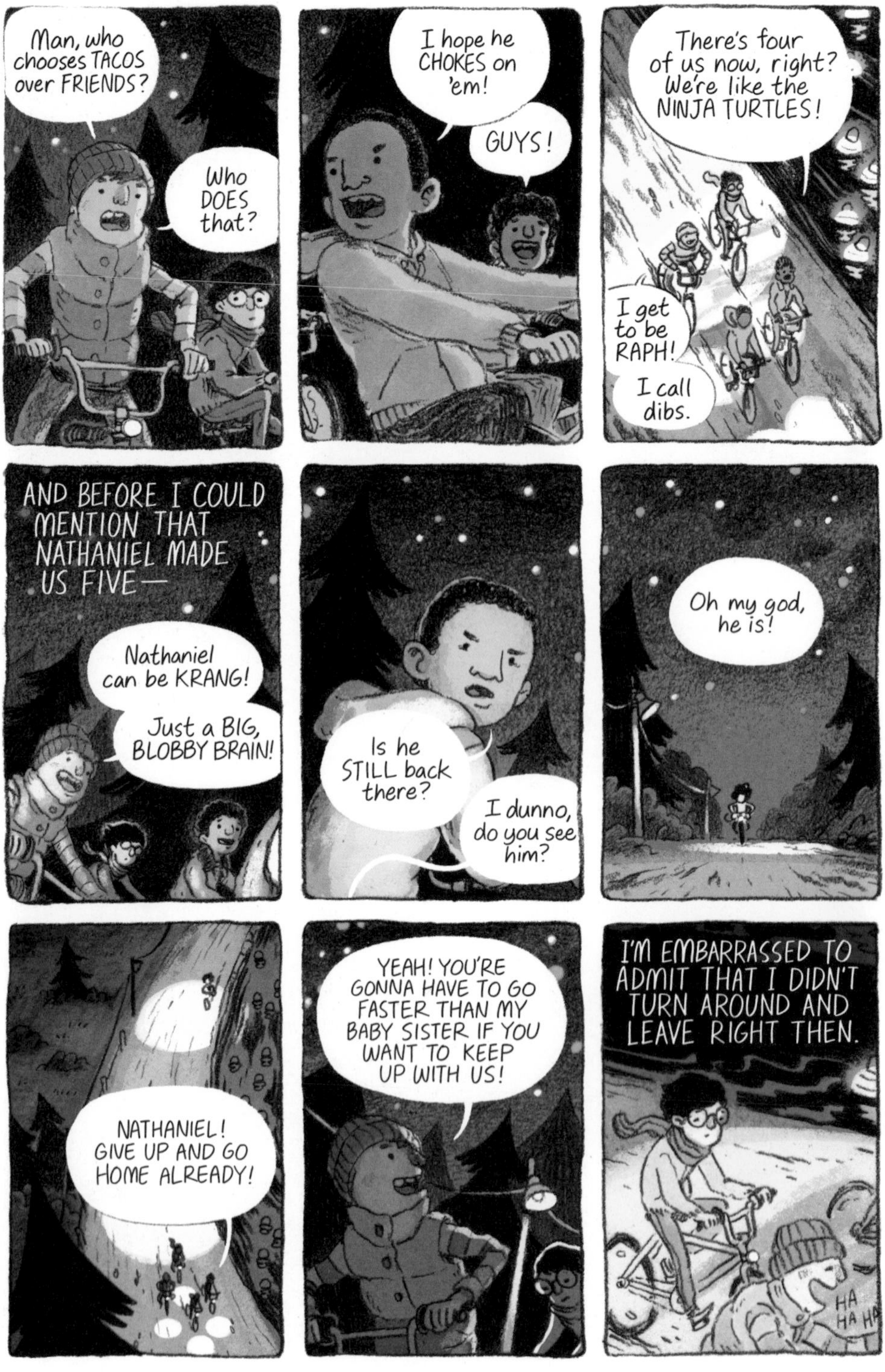
Man, who chooses TACOS over FRIENDS?
Who DOES that?
I hope he CHOKES on 'em!
GUYS!
There's four of us now, right? We're like the NINJA TURTLES!
I get to be RAPH!
I call dibs.
AND BEFORE I COULD MENTION THAT NATHANIEL MADE US FIVE—
Nathaniel can be KRANG!
Just a BIG, BLOBBY BRAIN!
Is he STILL back there?
I dunno, do you see him?
Oh my god, he is!
NATHANIEL! GIVE UP AND GO HOME ALREADY!
YEAH! YOU'RE GONNA HAVE TO GO FASTER THAN MY BABY SISTER IF YOU WANT TO KEEP UP WITH US!
I'M EMBARRASSED TO ADMIT THAT I DIDN'T TURN AROUND AND LEAVE RIGHT THEN.
HA HA HA

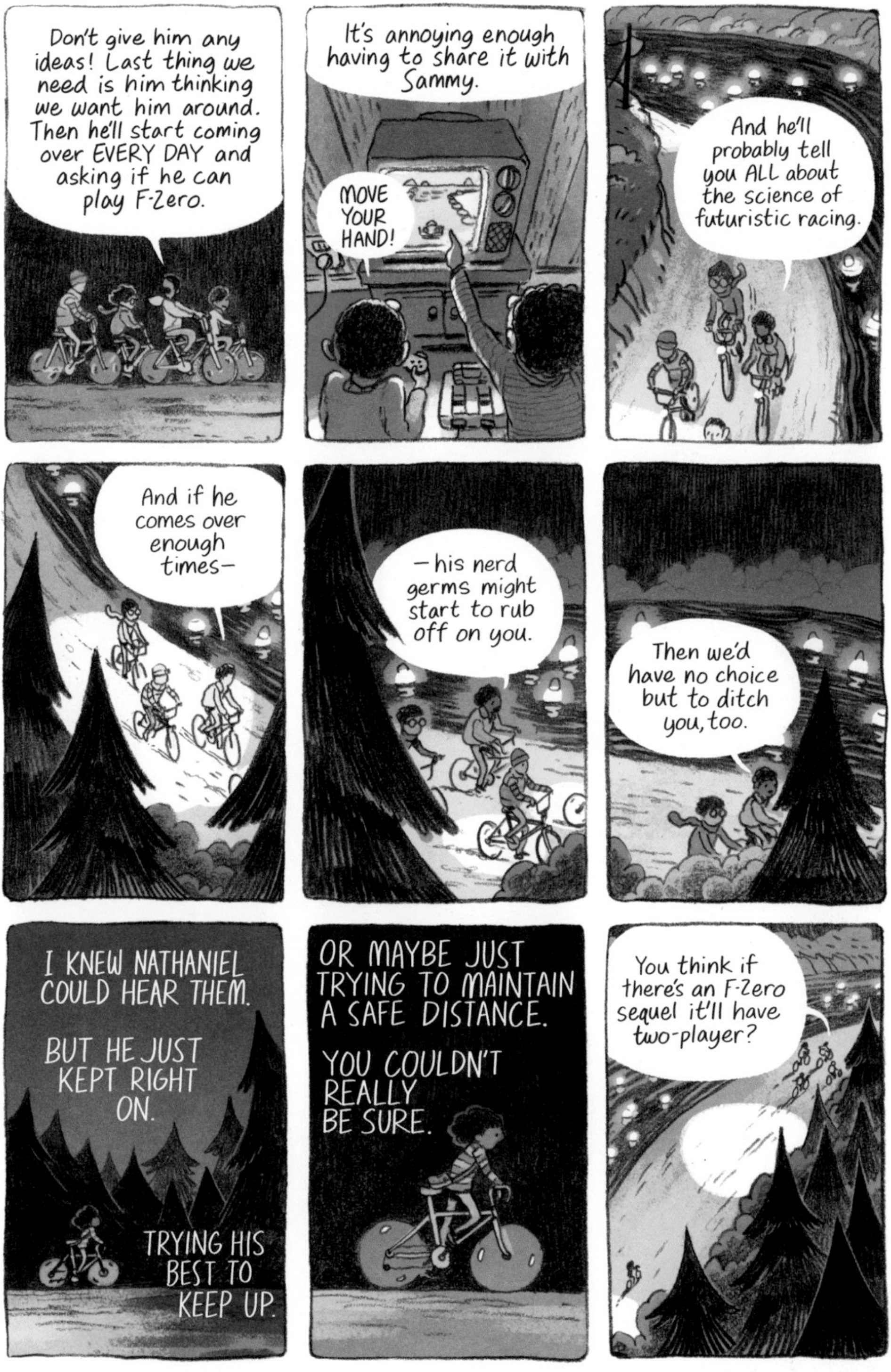

Don't give him any ideas! Last thing we need is him thinking we want him around. Then he'll start coming over EVERY DAY and asking if he can play F-Zero.
It's annoying enough having to share it with Sammy.
MOVE YOUR HAND!
And he'll probably tell you ALL about the science of futuristic racing.
And if he comes over enough times—
—his nerd germs might start to rub off on you.
Then we'd have no choice but to ditch you, too.
I KNEW NATHANIEL COULD HEAR THEM.
BUT HE JUST KEPT RIGHT ON.
TRYING HIS BEST TO KEEP UP.
OR MAYBE JUST TRYING TO MAINTAIN A SAFE DISTANCE.
YOU COULDN'T REALLY BE SURE.
You think if there's an F-Zero sequel it'll have two-player?

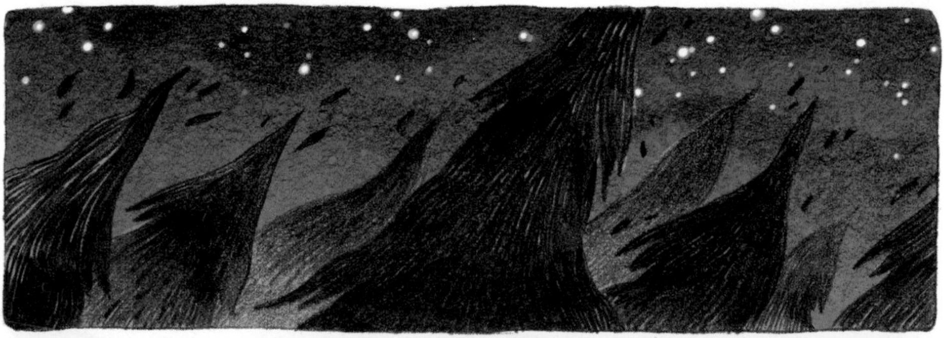

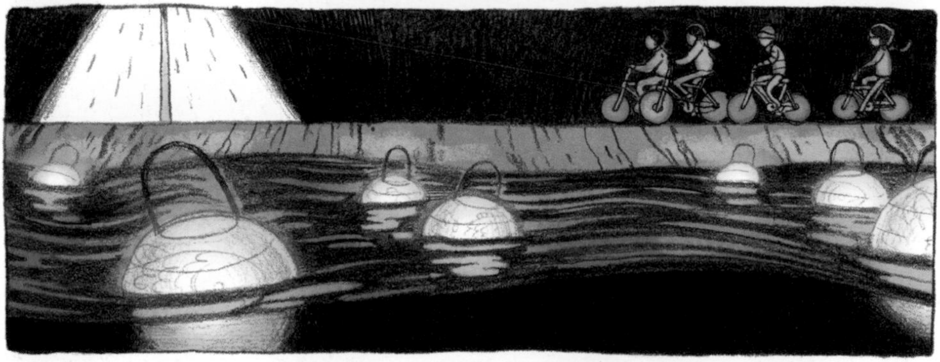

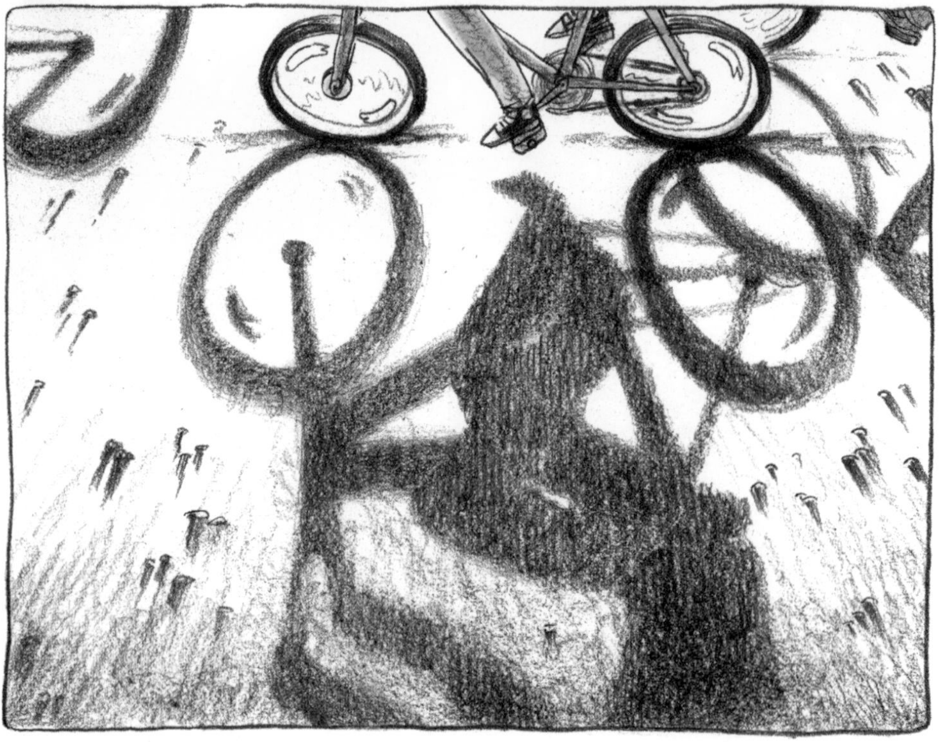

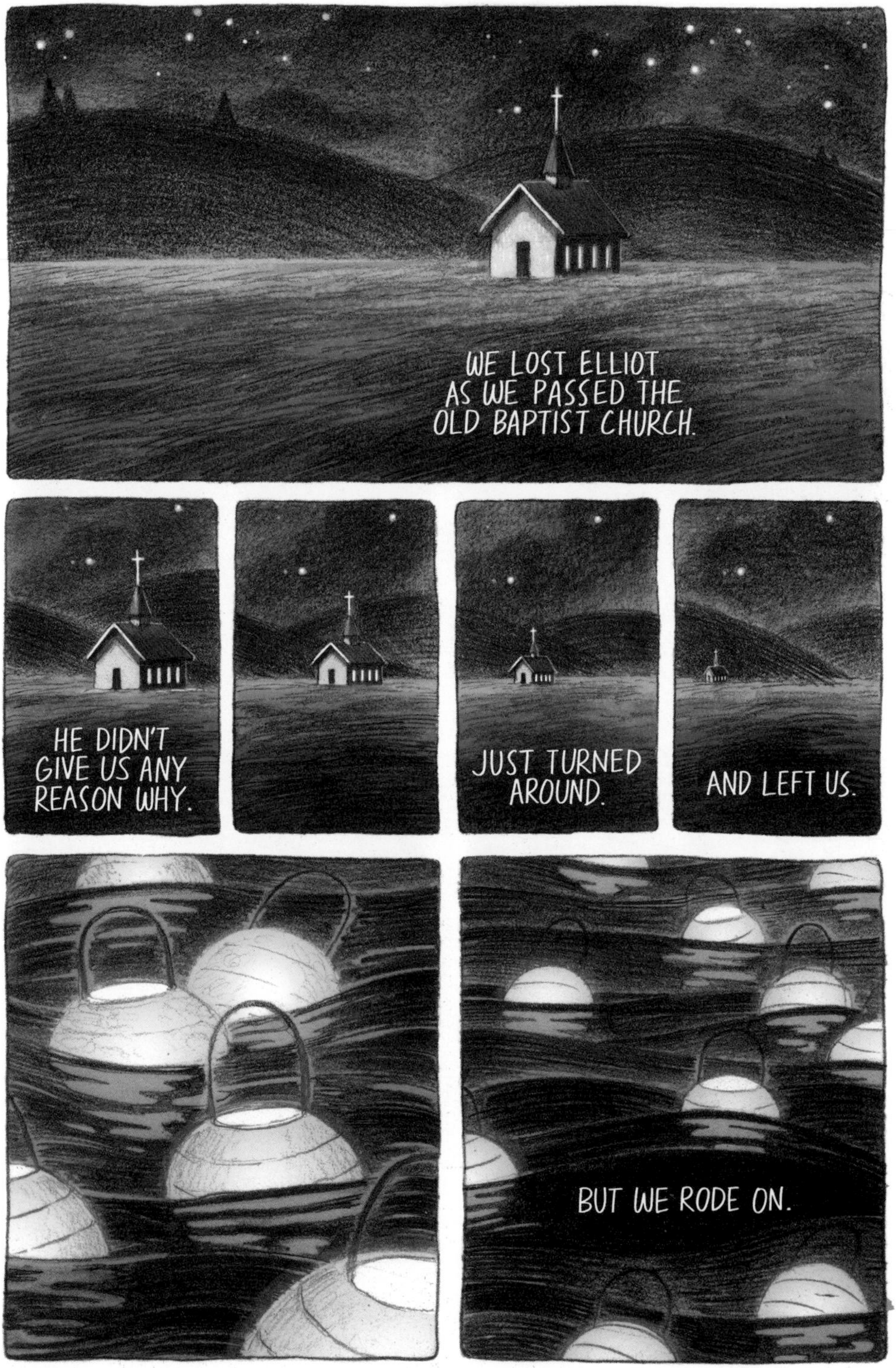
WE LOST ELLIOT AS WE PASSED THE OLD BAPTIST CHURCH.
HE DIDN'T GIVE US ANY REASON WHY.
JUST TURNED AROUND.
AND LEFT US.
BUT WE RODE ON.

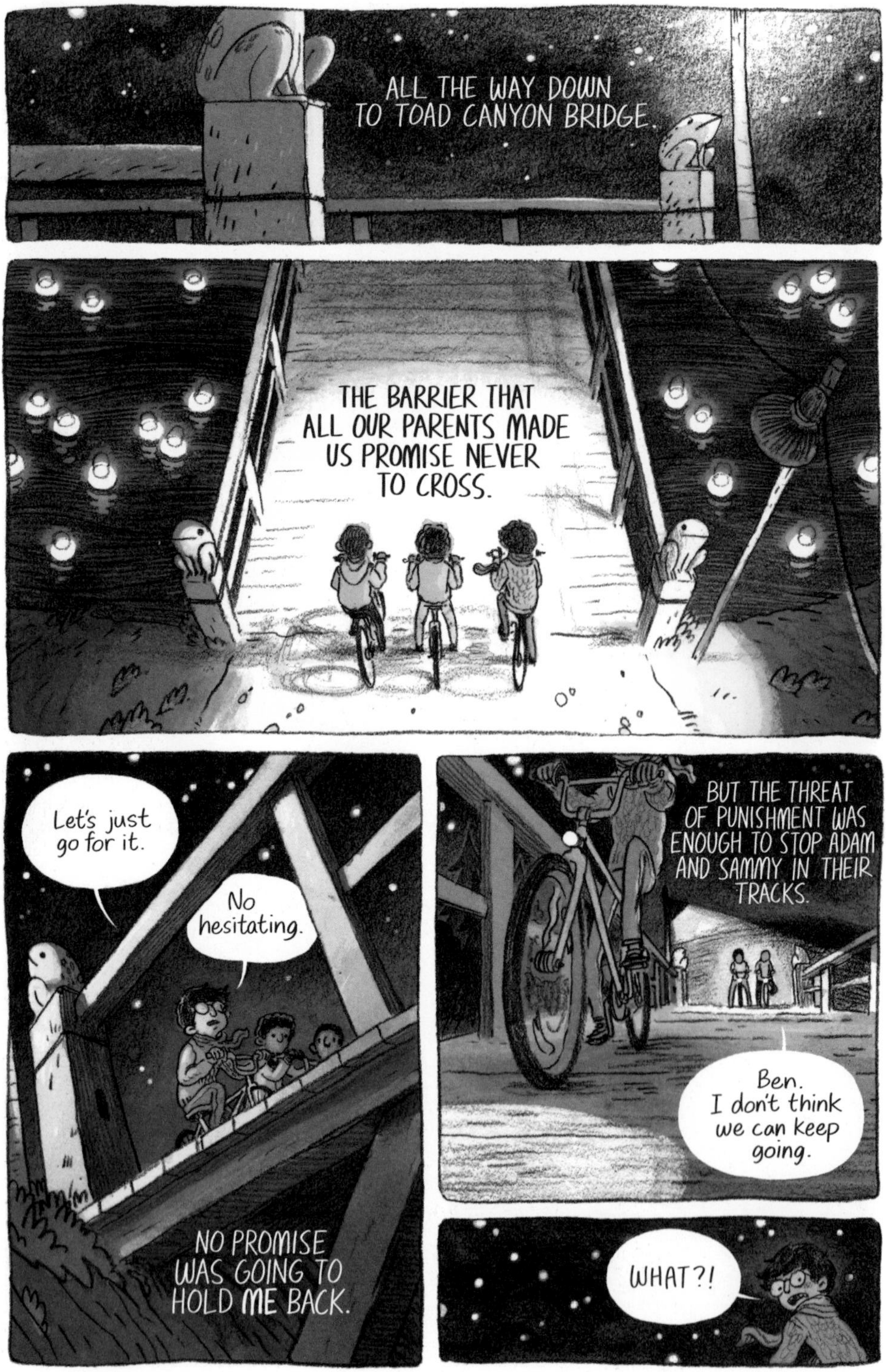
ALL THE WAY DOWN TO TOAD CANYON BRIDGE.
THE BARRIER THAT ALL OUR PARENTS MADE US PROMISE NEVER TO CROSS.
Let's just go for it.
No hesitating.
NO PROMISE WAS GOING TO HOLD ME BACK.
BUT THE THREAT OF PUNISHMENT WAS ENOUGH TO STOP ADAM AND SAMMY IN THEIR TRACKS.
Ben. I don't think we can keep going.
WHAT?!

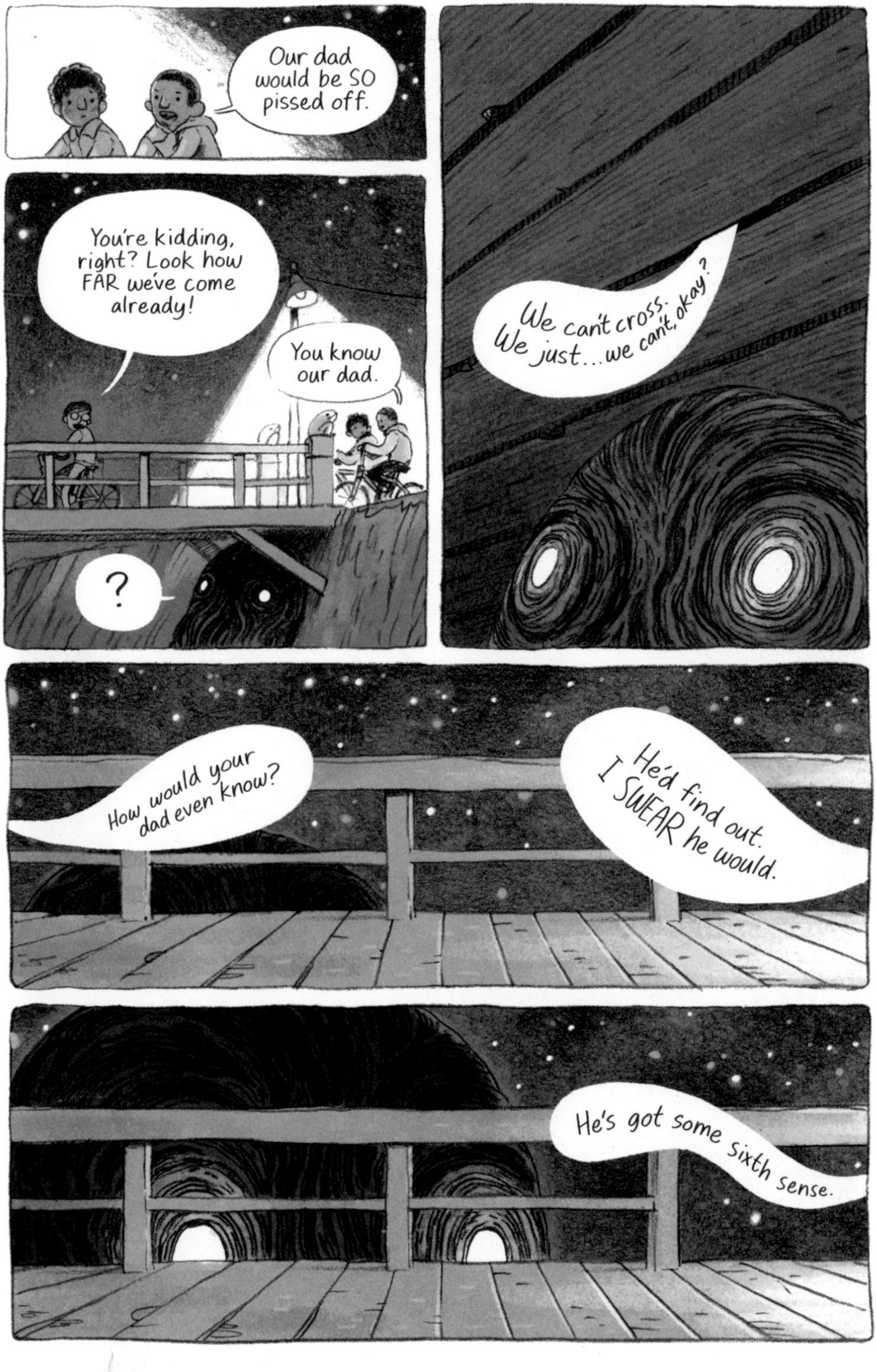
Our dad would be SO pissed off.
You're kidding, right? Look how FAR we've come already!
You know our dad.
?
We can't cross. We just... we can't, okay?
How would your dad even know?
He'd find out. I SWEAR he would.
He's got some sixth sense.

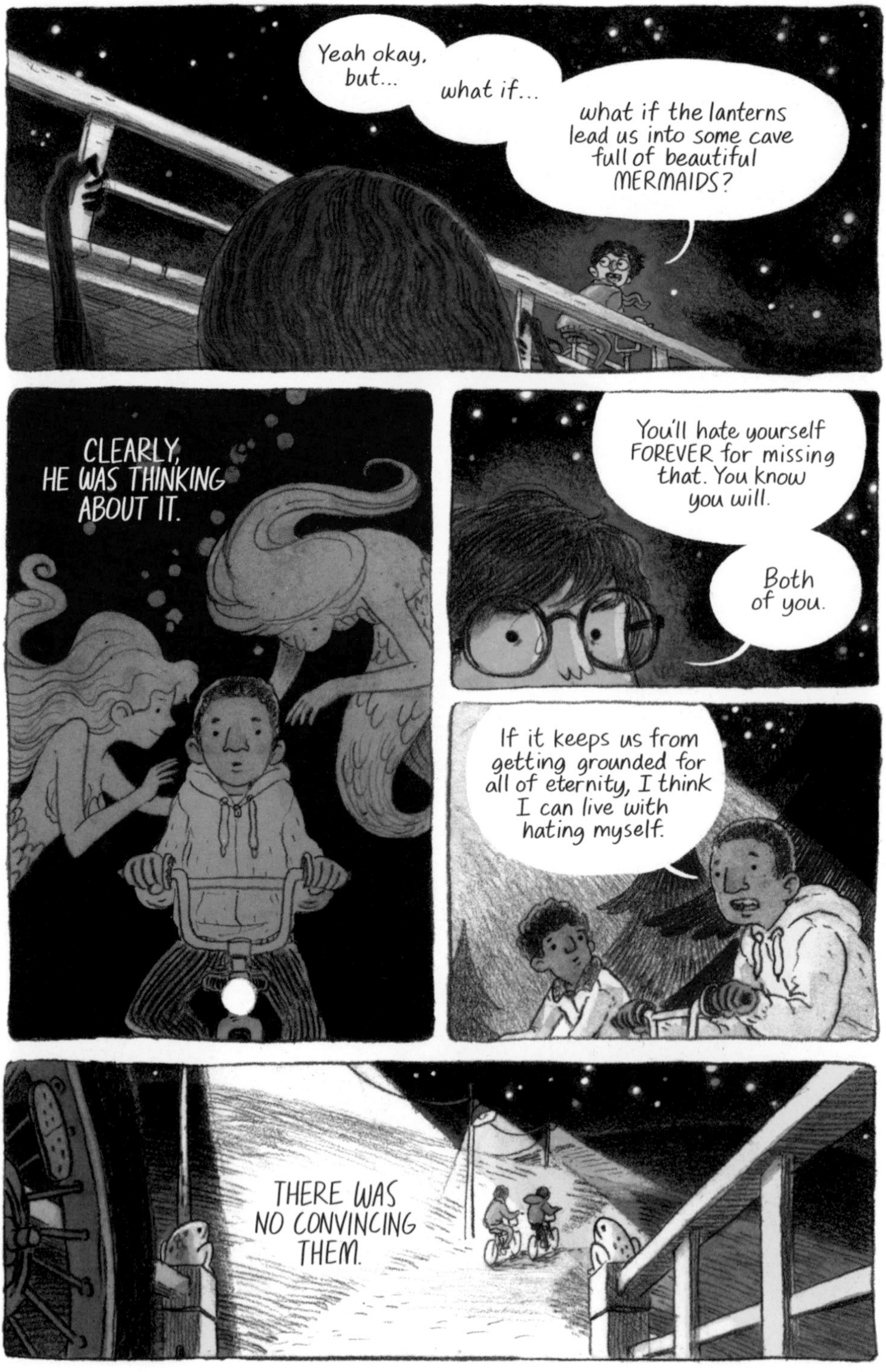

Yeah okay, but...
what if...
what if the lanterns lead us into some cave full of beautiful MERMAIDS?
CLEARLY, HE WAS THINKING ABOUT IT.
You'll hate yourself FOREVER for missing that. You know you will.
Both of you.
If it keeps us from getting grounded for all of eternity, I think I can live with hating myself.
THERE WAS NO CONVINCING THEM.

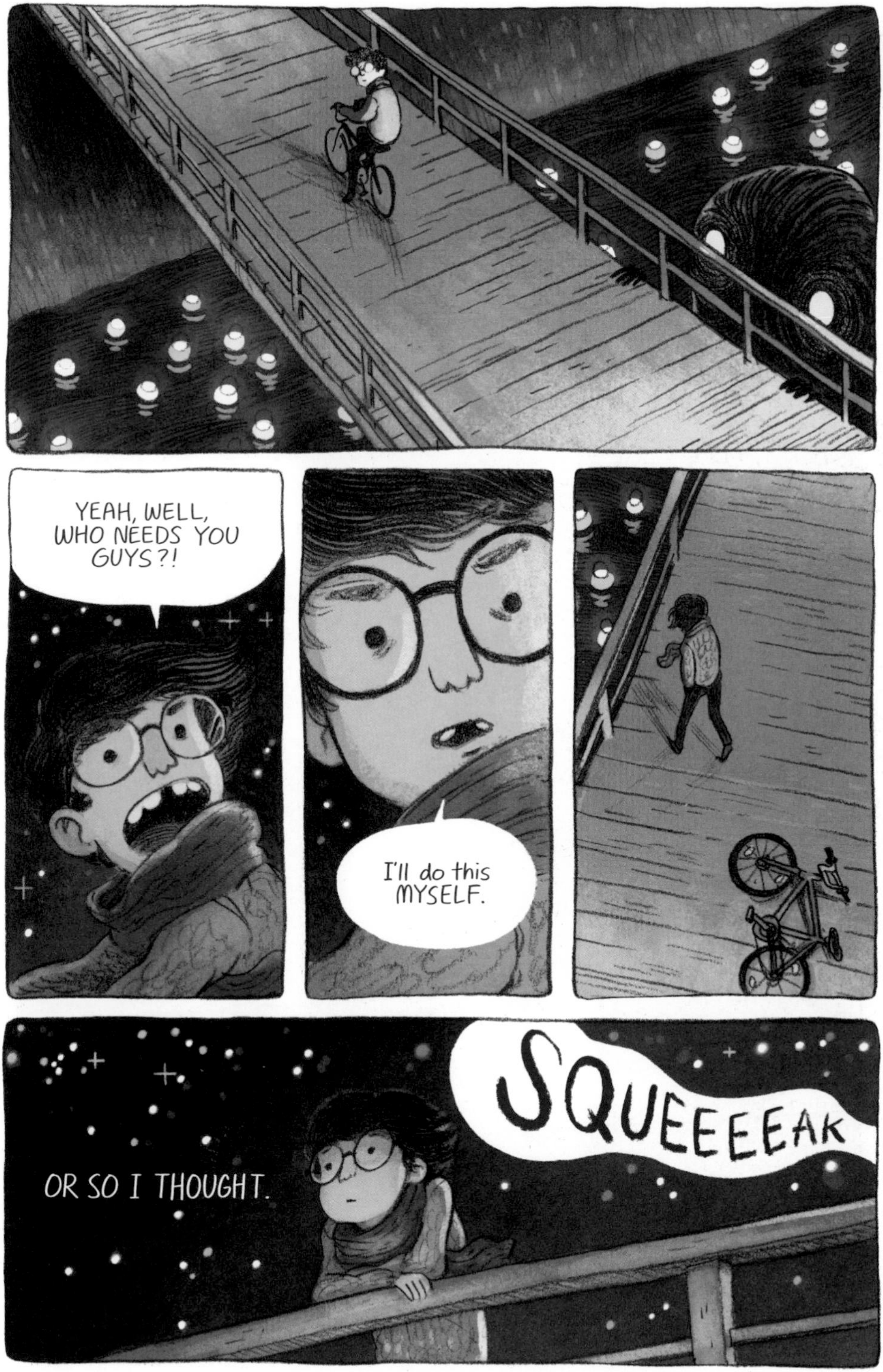
YEAH, WELL, WHO NEEDS YOU GUYS?!
I'll do this MYSELF.
SQUEEEEAK
OR SO I THOUGHT.

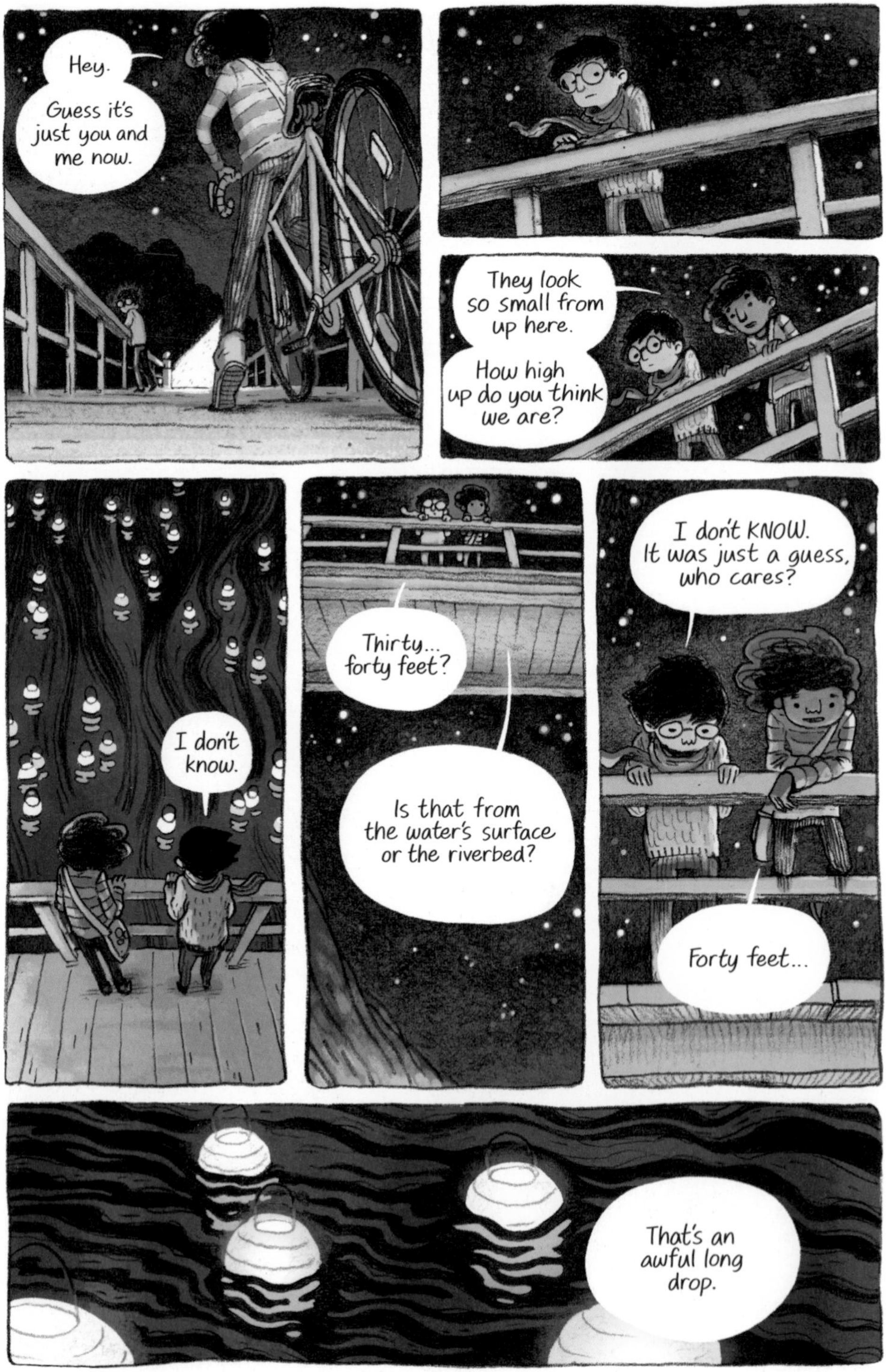
Hey.
Guess it's just you and me now.
They look so small from up here.
How high up do you think we are?
I don't know.
Thirty... forty feet?
Is that from the water's surface or the riverbed?
I don't KNOW. It was just a guess, who cares?
Forty feet...
That's an awful long drop.

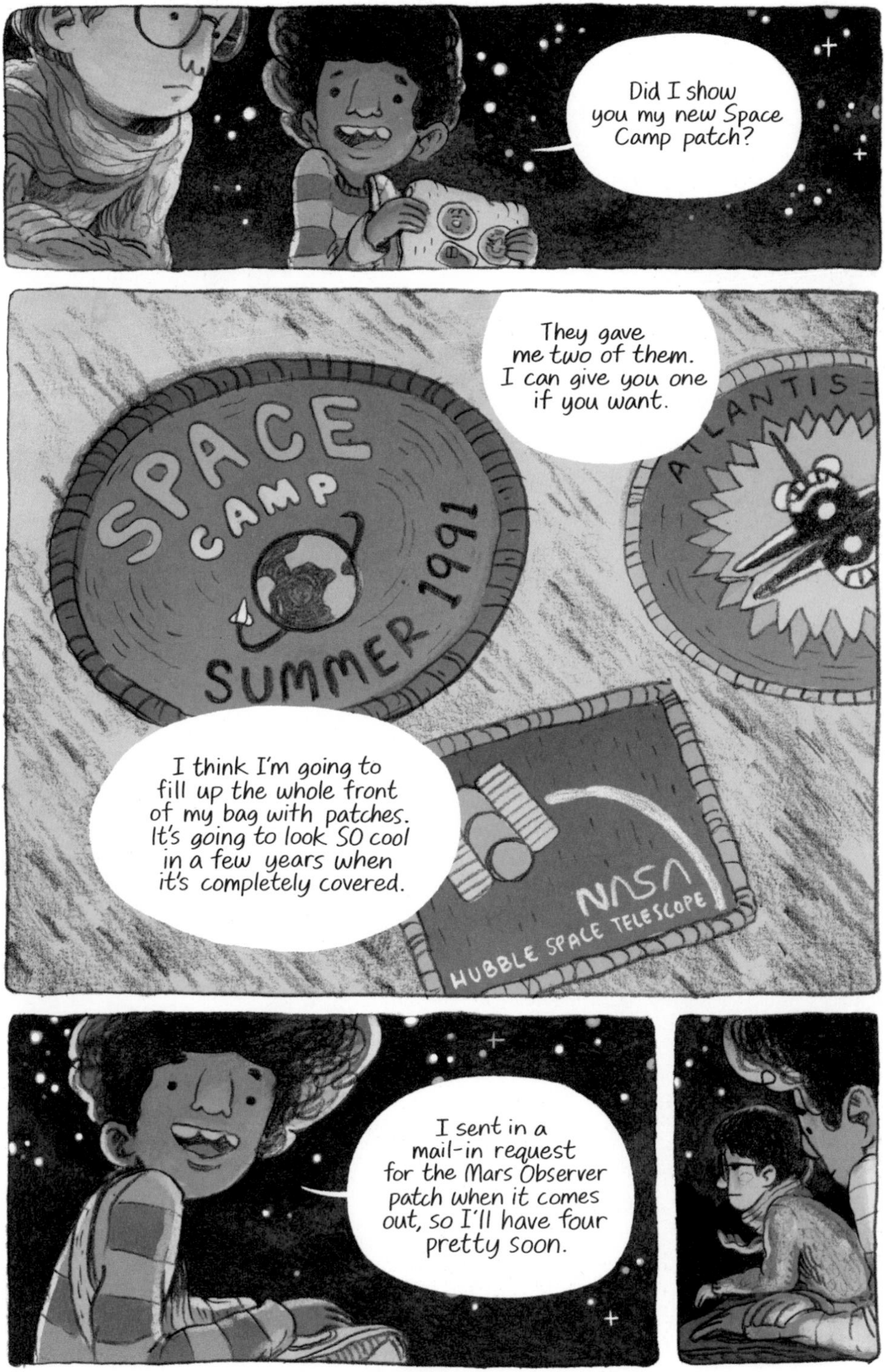
Did I show you my new Space Camp patch?
They gave me two of them. I can give you one if you want.
SPACE CAMP
SUMMER 1991
ATLANTIS
I think I'm going to fill up the whole front of my bag with patches. It's going to look SO cool in a few years when it's completely covered.
NASA
HUBBLE SPACE TELESCOPE
I sent in a mail-in request for the Mars Observer patch when it comes out, so I'll have four pretty soon.

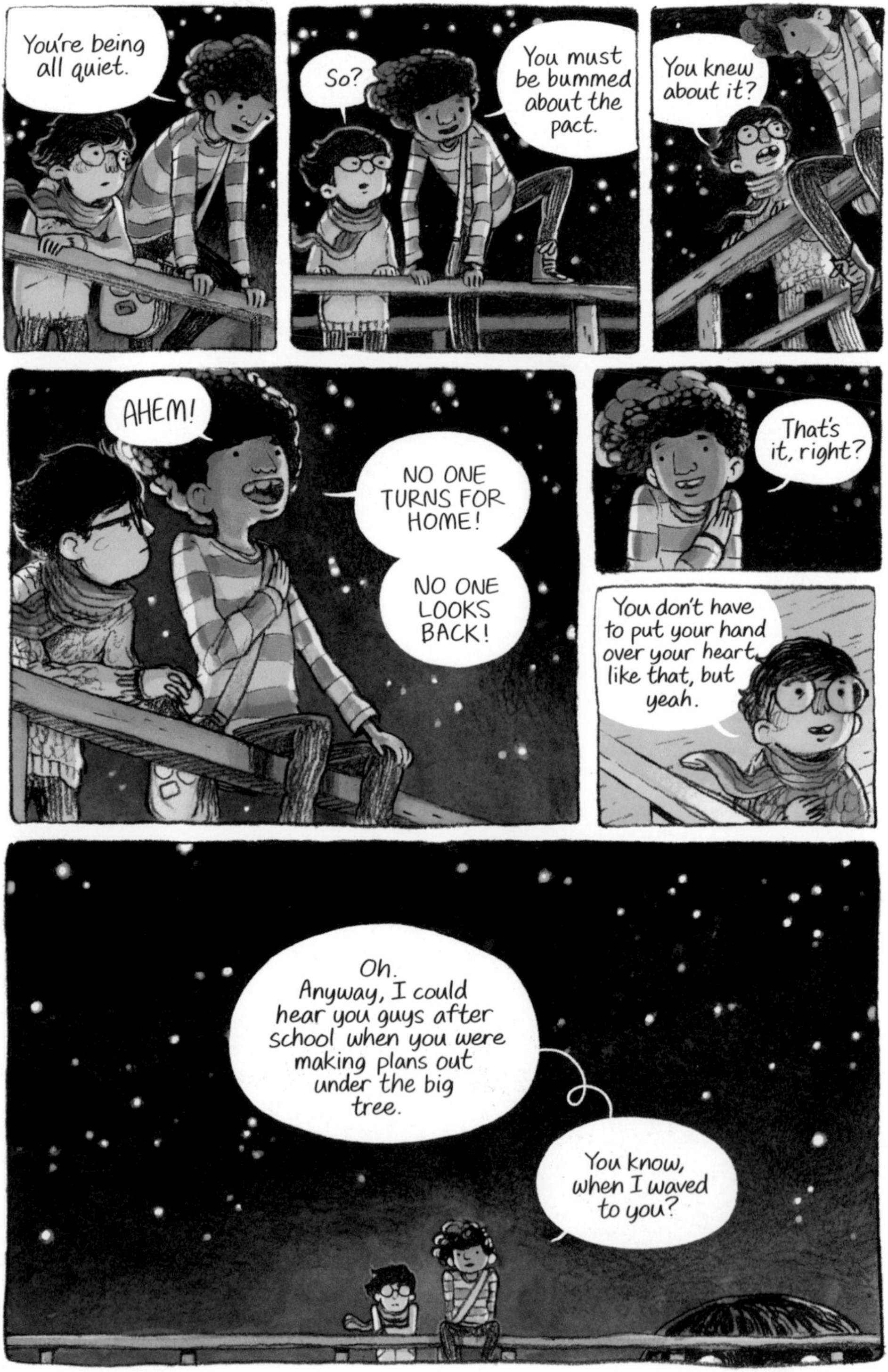

You're being all quiet.
So?
You must be bummed about the pact.
You knew about it?
AHEM!
NO ONE TURNS FOR HOME!
NO ONE LOOKS BACK!
That's it, right?
You don't have to put your hand over your heart like that, but yeah.
Oh. Anyway, I could hear you guys after school when you were making plans out under the big tree.
You know, when I waved to you?

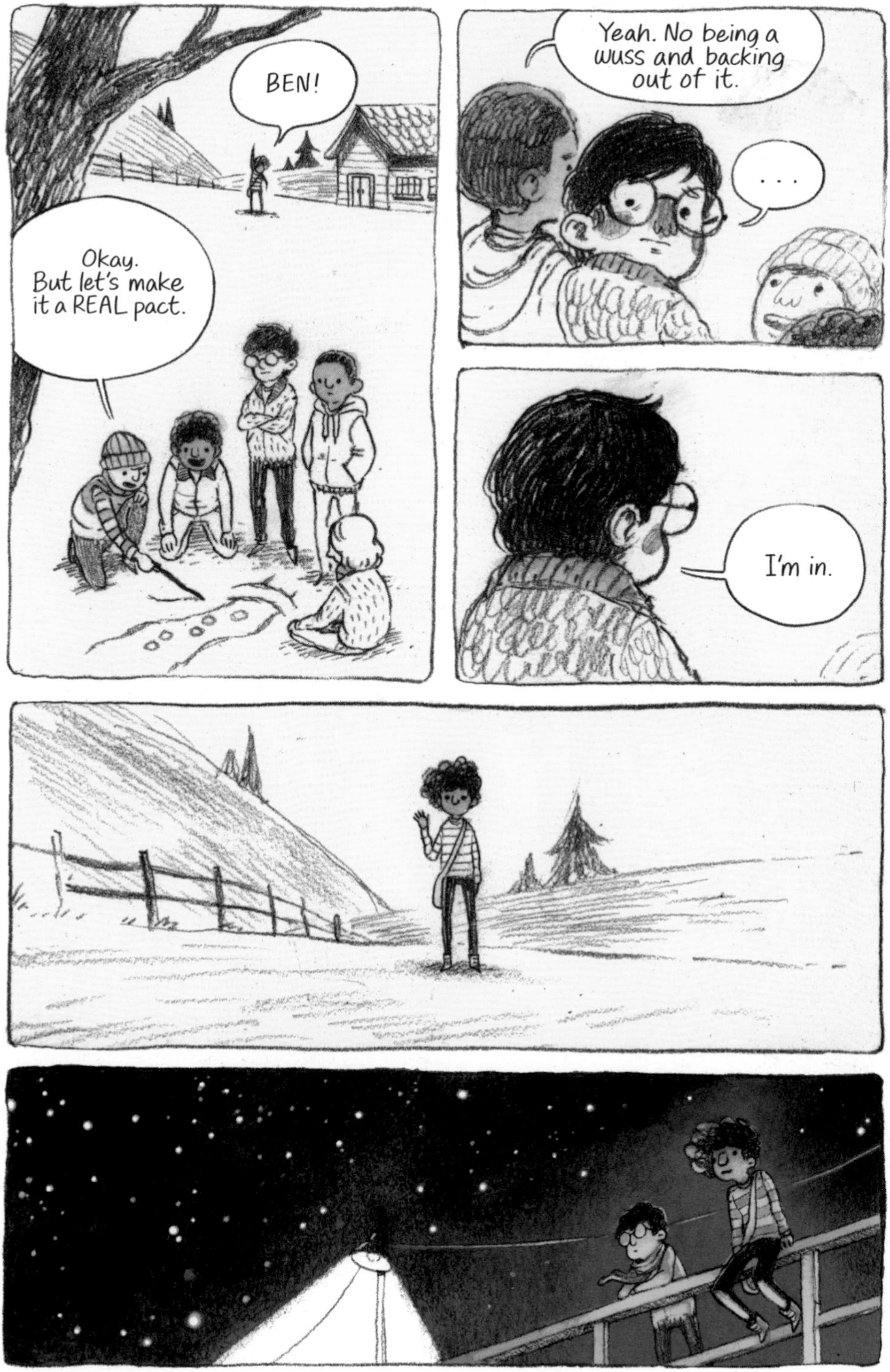
BEN!
Okay. But let's make it a REAL pact.
Yeah. No being a wuss and backing out of it.
. . .
I'm in.

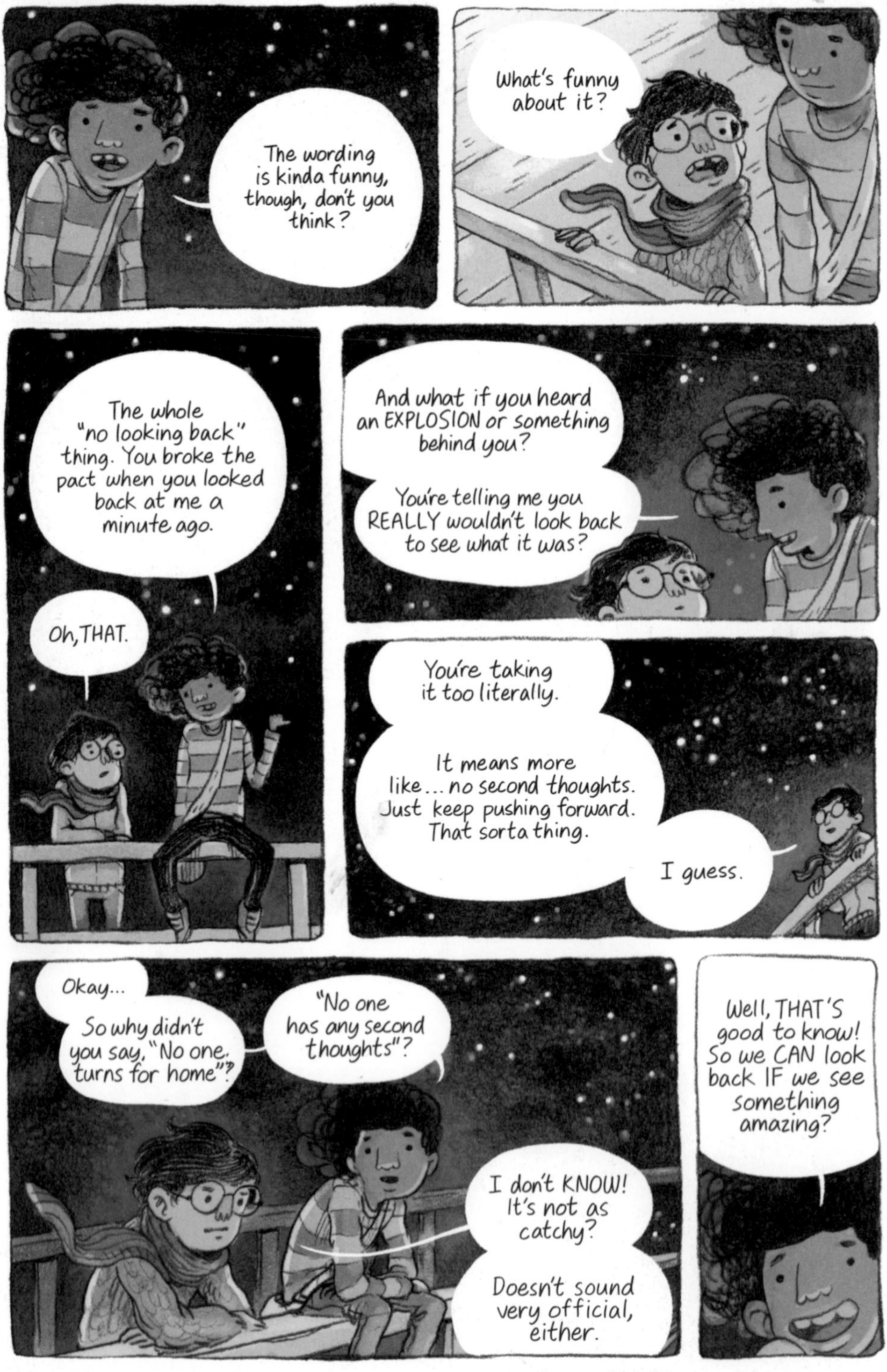
The wording is kinda funny, though, don't you think?
What's funny about it?
The whole "no looking back" thing. You broke the pact when you looked back at me a minute ago.
Oh, THAT.
And what if you heard an EXPLOSION or something behind you?
You're telling me you REALLY wouldn't look back to see what it was?
You're taking it too literally.
It means more like... no second thoughts. Just keep pushing forward. That sorta thing.
I guess.
Okay...
So why didn't you say, "No one turns for home"?
"No one has any second thoughts"?
I don't KNOW! It's not as catchy?
Doesn't sound very official, either.
Well, THAT'S good to know! So we CAN look back IF we see something amazing?

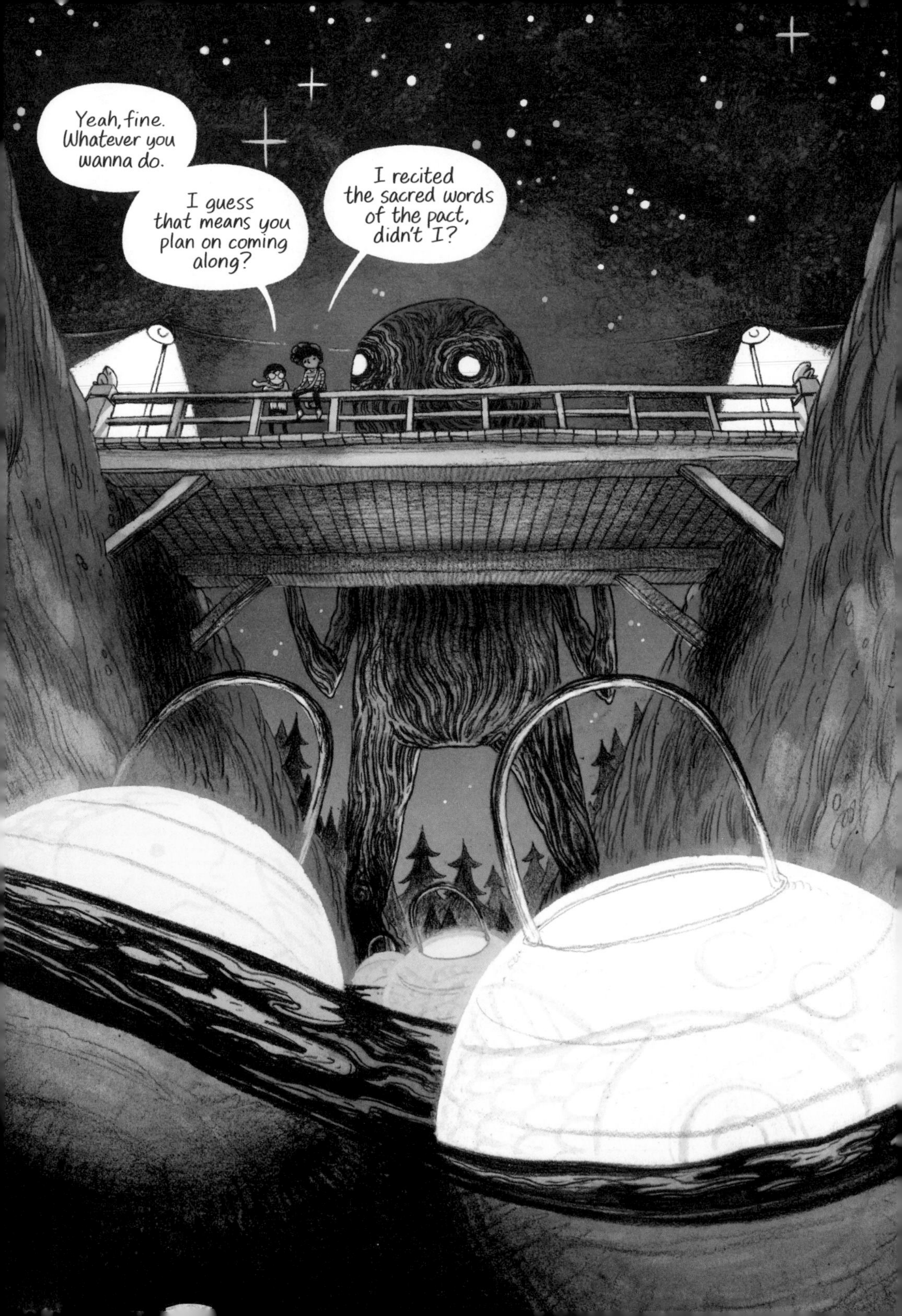
Yeah, fine. Whatever you wanna do.
I guess that means you plan on coming along?
I recited the sacred words of the pact, didn't I?

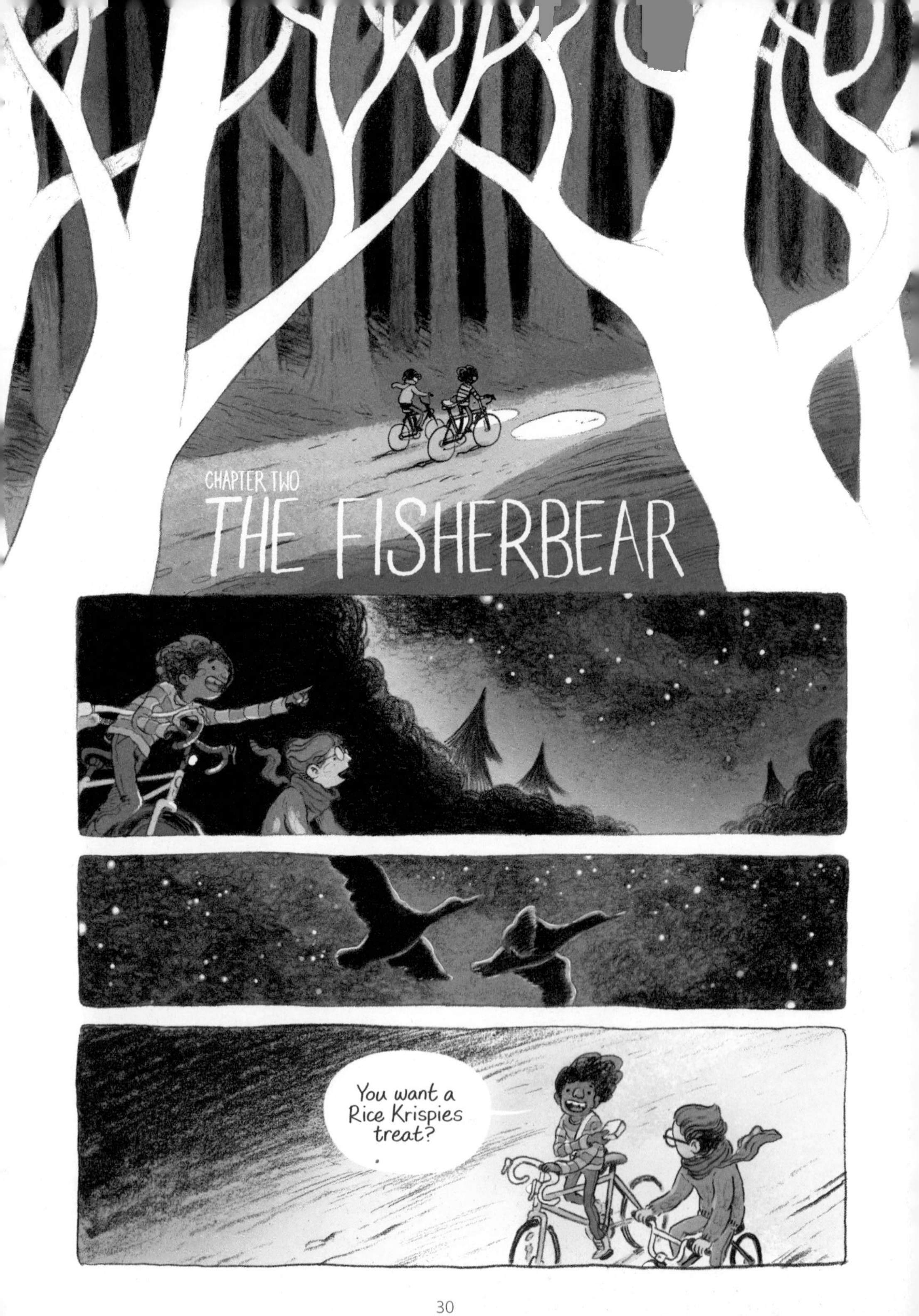
CHAPTER TWO
THE FISHERBEAR
You want a Rice Krispies treat?

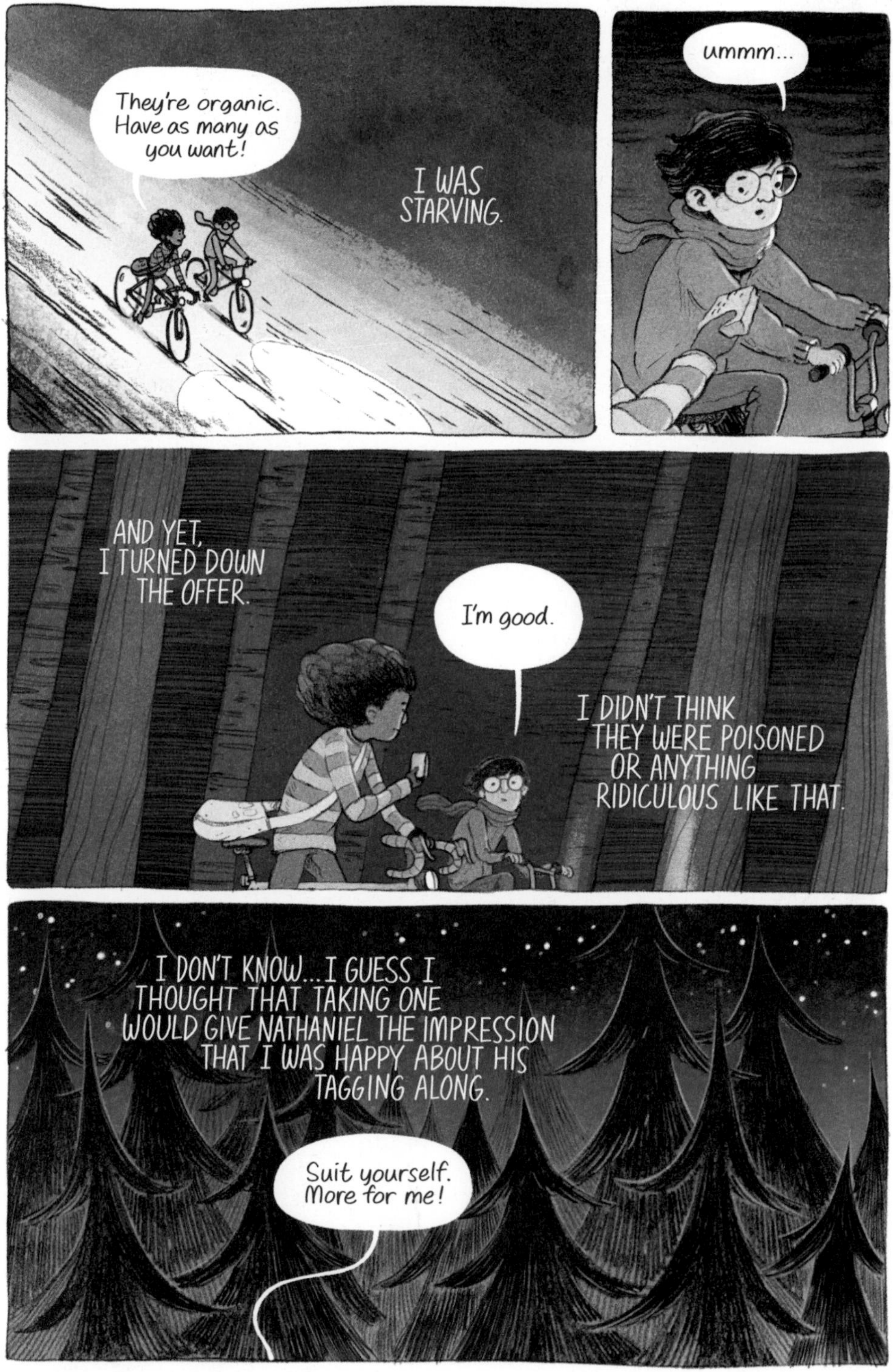
They're organic. Have as many as you want!
I WAS STARVING.
ummm...
AND YET, I TURNED DOWN THE OFFER.
I'm good.
I DIDN'T THINK THEY WERE POISONED OR ANYTHING RIDICULOUS LIKE THAT.
I DON'T KNOW...I GUESS I THOUGHT THAT TAKING ONE WOULD GIVE NATHANIEL THE IMPRESSION THAT I WAS HAPPY ABOUT HIS TAGGING ALONG.
Suit yourself. More for me!

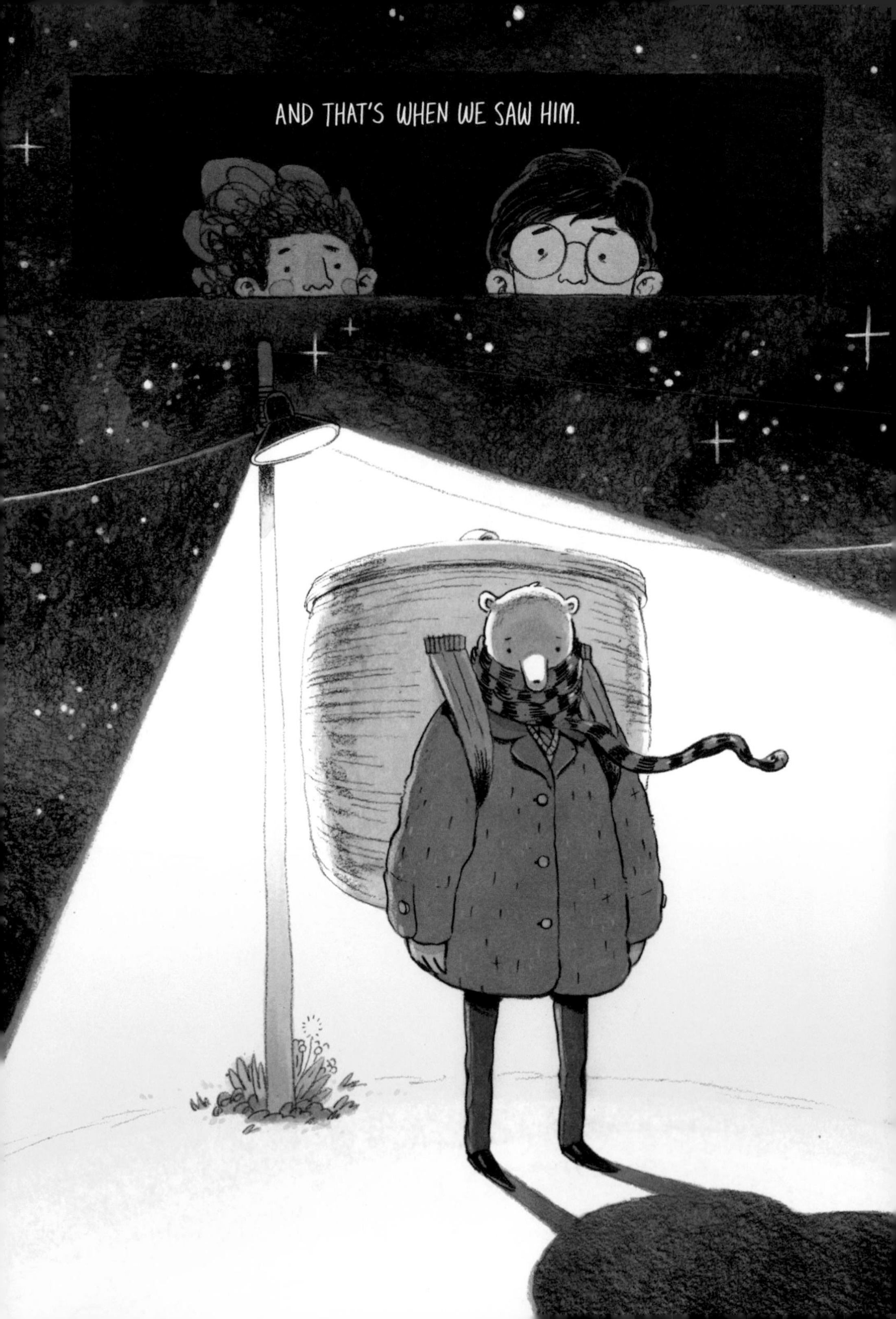
AND THAT'S WHEN WE SAW HIM.

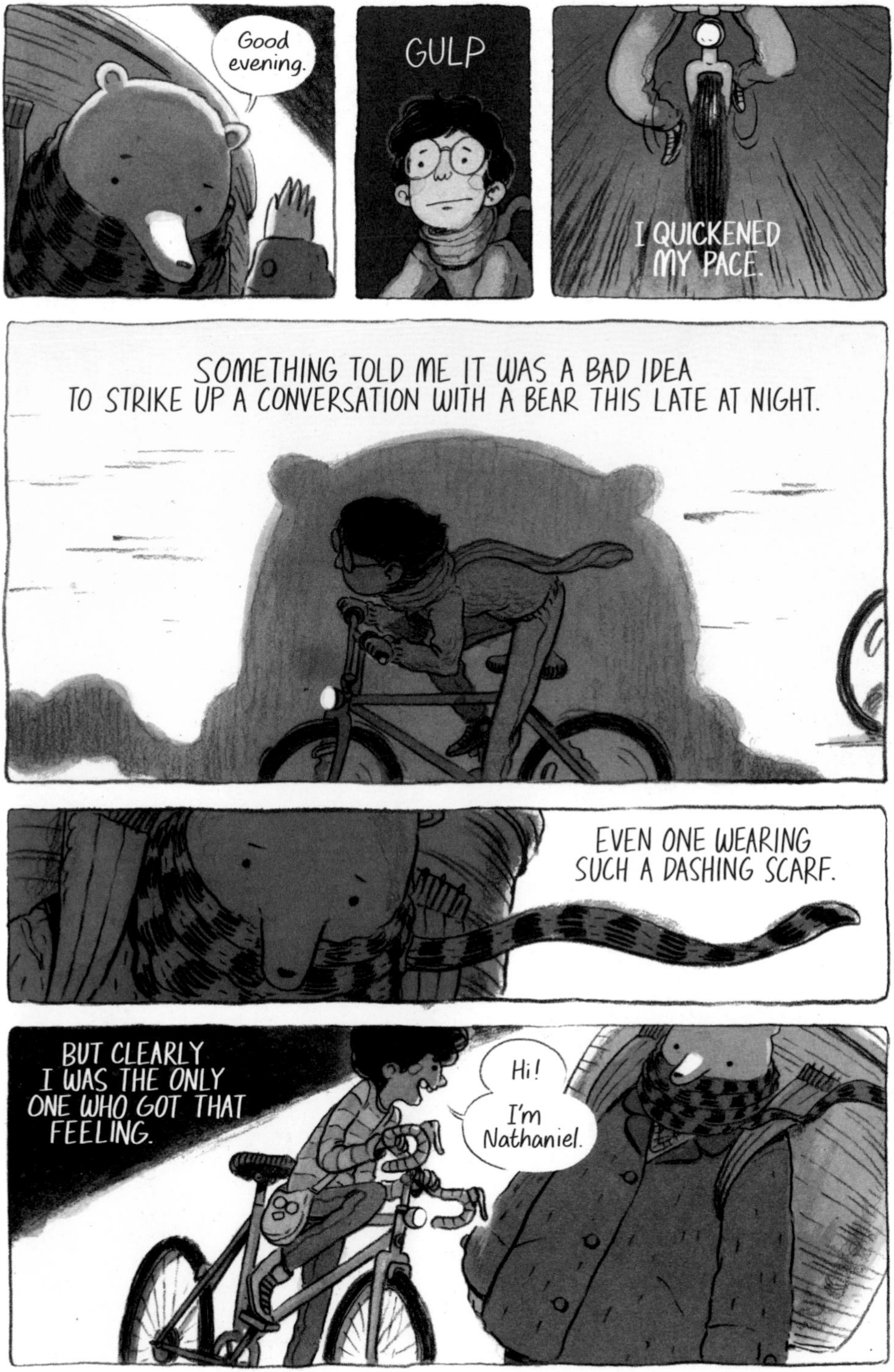
Good evening.
GULP
I QUICKENED MY PACE.
SOMETHING TOLD ME IT WAS A BAD IDEA TO STRIKE UP A CONVERSATION WITH A BEAR THIS LATE AT NIGHT.
EVEN ONE WEARING SUCH A DASHING SCARF.
BUT CLEARLY I WAS THE ONLY ONE WHO GOT THAT FEELING.
Hi!
I'm Nathaniel.

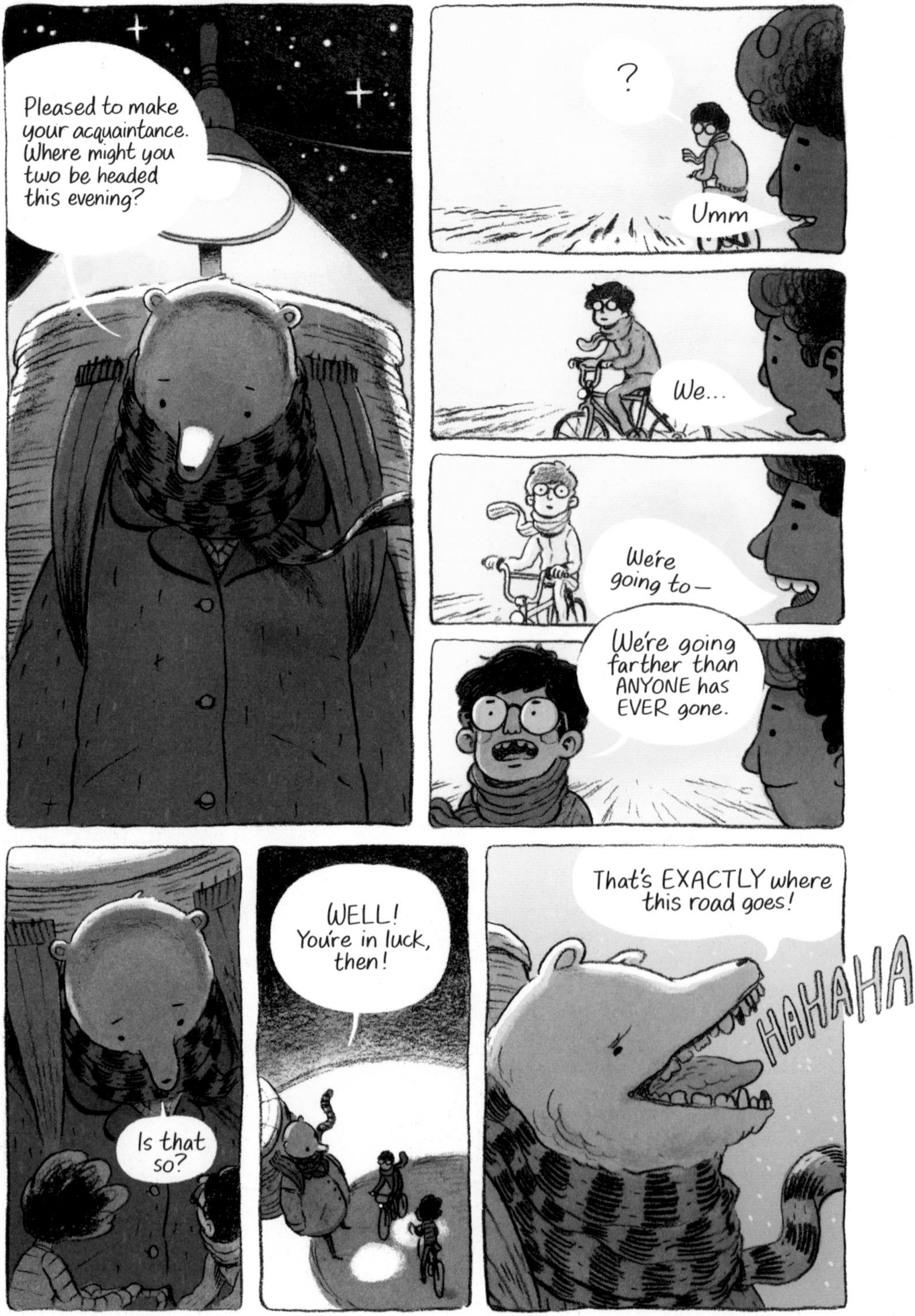
Pleased to make your acquaintance. Where might you two be headed this evening?
?
Umm
We...
We're going to—
We're going farther than ANYONE has EVER gone.
Is that so?
WELL! You're in luck, then!
That's EXACTLY where this road goes!
HAHAHA

...
So...
what's with the big basket?
Hm?
OH! You mean THIS old thing?
Is it not OBVIOUS?
A TERRIFYING THOUGHT CAME TO ME AT THAT MOMENT.
WHAT IF...
WHAT IF...

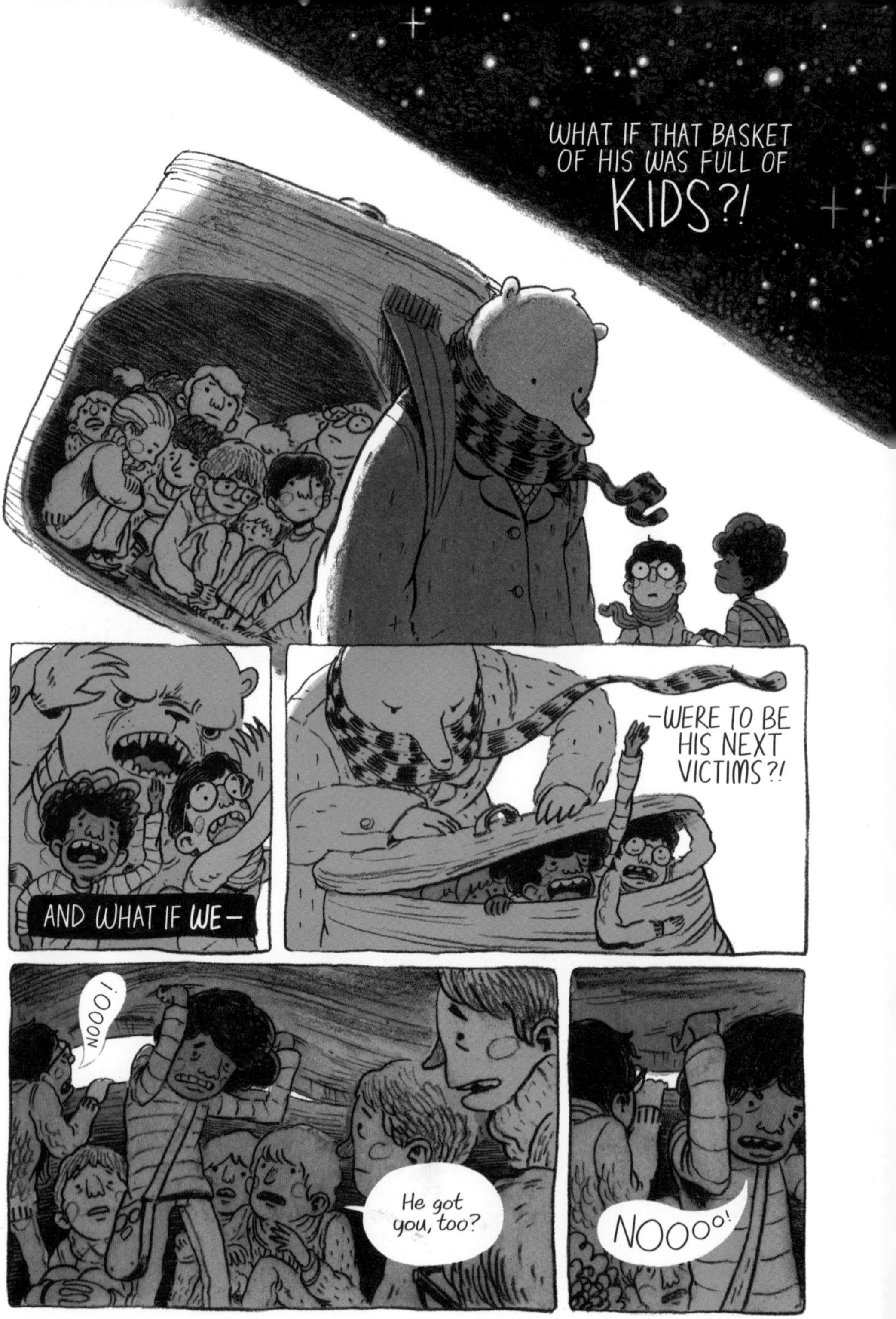

WHAT IF THAT BASKET OF HIS WAS FULL OF KIDS?!
AND WHAT IF WE—
—WERE TO BE HIS NEXT VICTIMS?!
NOOO!
He got you, too?
NOOOO!

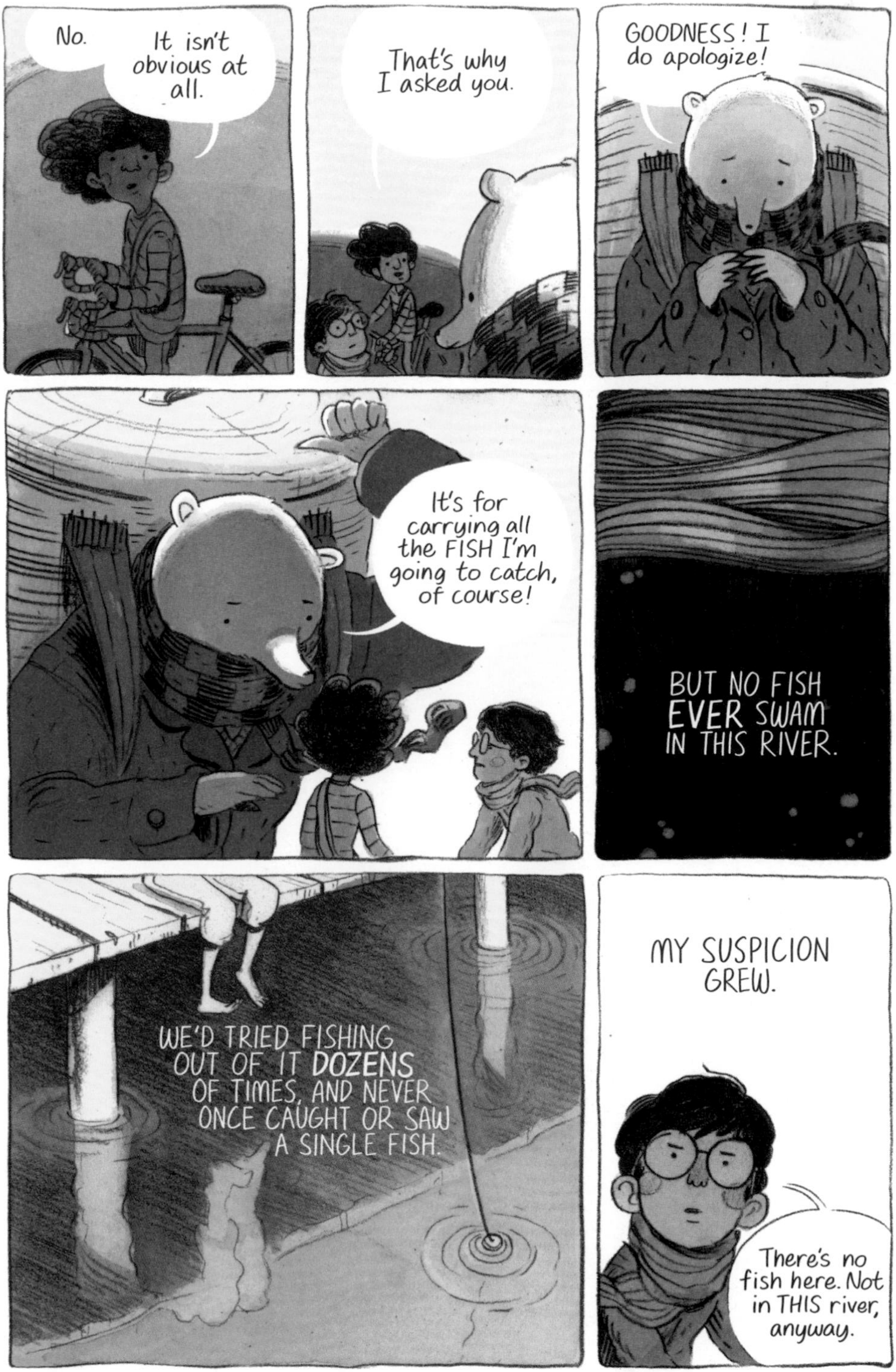
No.
It isn't obvious at all.
That's why I asked you.
GOODNESS! I do apologize!
It's for carrying all the FISH I'm going to catch, of course!
BUT NO FISH EVER SWAM IN THIS RIVER.
WE'D TRIED FISHING OUT OF IT DOZENS OF TIMES, AND NEVER ONCE CAUGHT OR SAW A SINGLE FISH.
MY SUSPICION GREW.
There's no fish here. Not in THIS river, anyway.

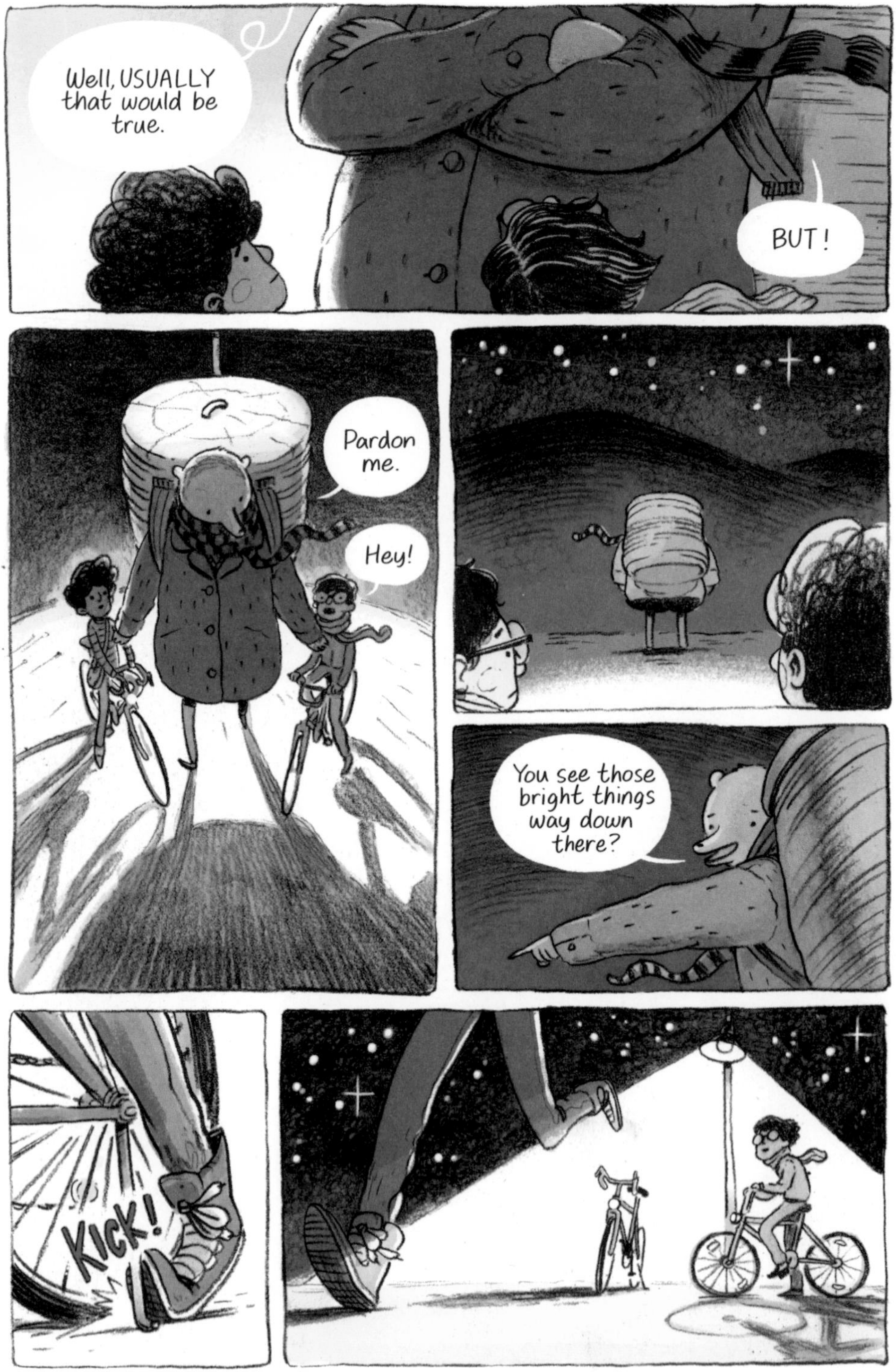
Well, USUALLY that would be true.
BUT!
Pardon me.
Hey!
You see those bright things way down there?
KICK!

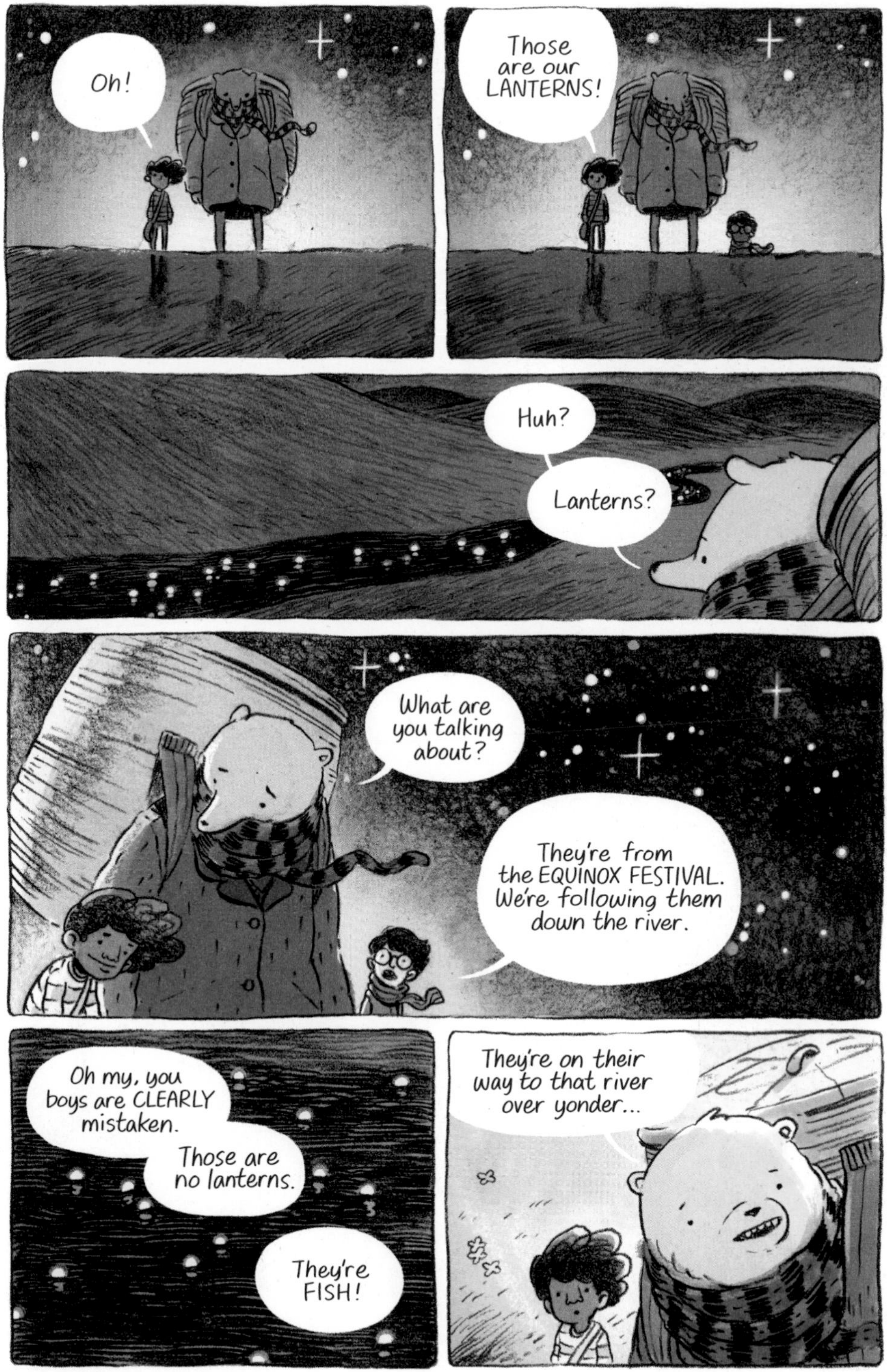
Oh!
Those are our LANTERNS!
Huh?
Lanterns?
What are you talking about?
They're from the EQUINOX FESTIVAL. We're following them down the river.
Oh my, you boys are CLEARLY mistaken.
Those are no lanterns.
They're FISH!
They're on their way to that river over yonder...

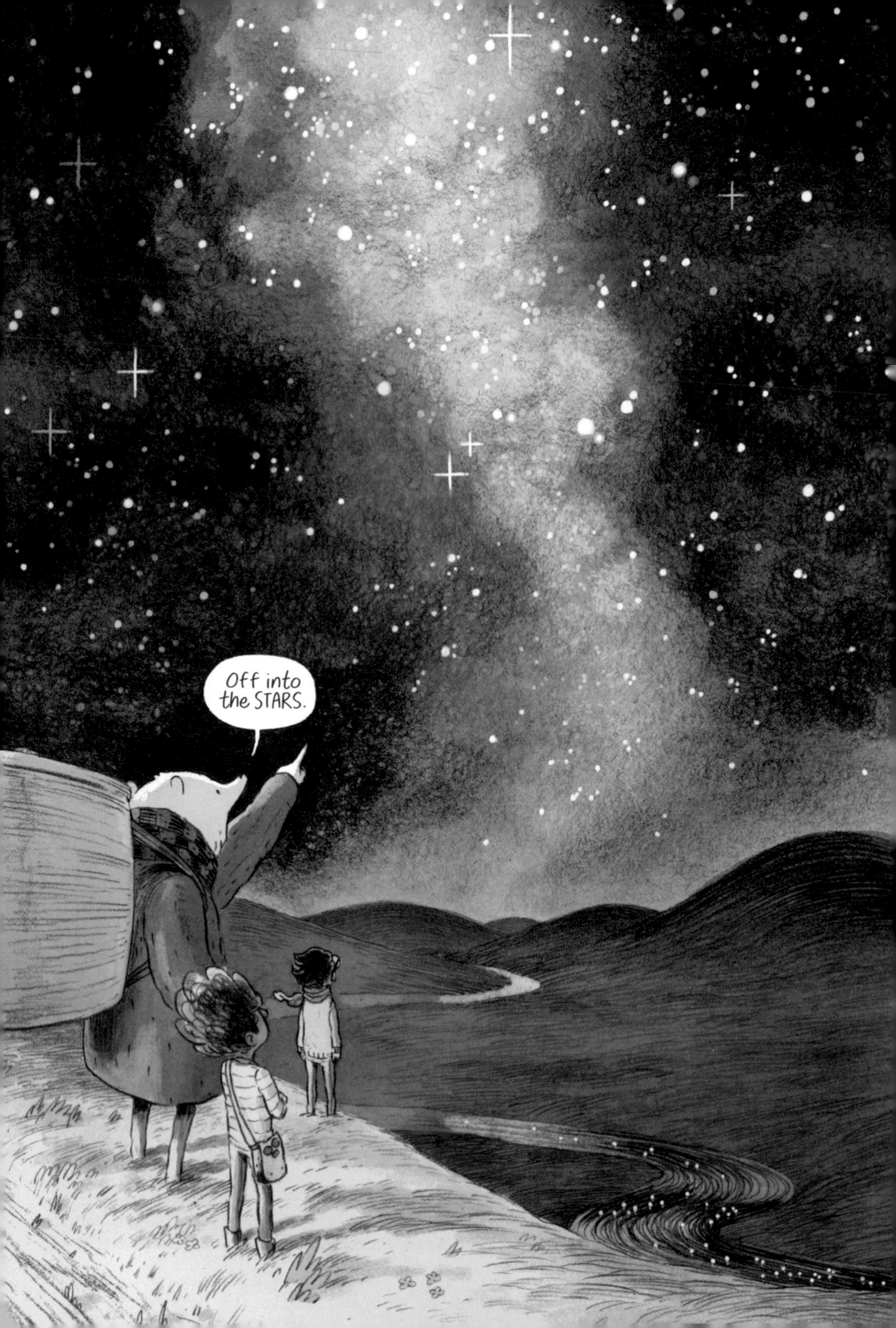
Off into the STARS.

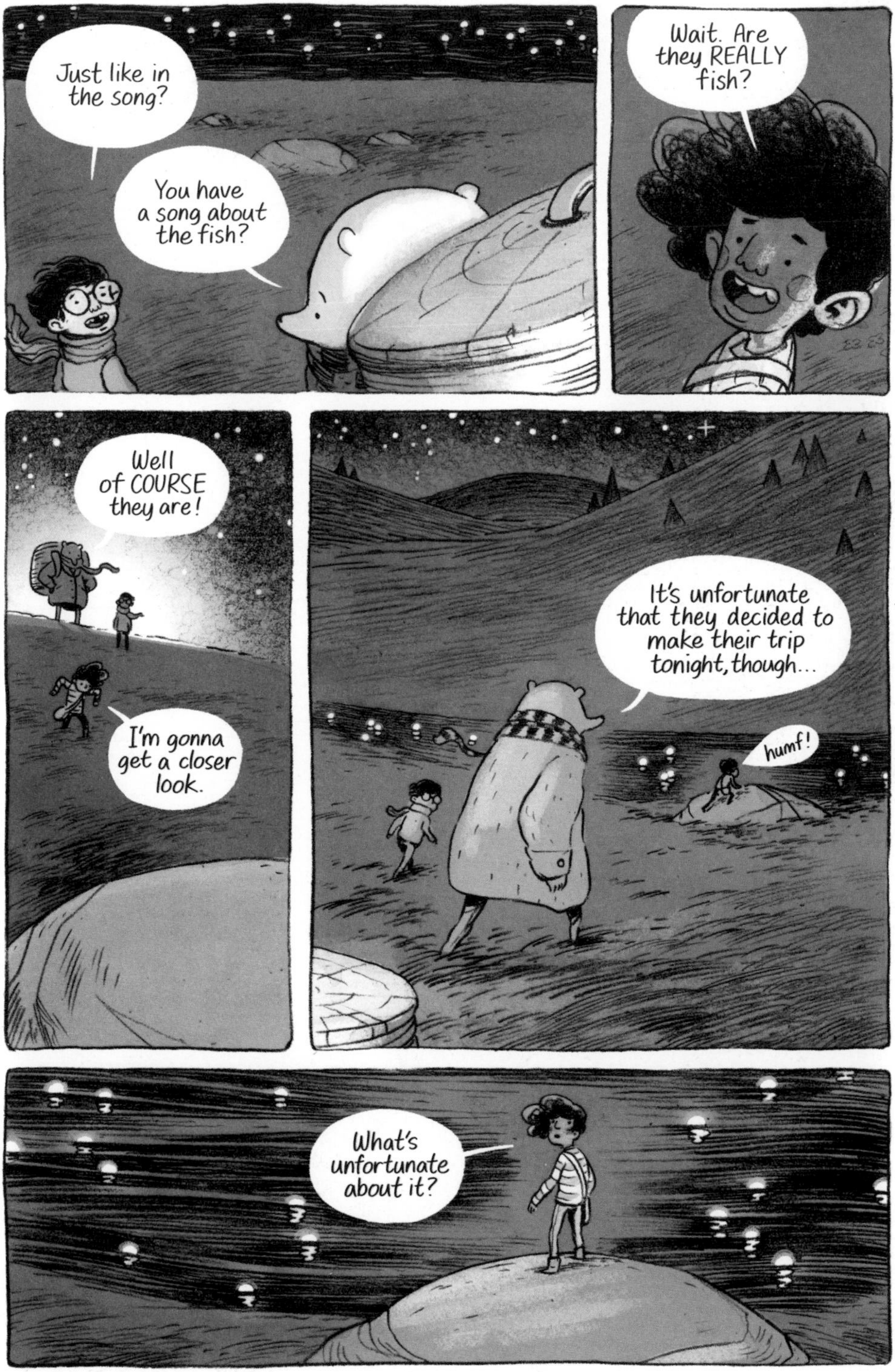
Just like in the song?
You have a song about the fish?
Wait. Are they REALLY fish?
Well of COURSE they are!
I'm gonna get a closer look.
It's unfortunate that they decided to make their trip tonight, though...
humf!
What's unfortunate about it?

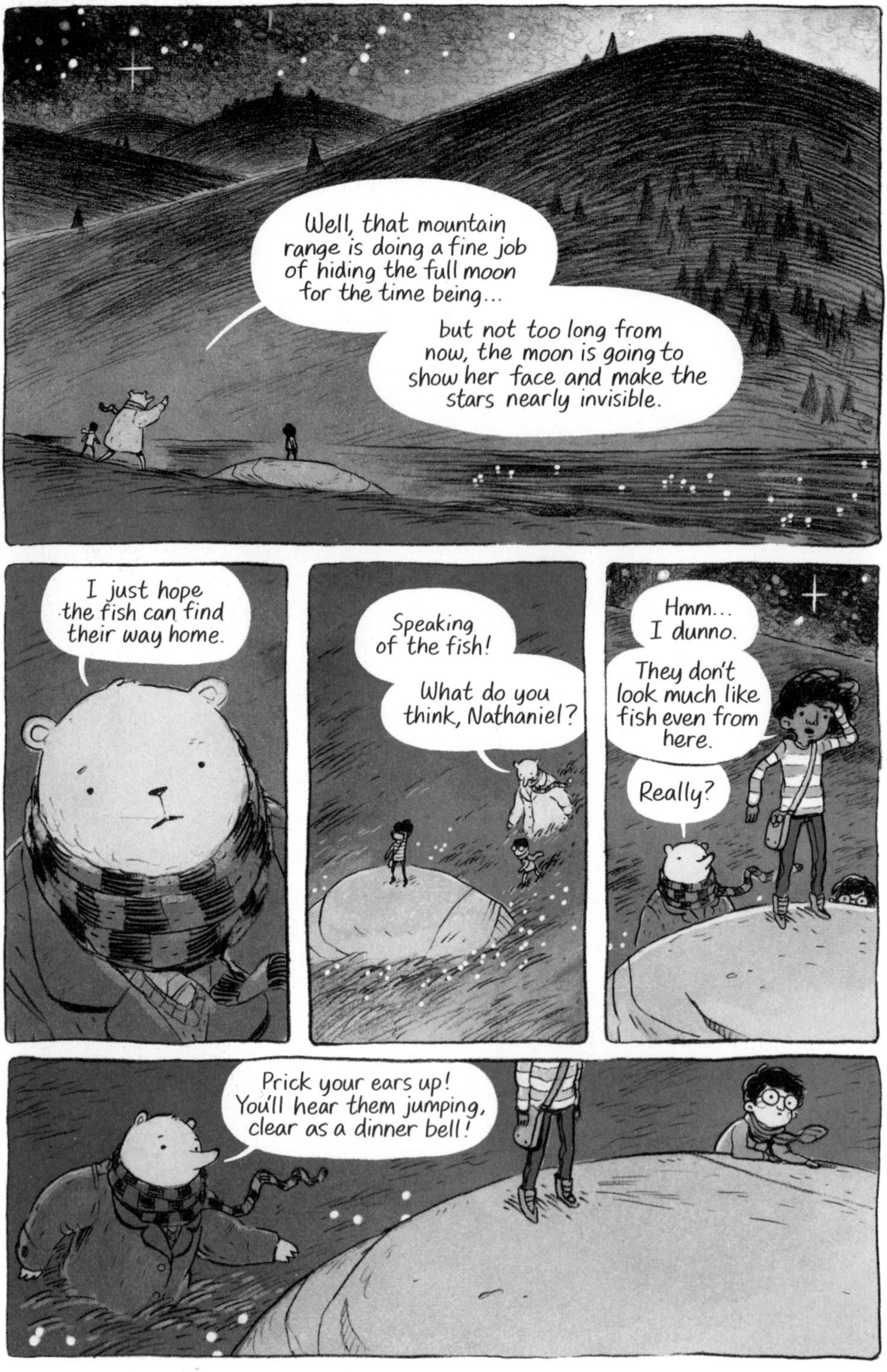
Well, that mountain range is doing a fine job of hiding the full moon for the time being...
but not too long from now, the moon is going to show her face and make the stars nearly invisible.
I just hope the fish can find their way home.
Speaking of the fish!
What do you think, Nathaniel?
Hmm... I dunno.
They don't look much like fish even from here.
Really?
Prick your ears up! You'll hear them jumping, clear as a dinner bell!

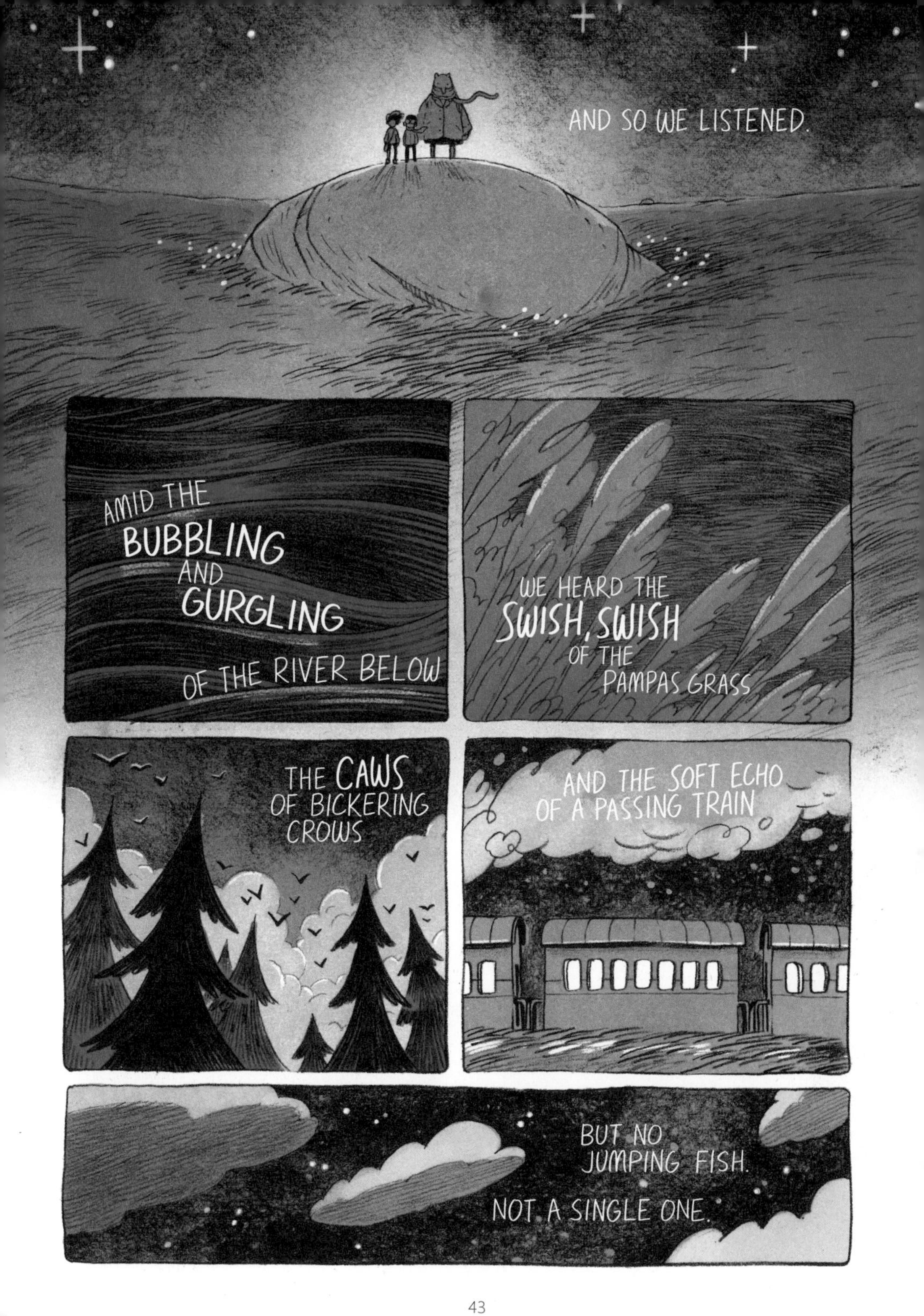
AND SO WE LISTENED.
AMID THE BUBBLING AND GURGLING OF THE RIVER BELOW
WE HEARD THE SWISH, SWISH OF THE PAMPAS GRASS
THE CAWS OF BICKERING CROWS
AND THE SOFT ECHO OF A PASSING TRAIN
BUT NO JUMPING FISH.
NOT A SINGLE ONE.

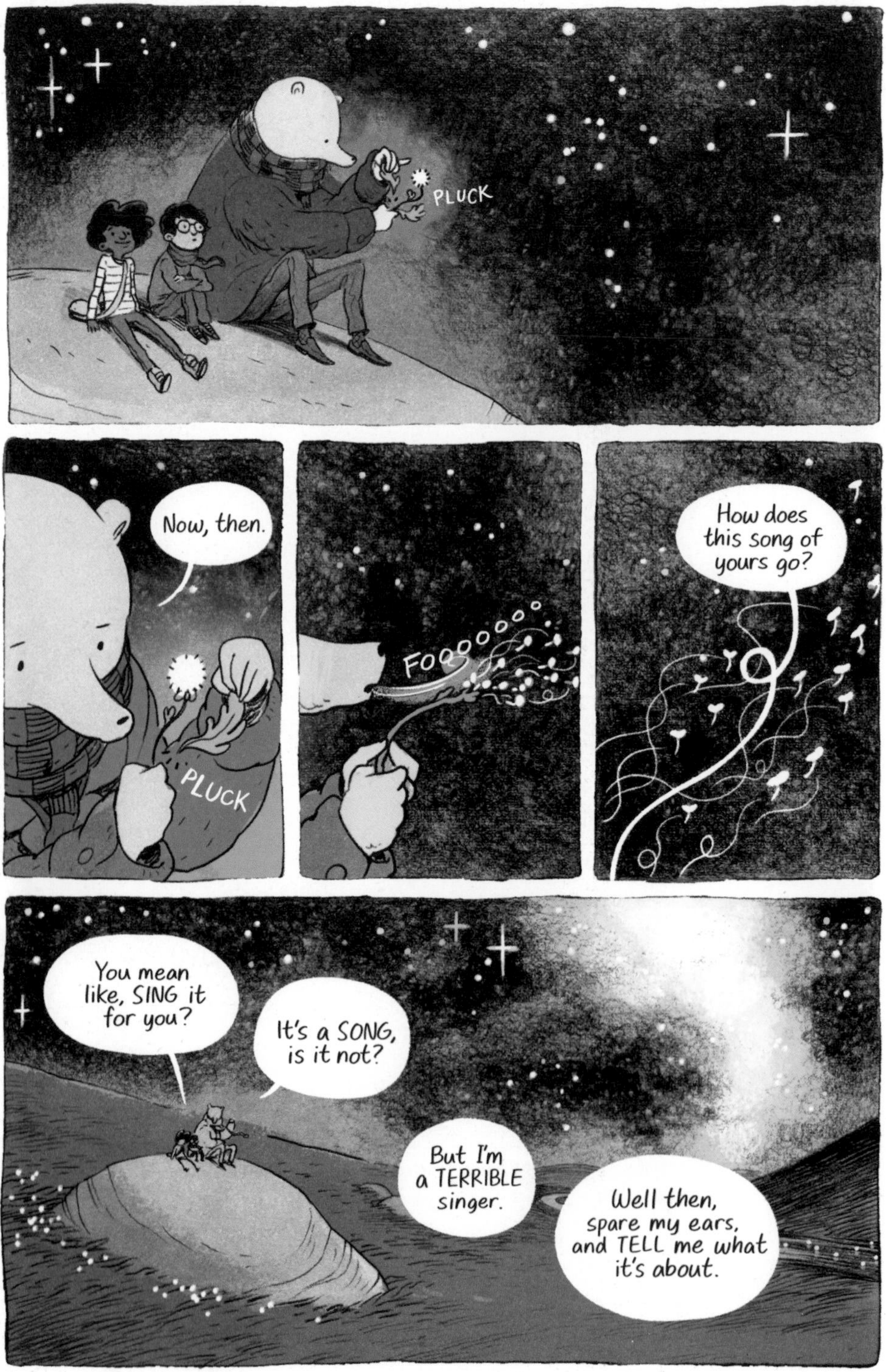
PLUCK
Now, then.
PLUCK
FOOOOOOOO
How does this song of yours go?
You mean like, SING it for you?
It's a SONG, is it not?
But I'm a TERRIBLE singer.
Well then, spare my ears, and TELL me what it's about.

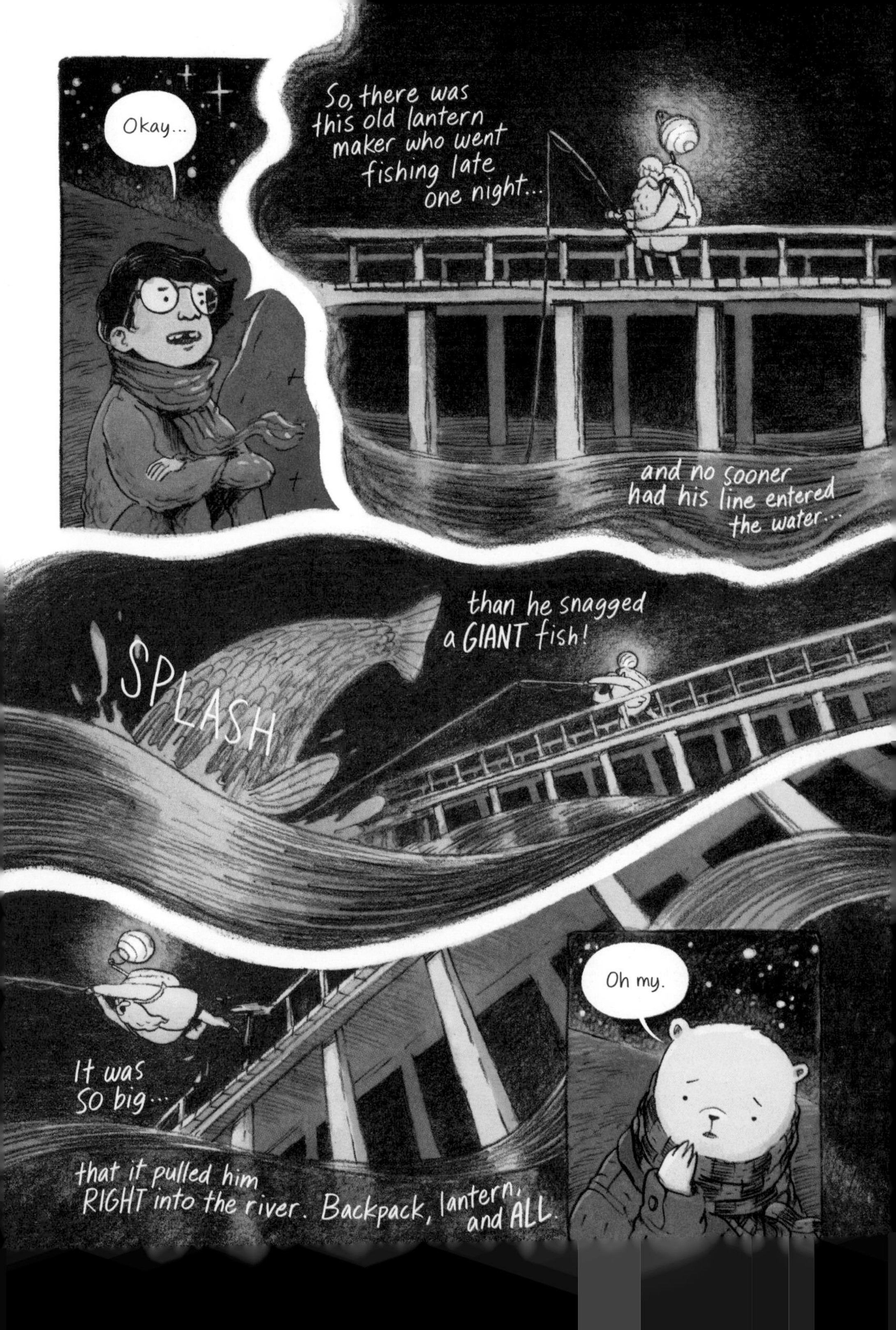
Okay...
So, there was this old lantern maker who went fishing late one night...
and no sooner had his line entered the water...
than he snagged a GIANT fish!
SPLASH
It was so big...
that it pulled him RIGHT into the river. Backpack, lantern, and ALL.
Oh my.

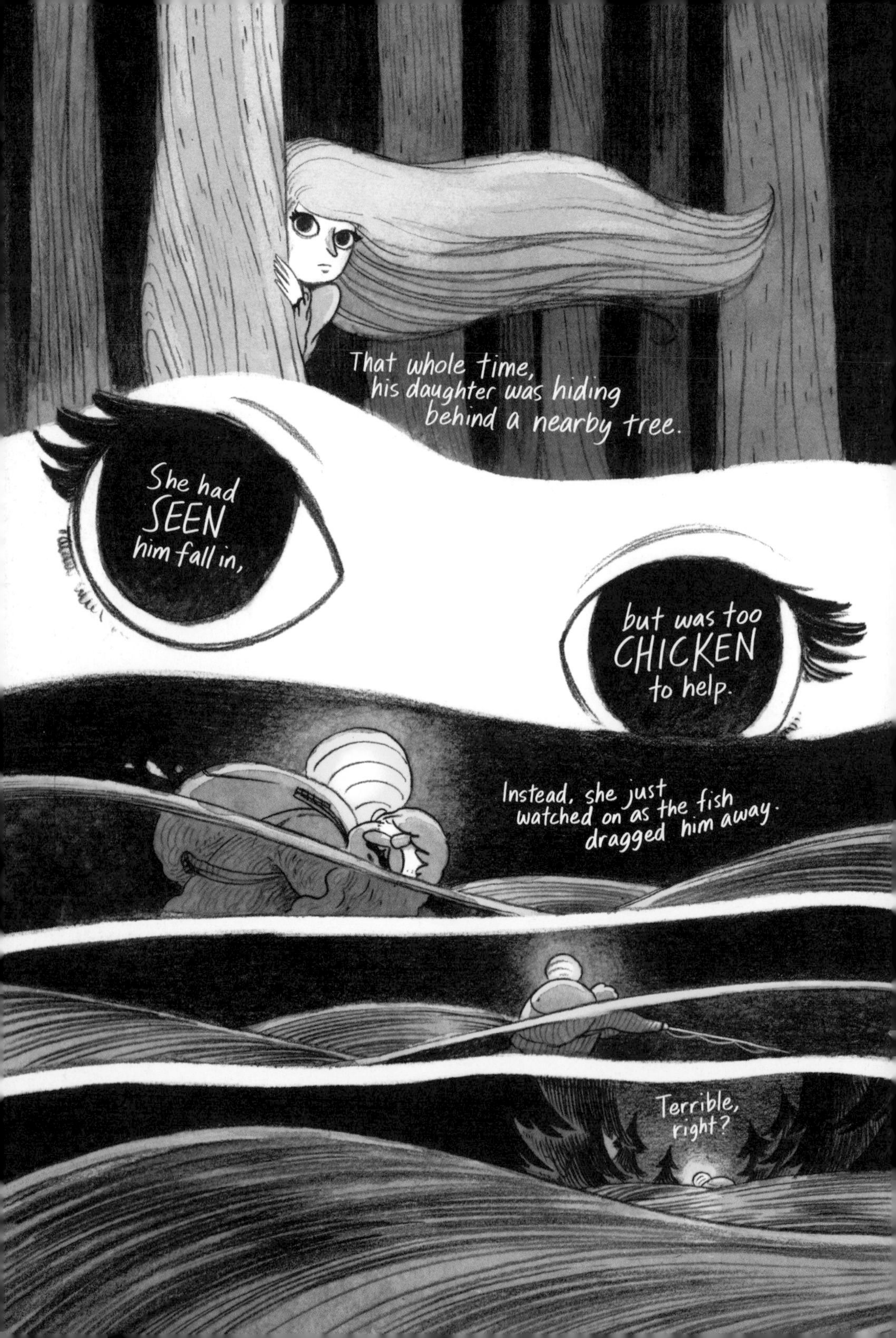
That whole time, his daughter was hiding behind a nearby tree.
She had SEEN him fall in,
but was too CHICKEN to help.
Instead, she just watched on as the fish dragged him away.
Terrible, right?

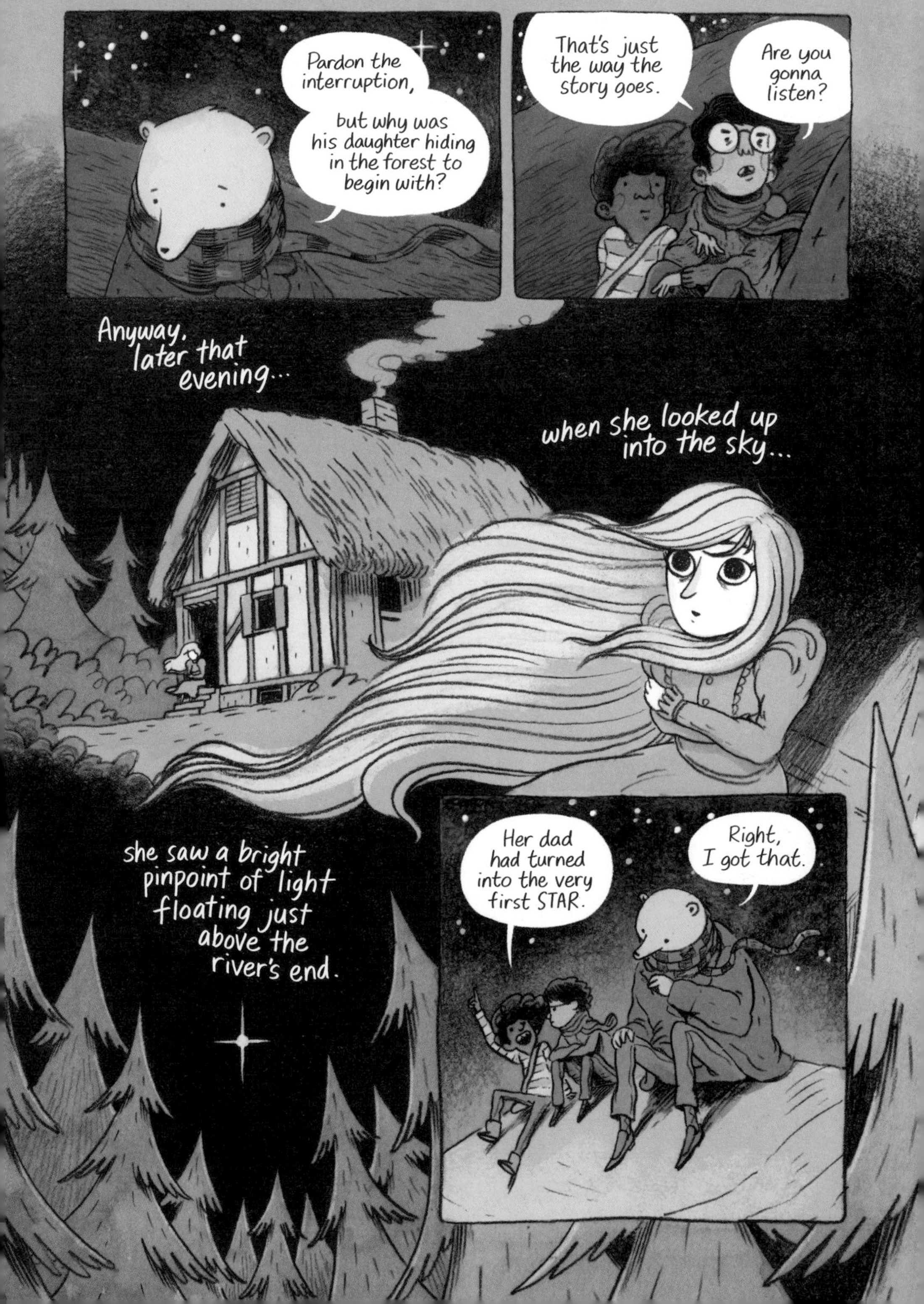

Pardon the interruption,
but why was his daughter hiding in the forest to begin with?
That's just the way the story goes.
Are you gonna listen?
Anyway, later that evening...
when she looked up into the sky...
she saw a bright pinpoint of light floating just above the river's end.
Her dad had turned into the very first STAR.
Right, I got that.

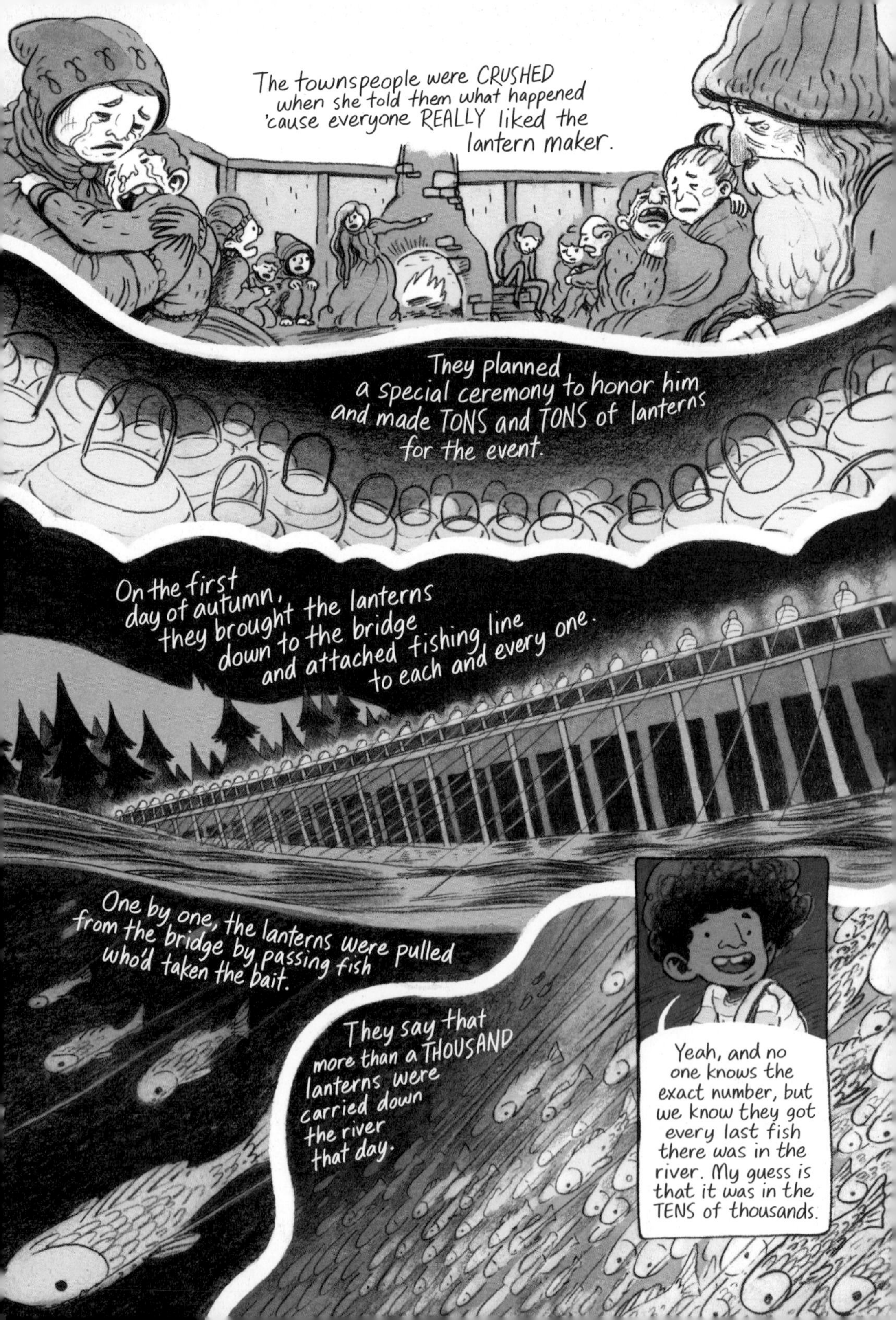
The townspeople were CRUSHED when she told them what happened 'cause everyone REALLY liked the lantern maker.
They planned a special ceremony to honor him and made TONS and TONS of lanterns for the event.
On the first day of autumn, they brought the lanterns down to the bridge and attached fishing line to each and every one.
One by one, the lanterns were pulled from the bridge by passing fish who'd taken the bait.
They say that more than a THOUSAND lanterns were carried down the river that day.
Yeah, and no one knows the exact number, but we know they got every last fish there was in the river. My guess is that it was in the TENS of thousands.

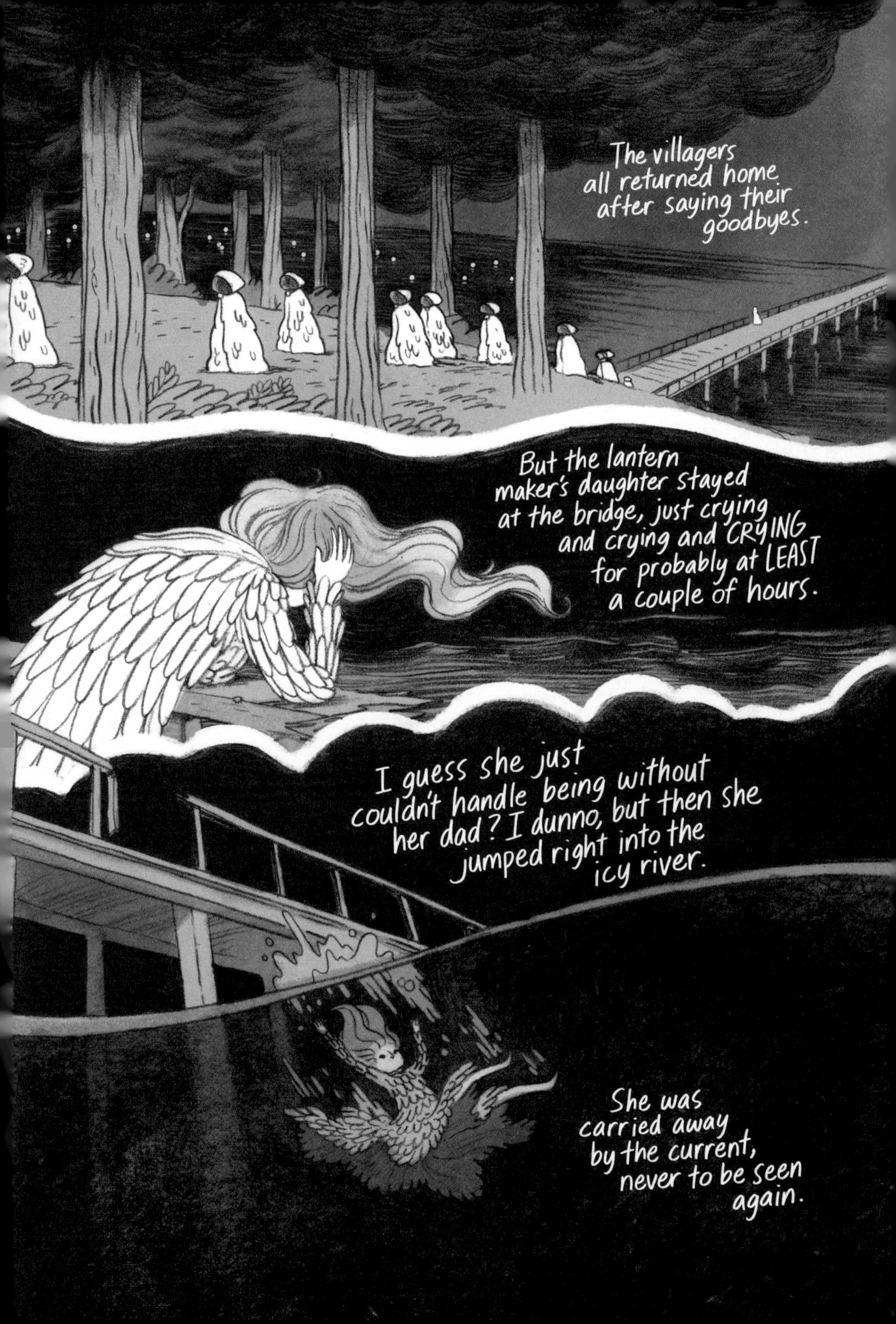
The villagers all returned home after saying their goodbyes.
But the lantern maker's daughter stayed at the bridge, just crying and crying and CRYING for probably at LEAST a couple of hours.
I guess she just couldn't handle being without her dad? I dunno, but then she jumped right into the icy river.
She was carried away by the current, never to be seen again.

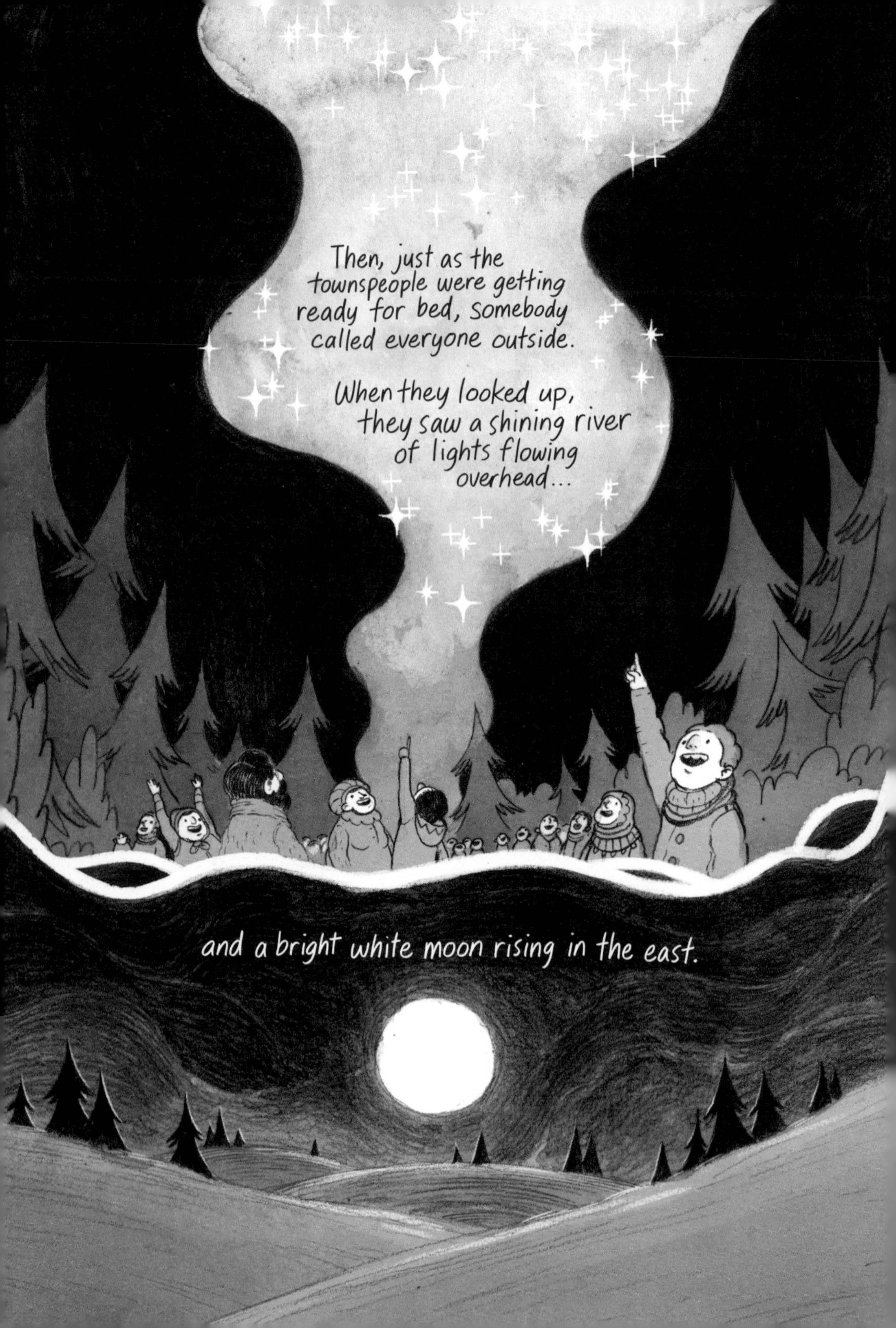
Then, just as the townspeople were getting ready for bed, somebody called everyone outside.
When they looked up, they saw a shining river of lights flowing overhead...
and a bright white moon rising in the east.

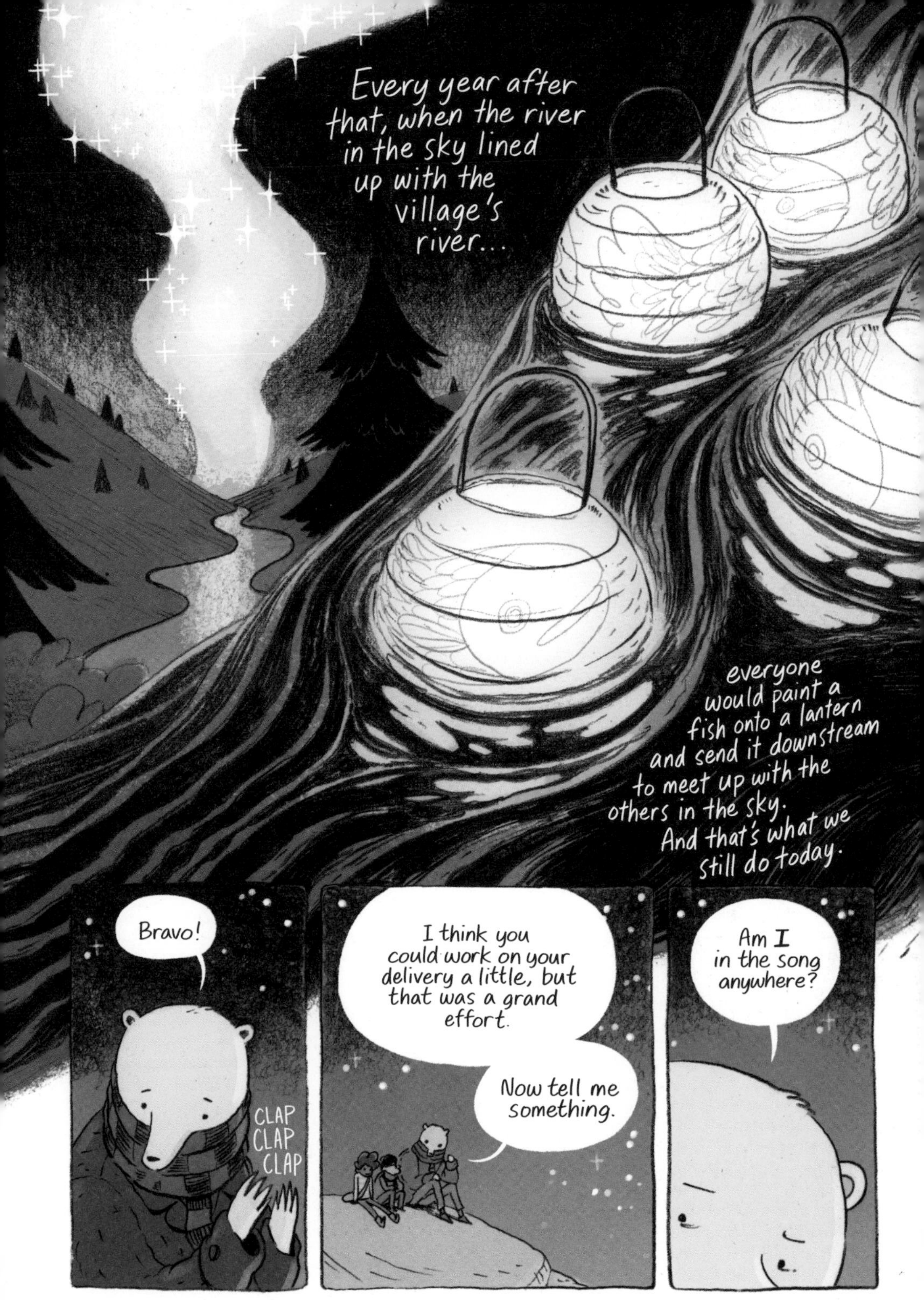
Every year after that, when the river in the sky lined up with the village's river...
everyone would paint a fish onto a lantern and send it downstream to meet up with the others in the sky. And that's what we still do today.
Bravo!
CLAP CLAP CLAP
I think you could work on your delivery a little, but that was a grand effort.
Now tell me something.
Am I in the song anywhere?

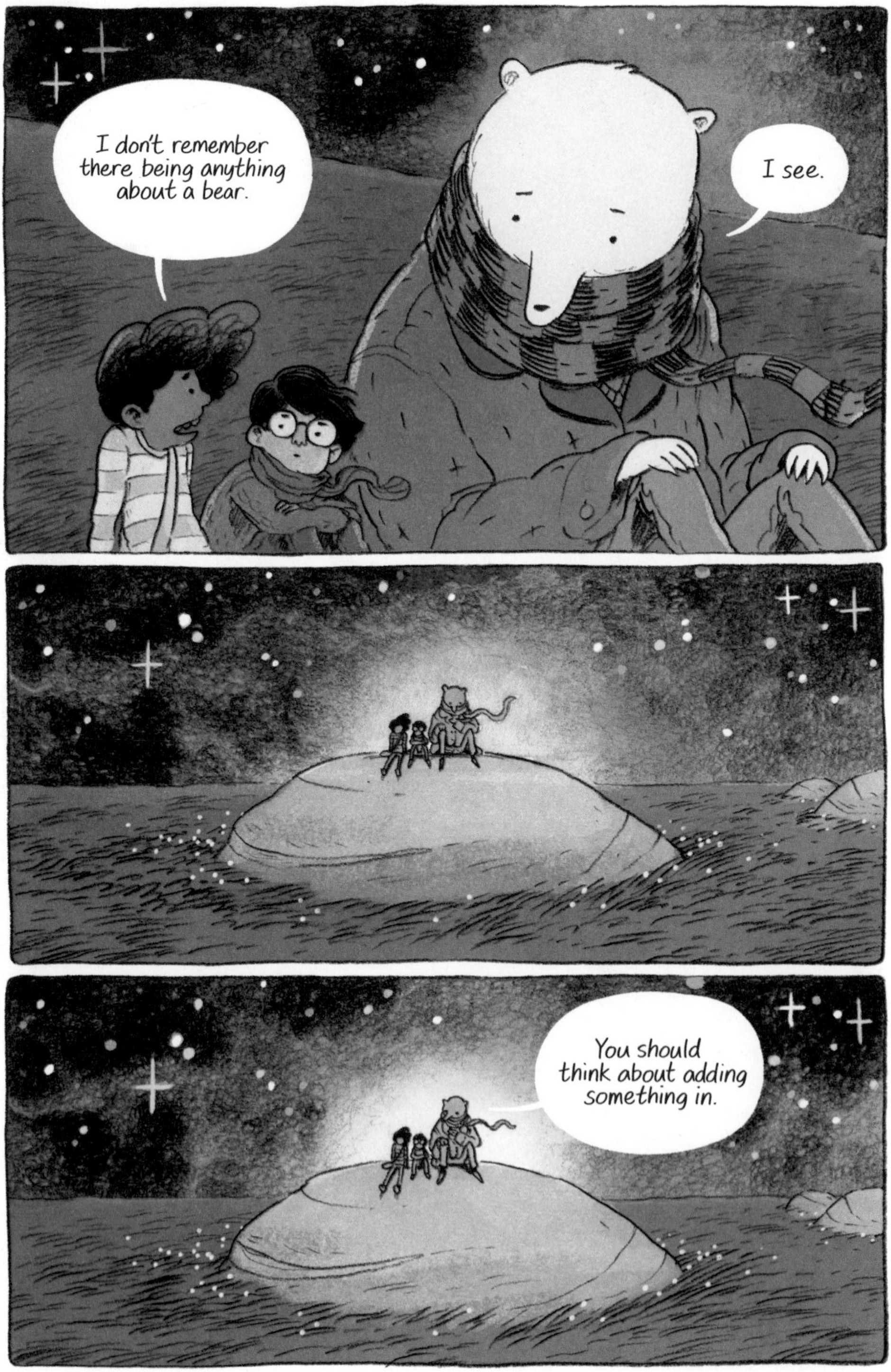
I don't remember there being anything about a bear.
I see.
You should think about adding something in.

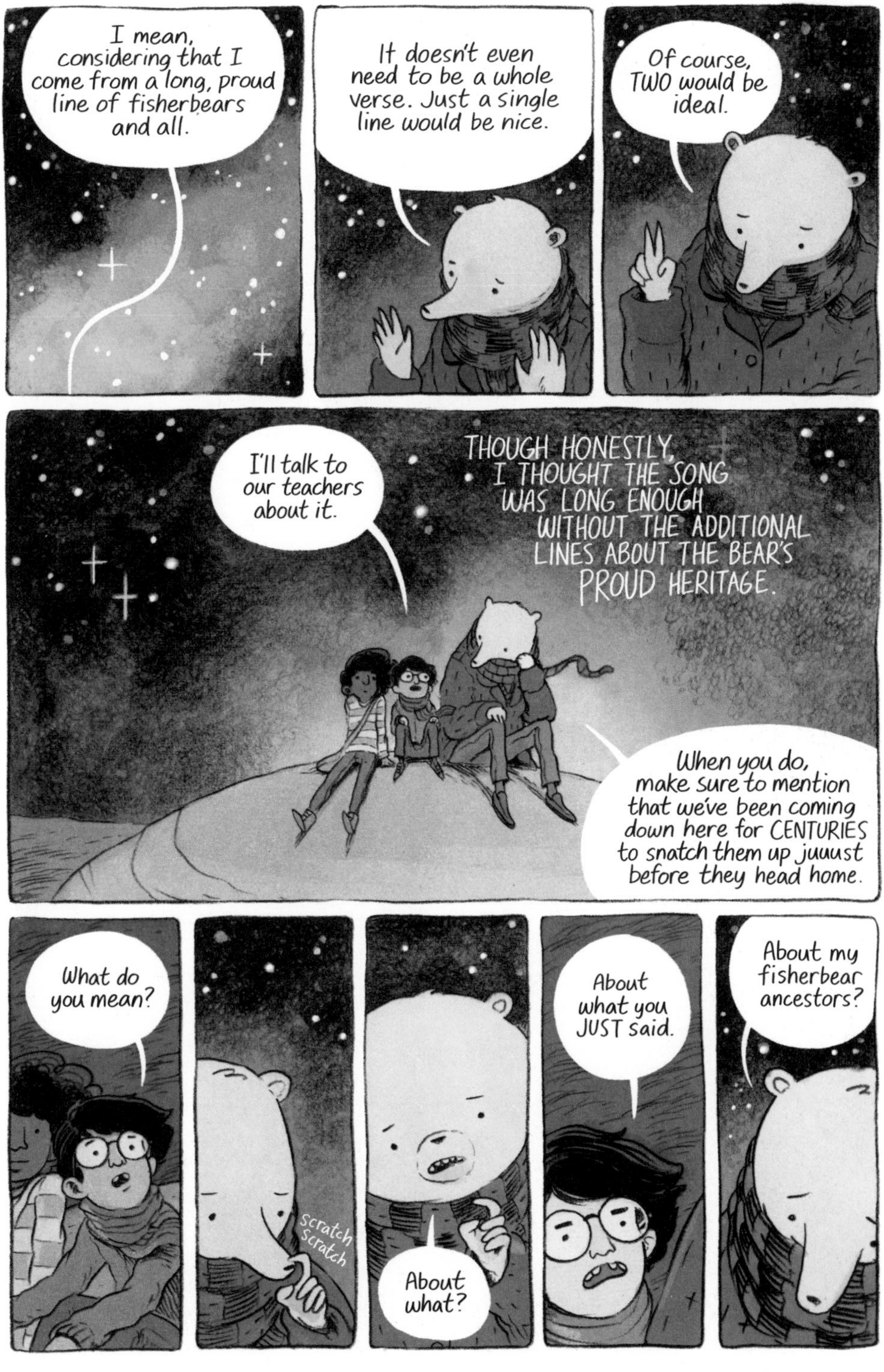
I mean, considering that I come from a long, proud line of fisherbears and all.
It doesn't even need to be a whole verse. Just a single line would be nice.
Of course, TWO would be ideal.
I'll talk to our teachers about it.
THOUGH HONESTLY, I THOUGHT THE SONG WAS LONG ENOUGH WITHOUT THE ADDITIONAL LINES ABOUT THE BEAR'S PROUD HERITAGE.
When you do, make sure to mention that we've been coming down here for CENTURIES to snatch them up juuust before they head home.
What do you mean?
scratch scratch
About what?
About what you JUST said.
About my fisherbear ancestors?

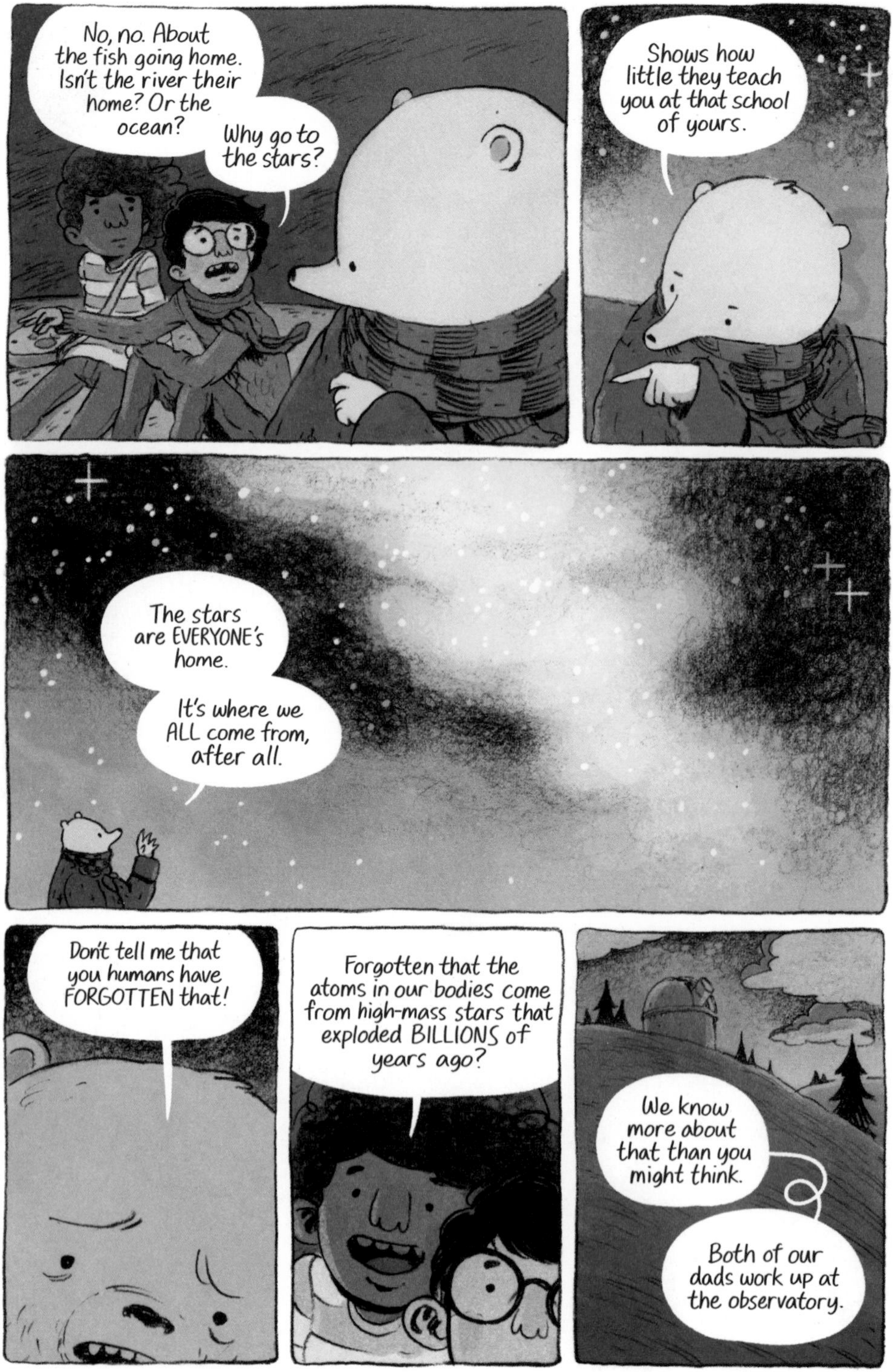
No, no. About the fish going home. Isn't the river their home? Or the ocean?
Why go to the stars?
Shows how little they teach you at that school of yours.
The stars are EVERYONE's home.
It's where we ALL come from, after all.
Don't tell me that you humans have FORGOTTEN that!
Forgotten that the atoms in our bodies come from high-mass stars that exploded BILLIONS of years ago?
We know more about that than you might think.
Both of our dads work up at the observatory.

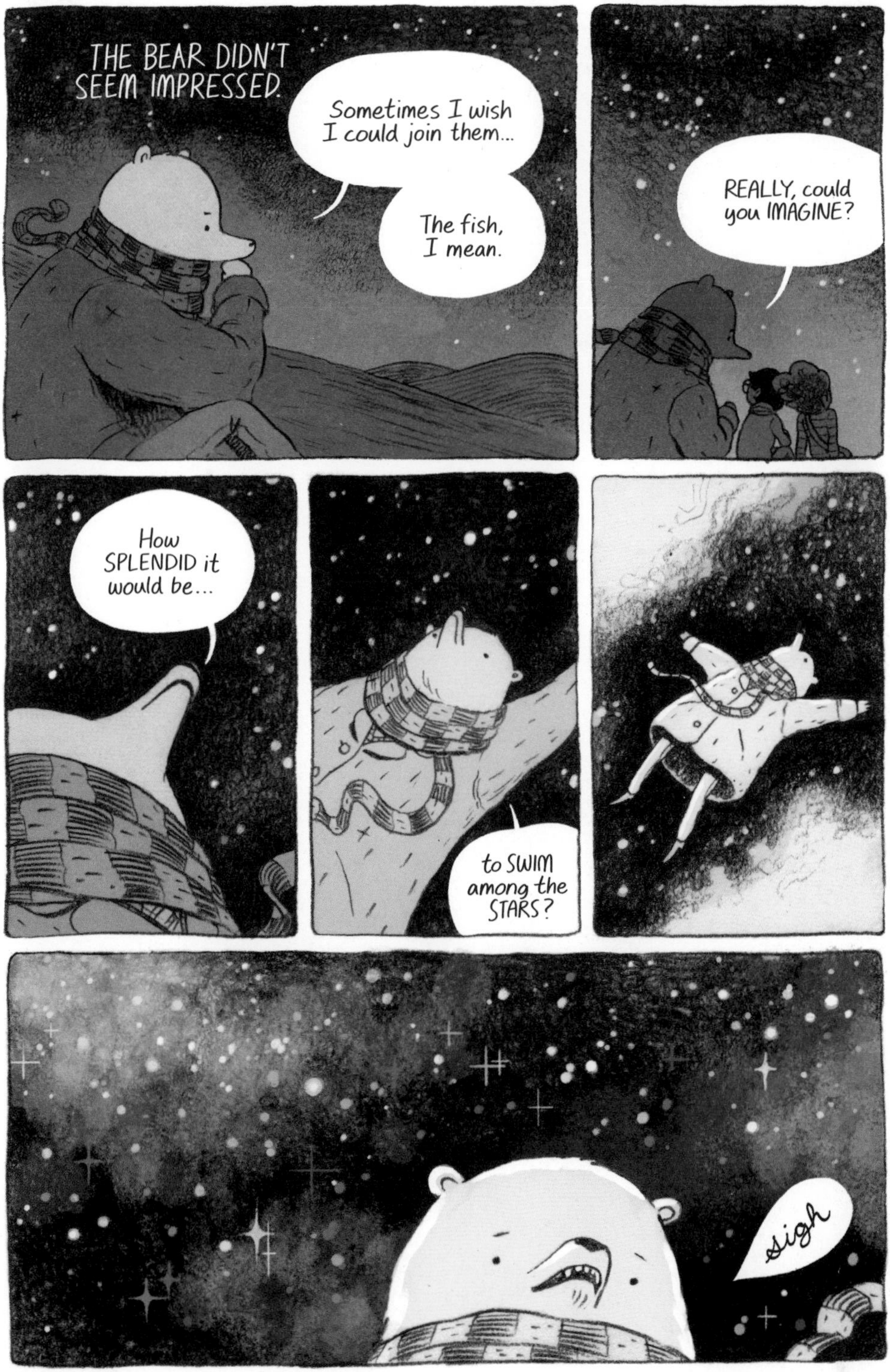
THE BEAR DIDN'T SEEM IMPRESSED.
Sometimes I wish I could join them...
The fish, I mean.
REALLY, could you IMAGINE?
How SPLENDID it would be...
to SWIM among the STARS?
Sigh

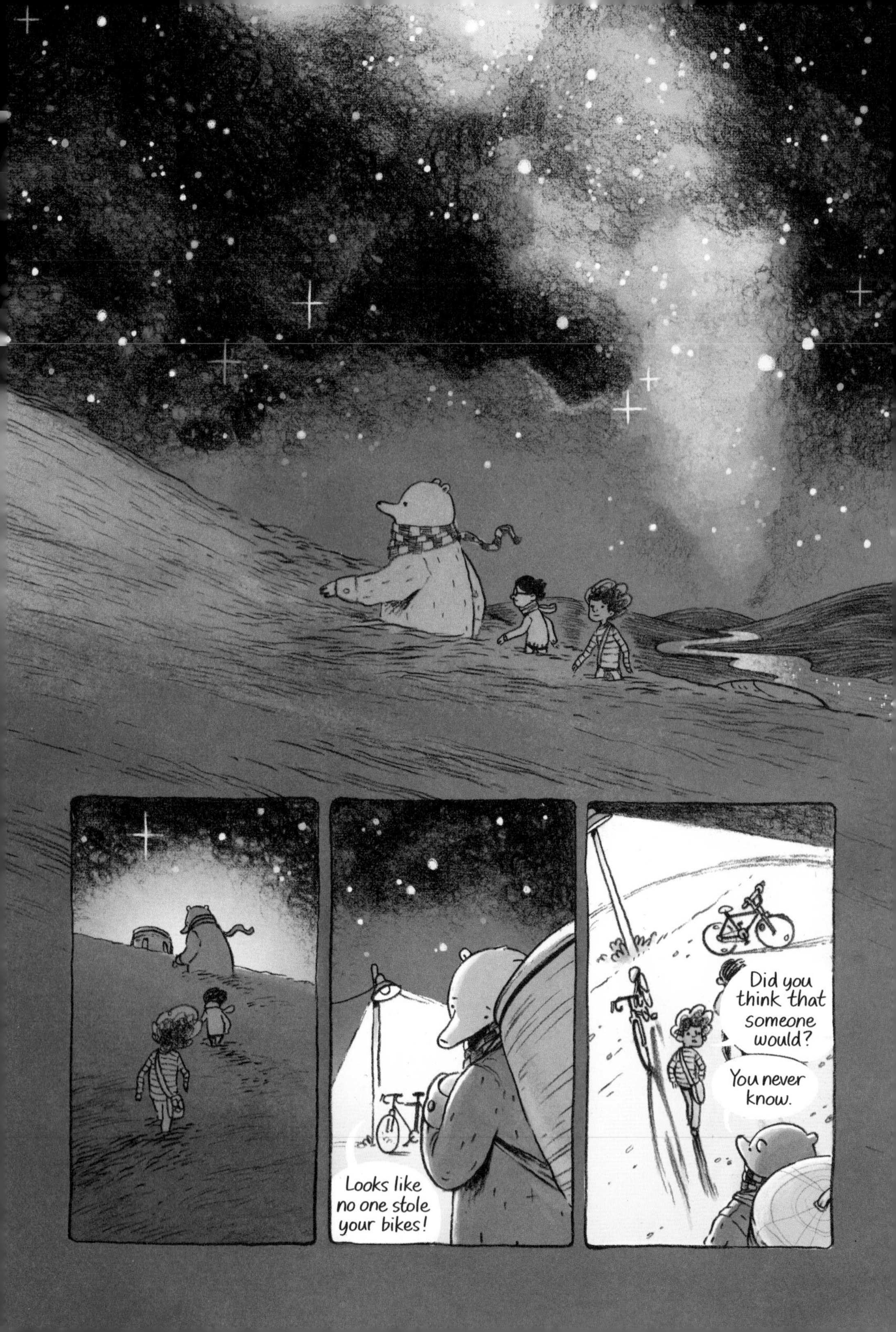
Looks like no one stole your bikes!
Did you think that someone would?
You never know.

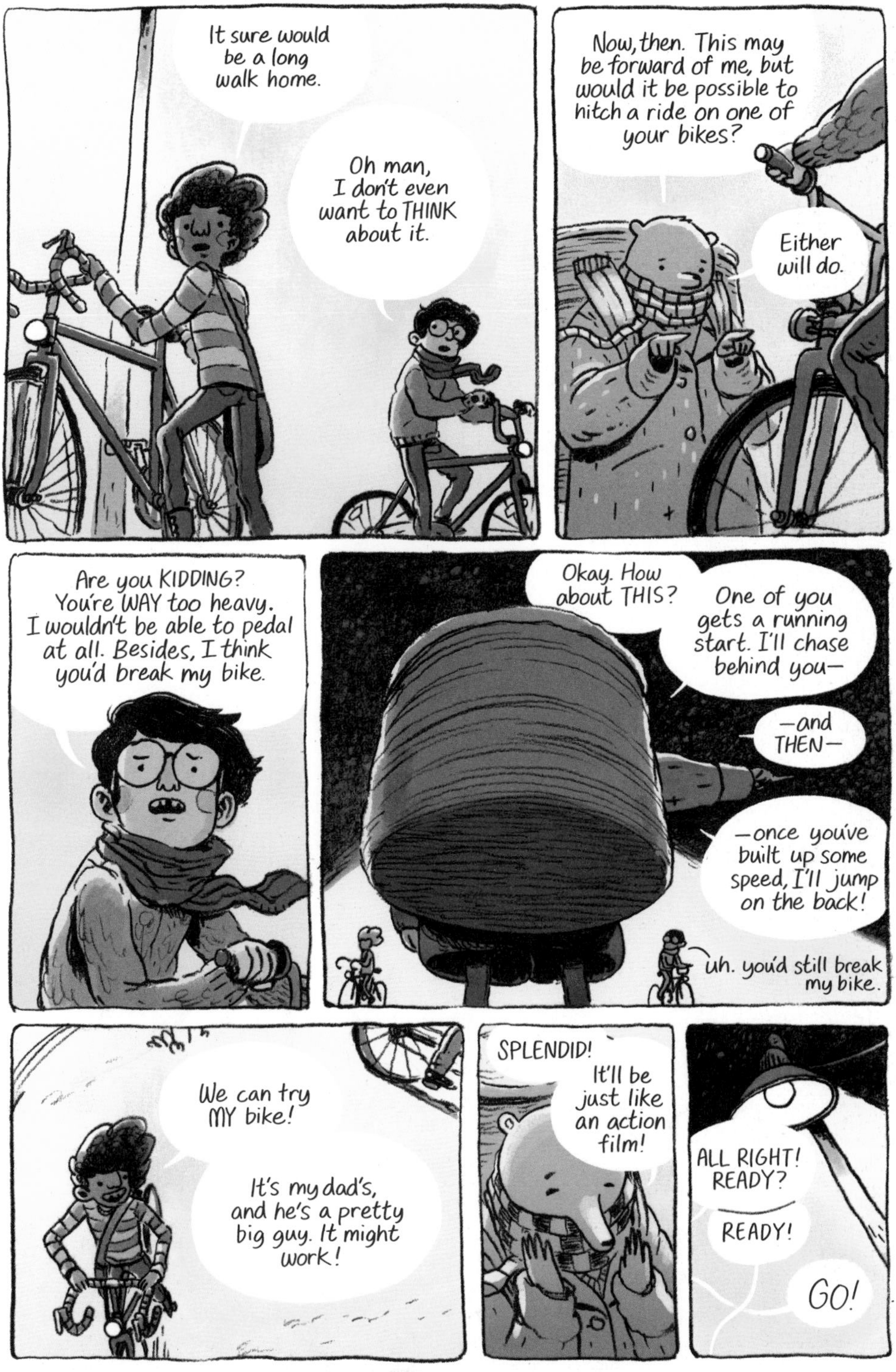
It sure would be a long walk home.
Oh man, I don't even want to THINK about it.
Now, then. This may be forward of me, but would it be possible to hitch a ride on one of your bikes?
Either will do.
Are you KIDDING? You're WAY too heavy. I wouldn't be able to pedal at all. Besides, I think you'd break my bike.
Okay. How about THIS?
One of you gets a running start. I'll chase behind you—
—and THEN—
—once you've built up some speed, I'll jump on the back!
uh. you'd still break my bike.
We can try MY bike!
It's my dad's, and he's a pretty big guy. It might work!
SPLENDID!
It'll be just like an action film!
ALL RIGHT! READY?
READY!
GO!

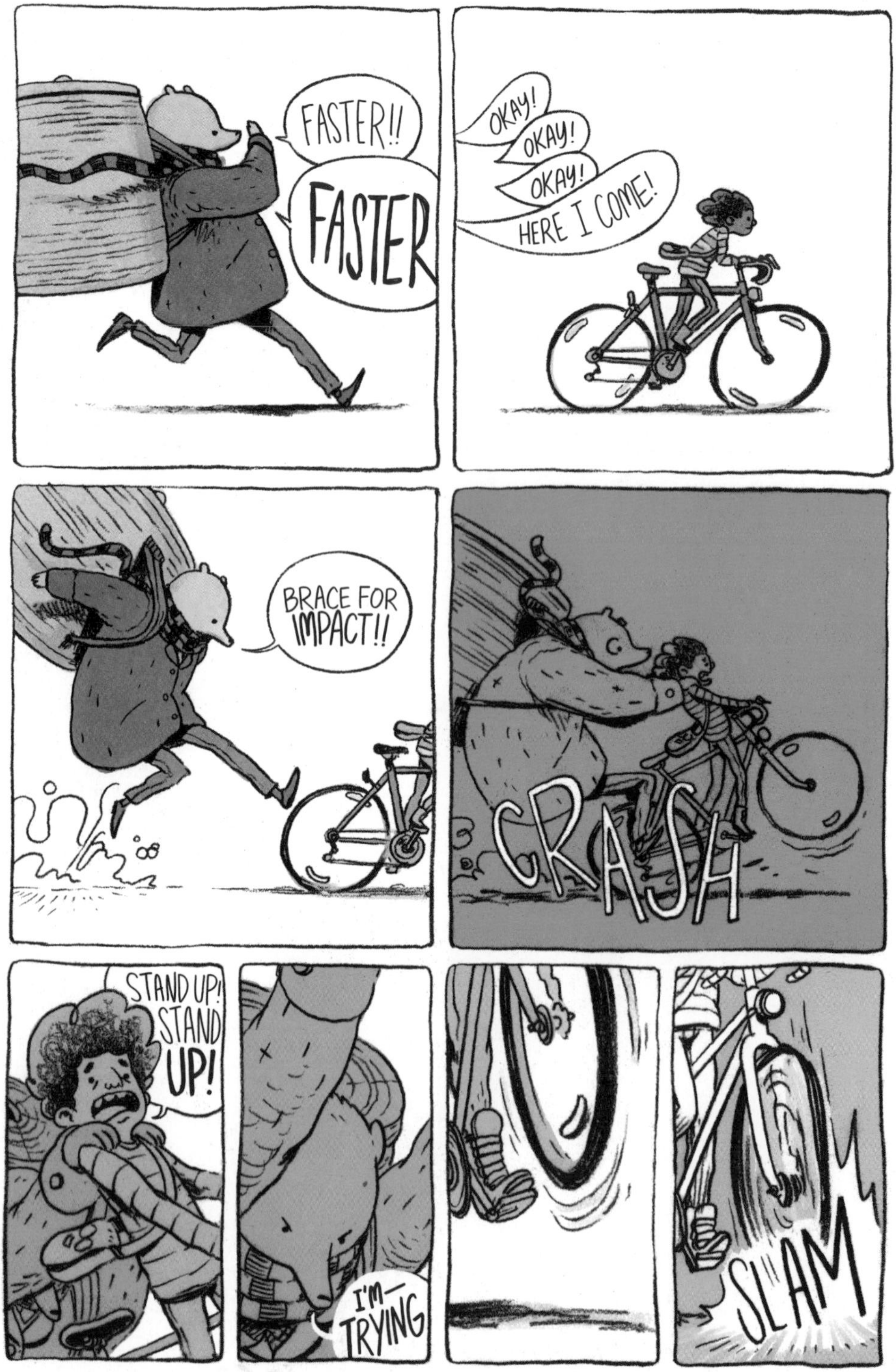
FASTER!!
FASTER
OKAY!
OKAY!
OKAY!
HERE I COME!
BRACE FOR IMPACT!!
CRASH
STAND UP! STAND UP!
I'M— TRYING
SLAM

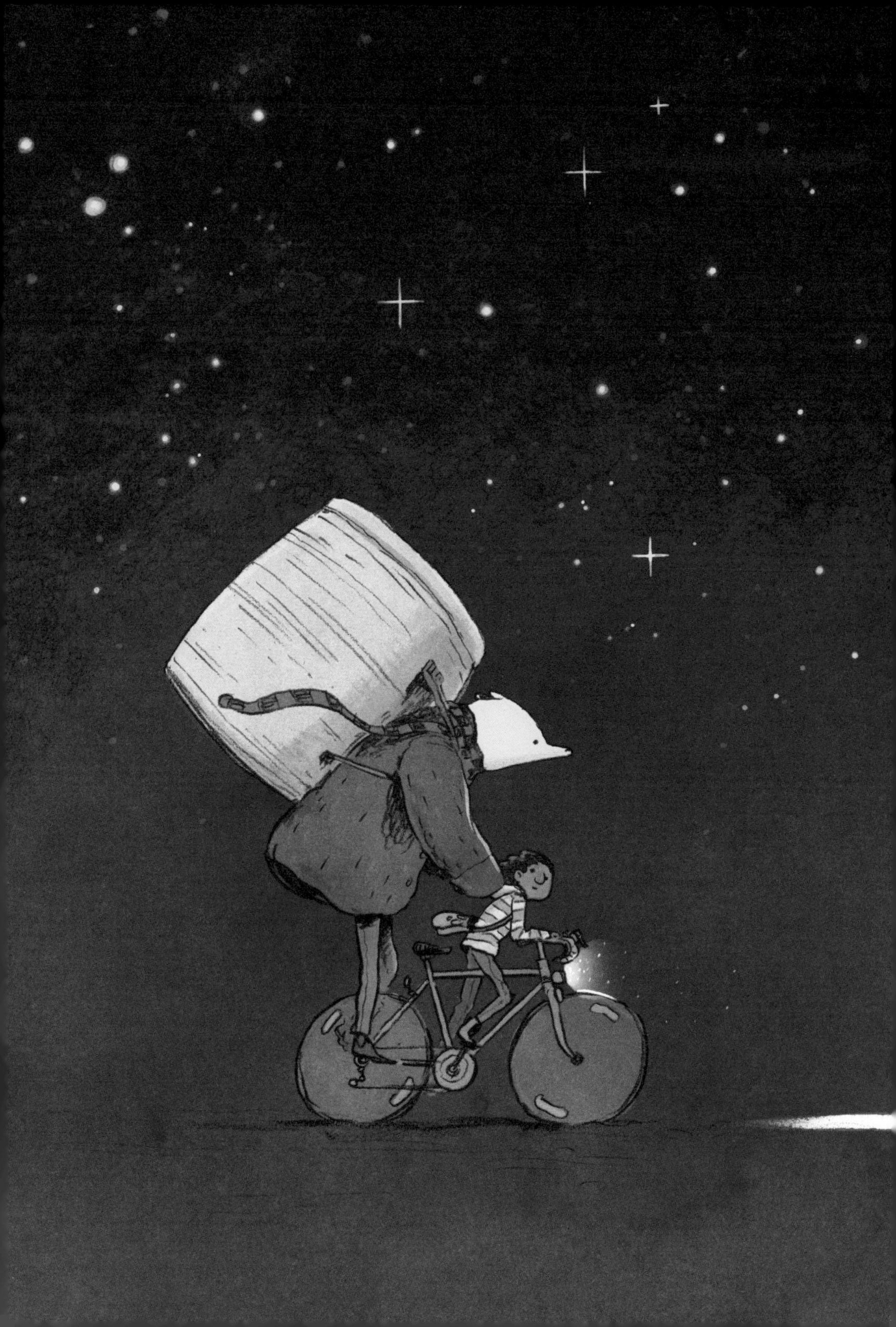

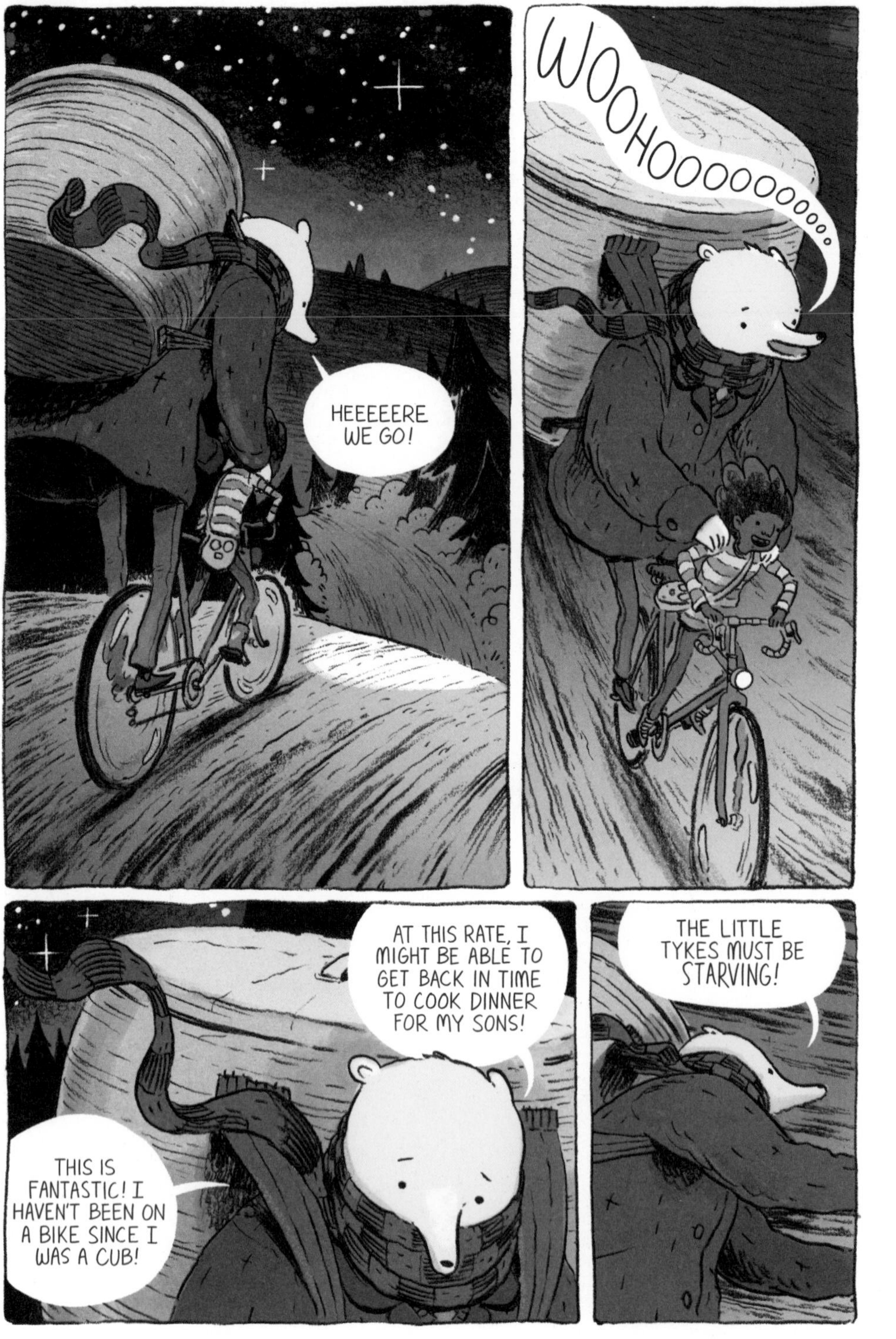
HEEEEERE WE GO!
WOOHOOOOOOOOoooo
AT THIS RATE, I MIGHT BE ABLE TO GET BACK IN TIME TO COOK DINNER FOR MY SONS!
THIS IS FANTASTIC! I HAVEN'T BEEN ON A BIKE SINCE I WAS A CUB!
THE LITTLE TYKES MUST BE STARVING!

WAIT UP!

hmm?

WHAT'S YOUR FRIEND'S NAME?

His n is Be

I CAN'T HEAR YOU! YOU'LL HAVE TO SHOUT!

I SAID, HIS NAME IS BEN!

BEN! YOU'VE GOT TO PEDAL FASTER THAN THAT IF YOU WANT TO KEEP UP!

HAHAH AHAHA AHAHAHAHAHAHAHAHAHH

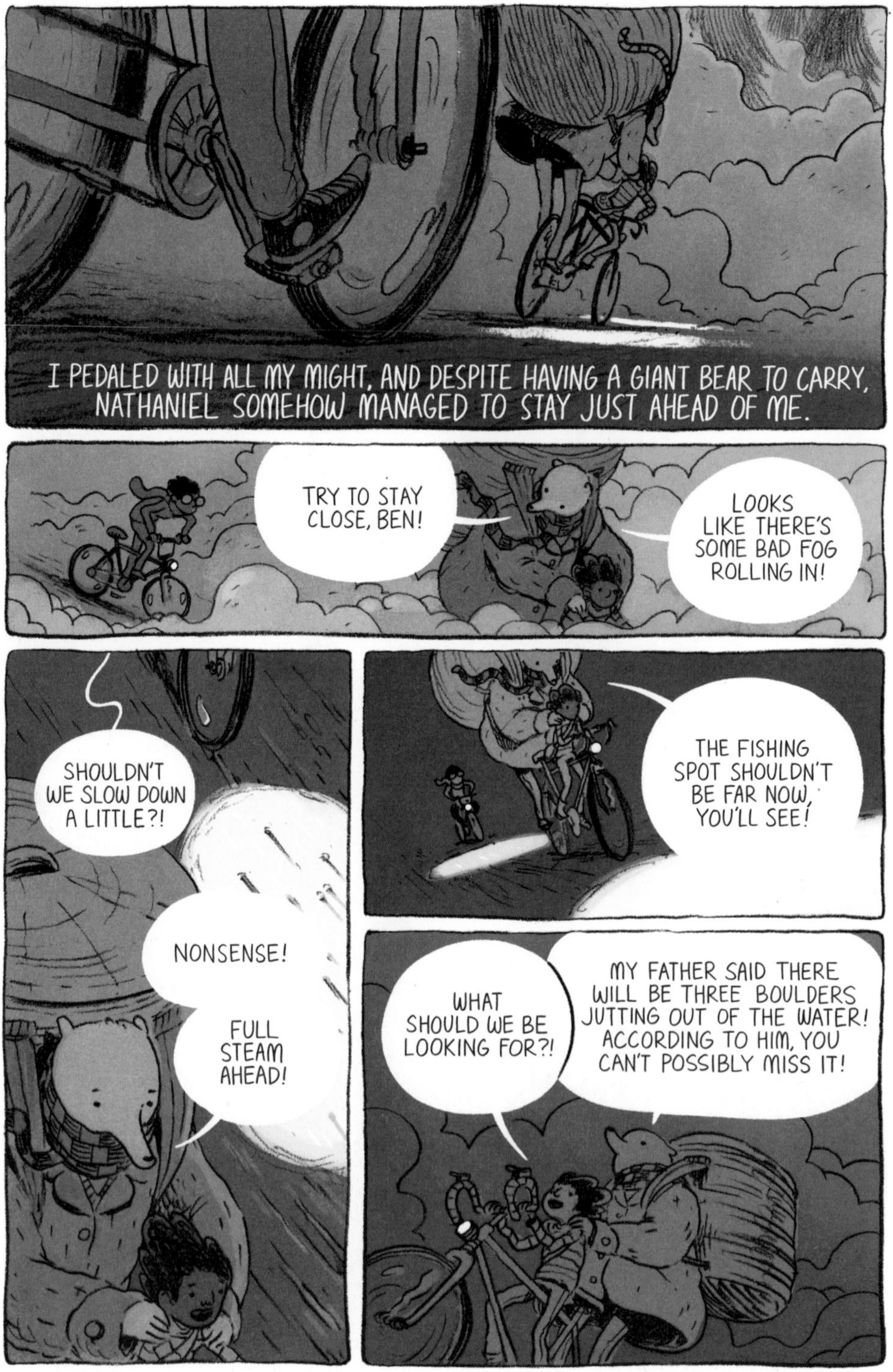
I PEDALED WITH ALL MY MIGHT, AND DESPITE HAVING A GIANT BEAR TO CARRY, NATHANIEL SOMEHOW MANAGED TO STAY JUST AHEAD OF ME.
TRY TO STAY CLOSE, BEN!
LOOKS LIKE THERE'S SOME BAD FOG ROLLING IN!
SHOULDN'T WE SLOW DOWN A LITTLE?!
NONSENSE!
FULL STEAM AHEAD!
THE FISHING SPOT SHOULDN'T BE FAR NOW, YOU'LL SEE!
WHAT SHOULD WE BE LOOKING FOR?!
MY FATHER SAID THERE WILL BE THREE BOULDERS JUTTING OUT OF THE WATER! ACCORDING TO HIM, YOU CAN'T POSSIBLY MISS IT!

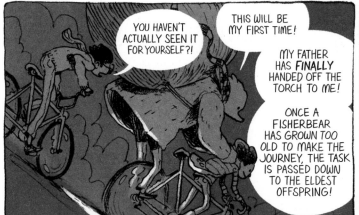

YOU HAVEN'T ACTUALLY SEEN IT FOR YOURSELF?!

THIS WILL BE MY FIRST TIME!

MY FATHER HAS **FINALLY** HANDED OFF THE TORCH TO ME!

ONCE A FISHERBEAR HAS GROWN TOO OLD TO MAKE THE JOURNEY, THE TASK IS PASSED DOWN TO THE ELDEST OFFSPRING!

AND THAT'S **ME**!

WHY DIDN'T HE EVER TAKE YOU WITH HIM WHEN YOU WERE LITTLE?!

THAT'S JUST NOT HOW IT'S DONE!

IT'S TRADITION TO HEAD OUT ALONE AND USE YOUR WITS TO FIND YOUR WAY!

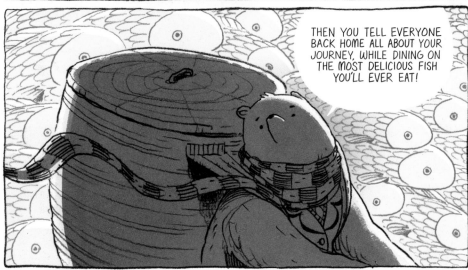

THEN YOU TELL EVERYONE BACK HOME ALL ABOUT YOUR JOURNEY, WHILE DINING ON THE MOST DELICIOUS FISH YOU'LL EVER EAT!

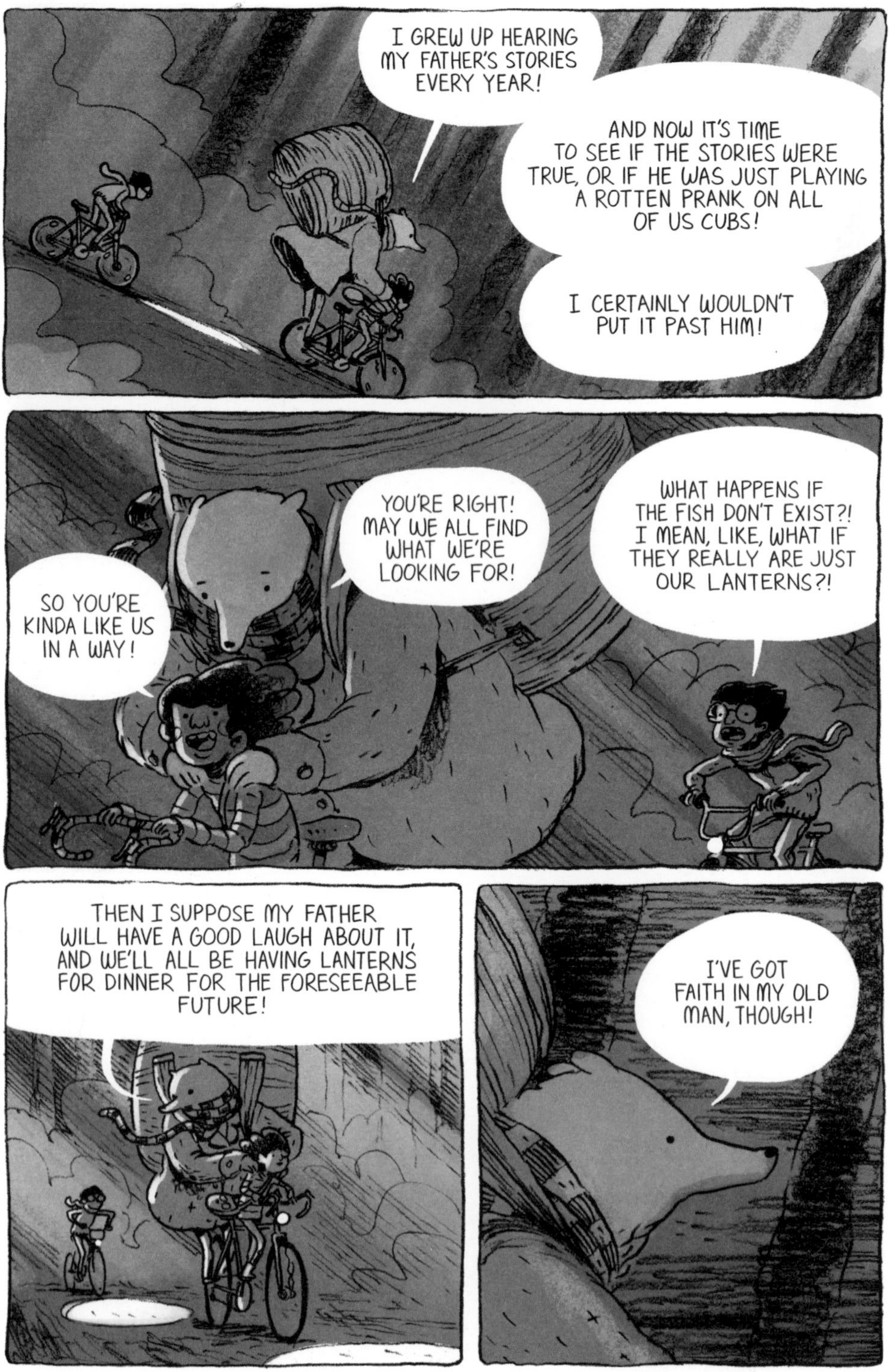
I GREW UP HEARING MY FATHER'S STORIES EVERY YEAR!
AND NOW IT'S TIME TO SEE IF THE STORIES WERE TRUE, OR IF HE WAS JUST PLAYING A ROTTEN PRANK ON ALL OF US CUBS!
I CERTAINLY WOULDN'T PUT IT PAST HIM!
SO YOU'RE KINDA LIKE US IN A WAY!
YOU'RE RIGHT! MAY WE ALL FIND WHAT WE'RE LOOKING FOR!
WHAT HAPPENS IF THE FISH DON'T EXIST?! I MEAN, LIKE, WHAT IF THEY REALLY ARE JUST OUR LANTERNS?!
THEN I SUPPOSE MY FATHER WILL HAVE A GOOD LAUGH ABOUT IT, AND WE'LL ALL BE HAVING LANTERNS FOR DINNER FOR THE FORESEEABLE FUTURE!
I'VE GOT FAITH IN MY OLD MAN, THOUGH!

SURELY HIS STORIES OF ADVENTURE WERE GREATLY EXAGGERATED, BUT THOSE FISH HE BROUGHT HOME WERE THE REAL DEAL! AND LIKE I SAID, WE'VE BEEN DOING THIS FOR GENERATIONS! NEARLY FOUR CENTURIES!

IT WAS MY GREAT GREAT GREAT GREAT GREAT GREAT GREAT GREAT GREAT GREAT GREAT GREAT GREAT GREAT GRANDFATHER DUNCAN THE THIRD WHO DISCOVERED THIS RIVER! IT WAS NO DOUBT WELL BEFORE THIS ROAD WAS HERE! HE HAD TO RELY ON HIS HIGHLY TRAINED NAVIGATIONAL ABILITIES IN ORDER TO MAKE HIS WAY THROUGH THE UNTAMED WILDERNESS ALONE! WE BEARS HAVE A FRIGHTENINGLY KEEN SENSE FOR WATER! OR, AT LEAST, WE USED TO! NOWADAYS, EVERYTHING — SO CONVENIENT! WHY BOTHER GOING OUT TO LOOK FOR — HAVE IT DELIVERED TO YOUR CAVE IN A PLAST— WHEN YOU HAVE A FRESH JUG —— NO U——

BEN! LOOK HOW THE MOONLIGHT FILTERS IN THROUGH THE TREES!

HAAAAHAHAHAHAHAHAHAH

?

HAHAHAHAHAHAH

HAHAHAAAAHAHAHAHAHAHAHAHAHAH

YOU THINK YOU KNOW MORE MOON FACTS THAN I DO?! IMPOSSIBLE!

I'LL PROVE IT!

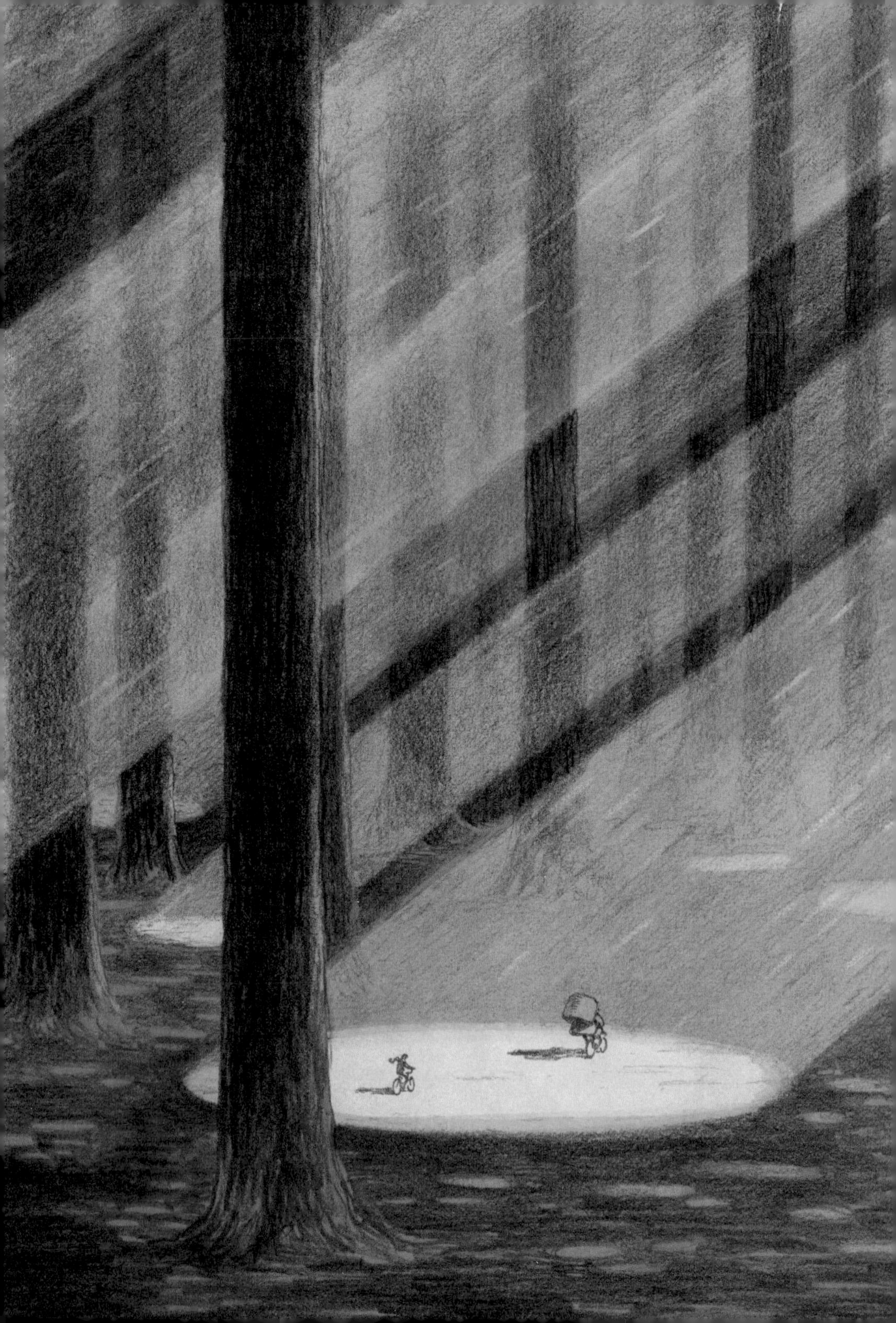

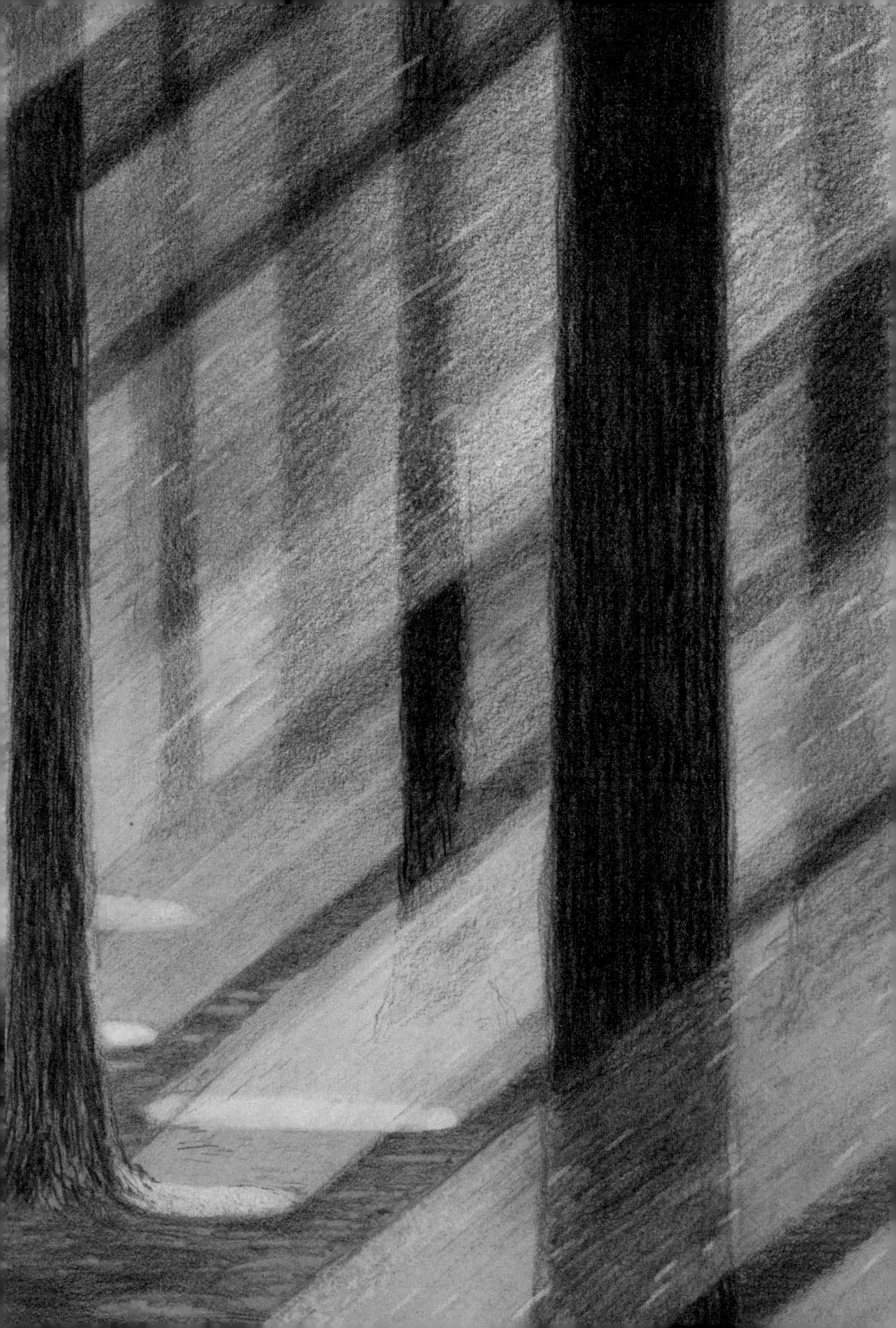

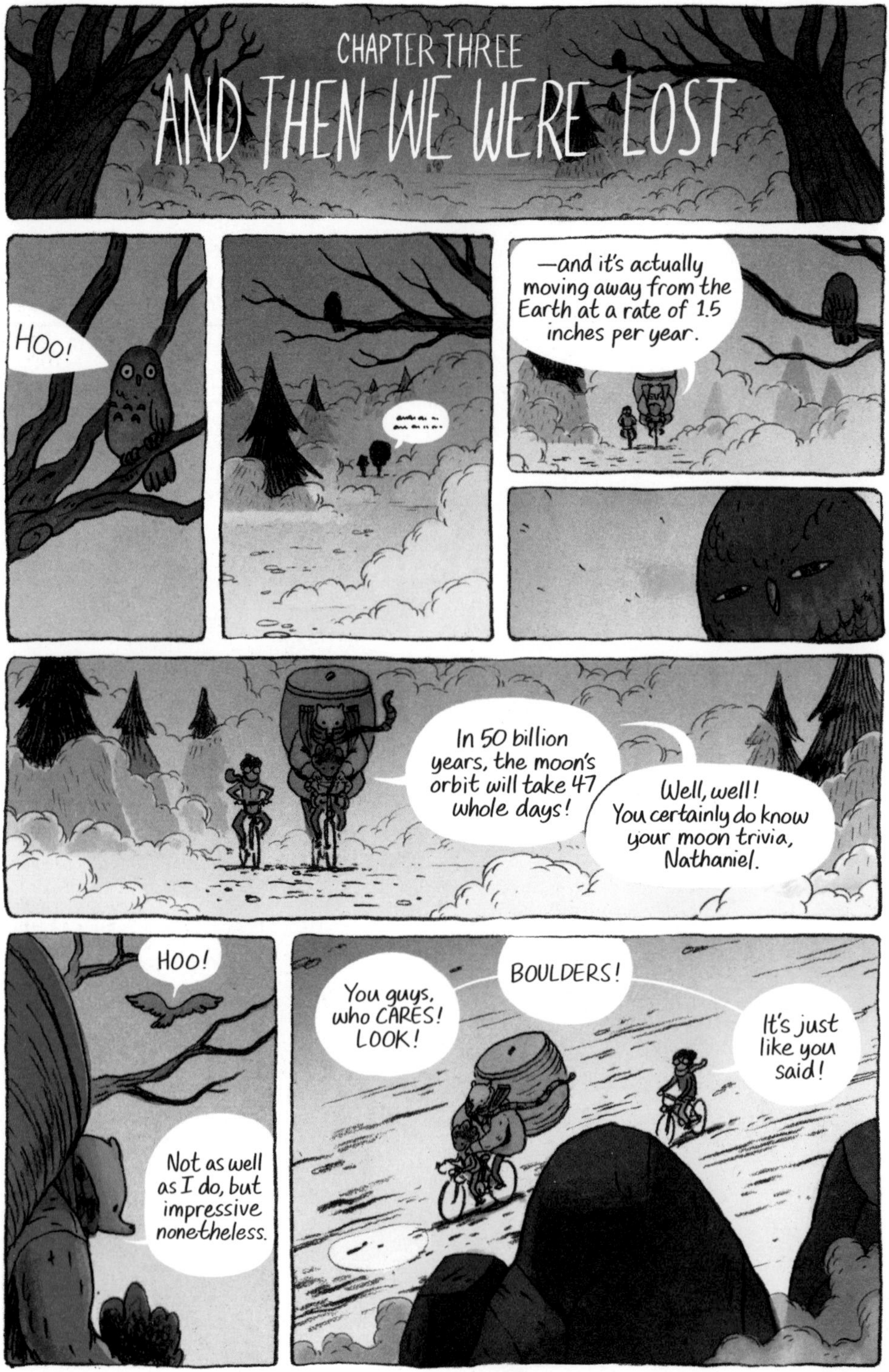
CHAPTER THREE
AND THEN WE WERE LOST
HOO!
—and it's actually moving away from the Earth at a rate of 1.5 inches per year.
In 50 billion years, the moon's orbit will take 47 whole days!
Well, well! You certainly do know your moon trivia, Nathaniel.
HOO!
Not as well as I do, but impressive nonetheless.
You guys, who CARES! LOOK!
BOULDERS!
It's just like you said!

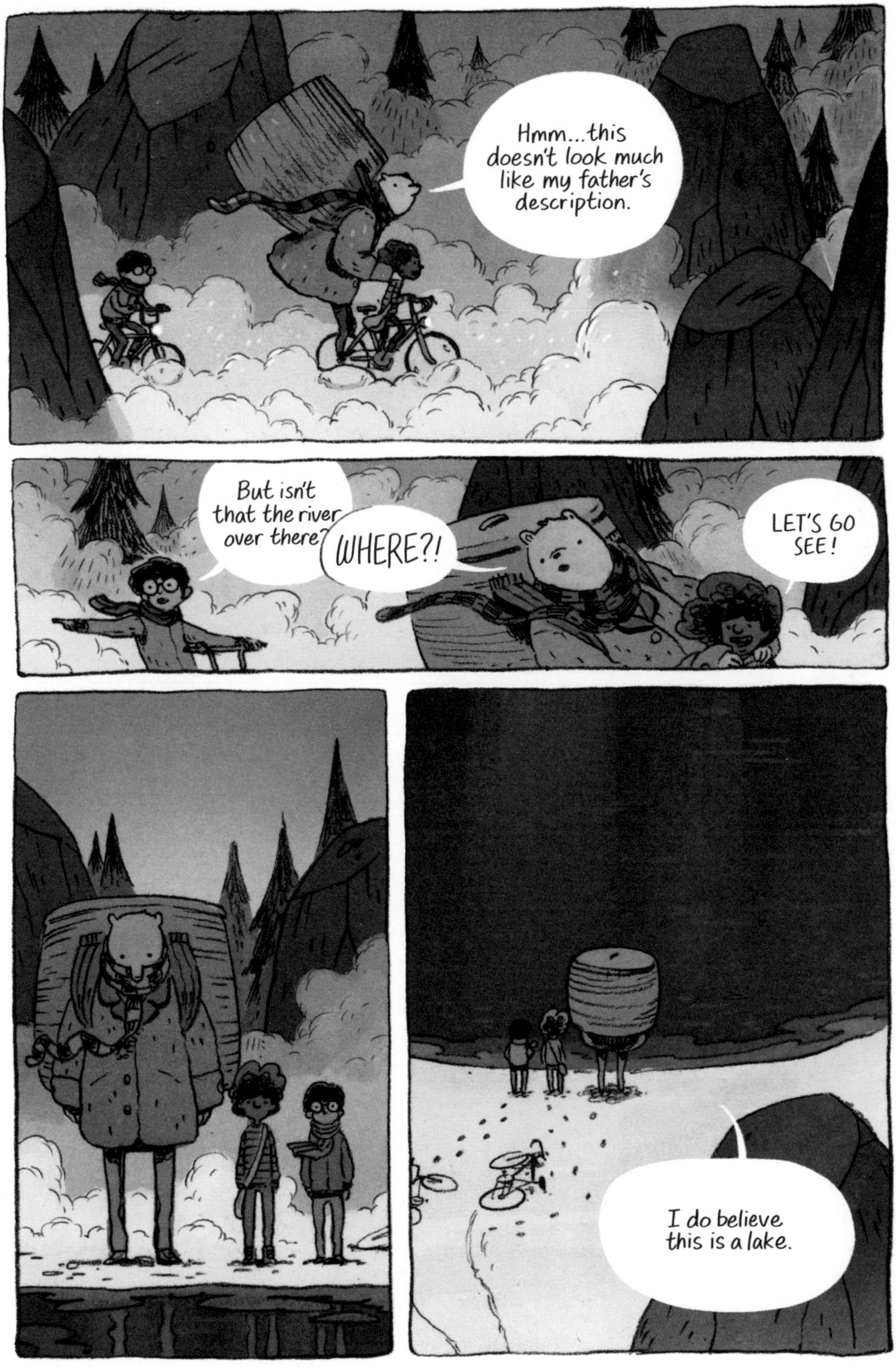
Hmm...this doesn't look much like my father's description.
But isn't that the river over there?
WHERE?!
LET'S GO SEE!
I do believe this is a lake.

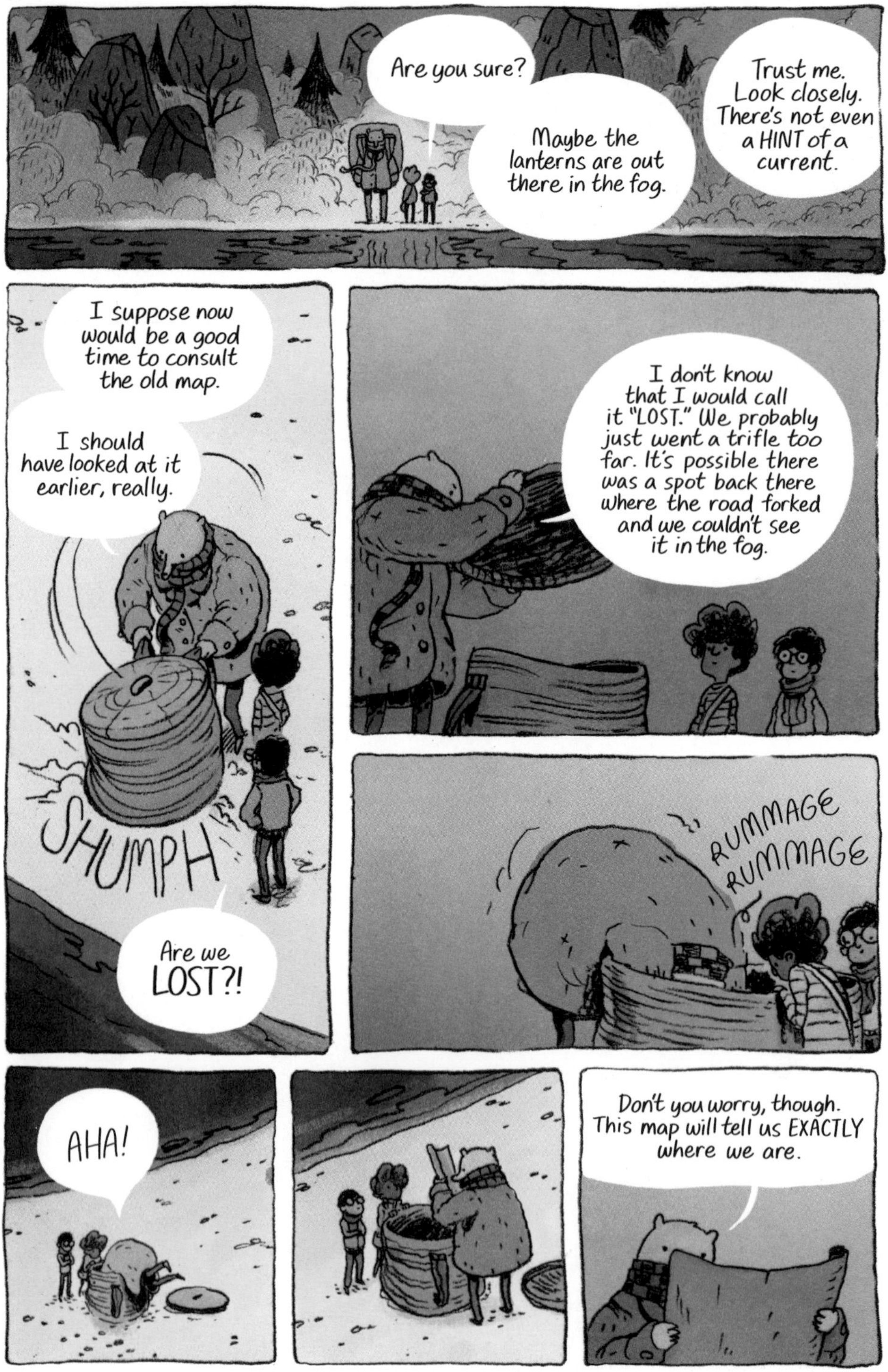
Are you sure?
Maybe the lanterns are out there in the fog.
Trust me. Look closely. There's not even a HINT of a current.
I suppose now would be a good time to consult the old map.
I should have looked at it earlier, really.
SHUMPH
Are we LOST?!
I don't know that I would call it "LOST." We probably just went a trifle too far. It's possible there was a spot back there where the road forked and we couldn't see it in the fog.
RUMMAGE RUMMAGE
AHA!
Don't you worry, though. This map will tell us EXACTLY where we are.

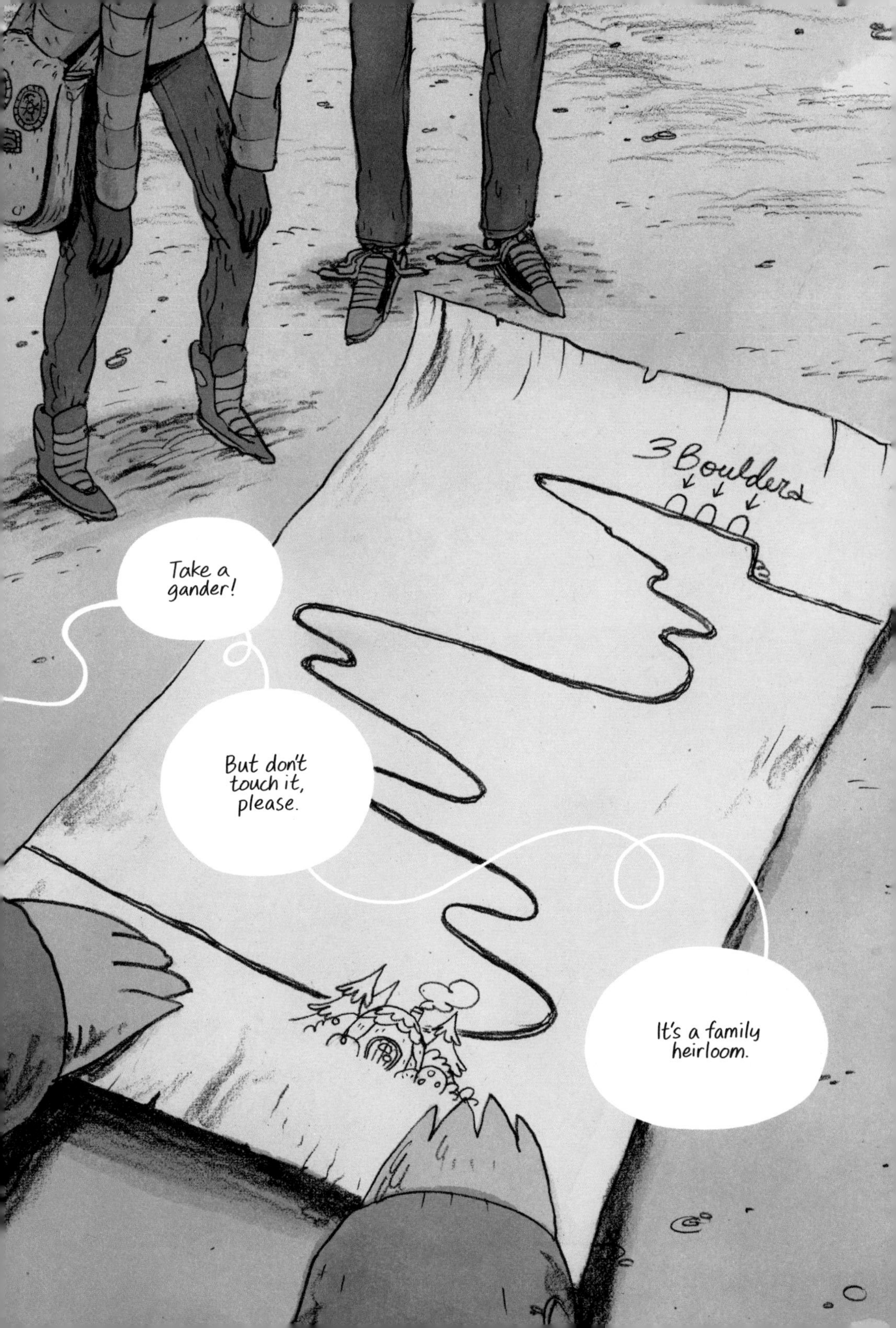
3 Boulders
Take a gander!
But don't touch it, please.
It's a family heirloom.

Here's my house. Quite lovely in the spring, I might add.

This line here is the river. All we need to do is follow it north.

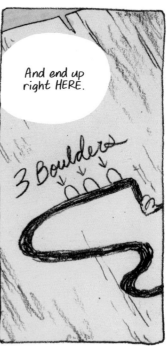

And end up right HERE.

3 Boulders

Wait, is this a joke? There's nothing on here but the river! How is this gonna help us? Where are the ROADS? Better yet, where's this GIANT LAKE?!

WELL—

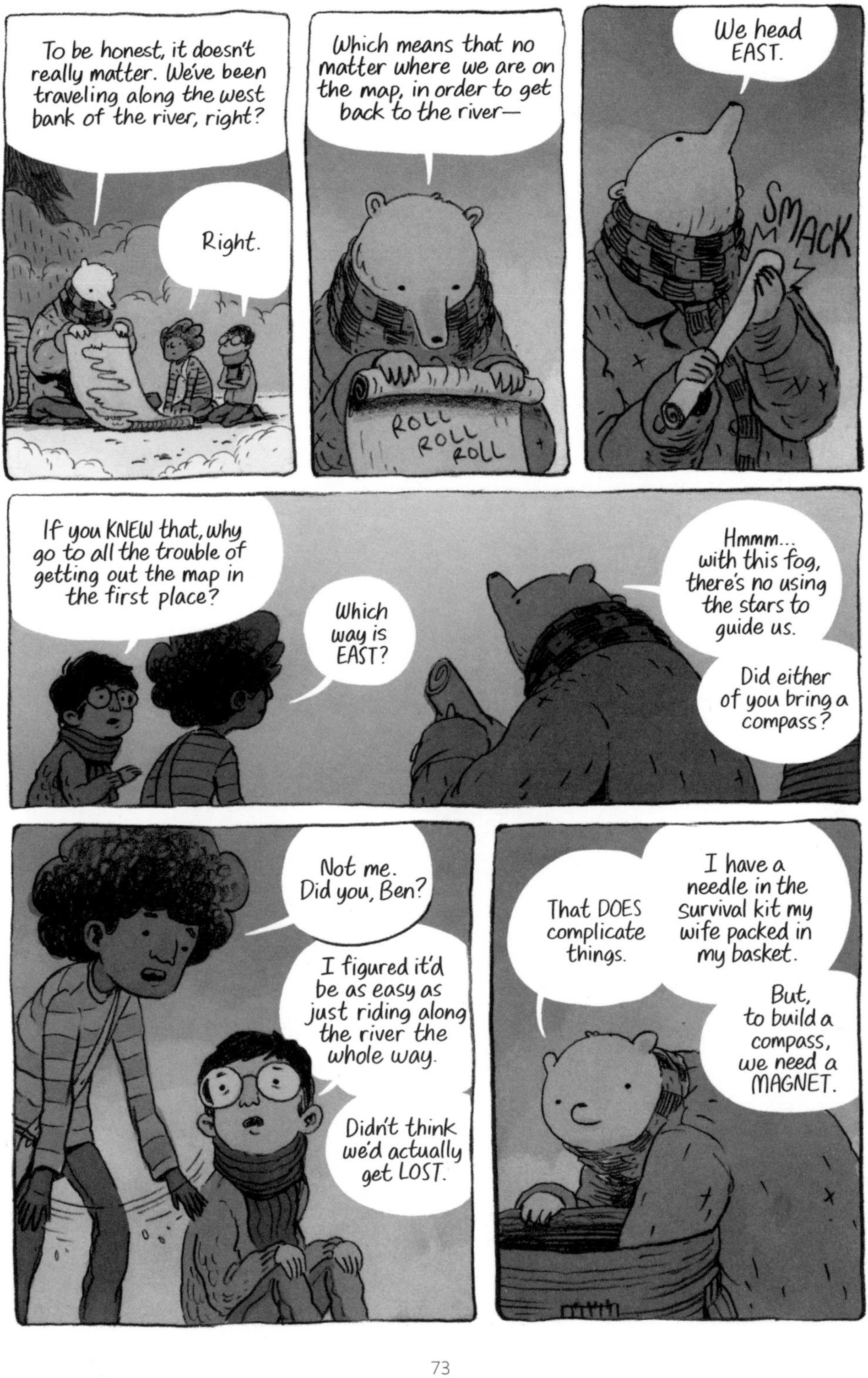
To be honest, it doesn't really matter. We've been traveling along the west bank of the river, right?
Right.
Which means that no matter where we are on the map, in order to get back to the river—
ROLL ROLL ROLL
We head EAST.
SMACK
If you KNEW that, why go to all the trouble of getting out the map in the first place?
Which way is EAST?
Hmmm... with this fog, there's no using the stars to guide us.
Did either of you bring a compass?
Not me. Did you, Ben?
I figured it'd be as easy as just riding along the river the whole way.
Didn't think we'd actually get LOST.
That DOES complicate things.
I have a needle in the survival kit my wife packed in my basket.
But, to build a compass, we need a MAGNET.

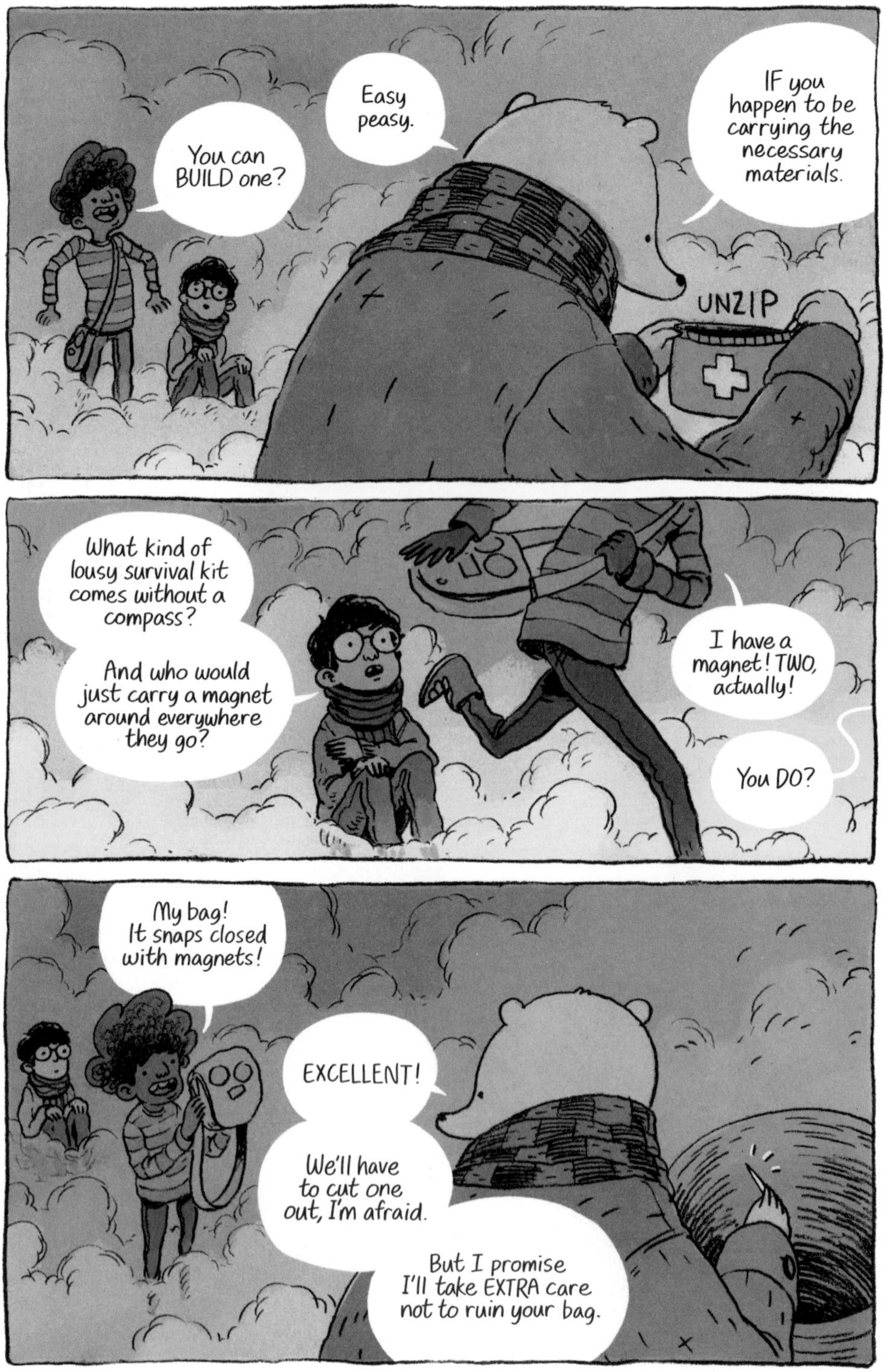
You can BUILD one?
Easy peasy.
IF you happen to be carrying the necessary materials.
UNZIP
What kind of lousy survival kit comes without a compass?
And who would just carry a magnet around everywhere they go?
I have a magnet! TWO, actually!
You DO?
My bag! It snaps closed with magnets!
EXCELLENT!
We'll have to cut one out, I'm afraid.
But I promise I'll take EXTRA care not to ruin your bag.

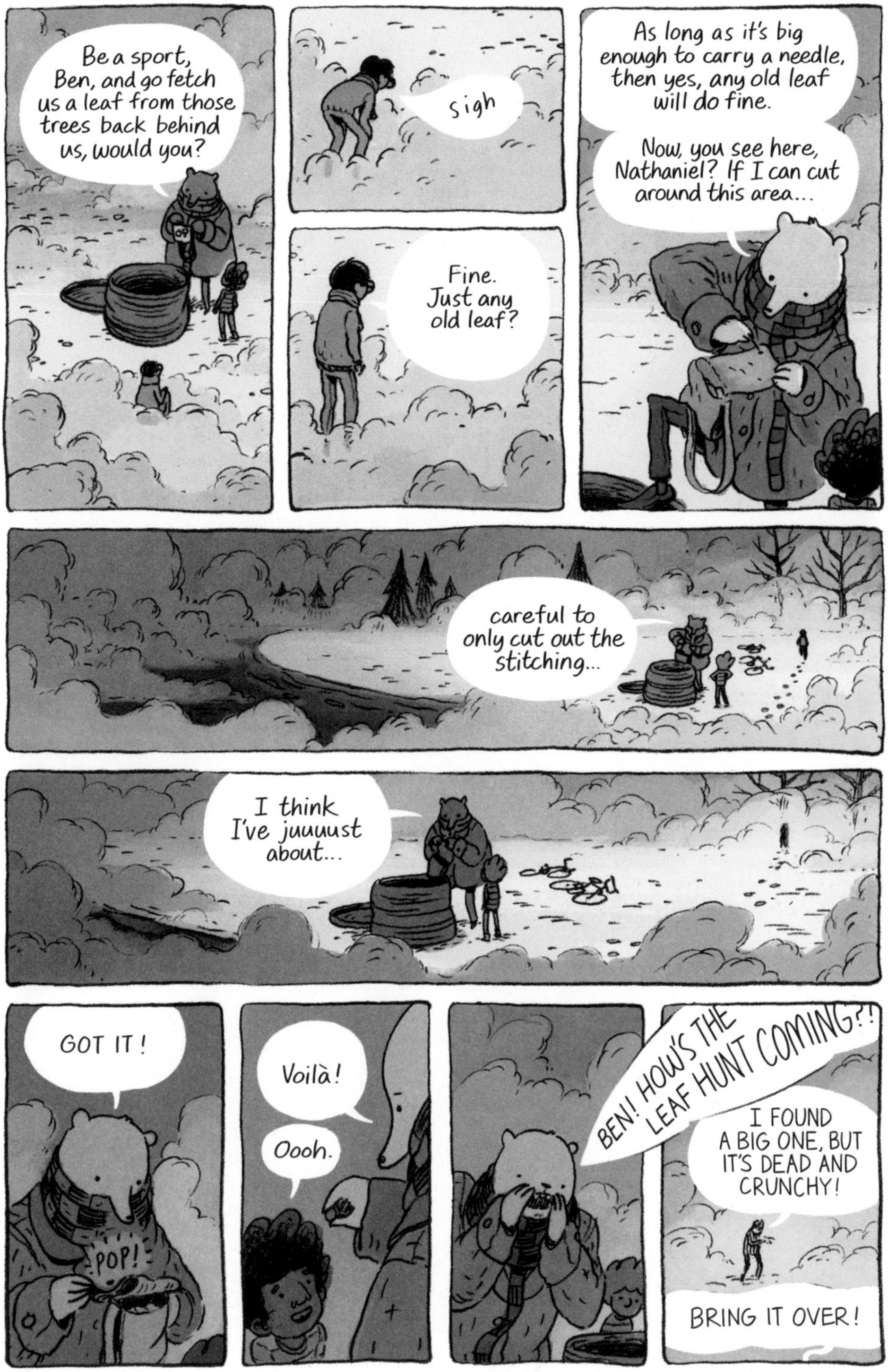
Be a sport, Ben, and go fetch us a leaf from those trees back behind us, would you?
sigh
Fine. Just any old leaf?
As long as it's big enough to carry a needle, then yes, any old leaf will do fine.
Now, you see here, Nathaniel? If I can cut around this area...
careful to only cut out the stitching...
I think I've juuuust about...
GOT IT!
POP!
Voilà!
Oooh.
BEN! HOW'S THE LEAF HUNT COMING?!
I FOUND A BIG ONE, BUT IT'S DEAD AND CRUNCHY!
BRING IT OVER!

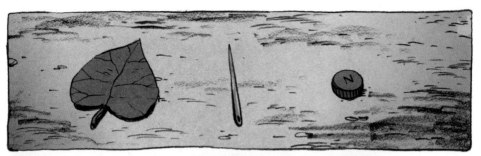

How's it work?

Right. It's quite simple.

STEP 1

SWIPE THE NORTH SIDE OF THE MAGNET OVER ONE END OF THE NEEDLE.

Fifty times should suffice.

STEP 2
PLACE THE NEEDLE ON THE LEAF LIKE SO.

For step three, we need a puddle.

There's one!

STEP 3

Now what?
Now we let the needle point to the magnetic north pole.
It's WORKING!
Well, of COURSE it is.
And there you have it.
If that's NORTH, then EAST is...
That way.
How'd you know that would work?
My father taught me that trick.
He's quite the knowledgeable fellow.

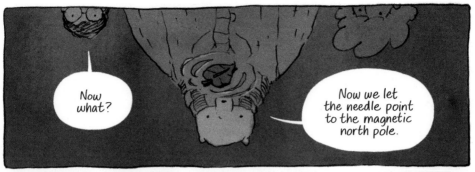

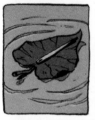

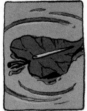

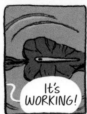

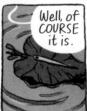

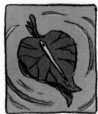

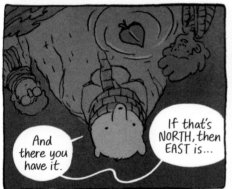

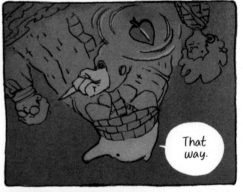

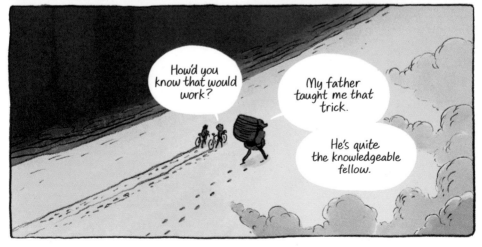

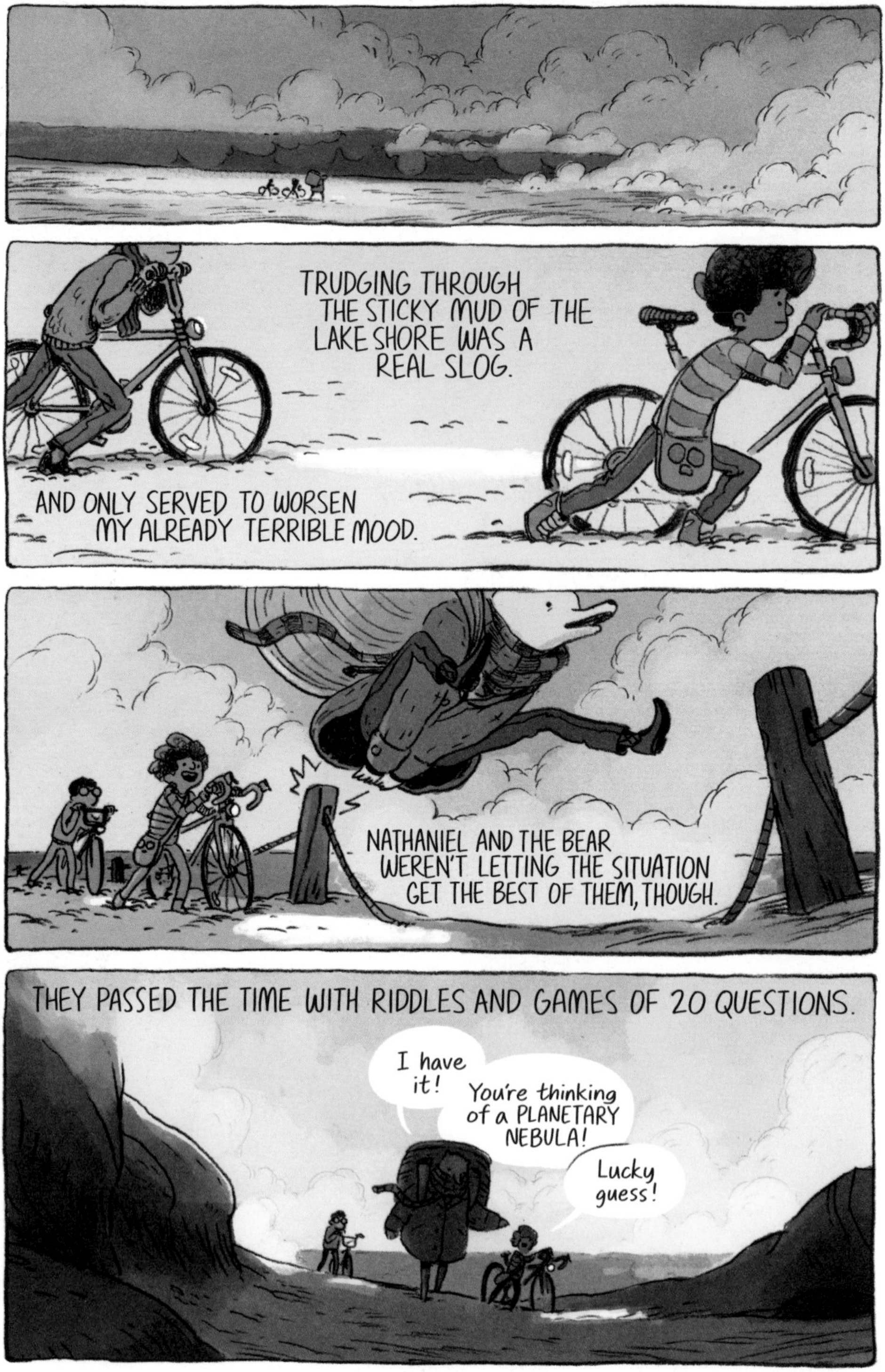
TRUDGING THROUGH THE STICKY MUD OF THE LAKE SHORE WAS A REAL SLOG.
AND ONLY SERVED TO WORSEN MY ALREADY TERRIBLE MOOD.
NATHANIEL AND THE BEAR WEREN'T LETTING THE SITUATION GET THE BEST OF THEM, THOUGH.
THEY PASSED THE TIME WITH RIDDLES AND GAMES OF 20 QUESTIONS.
I have it!
You're thinking of a PLANETARY NEBULA!
Lucky guess!

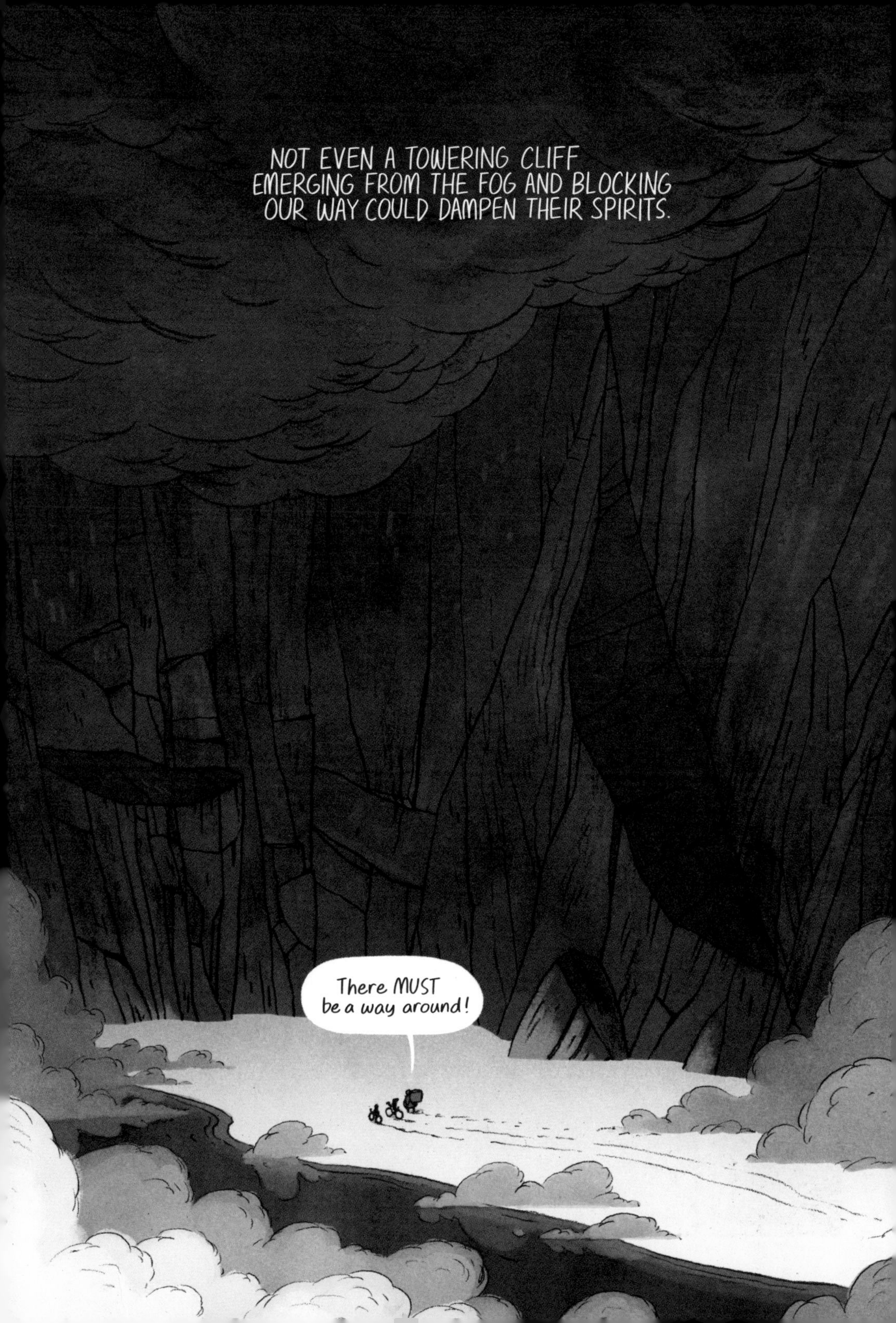
NOT EVEN A TOWERING CLIFF EMERGING FROM THE FOG AND BLOCKING OUR WAY COULD DAMPEN THEIR SPIRITS.
There MUST be a way around!

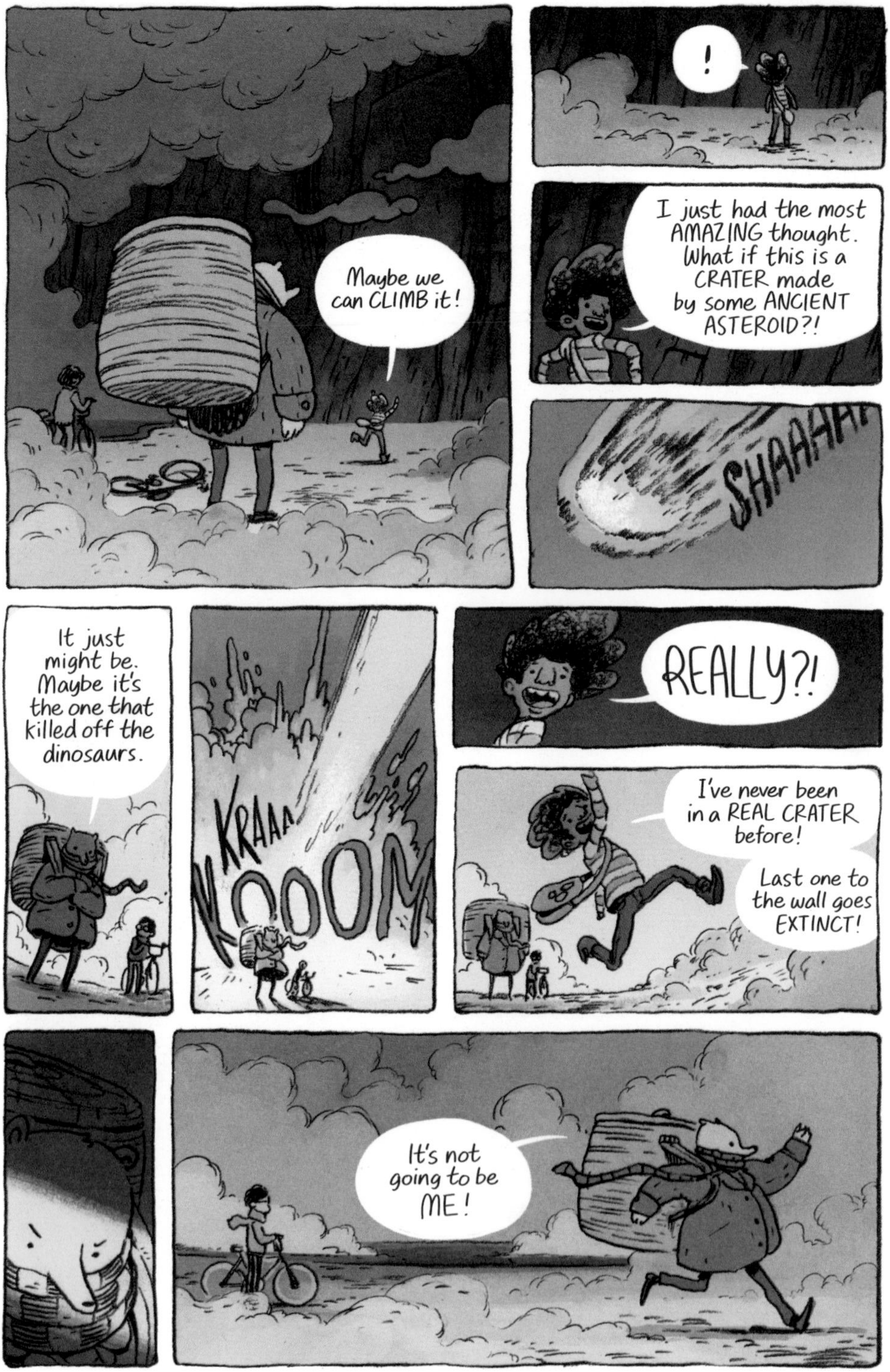
Maybe we can CLIMB it!
!
I just had the most AMAZING thought. What if this is a CRATER made by some ANCIENT ASTEROID?!
SHAAAA
It just might be. Maybe it's the one that killed off the dinosaurs.
KRAAA
KOOOM
REALLY?!
I've never been in a REAL CRATER before!
Last one to the wall goes EXTINCT!
It's not going to be ME!

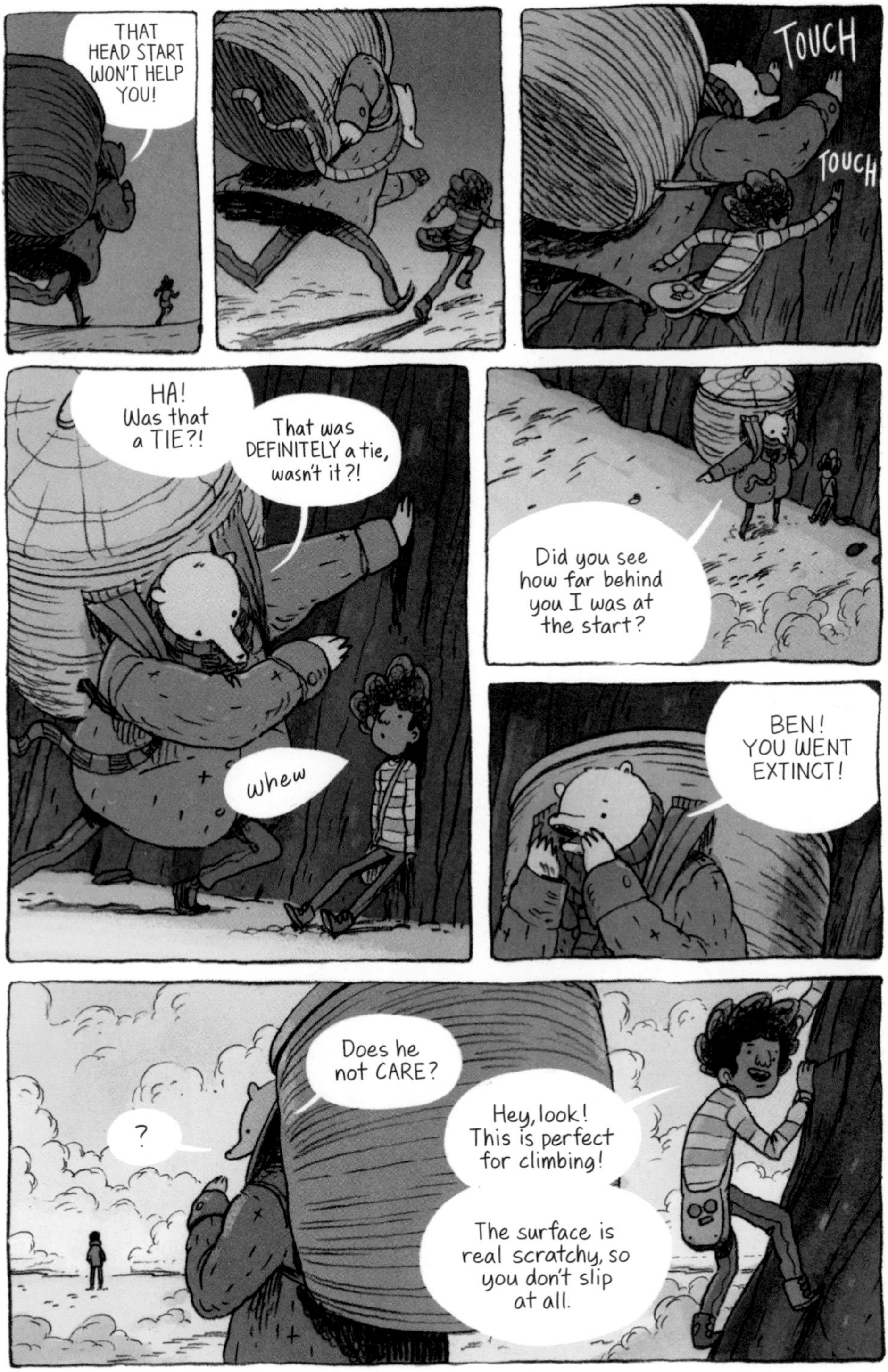
THAT HEAD START WON'T HELP YOU!
TOUCH
TOUCH
HA! Was that a TIE?!
That was DEFINITELY a tie, wasn't it?!
whew
Did you see how far behind you I was at the start?
BEN! YOU WENT EXTINCT!
?
Does he not CARE?
Hey, look! This is perfect for climbing!
The surface is real scratchy, so you don't slip at all.

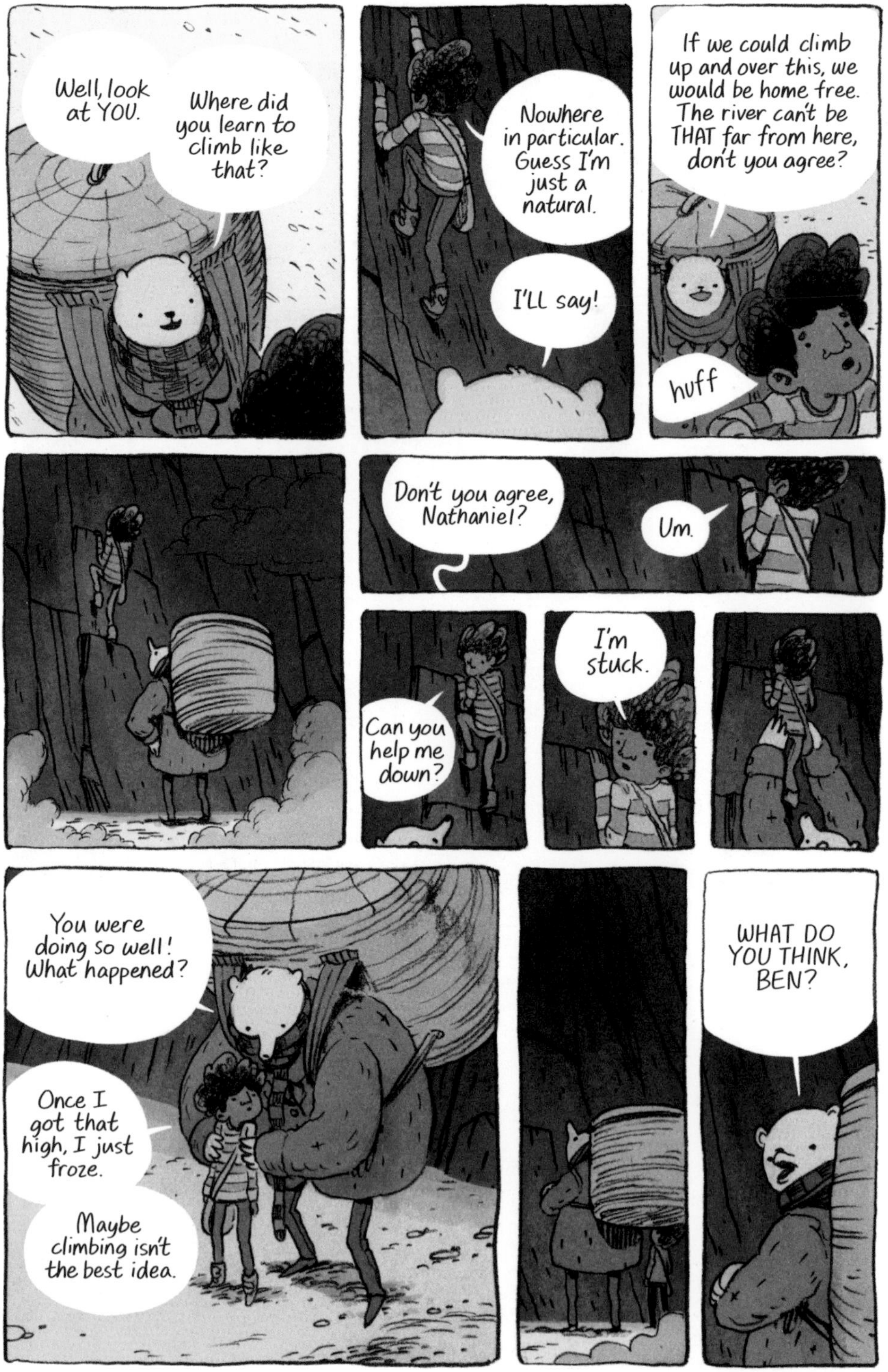
Well, look at YOU.
Where did you learn to climb like that?
Nowhere in particular. Guess I'm just a natural.
I'LL say!
If we could climb up and over this, we would be home free. The river can't be THAT far from here, don't you agree?
huff
Don't you agree, Nathaniel?
Um.
Can you help me down?
I'm stuck.
You were doing so well! What happened?
Once I got that high, I just froze.
Maybe climbing isn't the best idea.
WHAT DO YOU THINK, BEN?

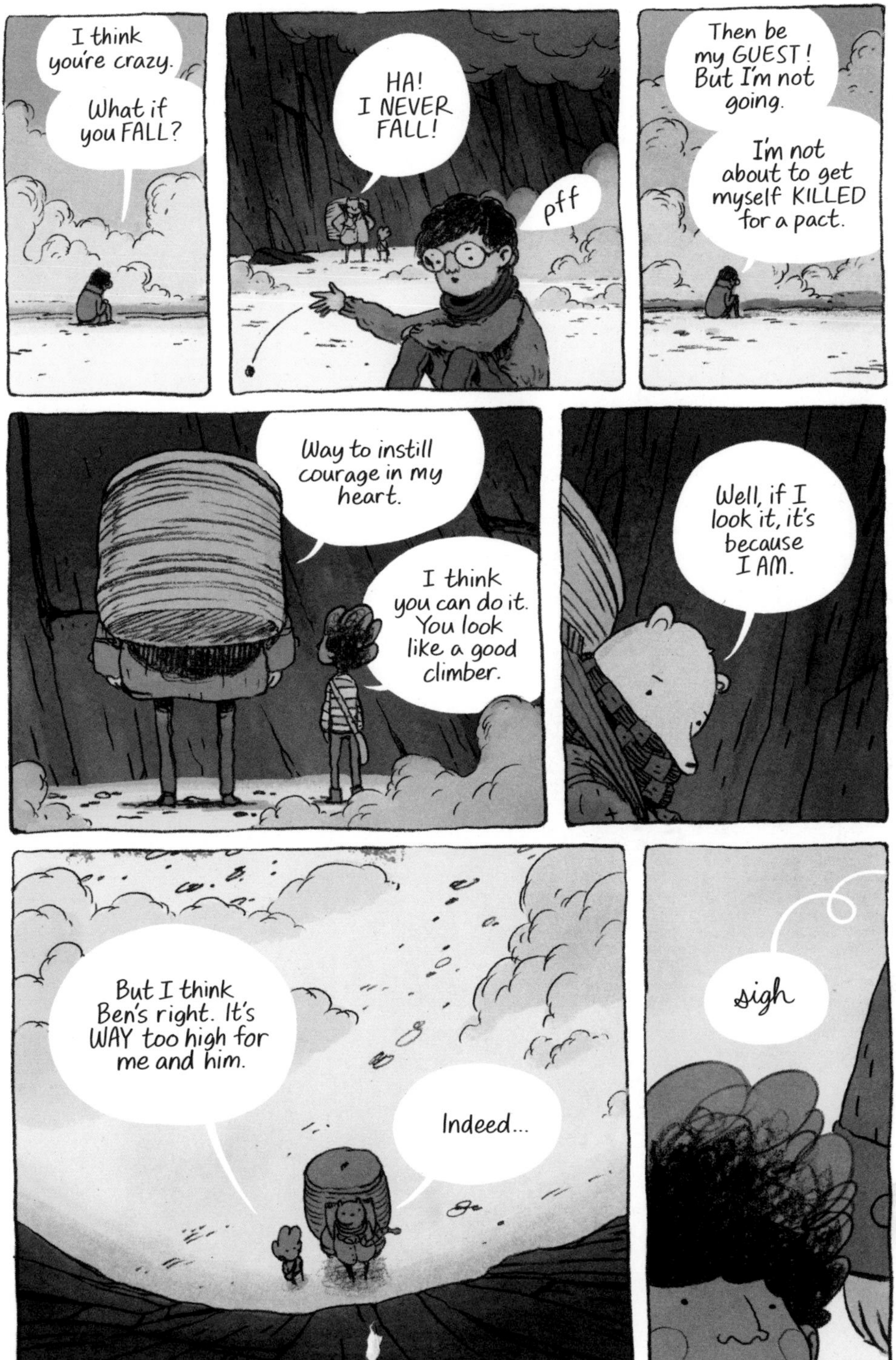
I think you're crazy.
What if you FALL?
HA! I NEVER FALL!
pff
Then be my GUEST! But I'm not going.
I'm not about to get myself KILLED for a pact.
Way to instill courage in my heart.
I think you can do it. You look like a good climber.
Well, if I look it, it's because I AM.
But I think Ben's right. It's WAY too high for me and him.
Indeed...
sigh

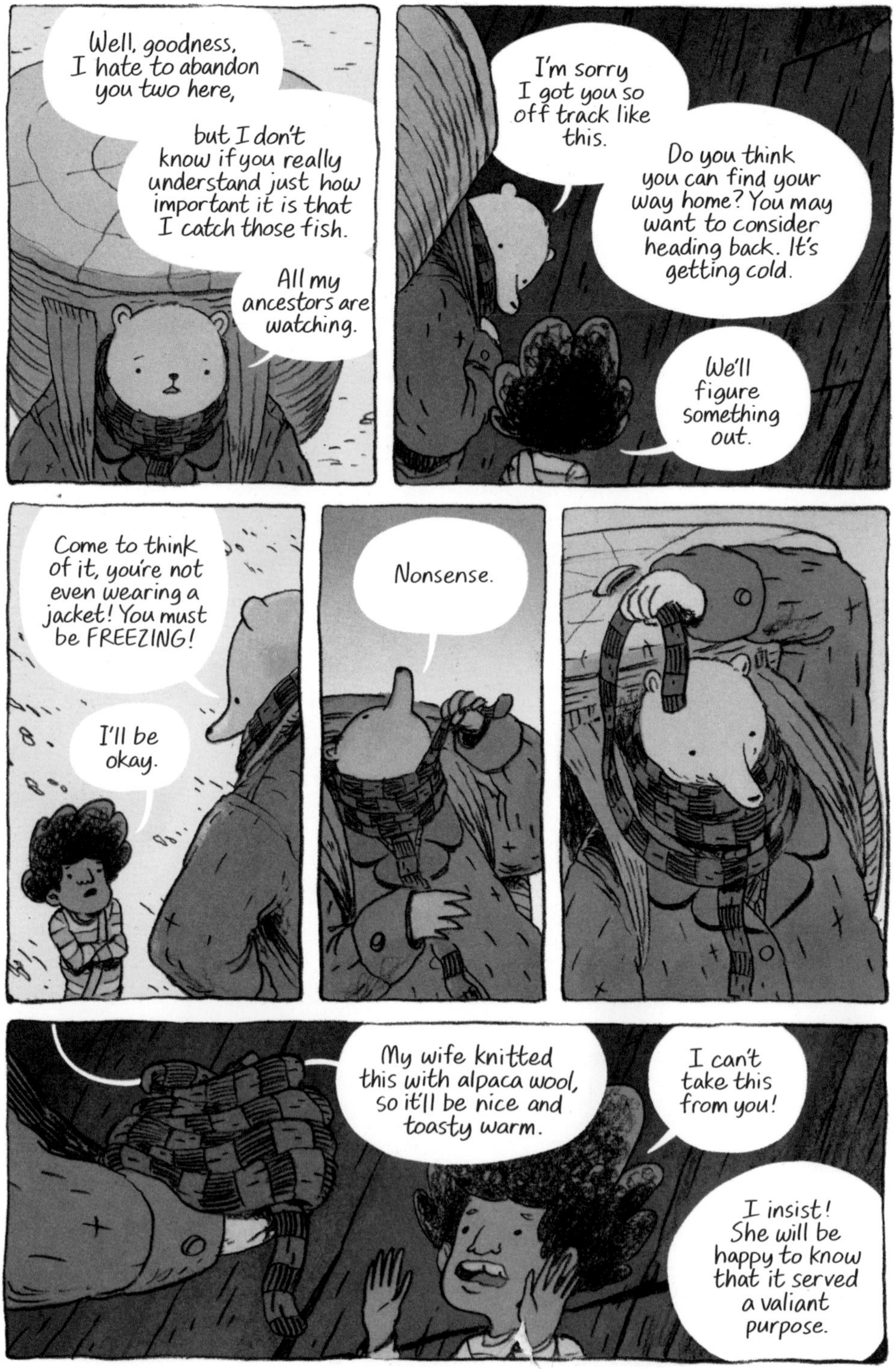
Well, goodness, I hate to abandon you two here,
but I don't know if you really understand just how important it is that I catch those fish.
All my ancestors are watching.
I'm sorry I got you so off track like this.
Do you think you can find your way home? You may want to consider heading back. It's getting cold.
We'll figure something out.
Come to think of it, you're not even wearing a jacket! You must be FREEZING!
I'll be okay.
Nonsense.
My wife knitted this with alpaca wool, so it'll be nice and toasty warm.
I can't take this from you!
I insist! She will be happy to know that it served a valiant purpose.

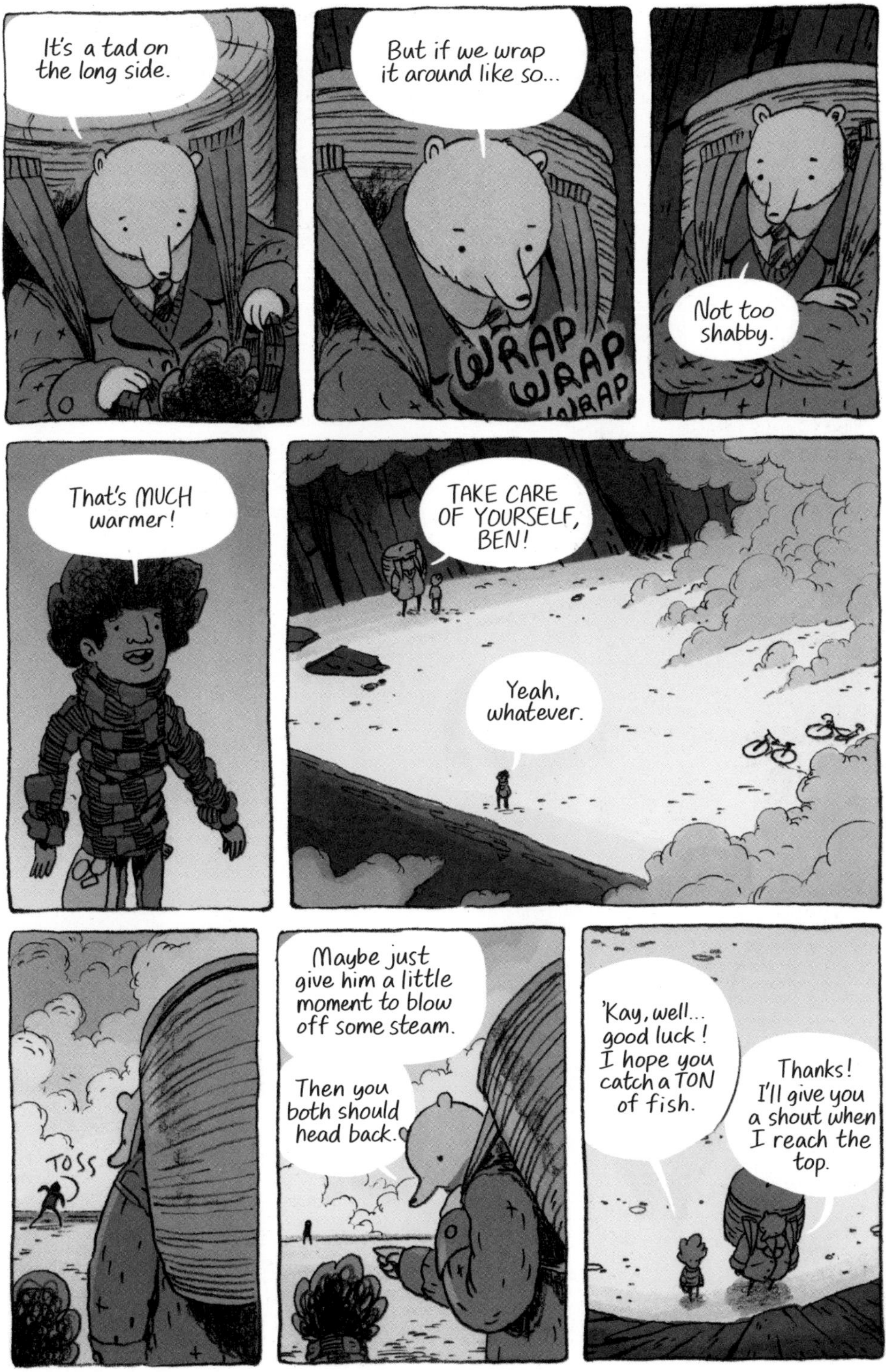
It's a tad on the long side.
But if we wrap it around like so...
WRAP WRAP WRAP
Not too shabby.
That's MUCH warmer!
TAKE CARE OF YOURSELF, BEN!
Yeah, whatever.
TOSS
Maybe just give him a little moment to blow off some steam.
Then you both should head back.
'Kay, well... good luck! I hope you catch a TON of fish.
Thanks! I'll give you a shout when I reach the top.

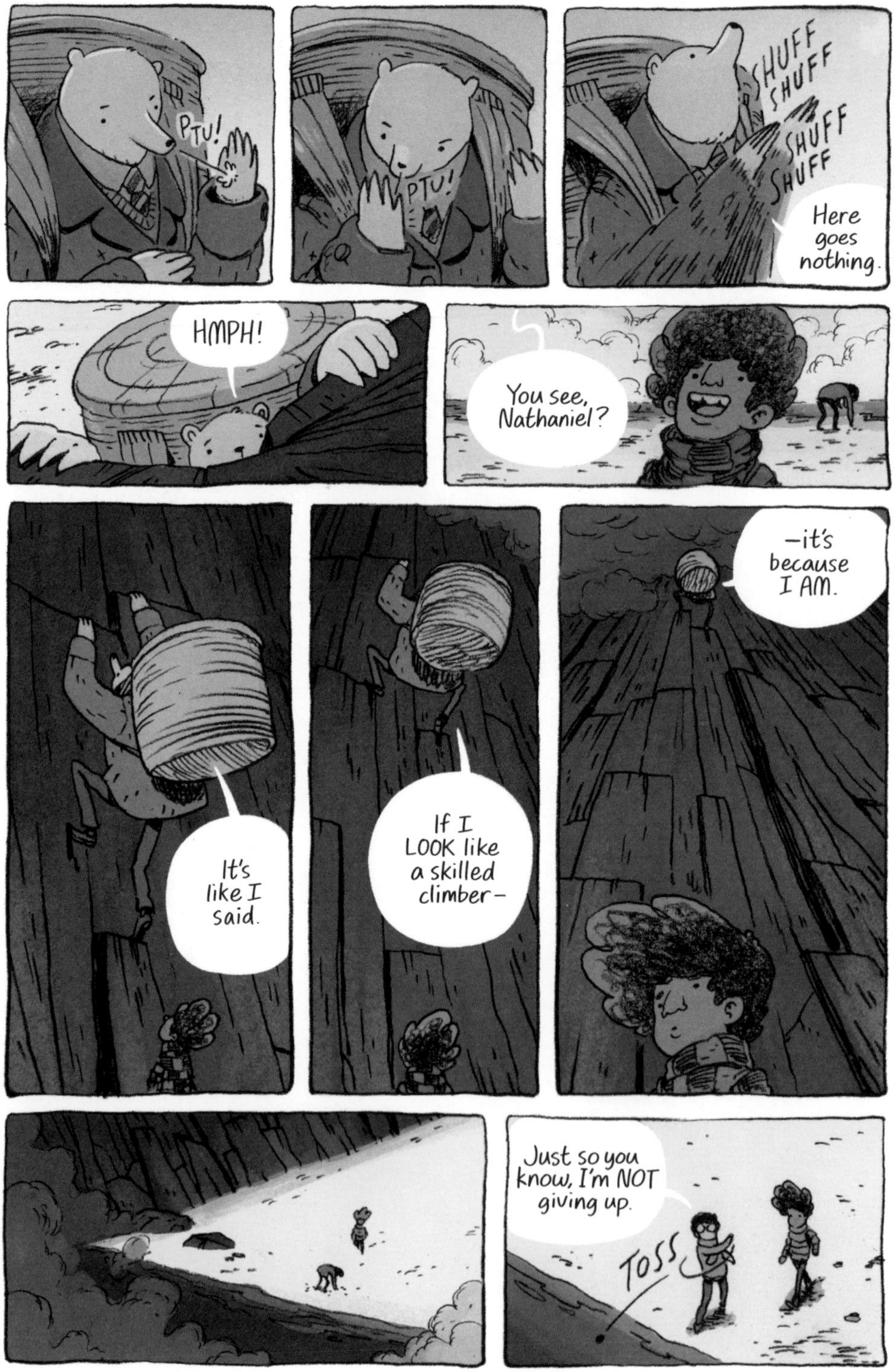
PTU!
PTU!
SHUFF SHUFF
SHUFF SHUFF
Here goes nothing.
HMPH!
You see, Nathaniel?
It's like I said.
If I LOOK like a skilled climber-
-it's because I AM.
Just so you know, I'm NOT giving up.
TOSS

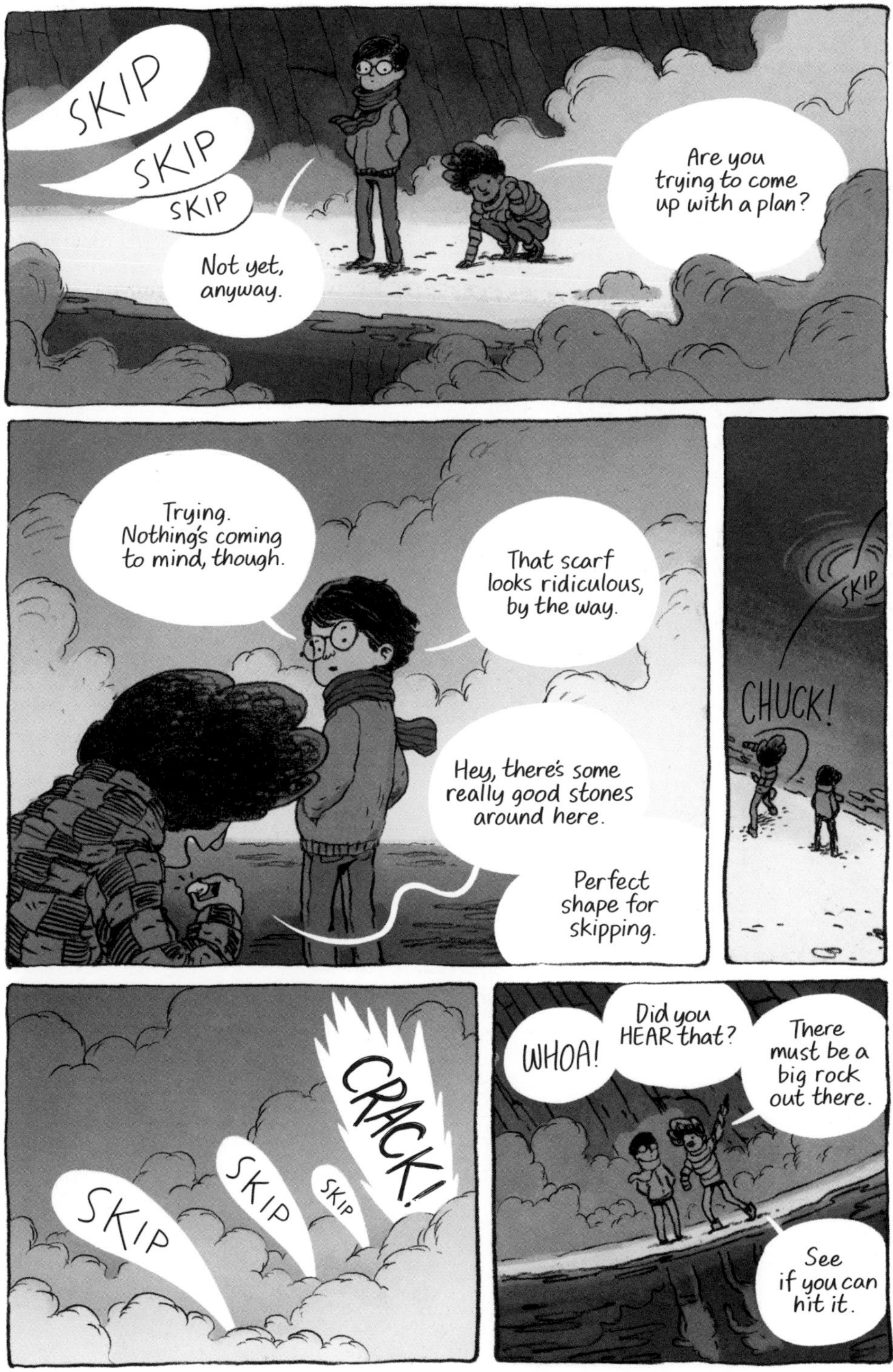
SKIP
SKIP
SKIP
Not yet, anyway.
Are you trying to come up with a plan?
Trying. Nothing's coming to mind, though.
That scarf looks ridiculous, by the way.
Hey, there's some really good stones around here.
Perfect shape for skipping.
SKIP
CHUCK!
SKIP
SKIP
SKIP
CRACK!
WHOA!
Did you HEAR that?
There must be a big rock out there.
See if you can hit it.

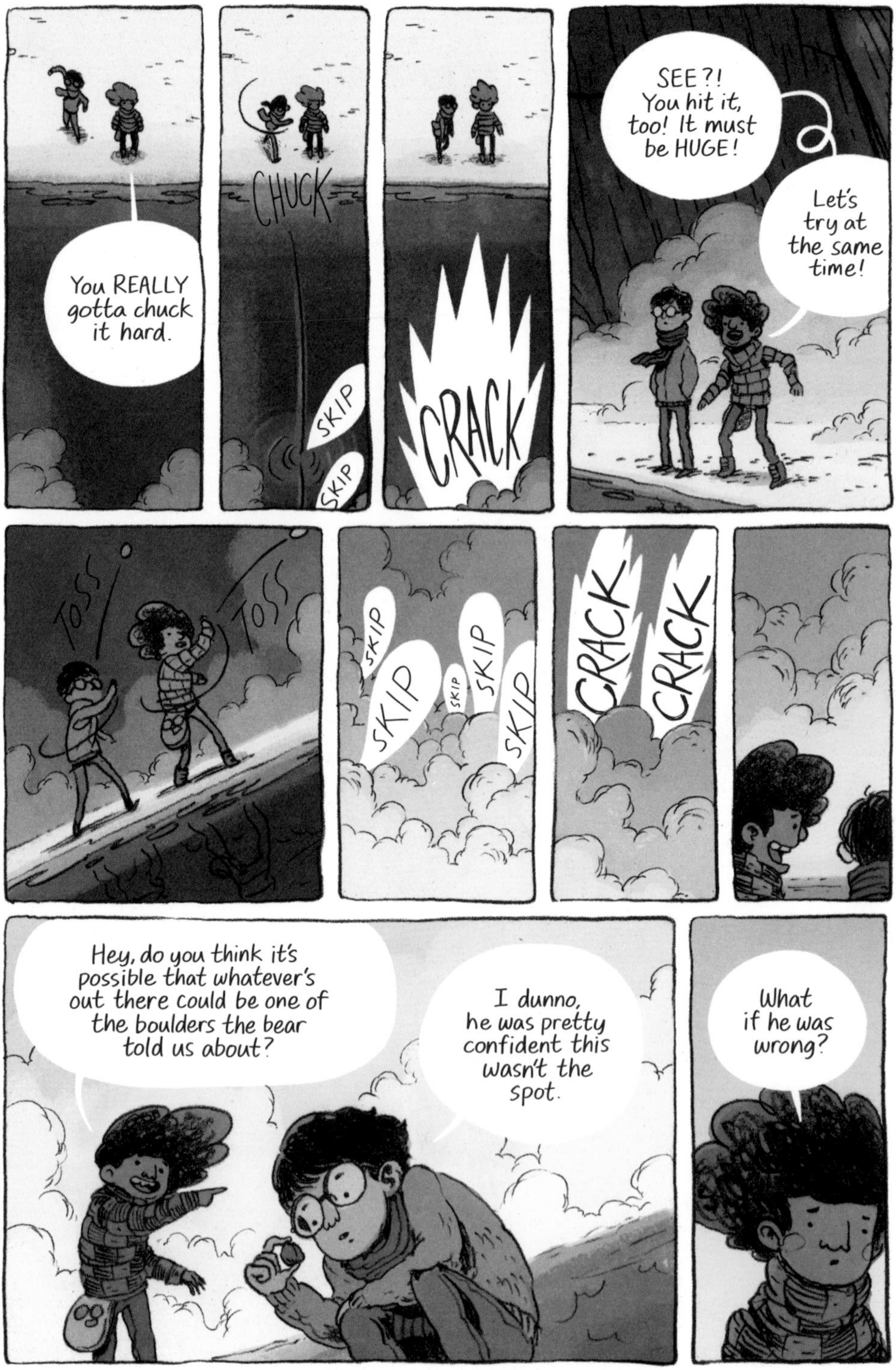
You REALLY gotta chuck it hard.
CHUCK
SKIP
SKIP
CRACK
SEE?! You hit it, too! It must be HUGE!
Let's try at the same time!
TOSS
TOSS
SKIP
SKIP
SKIP
SKIP
SKIP
CRACK
CRACK
Hey, do you think it's possible that whatever's out there could be one of the boulders the bear told us about?
I dunno, he was pretty confident this wasn't the spot.
What if he was wrong?

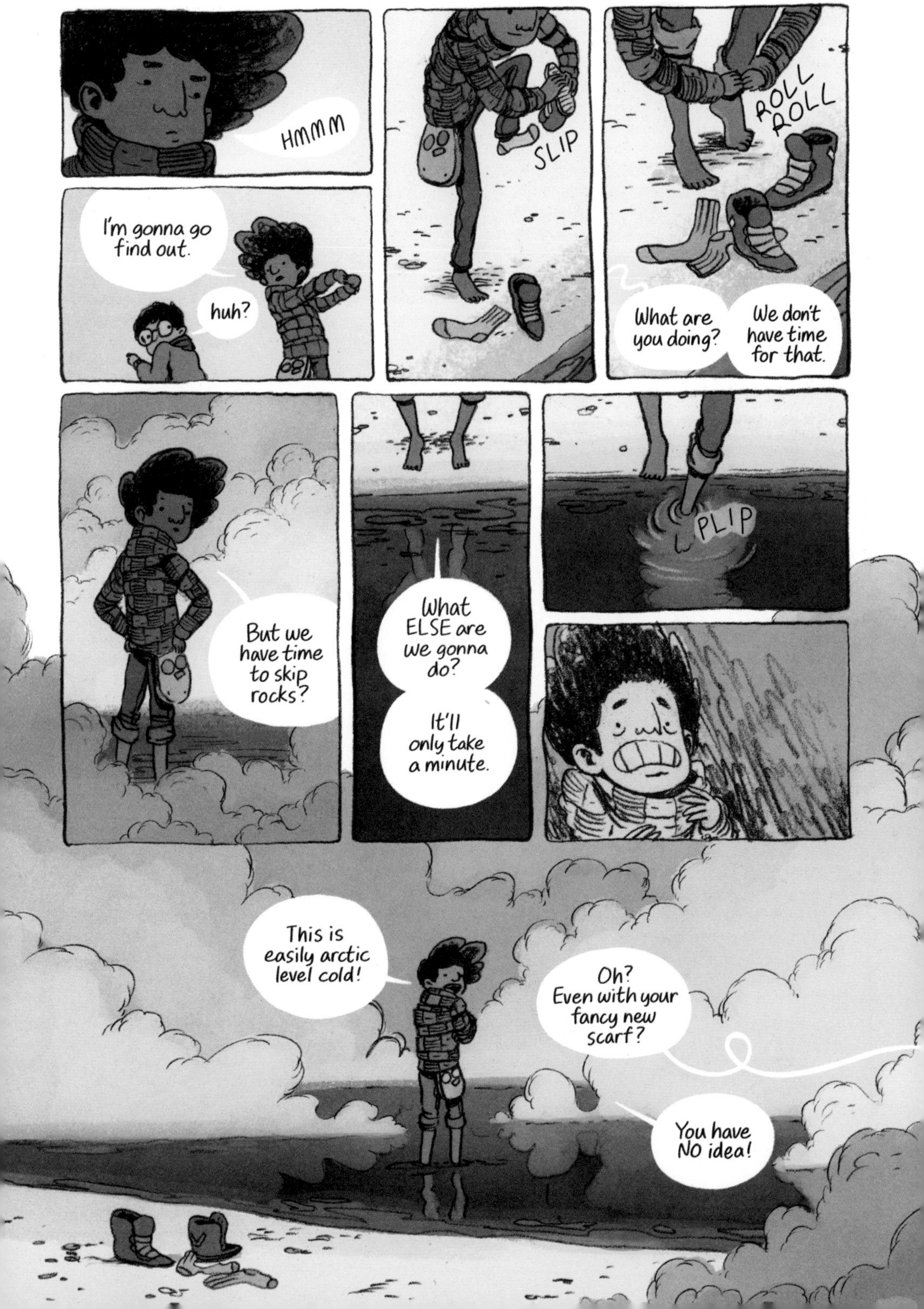
HMMM
I'm gonna go find out.
huh?
SLIP
ROLL ROLL
What are you doing?
We don't have time for that.
But we have time to skip rocks?
What ELSE are we gonna do?
It'll only take a minute.
PLIP
This is easily arctic level cold!
Oh? Even with your fancy new scarf?
You have NO idea!

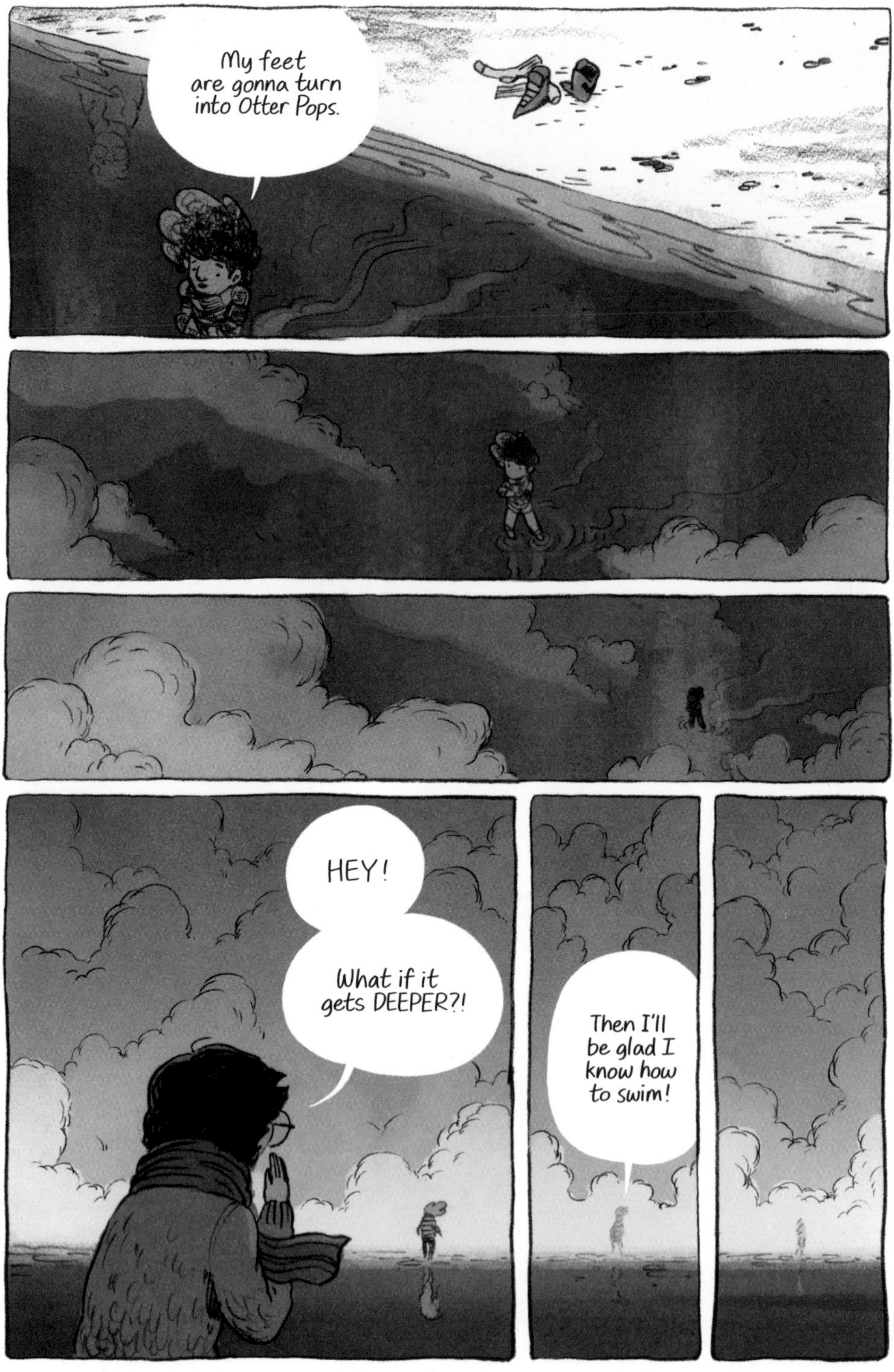
My feet are gonna turn into Otter Pops.
HEY!
What if it gets DEEPER?!
Then I'll be glad I know how to swim!

NATHANIEL!
DID YOU FIND WHAT WE HIT?!
Nathaniel?

Are you there?

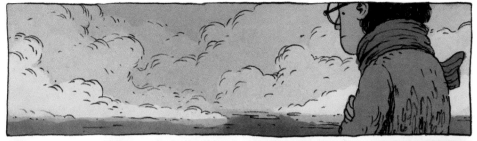

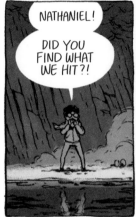

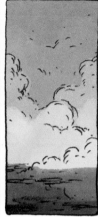

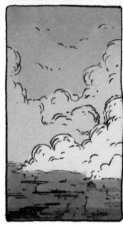

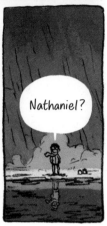

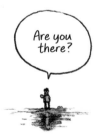

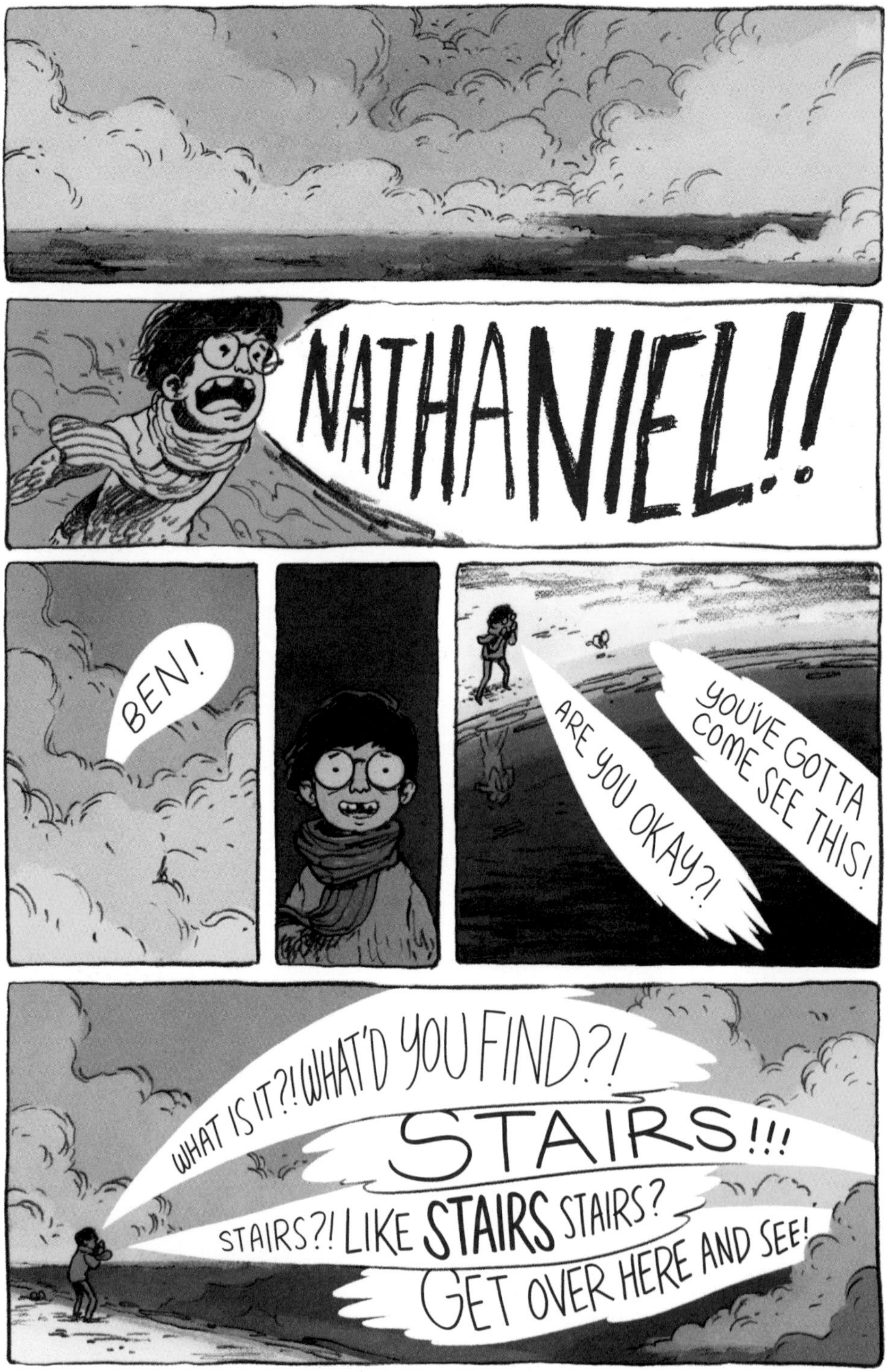
NATHANIEL!!
BEN!
ARE YOU OKAY?!
YOU'VE GOTTA COME SEE THIS!
WHAT IS IT?! WHAT'D YOU FIND?!
STAIRS!!!
STAIRS?! LIKE STAIRS STAIRS?
GET OVER HERE AND SEE!

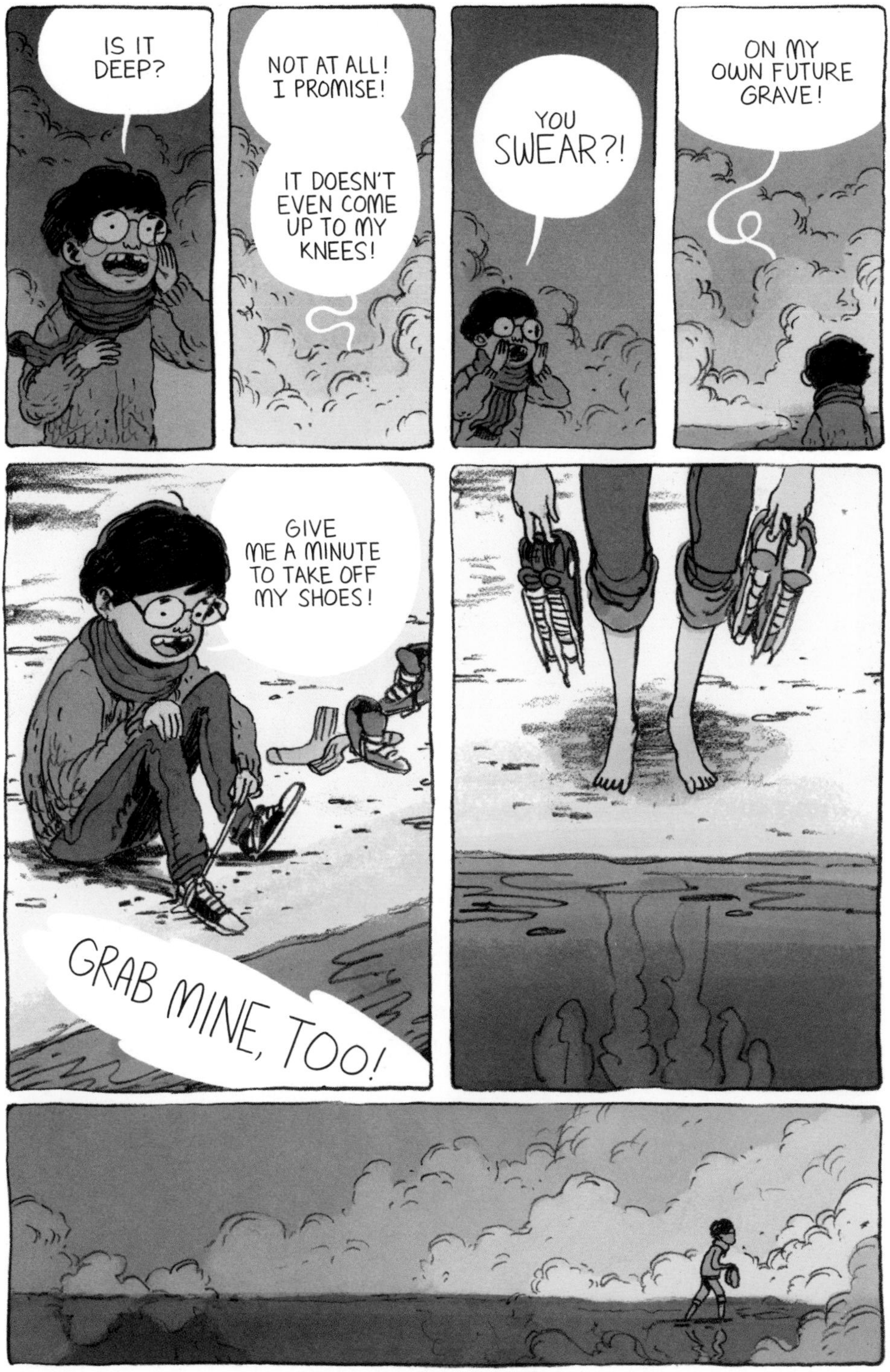
IS IT DEEP?
NOT AT ALL! I PROMISE!
IT DOESN'T EVEN COME UP TO MY KNEES!
YOU SWEAR?!
ON MY OWN FUTURE GRAVE!
GIVE ME A MINUTE TO TAKE OFF MY SHOES!
GRAB MINE, TOO!

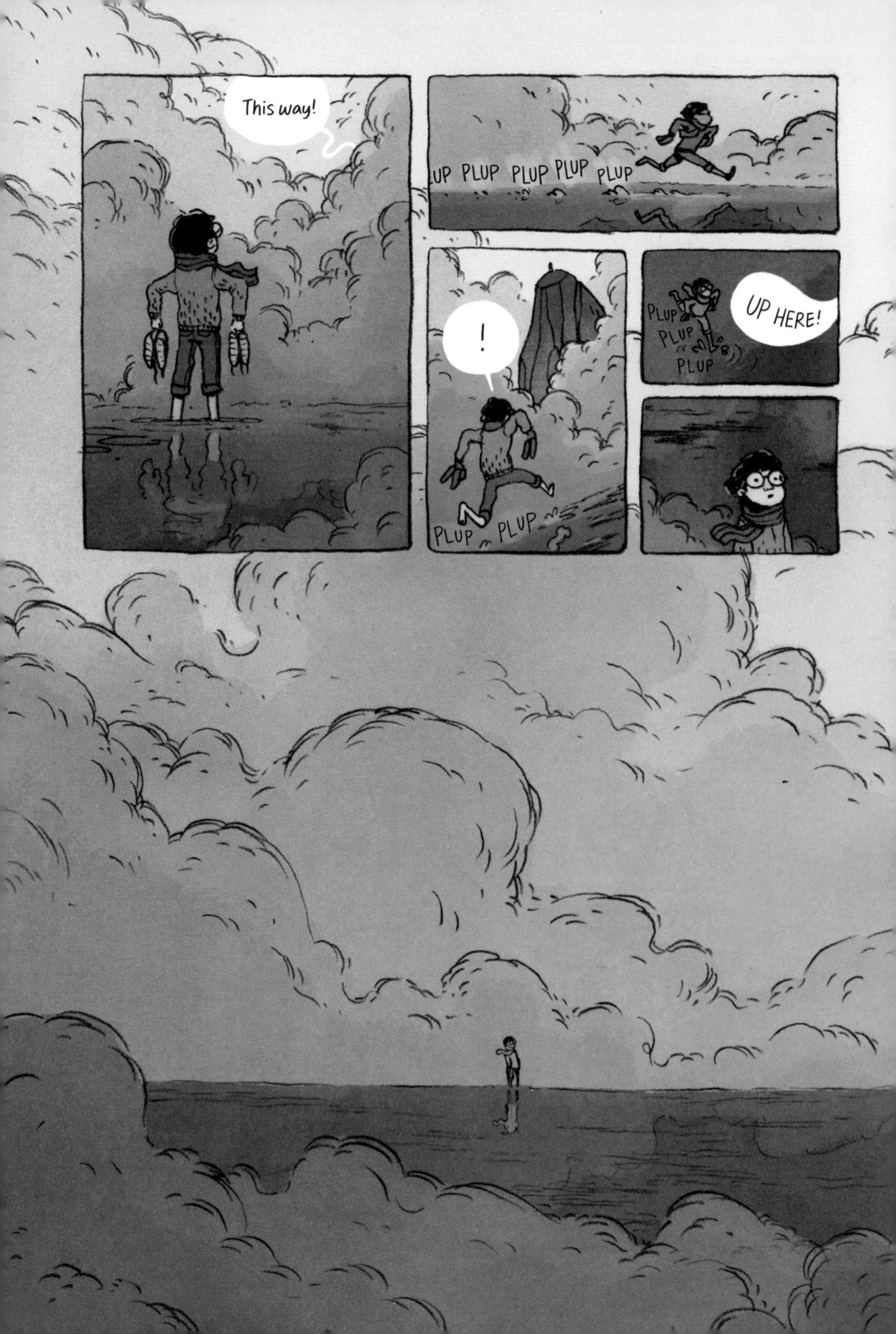
This way!
PLUP PLUP PLUP PLUP PLUP
!
PLUP PLUP
PLUP PLUP PLUP
UP HERE!

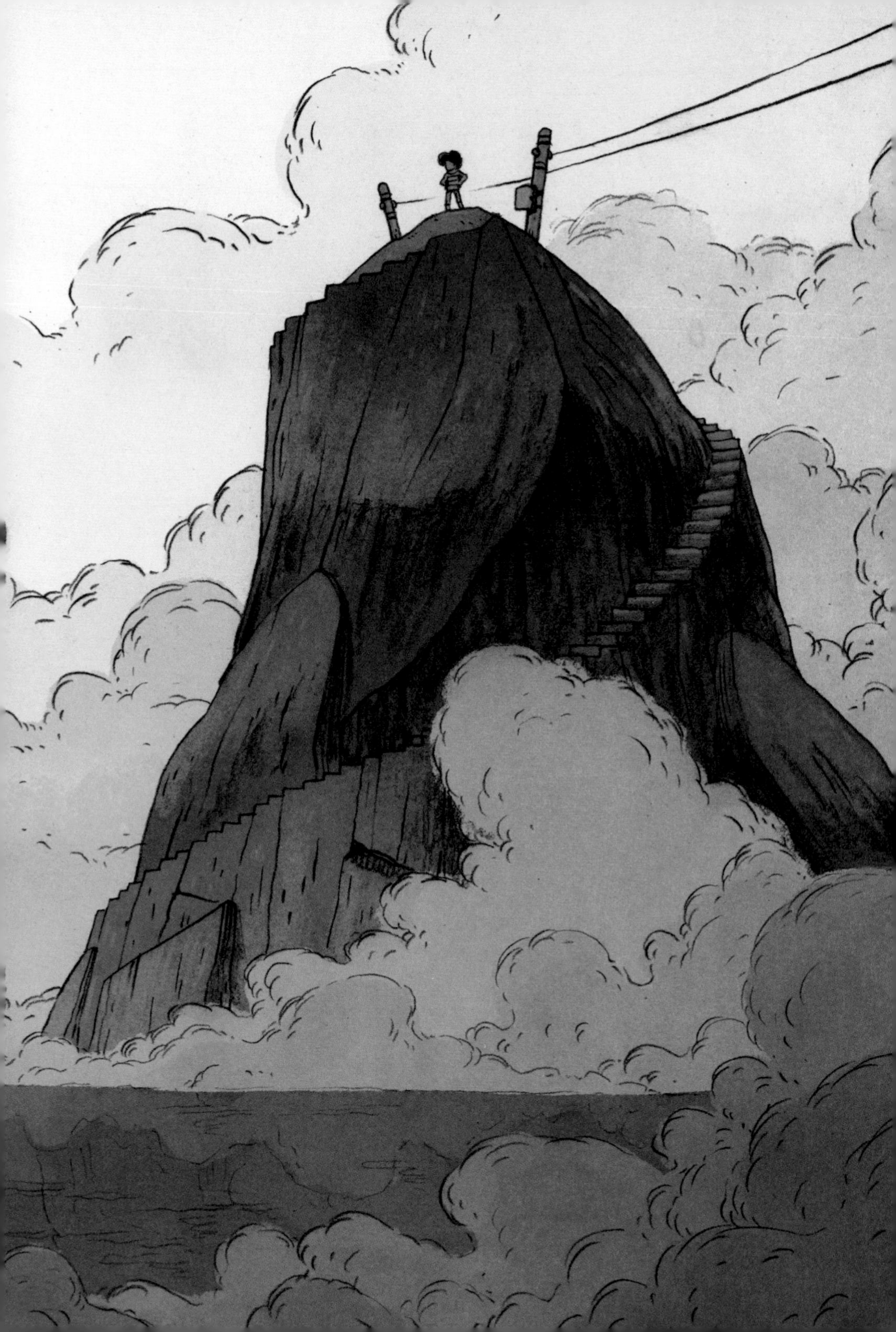

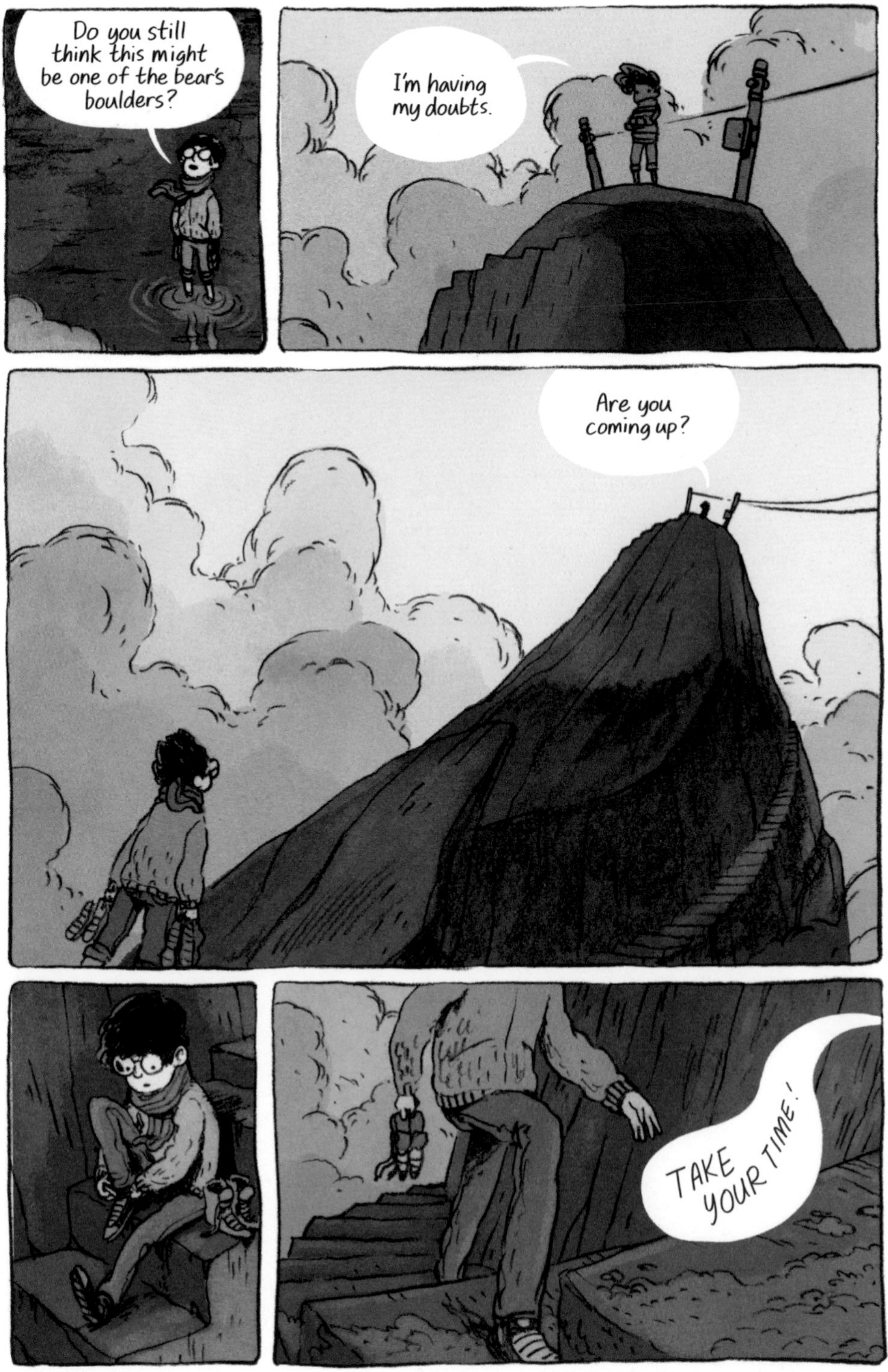
Do you still think this might be one of the bear's boulders?
I'm having my doubts.
Are you coming up?
TAKE YOUR TIME!

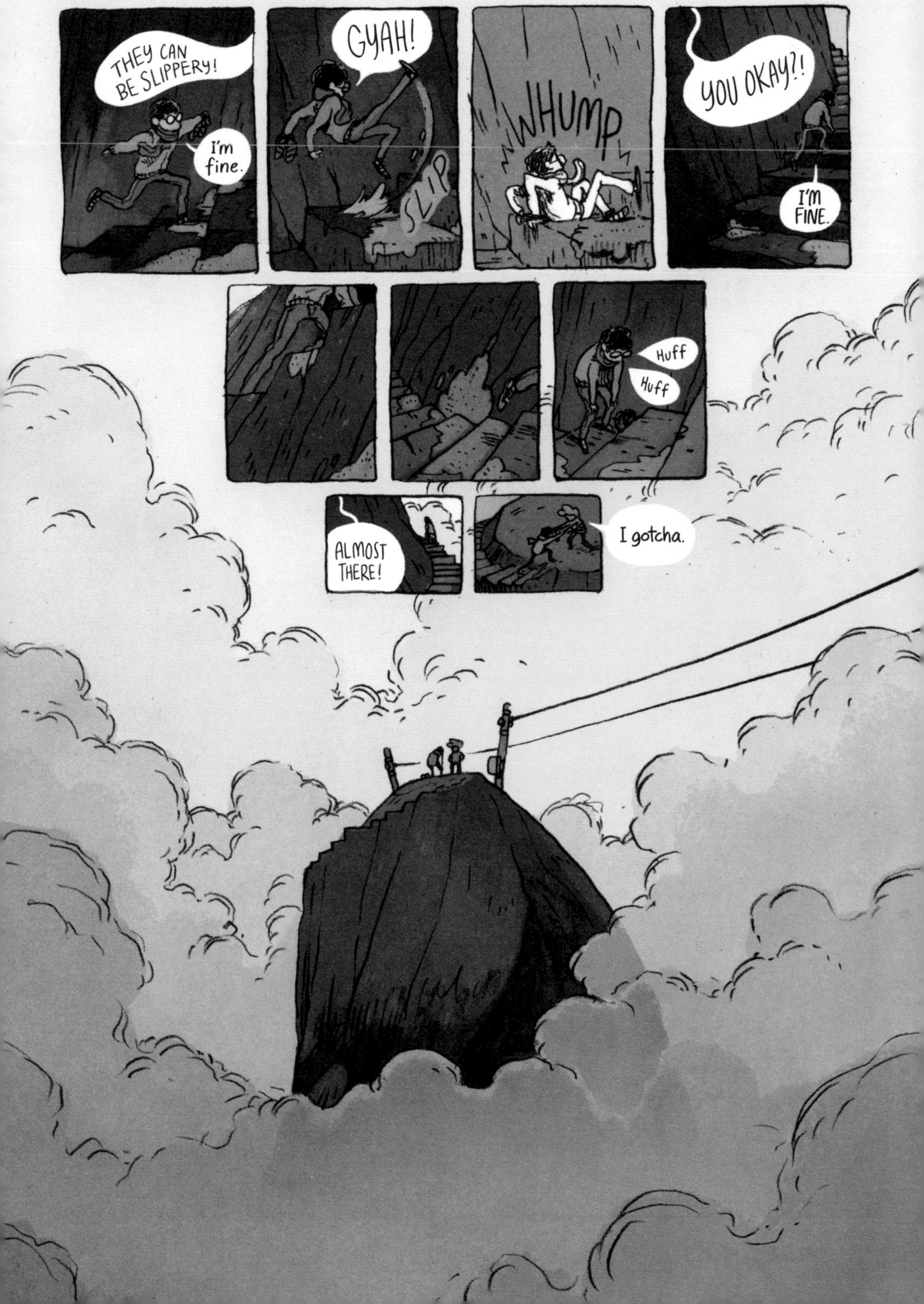
THEY CAN BE SLIPPERY!
I'm fine.
GYAH!
SLIP
WHUMP
YOU OKAY?!
I'M FINE.
Huff
Huff
ALMOST THERE!
I gotcha.

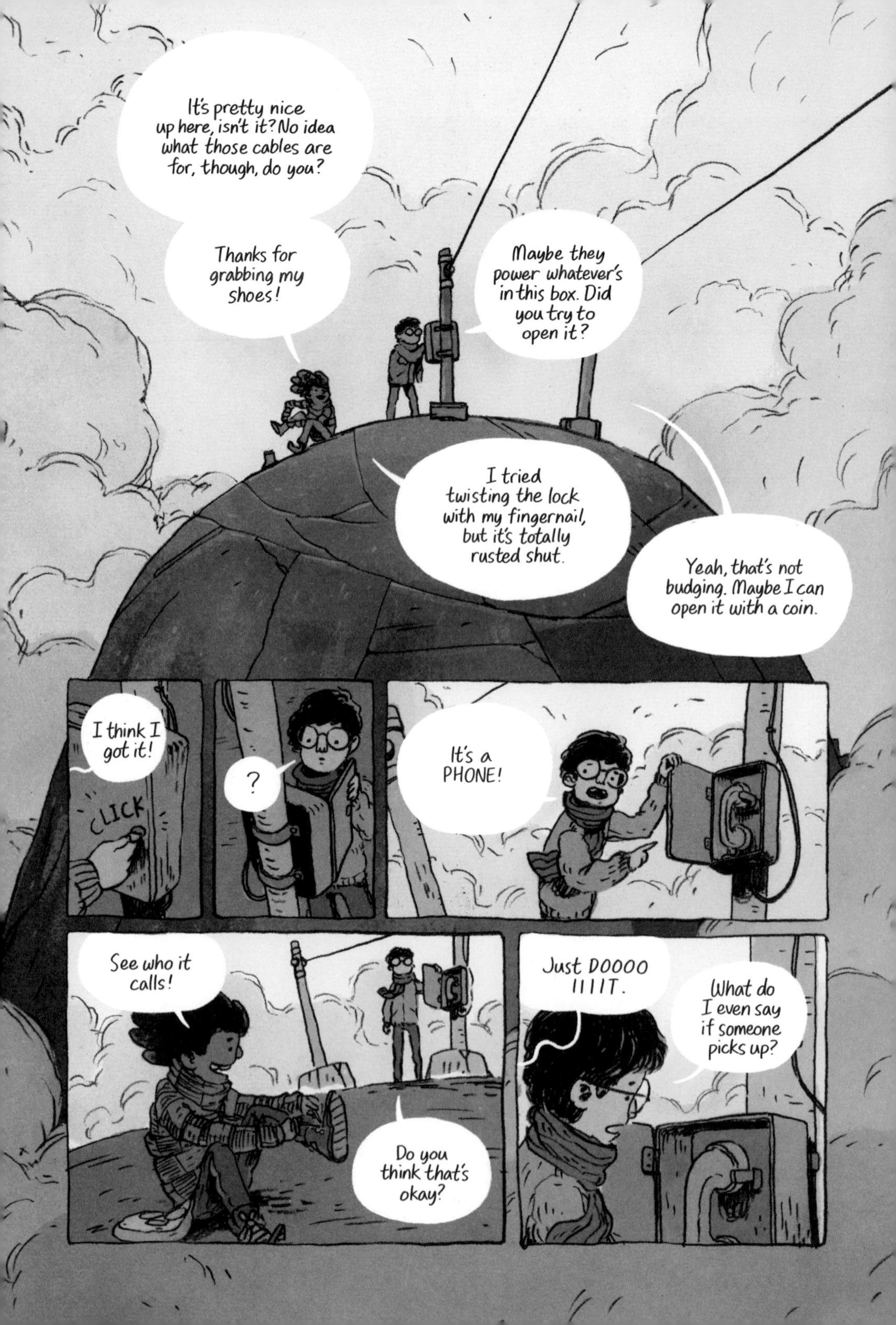
It's pretty nice up here, isn't it? No idea what those cables are for, though, do you?
Thanks for grabbing my shoes!
Maybe they power whatever's in this box. Did you try to open it?
I tried twisting the lock with my fingernail, but it's totally rusted shut.
Yeah, that's not budging. Maybe I can open it with a coin.
I think I got it!
CLICK
?
It's a PHONE!
See who it calls!
Do you think that's okay?
Just DOOOO IIIIT.
What do I even say if someone picks up?

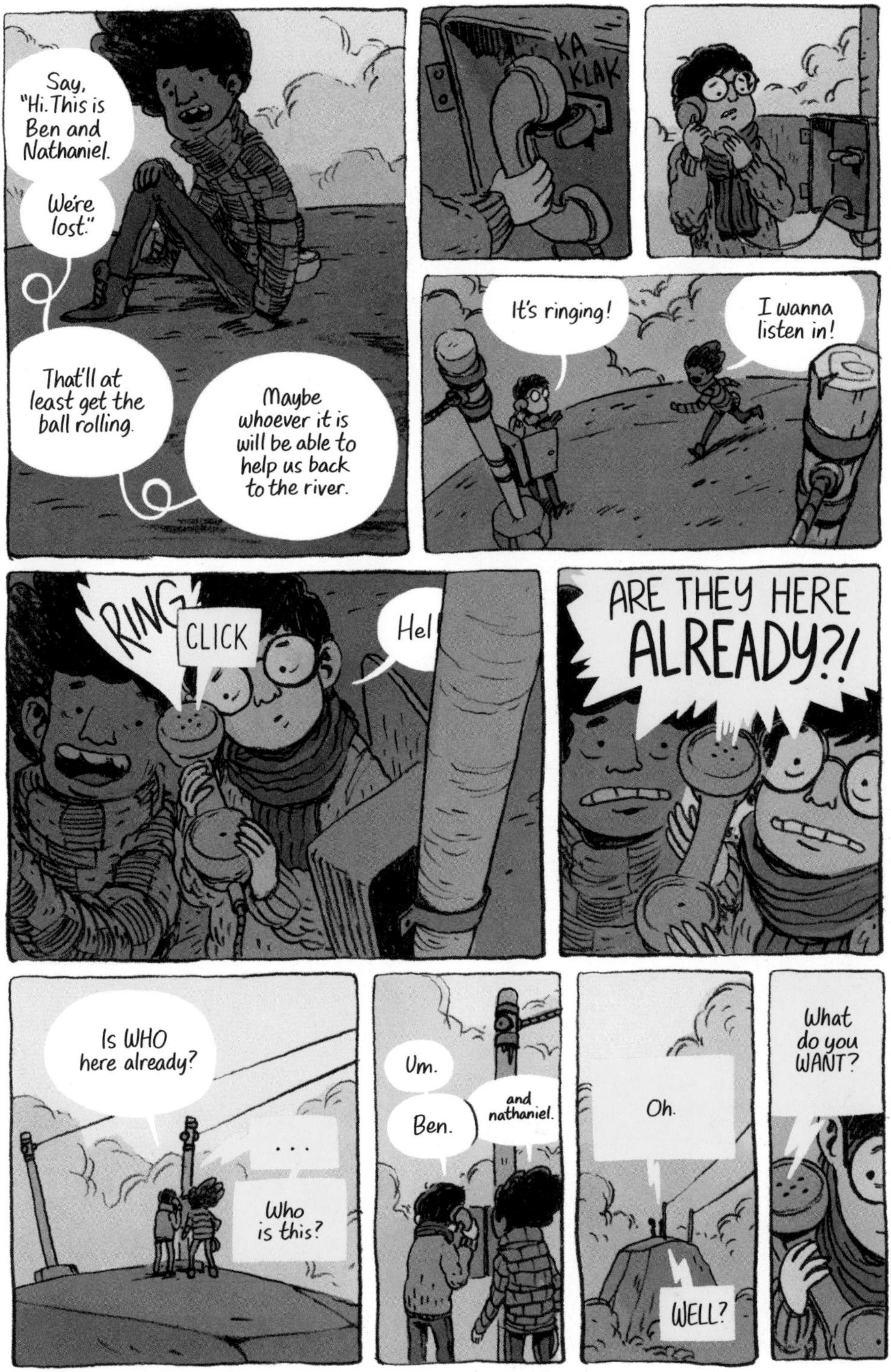

Say, "Hi. This is Ben and Nathaniel.
We're lost."
That'll at least get the ball rolling.
Maybe whoever it is will be able to help us back to the river.
KA KLAK
It's ringing!
I wanna listen in!
RING
CLICK
Hel
ARE THEY HERE ALREADY?!
Is WHO here already?
. . .
Who is this?
Um.
Ben.
and nathaniel.
Oh.
WELL?
What do you WANT?

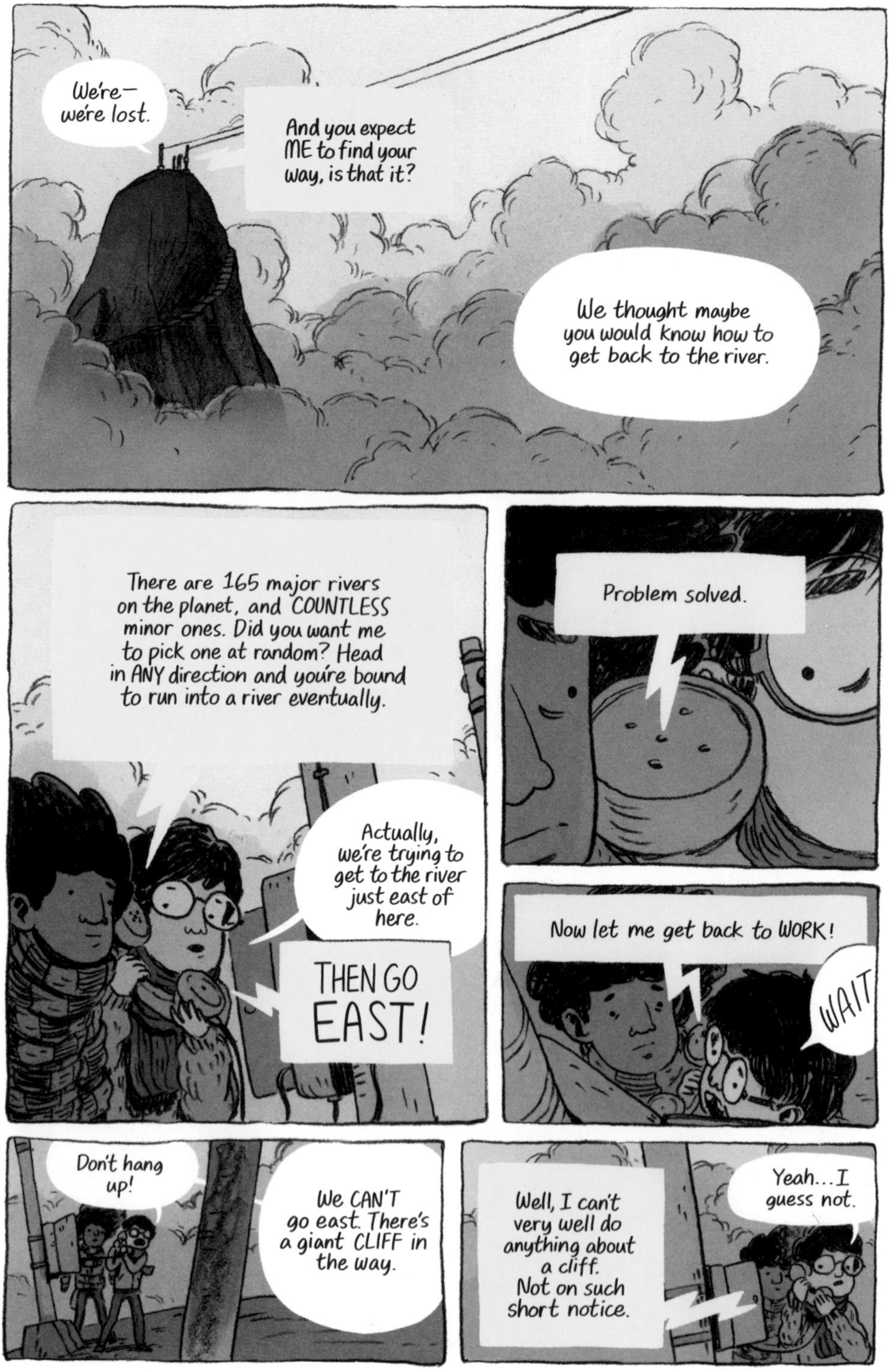
We're—
we're lost.
And you expect ME to find your way, is that it?
We thought maybe you would know how to get back to the river.
There are 165 major rivers on the planet, and COUNTLESS minor ones. Did you want me to pick one at random? Head in ANY direction and you're bound to run into a river eventually.
Actually, we're trying to get to the river just east of here.
THEN GO EAST!
Problem solved.
Now let me get back to WORK!
WAIT
Don't hang up!
We CAN'T go east. There's a giant CLIFF in the way.
Well, I can't very well do anything about a cliff. Not on such short notice.
Yeah... I guess not.

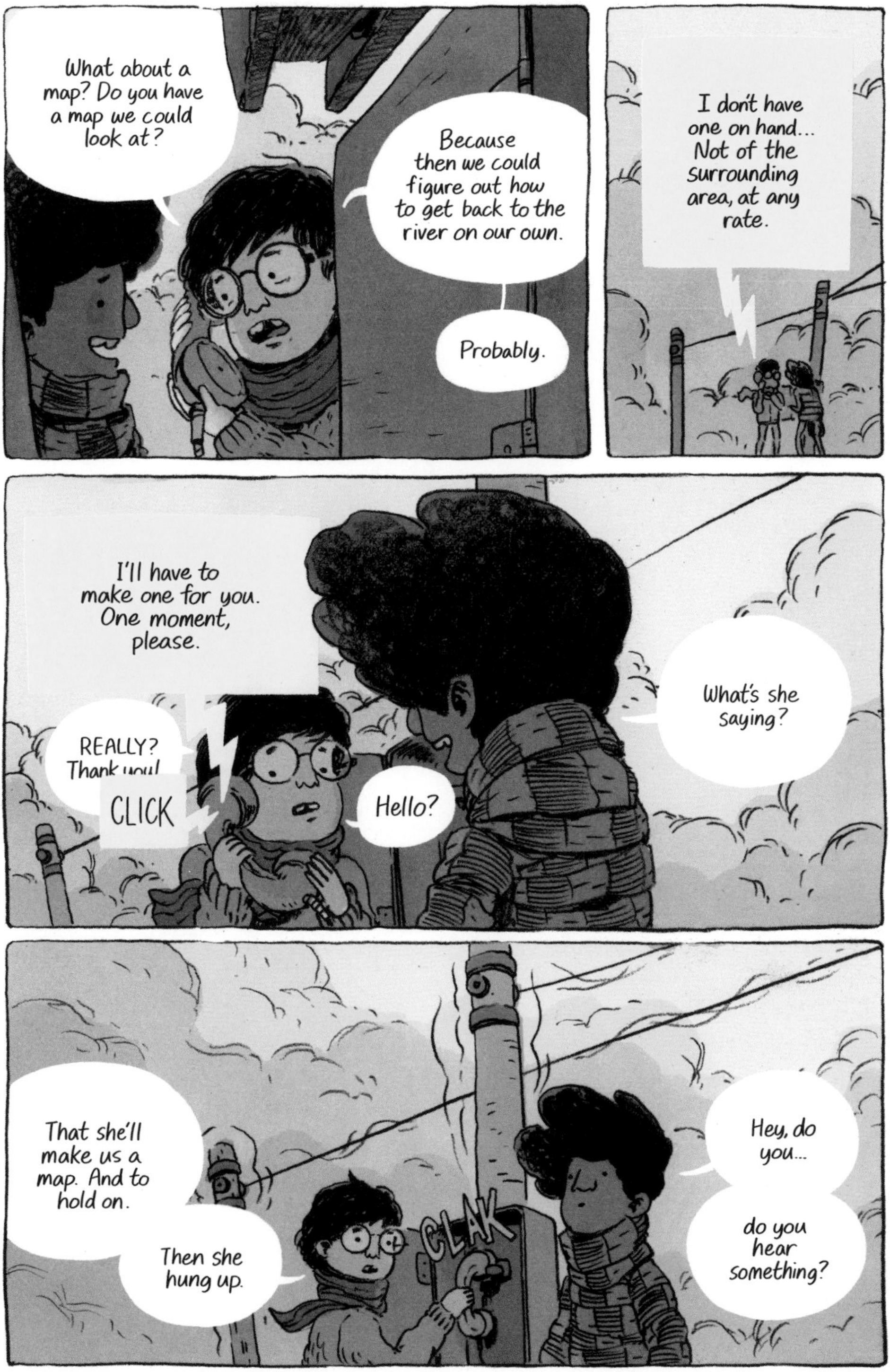
What about a map? Do you have a map we could look at?
Because then we could figure out how to get back to the river on our own.
Probably.
I don't have one on hand... Not of the surrounding area, at any rate.
I'll have to make one for you. One moment, please.
REALLY? Thank you!
CLICK
Hello?
What's she saying?
That she'll make us a map. And to hold on.
Then she hung up.
CLAK
Hey, do you...
do you hear something?

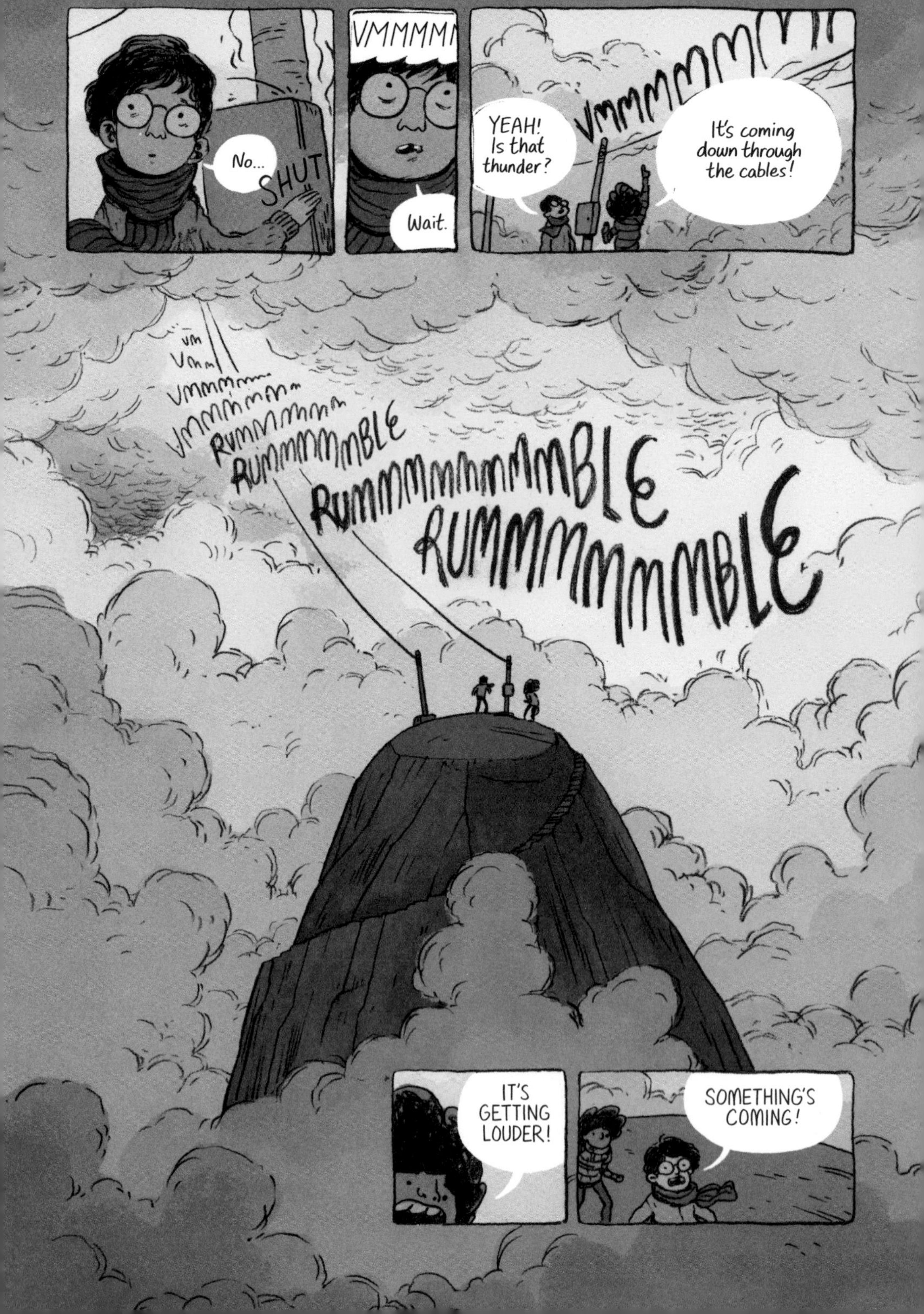
No...
SHUT
VMMMM
Wait.
YEAH! Is that thunder?
VMMMMMM
It's coming down through the cables!
vm
Vmm
VMMMmmm
VMMMMmmm
VMMMMmmm
RUMMMMMM
RUMMMMMBLE
RUMMMMMMMMBLE
RUMMMMMMBLE
IT'S GETTING LOUDER!
SOMETHING'S COMING!

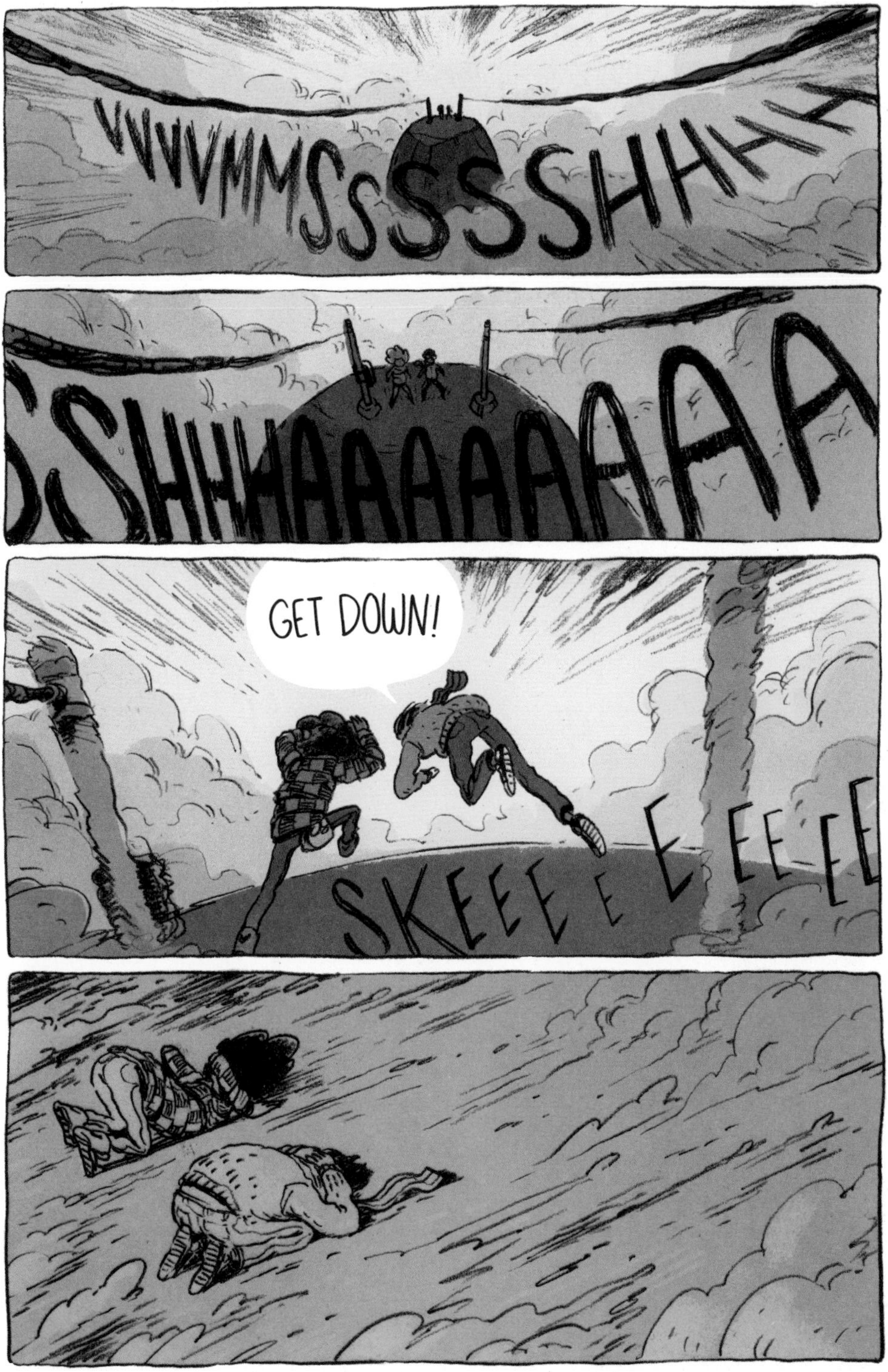
VVVVMMSSSSSSHHAAH
SSHHAAAAAAAAA
GET DOWN!
SKEEEEEEEE

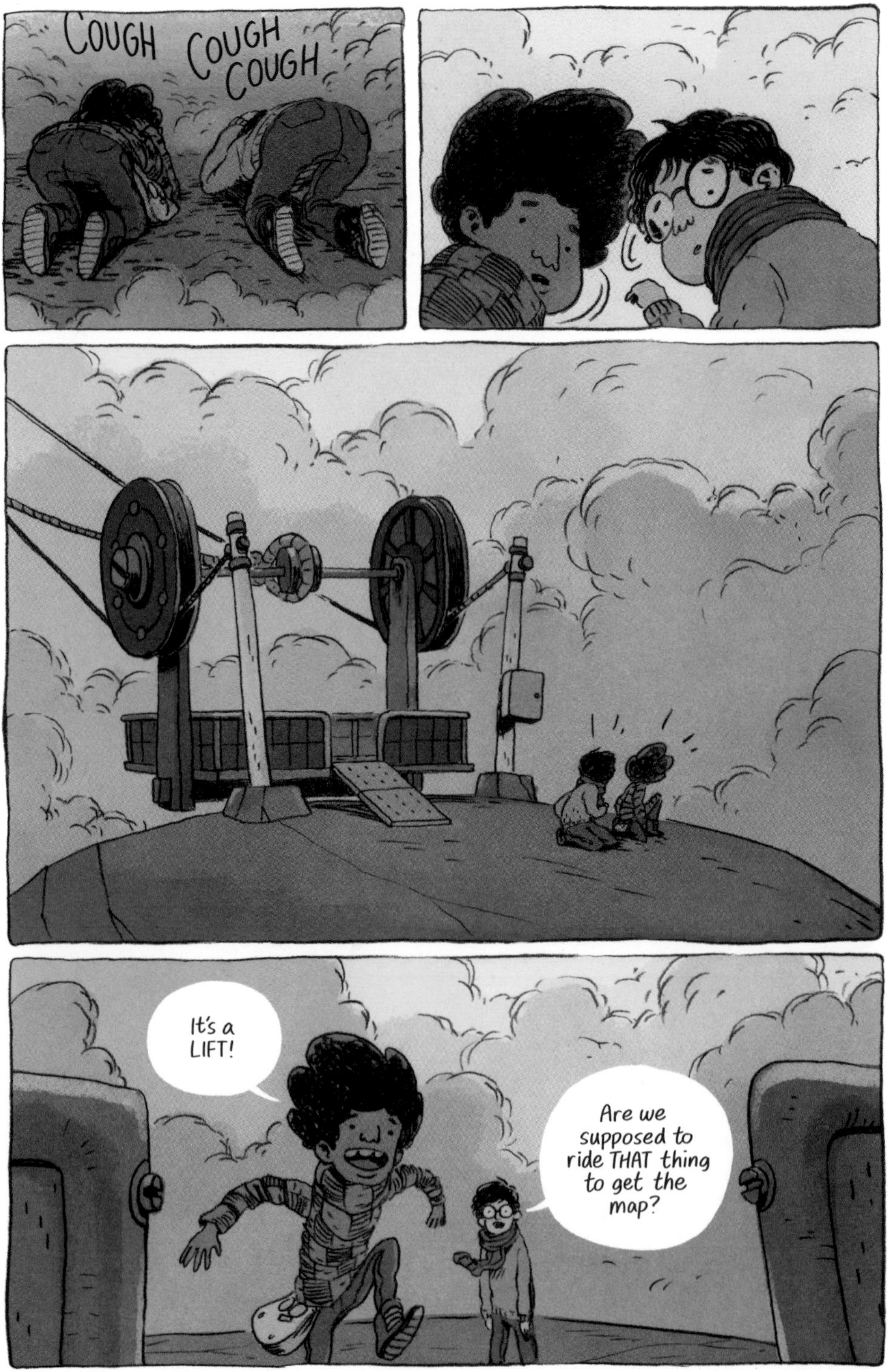
COUGH
COUGH
COUGH
It's a LIFT!
Are we supposed to ride THAT thing to get the map?

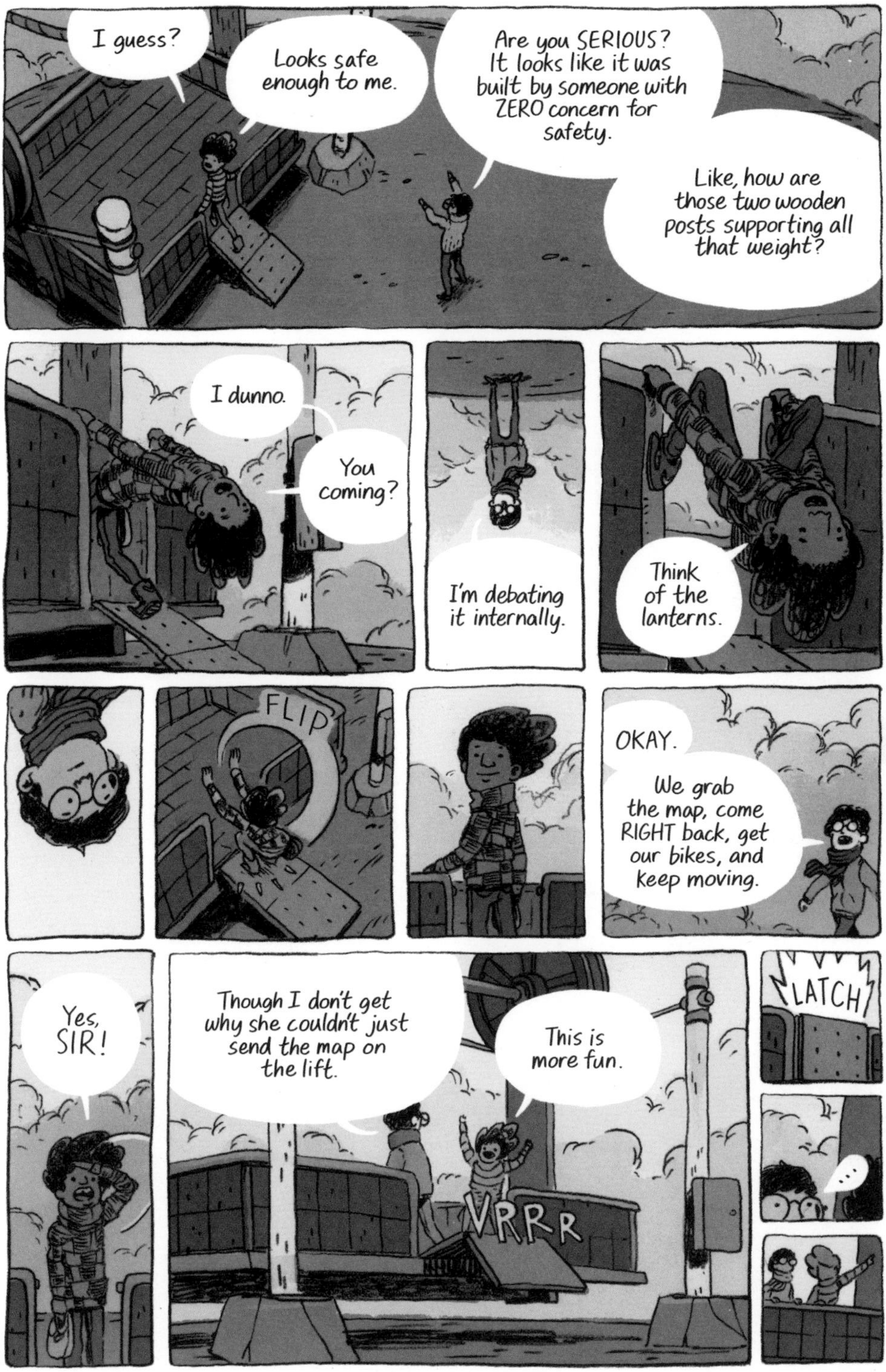
I guess?
Looks safe enough to me.
Are you SERIOUS? It looks like it was built by someone with ZERO concern for safety.
Like, how are those two wooden posts supporting all that weight?
I dunno.
You coming?
I'm debating it internally.
Think of the lanterns.
FLIP
OKAY.
We grab the map, come RIGHT back, get our bikes, and keep moving.
Yes, SIR!
Though I don't get why she couldn't just send the map on the lift.
This is more fun.
VRRR
LATCH
...

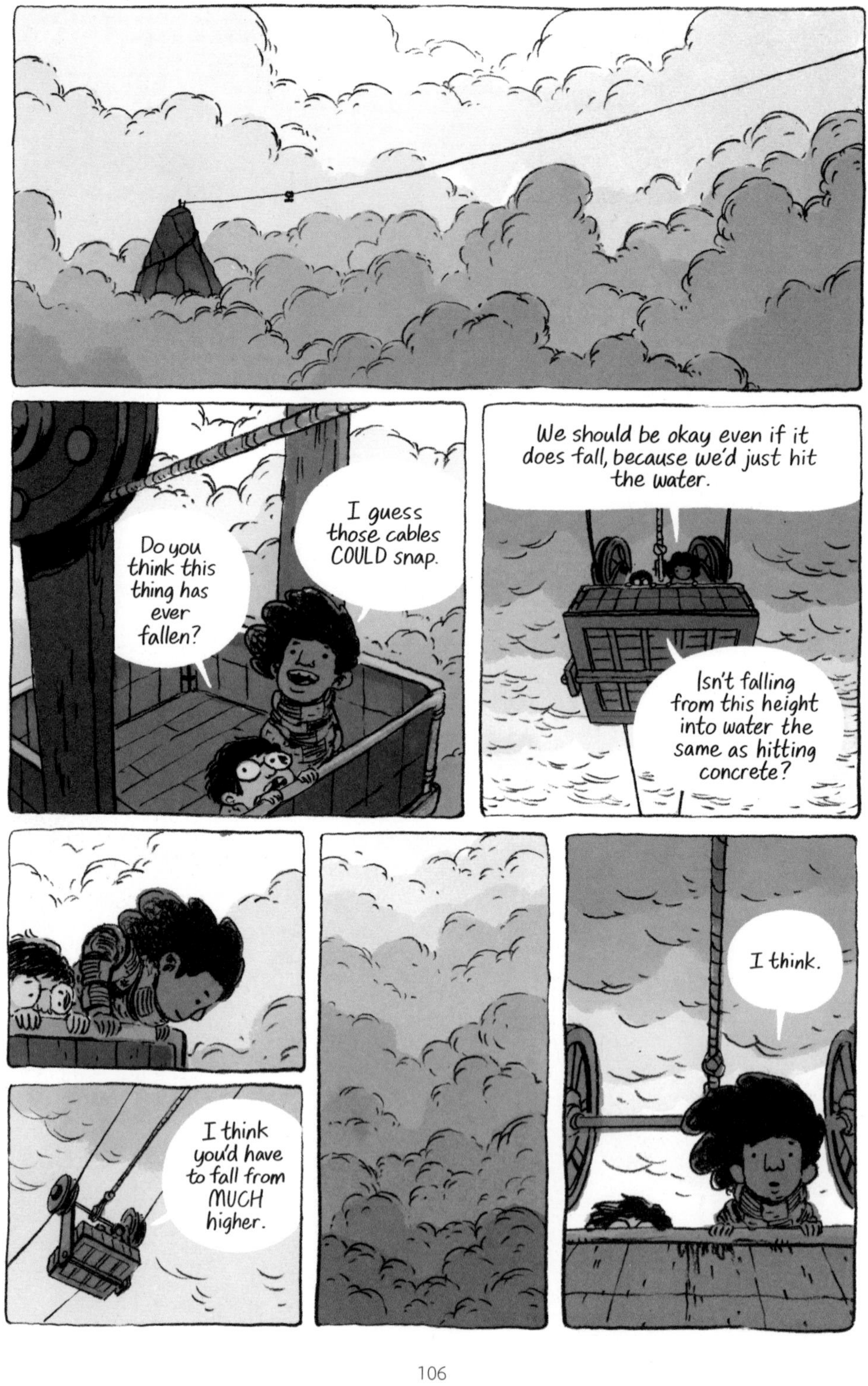
Do you think this thing has ever fallen?
I guess those cables COULD snap.
We should be okay even if it does fall, because we'd just hit the water.
Isn't falling from this height into water the same as hitting concrete?
I think you'd have to fall from MUCH higher.
I think.

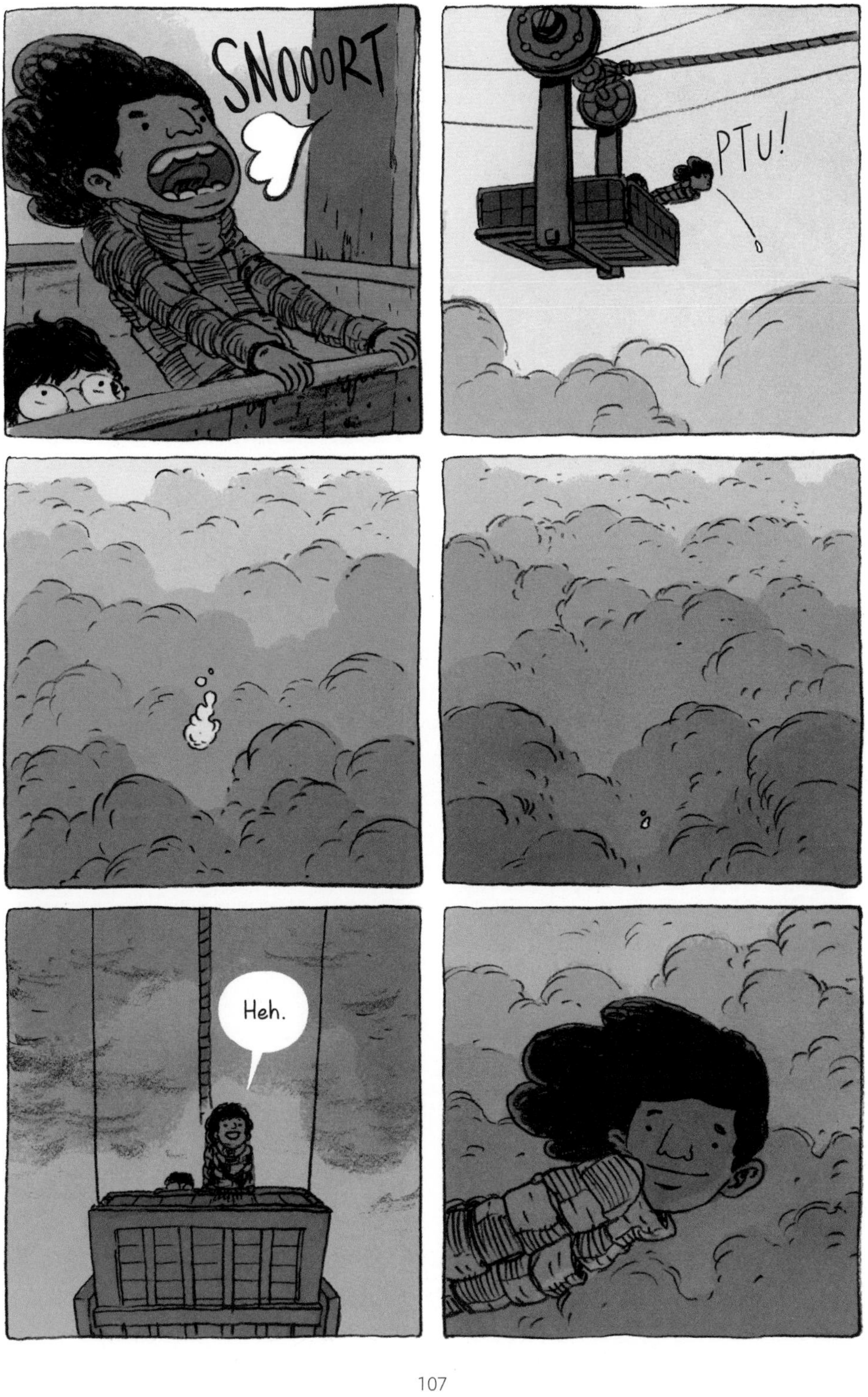
SNOOORT
PTU!
Heh.

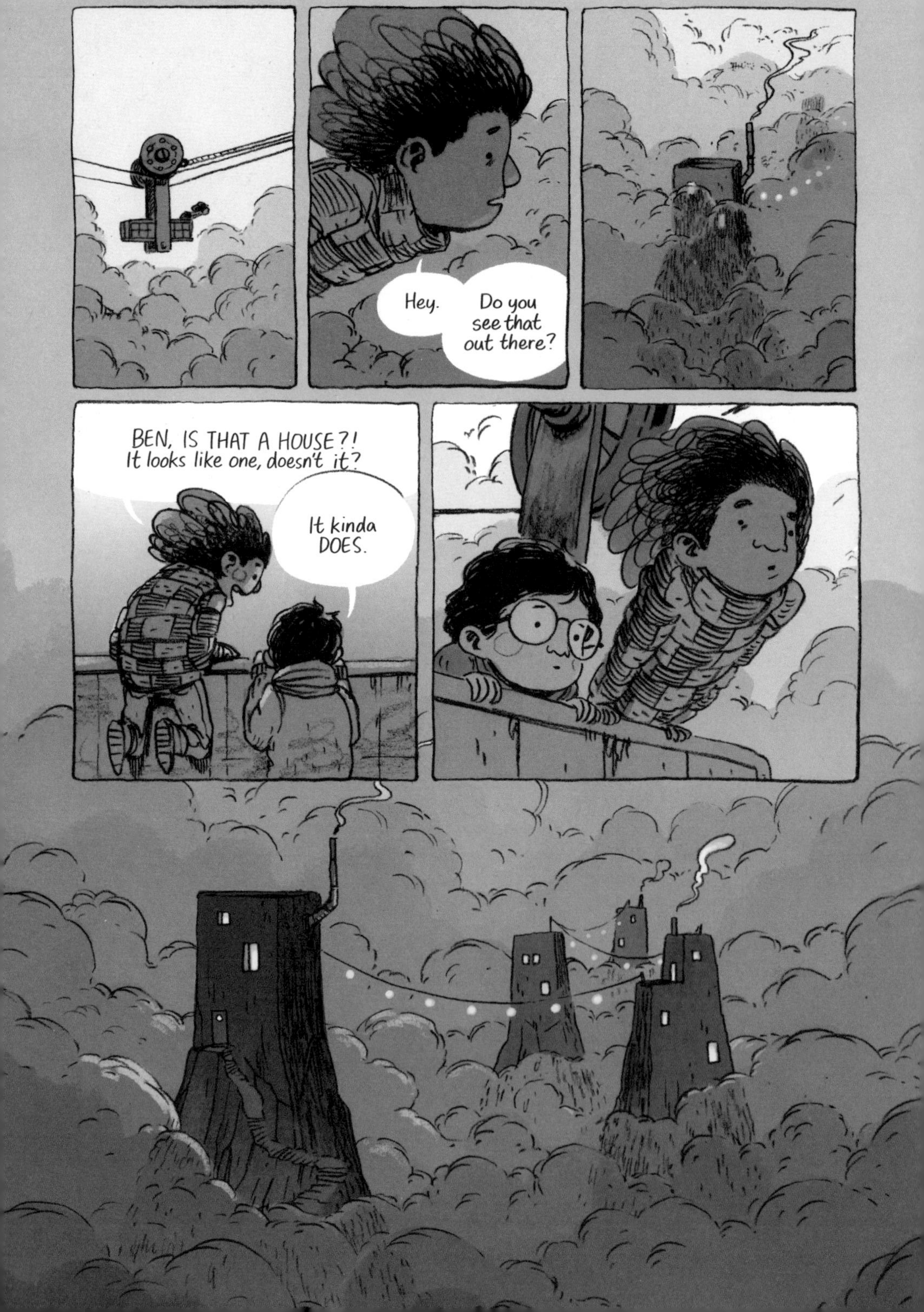
Hey.
Do you see that out there?
BEN, IS THAT A HOUSE?!
It looks like one, doesn't it?
It kinda DOES.

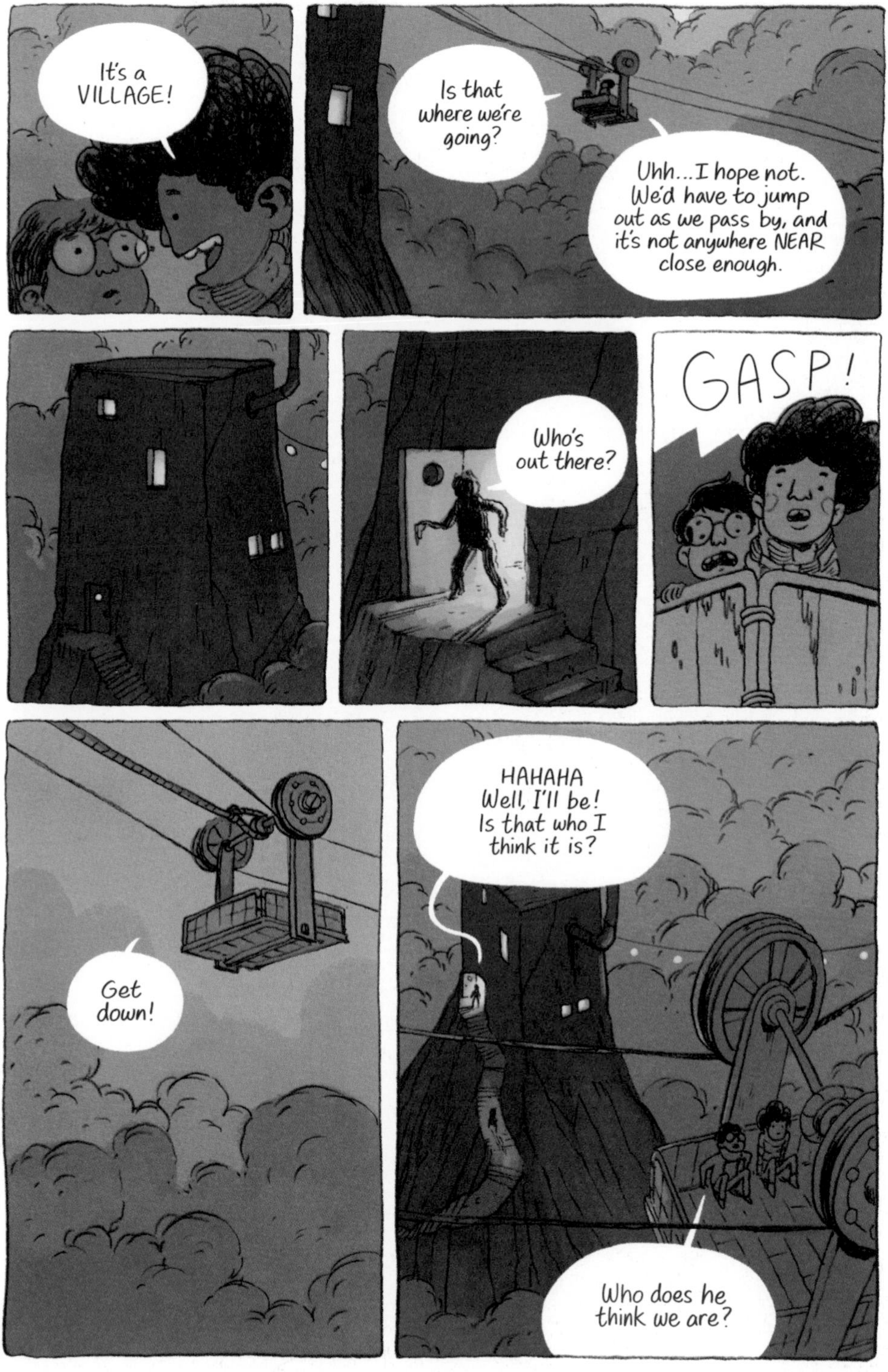
It's a VILLAGE!
Is that where we're going?
Uhh... I hope not. We'd have to jump out as we pass by, and it's not anywhere NEAR close enough.
Who's out there?
GASP!
Get down!
HAHAHA Well, I'll be! Is that who I think it is?
Who does he think we are?

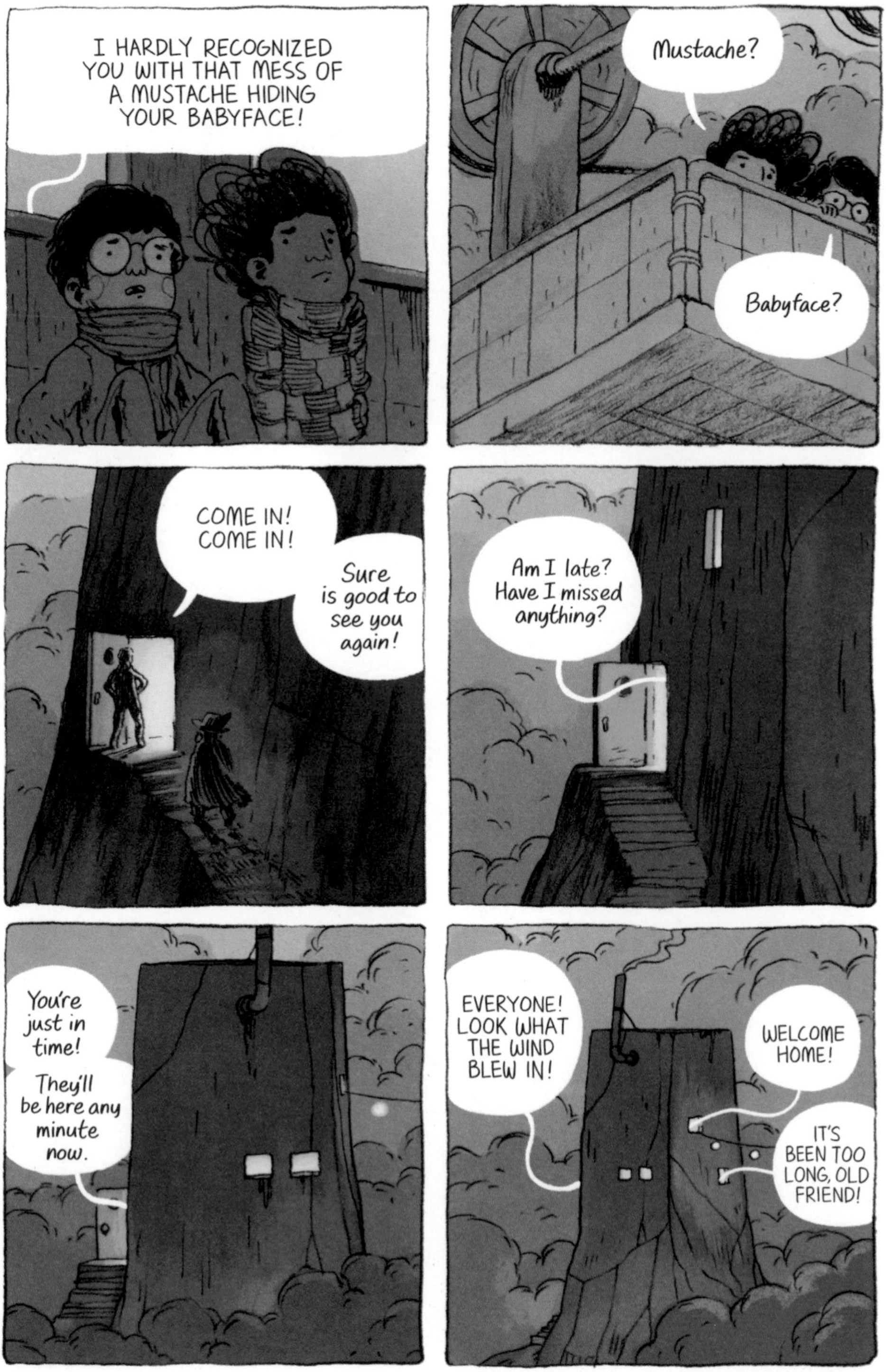
I HARDLY RECOGNIZED YOU WITH THAT MESS OF A MUSTACHE HIDING YOUR BABYFACE!
Mustache?
Babyface?
COME IN! COME IN!
Sure is good to see you again!
Am I late? Have I missed anything?
You're just in time!
They'll be here any minute now.
EVERYONE! LOOK WHAT THE WIND BLEW IN!
WELCOME HOME!
IT'S BEEN TOO LONG, OLD FRIEND!

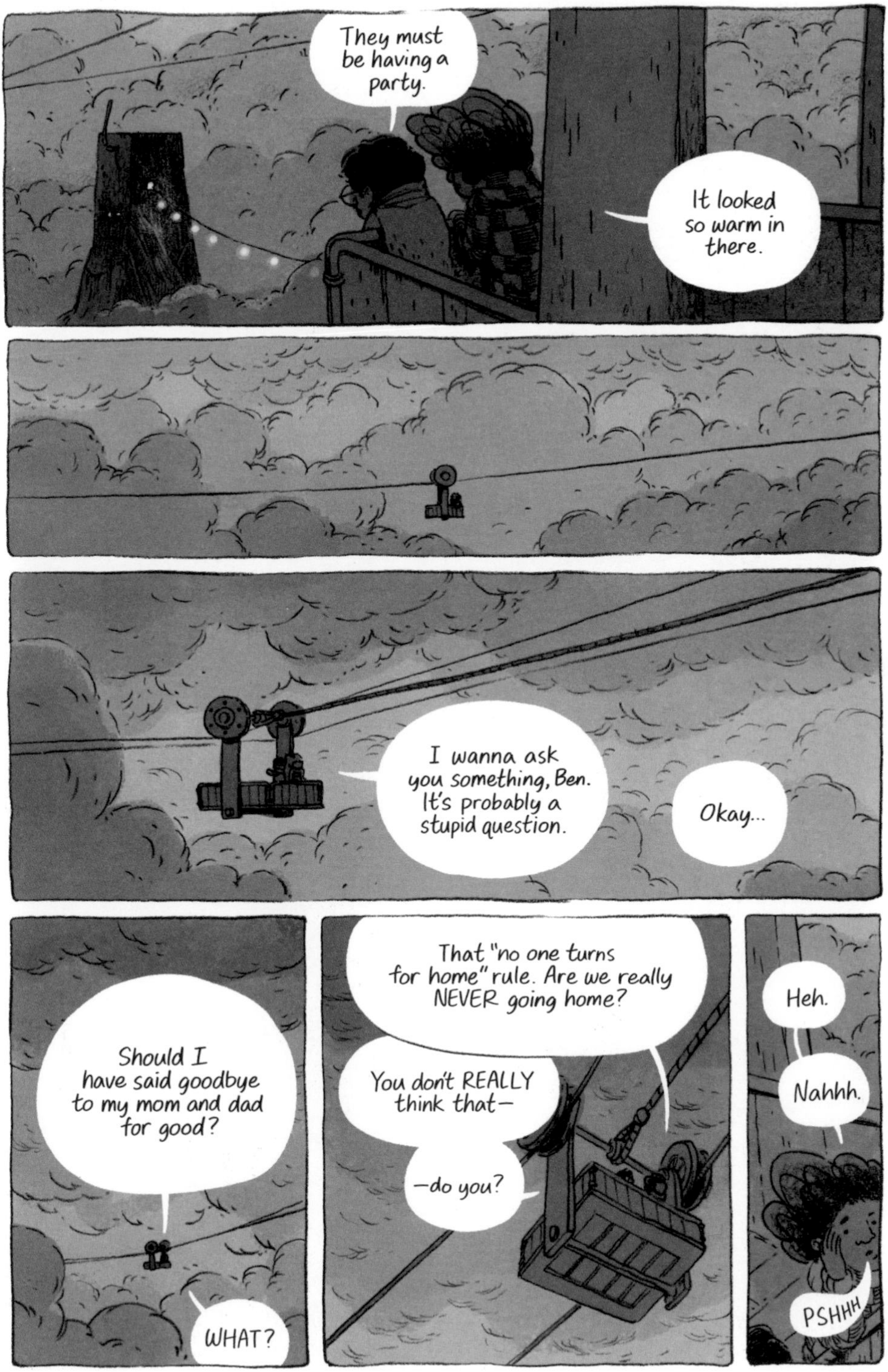
They must be having a party.
It looked so warm in there.
I wanna ask you something, Ben. It's probably a stupid question.
Okay...
Should I have said goodbye to my mom and dad for good?
WHAT?
That "no one turns for home" rule. Are we really NEVER going home?
You don't REALLY think that—
—do you?
Heh.
Nahhh.
PSHHH

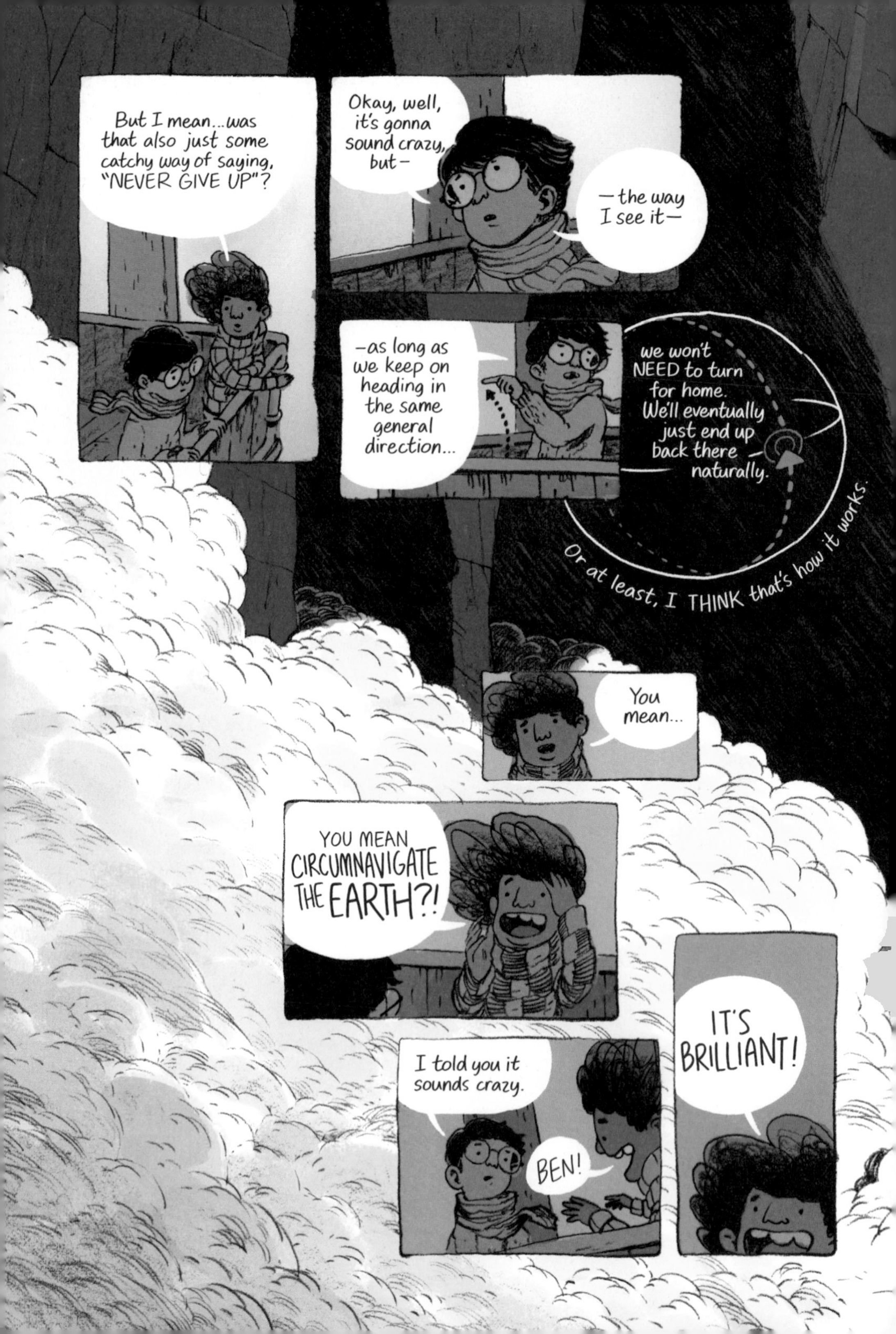

But I mean...was that also just some catchy way of saying, "NEVER GIVE UP"?
Okay, well, it's gonna sound crazy, but–
–the way I see it–
–as long as we keep on heading in the same general direction...
we won't NEED to turn for home. We'll eventually just end up back there naturally.
Or at least, I THINK that's how it works.
You mean...
YOU MEAN CIRCUMNAVIGATE THE EARTH?!
I told you it sounds crazy.
BEN!
IT'S BRILLIANT!

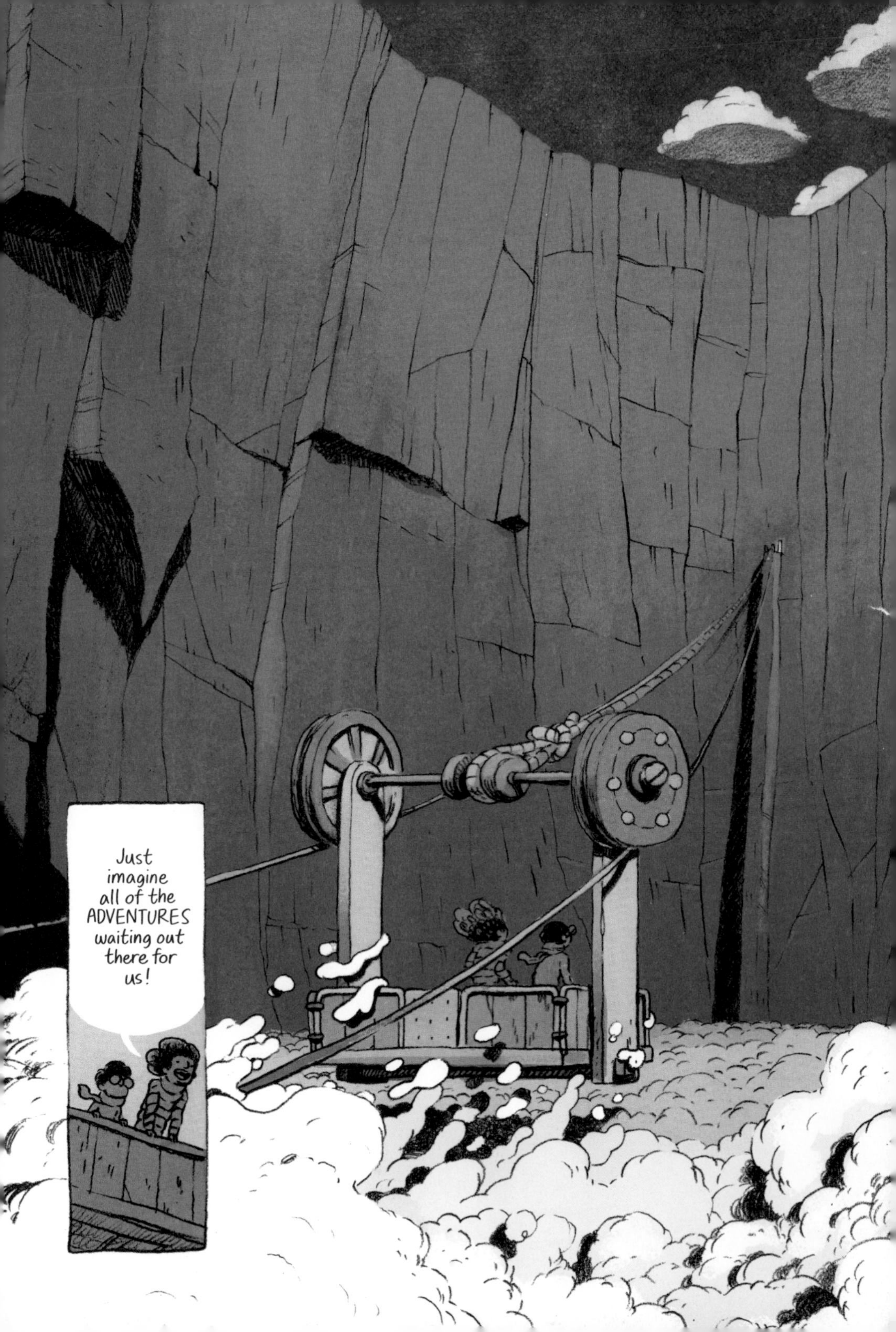
Just imagine all of the ADVENTURES waiting out there for us!

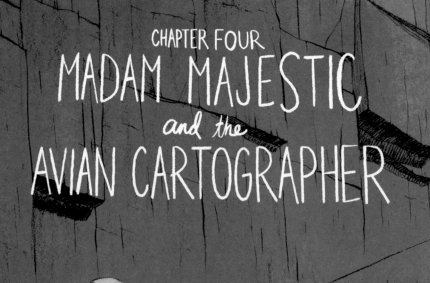

CHAPTER FOUR
MADAM MAJESTIC
and the
AVIAN CARTOGRAPHER

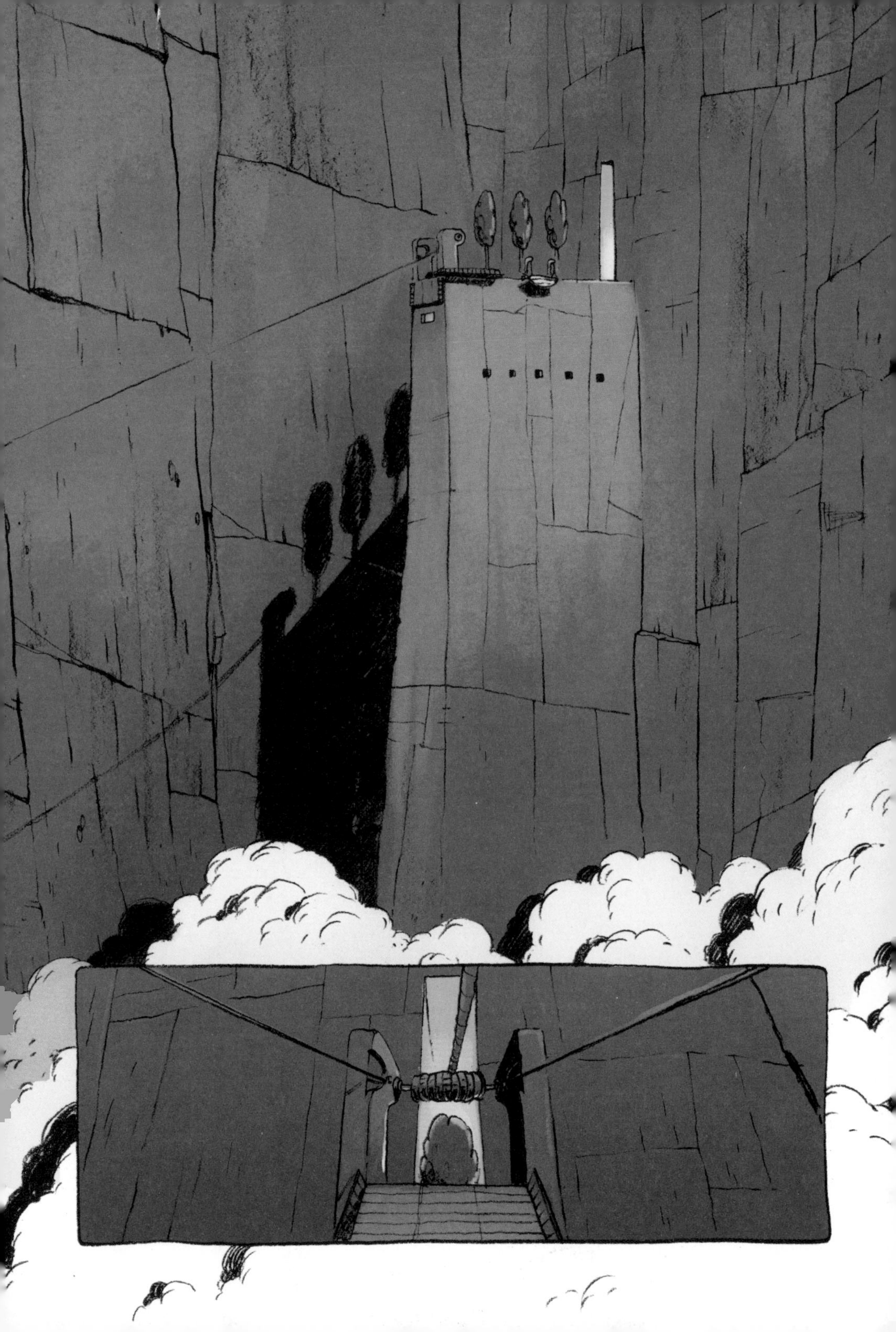

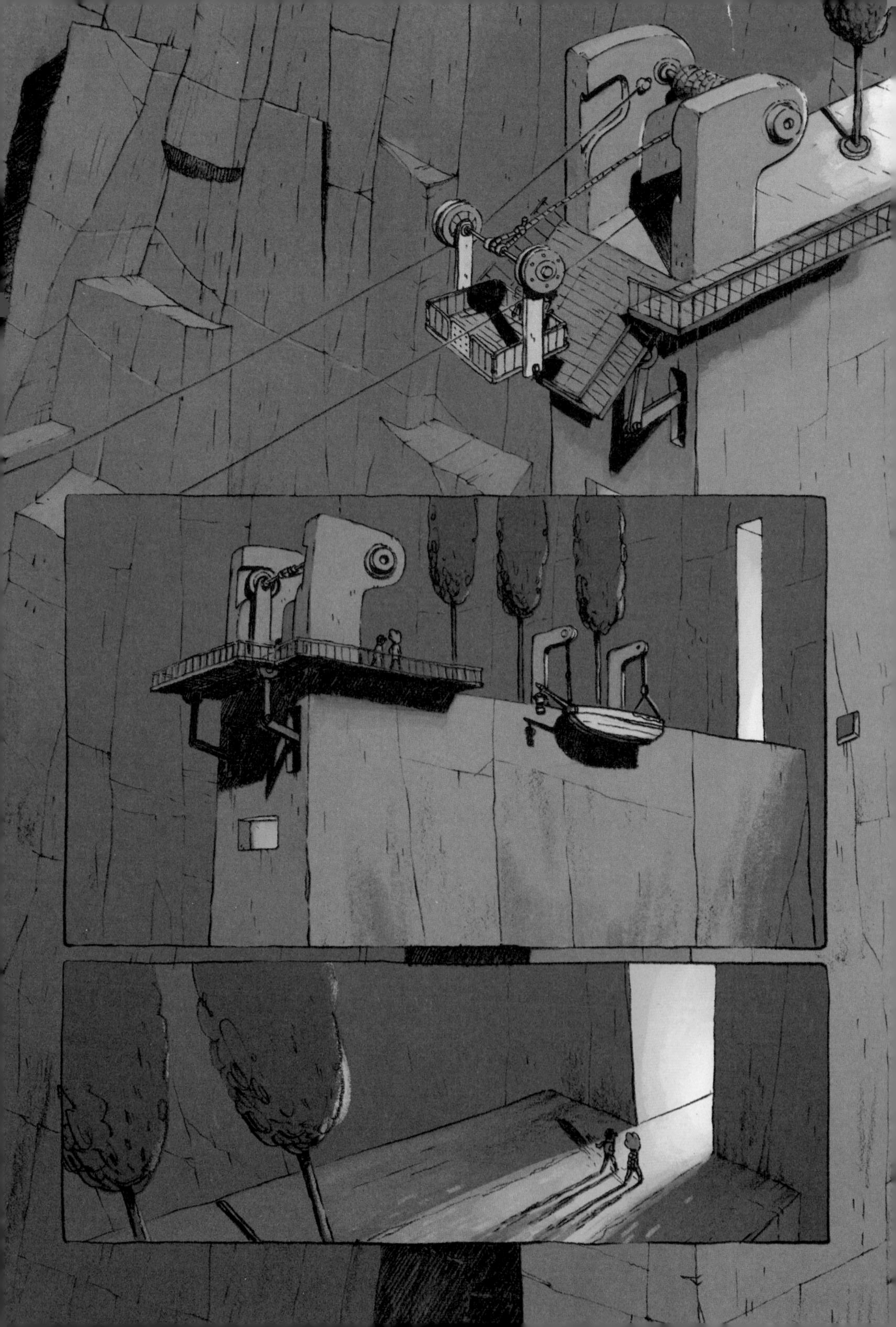

Madam Majestic...
MADAMMAJESTIC
You wanna knock?
MADAMMAJESTIC
You knock.
Let's BOTH knock.
NOD

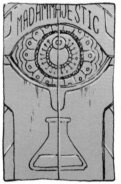

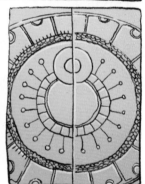

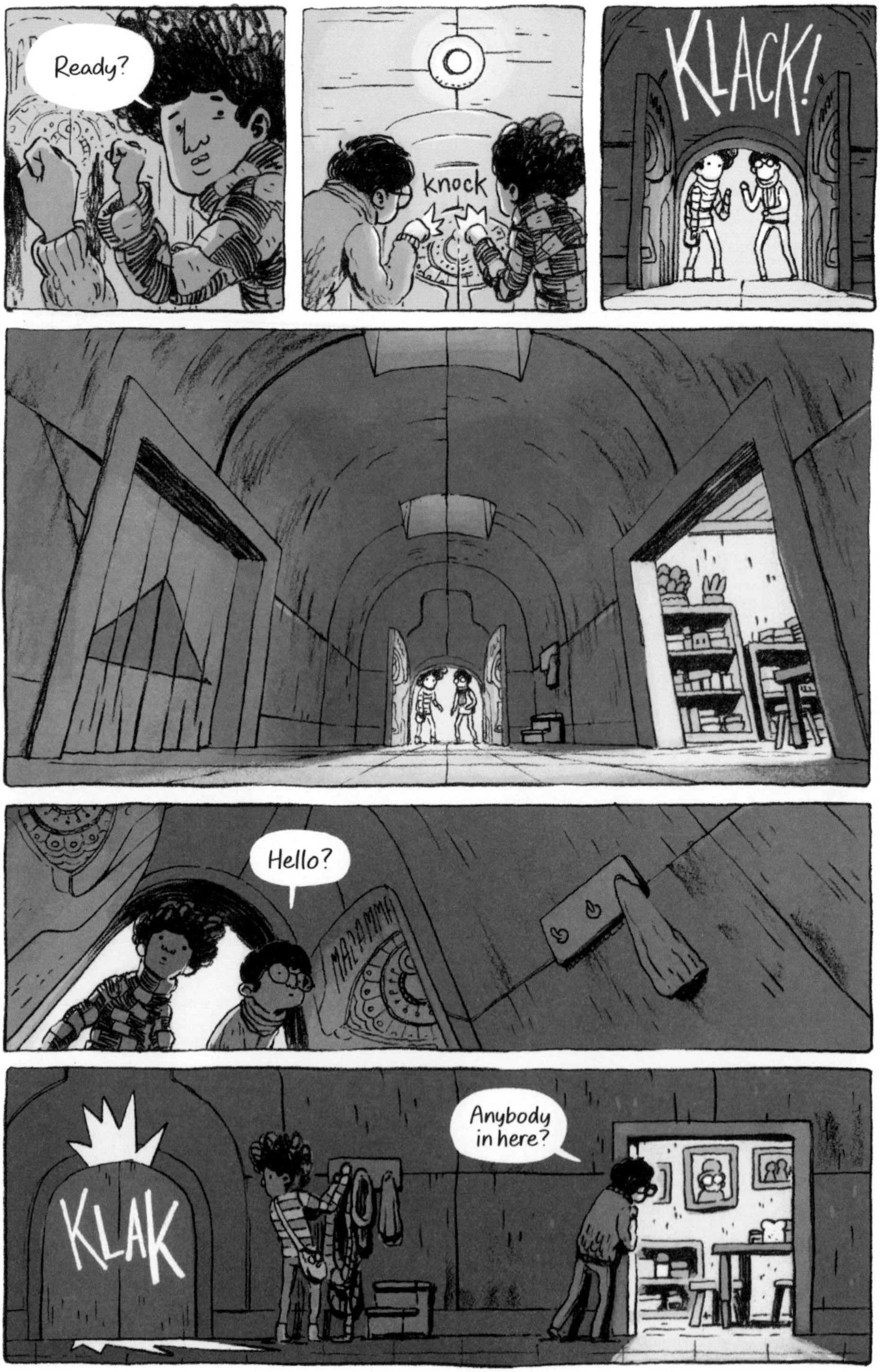
Ready?
knock
KLACK!
Hello?
KLAK
Anybody in here?

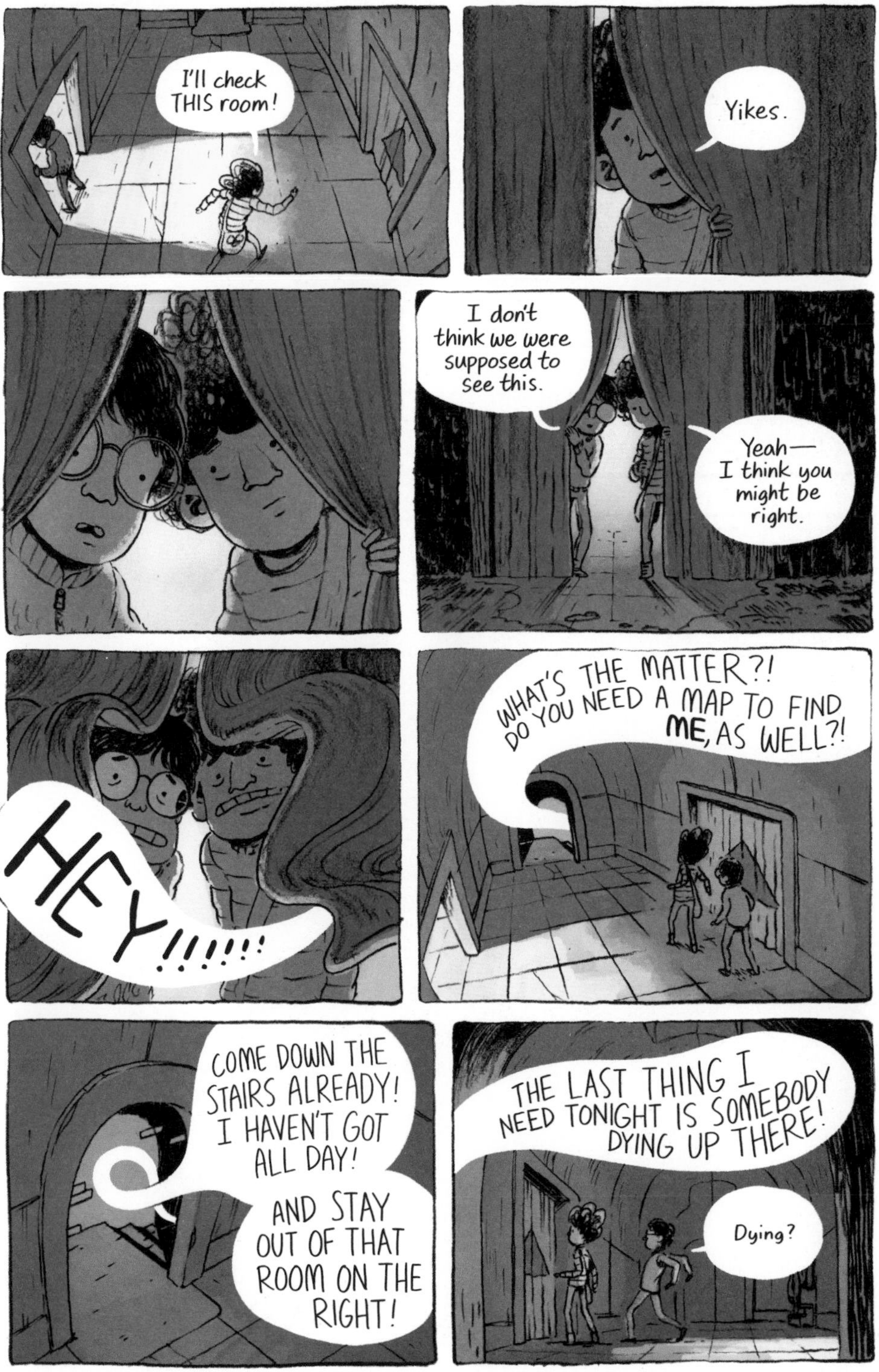
I'll check THIS room!
Yikes.
I don't think we were supposed to see this.
Yeah— I think you might be right.
HEY!!!!!!
WHAT'S THE MATTER?! DO YOU NEED A MAP TO FIND **ME**, AS WELL?!
COME DOWN THE STAIRS ALREADY! I HAVEN'T GOT ALL DAY!
AND STAY OUT OF THAT ROOM ON THE RIGHT!
THE LAST THING I NEED TONIGHT IS SOMEBODY DYING UP THERE!
Dying?

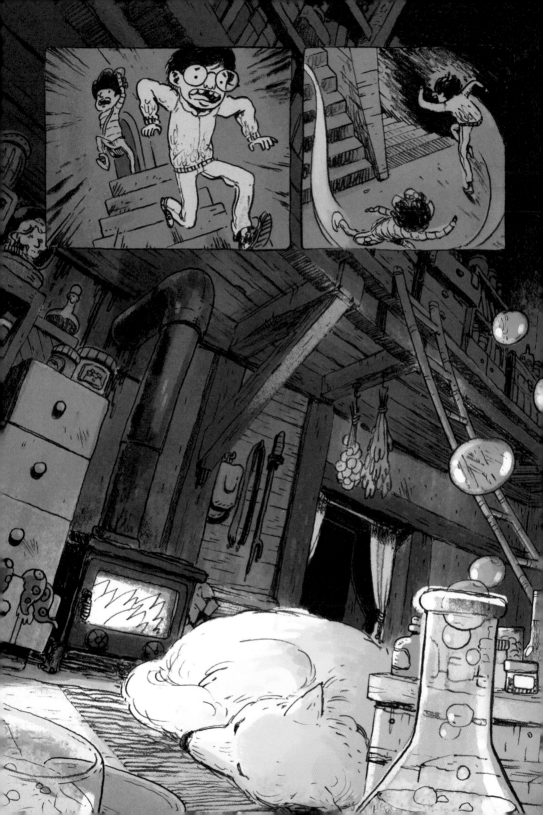

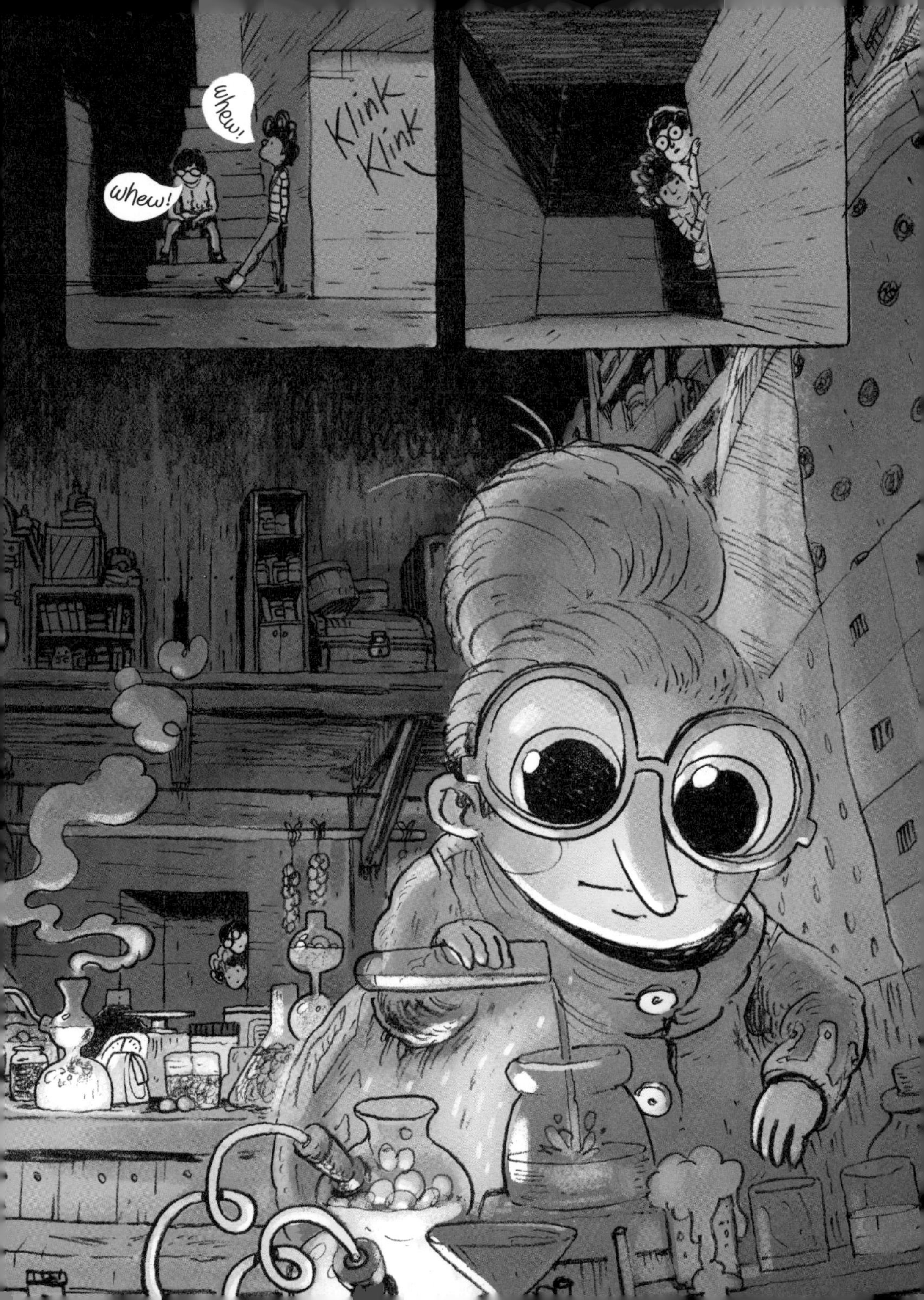
whew!
whew!
Klink
Klink

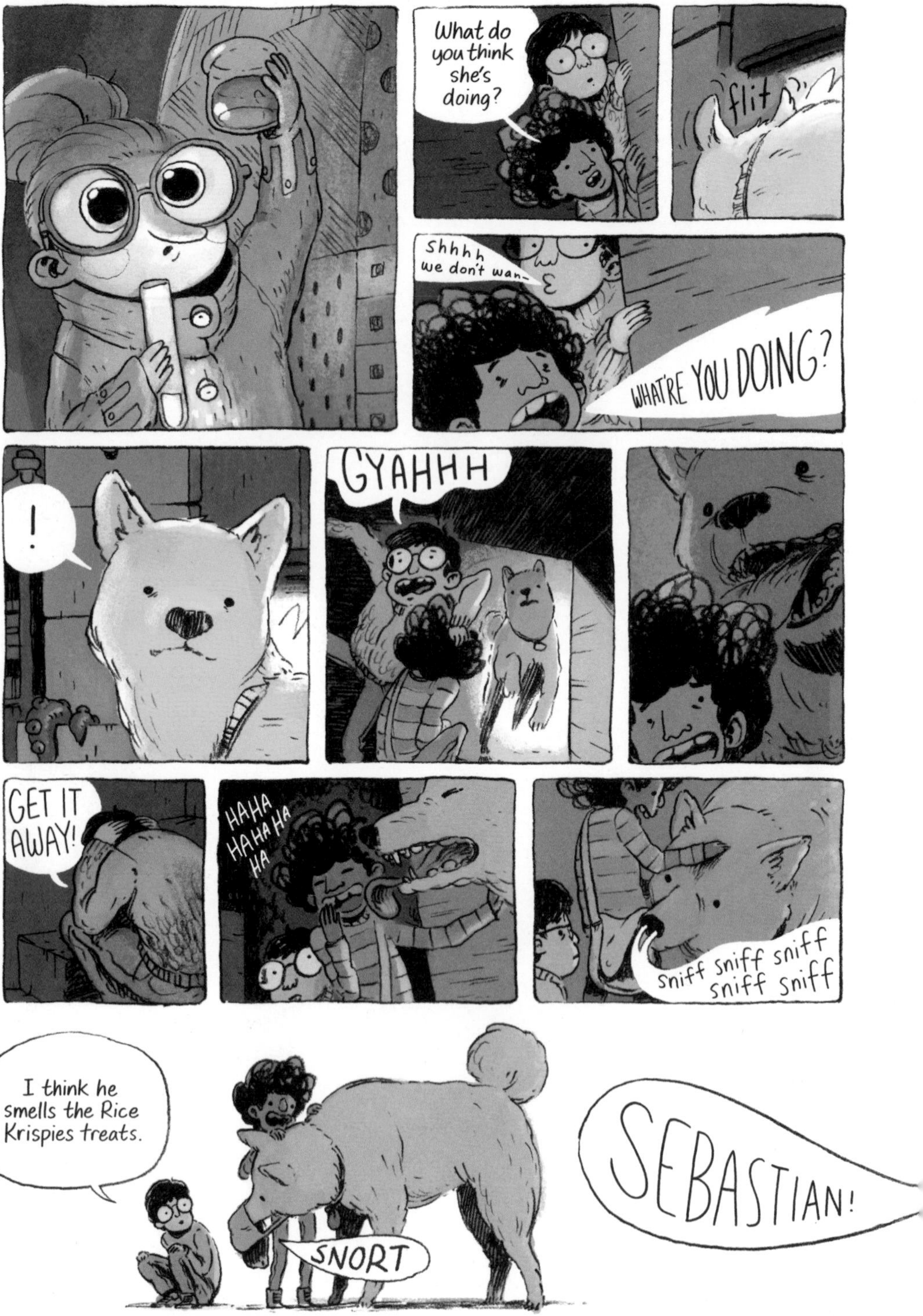
What do you think she's doing?
flit
Shhhh we don't wan–
WHAT'RE YOU DOING?
!
GYAHHH
GET IT AWAY!
HAHA HAHAHA HA
sniff sniff sniff sniff sniff
I think he smells the Rice Krispies treats.
SNORT
SEBASTIAN!

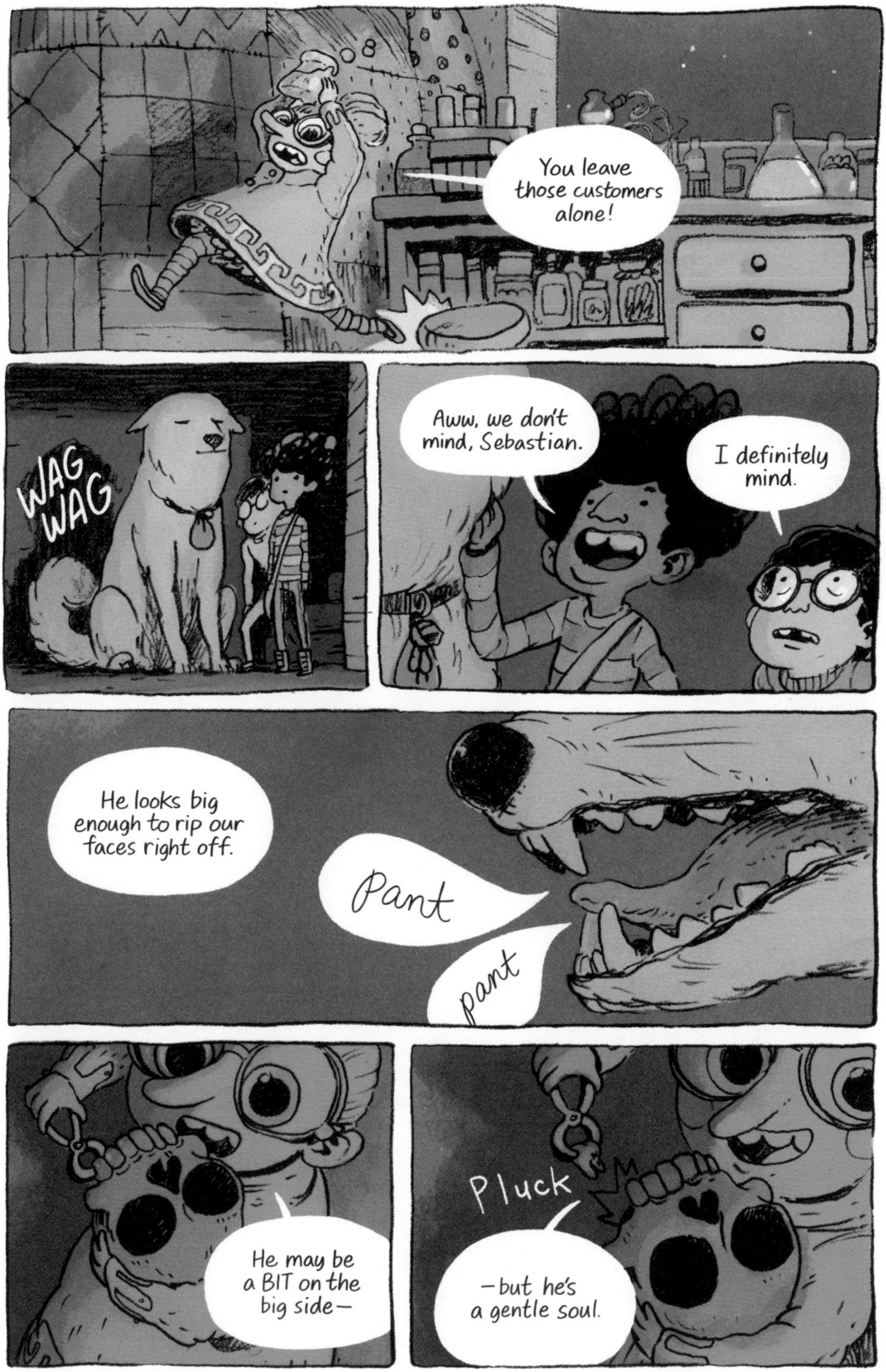
You leave those customers alone!
WAG WAG
Aww, we don't mind, Sebastian.
I definitely mind.
He looks big enough to rip our faces right off.
Pant
pant
He may be a BIT on the big side—
Pluck
—but he's a gentle soul.

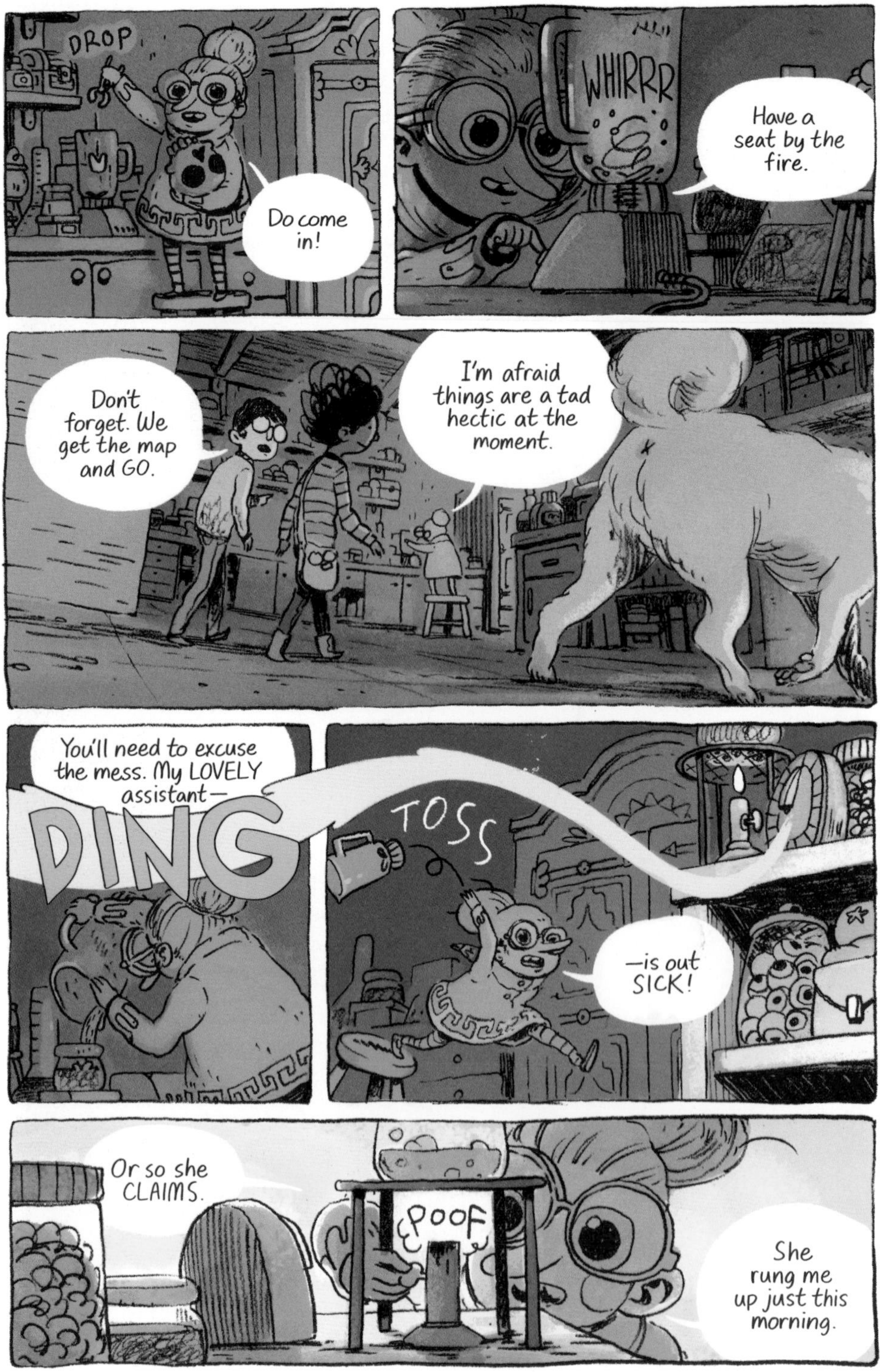
DROP
Do come in!
WHIRRR
Have a seat by the fire.
Don't forget. We get the map and GO.
I'm afraid things are a tad hectic at the moment.
You'll need to excuse the mess. My LOVELY assistant—
DING
TOSS
—is out SICK!
Or so she CLAIMS.
POOF
She rung me up just this morning.

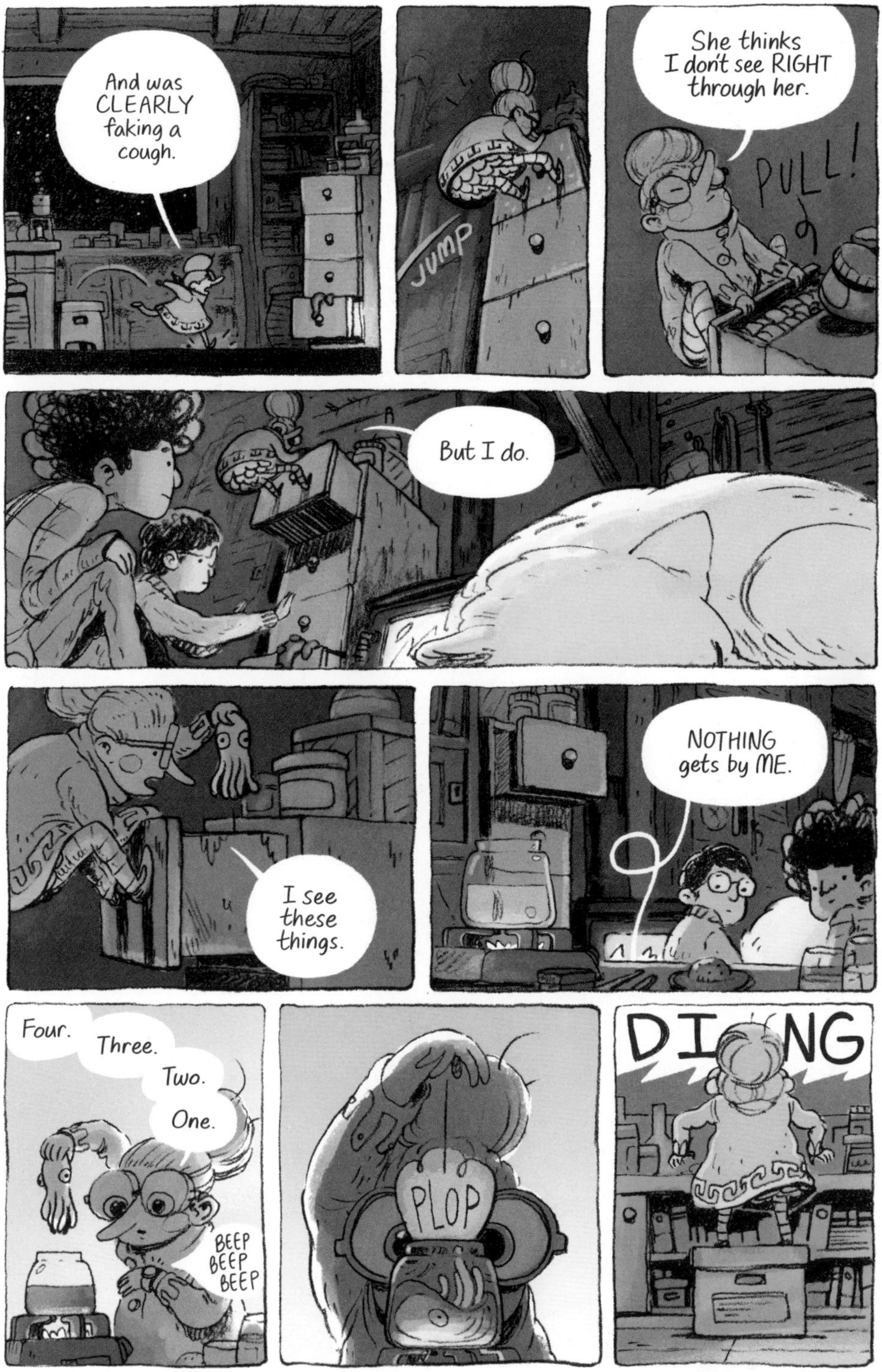
And was CLEARLY faking a cough.
JUMP
She thinks I don't see RIGHT through her.
PULL!
But I do.
I see these things.
NOTHING gets by ME.
Four.
Three.
Two.
One.
BEEP BEEP BEEP
PLOP
DING

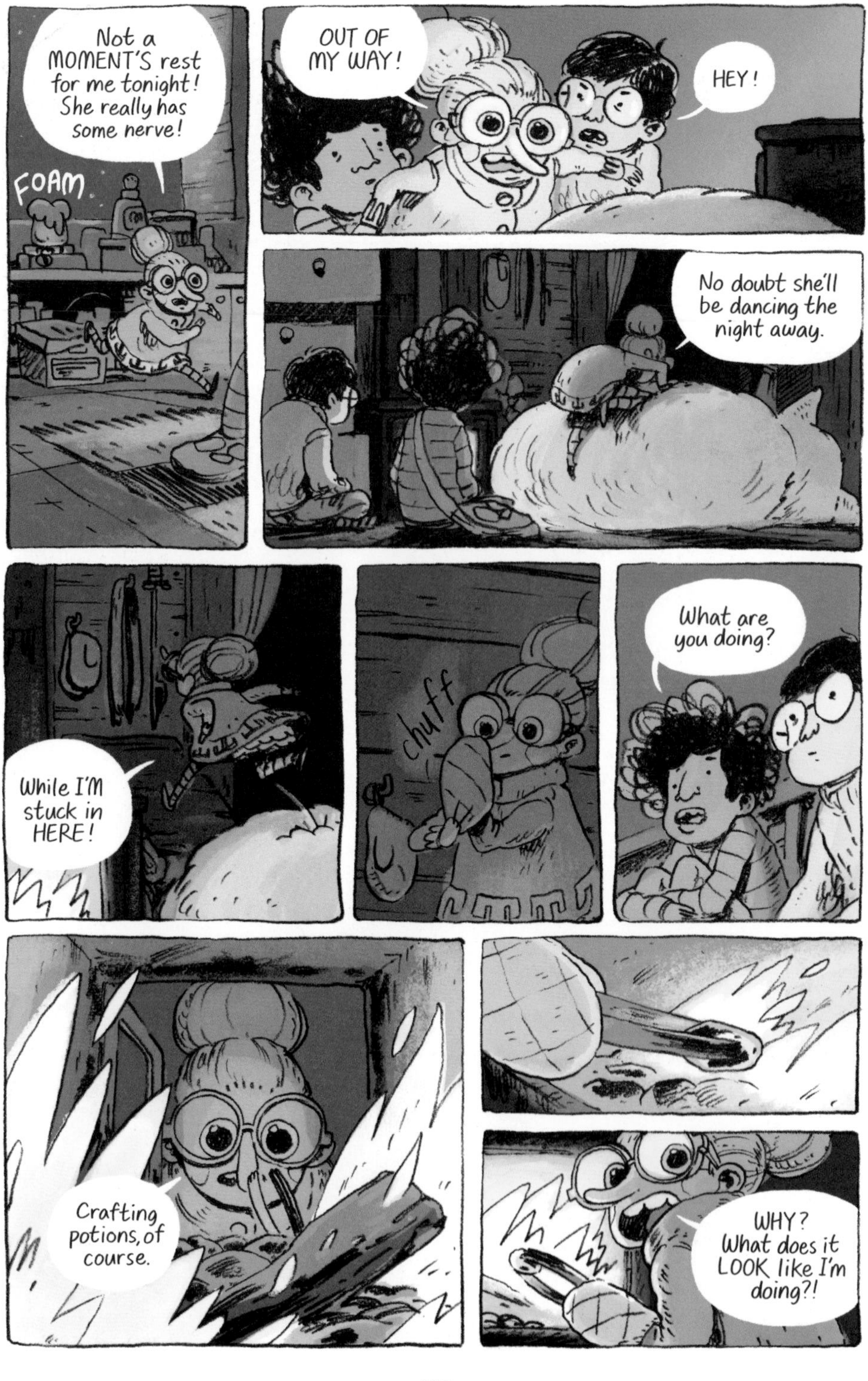
Not a MOMENT'S rest for me tonight! She really has some nerve!
FOAM
OUT OF MY WAY!
HEY!
No doubt she'll be dancing the night away.
While I'M stuck in HERE!
chuff
What are you doing?
Crafting potions, of course.
WHY? What does it LOOK like I'm doing?!

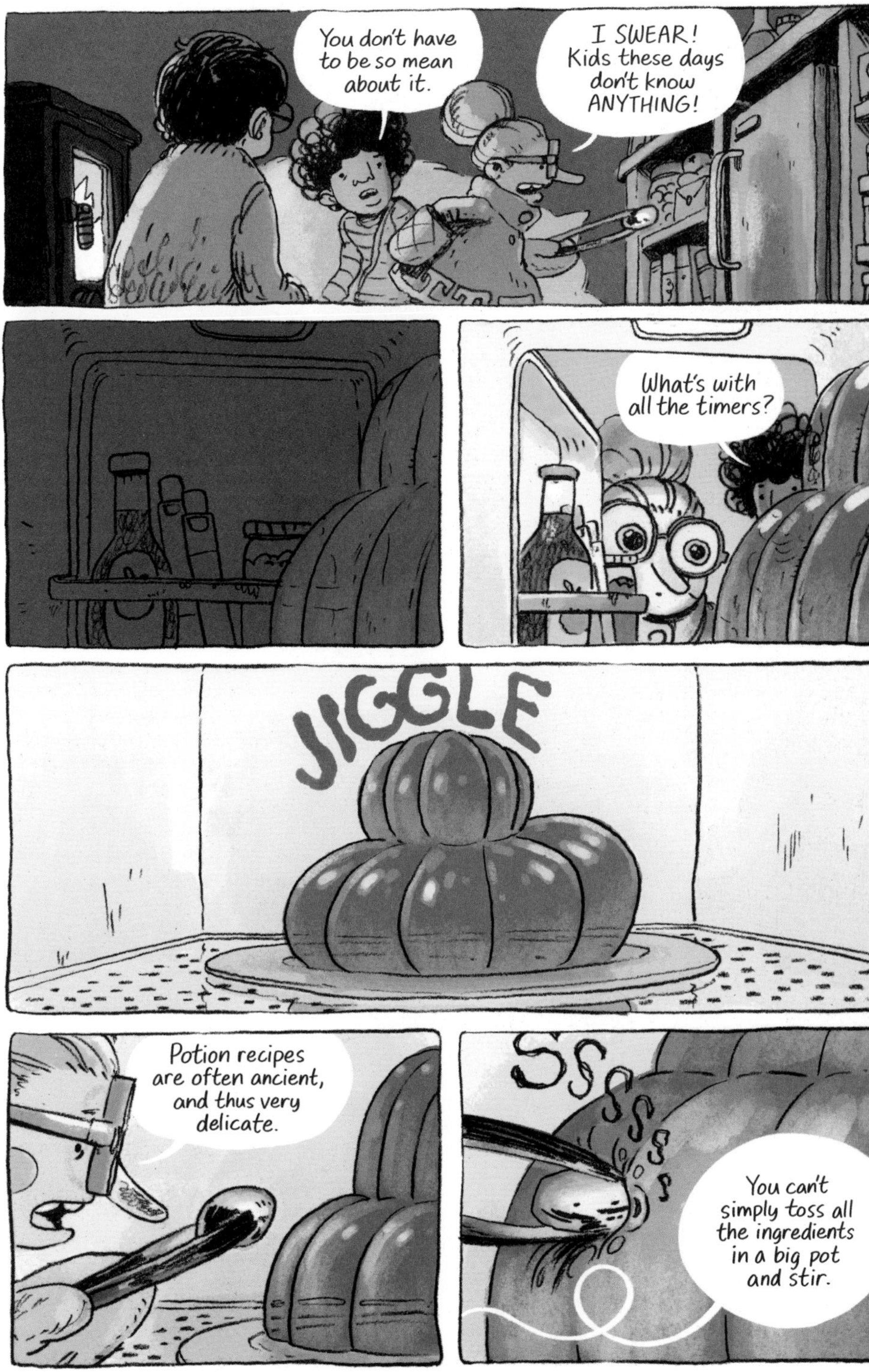
You don't have to be so mean about it.
I SWEAR! Kids these days don't know ANYTHING!
What's with all the timers?
JIGGLE
Potion recipes are often ancient, and thus very delicate.
SSSSSS
You can't simply toss all the ingredients in a big pot and stir.

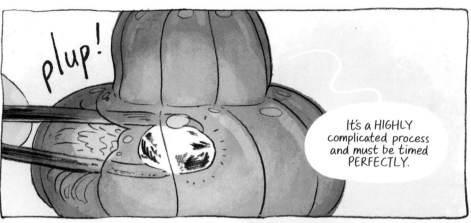

plup!

It's a HIGHLY complicated process and must be timed PERFECTLY.

WIGGLE WIGGLE

SHUT

Don't you fret, though. I haven't forgotten about your map.

DING

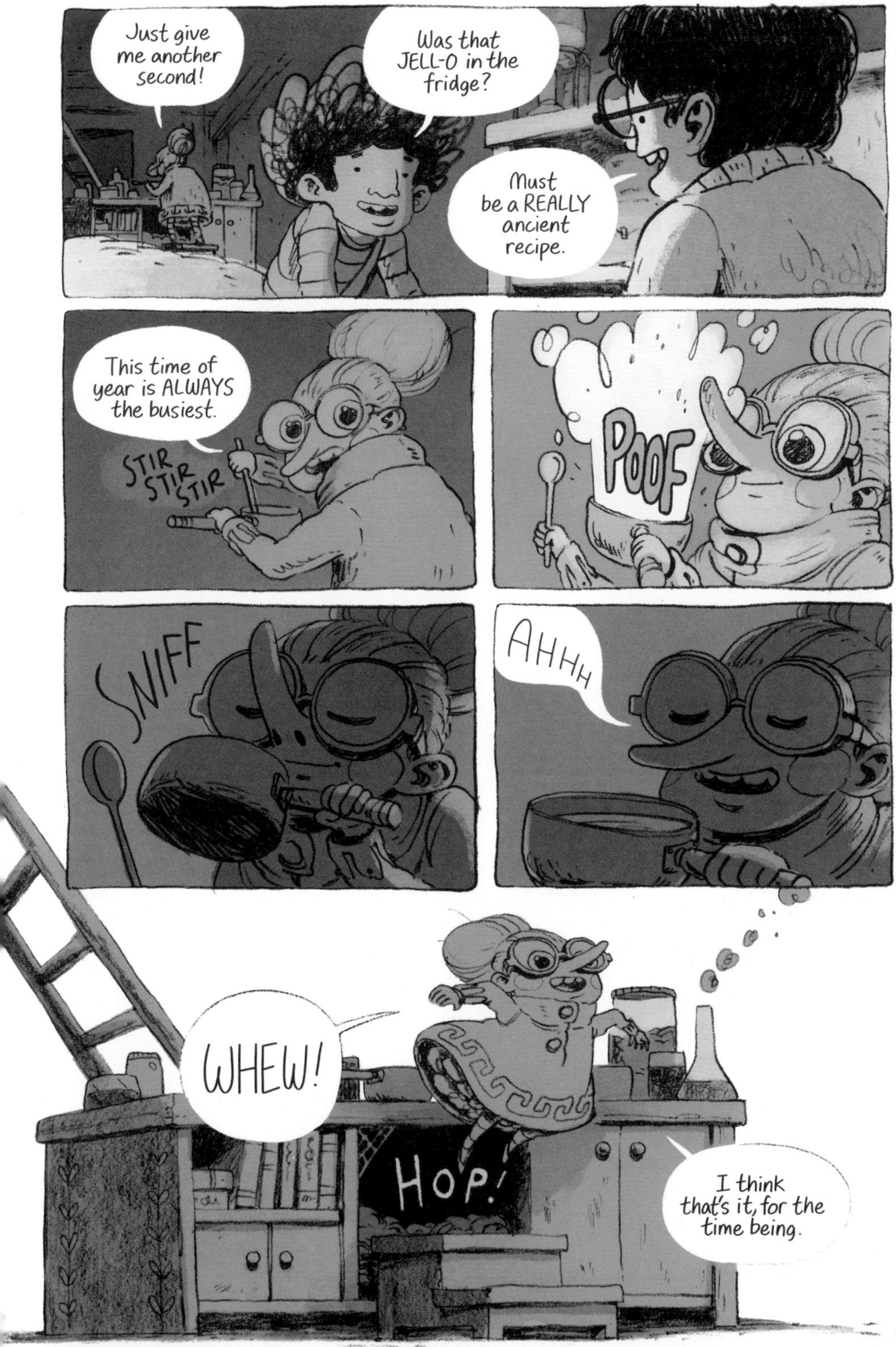
Just give me another second!
Was that JELL-O in the fridge?
Must be a REALLY ancient recipe.
This time of year is ALWAYS the busiest.
STIR STIR STIR
POOF
SNIFF
AHHH
WHEW!
HOP!
I think that's it, for the time being.

Now for your MAP!

Finally.

Fortunately, that's an easy one!

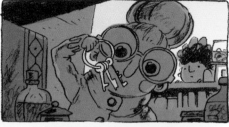

I SHOULD still have a few drops of Eye of the Cartographer extract left.

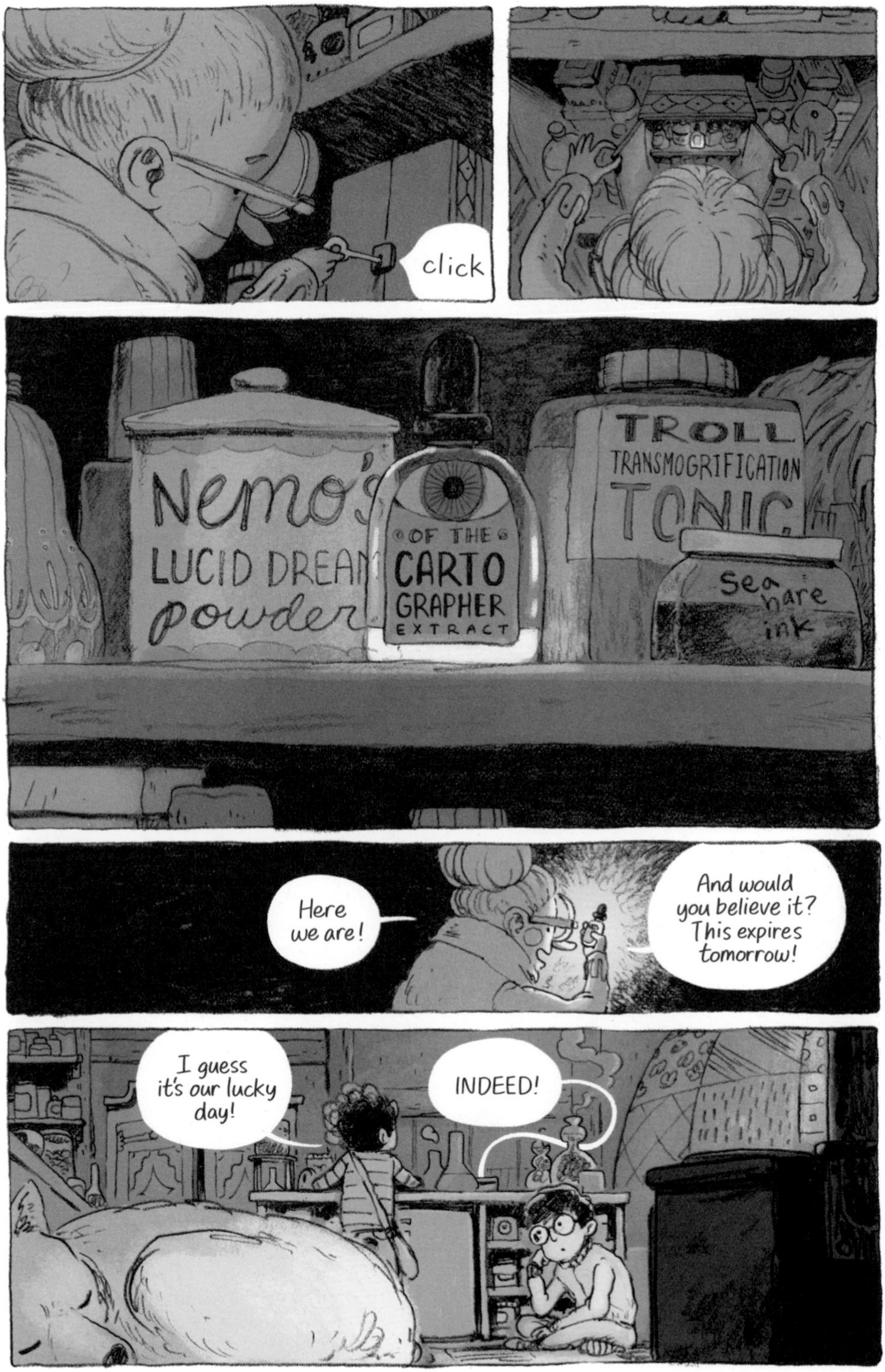
click
Nemo's
LUCID DREAM
powder
OF THE
CARTO
GRAPHER
EXTRACT
TROLL
TRANSMOGRIFICATION
TONIC
sea hare ink
Here we are!
And would you believe it? This expires tomorrow!
I guess it's our lucky day!
INDEED!

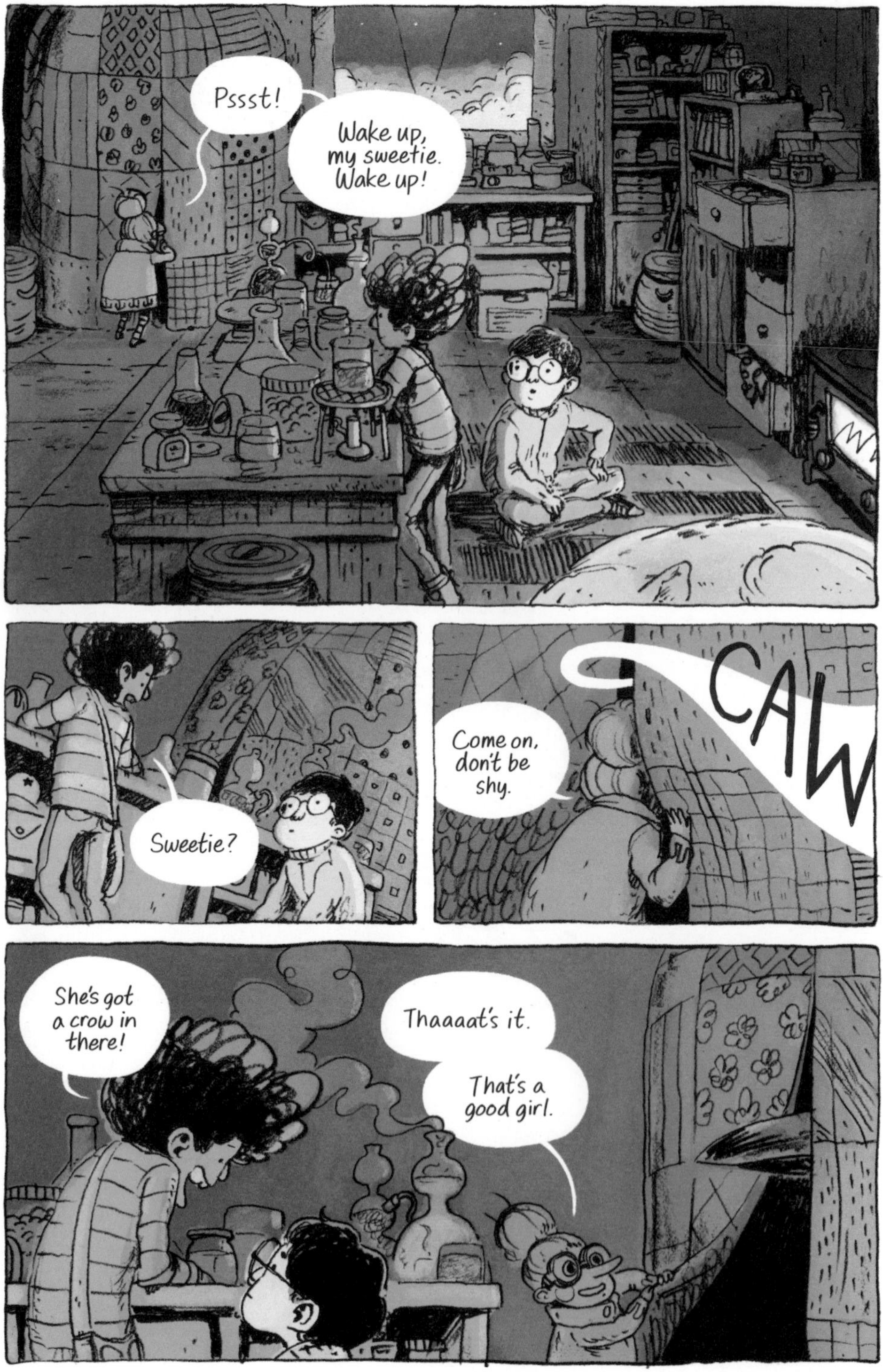
Pssst!
Wake up, my sweetie. Wake up!
Sweetie?
Come on, don't be shy.
CAW
She's got a crow in there!
Thaaaat's it.
That's a good girl.

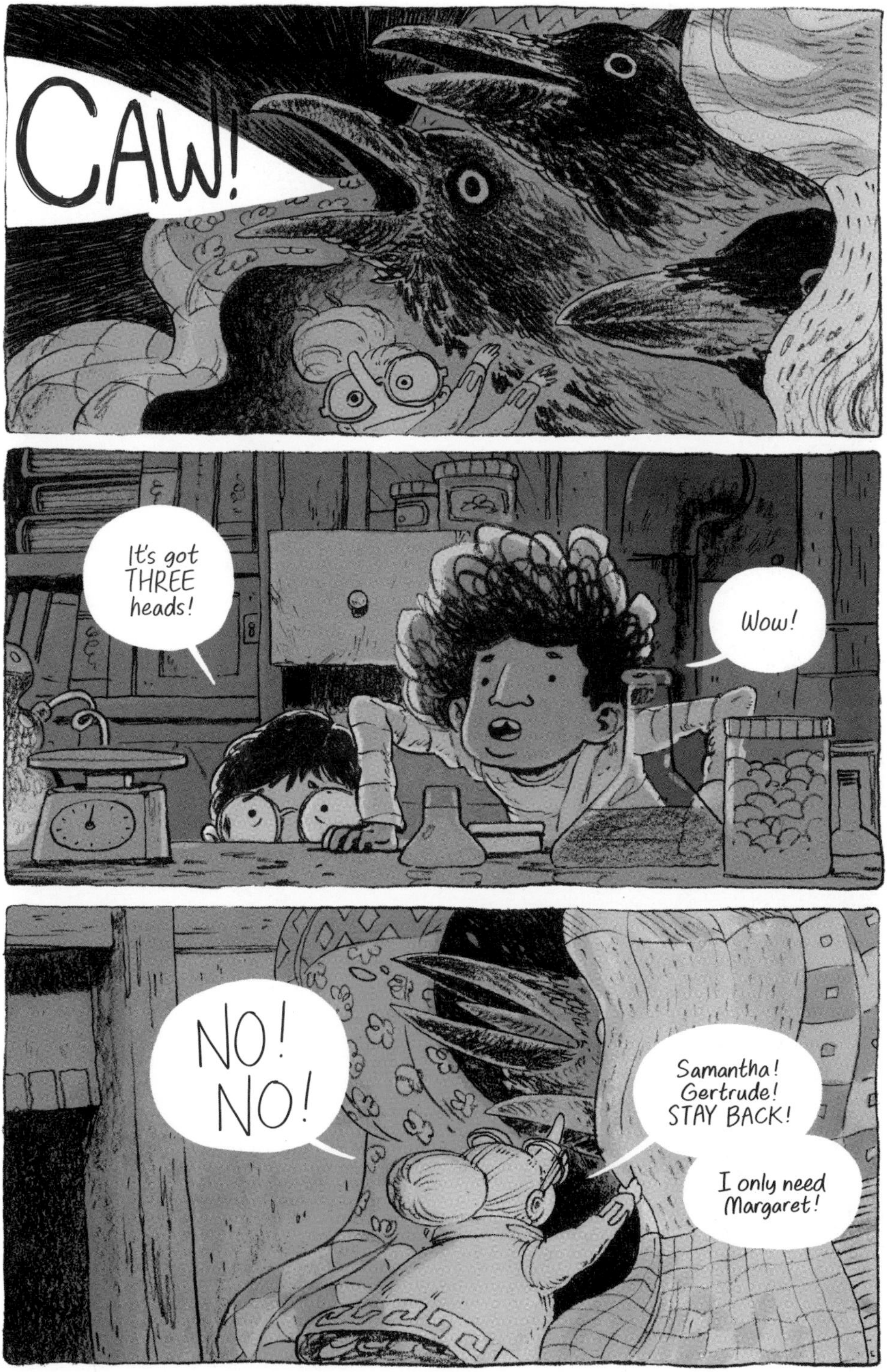
CAW!
It's got THREE heads!
Wow!
NO! NO!
Samantha! Gertrude! STAY BACK!
I only need Margaret!

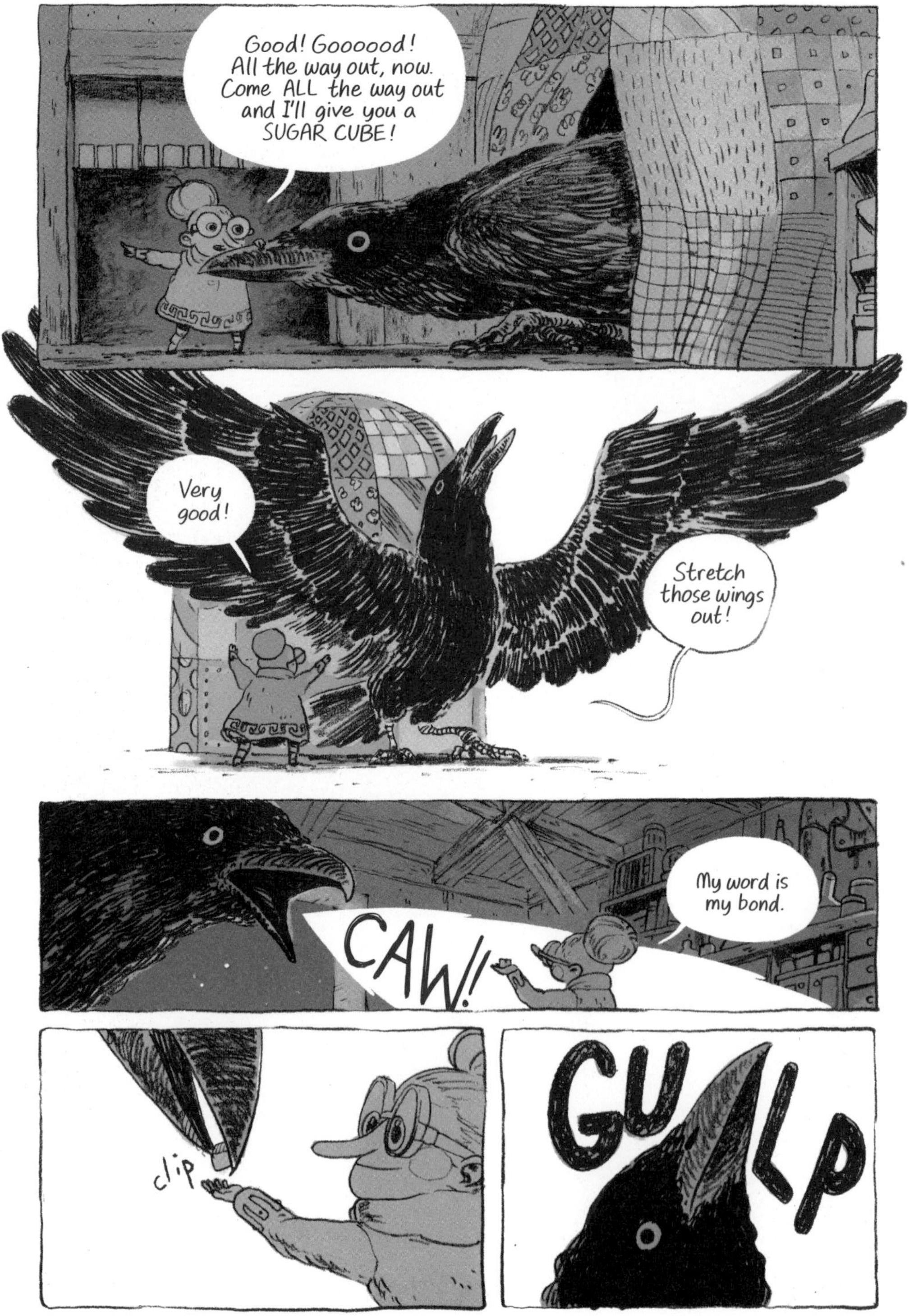
Good! Goooood! All the way out, now. Come ALL the way out and I'll give you a SUGAR CUBE!
Very good!
Stretch those wings out!
CAW!!
My word is my bond.
clip
GULP

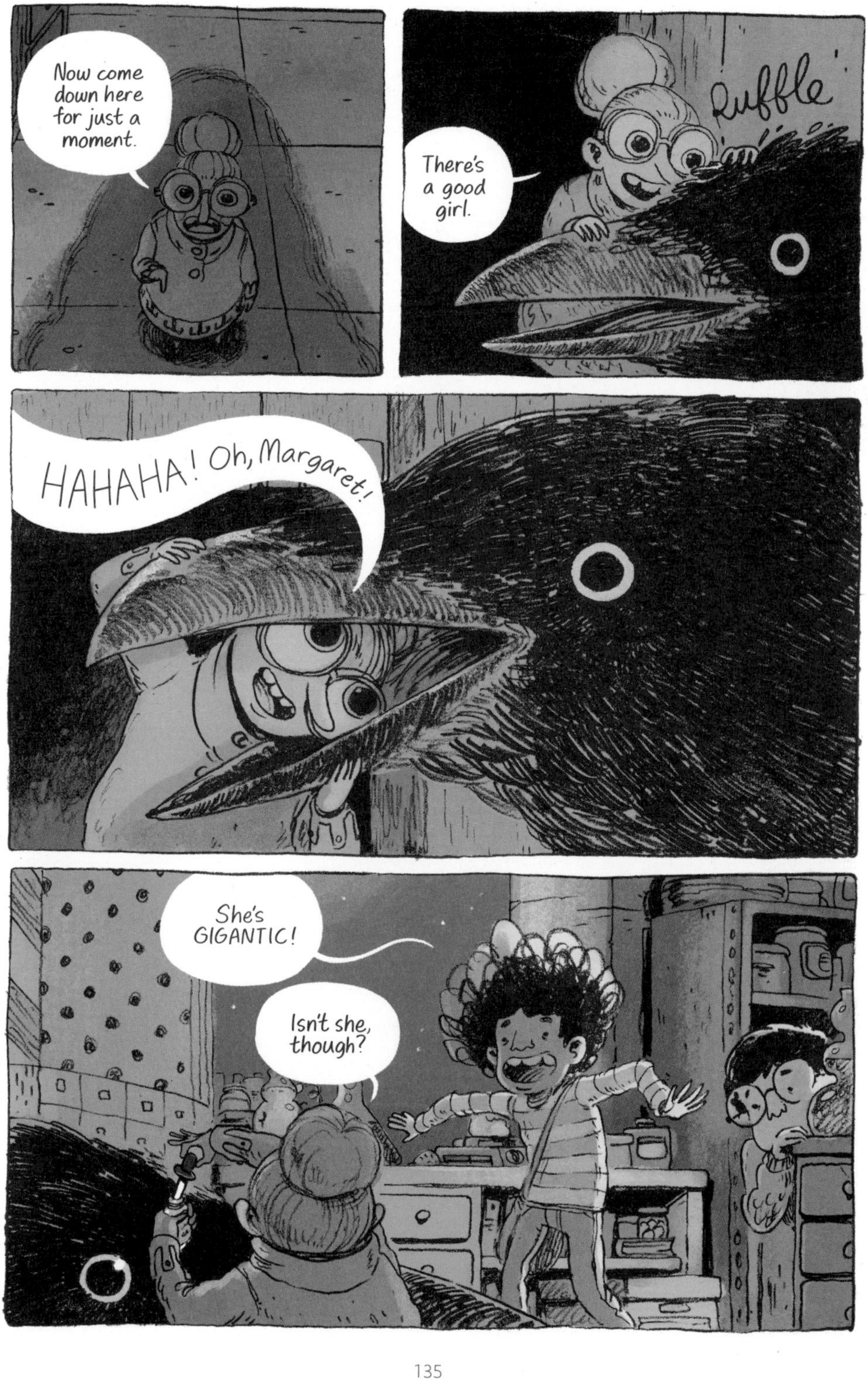
Now come down here for just a moment.
There's a good girl.
Ruffle
HAHAHA! Oh, Margaret!
She's GIGANTIC!
Isn't she, though?

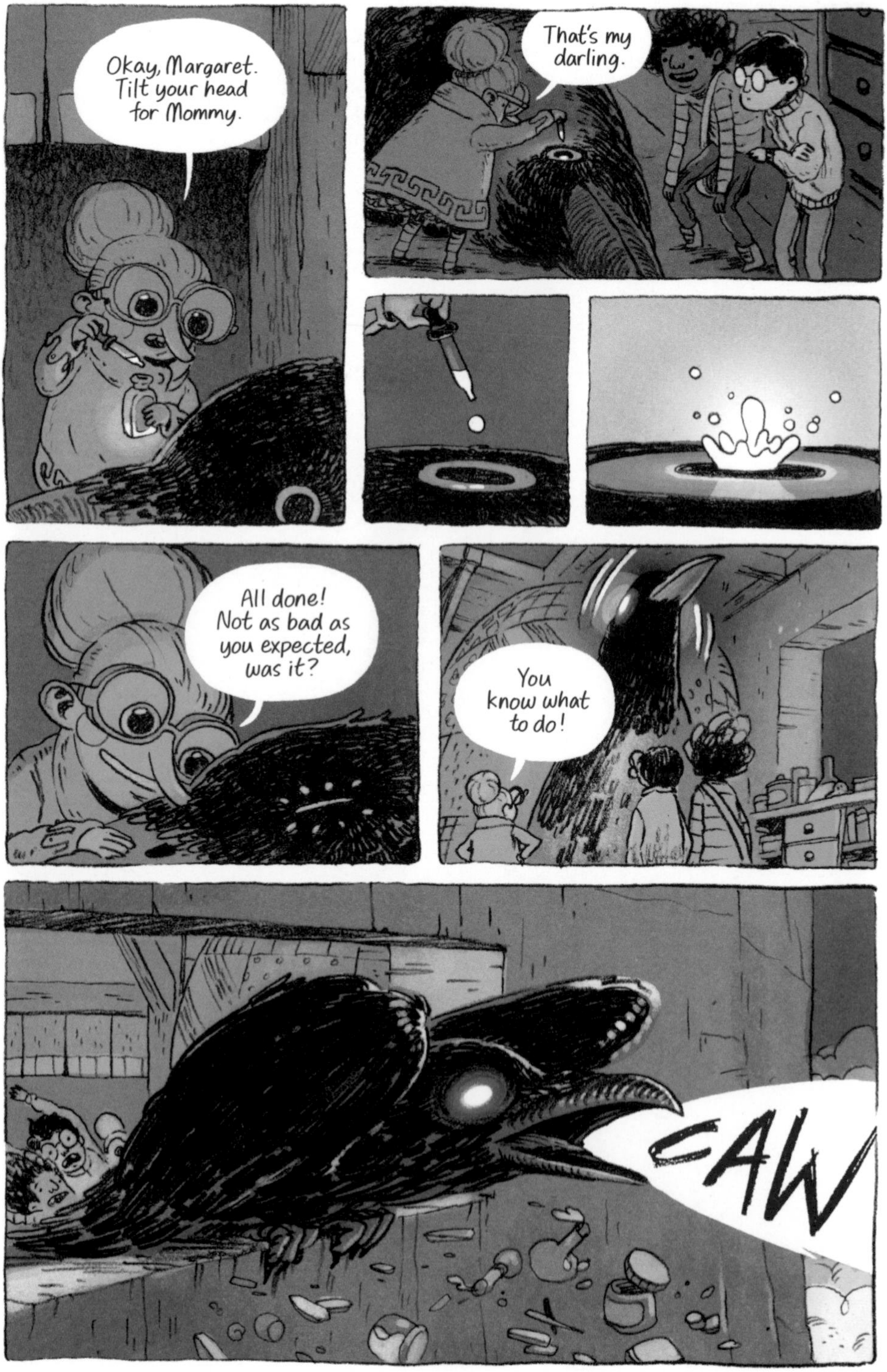
Okay, Margaret. Tilt your head for Mommy.
That's my darling.
All done! Not as bad as you expected, was it?
You know what to do!
CAW

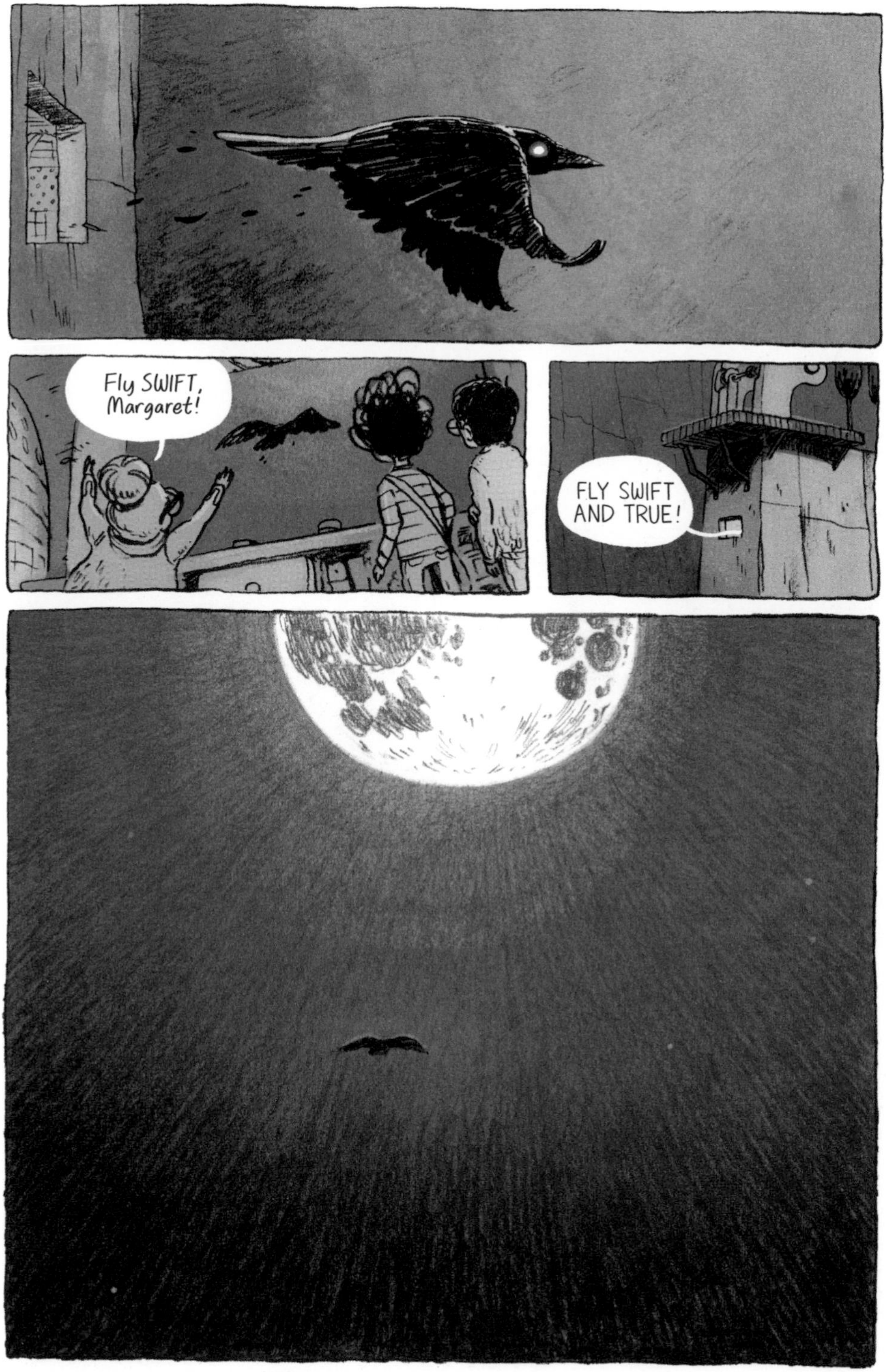
Fly SWIFT, Margaret!
FLY SWIFT AND TRUE!

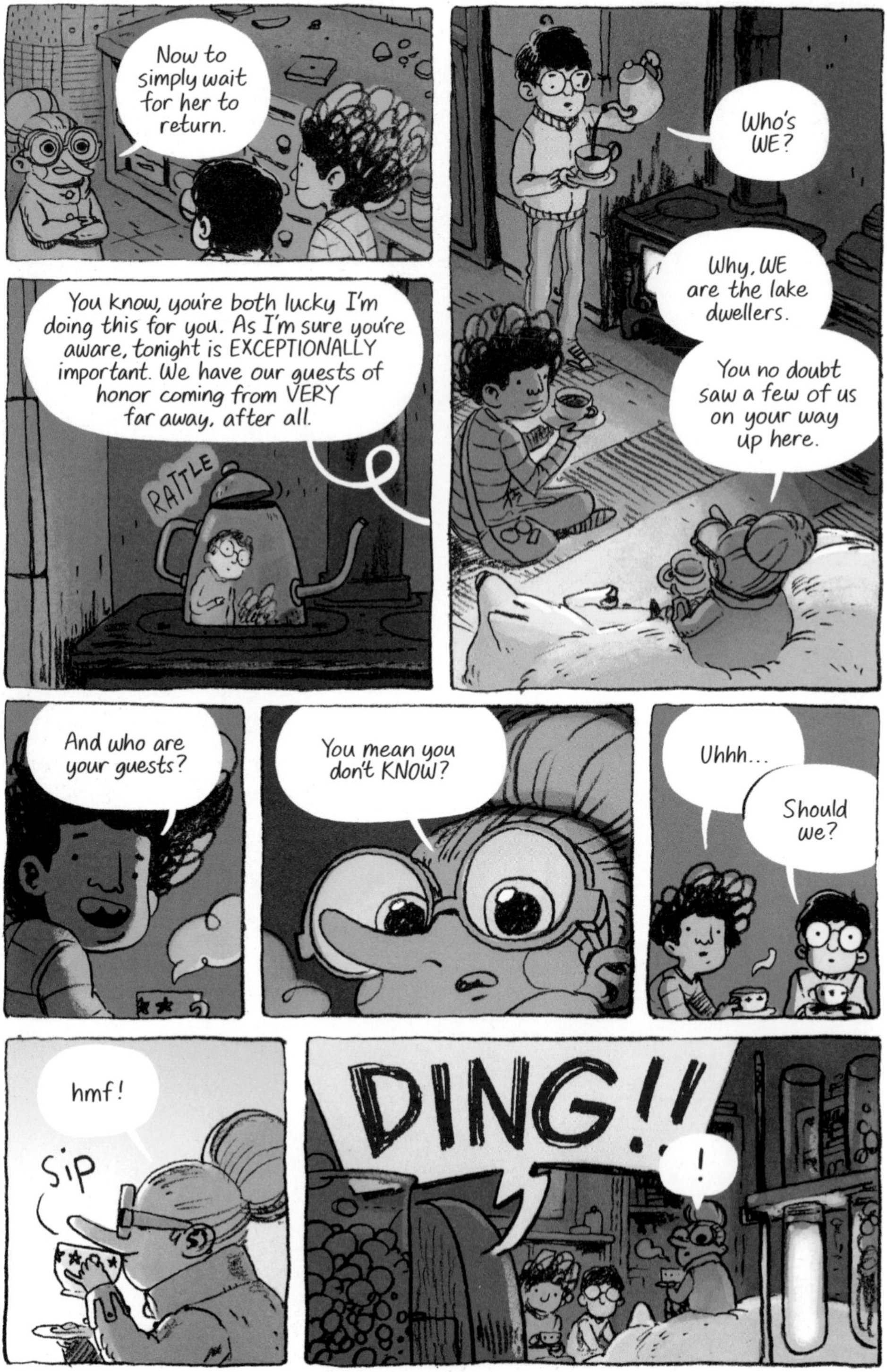
Now to simply wait for her to return.
Who's WE?
You know, you're both lucky I'm doing this for you. As I'm sure you're aware, tonight is EXCEPTIONALLY important. We have our guests of honor coming from VERY far away, after all.
RATTLE
Why, WE are the lake dwellers.
You no doubt saw a few of us on your way up here.
And who are your guests?
You mean you don't KNOW?
Uhhh...
Should we?
hmf!
Sip
DING!!
!

OUR VILLAGE IS TO BE VISITED BY THE ENLIGHTENED ONES!

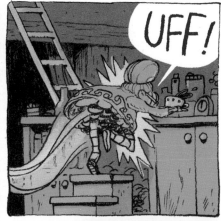

UFF!

They grace us with their presence only once per year!

To mark the first day of autumn and the ensuing harvest!

...

I thought EVERYONE knew that!

hup!

That's pretty neat, I guess.

Sip

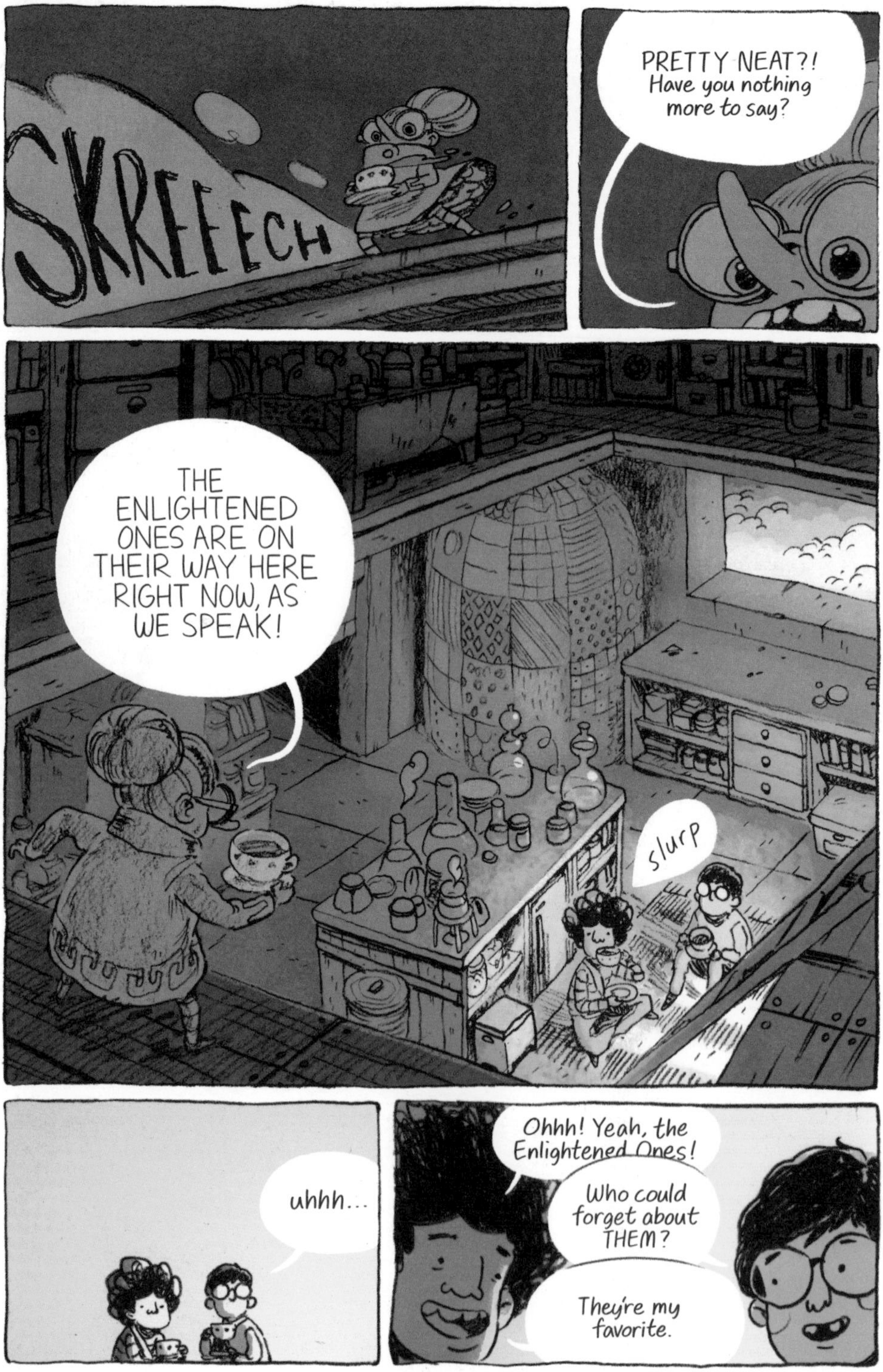
SKREEECH
PRETTY NEAT?! Have you nothing more to say?
THE ENLIGHTENED ONES ARE ON THEIR WAY HERE RIGHT NOW, AS WE SPEAK!
slurp
uhhh...
Ohhh! Yeah, the Enlightened Ones!
Who could forget about THEM?
They're my favorite.

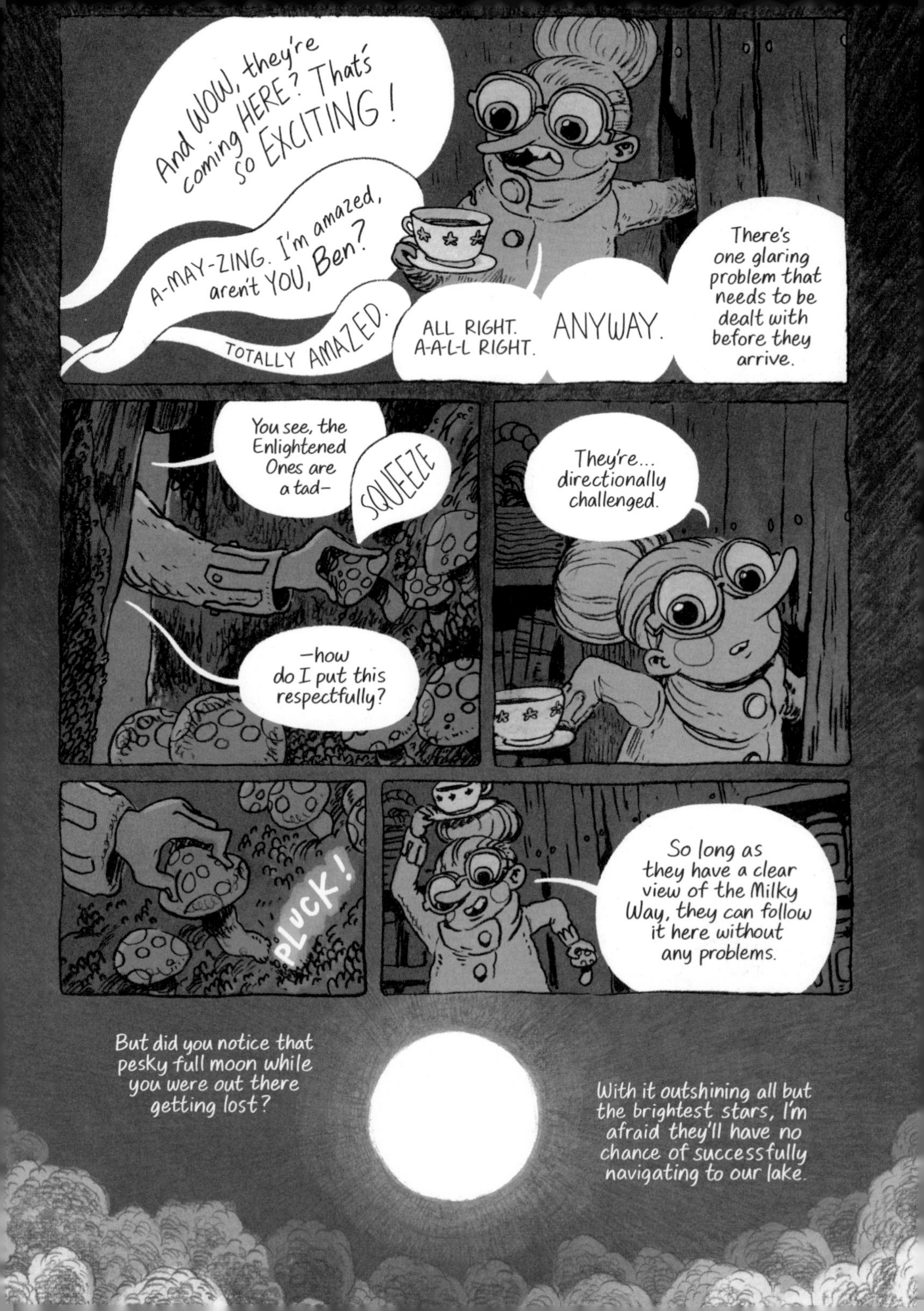
And WOW, they're coming HERE? That's so EXCITING!
A-MAY-ZING. I'm amazed, aren't YOU, Ben?
TOTALLY AMAZED.
ALL RIGHT. A-A-L-L RIGHT.
ANYWAY.
There's one glaring problem that needs to be dealt with before they arrive.
You see, the Enlightened Ones are a tad–
SQUEEZE
–how do I put this respectfully?
They're... directionally challenged.
PLUCK!
So long as they have a clear view of the Milky Way, they can follow it here without any problems.
But did you notice that pesky full moon while you were out there getting lost?
With it outshining all but the brightest stars, I'm afraid they'll have no chance of successfully navigating to our lake.

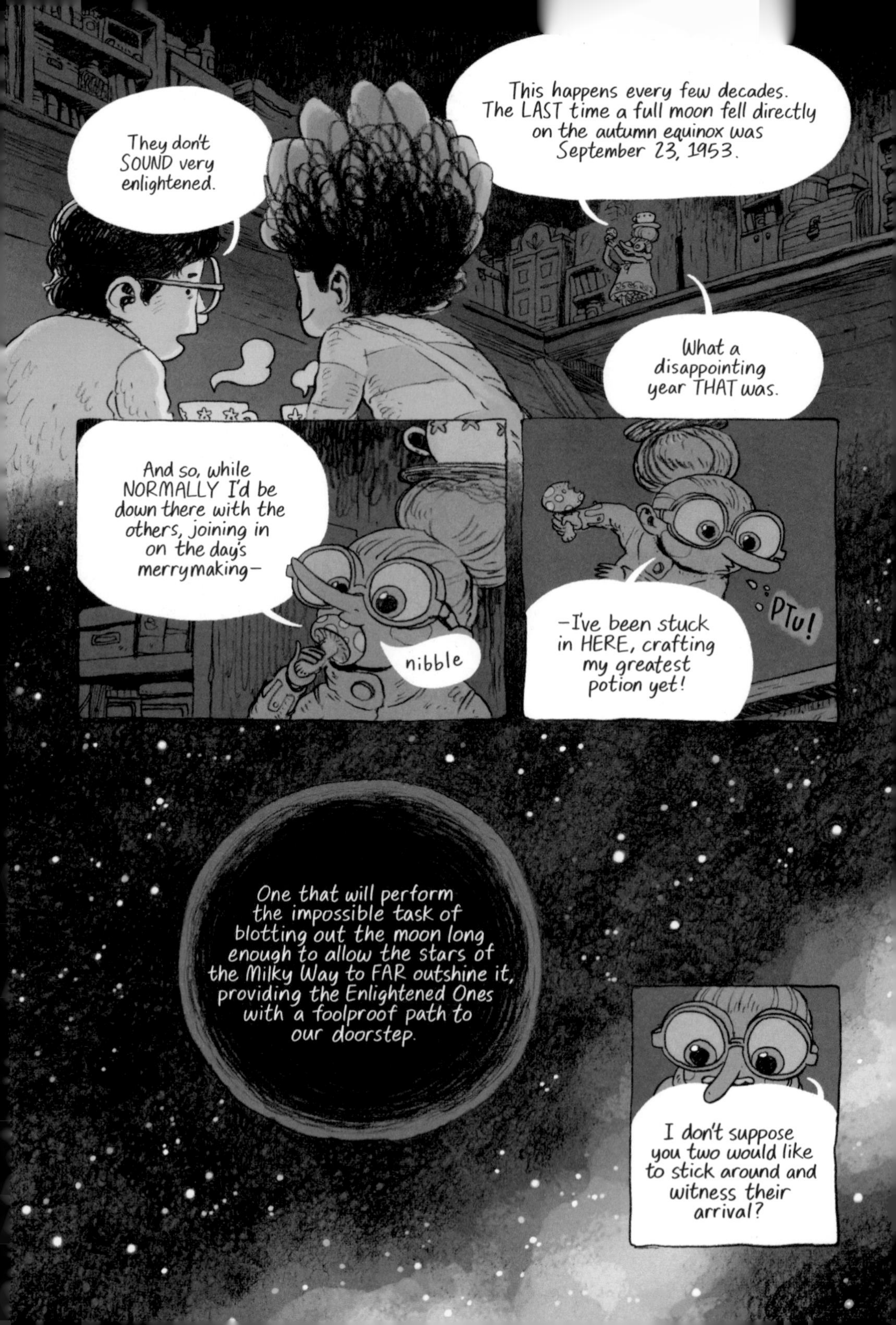
They don't SOUND very enlightened.
This happens every few decades. The LAST time a full moon fell directly on the autumn equinox was September 23, 1953.
What a disappointing year THAT was.
And so, while NORMALLY I'd be down there with the others, joining in on the day's merrymaking—
nibble
—I've been stuck in HERE, crafting my greatest potion yet!
PTU!
One that will perform the impossible task of blotting out the moon long enough to allow the stars of the Milky Way to FAR outshine it, providing the Enlightened Ones with a foolproof path to our doorstep.
I don't suppose you two would like to stick around and witness their arrival?

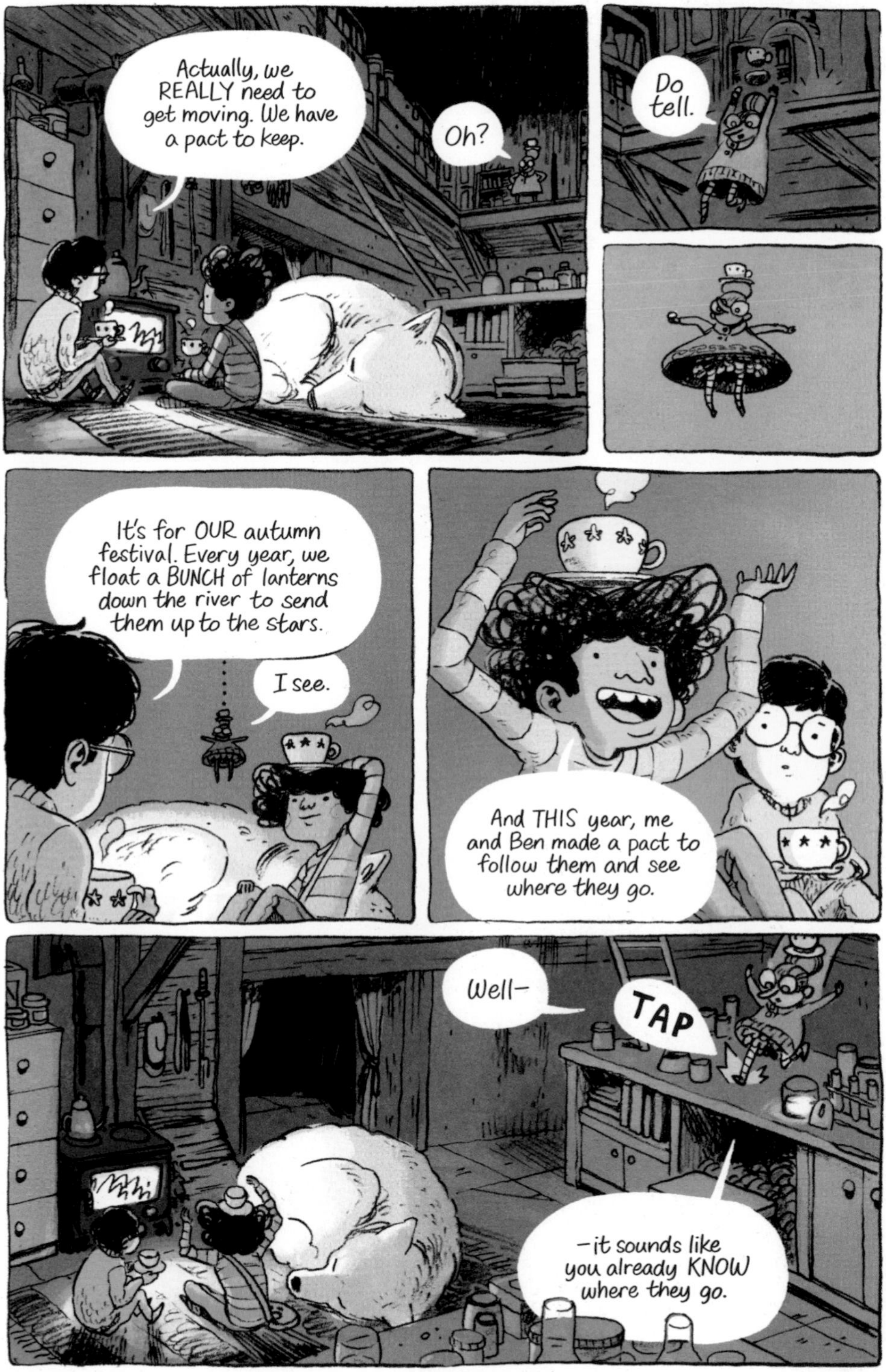
Actually, we REALLY need to get moving. We have a pact to keep.
Oh?
Do tell.
It's for OUR autumn festival. Every year, we float a BUNCH of lanterns down the river to send them up to the stars.
I see.
And THIS year, me and Ben made a pact to follow them and see where they go.
Well—
TAP
—it sounds like you already KNOW where they go.

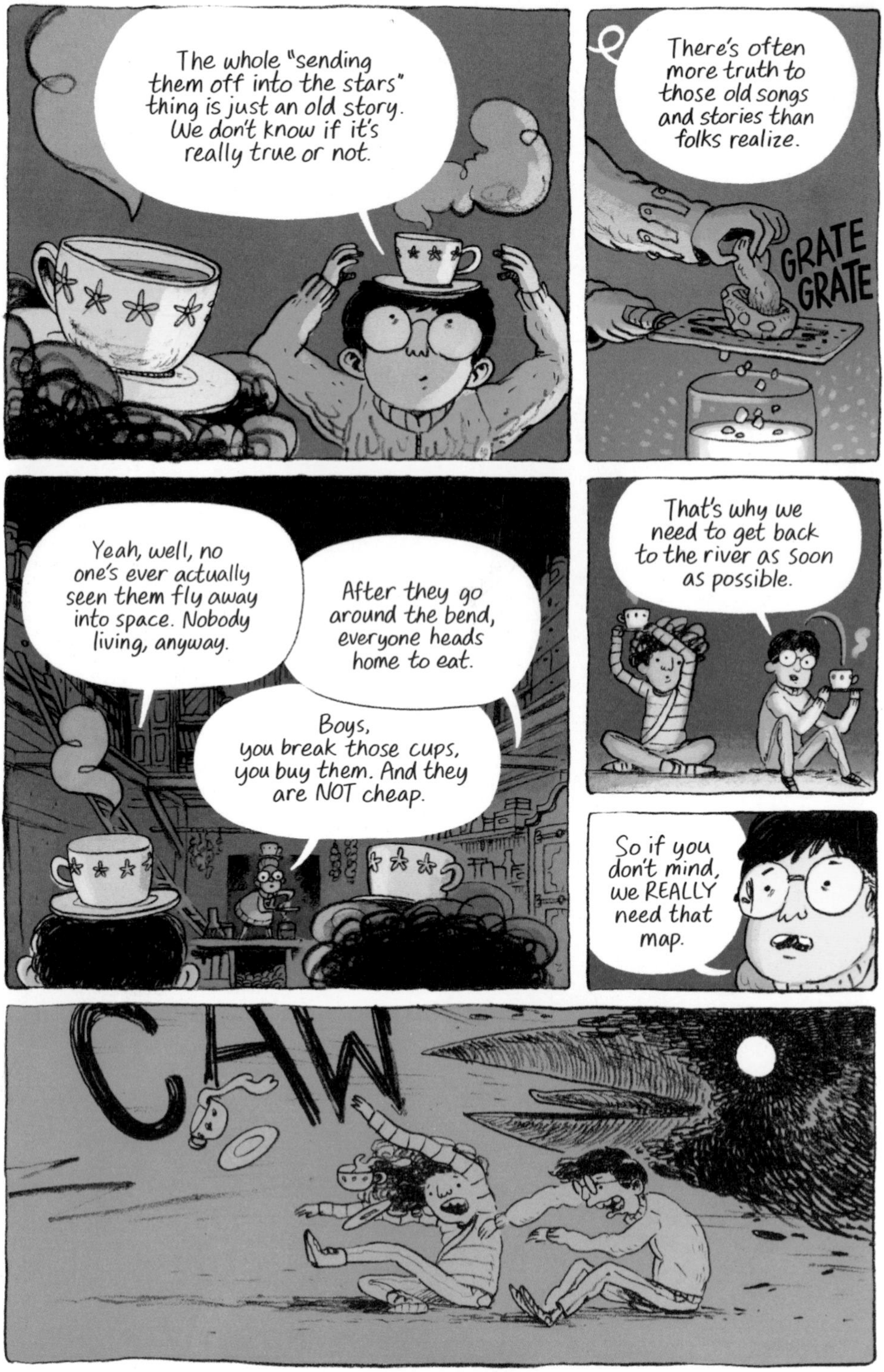
The whole "sending them off into the stars" thing is just an old story. We don't know if it's really true or not.
There's often more truth to those old songs and stories than folks realize.
GRATE GRATE
Yeah, well, no one's ever actually seen them fly away into space. Nobody living, anyway.
After they go around the bend, everyone heads home to eat.
Boys, you break those cups, you buy them. And they are NOT cheap.
That's why we need to get back to the river as soon as possible.
So if you don't mind, we REALLY need that map.
CAW

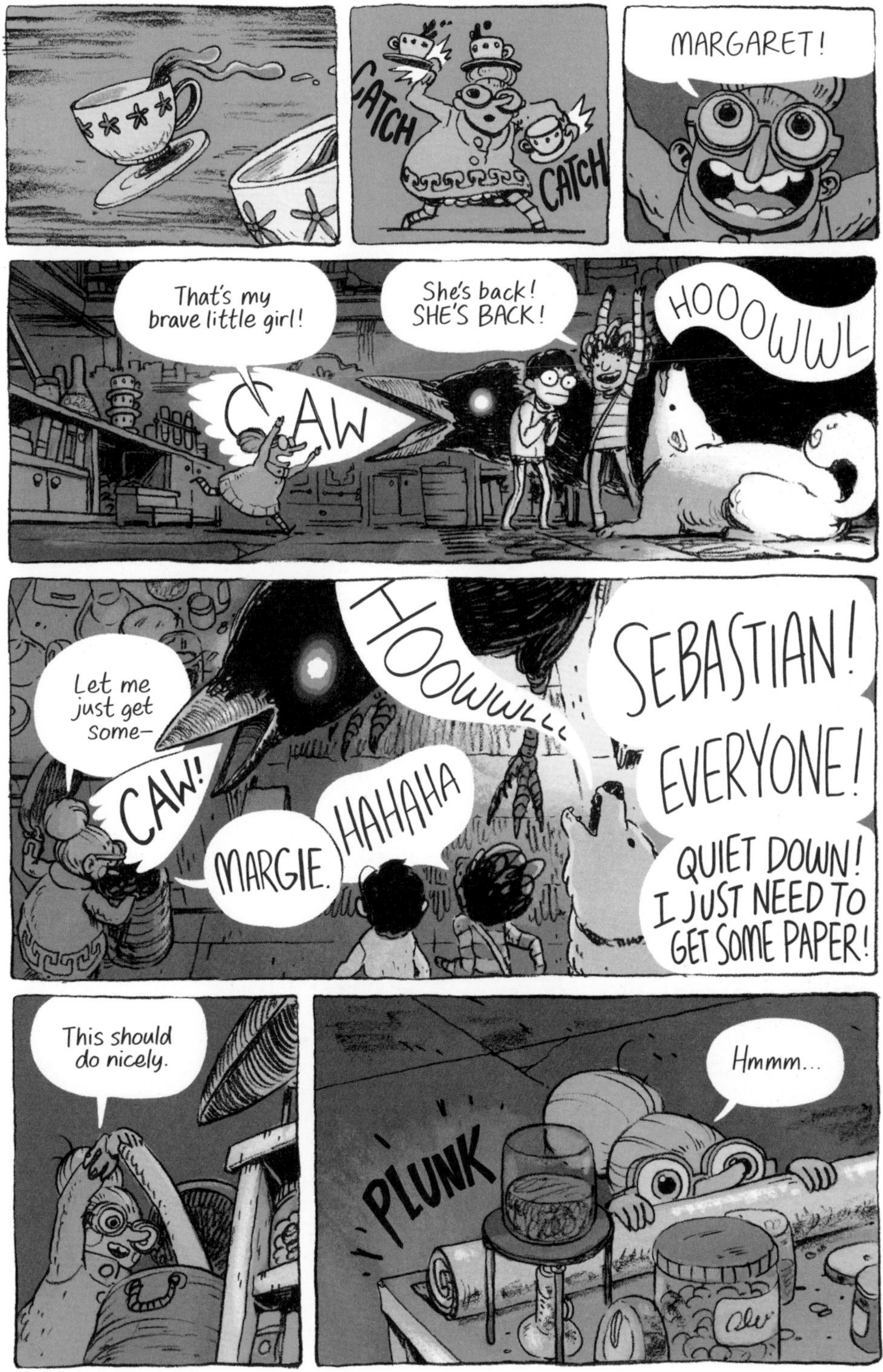
CATCH
CATCH
MARGARET!
That's my brave little girl!
She's back! SHE'S BACK!
HOOOWWL
CAW
Let me just get some–
CAW!
HOOWWLL
SEBASTIAN!
EVERYONE!
MARGIE.
HAHAHA
QUIET DOWN! I JUST NEED TO GET SOME PAPER!
This should do nicely.
Hmmm...
PLUNK

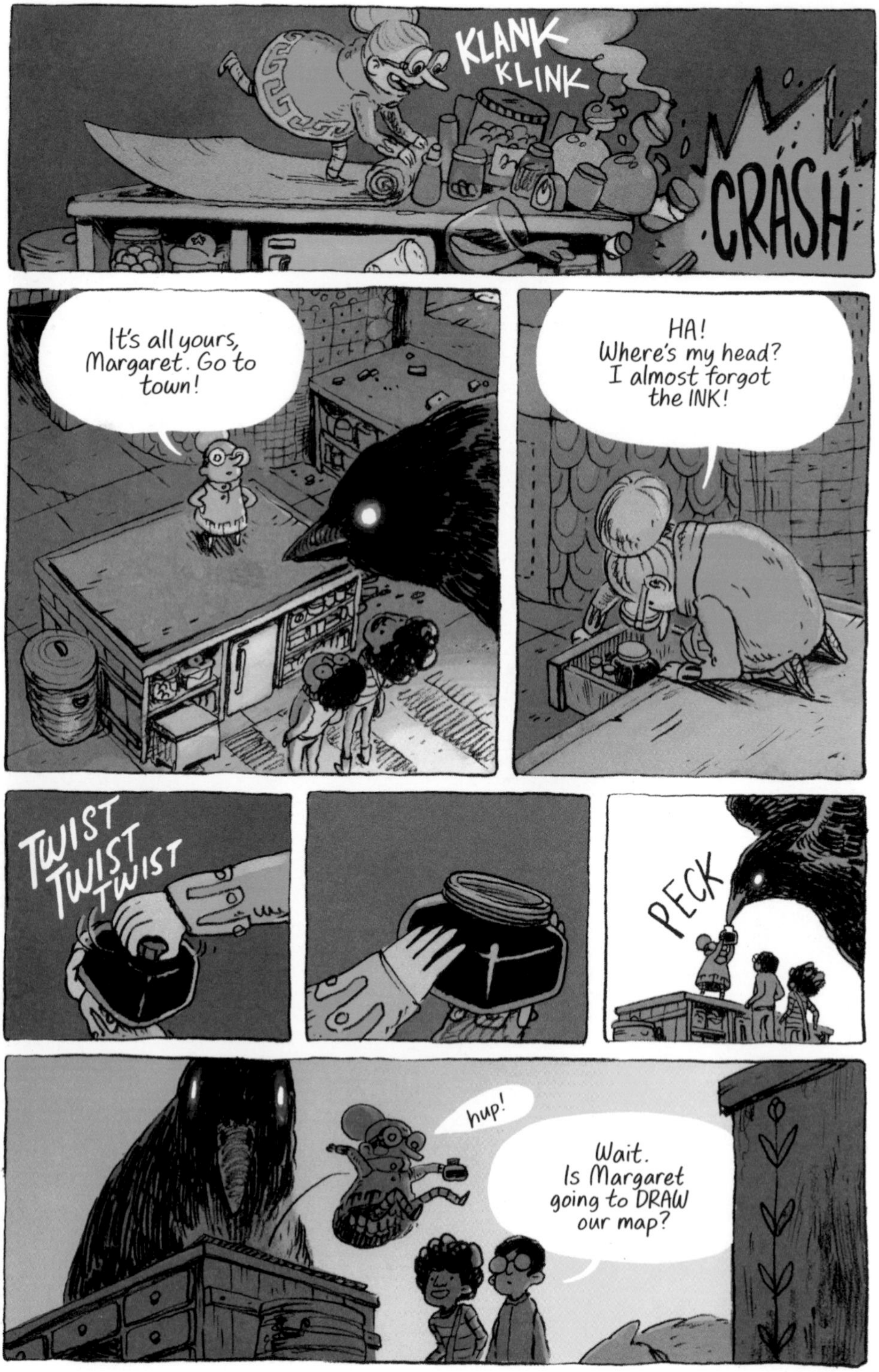
KLANK
KLINK
CRASH
It's all yours, Margaret. Go to town!
HA! Where's my head? I almost forgot the INK!
TWIST TWIST TWIST
PECK
hup!
Wait. Is Margaret going to DRAW our map?

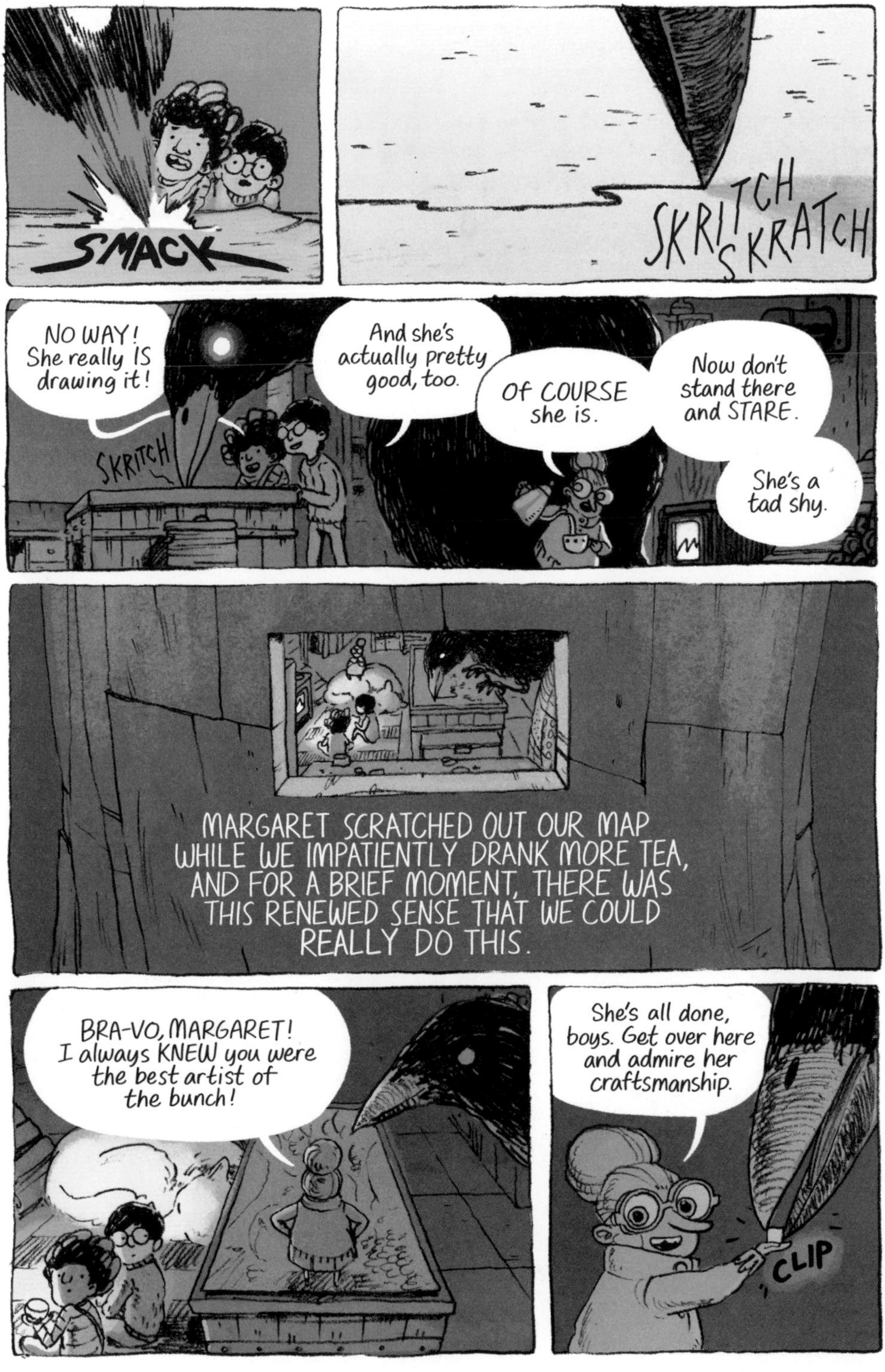
SMACK
SKRITCH SKRATCH
NO WAY! She really IS drawing it!
SKRITCH
And she's actually pretty good, too.
OF COURSE she is.
Now don't stand there and STARE.
She's a tad shy.
MARGARET SCRATCHED OUT OUR MAP WHILE WE IMPATIENTLY DRANK MORE TEA, AND FOR A BRIEF MOMENT, THERE WAS THIS RENEWED SENSE THAT WE COULD REALLY DO THIS.
BRA-VO, MARGARET! I always KNEW you were the best artist of the bunch!
She's all done, boys. Get over here and admire her craftsmanship.
CLIP

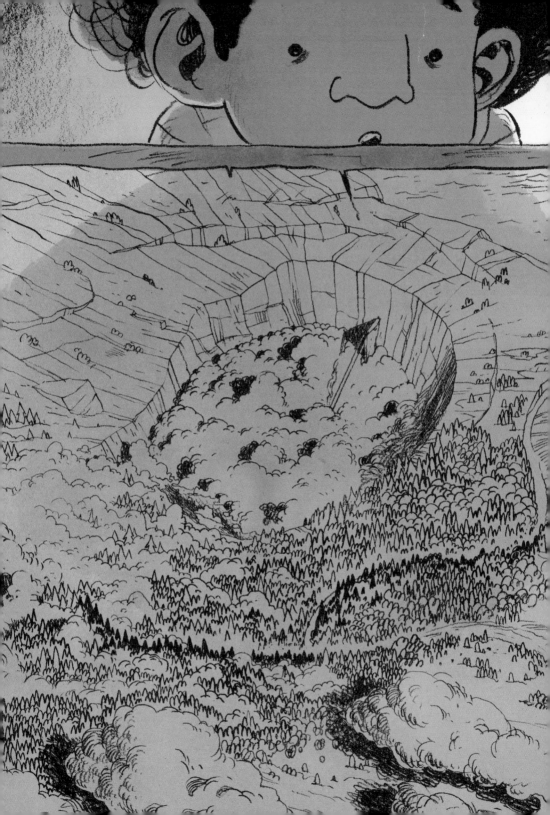

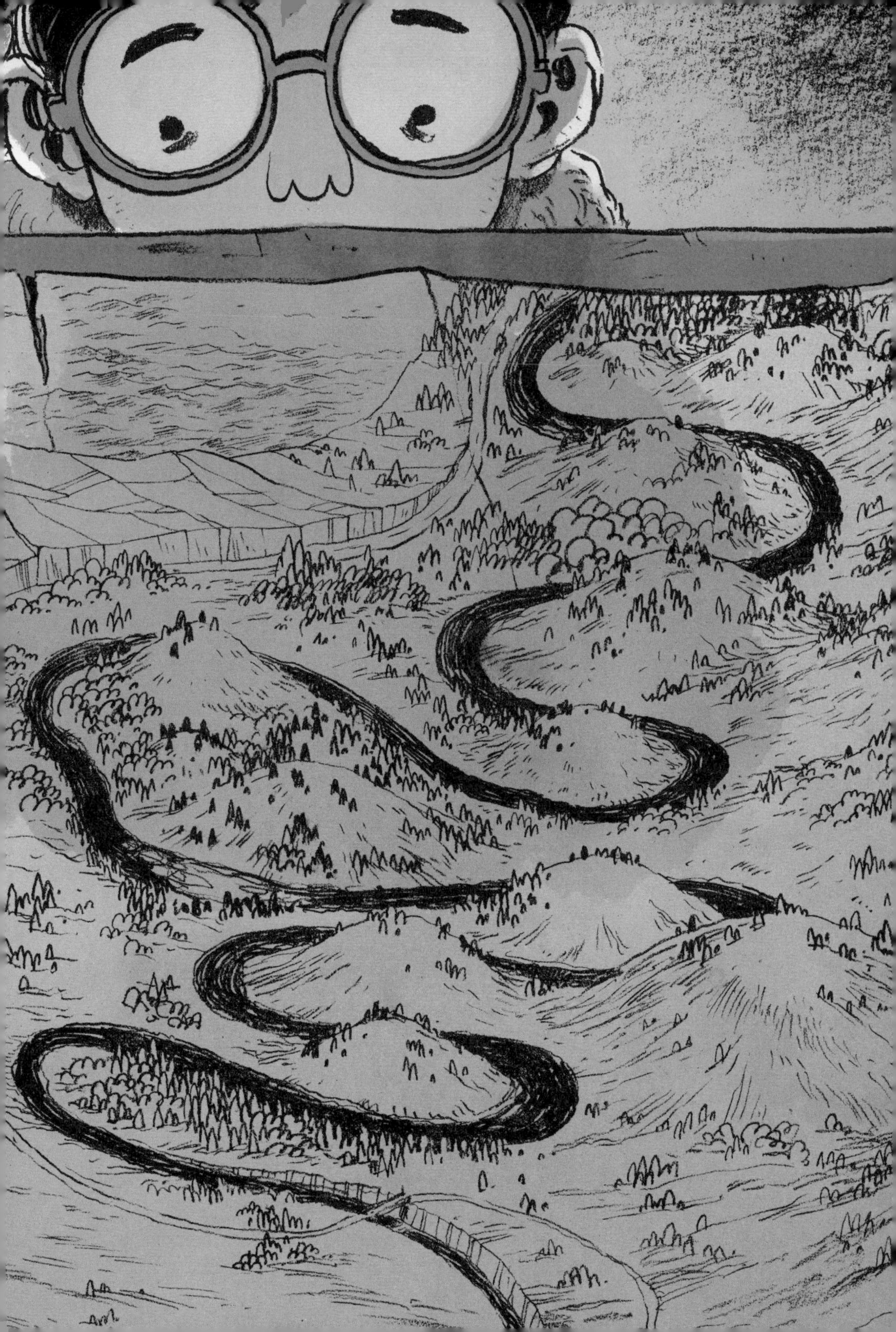

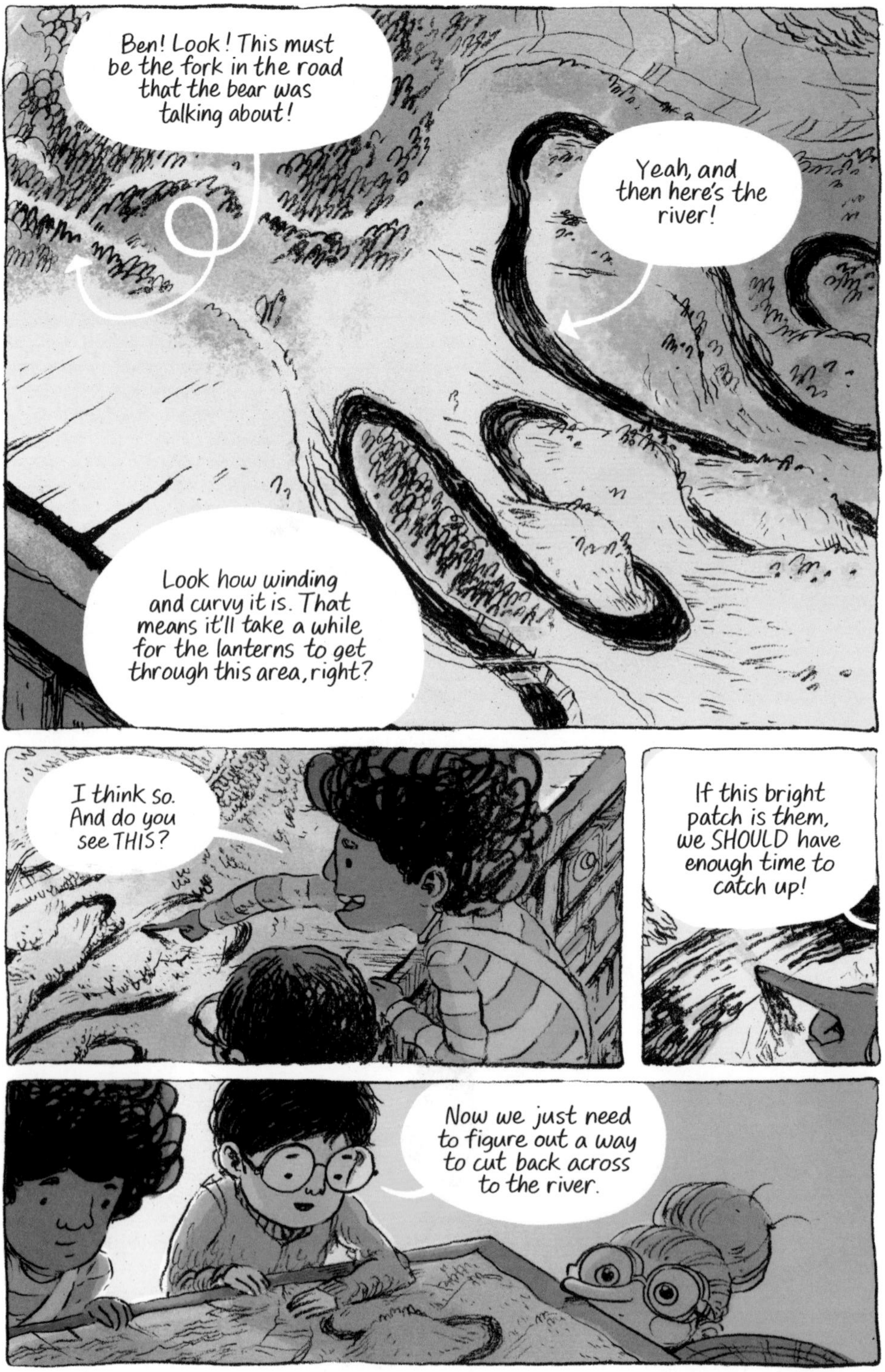
Ben! Look! This must be the fork in the road that the bear was talking about!
Yeah, and then here's the river!
Look how winding and curvy it is. That means it'll take a while for the lanterns to get through this area, right?
I think so. And do you see THIS?
If this bright patch is them, we SHOULD have enough time to catch up!
Now we just need to figure out a way to cut back across to the river.

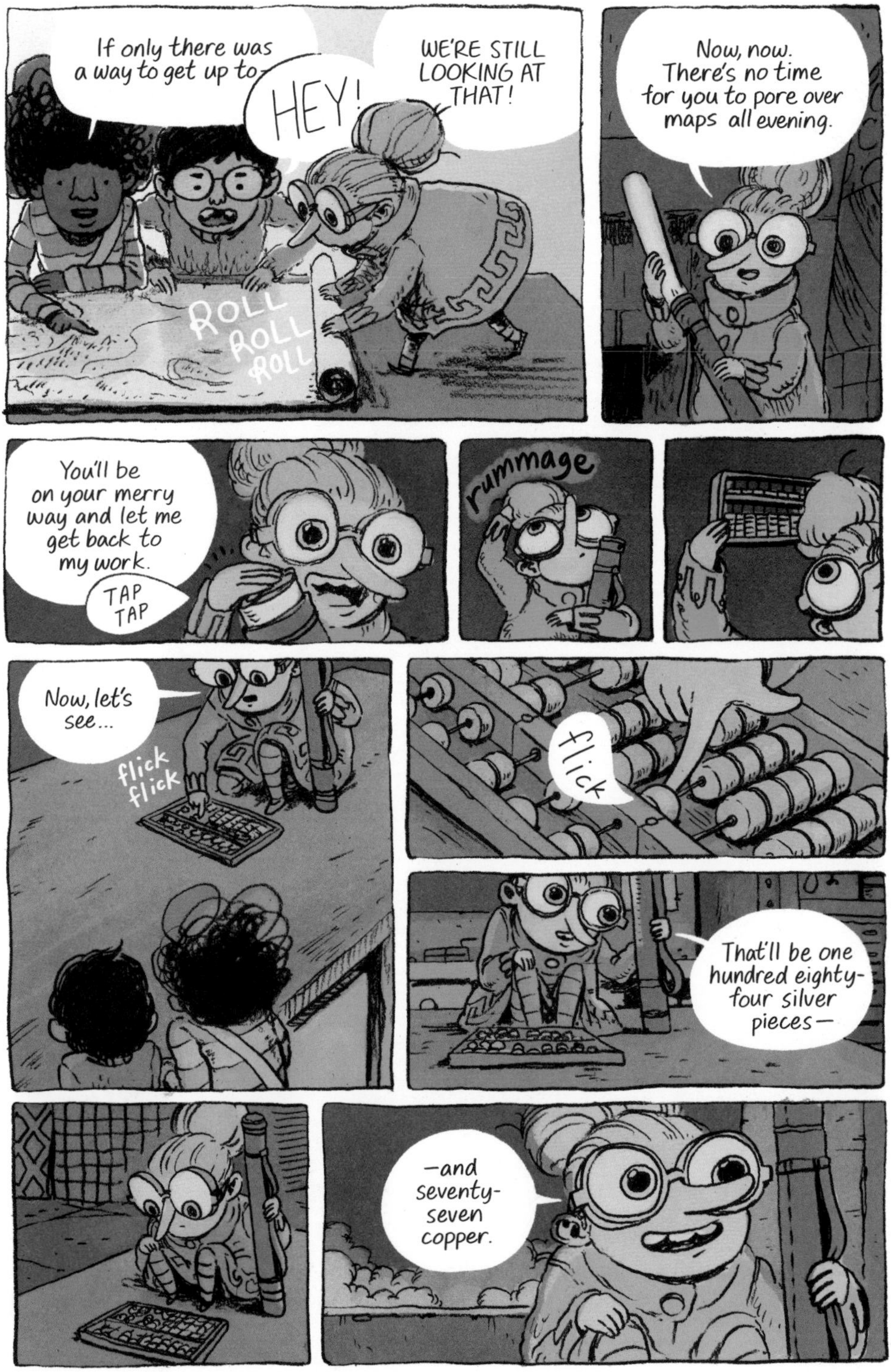

If only there was a way to get up to—
HEY!
WE'RE STILL LOOKING AT THAT!
ROLL ROLL ROLL
Now, now. There's no time for you to pore over maps all evening.
You'll be on your merry way and let me get back to my work.
TAP TAP
rummage
Now, let's see...
flick flick
flick
That'll be one hundred eighty-four silver pieces—
—and seventy-seven copper.

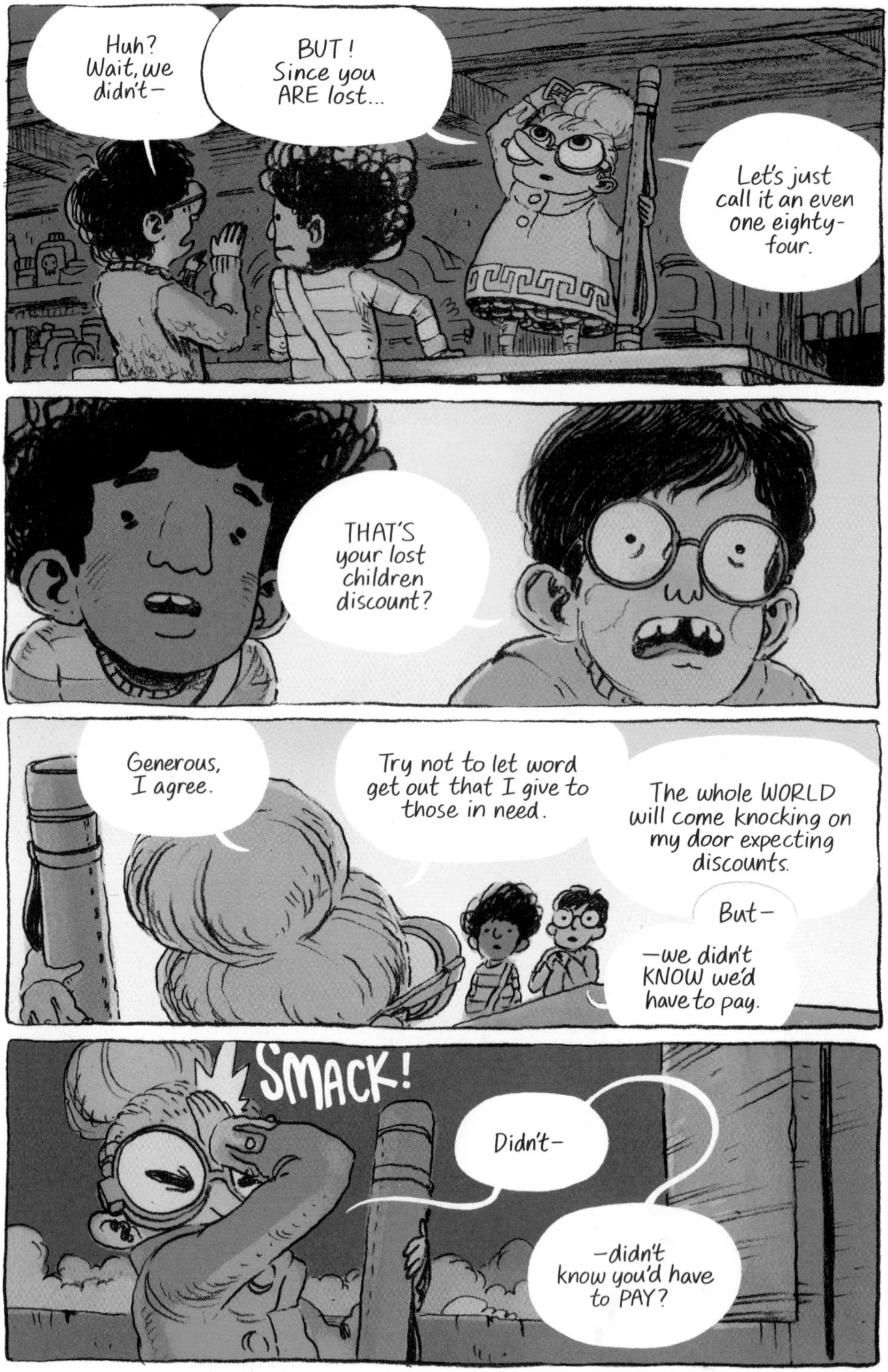
Huh? Wait, we didn't–
BUT! Since you ARE lost...
Let's just call it an even one eighty-four.
THAT'S your lost children discount?
Generous, I agree.
Try not to let word get out that I give to those in need.
The whole WORLD will come knocking on my door expecting discounts.
But–
–we didn't KNOW we'd have to pay.
SMACK!
Didn't–
–didn't know you'd have to PAY?

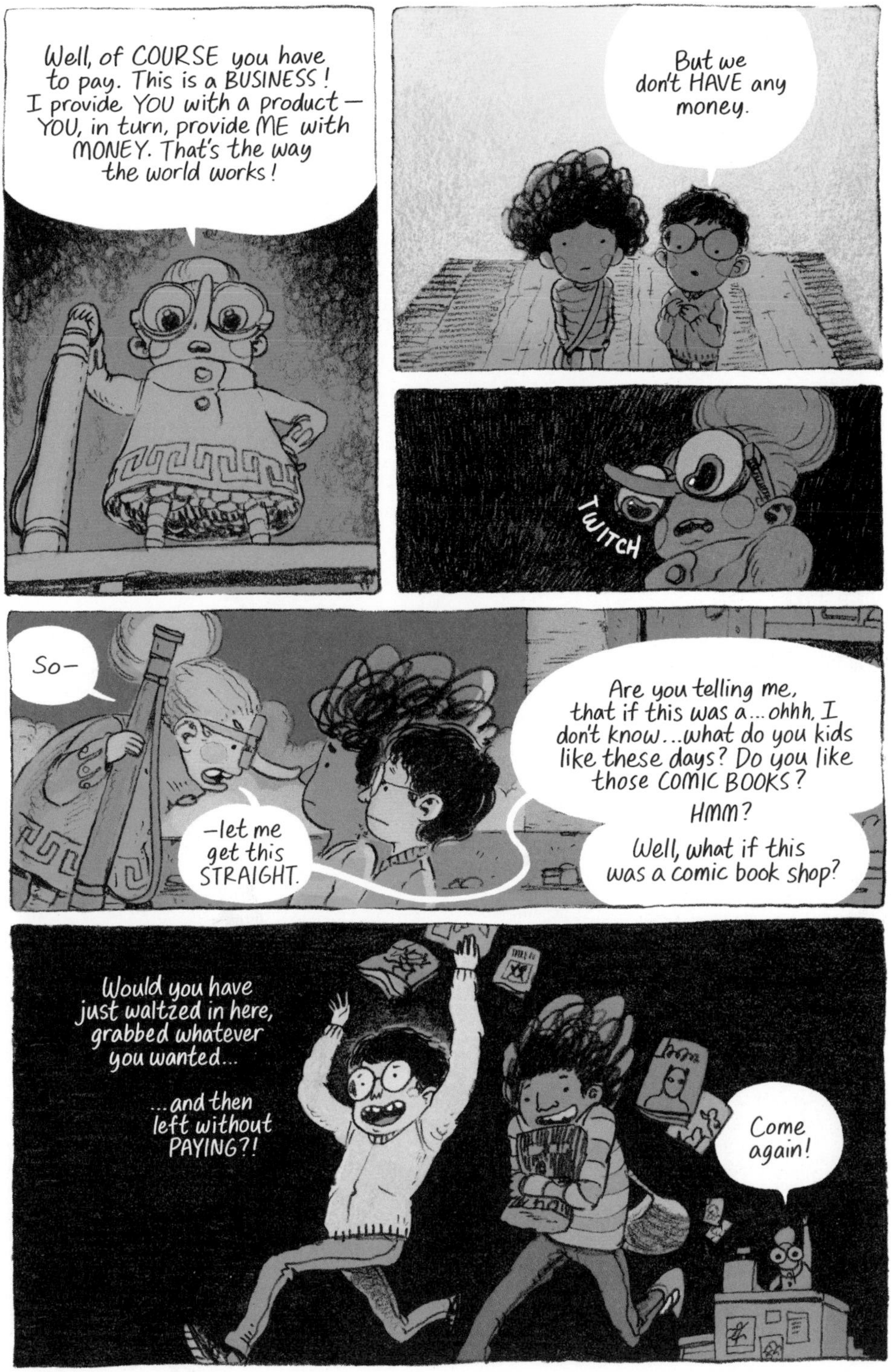
Well, of COURSE you have to pay. This is a BUSINESS! I provide YOU with a product— YOU, in turn, provide ME with MONEY. That's the way the world works!
But we don't HAVE any money.
TWITCH
So—
—let me get this STRAIGHT.
Are you telling me, that if this was a...ohhh, I don't know...what do you kids like these days? Do you like those COMIC BOOKS?
HMM?
Well, what if this was a comic book shop?
Would you have just waltzed in here, grabbed whatever you wanted...
...and then left without PAYING?!
Come again!

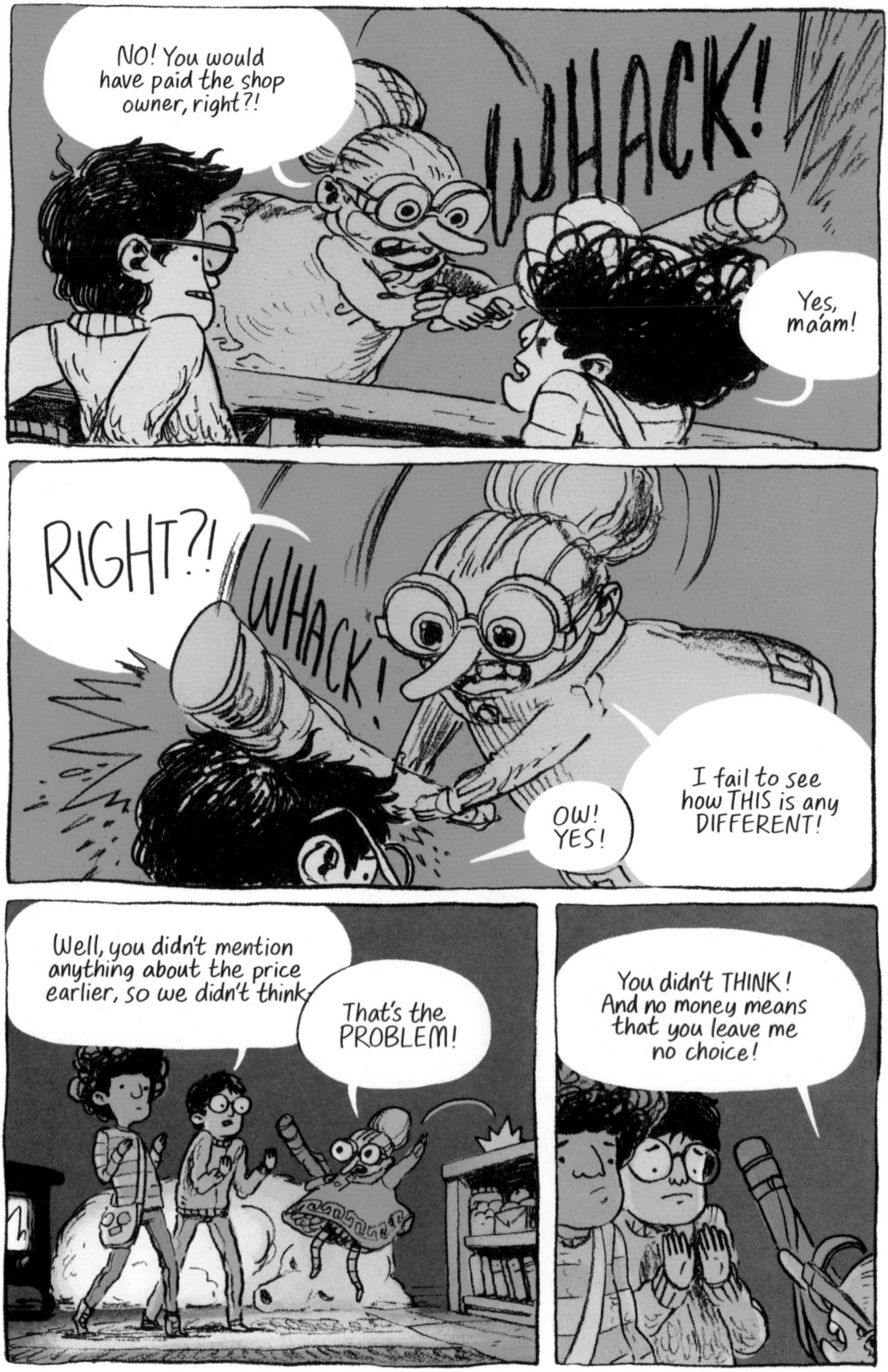
NO! You would have paid the shop owner, right?!
WHACK!
Yes, ma'am!
RIGHT?!
WHACK!
I fail to see how THIS is any DIFFERENT!
OW! YES!
Well, you didn't mention anything about the price earlier, so we didn't think-
That's the PROBLEM!
You didn't THINK! And no money means that you leave me no choice!

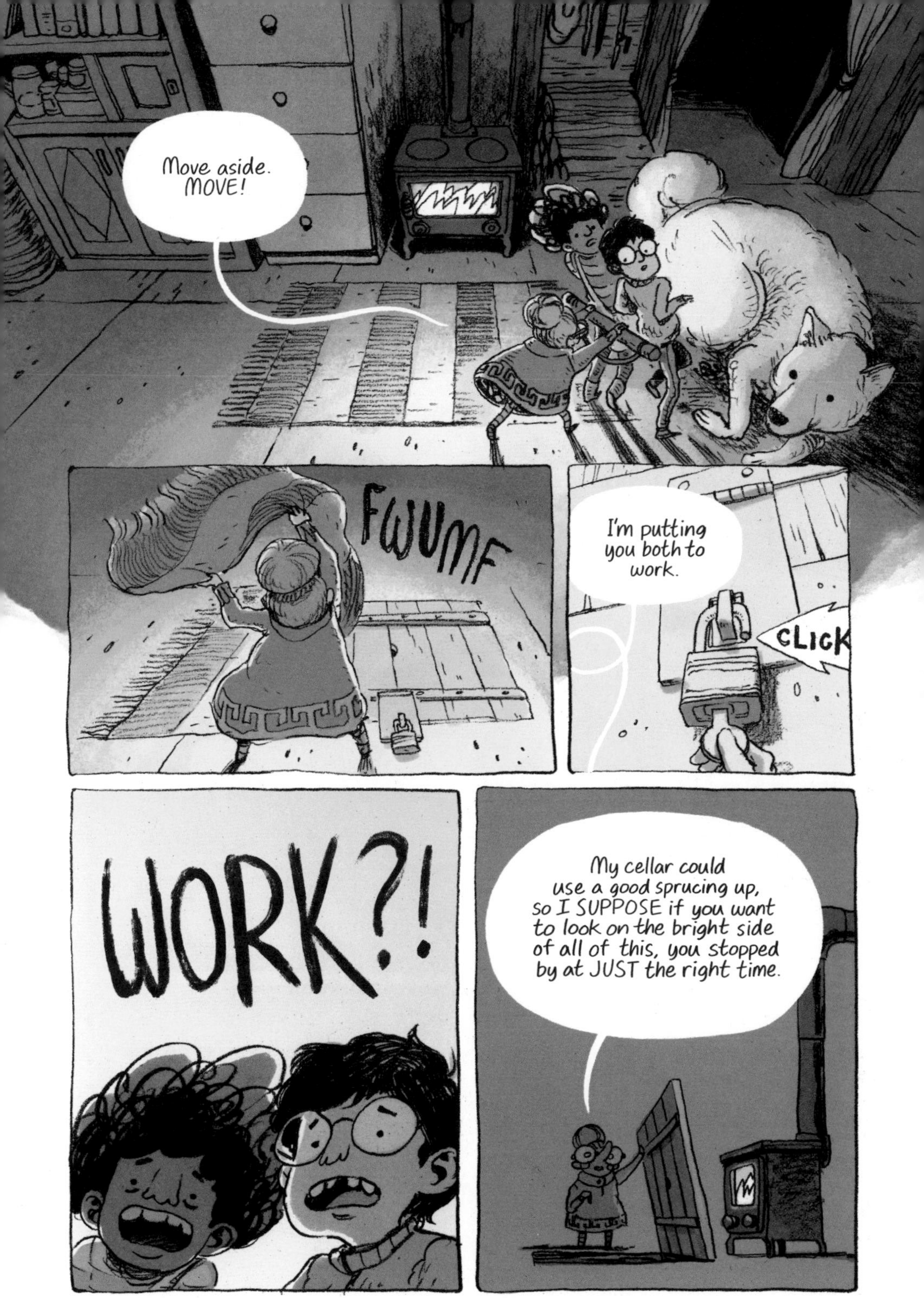
Move aside. MOVE!
FWUMF
I'm putting you both to work.
CLICK
WORK?!
My cellar could use a good sprucing up, so I SUPPOSE if you want to look on the bright side of all of this, you stopped by at JUST the right time.

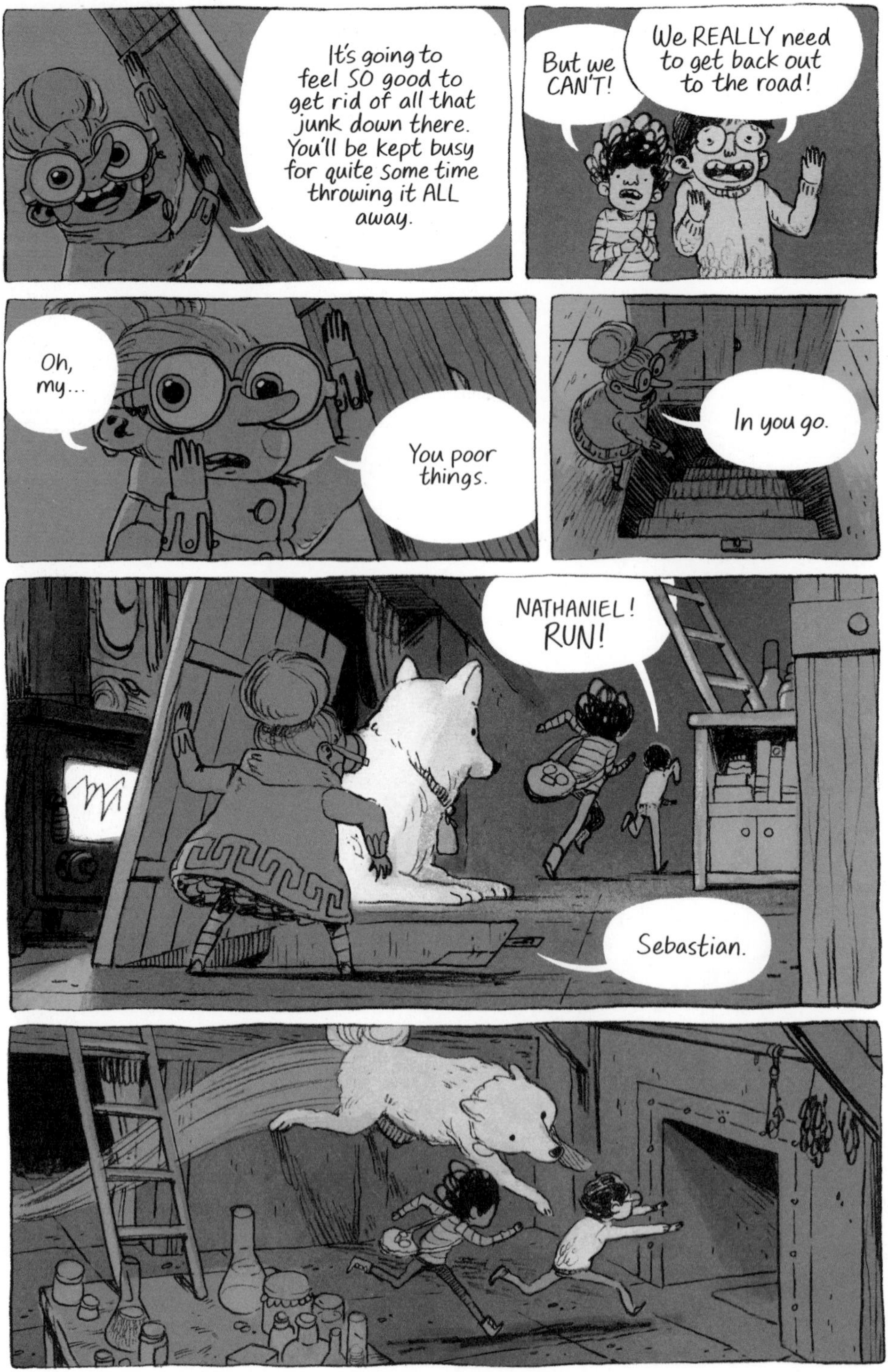
It's going to feel SO good to get rid of all that junk down there. You'll be kept busy for quite some time throwing it ALL away.
But we CAN'T!
We REALLY need to get back out to the road!
Oh, my...
You poor things.
In you go.
NATHANIEL! RUN!
Sebastian.

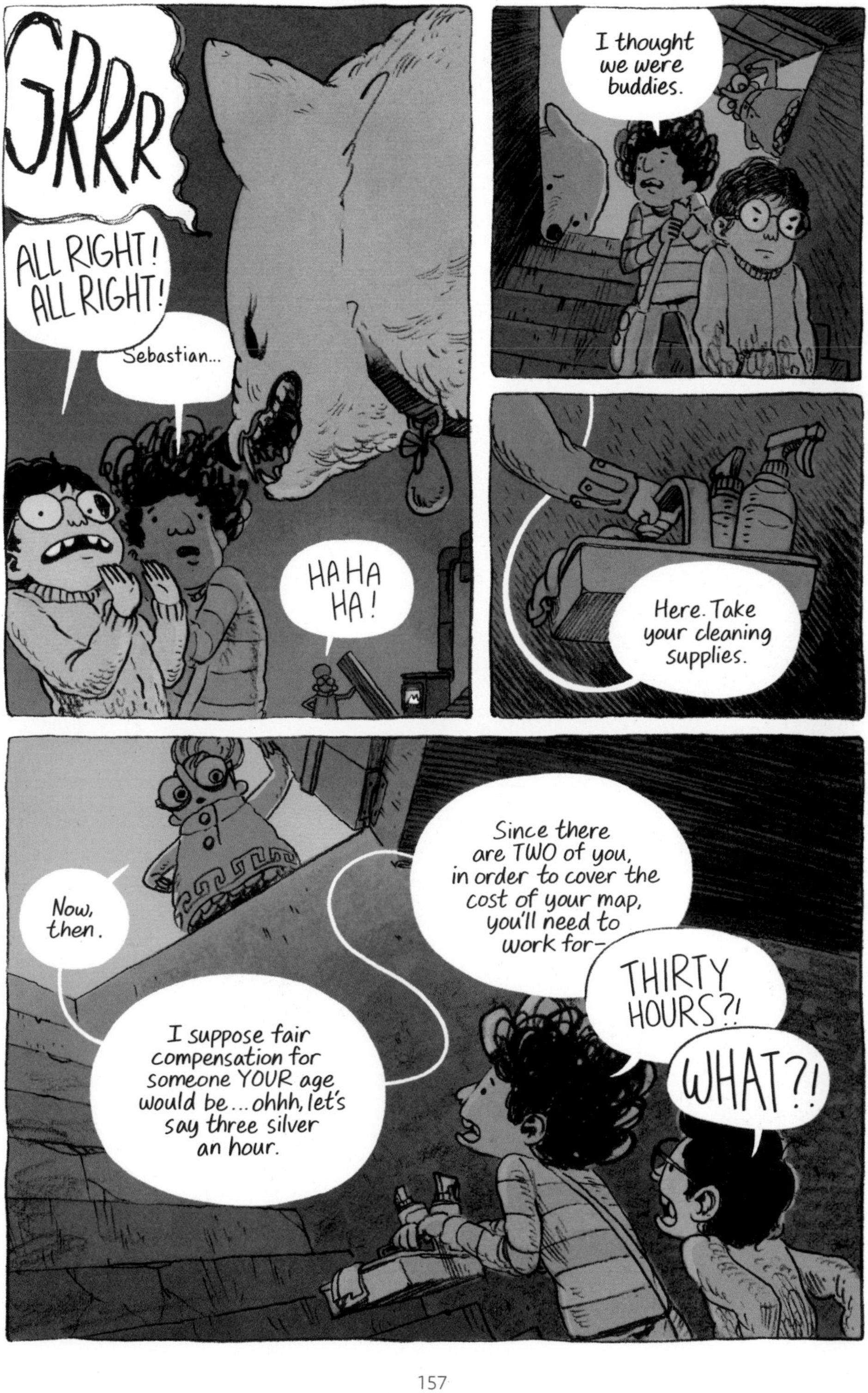
GRRR
ALL RIGHT! ALL RIGHT!
Sebastian...
HA HA HA!
I thought we were buddies.
Here. Take your cleaning supplies.
Now, then.
Since there are TWO of you, in order to cover the cost of your map, you'll need to work for–
I suppose fair compensation for someone YOUR age would be...ohhh, let's say three silver an hour.
THIRTY HOURS?!
WHAT?!

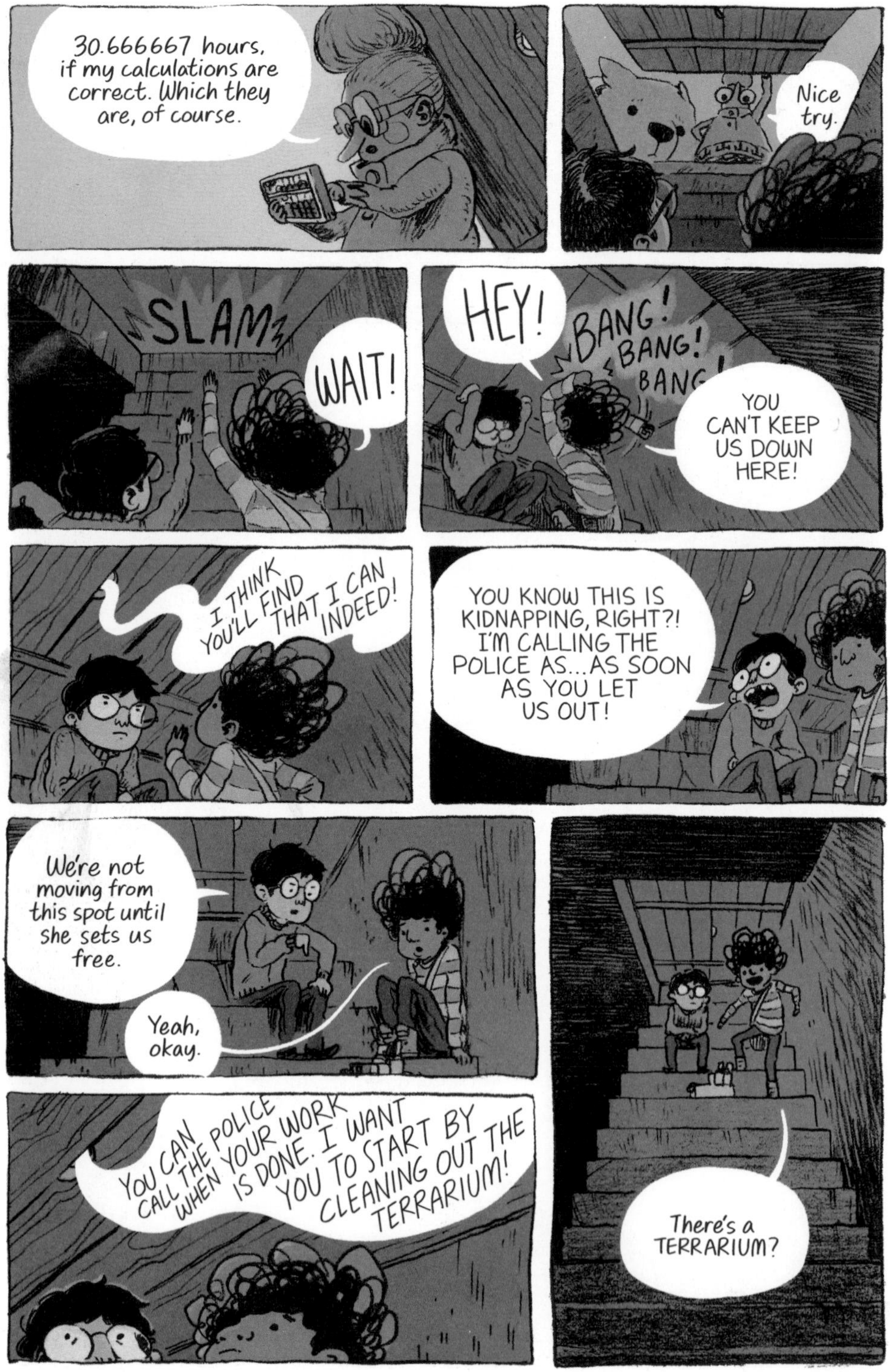
30.666667 hours, if my calculations are correct. Which they are, of course.
Nice try.
SLAM
WAIT!
HEY!
BANG! BANG! BANG!
YOU CAN'T KEEP US DOWN HERE!
I THINK YOU'LL FIND THAT I CAN INDEED!
YOU KNOW THIS IS KIDNAPPING, RIGHT?! I'M CALLING THE POLICE AS...AS SOON AS YOU LET US OUT!
We're not moving from this spot until she sets us free.
Yeah, okay.
YOU CAN CALL THE POLICE WHEN YOUR WORK IS DONE. I WANT YOU TO START BY CLEANING OUT THE TERRARIUM!
There's a TERRARIUM?

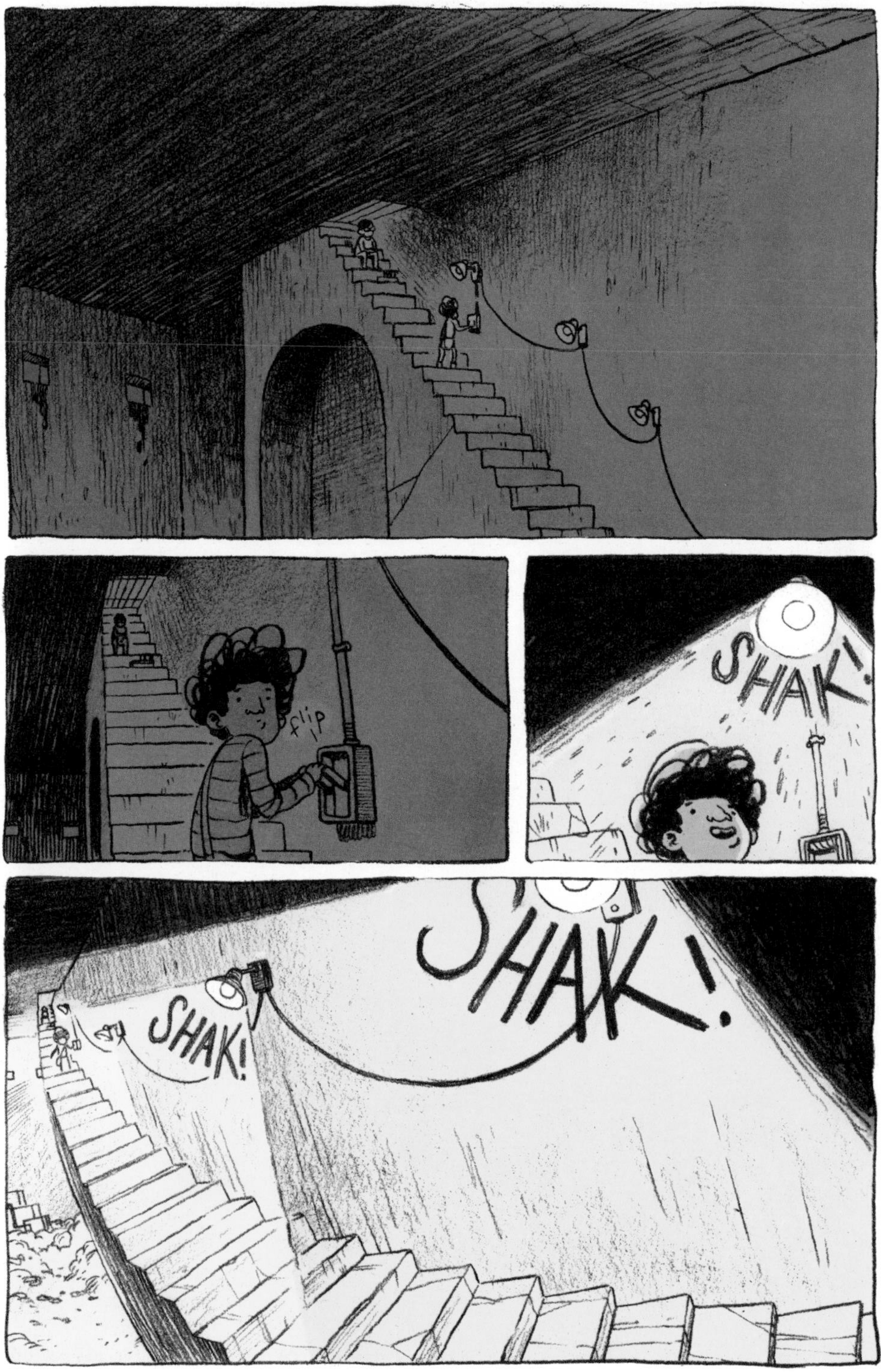
flip
SHAK!
SHAK!
SHAK!

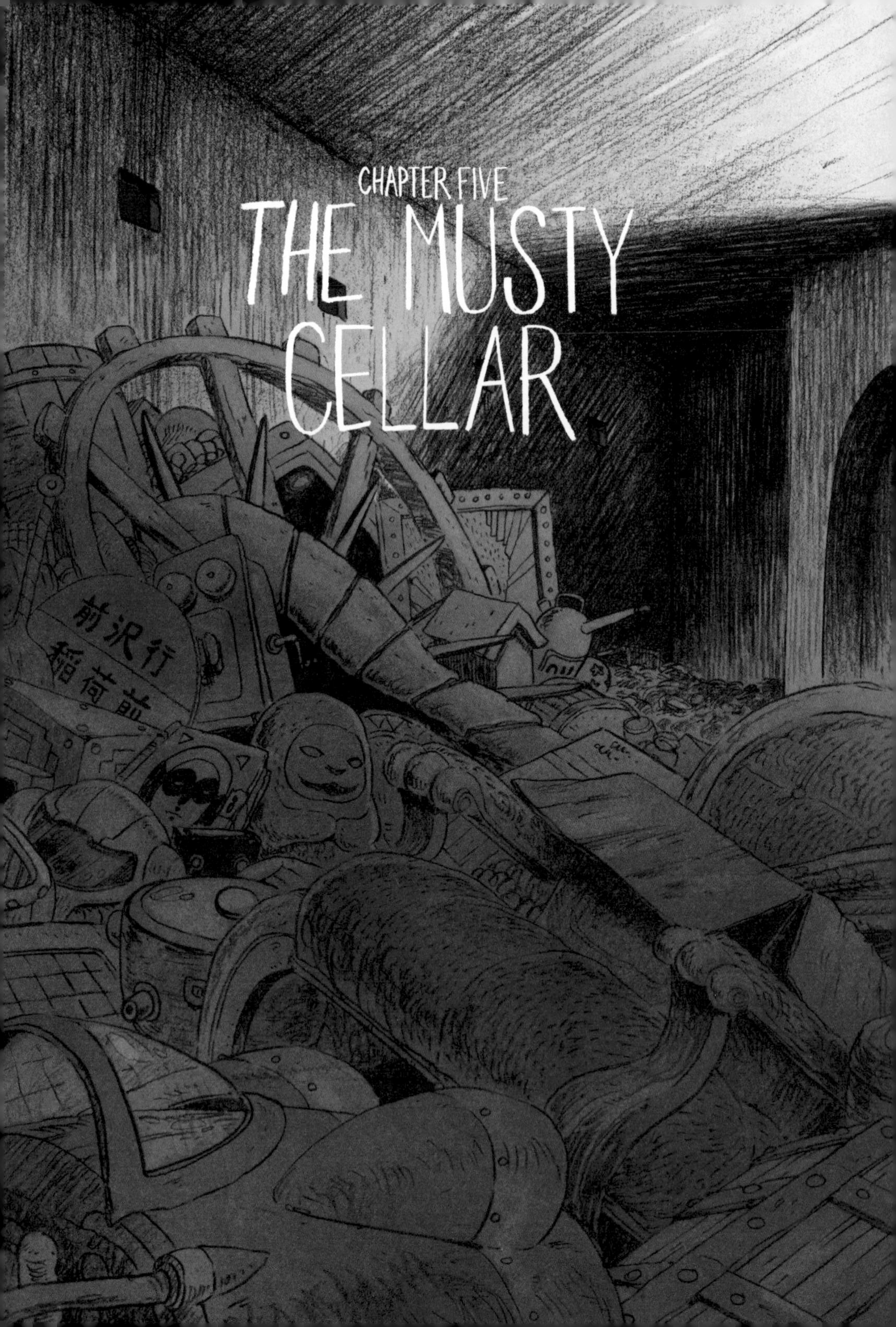
CHAPTER FIVE
THE MUSTY CELLAR
前沢行
稲荷前

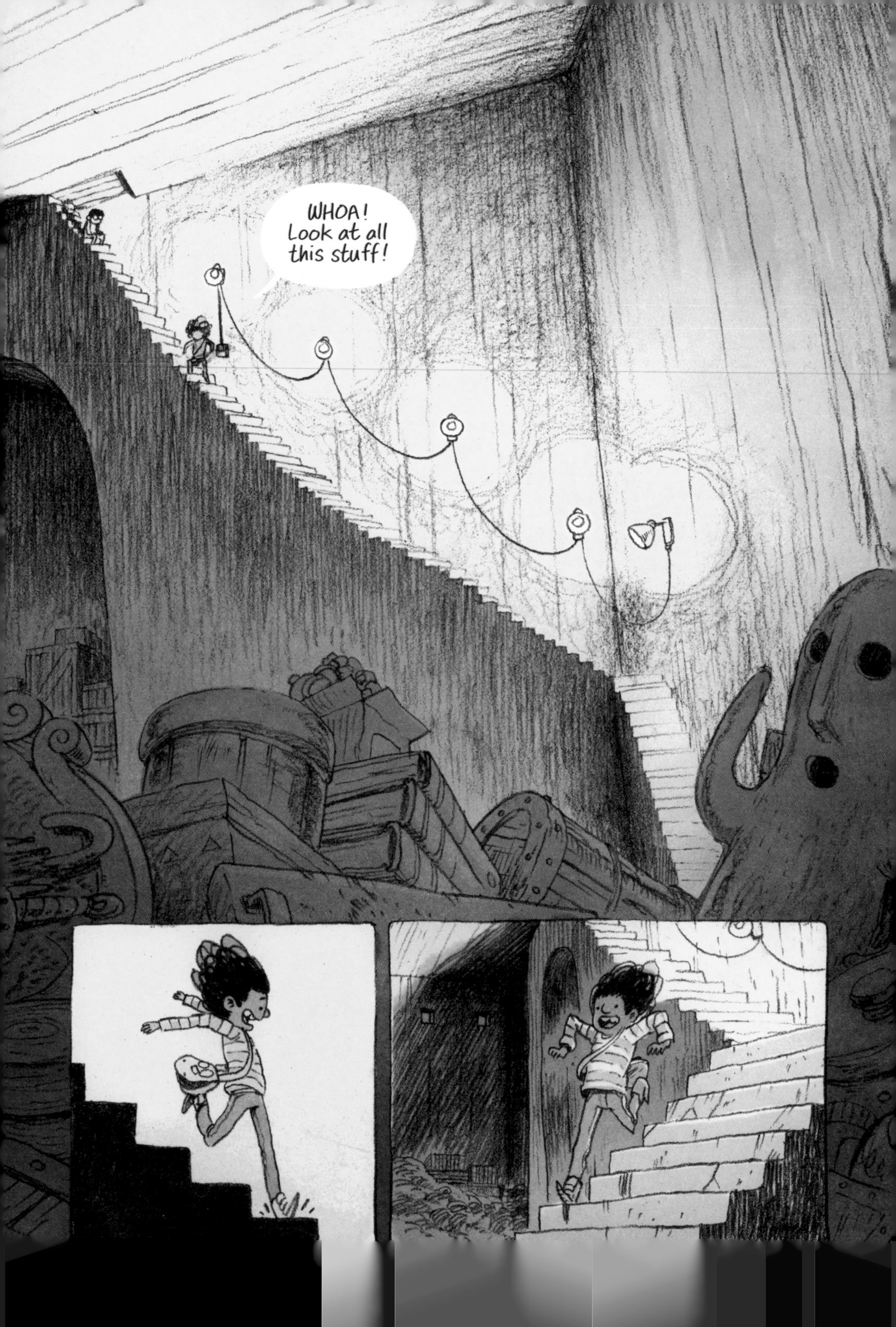
WHOA! Look at all this stuff!

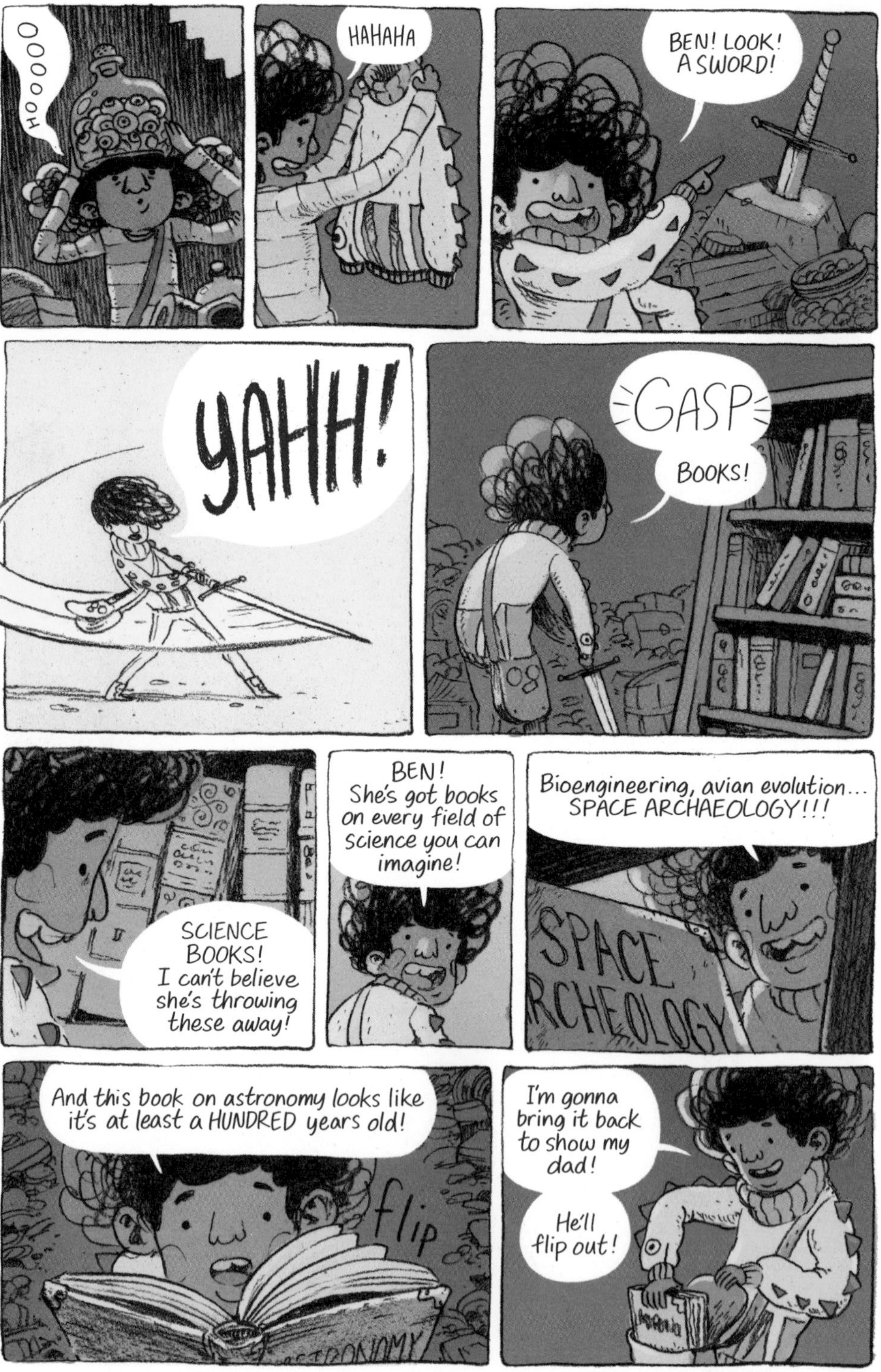
HOOOOOO
HAHAHA
BEN! LOOK! A SWORD!
YAHH!
GASP
BOOKS!
SCIENCE BOOKS! I can't believe she's throwing these away!
BEN! She's got books on every field of science you can imagine!
Bioengineering, avian evolution... SPACE ARCHAEOLOGY!!!
SPACE ARCHEOLOGY
And this book on astronomy looks like it's at least a HUNDRED years old!
flip
I'm gonna bring it back to show my dad!
He'll flip out!

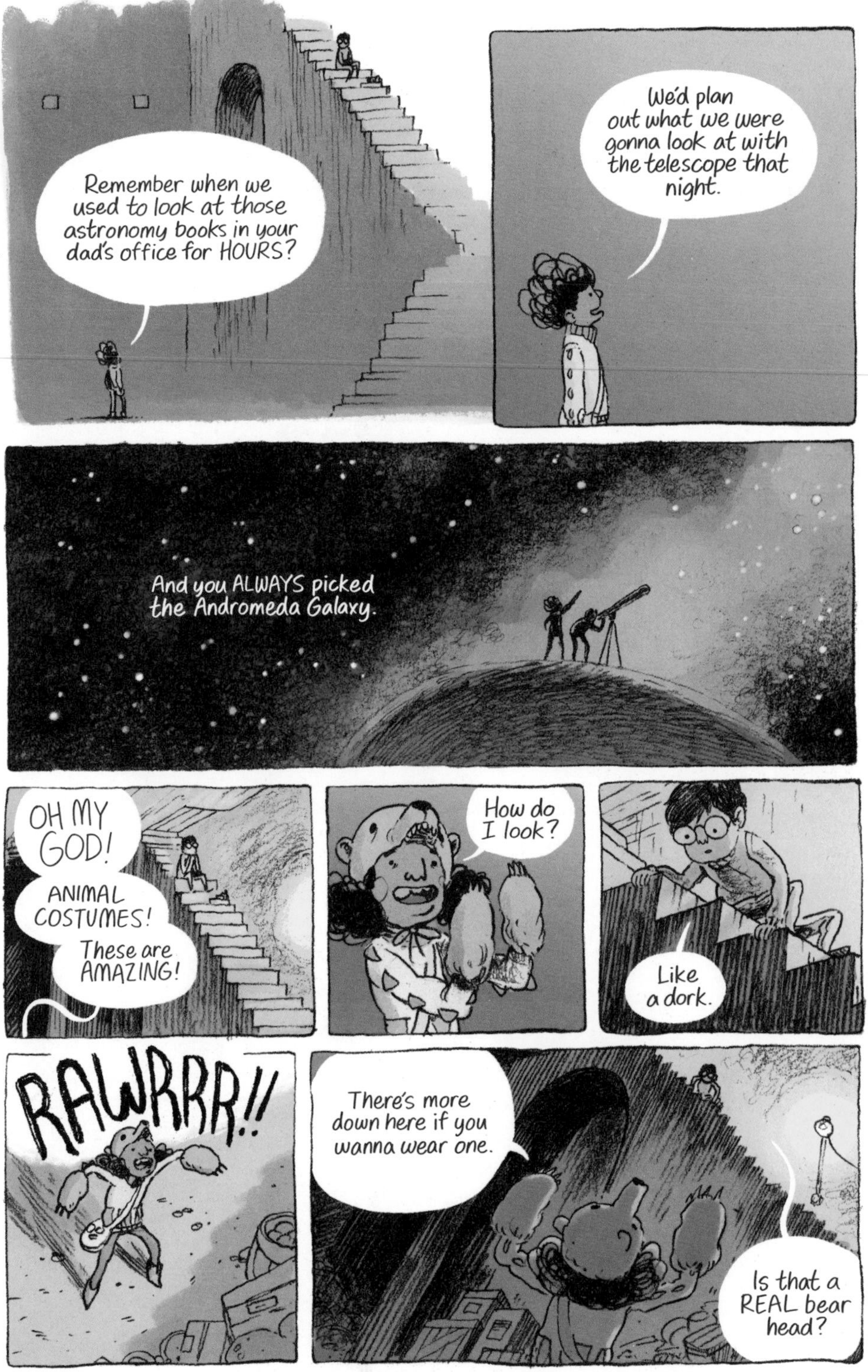
Remember when we used to look at those astronomy books in your dad's office for HOURS?
We'd plan out what we were gonna look at with the telescope that night.
And you ALWAYS picked the Andromeda Galaxy.
OH MY GOD!
ANIMAL COSTUMES!
These are AMAZING!
How do I look?
Like a dork.
RAWRRR!!
There's more down here if you wanna wear one.
Is that a REAL bear head?

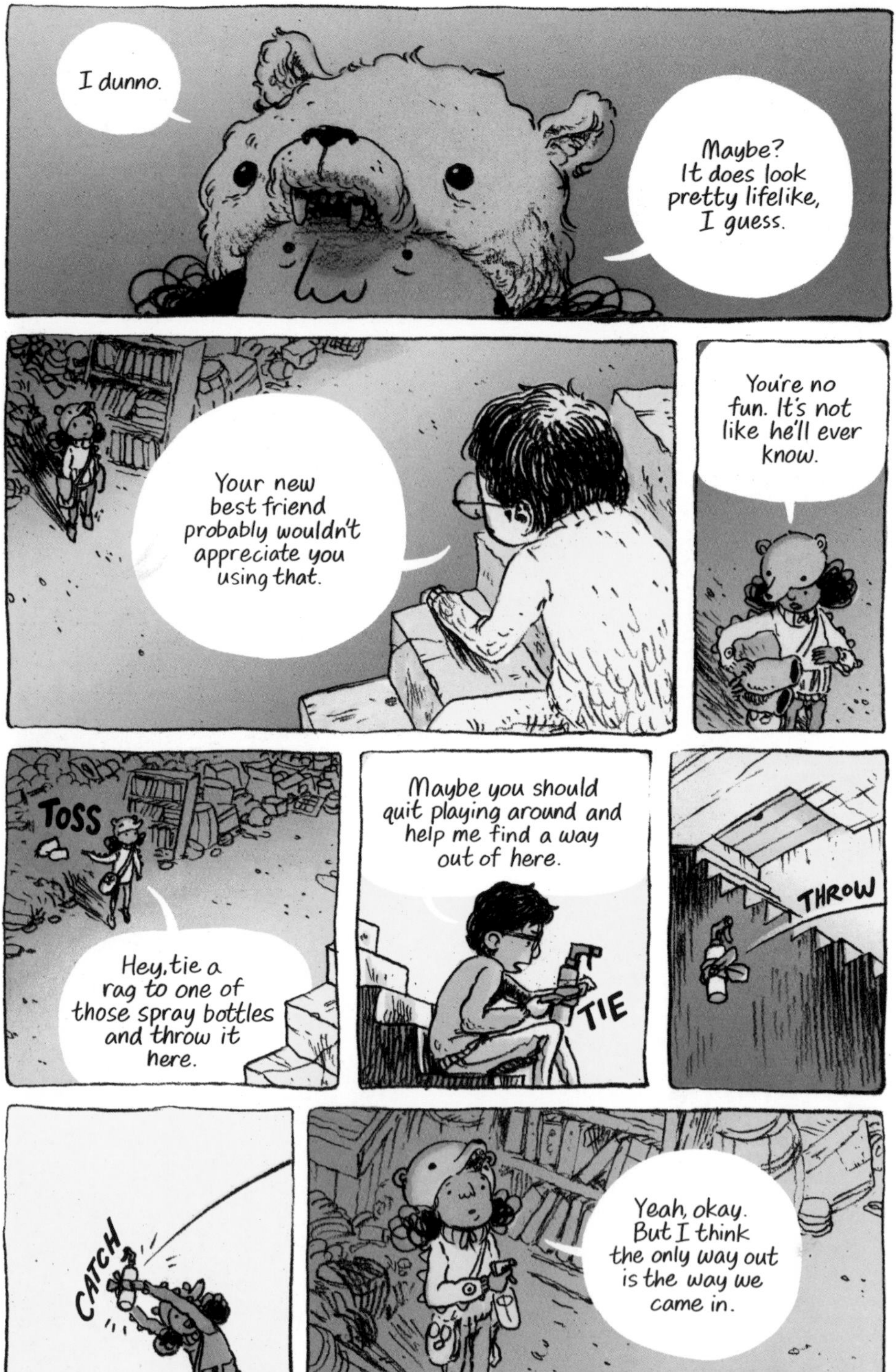
I dunno.
Maybe? It does look pretty lifelike, I guess.
Your new best friend probably wouldn't appreciate you using that.
You're no fun. It's not like he'll ever know.
TOSS
Hey, tie a rag to one of those spray bottles and throw it here.
Maybe you should quit playing around and help me find a way out of here.
TIE
THROW
CATCH
Yeah, okay. But I think the only way out is the way we came in.

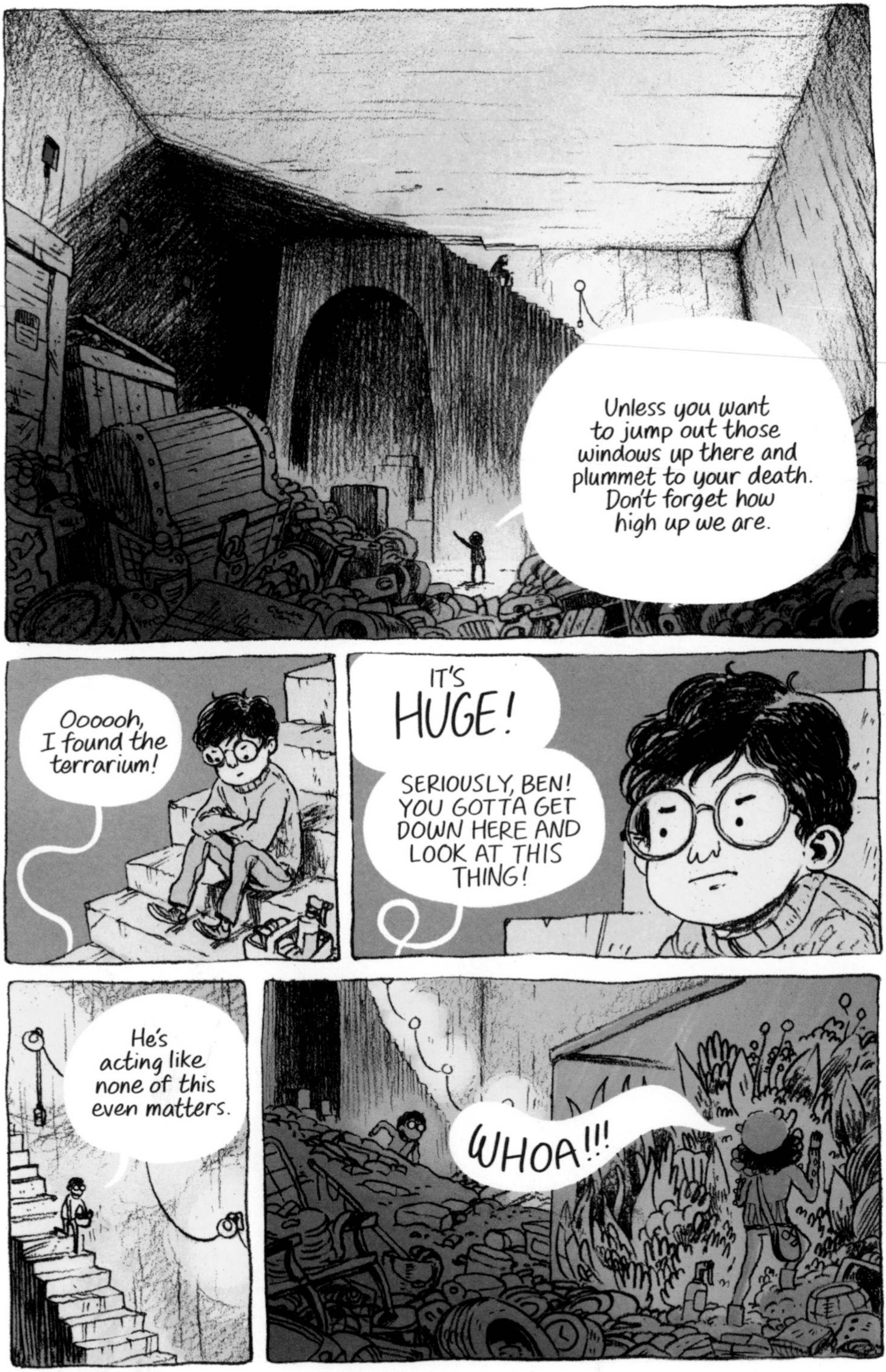
Unless you want to jump out those windows up there and plummet to your death. Don't forget how high up we are.
Oooooh, I found the terrarium!
IT'S HUGE!
SERIOUSLY, BEN! YOU GOTTA GET DOWN HERE AND LOOK AT THIS THING!
He's acting like none of this even matters.
WHOA!!!

BEN! YOU'VE ABSOLUTELY GOT TO SEE THIS...LIZARD...OR WHATEVER IT IS!

You know, for being the one who got us into this mess, you sure aren't doing much to help us out of it.

What do you mean, I'M the one who got us into this?

YOU found this place.

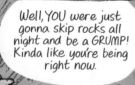

Well, YOU were just gonna skip rocks all night and be a GRUMP! Kinda like you're being right now.

At least I made the decision to do SOMETHING!

Yeah, and look how THAT turned out! About as well as your decision to talk to that bear! It took him what, TEN MINUTES to get us completely lost?

He didn't do it on PURPOSE. And ever since, you've been a total JERK to him.

Well EXCUSE ME for getting mad about the main event of this trip being RUINED!

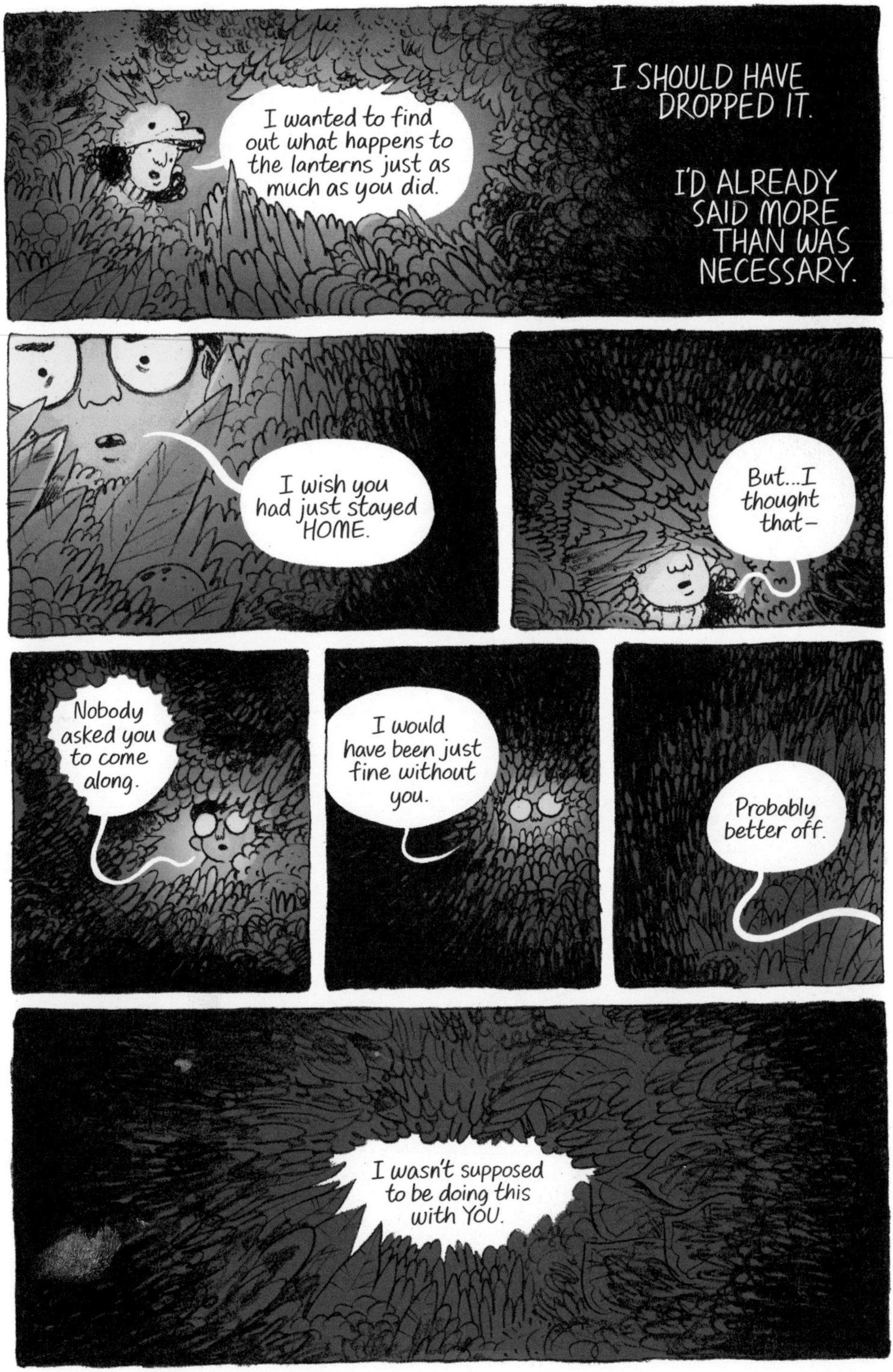

I wanted to find out what happens to the lanterns just as much as you did.
I SHOULD HAVE DROPPED IT.
I'D ALREADY SAID MORE THAN WAS NECESSARY.
I wish you had just stayed HOME.
But...I thought that–
Nobody asked you to come along.
I would have been just fine without you.
Probably better off.
I wasn't supposed to be doing this with YOU.

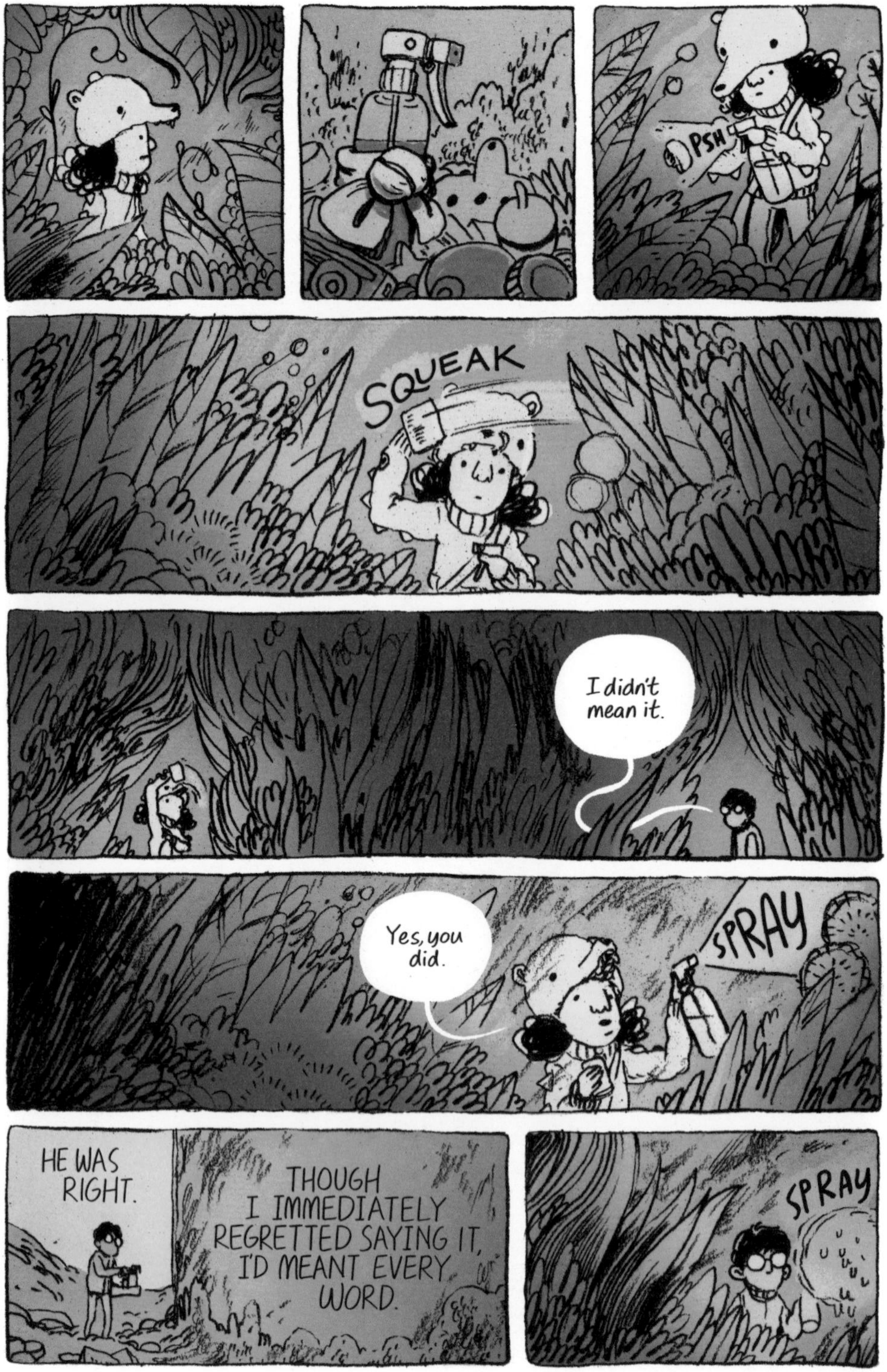
PSH
SQUEAK
I didn't mean it.
Yes, you did.
SPRAY
HE WAS RIGHT.
THOUGH I IMMEDIATELY REGRETTED SAYING IT, I'D MEANT EVERY WORD.
SPRAY

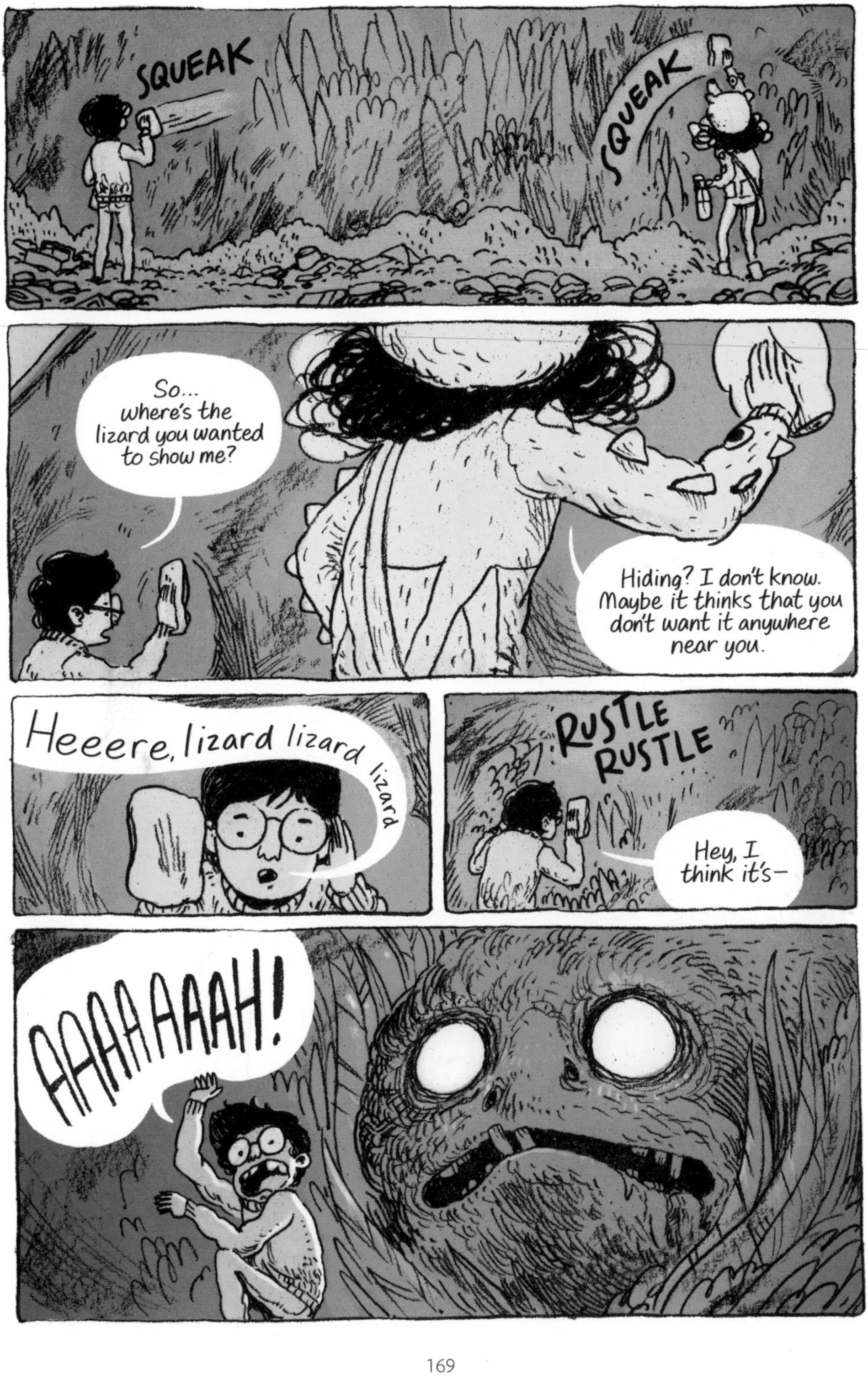
SQUEAK
SQUEAK
So... where's the lizard you wanted to show me?
Hiding? I don't know. Maybe it thinks that you don't want it anywhere near you.
Heeere, lizard lizard lizard
RUSTLE RUSTLE
Hey, I think it's—
AAAAAAAH!

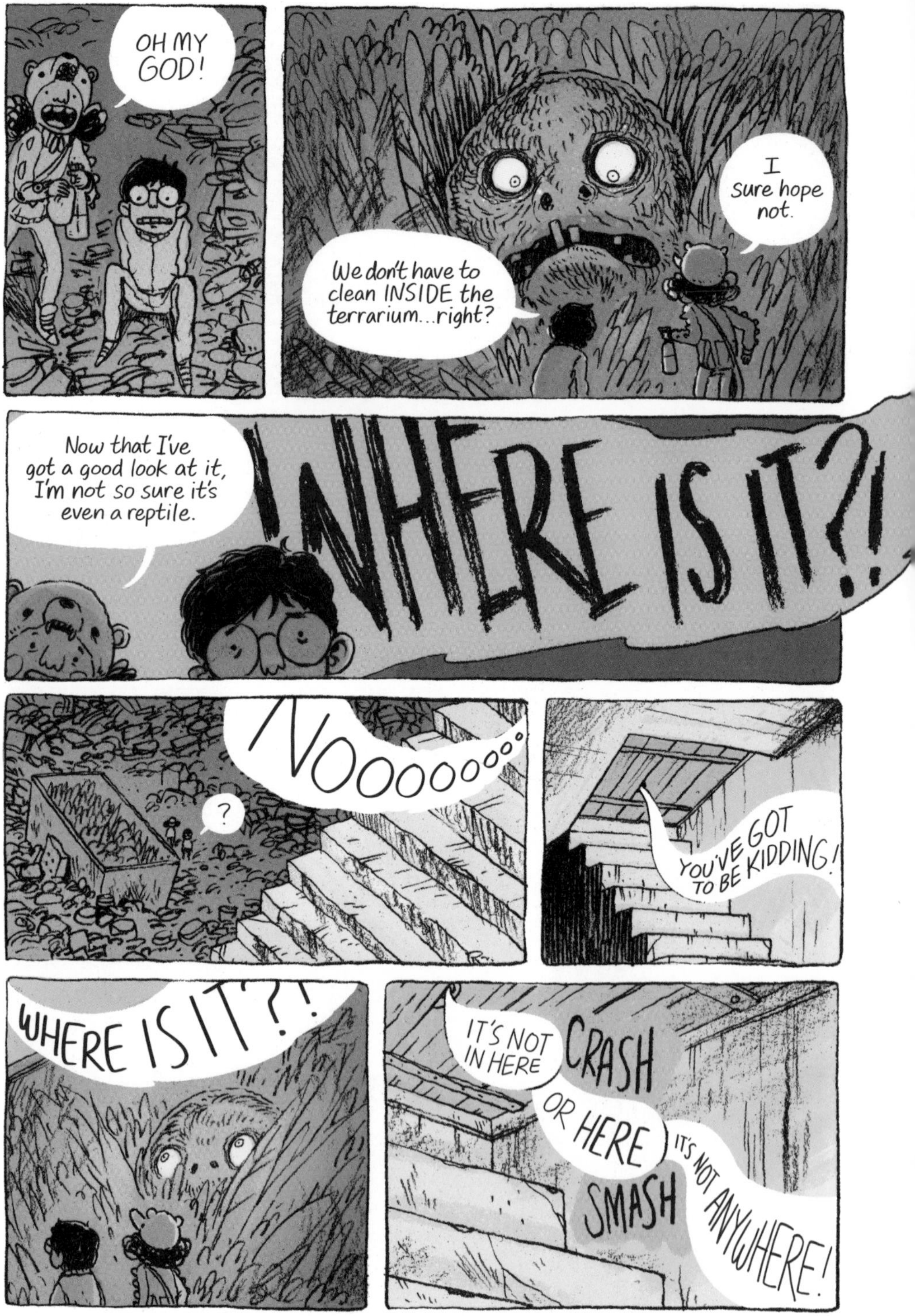
OH MY GOD!
We don't have to clean INSIDE the terrarium...right?
I sure hope not.
Now that I've got a good look at it, I'm not so sure it's even a reptile.
WHERE IS IT?!
NOOOOOOooo
?
YOU'VE GOT TO BE KIDDING!
WHERE IS IT?!
IT'S NOT IN HERE
CRASH
OR HERE
SMASH
IT'S NOT ANYWHERE!

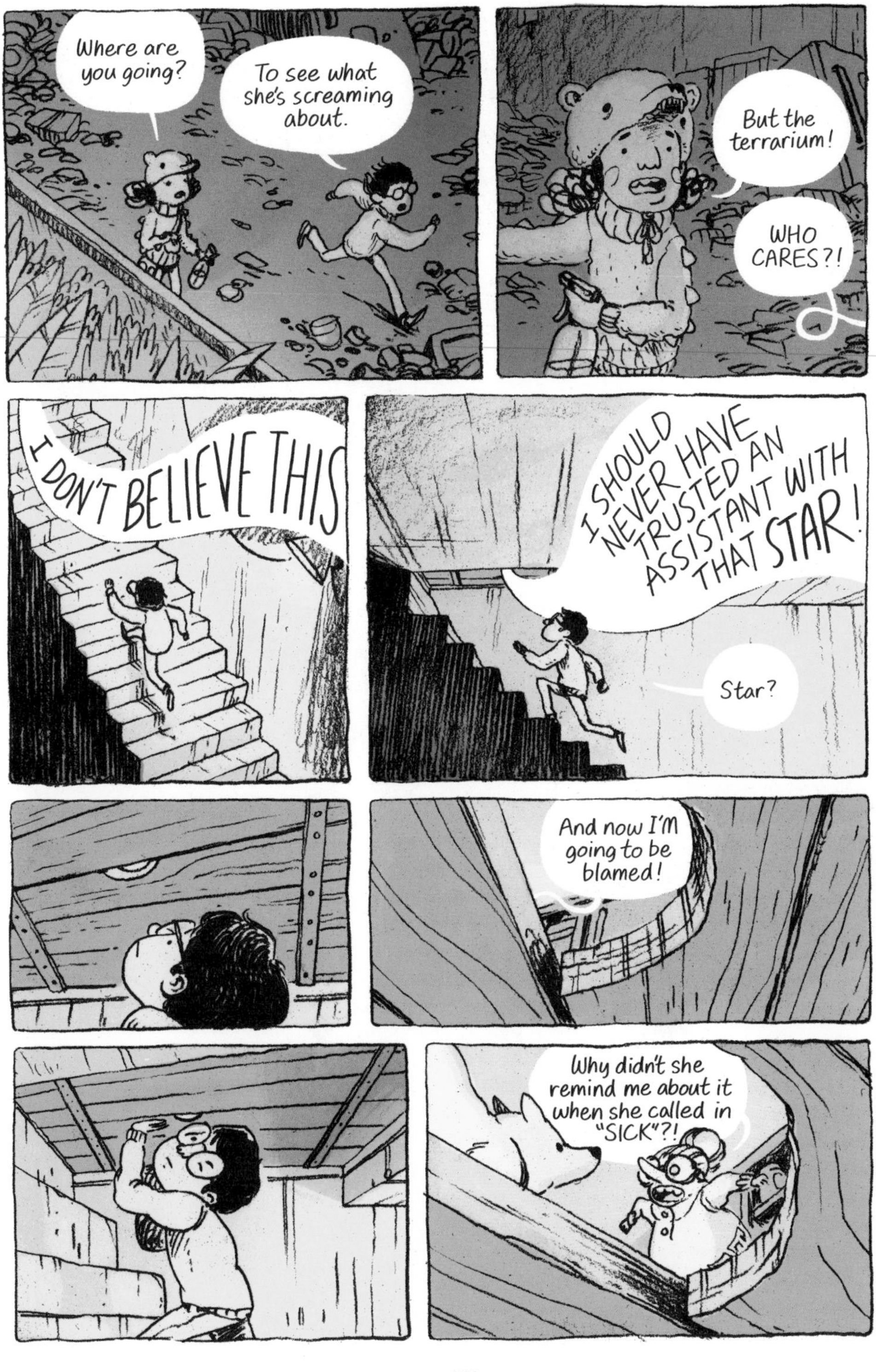
Where are you going?
To see what she's screaming about.
But the terrarium!
WHO CARES?!
I DON'T BELIEVE THIS
I SHOULD NEVER HAVE TRUSTED AN ASSISTANT WITH THAT STAR!
Star?
And now I'M going to be blamed!
Why didn't she remind me about it when she called in "SICK"?!

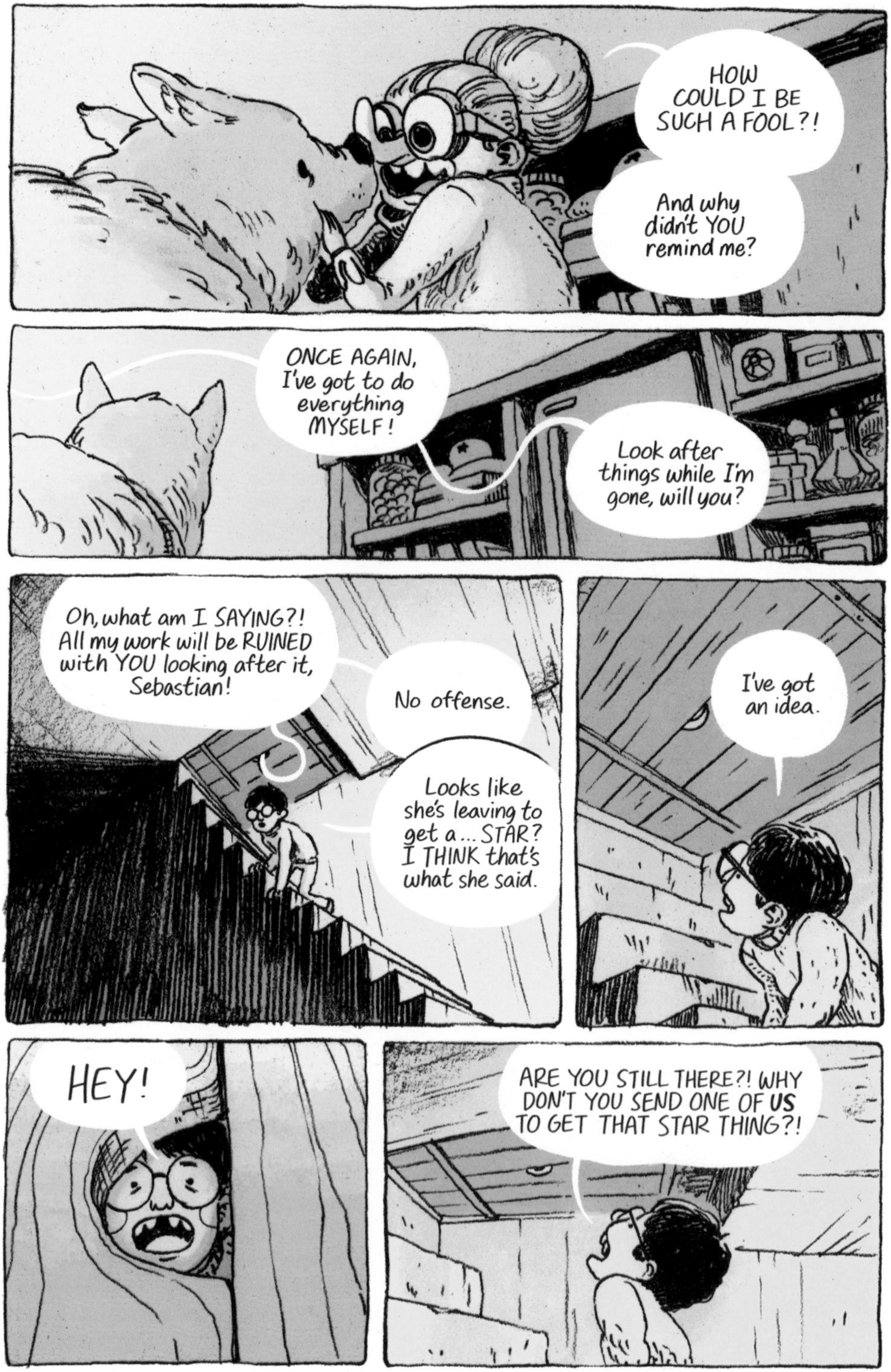
HOW COULD I BE SUCH A FOOL?!
And why didn't YOU remind me?
ONCE AGAIN, I've got to do everything MYSELF!
Look after things while I'm gone, will you?
Oh, what am I SAYING?! All my work will be RUINED with YOU looking after it, Sebastian!
No offense.
Looks like she's leaving to get a... STAR? I THINK that's what she said.
I've got an idea.
HEY!
ARE YOU STILL THERE?! WHY DON'T YOU SEND ONE OF US TO GET THAT STAR THING?!

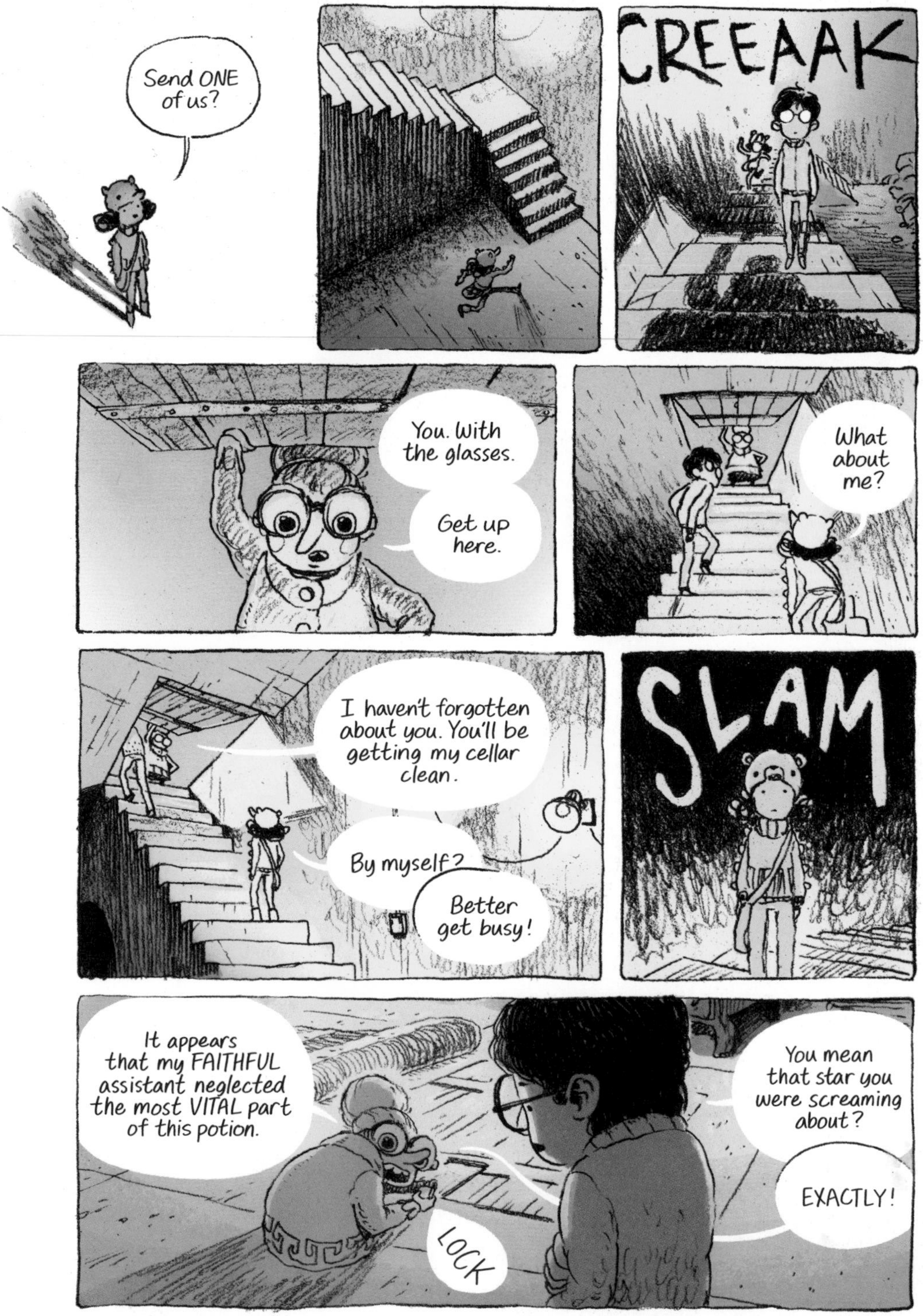

Send ONE of us?
CREEAK
You. With the glasses.
Get up here.
What about me?
I haven't forgotten about you. You'll be getting my cellar clean.
By myself?
Better get busy!
SLAM
It appears that my FAITHFUL assistant neglected the most VITAL part of this potion.
You mean that star you were screaming about?
EXACTLY!
LOCK

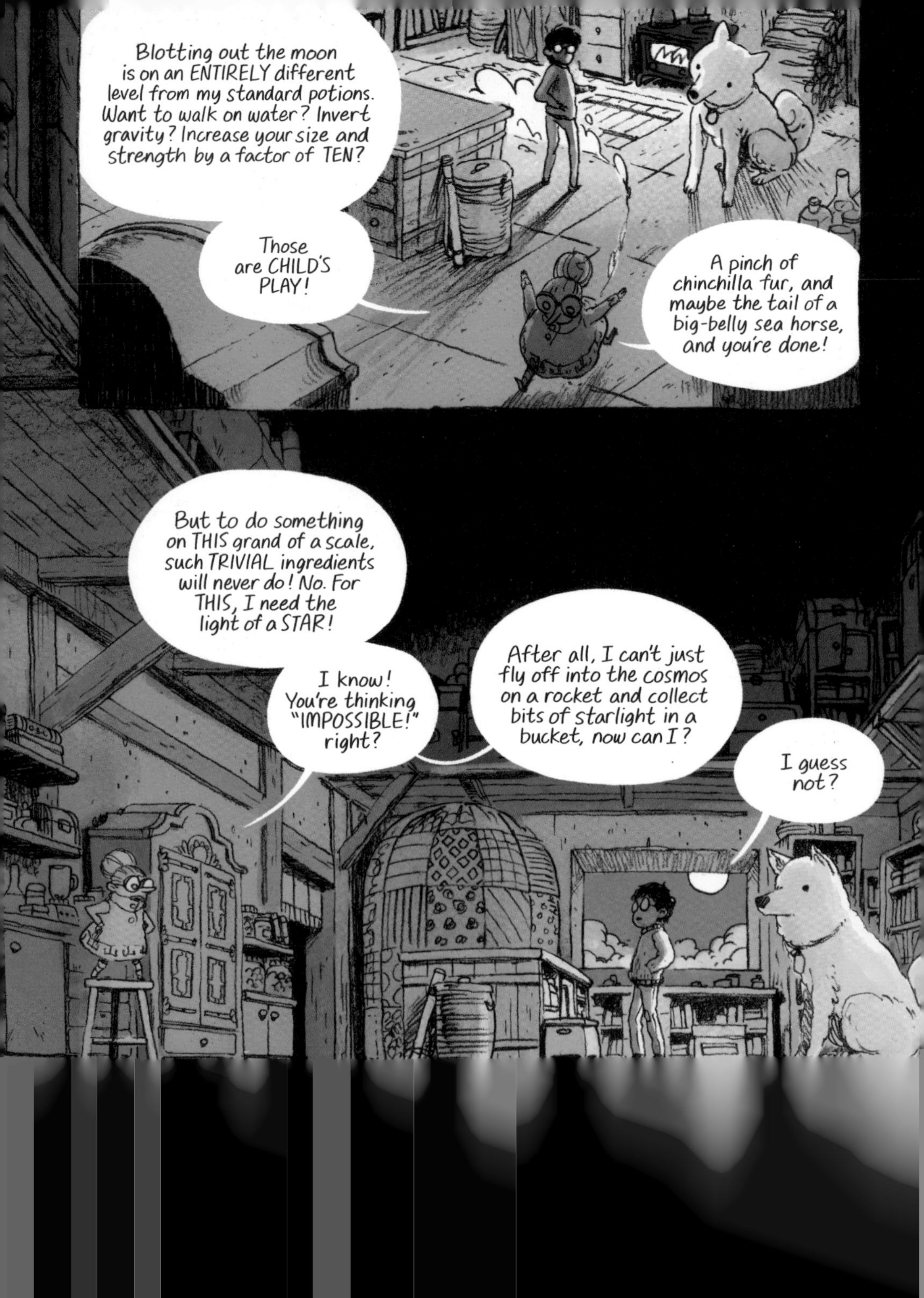
Blotting out the moon is on an ENTIRELY different level from my standard potions. Want to walk on water? Invert gravity? Increase your size and strength by a factor of TEN?
Those are CHILD'S PLAY!
A pinch of chinchilla fur, and maybe the tail of a big-belly sea horse, and you're done!
But to do something on THIS grand of a scale, such TRIVIAL ingredients will never do! No. For THIS, I need the light of a STAR!
I know! You're thinking "IMPOSSIBLE!" right?
After all, I can't just fly off into the cosmos on a rocket and collect bits of starlight in a bucket, now can I?
I guess not?

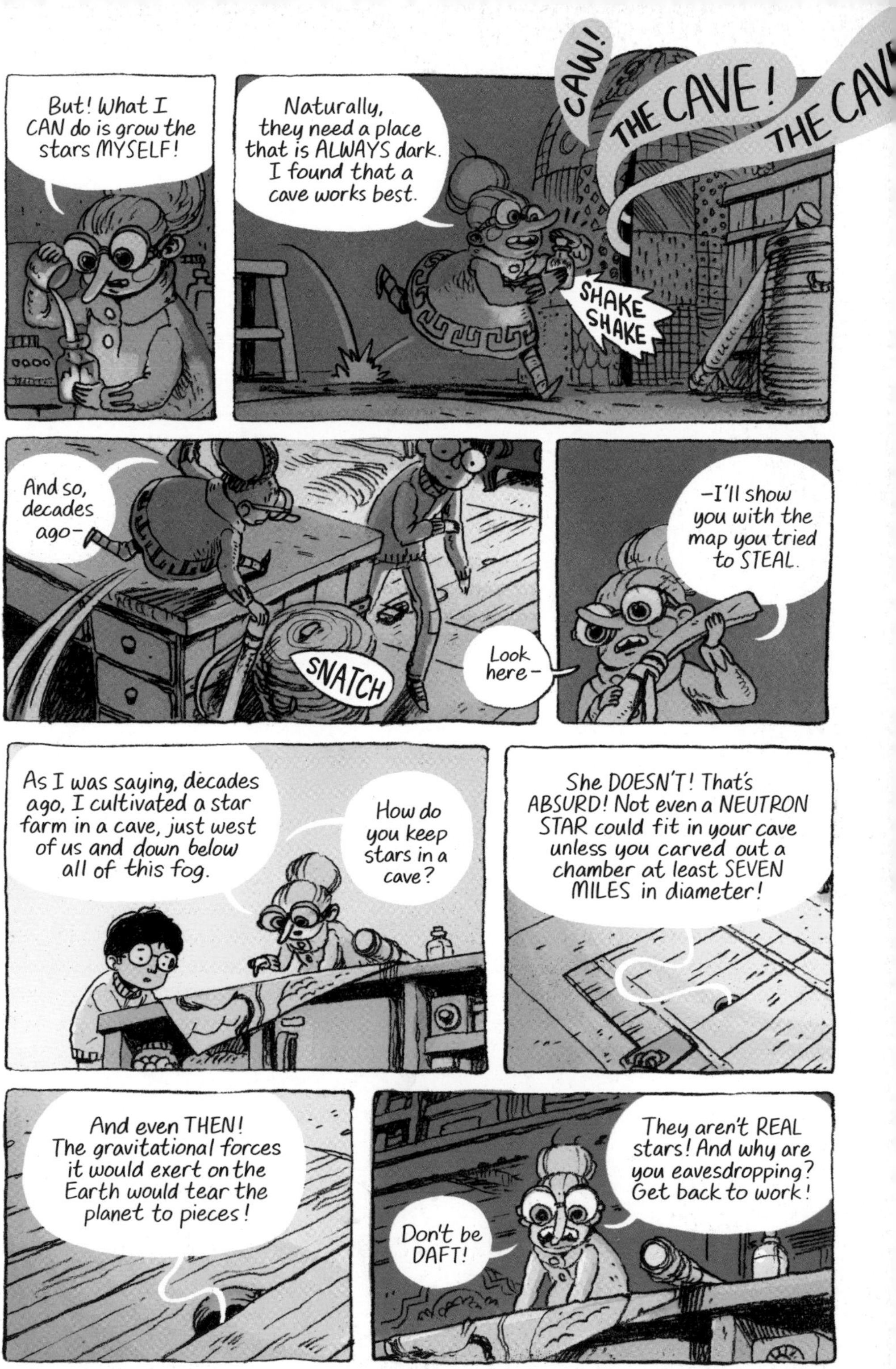

But! What I CAN do is grow the stars MYSELF!
Naturally, they need a place that is ALWAYS dark. I found that a cave works best.
CAW!
THE CAVE!
THE CAV
SHAKE SHAKE
And so, decades ago—
SNATCH
Look here—
—I'll show you with the map you tried to STEAL.
As I was saying, decades ago, I cultivated a star farm in a cave, just west of us and down below all of this fog.
How do you keep stars in a cave?
She DOESN'T! That's ABSURD! Not even a NEUTRON STAR could fit in your cave unless you carved out a chamber at least SEVEN MILES in diameter!
And even THEN! The gravitational forces it would exert on the Earth would tear the planet to pieces!
Don't be DAFT!
They aren't REAL stars! And why are you eavesdropping? Get back to work!

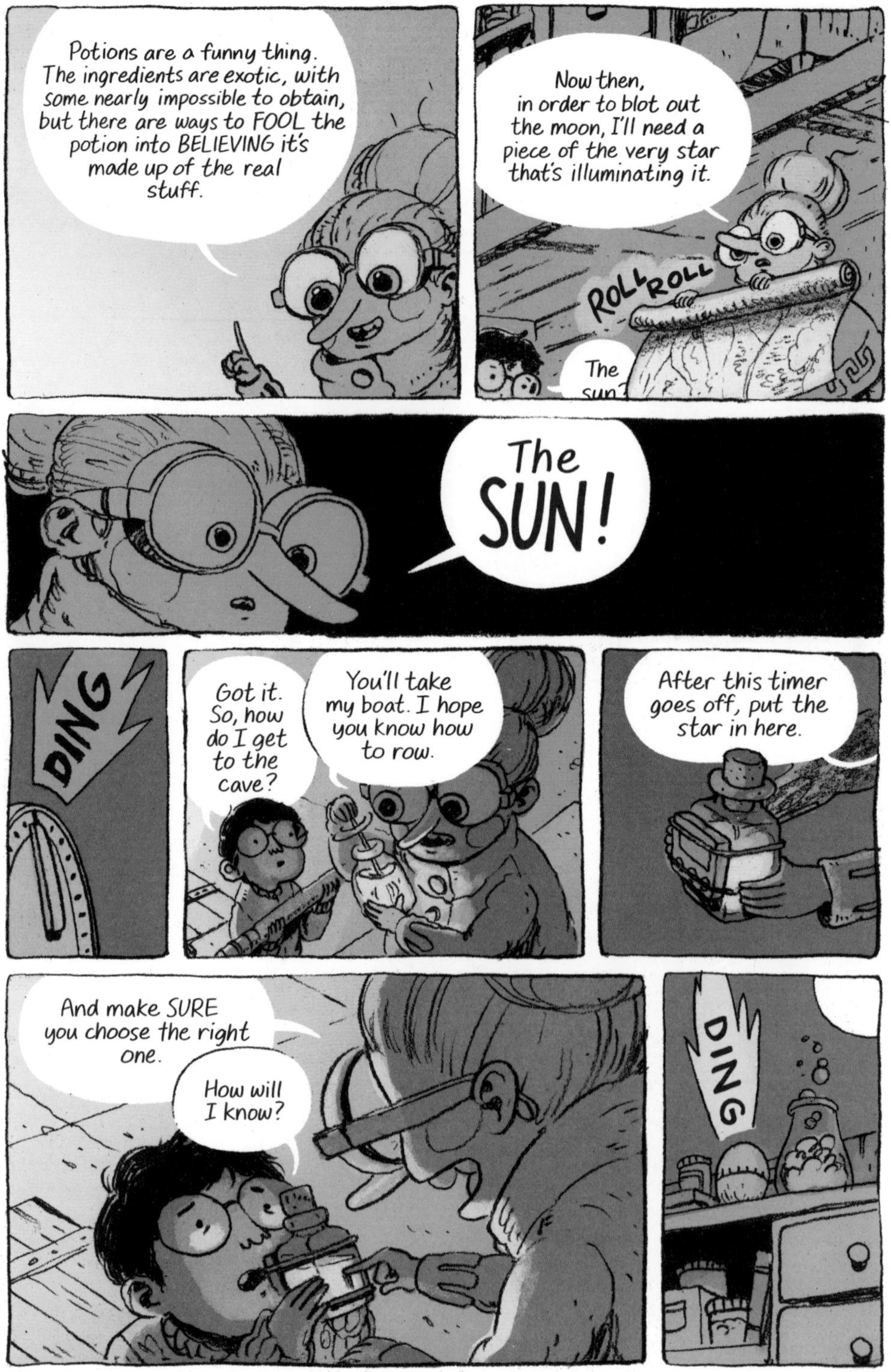

Potions are a funny thing. The ingredients are exotic, with some nearly impossible to obtain, but there are ways to FOOL the potion into BELIEVING it's made up of the real stuff.
Now then, in order to blot out the moon, I'll need a piece of the very star that's illuminating it.
ROLL ROLL
The sun?
The SUN!
DING
Got it. So, how do I get to the cave?
You'll take my boat. I hope you know how to row.
After this timer goes off, put the star in here.
And make SURE you choose the right one.
How will I know?
DING

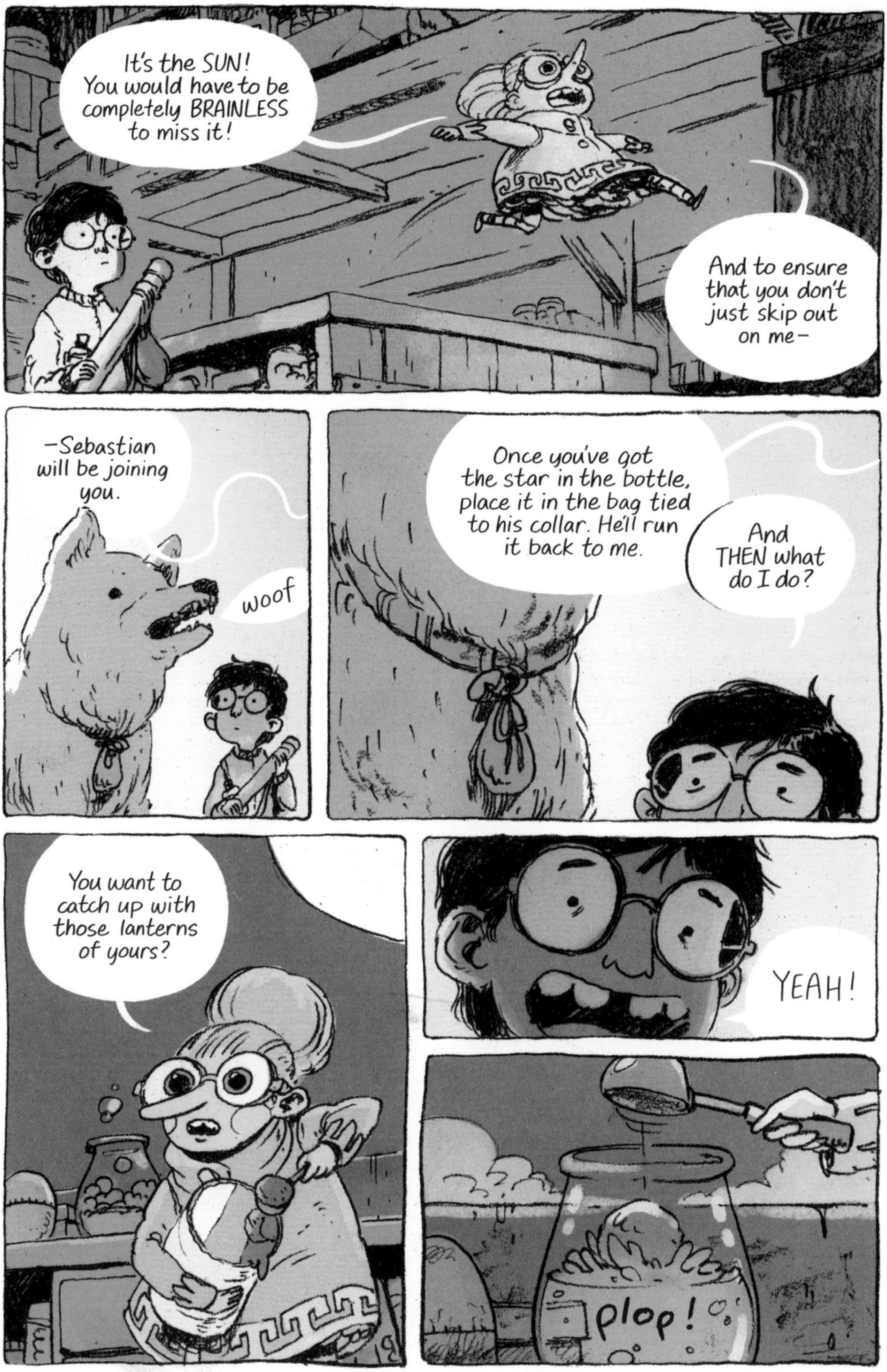
It's the SUN! You would have to be completely BRAINLESS to miss it!
And to ensure that you don't just skip out on me–
–Sebastian will be joining you.
woof
Once you've got the star in the bottle, place it in the bag tied to his collar. He'll run it back to me.
And THEN what do I do?
You want to catch up with those lanterns of yours?
YEAH!
plop!

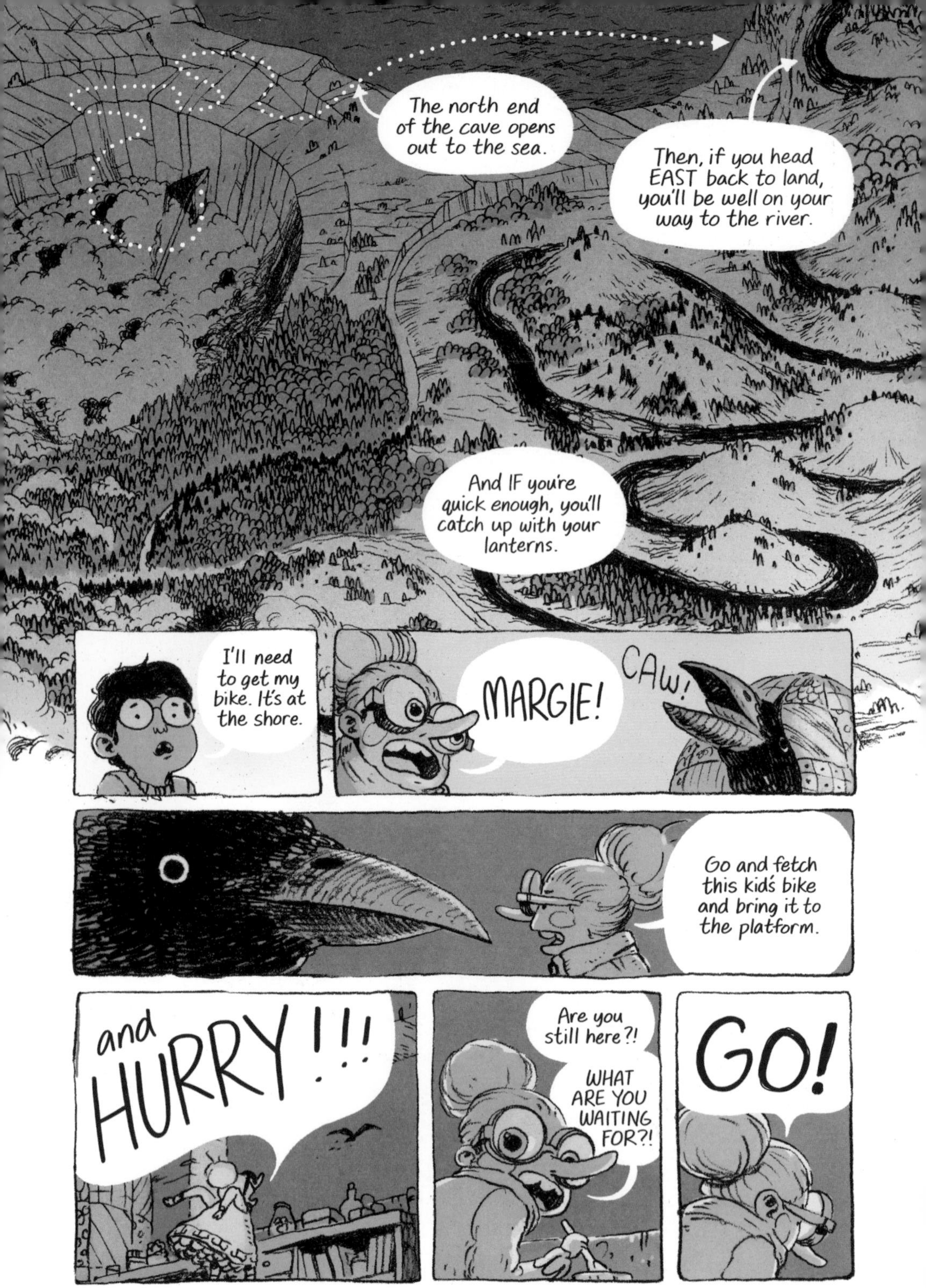
The north end of the cave opens out to the sea.
Then, if you head EAST back to land, you'll be well on your way to the river.
And IF you're quick enough, you'll catch up with your lanterns.
I'll need to get my bike. It's at the shore.
MARGIE!
CAW!
Go and fetch this kid's bike and bring it to the platform.
and HURRY!!!
Are you still here?!
WHAT ARE YOU WAITING FOR?!
GO!

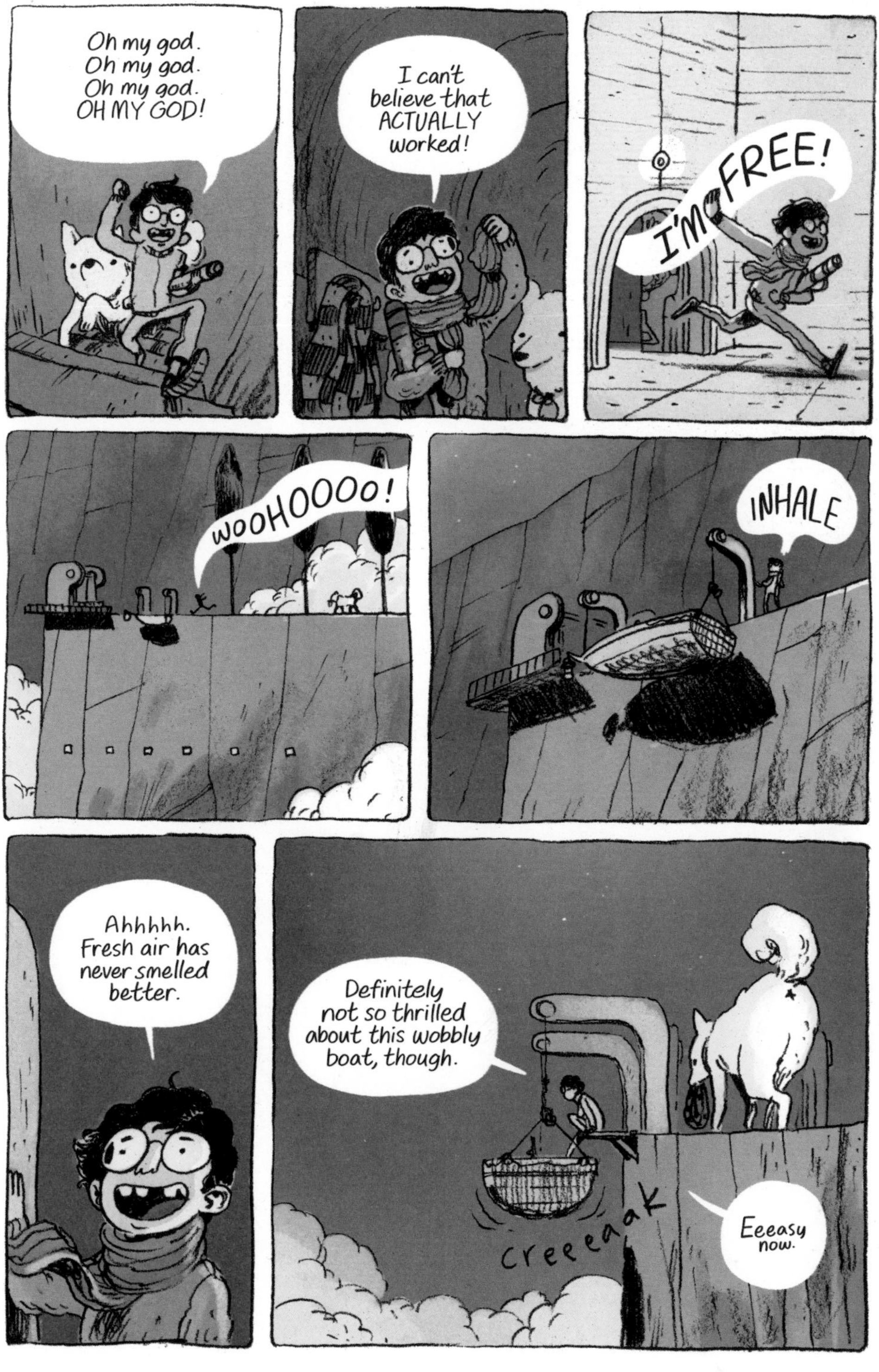
Oh my god.
Oh my god.
Oh my god.
OH MY GOD!
I can't believe that ACTUALLY worked!
I'M FREE!
wooHOOOO!
INHALE
Ahhhhh. Fresh air has never smelled better.
Definitely not so thrilled about this wobbly boat, though.
creeeaak
Eeeasy now.

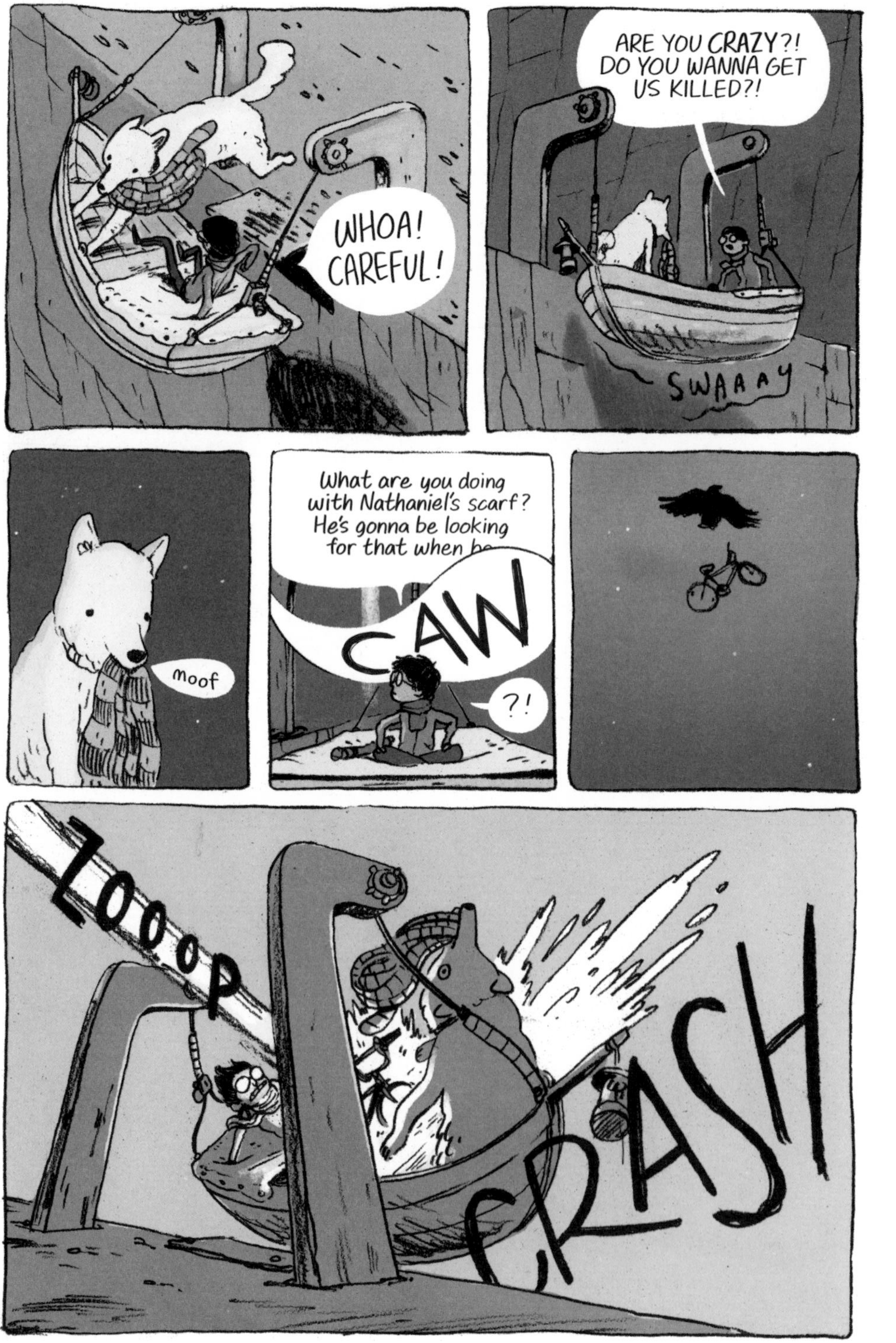
WHOA! CAREFUL!
ARE YOU CRAZY?! DO YOU WANNA GET US KILLED?!
SWAAAY
moof
What are you doing with Nathaniel's scarf? He's gonna be looking for that when
CAW
?!
ZOOOP
CRASH

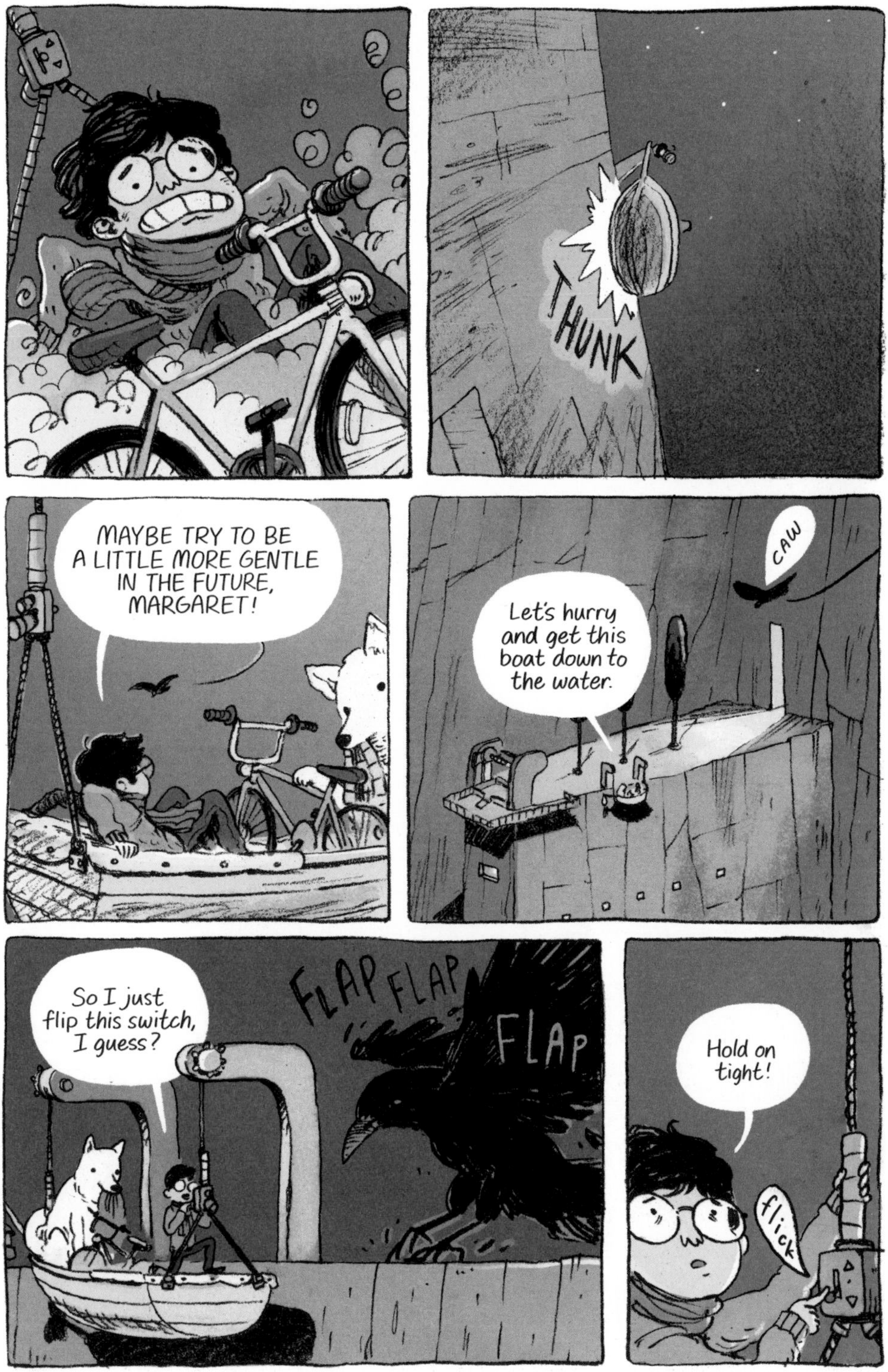
THUNK
MAYBE TRY TO BE A LITTLE MORE GENTLE IN THE FUTURE, MARGARET!
CAW
Let's hurry and get this boat down to the water.
So I just flip this switch, I guess?
FLAP FLAP
FLAP
Hold on tight!
flick

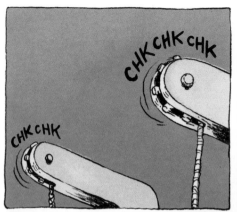

CHK CHK CHK

CHK CHK

PUTT

PUTT

At least it's nice and slow.

The CELLAR!

flip

POP!

SQUEAK

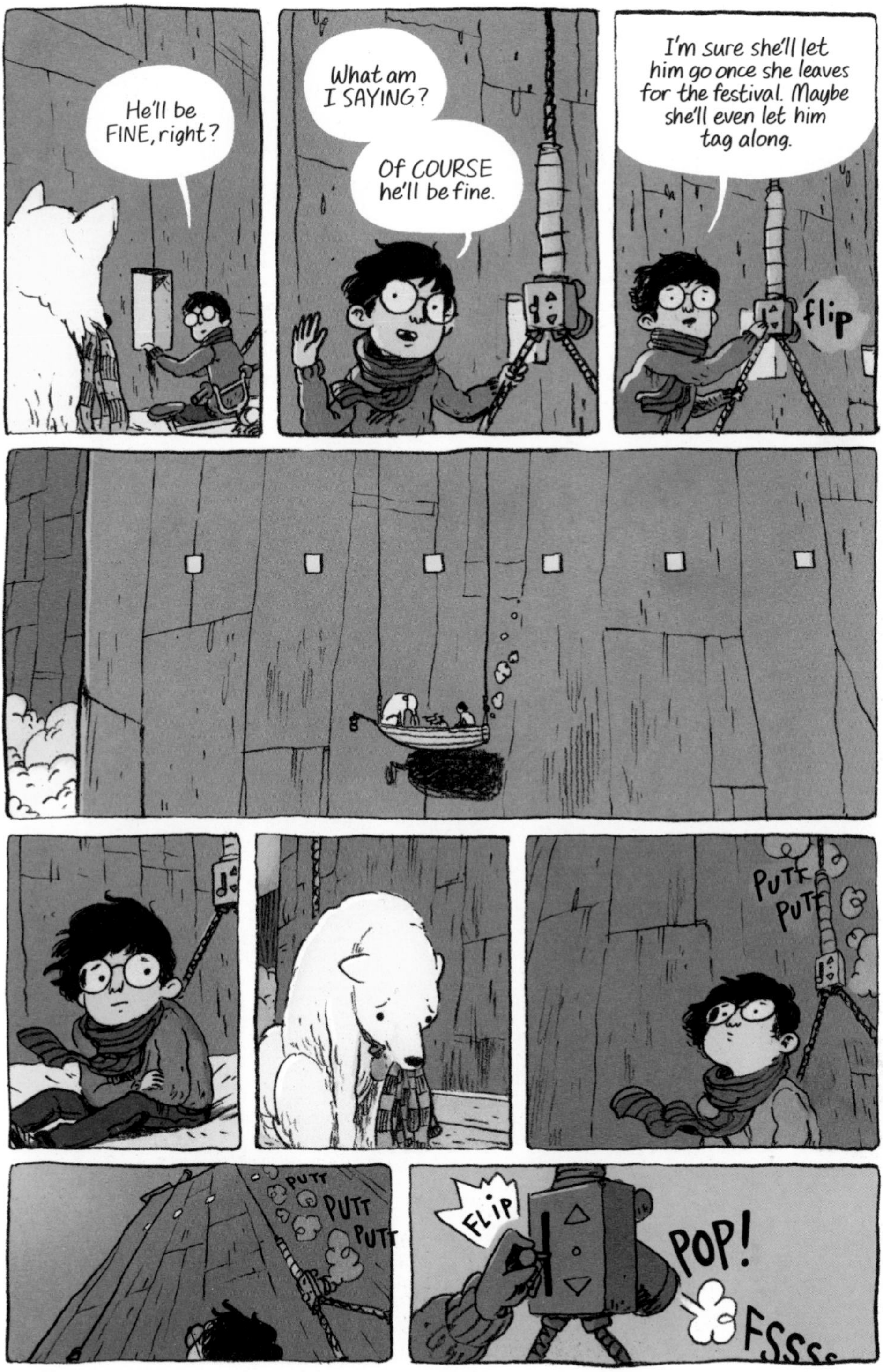
He'll be FINE, right?
What am I SAYING?
Of COURSE he'll be fine.
I'm sure she'll let him go once she leaves for the festival. Maybe she'll even let him tag along.
flip
PUTT PUTT
PUTT PUTT PUTT
FLIP
POP!
FSSSS

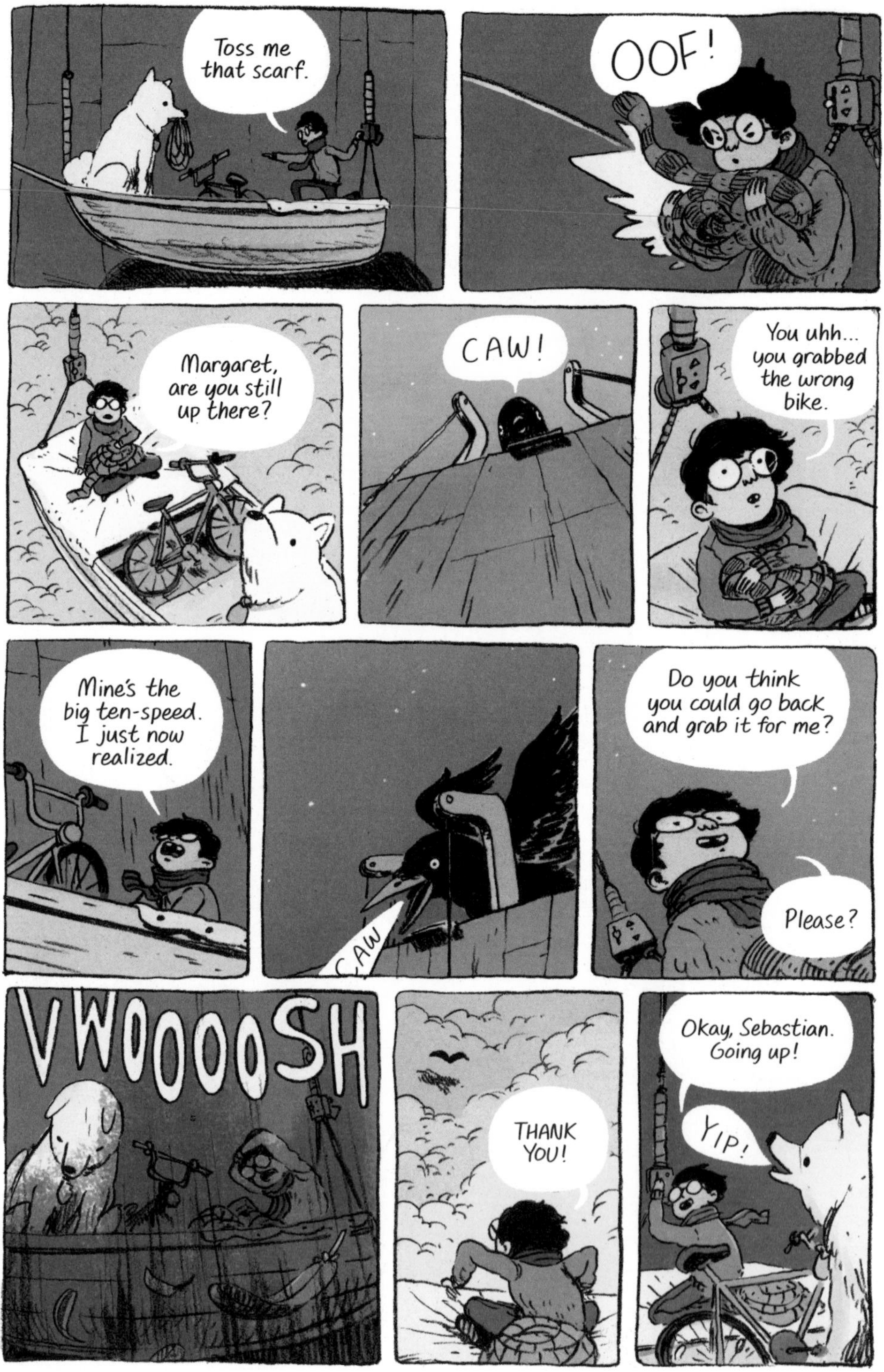
Toss me that scarf.
OOF!
Margaret, are you still up there?
CAW!
You uhh... you grabbed the wrong bike.
Mine's the big ten-speed. I just now realized.
CAW
Do you think you could go back and grab it for me?
Please?
VWOOOOSH
THANK YOU!
Okay, Sebastian. Going up!
YIP!

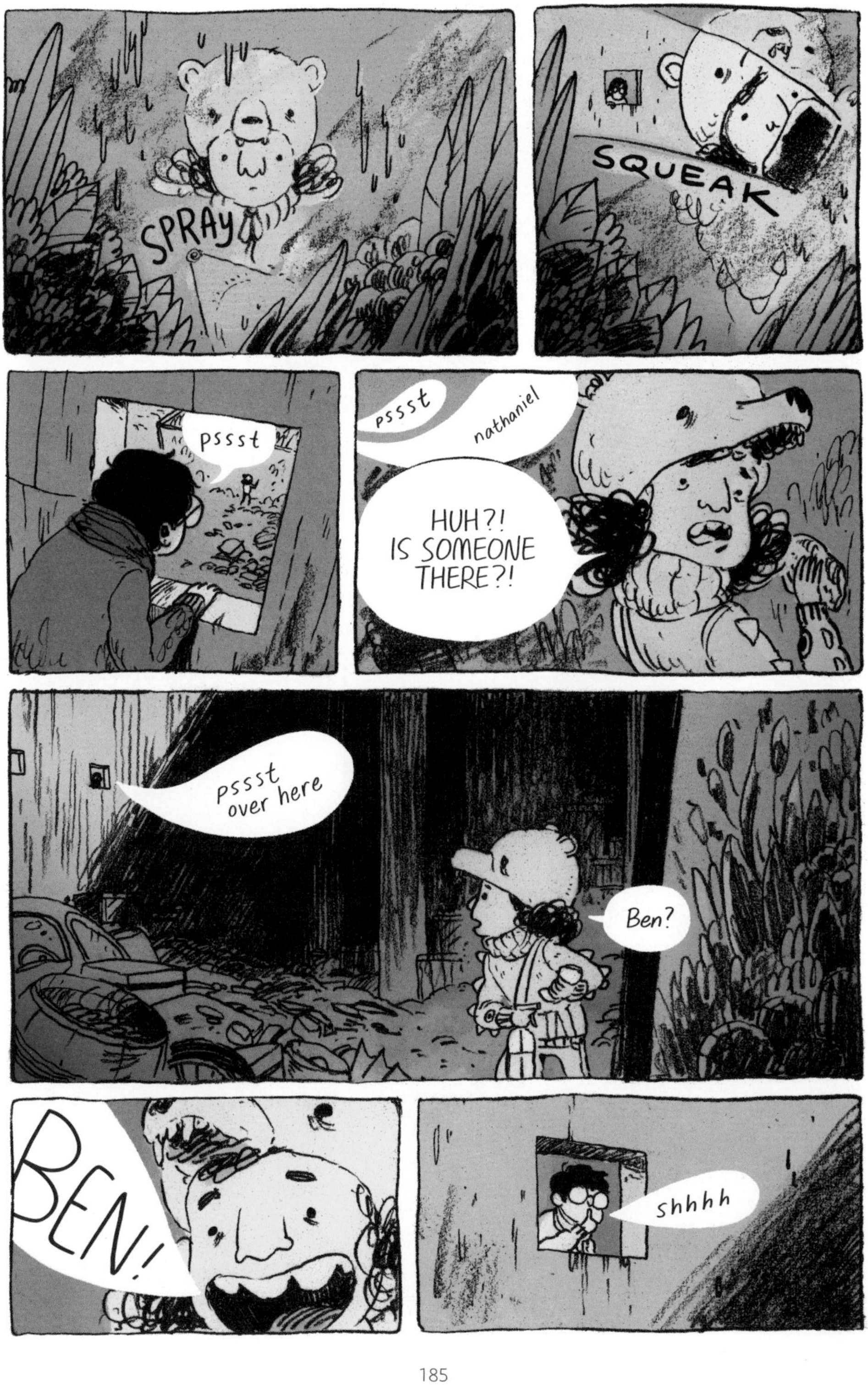
SPRAY
SQUEAK
pssst
pssst
nathaniel
HUH?! IS SOMEONE THERE?!
pssst over here
Ben?
BEN!
shhhh

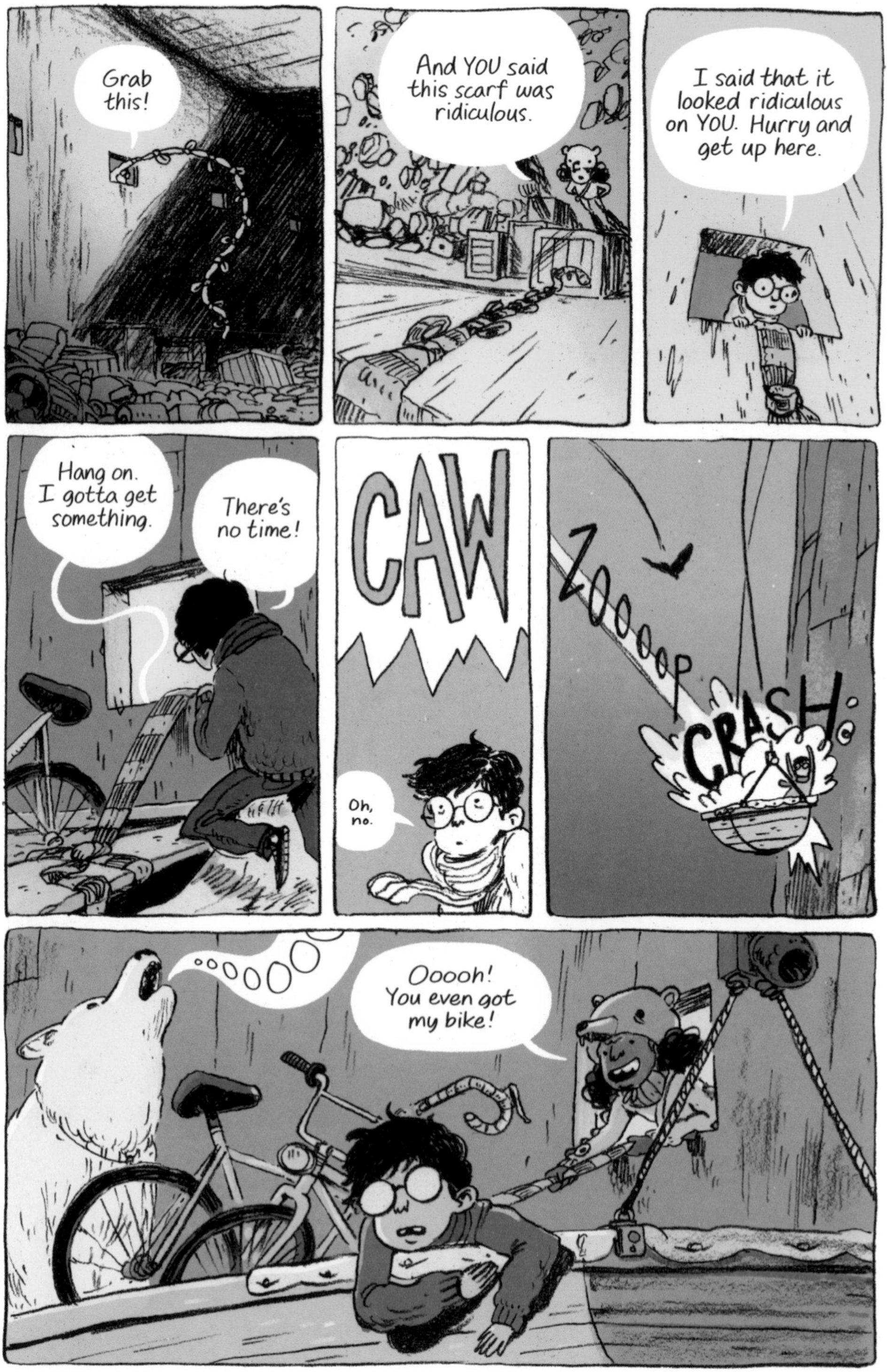

Grab this!
And YOU said this scarf was ridiculous.
I said that it looked ridiculous on YOU. Hurry and get up here.
Hang on. I gotta get something.
There's no time!
CAW
Oh, no.
ZOOOOOP
CRASH!
OOOOOO
Ooooh! You even got my bike!

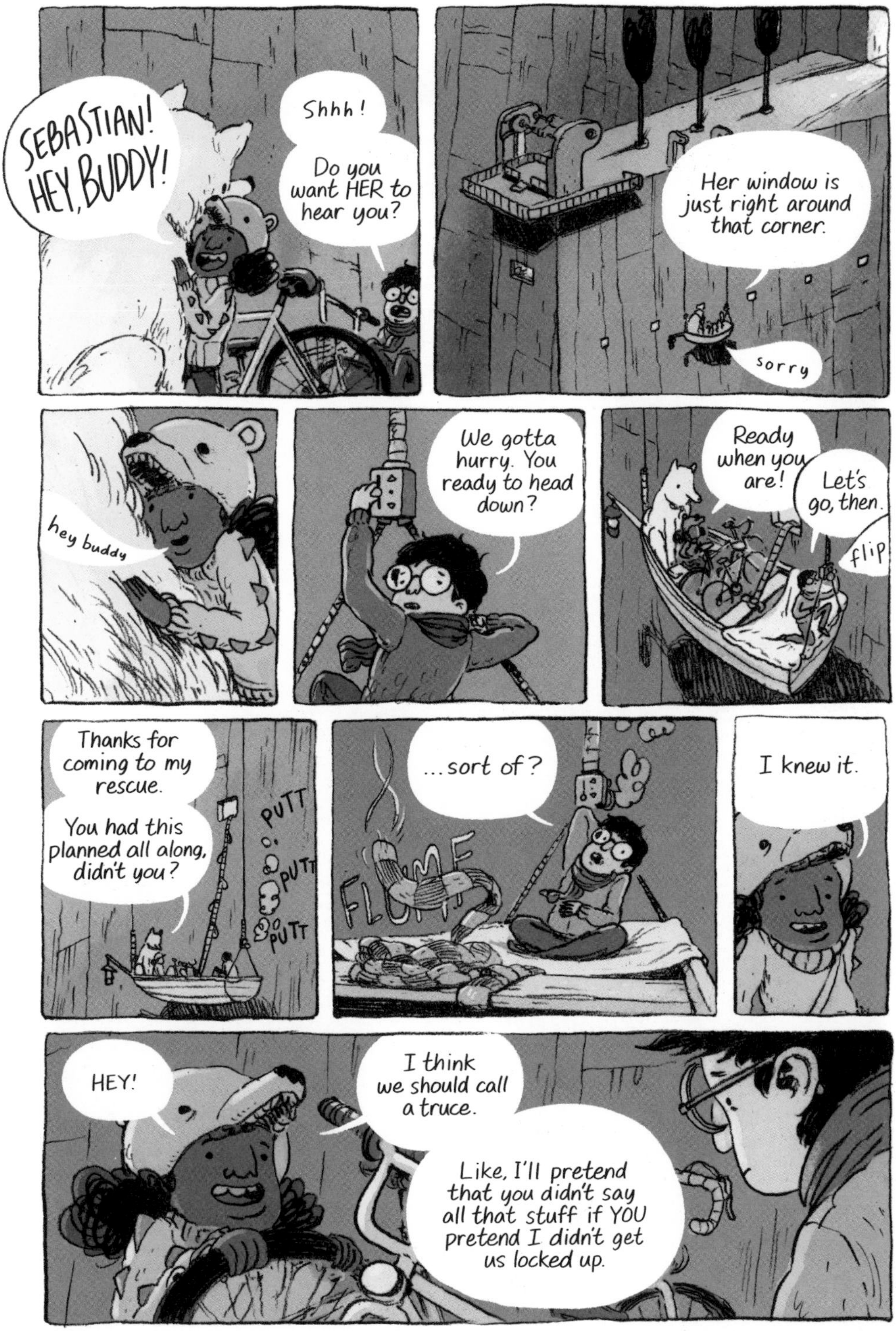
SEBASTIAN! HEY, BUDDY!
Shhh!
Do you want HER to hear you?
Her window is just right around that corner.
sorry
hey buddy
We gotta hurry. You ready to head down?
Ready when you are!
Let's go, then.
flip
Thanks for coming to my rescue.
You had this planned all along, didn't you?
PUTT
PUTT
PUTT
...sort of?
FLUMF
I knew it.
HEY!
I think we should call a truce.
Like, I'll pretend that you didn't say all that stuff if YOU pretend I didn't get us locked up.

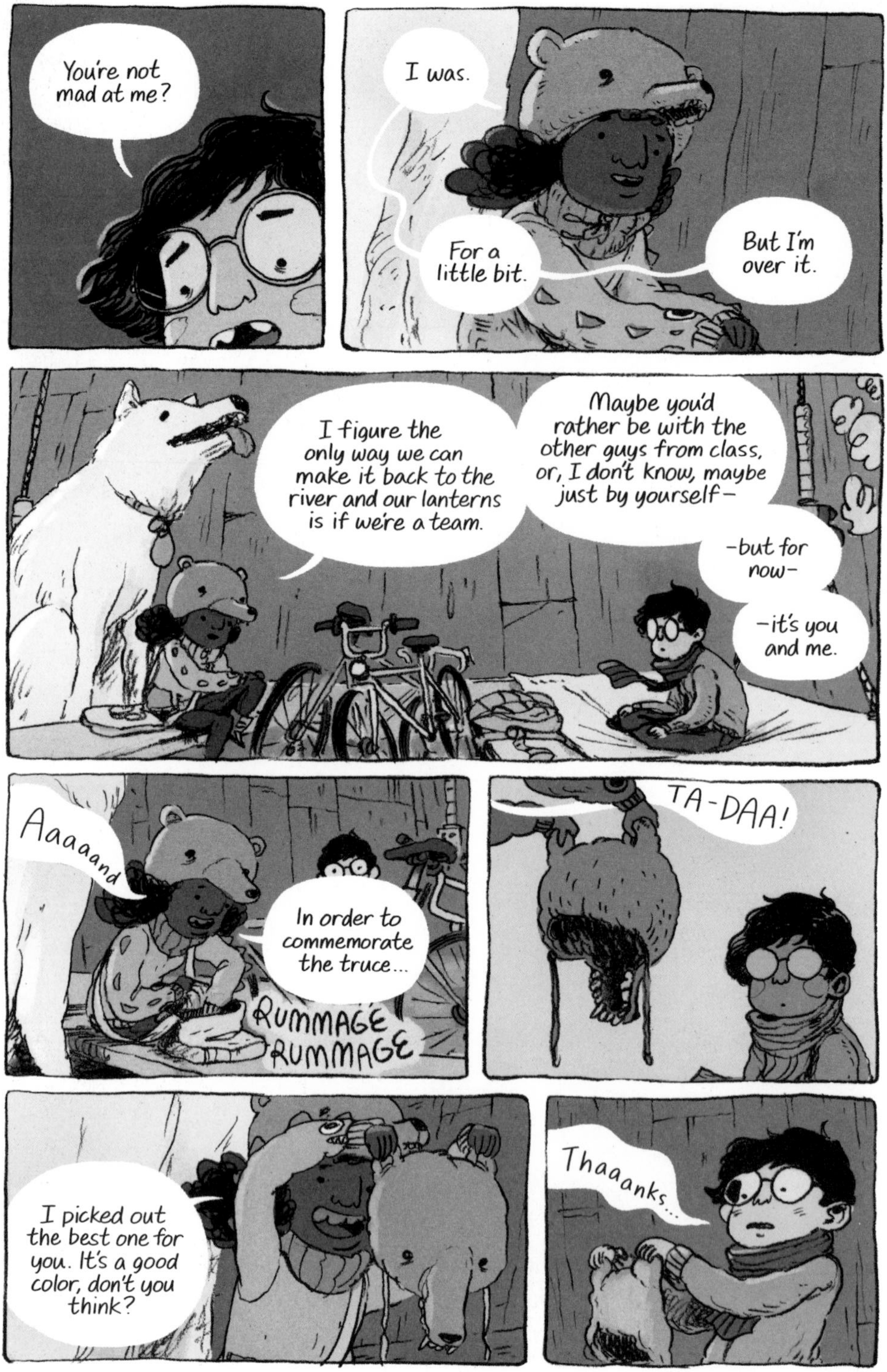
You're not mad at me?
I was.
For a little bit.
But I'm over it.
I figure the only way we can make it back to the river and our lanterns is if we're a team.
Maybe you'd rather be with the other guys from class, or, I don't know, maybe just by yourself–
–but for now–
–it's you and me.
Aaaaand
In order to commemorate the truce...
RUMMAGE RUMMAGE
TA-DAA!
I picked out the best one for you. It's a good color, don't you think?
Thaaanks...

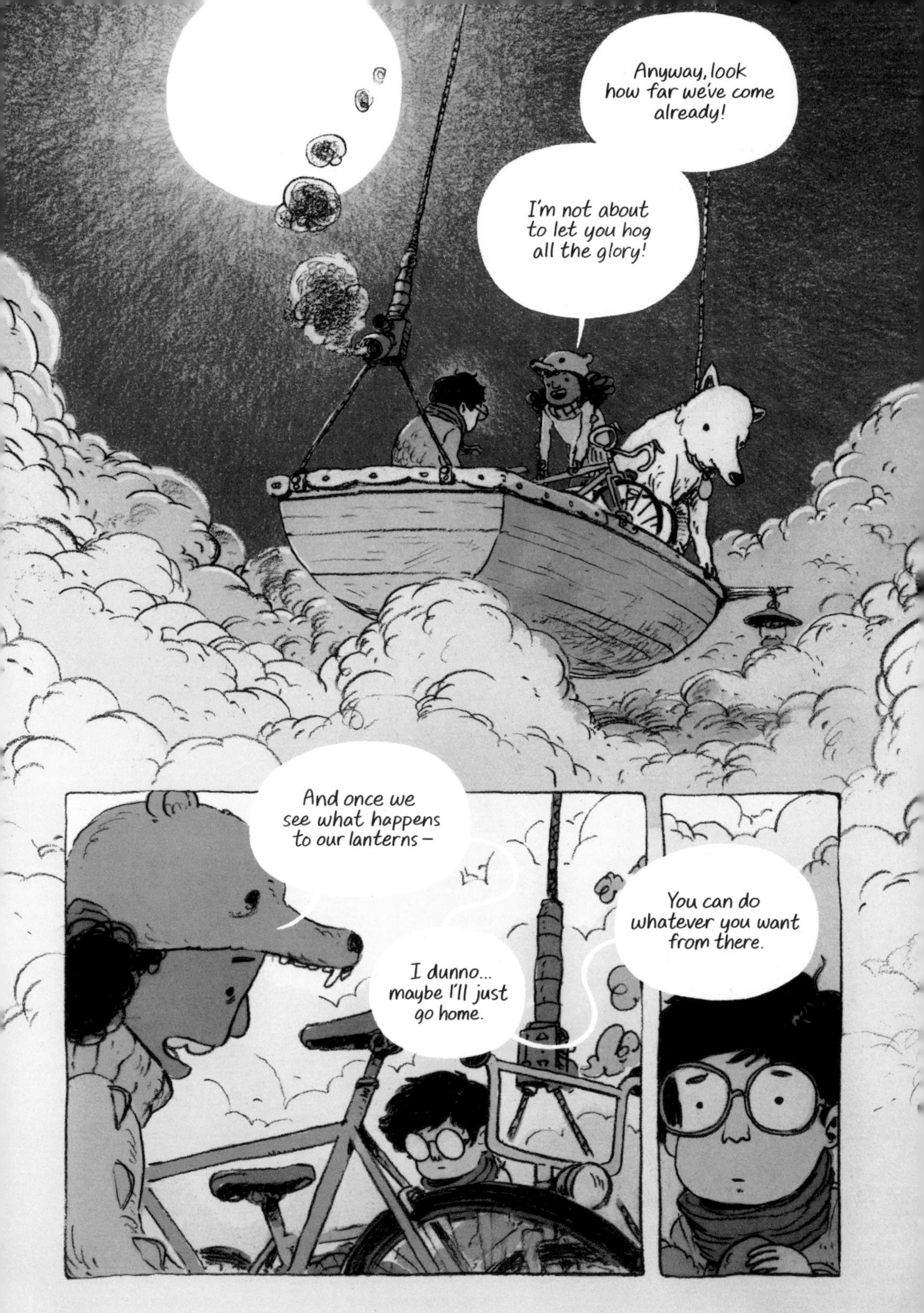
Anyway, look how far we've come already!
I'm not about to let you hog all the glory!
And once we see what happens to our lanterns –
I dunno... maybe I'll just go home.
You can do whatever you want from there.

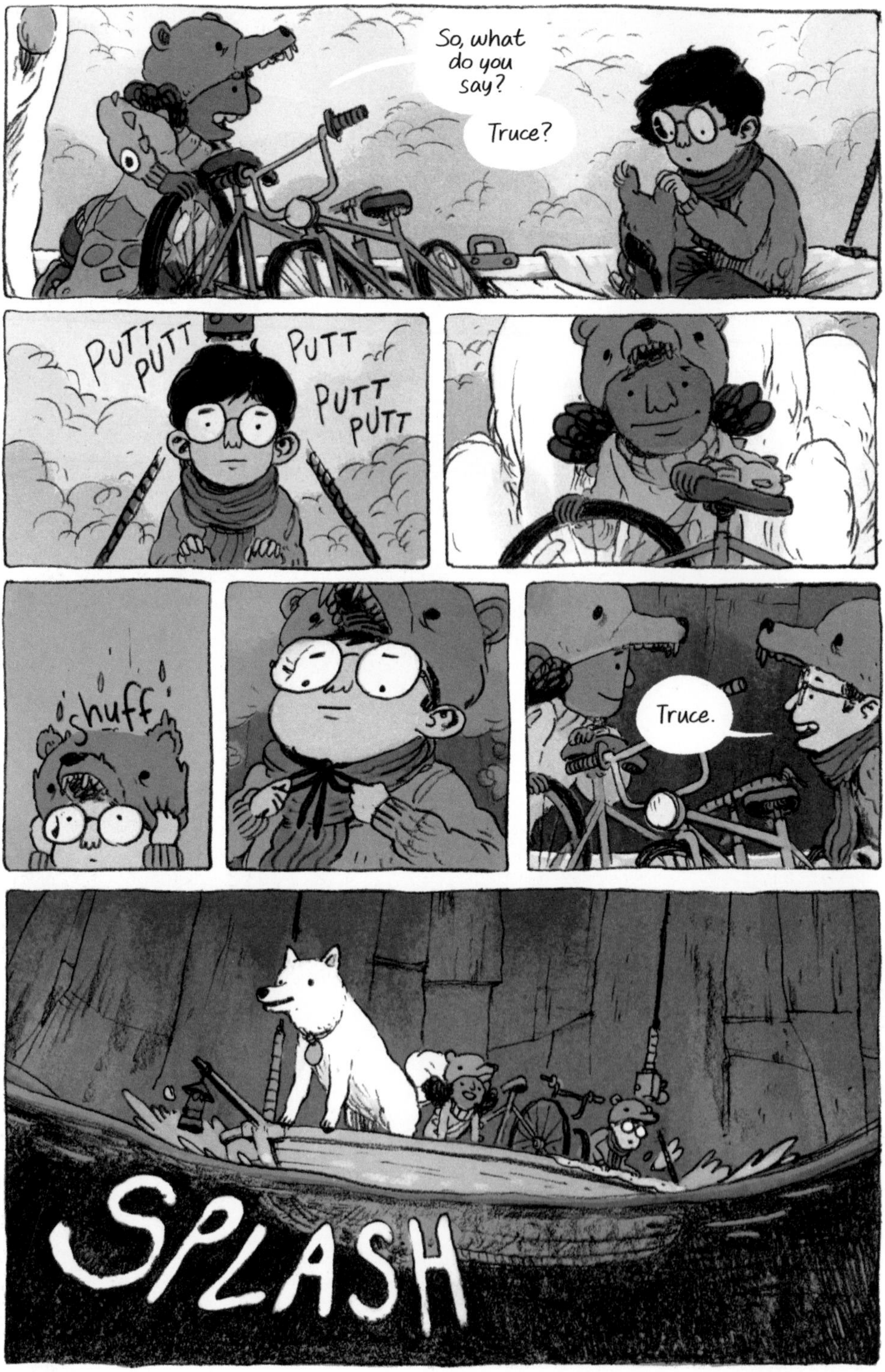
So, what do you say?
Truce?
PUTT PUTT
PUTT
PUTT PUTT
shuff
Truce.
SPLASH

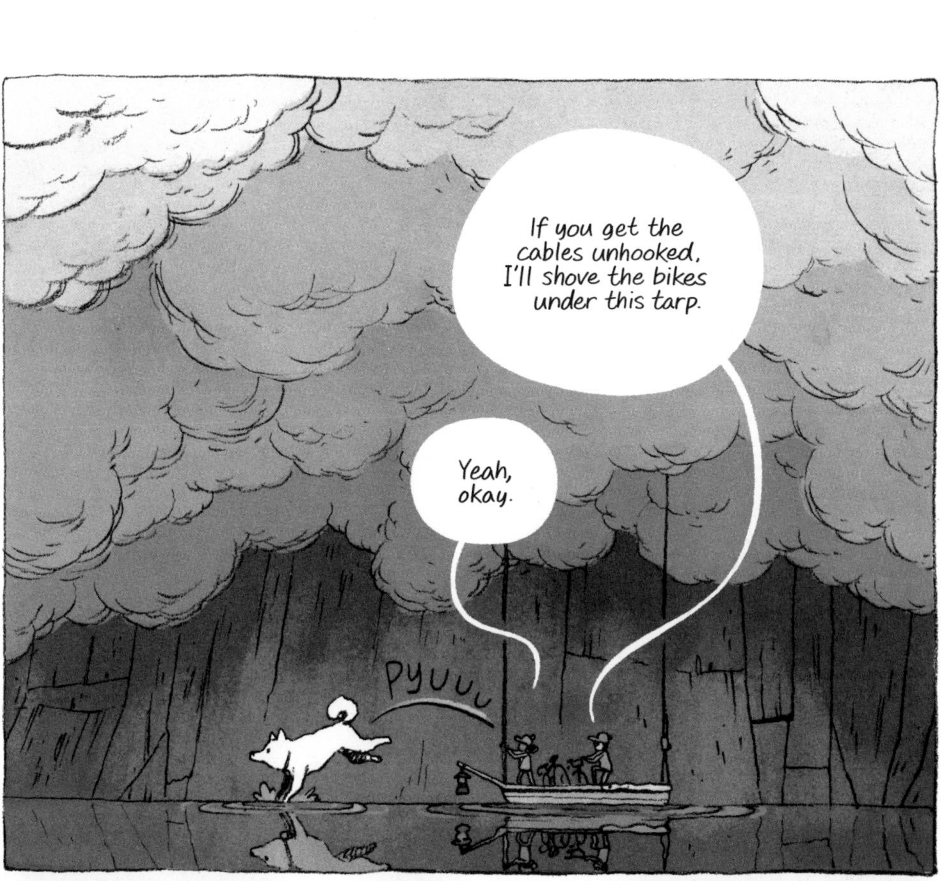
If you get the cables unhooked, I'll shove the bikes under this tarp.
Yeah, okay.
PYUUU

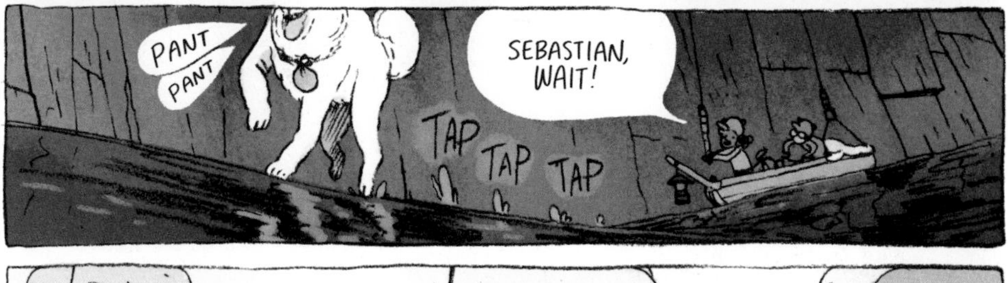
PANT
PANT
SEBASTIAN, WAIT!
TAP
TAP
TAP

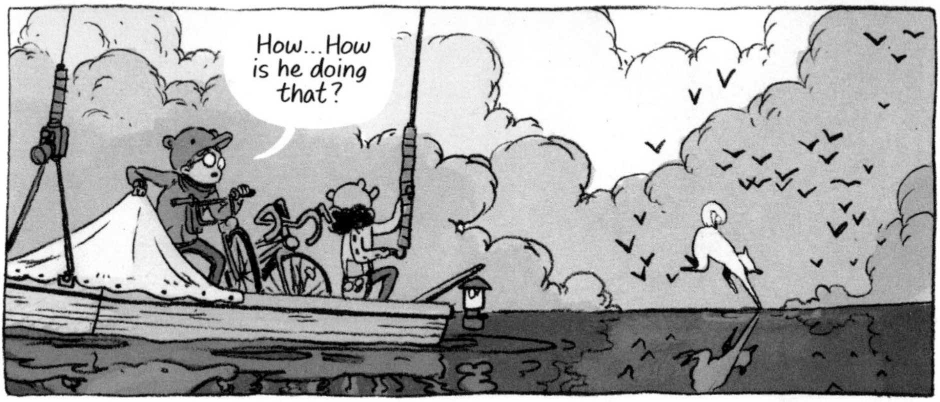
How... How is he doing that?

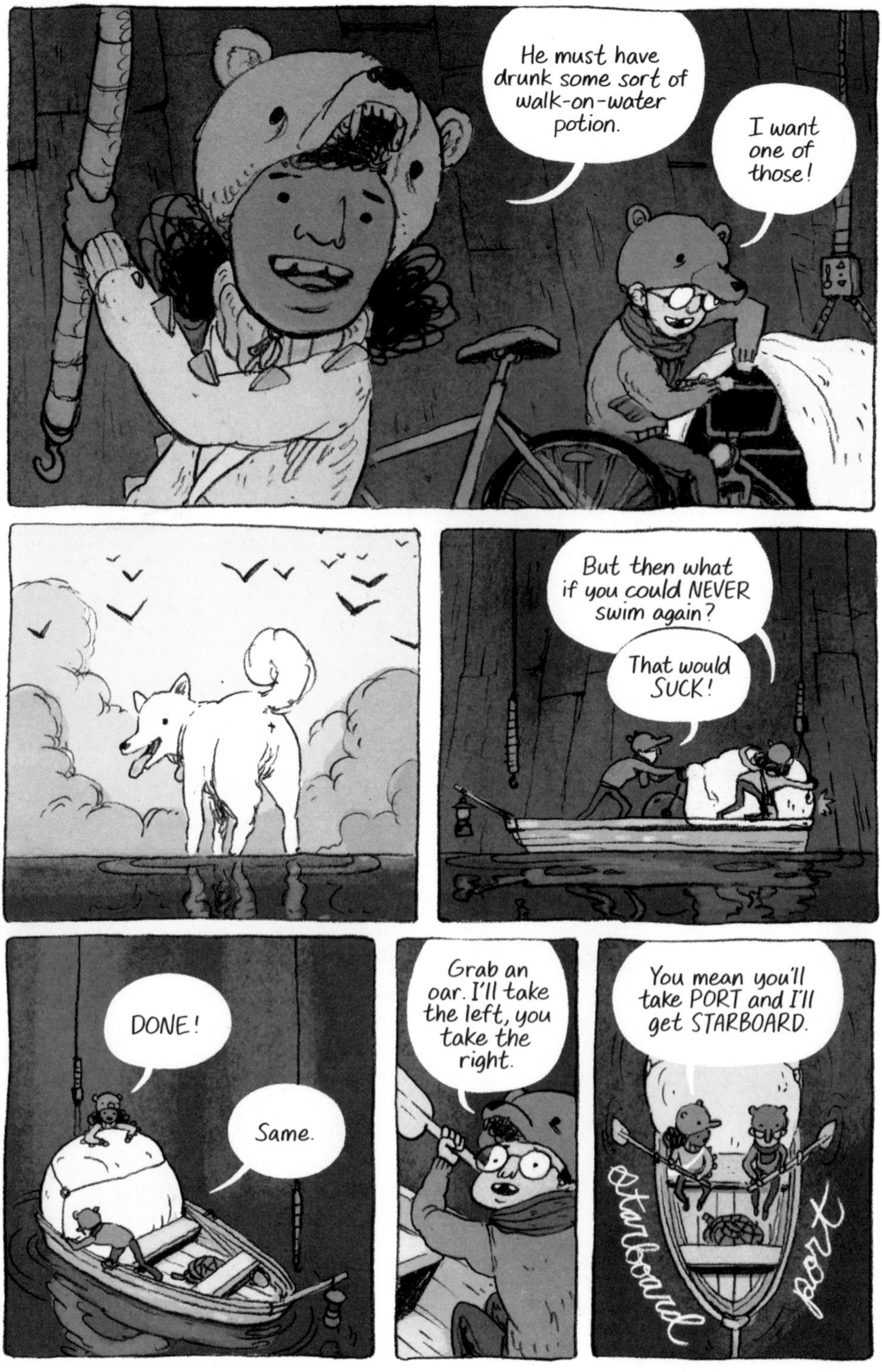
He must have drunk some sort of walk-on-water potion.
I want one of those!
But then what if you could NEVER swim again?
That would SUCK!
DONE!
Same.
Grab an oar. I'll take the left, you take the right.
You mean you'll take PORT and I'll get STARBOARD.
starboard
port

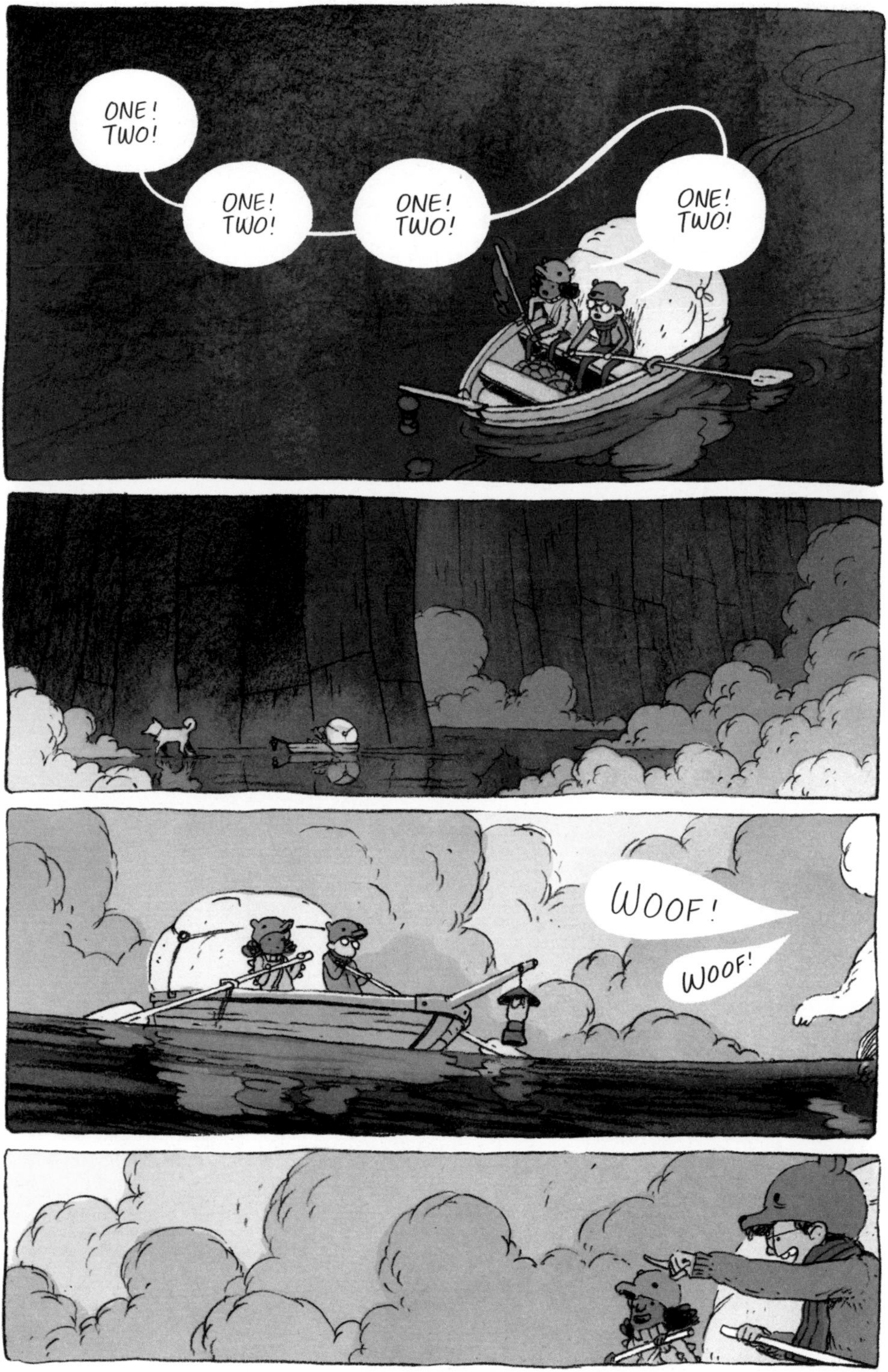
ONE! TWO!
ONE! TWO!
ONE! TWO!
ONE! TWO!
WOOF!
WOOF!

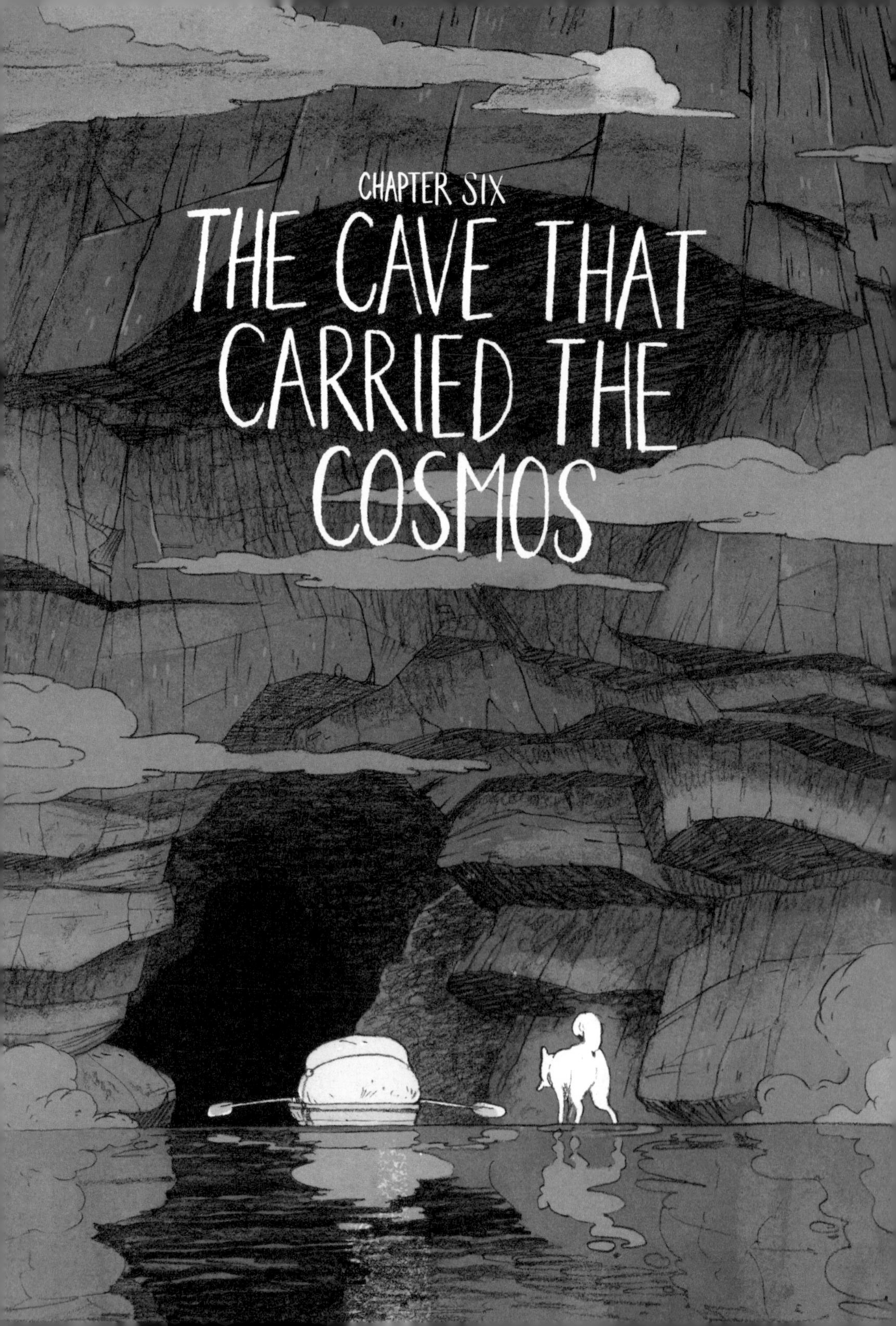
CHAPTER SIX
THE CAVE THAT CARRIED THE COSMOS

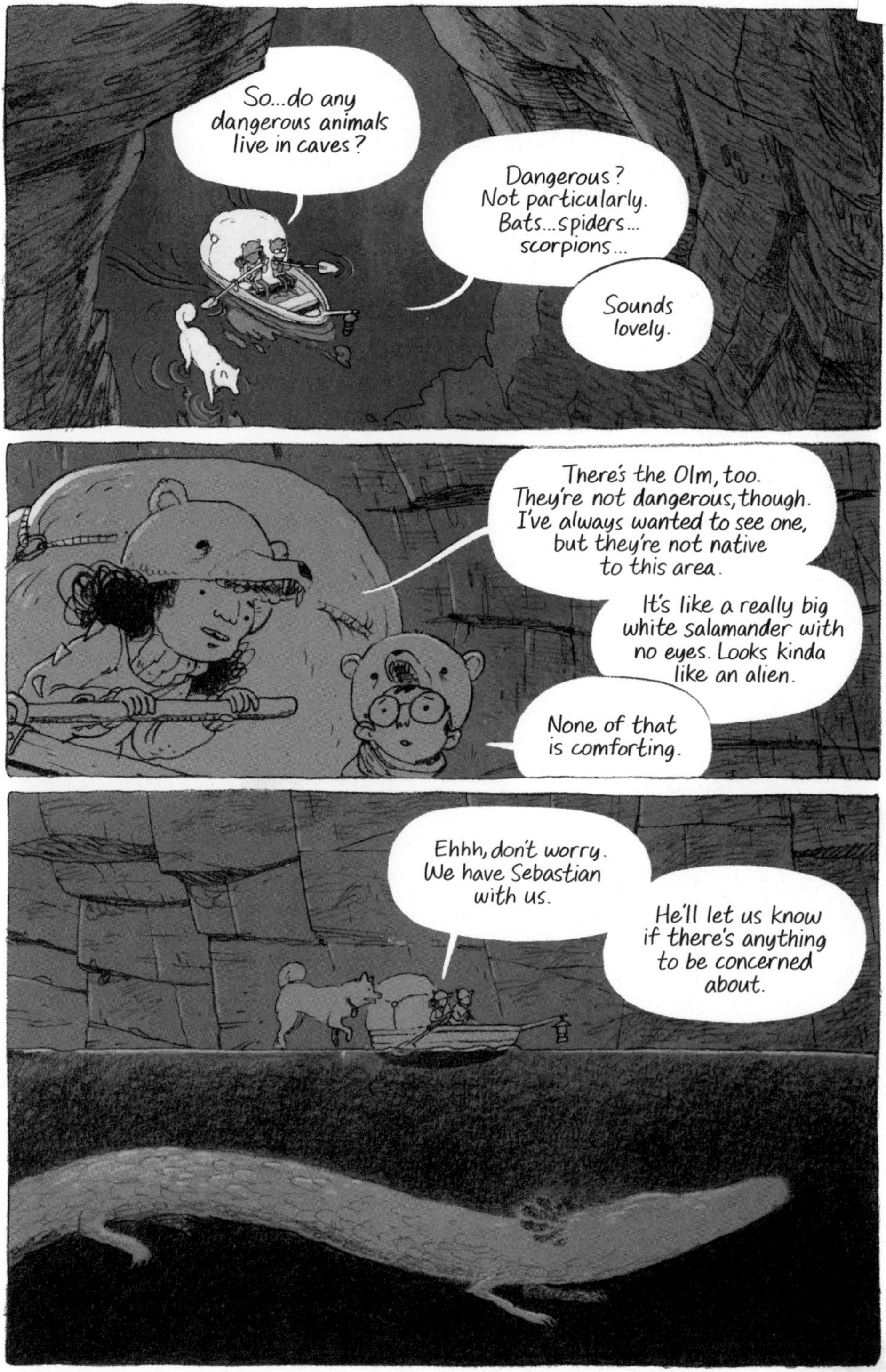
So...do any dangerous animals live in caves?
Dangerous? Not particularly. Bats...spiders... scorpions...
Sounds lovely.
There's the Olm, too. They're not dangerous, though. I've always wanted to see one, but they're not native to this area.
It's like a really big white salamander with no eyes. Looks kinda like an alien.
None of that is comforting.
Ehhh, don't worry. We have Sebastian with us.
He'll let us know if there's anything to be concerned about.

I think it's about time we light up this little guy.

Do you know how?

My uncle showed me how. He still uses one because he doesn't believe in electricity, or something crazy like that.

PUMP PUMP PUMP

PULL

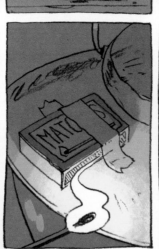

MATC

Do you think it leads anywhere?

There's a lot more up ahead!

I wonder if anything lives inside them.

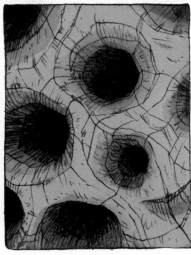

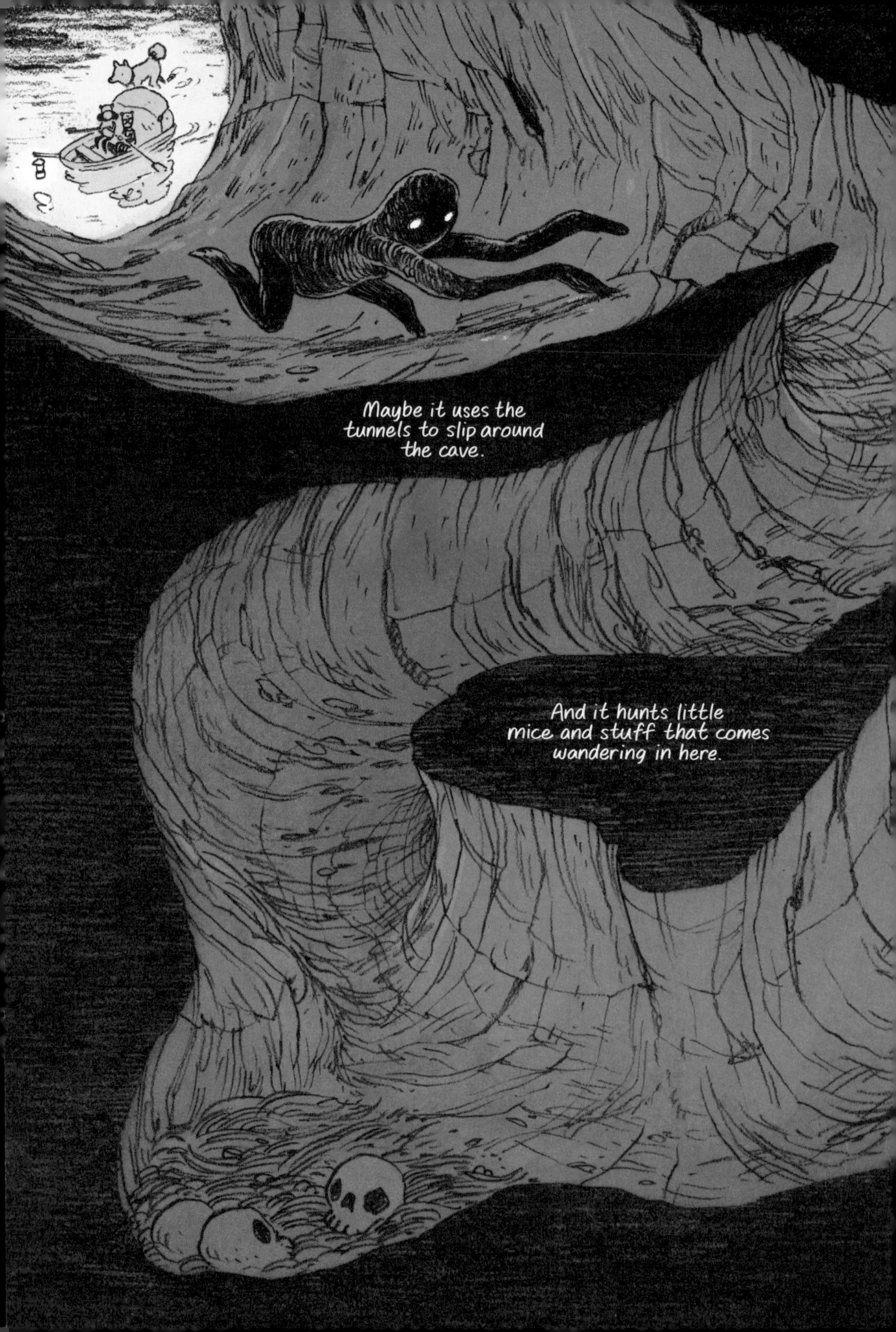
Maybe it uses the tunnels to slip around the cave.
And it hunts little mice and stuff that comes wandering in here.

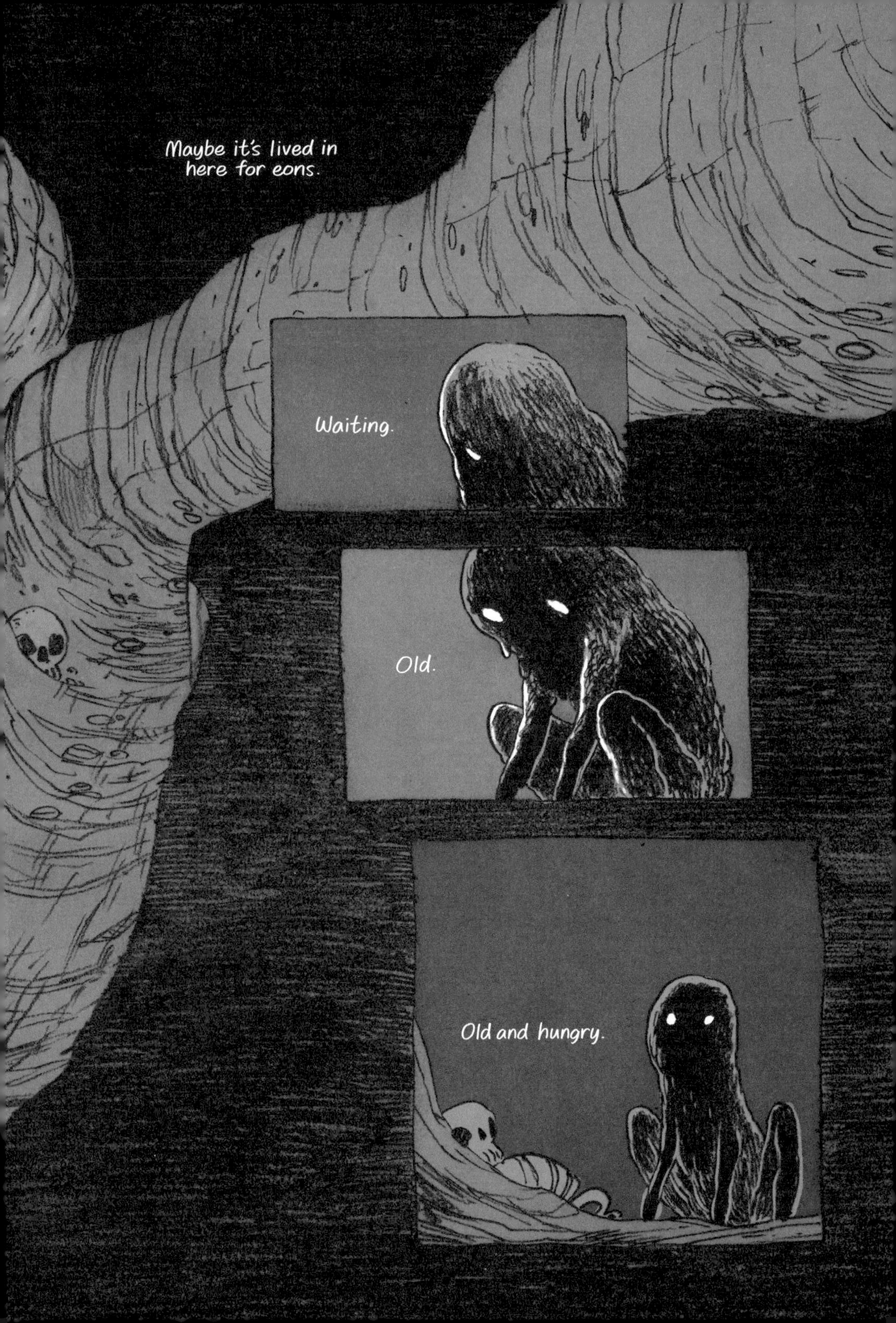
Maybe it's lived in here for eons.
Waiting.
Old.
Old and hungry.

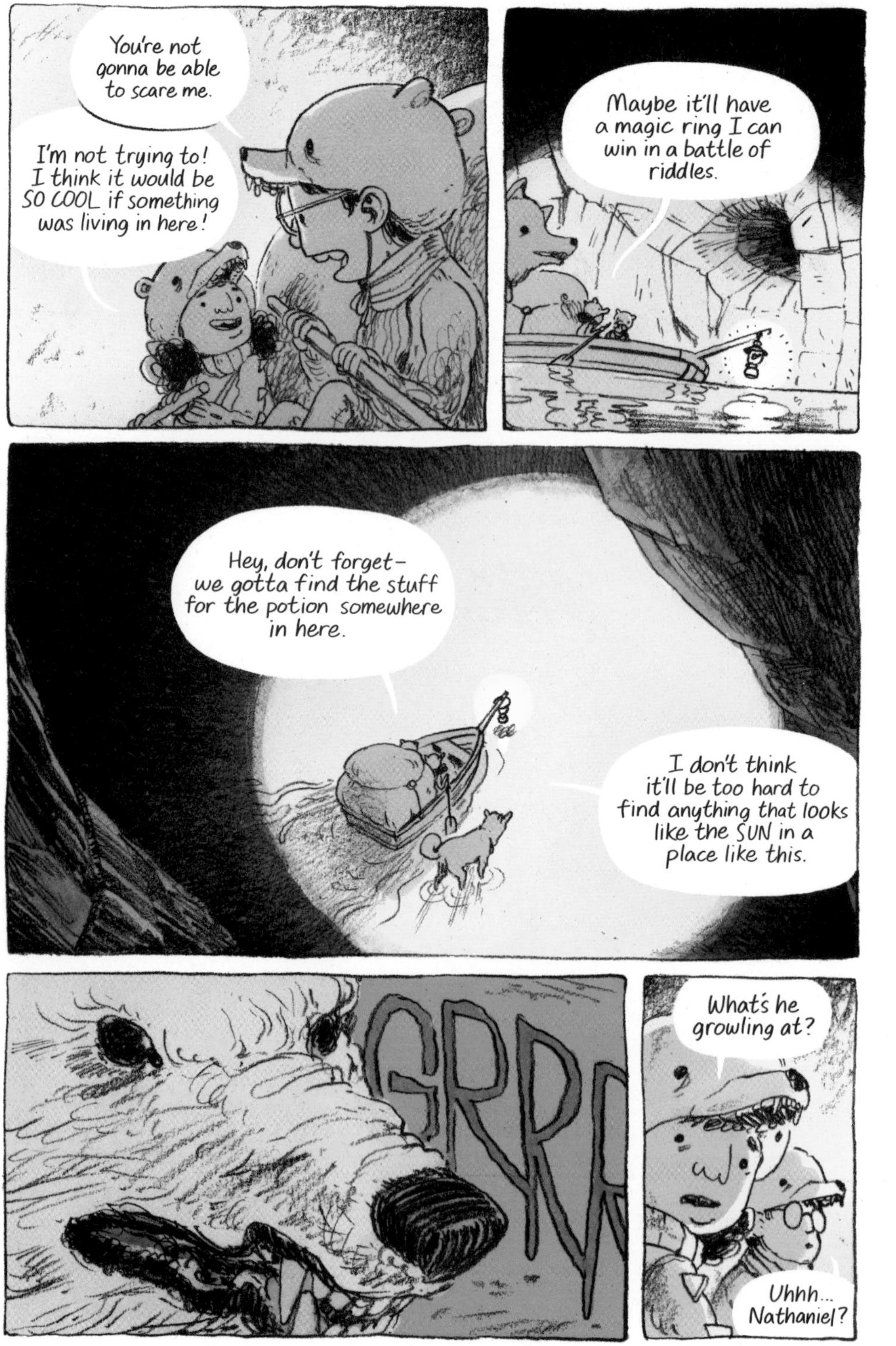
You're not gonna be able to scare me.
I'm not trying to! I think it would be SO COOL if something was living in here!
Maybe it'll have a magic ring I can win in a battle of riddles.
Hey, don't forget– we gotta find the stuff for the potion somewhere in here.
I don't think it'll be too hard to find anything that looks like the SUN in a place like this.
GRRR
What's he growling at?
Uhhh... Nathaniel?

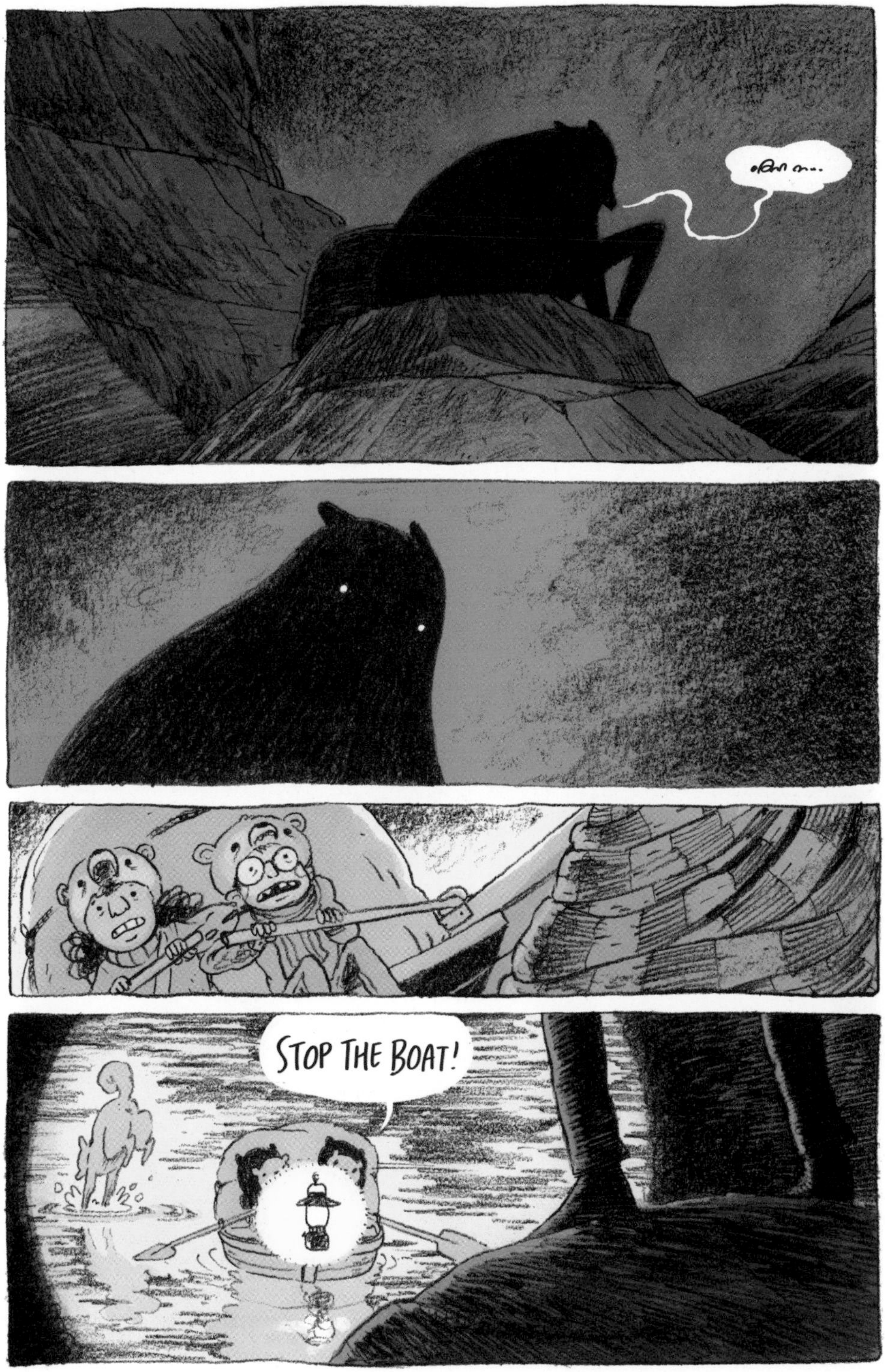
STOP THE BOAT!

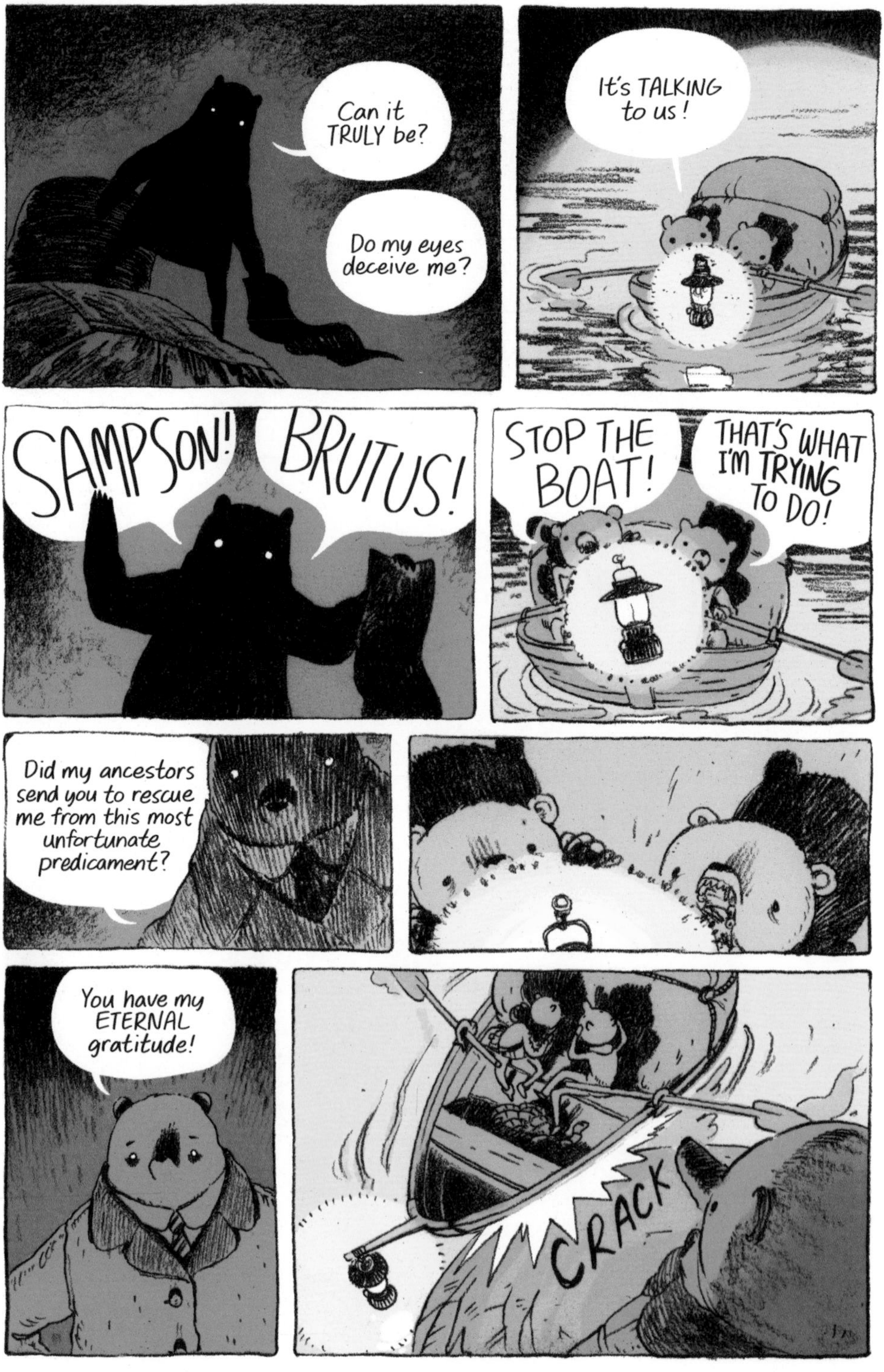
Can it TRULY be?
Do my eyes deceive me?
It's TALKING to us!
SAMPSON!
BRUTUS!
STOP THE BOAT!
THAT'S WHAT I'M TRYING TO DO!
Did my ancestors send you to rescue me from this most unfortunate predicament?
You have my ETERNAL gratitude!
CRACK

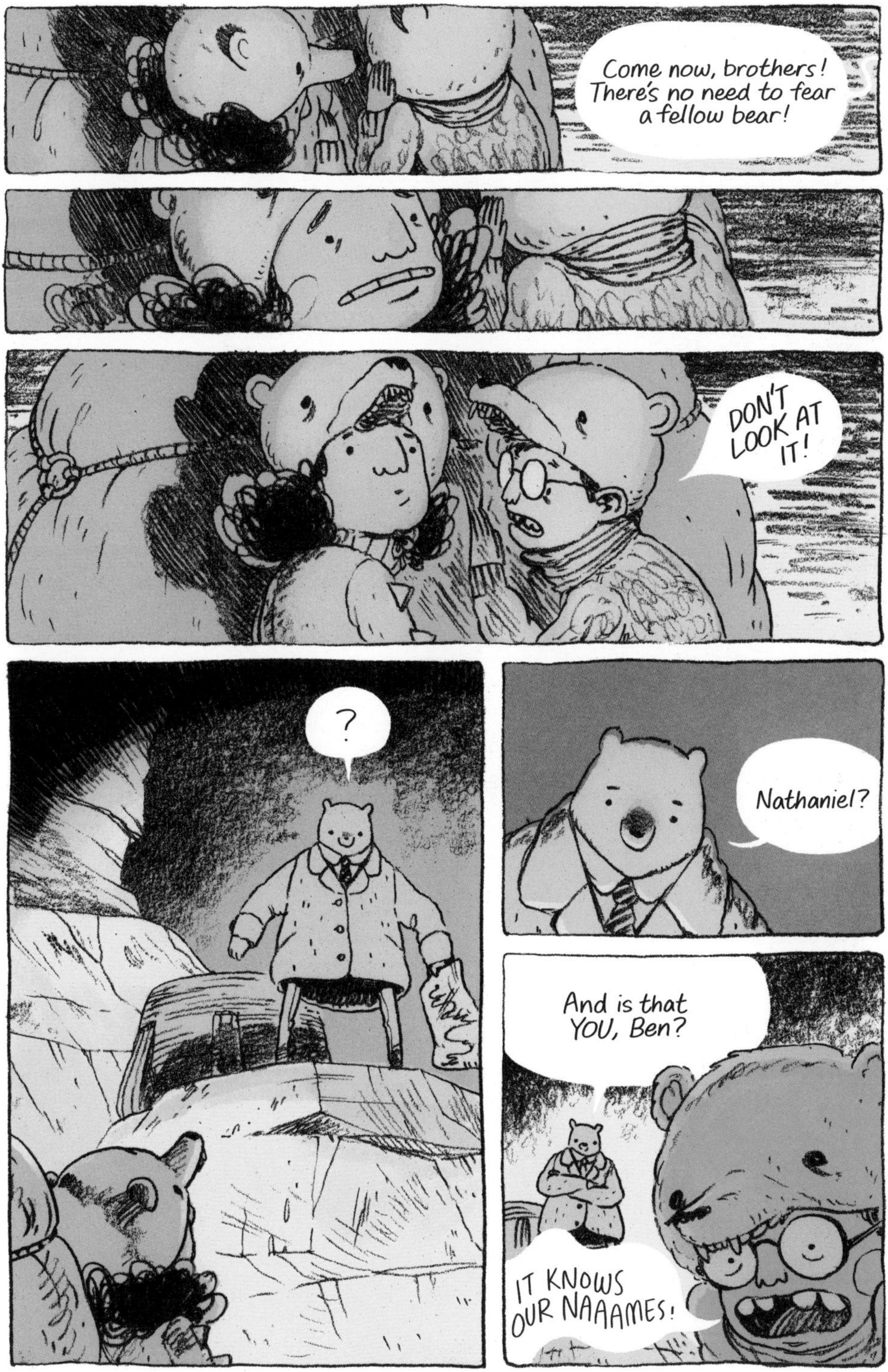

Come now, brothers! There's no need to fear a fellow bear!
DON'T LOOK AT IT!
?
Nathaniel?
And is that YOU, Ben?
IT KNOWS OUR NAAAMES!

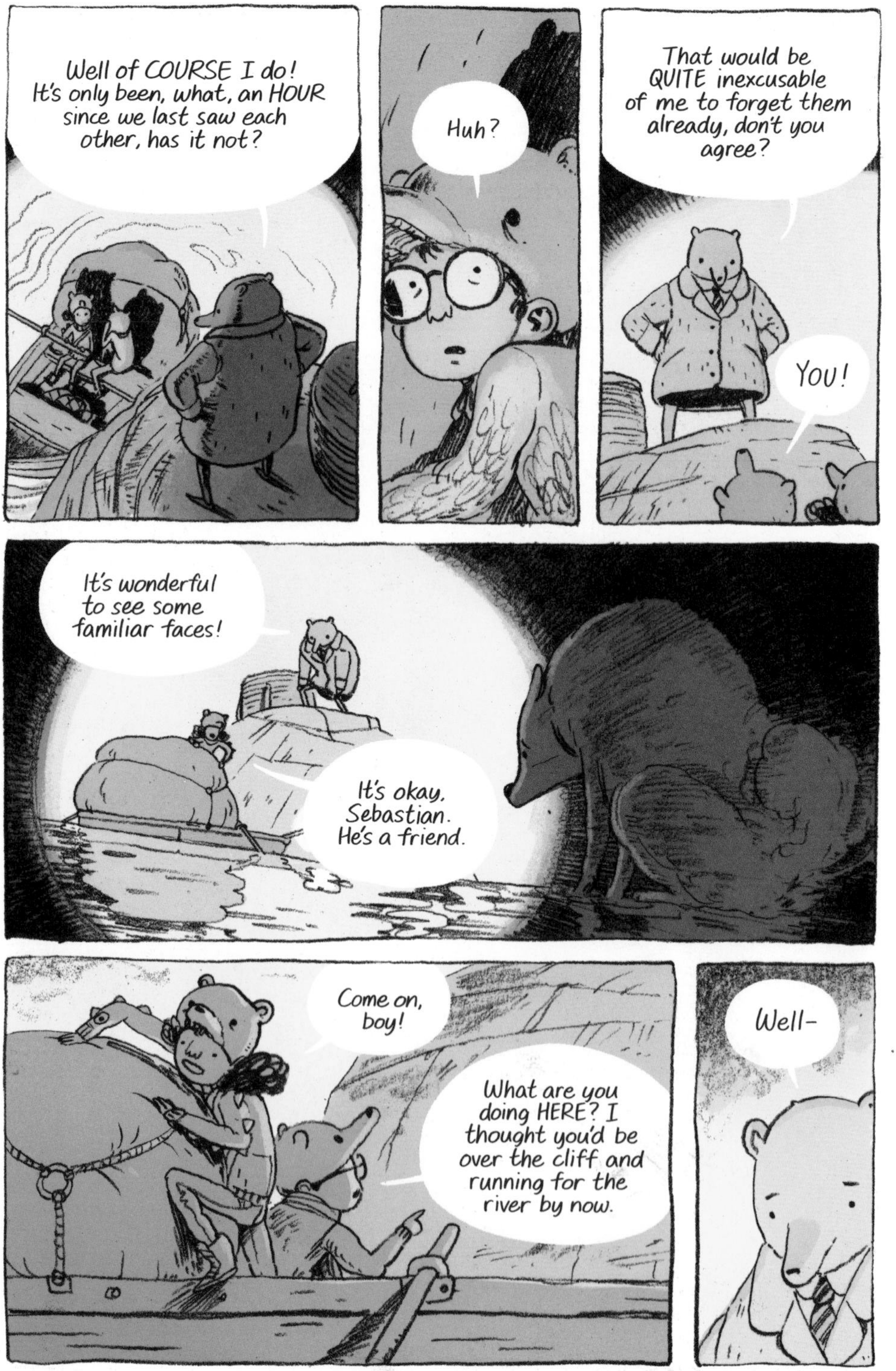
Well of COURSE I do! It's only been, what, an HOUR since we last saw each other, has it not?
Huh?
That would be QUITE inexcusable of me to forget them already, don't you agree?
YOU!
It's wonderful to see some familiar faces!
It's okay, Sebastian. He's a friend.
Come on, boy!
What are you doing HERE? I thought you'd be over the cliff and running for the river by now.
Well-

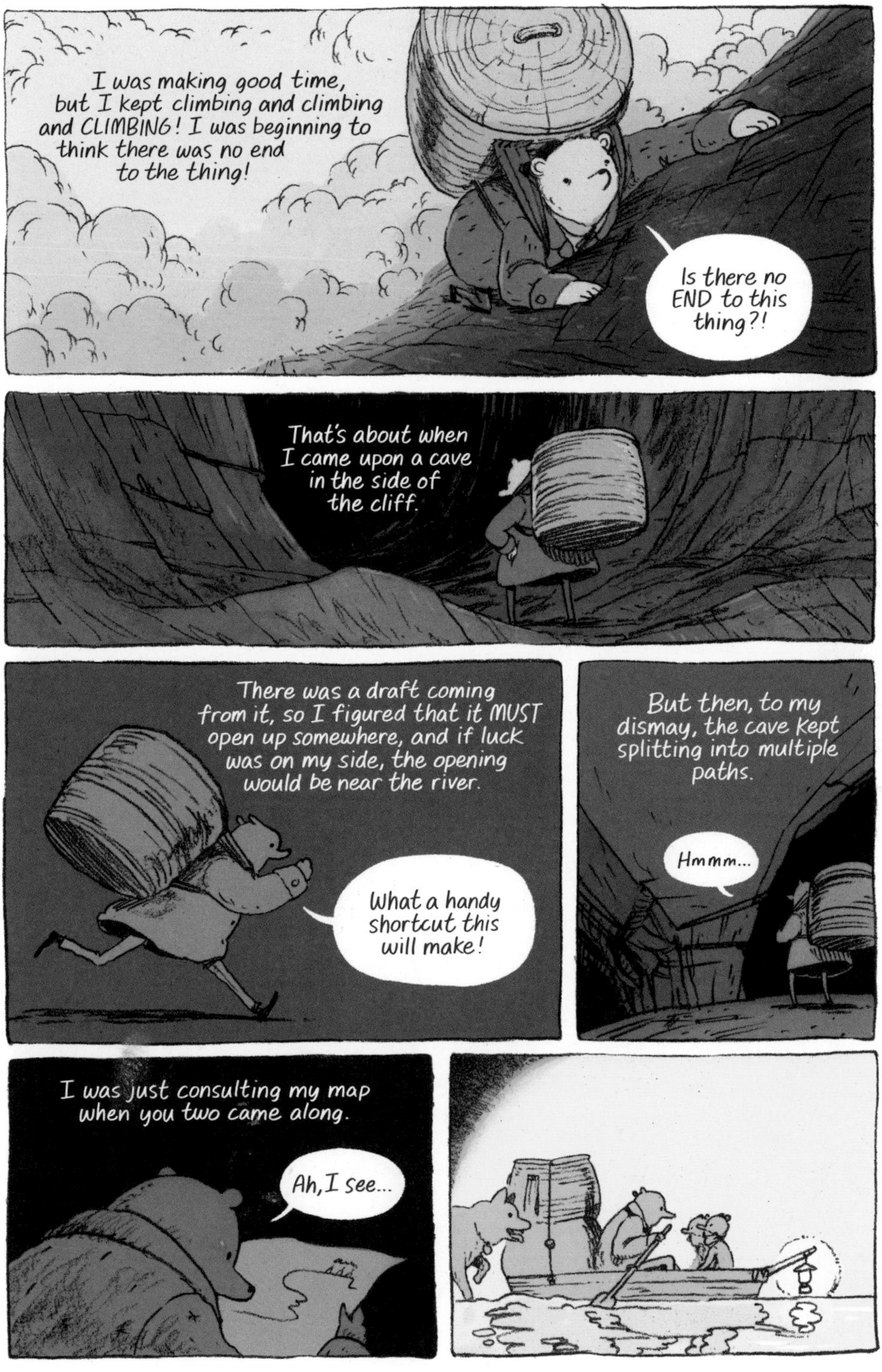
I was making good time, but I kept climbing and climbing and CLIMBING! I was beginning to think there was no end to the thing!
Is there no END to this thing?!
That's about when I came upon a cave in the side of the cliff.
There was a draft coming from it, so I figured that it MUST open up somewhere, and if luck was on my side, the opening would be near the river.
What a handy shortcut this will make!
But then, to my dismay, the cave kept splitting into multiple paths.
Hmmm...
I was just consulting my map when you two came along.
Ah, I see...

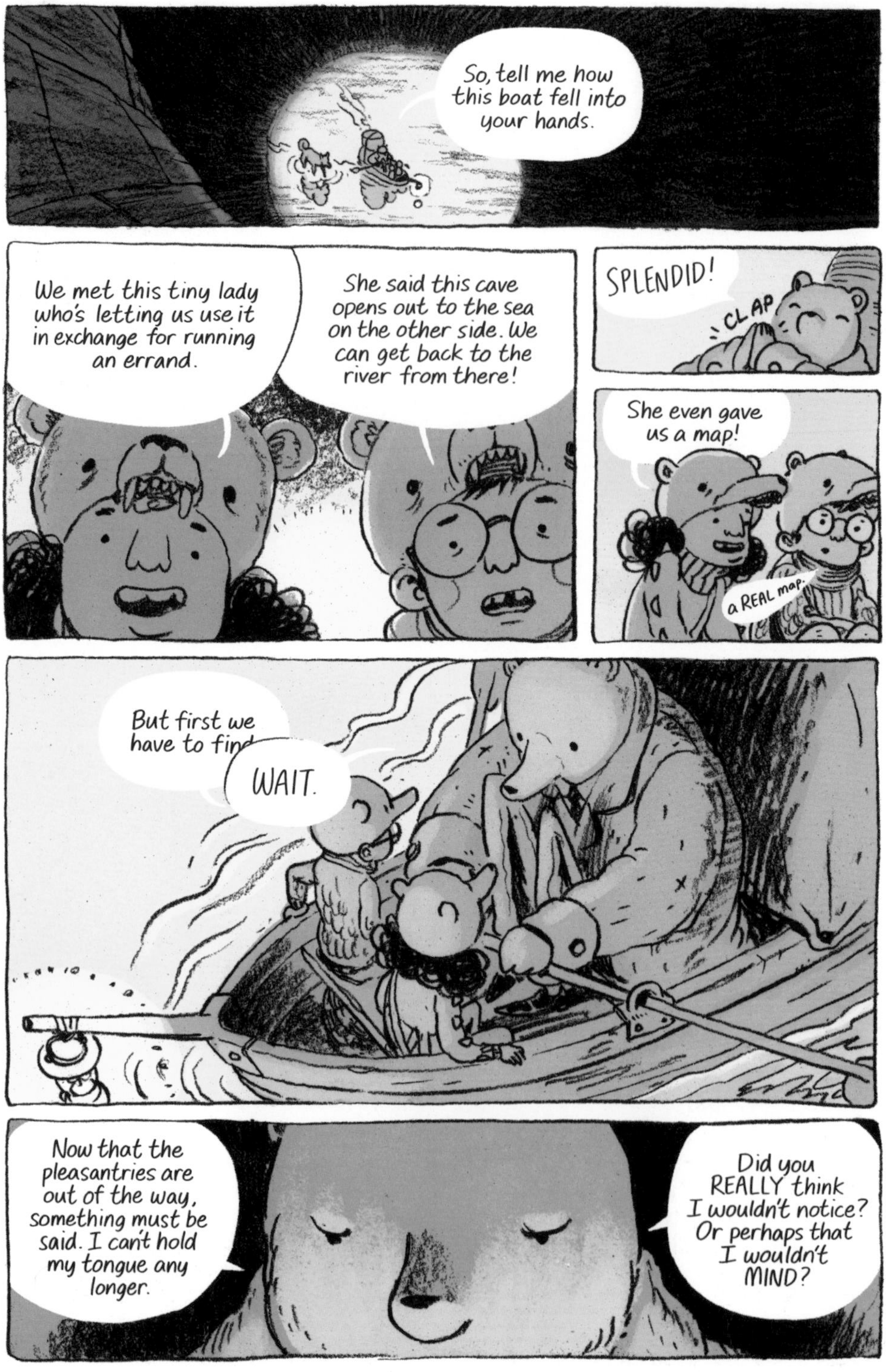

So, tell me how this boat fell into your hands.
We met this tiny lady who's letting us use it in exchange for running an errand.
She said this cave opens out to the sea on the other side. We can get back to the river from there!
SPLENDID!
CLAP
She even gave us a map!
a REAL map.
But first we have to fin
WAIT.
Now that the pleasantries are out of the way, something must be said. I can't hold my tongue any longer.
Did you REALLY think I wouldn't notice? Or perhaps that I wouldn't MIND?

Is that not the scarf I gave you? The scarf my wife painstakingly made with her own hands?

Ohhhh! Yeah! It ended up really coming in handy!

Yeah! Ben rescued me, and I had to climb out of this really high window—

Not only did you carelessly toss it on the wet floor of the boat... but you even tied it in KNOTS!

She would be HEARTBROKEN if she saw this!

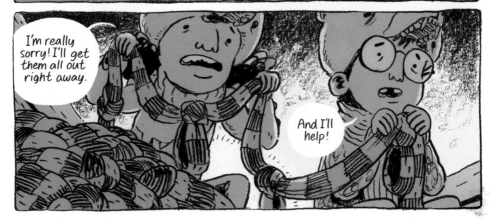

I'm really sorry! I'll get them all out right away.

And I'll help!

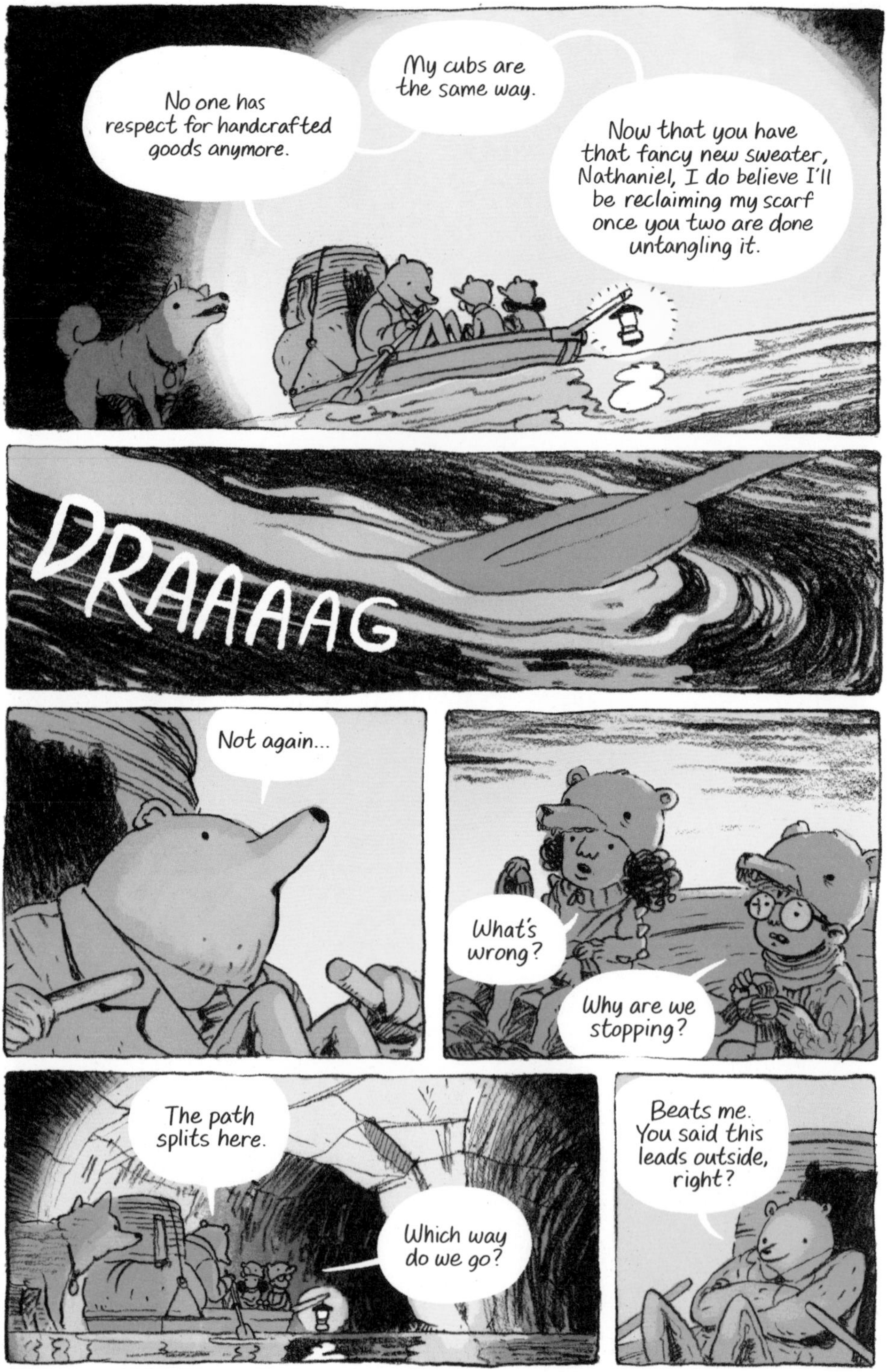
No one has respect for handcrafted goods anymore.
My cubs are the same way.
Now that you have that fancy new sweater, Nathaniel, I do believe I'll be reclaiming my scarf once you two are done untangling it.
DRAAAAG
Not again...
What's wrong?
Why are we stopping?
The path splits here.
Which way do we go?
Beats me. You said this leads outside, right?

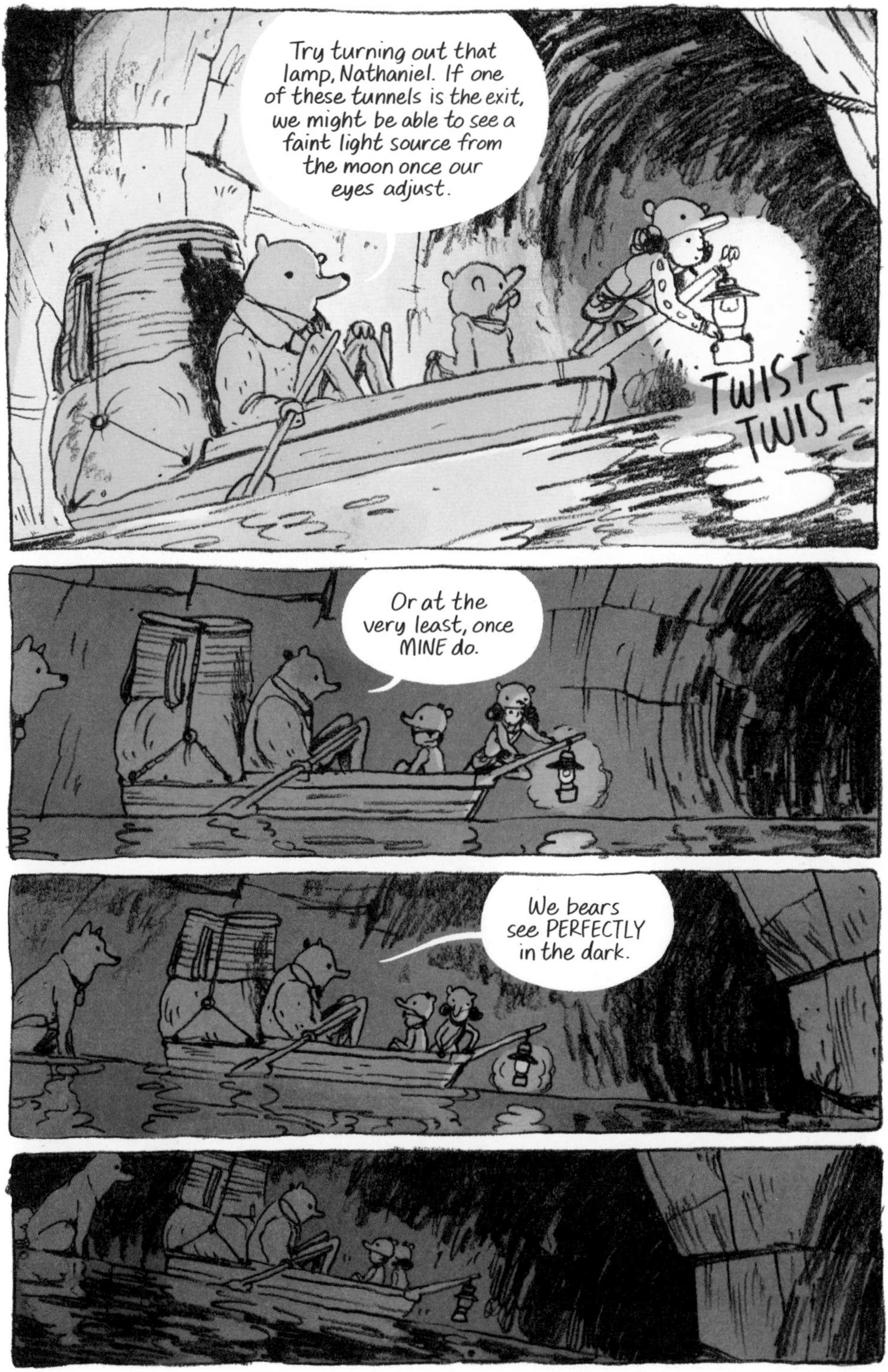
Try turning out that lamp, Nathaniel. If one of these tunnels is the exit, we might be able to see a faint light source from the moon once our eyes adjust.
TWIST
TWIST
Or at the very least, once MINE do.
We bears see PERFECTLY in the dark.

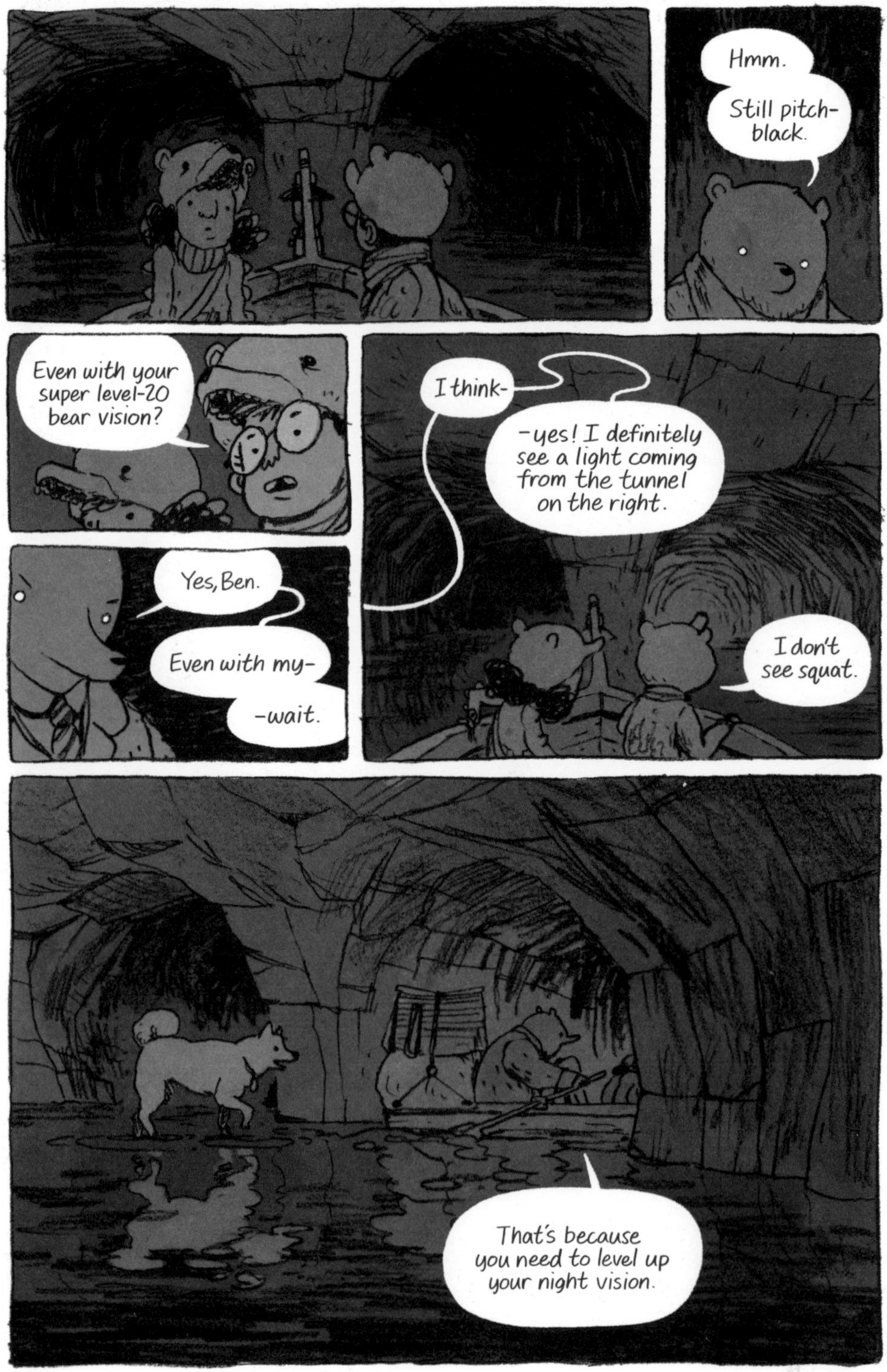
Hmm.
Still pitch-black.
Even with your super level-20 bear vision?
Yes, Ben.
Even with my-
-wait.
I think-
-yes! I definitely see a light coming from the tunnel on the right.
I don't see squat.
That's because you need to level up your night vision.

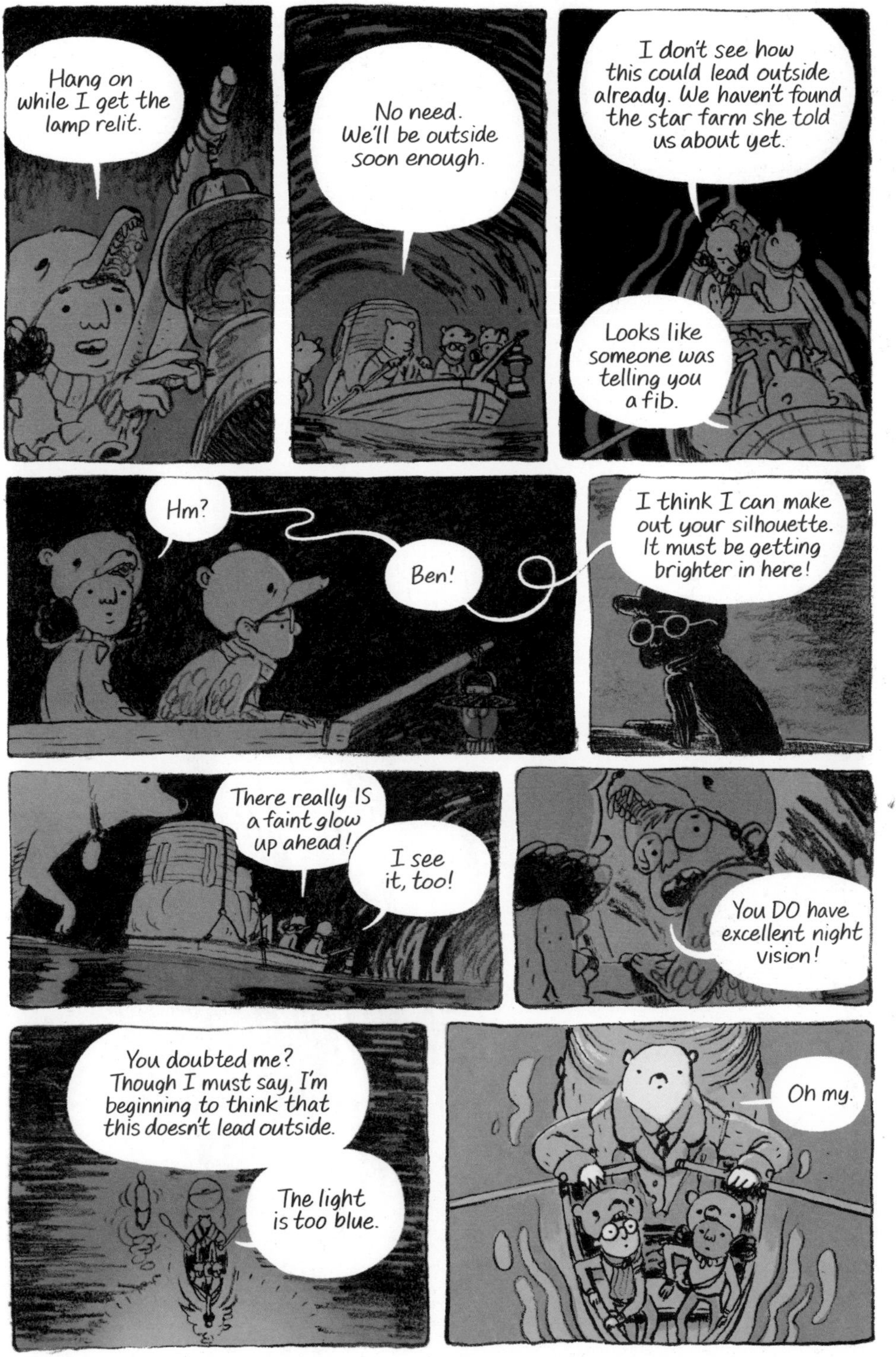
Hang on while I get the lamp relit.
No need. We'll be outside soon enough.
I don't see how this could lead outside already. We haven't found the star farm she told us about yet.
Looks like someone was telling you a fib.
Hm?
Ben!
I think I can make out your silhouette. It must be getting brighter in here!
There really IS a faint glow up ahead!
I see it, too!
You DO have excellent night vision!
You doubted me? Though I must say, I'm beginning to think that this doesn't lead outside.
The light is too blue.
Oh my.

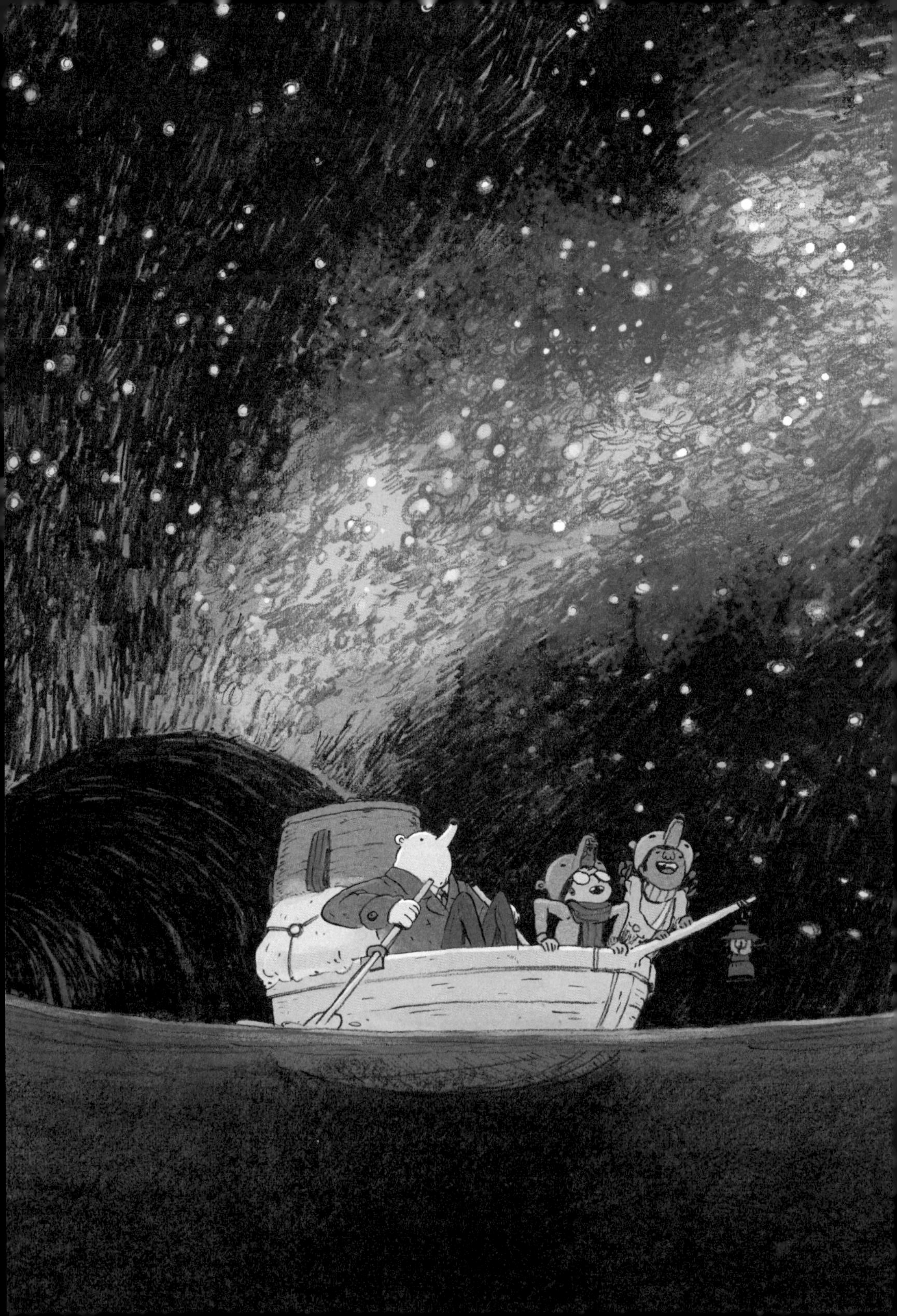

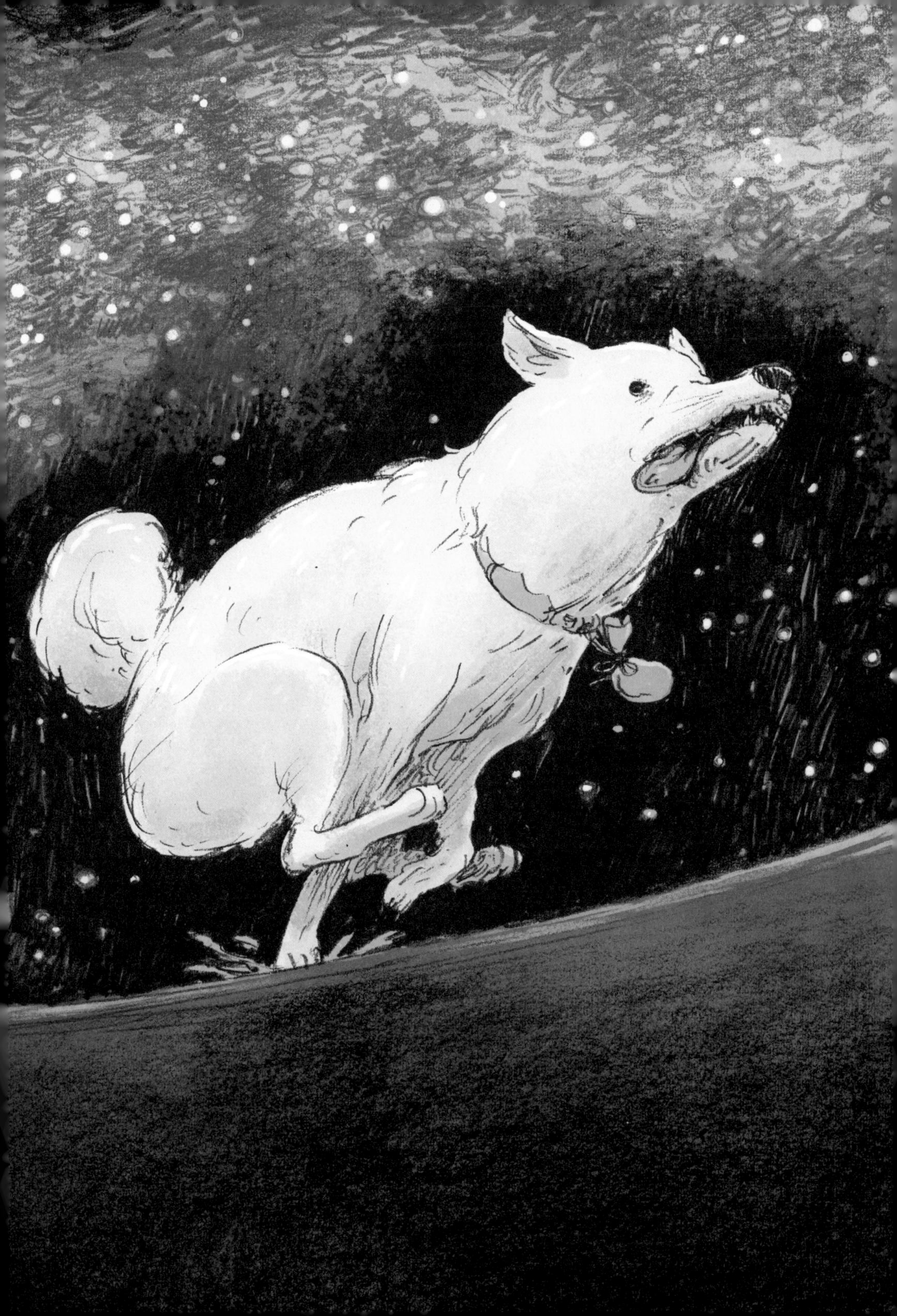

The star
farm...

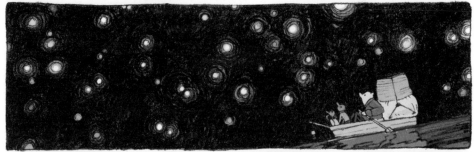

I've never
seen anything
like it.

Take us out
to the middle.
I want to check
something.

Okay, stop.
This looks about
right.

How on earth did she DO this?

Hmm...

It must have taken FOREVER.

Is that...

GASP

BEN! Now I understand what she meant! She's a GENIUS!

She said she had to fool the potion into believing that these were REAL stars, right?

Yyyeah...

Look over there. Do you see it?

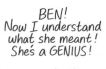

!

THE BIG DIPPER! THIS IS A STAR MAP!

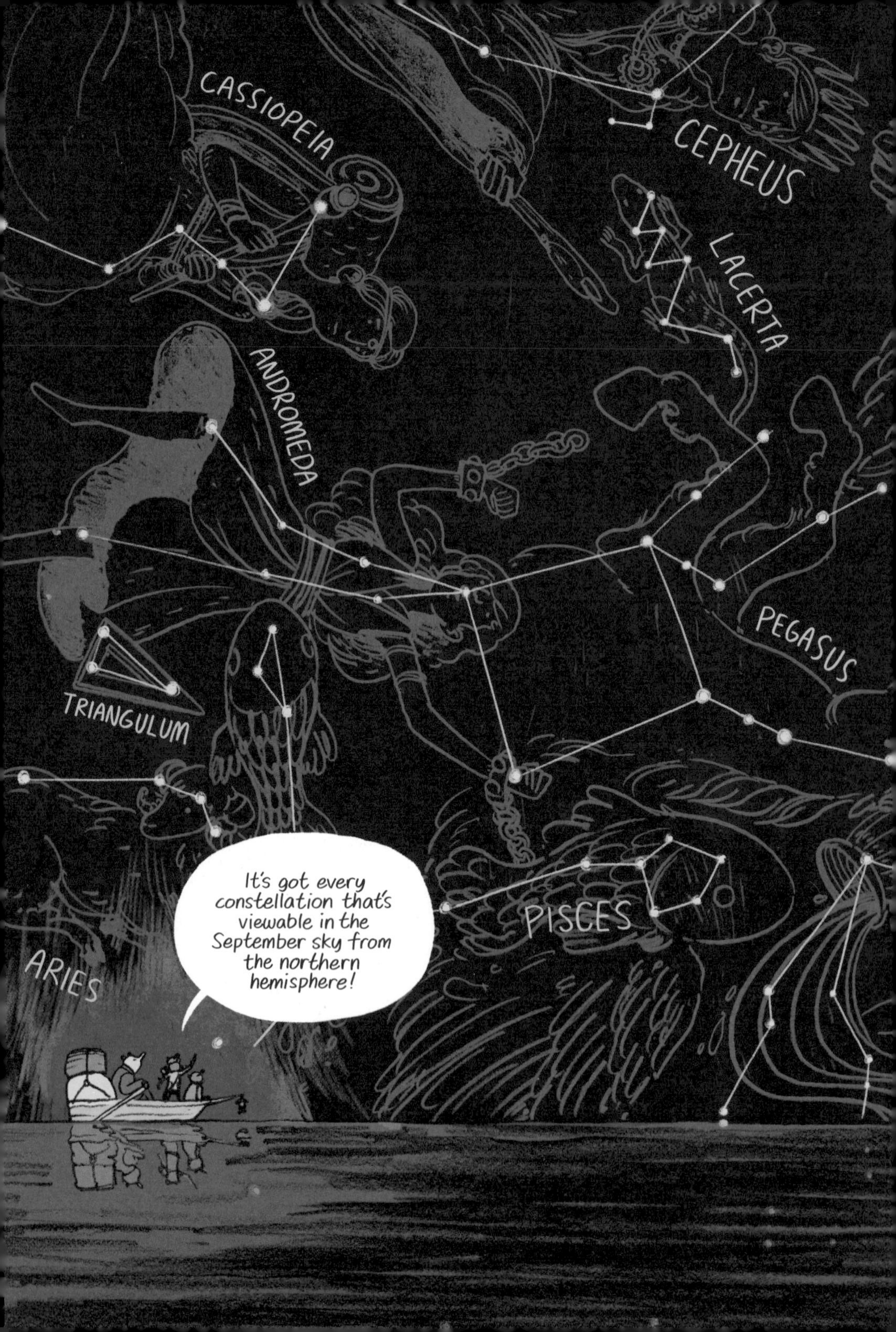
CASSIOPEIA
CEPHEUS
LACERTA
ANDROMEDA
PEGASUS
TRIANGULUM
PISCES
ARIES
It's got every constellation that's viewable in the September sky from the northern hemisphere!

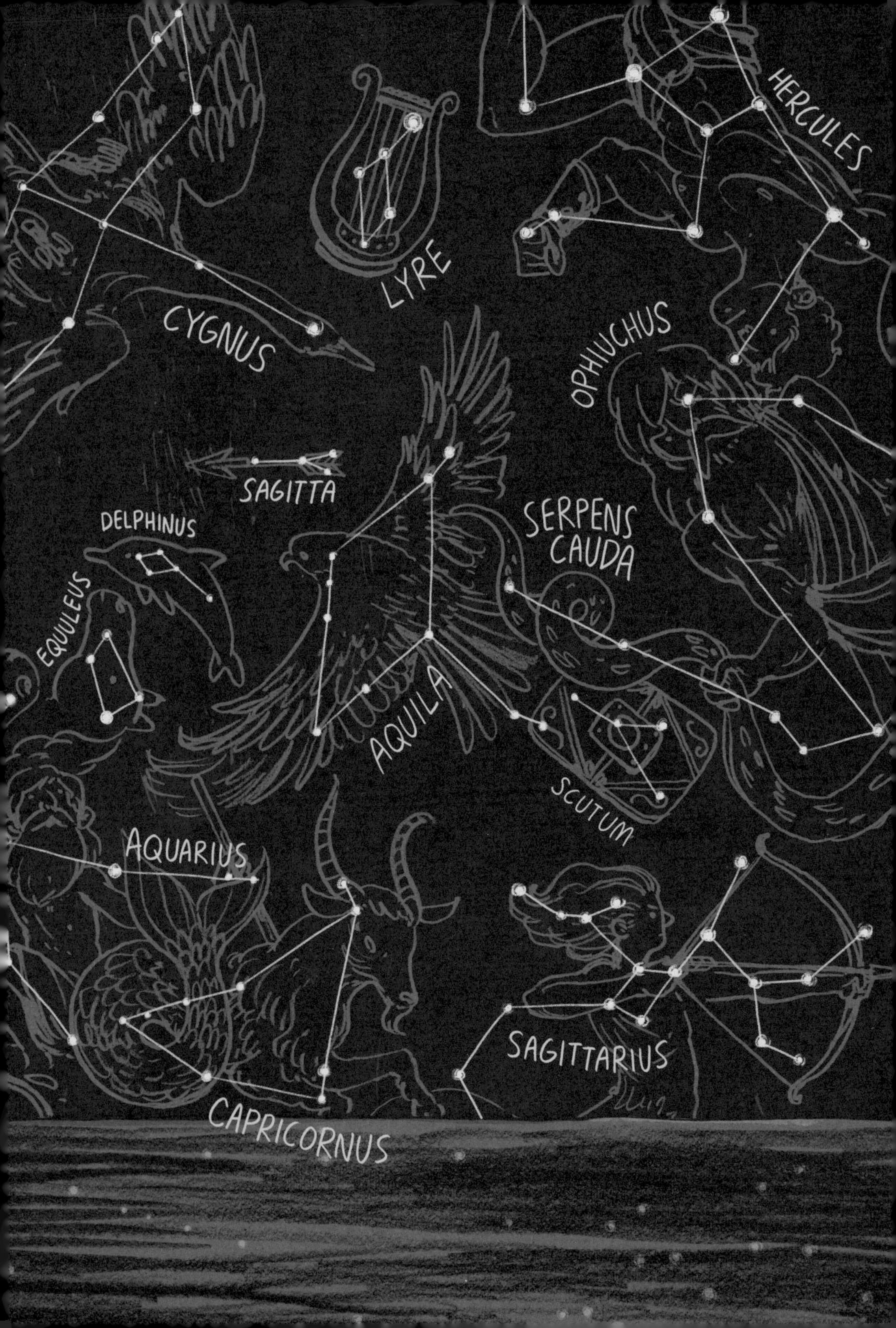
CYGNUS
LYRE
HERCULES
OPHIUCHUS
SAGITTA
DELPHINUS
EQUULEUS
SERPENS
CAUDA
AQUILA
SCUTUM
AQUARIUS
SAGITTARIUS
CAPRICORNUS

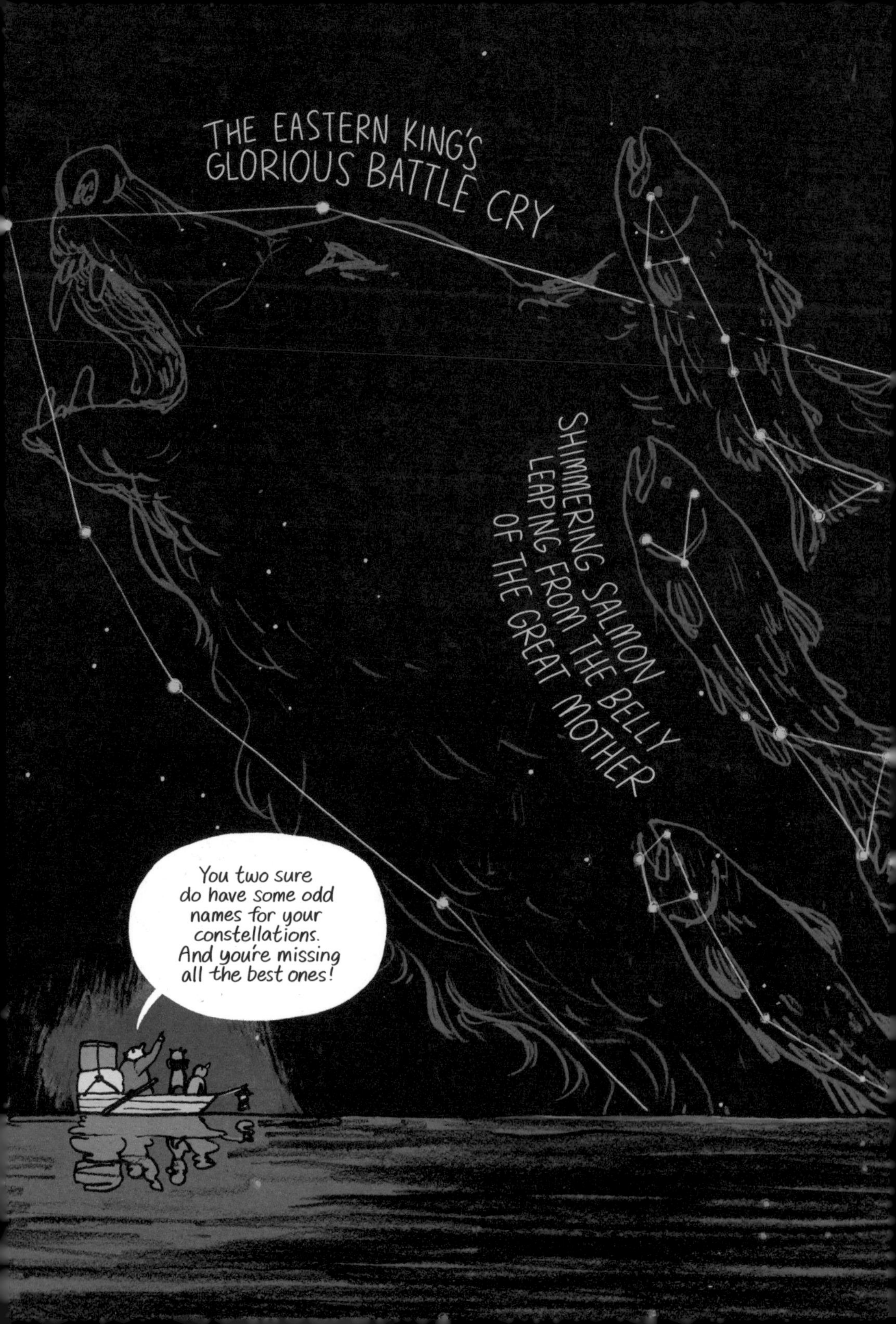
THE EASTERN KING'S GLORIOUS BATTLE CRY
SHIMMERING SALMON LEAPING FROM THE BELLY OF THE GREAT MOTHER
You two sure do have some odd names for your constellations. And you're missing all the best ones!

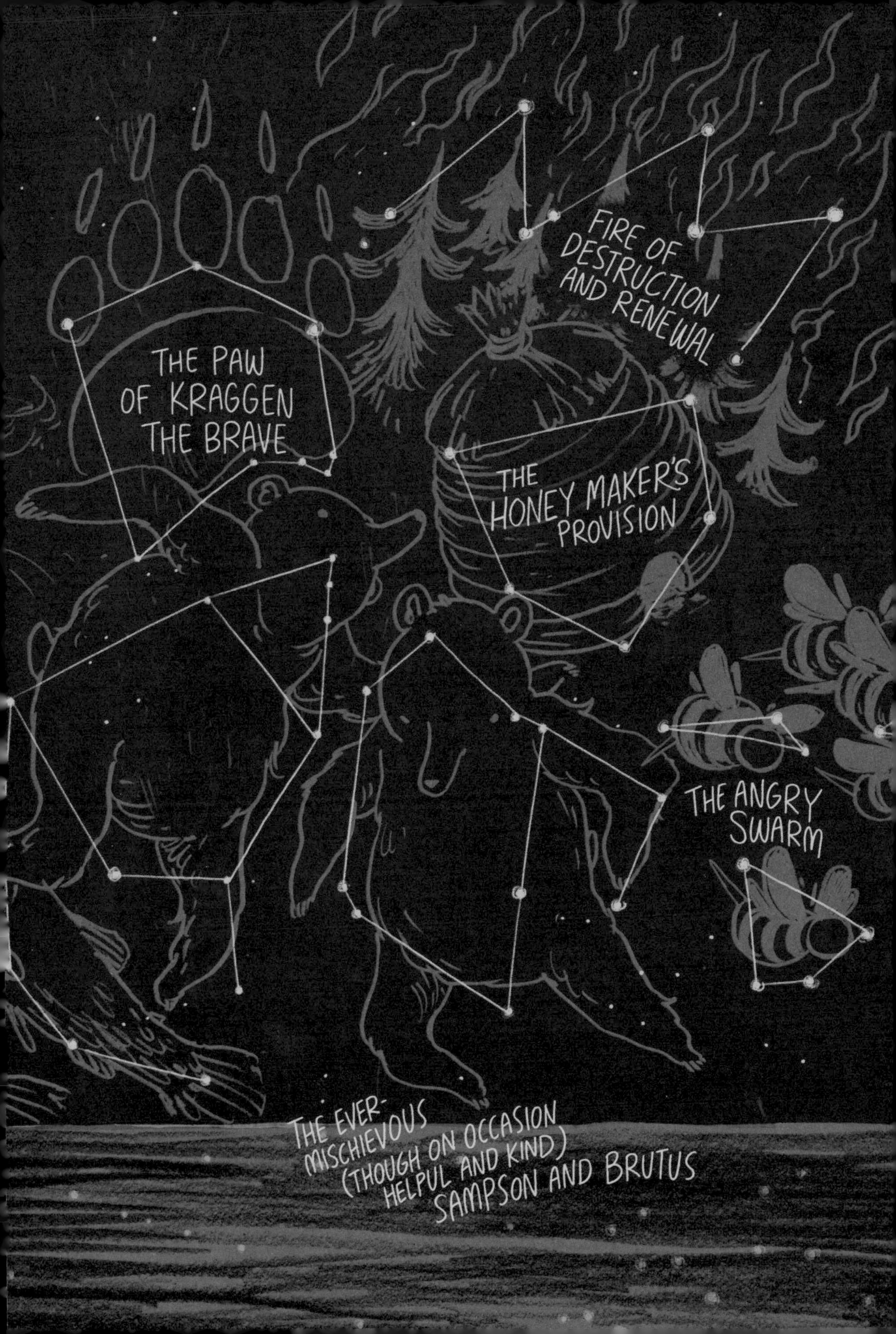

THE PAW OF KRAGGEN THE BRAVE
FIRE OF DESTRUCTION AND RENEWAL
THE HONEY MAKER'S PROVISION
THE ANGRY SWARM
THE EVER-MISCHIEVOUS (THOUGH ON OCCASION HELPUL AND KIND) SAMPSON AND BRUTUS

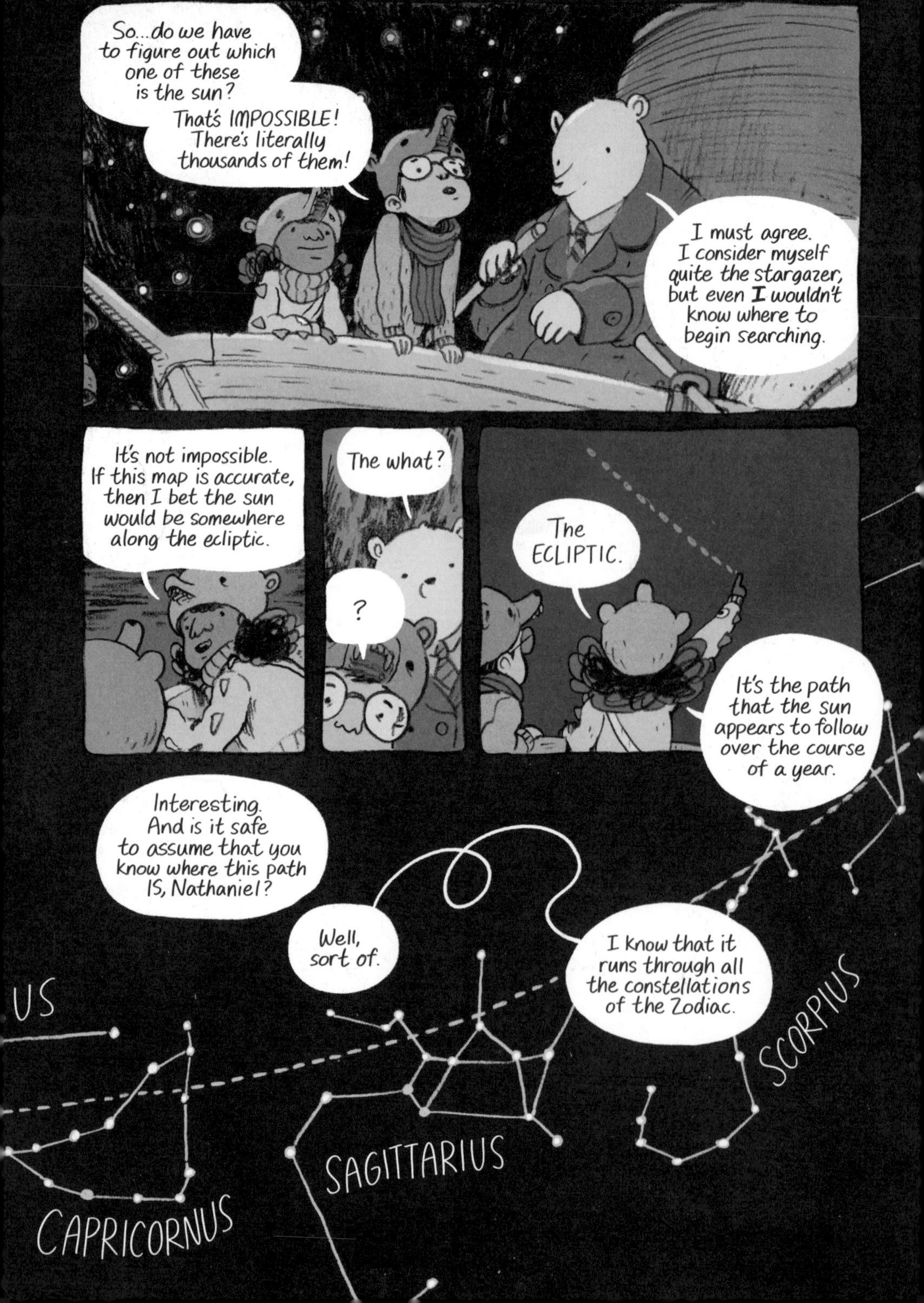

So...do we have to figure out which one of these is the sun?
That's IMPOSSIBLE! There's literally thousands of them!
I must agree. I consider myself quite the stargazer, but even **I** wouldn't know where to begin searching.
It's not impossible. If this map is accurate, then I bet the sun would be somewhere along the ecliptic.
The what?
?
The ECLIPTIC.
It's the path that the sun appears to follow over the course of a year.
Interesting. And is it safe to assume that you know where this path IS, Nathaniel?
Well, sort of.
I know that it runs through all the constellations of the Zodiac.
US
SCORPIUS
SAGITTARIUS
CAPRICORNUS

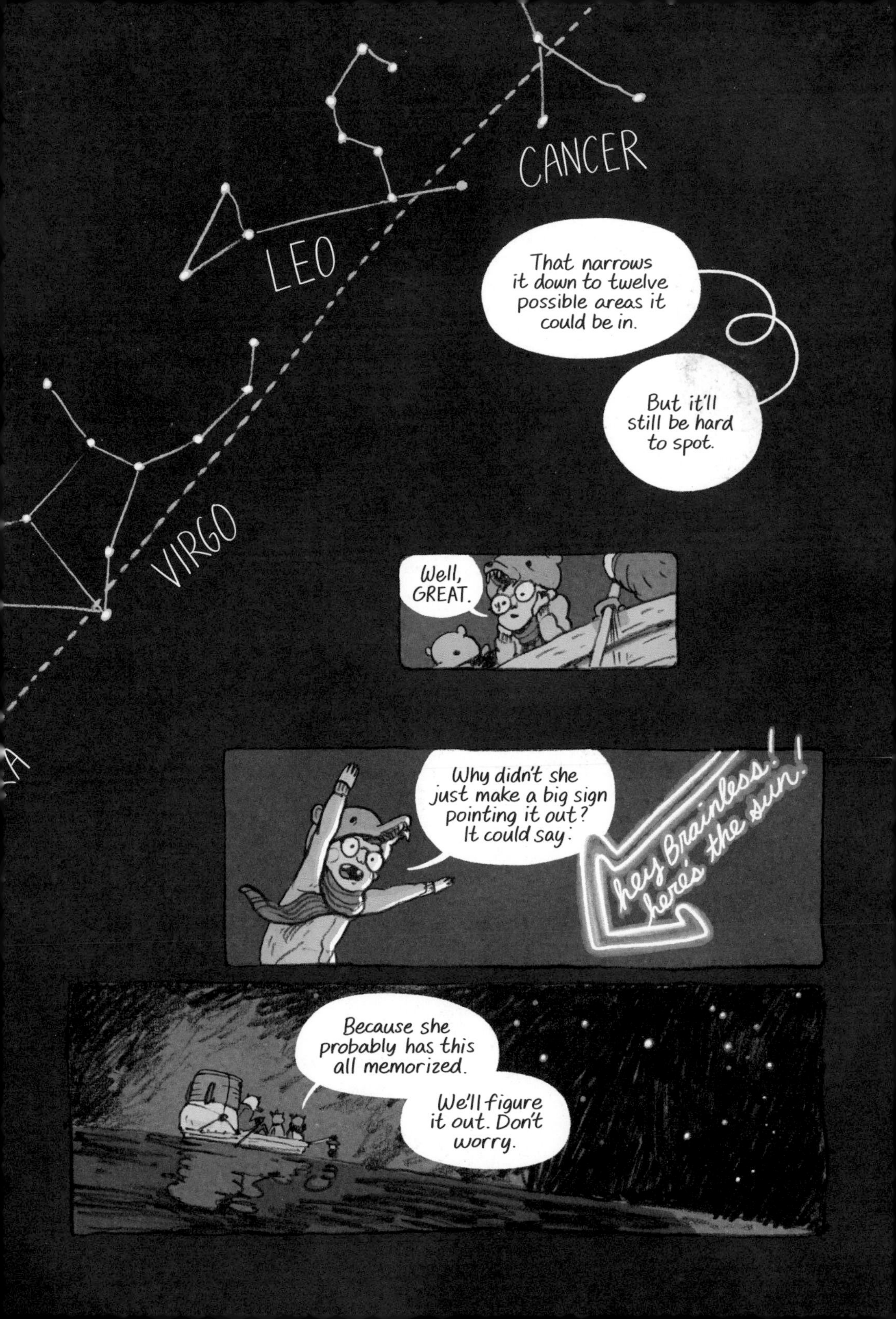
CANCER
LEO
VIRGO
That narrows it down to twelve possible areas it could be in.
But it'll still be hard to spot.
Well, GREAT.
Why didn't she just make a big sign pointing it out? It could say:
hey Brainless! here's the sun!
Because she probably has this all memorized.
We'll figure it out. Don't worry.

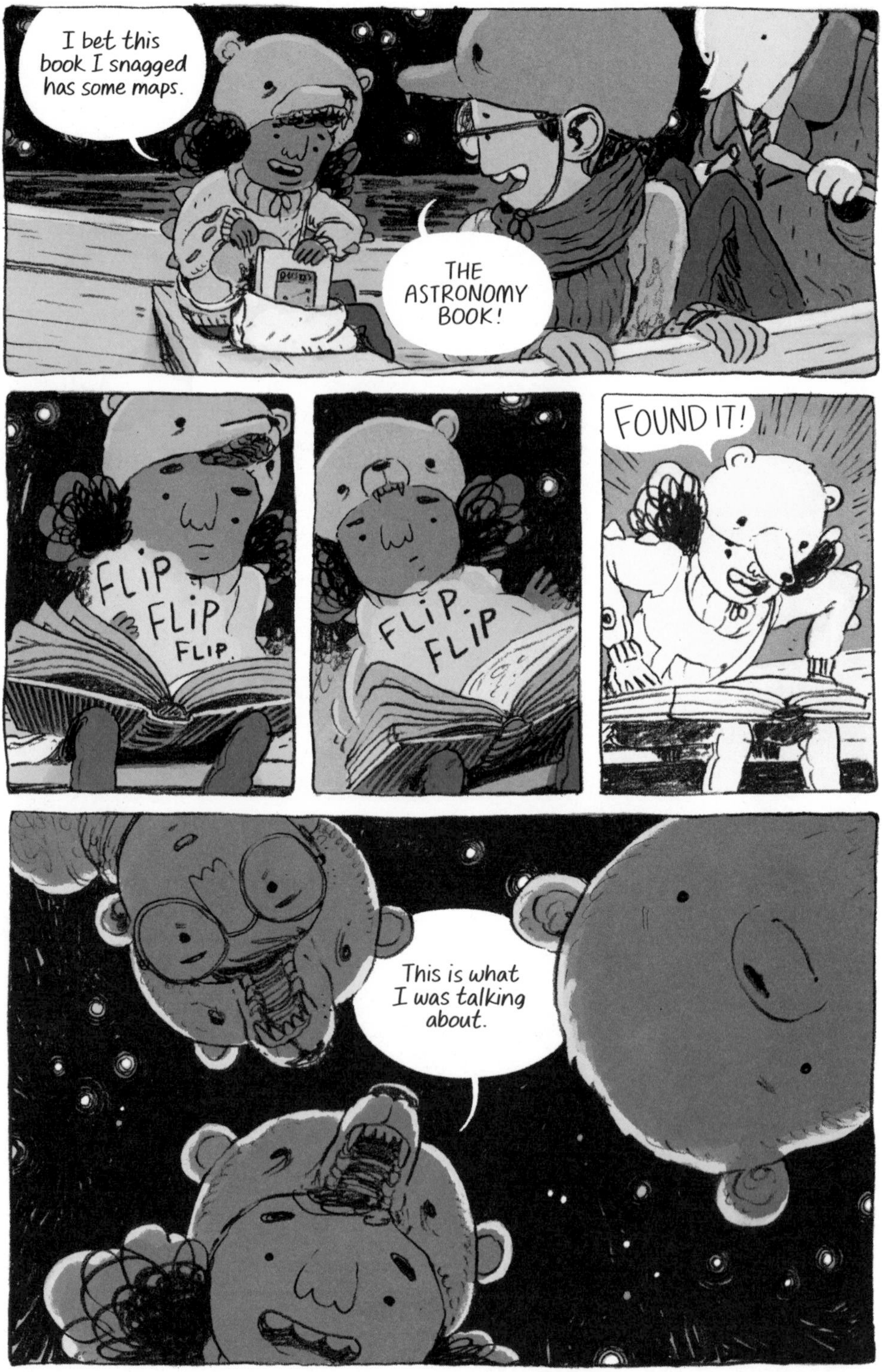
I bet this book I snagged has some maps.
THE ASTRONOMY BOOK!
FLIP FLIP FLIP
FLIP FLIP
FOUND IT!
This is what I was talking about.

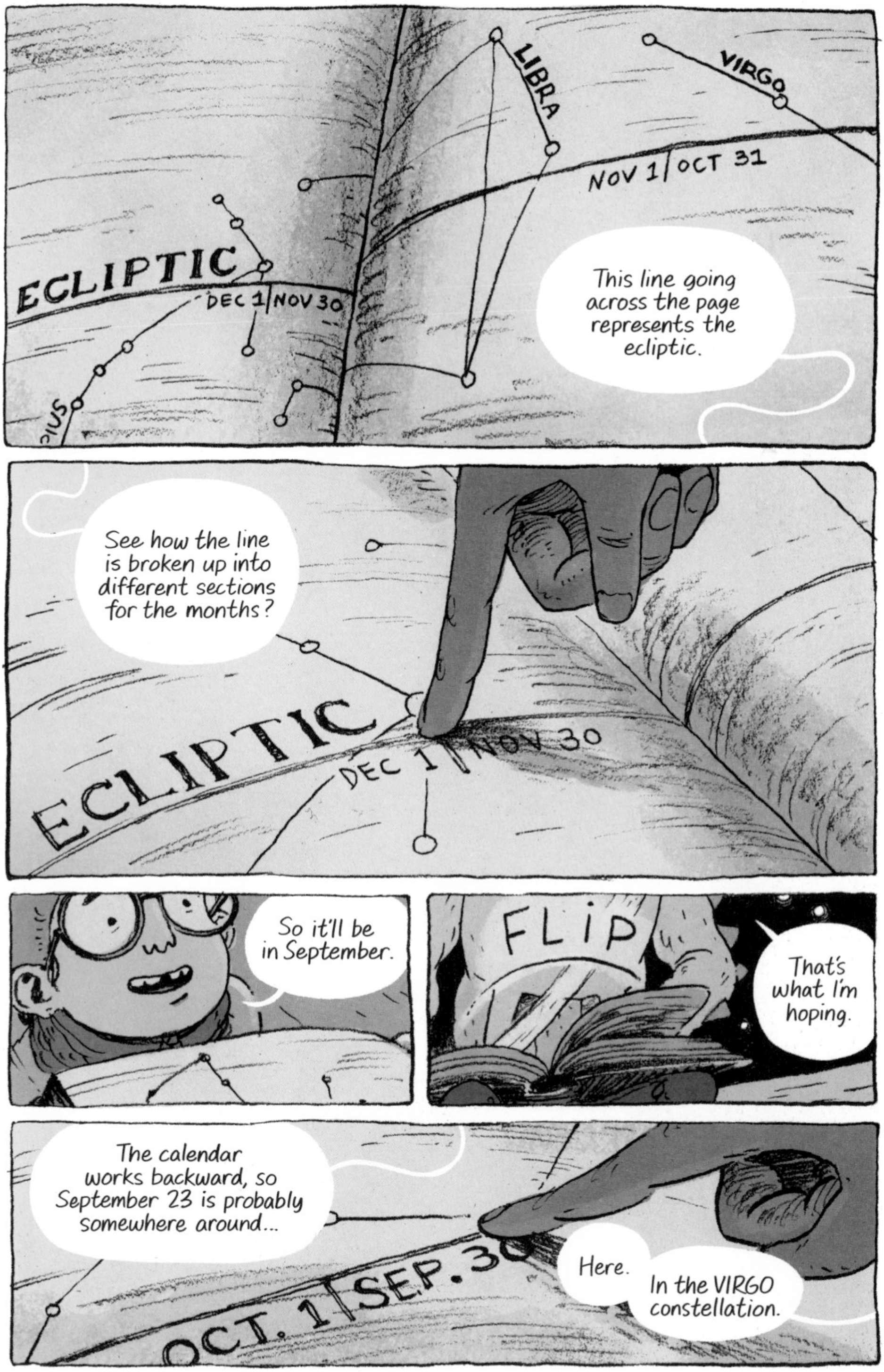
LIBRA
VIRGO
NOV 1 | OCT 31
ECLIPTIC
DEC 1 | NOV 30
This line going across the page represents the ecliptic.
See how the line is broken up into different sections for the months?
ECLIPTIC
DEC 1 | NOV 30
So it'll be in September.
FLIP
That's what I'm hoping.
The calendar works backward, so September 23 is probably somewhere around...
OCT. 1 | SEP. 30
Here.
In the VIRGO constellation.

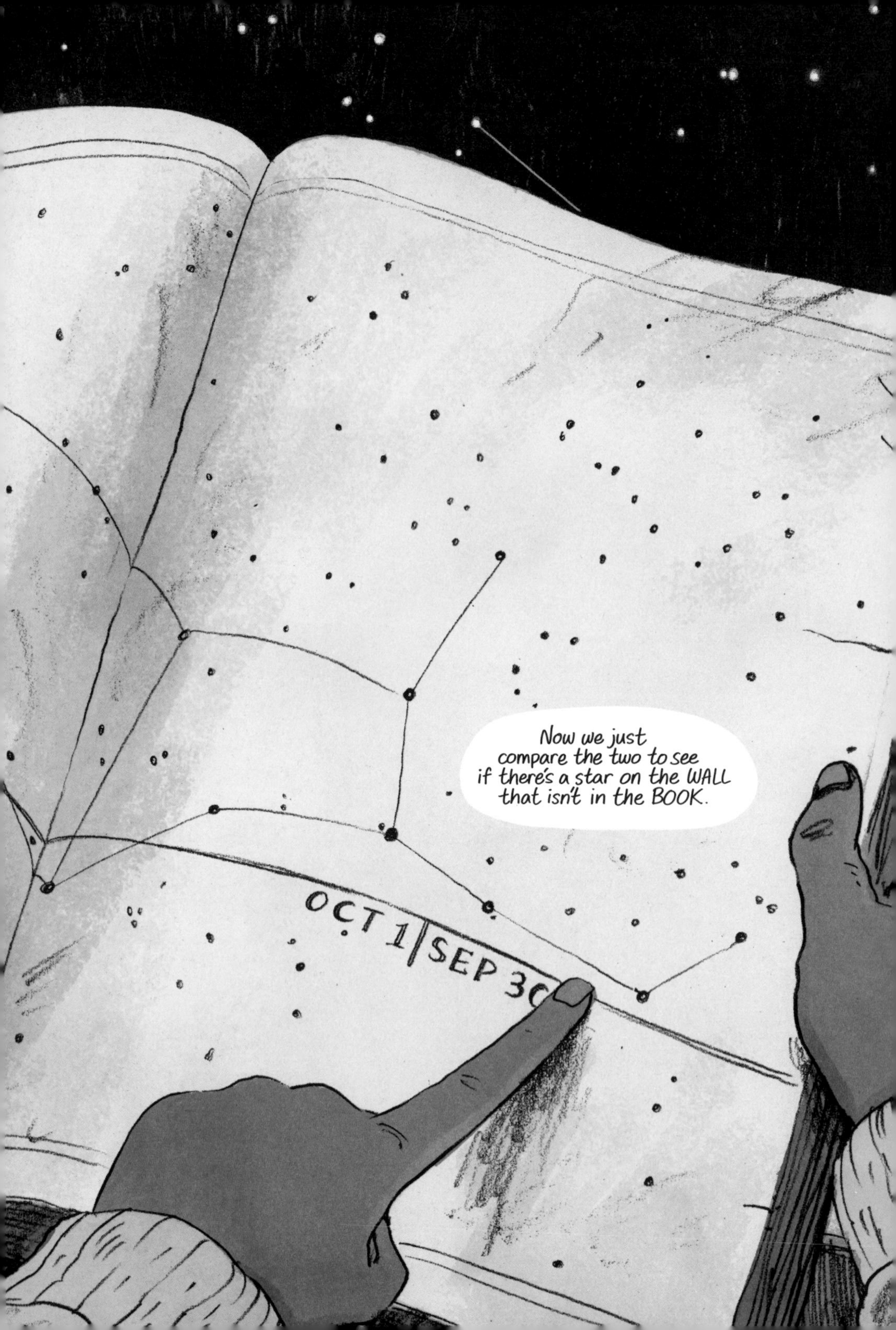

OCT 1
SEP 30
Now we just compare the two to see if there's a star on the WALL that isn't in the BOOK.

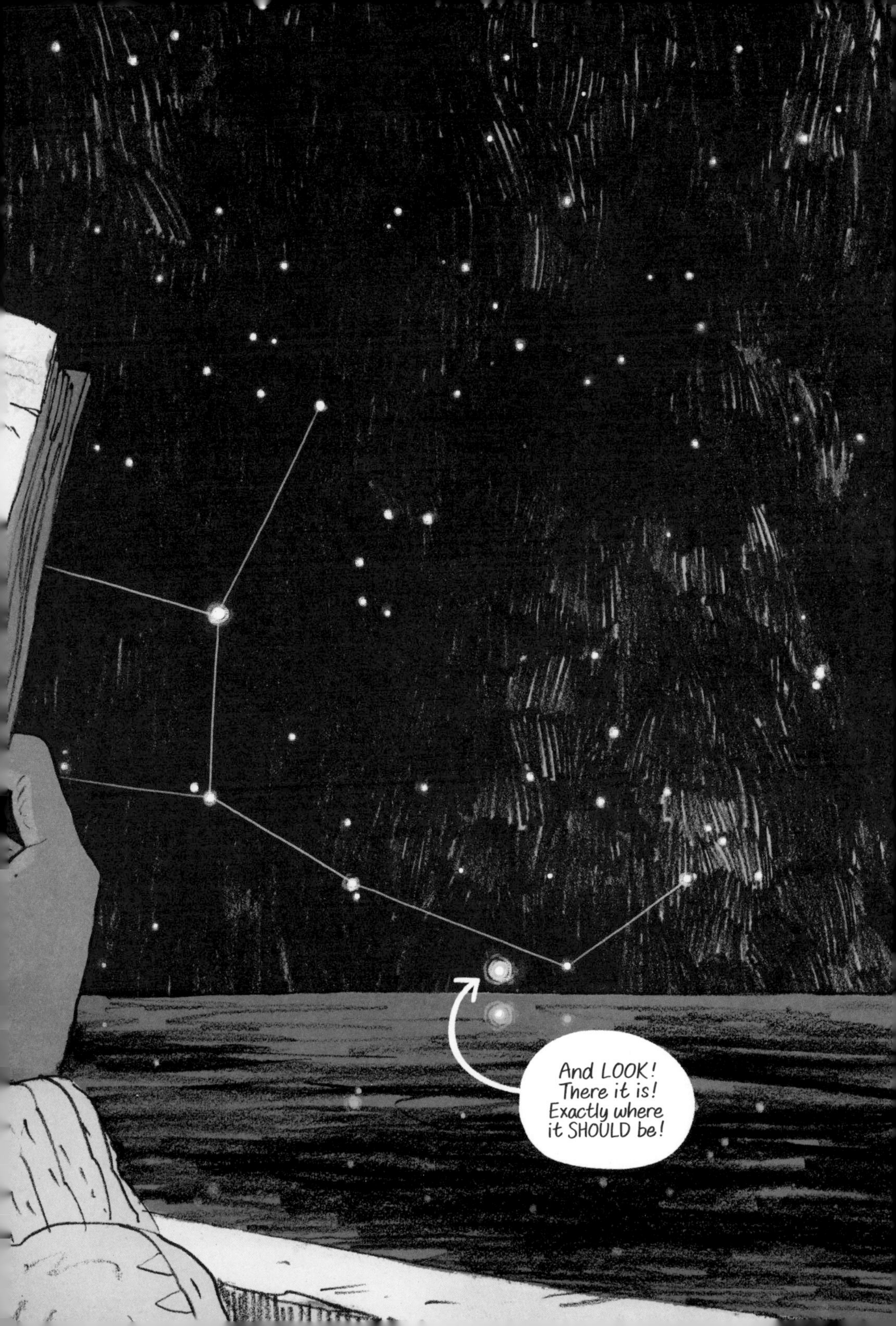
And LOOK! There it is! Exactly where it SHOULD be!

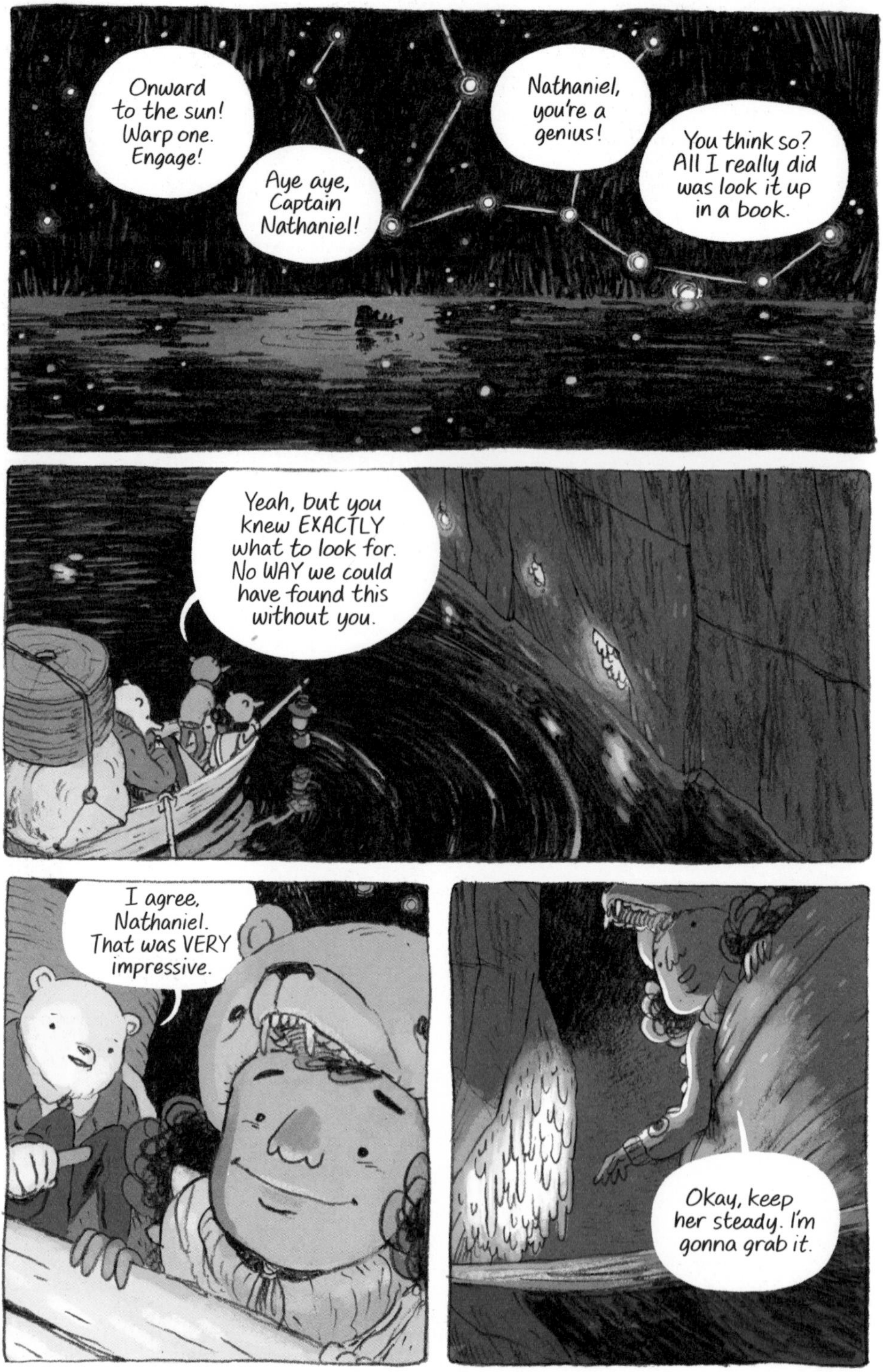

Onward to the sun! Warp one. Engage!
Aye aye, Captain Nathaniel!
Nathaniel, you're a genius!
You think so? All I really did was look it up in a book.
Yeah, but you knew EXACTLY what to look for. No WAY we could have found this without you.
I agree, Nathaniel. That was VERY impressive.
Okay, keep her steady. I'm gonna grab it.

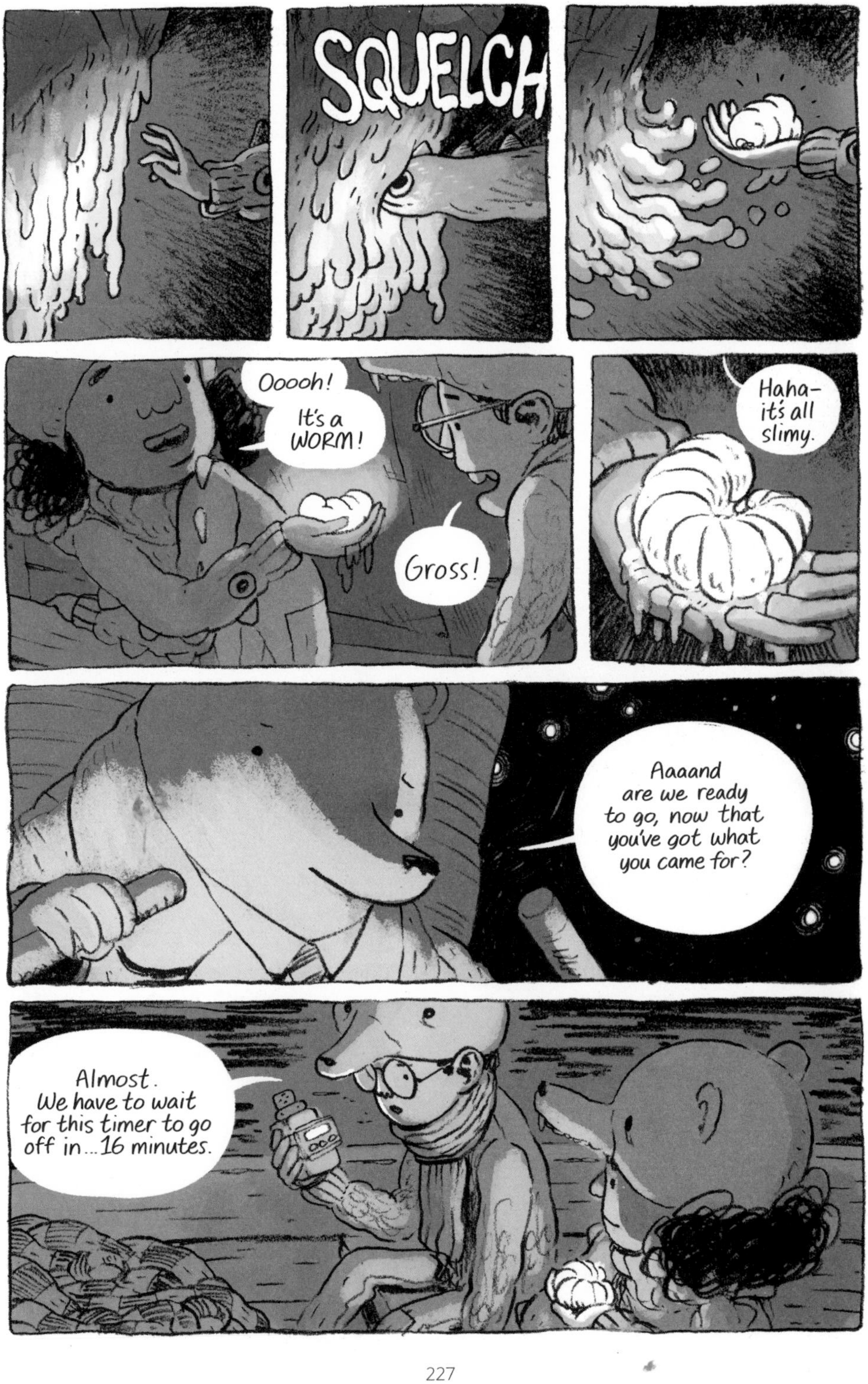
SQUELCH
Ooooh!
It's a WORM!
Gross!
Haha- it's all slimy.
Aaaand are we ready to go, now that you've got what you came for?
Almost. We have to wait for this timer to go off in... 16 minutes.

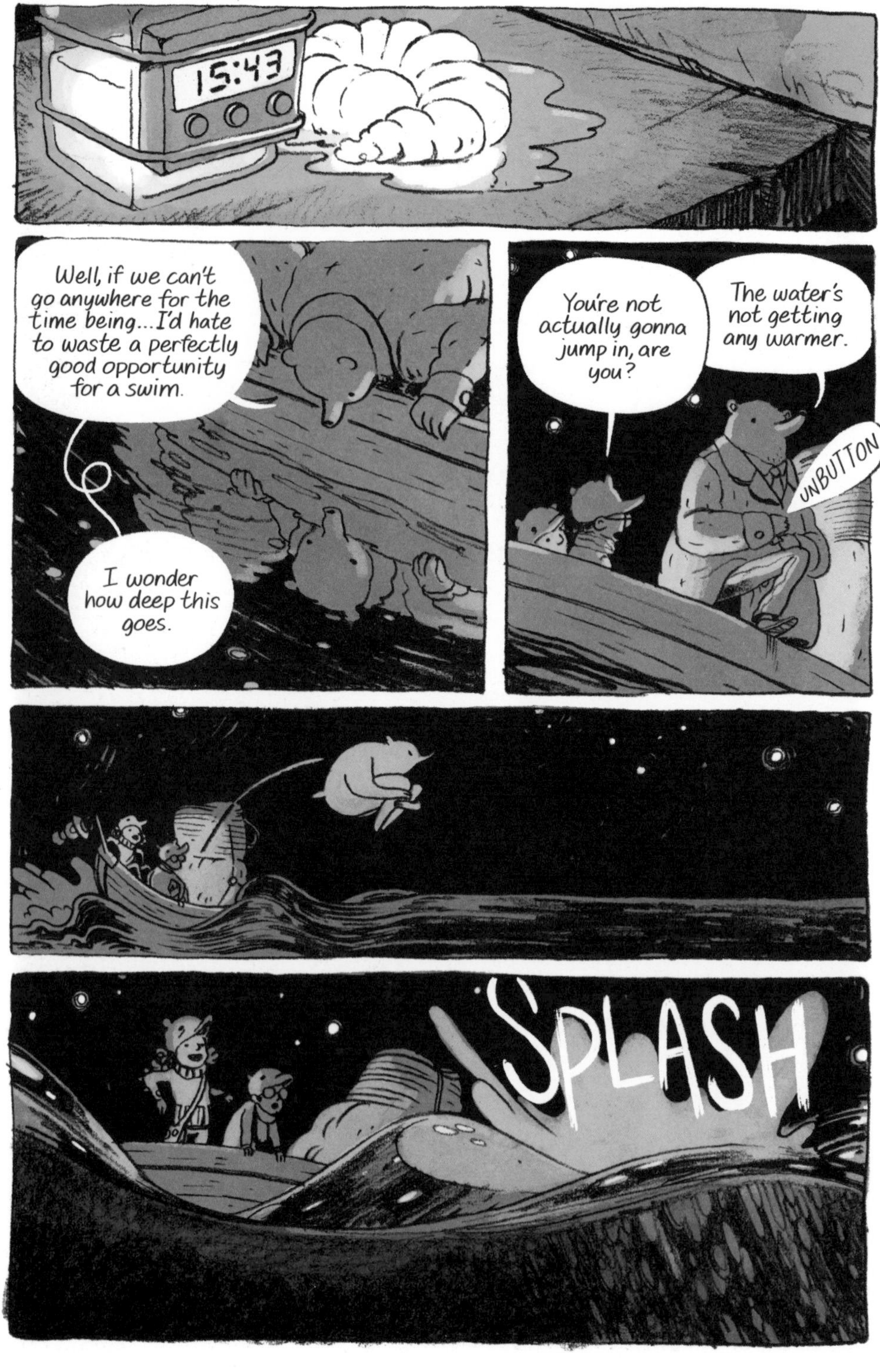
15:43
Well, if we can't go anywhere for the time being...I'd hate to waste a perfectly good opportunity for a swim.
I wonder how deep this goes.
You're not actually gonna jump in, are you?
The water's not getting any warmer.
UNBUTTON
SPLASH

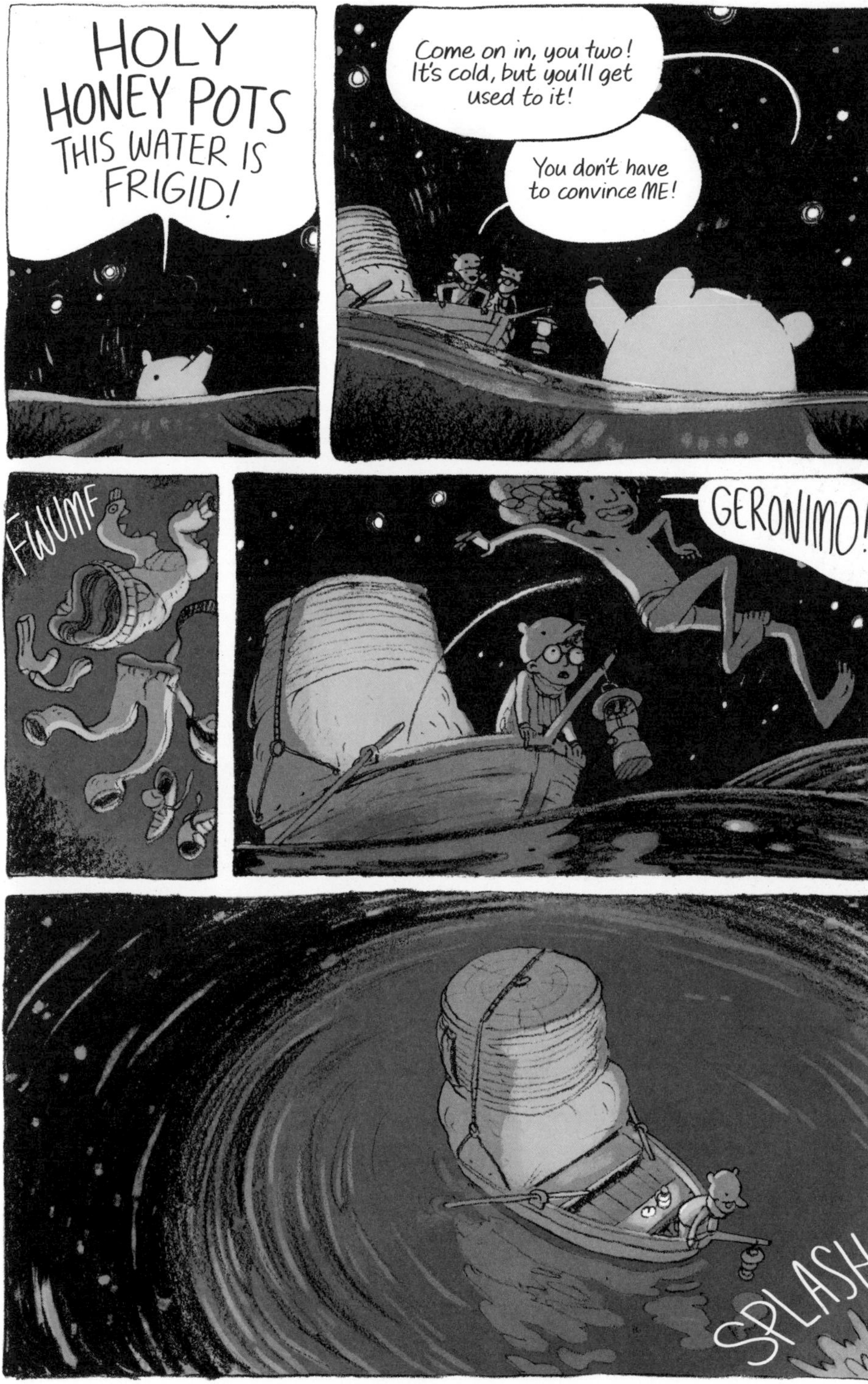
HOLY HONEY POTS THIS WATER IS FRIGID!
Come on in, you two! It's cold, but you'll get used to it!
You don't have to convince ME!
FWUMF
GERONIMO!
SPLASH

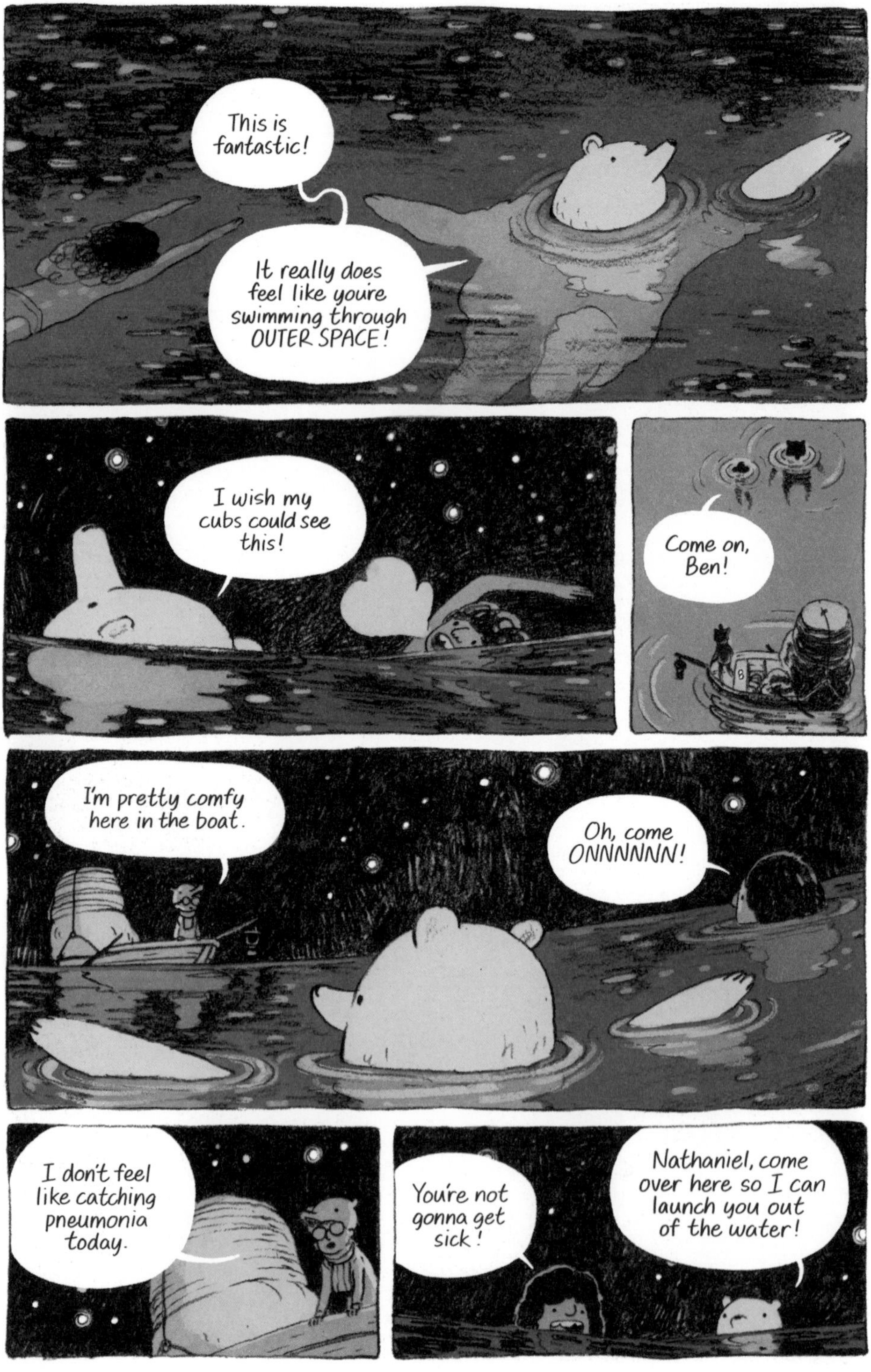
This is fantastic!
It really does feel like youre swimming through OUTER SPACE!
I wish my cubs could see this!
Come on, Ben!
I'm pretty comfy here in the boat.
Oh, come ONNNNNN!
I don't feel like catching pneumonia today.
You're not gonna get sick!
Nathaniel, come over here so I can launch you out of the water!

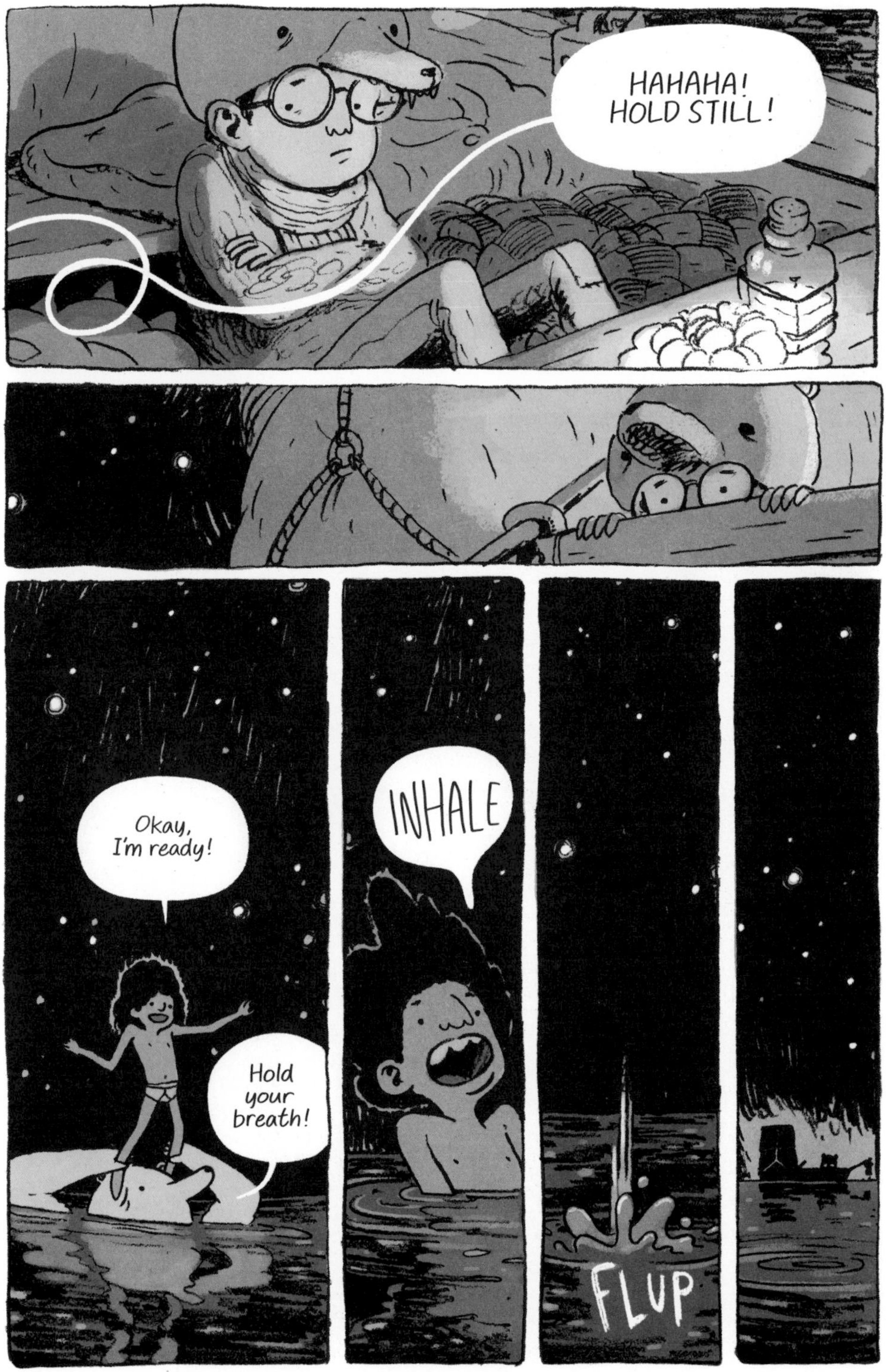
HAHAHA! HOLD STILL!
Okay, I'm ready!
Hold your breath!
INHALE
FLUP

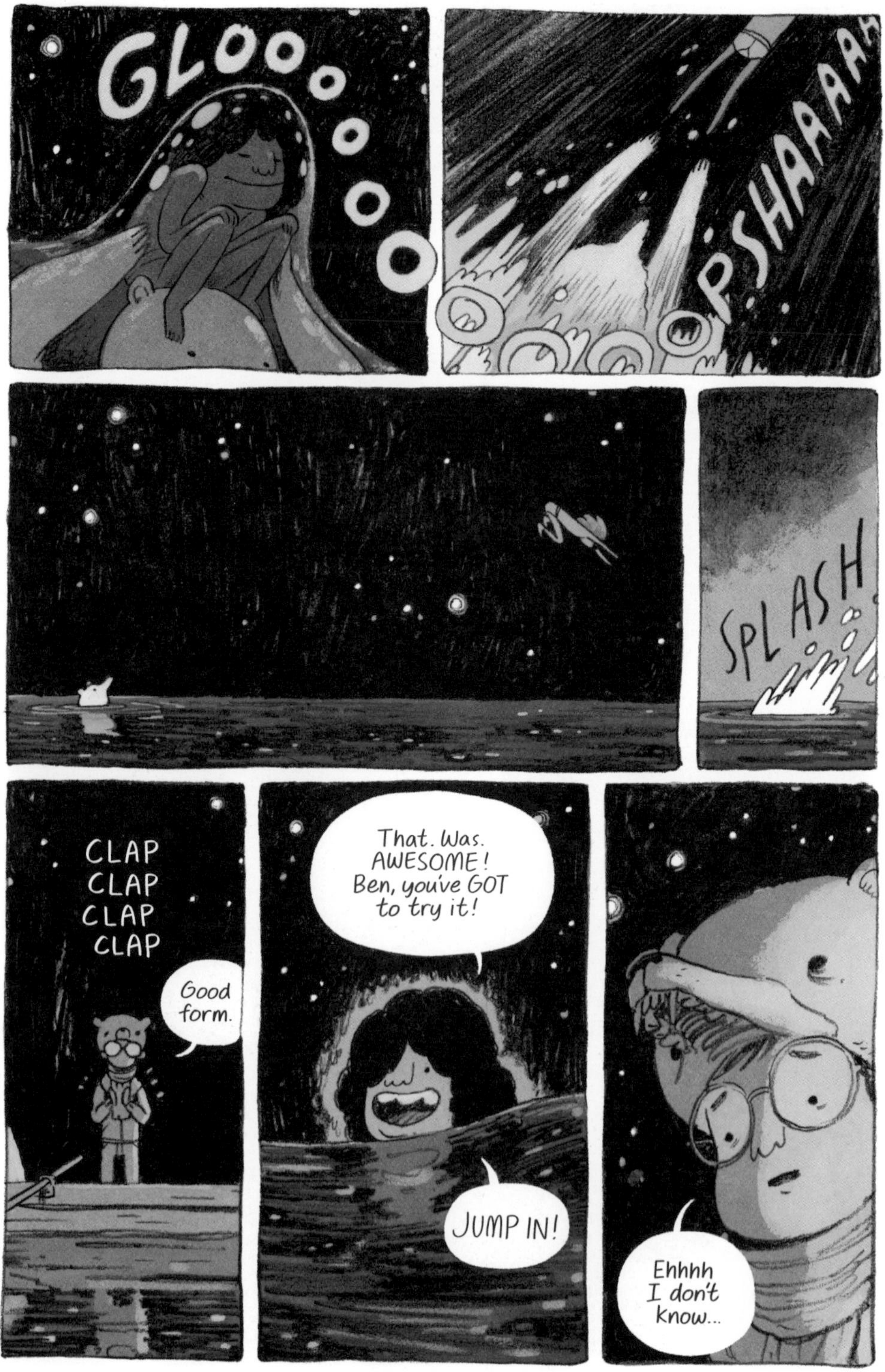
GLOOOOOOO
PSHAAAAA
SPLASH
CLAP
CLAP
CLAP
CLAP
Good form.
That. Was. AWESOME! Ben, you've GOT to try it!
JUMP IN!
Ehhhh I don't know...

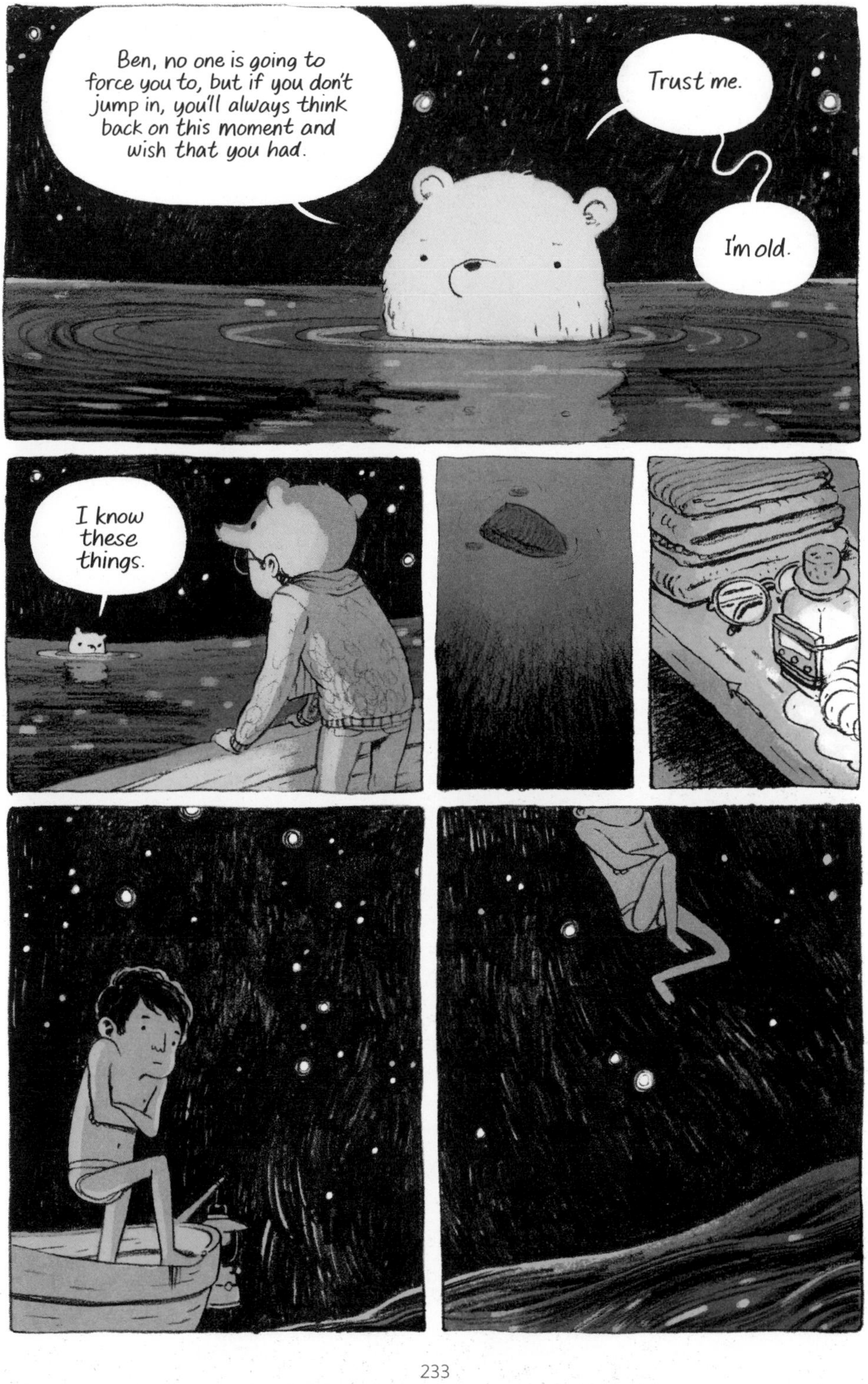
Ben, no one is going to force you to, but if you don't jump in, you'll always think back on this moment and wish that you had.
Trust me.
I'm old.
I know these things.

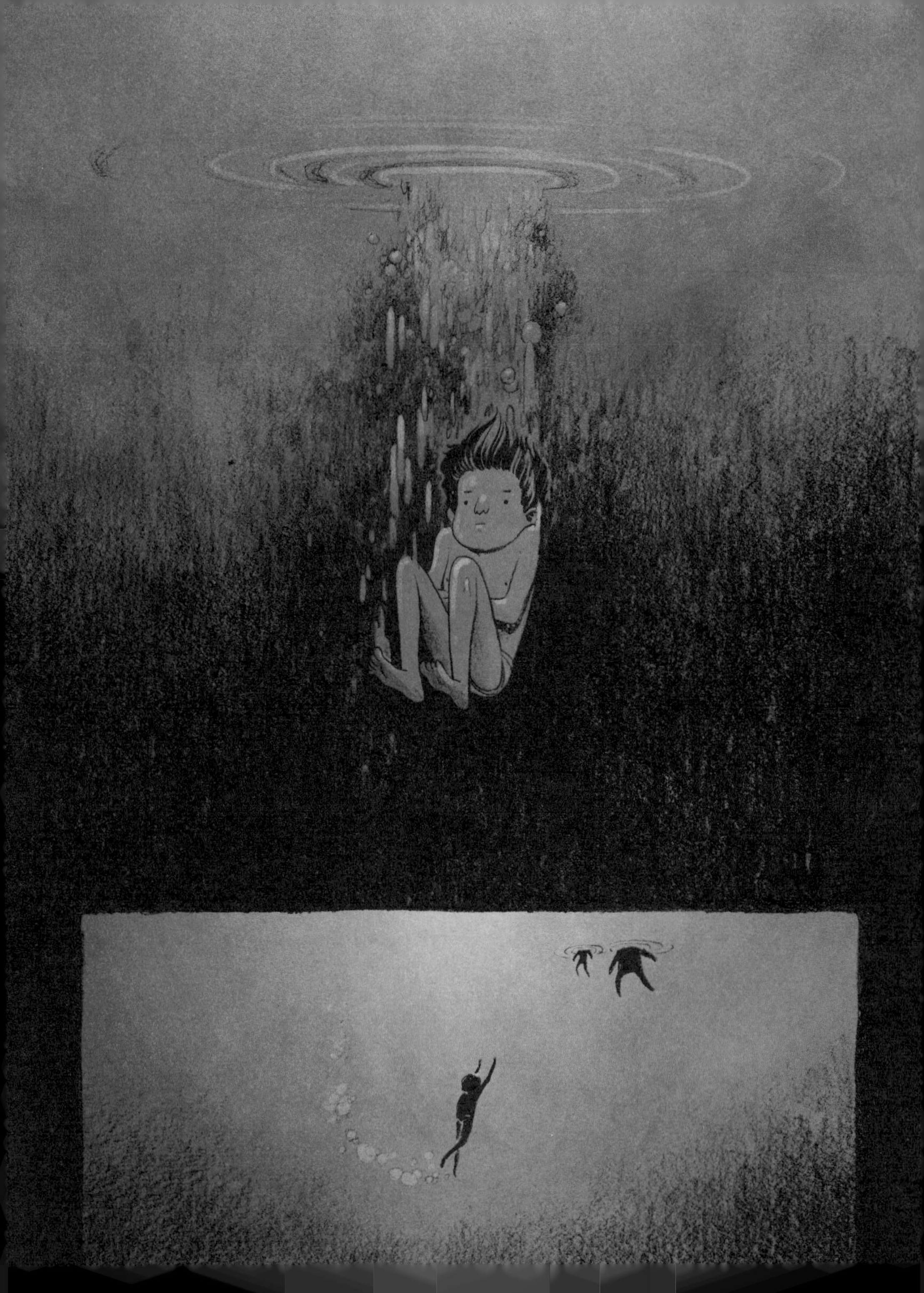

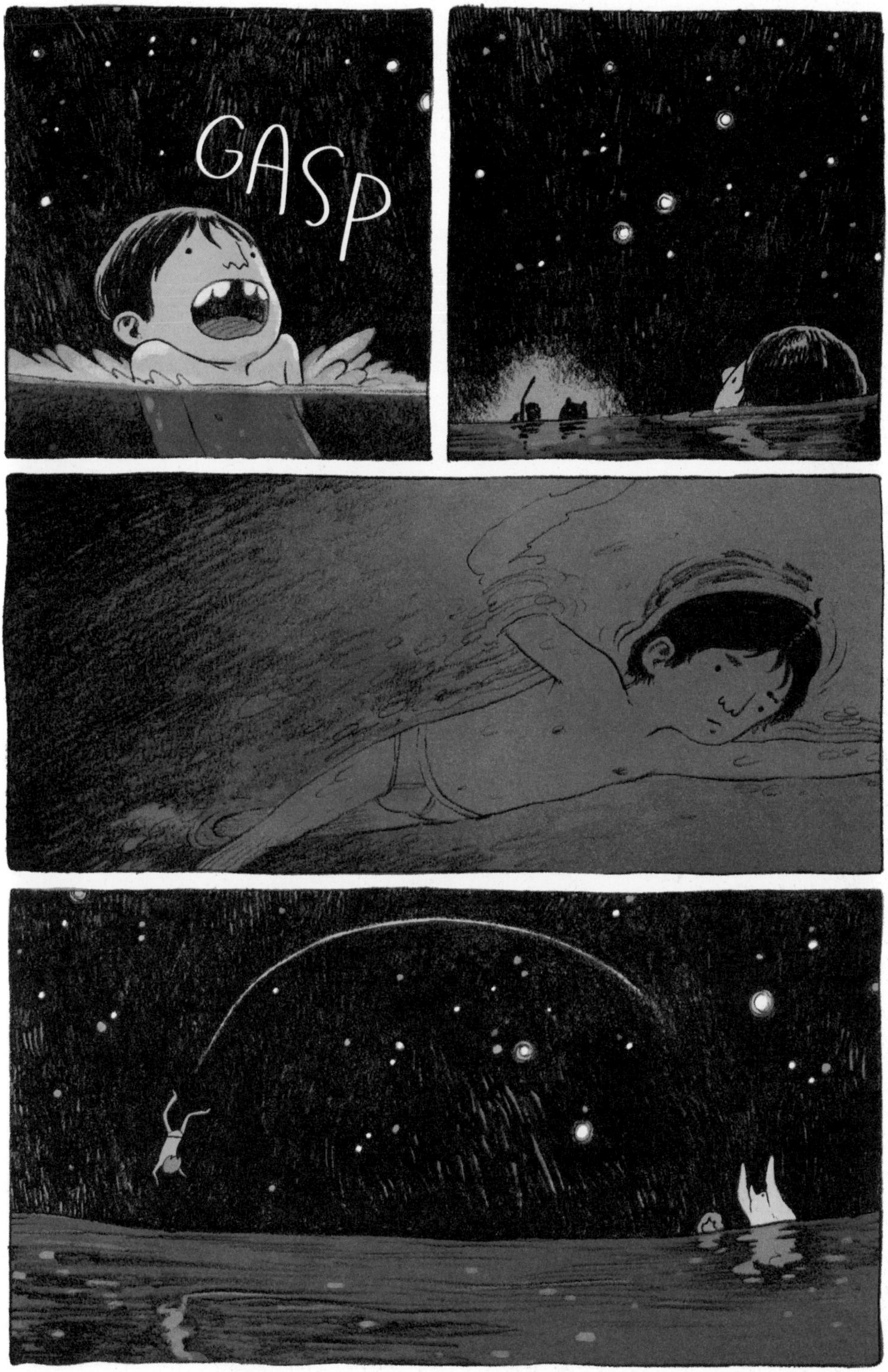
GASP

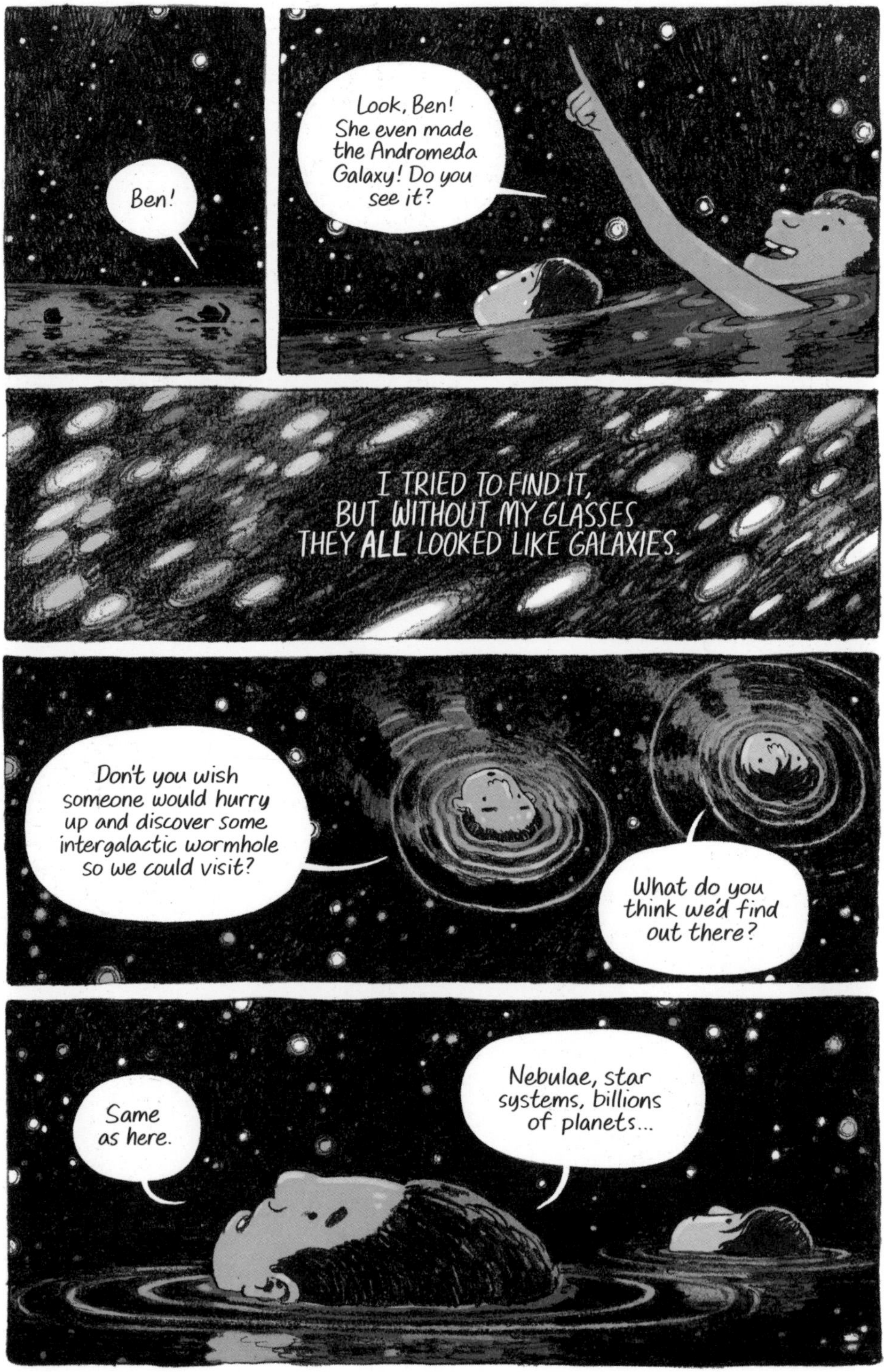
Ben!
Look, Ben! She even made the Andromeda Galaxy! Do you see it?
I TRIED TO FIND IT, BUT WITHOUT MY GLASSES THEY ALL LOOKED LIKE GALAXIES.
Don't you wish someone would hurry up and discover some intergalactic wormhole so we could visit?
What do you think we'd find out there?
Nebulae, star systems, billions of planets...
Same as here.

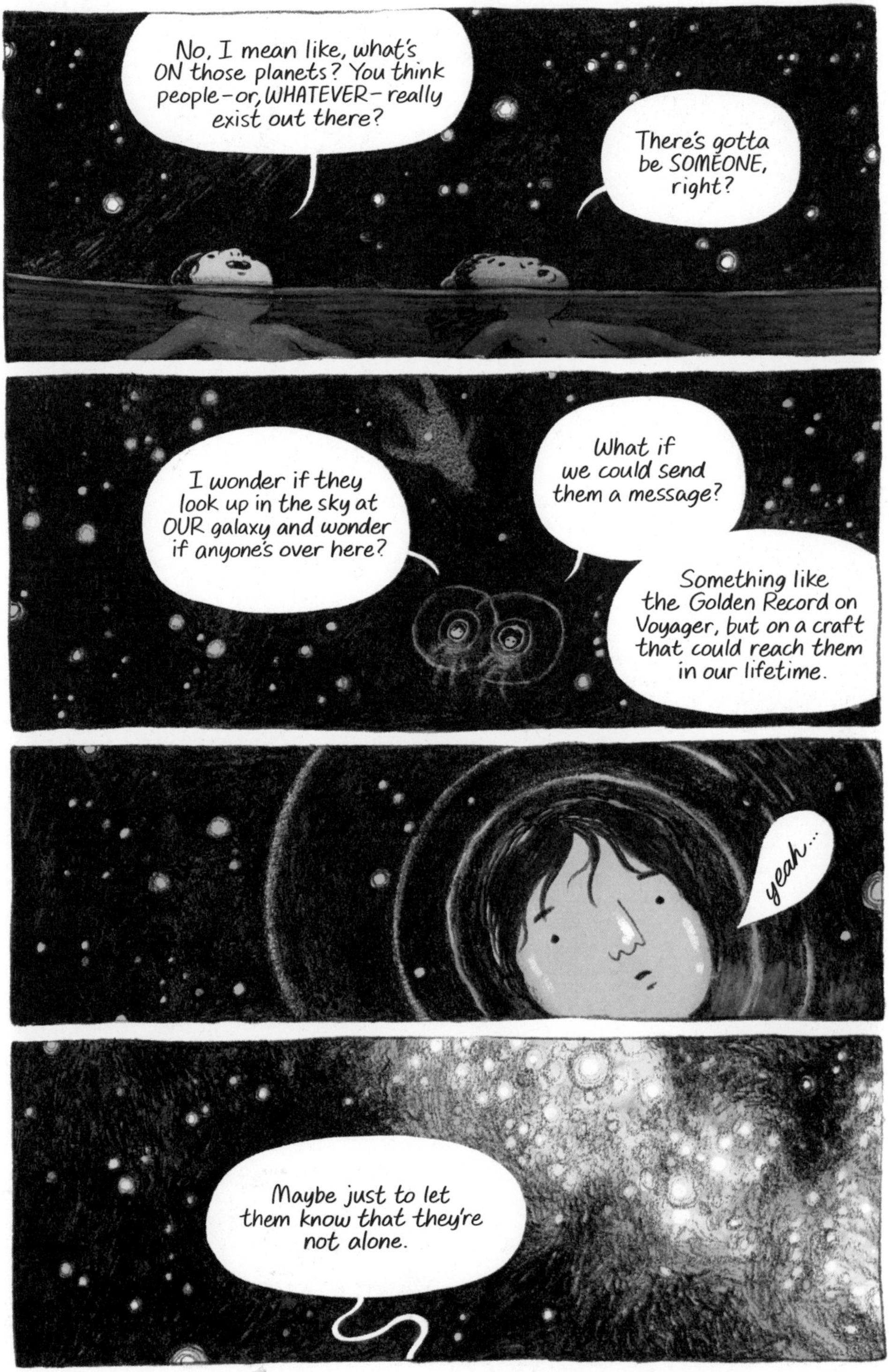
No, I mean like, what's ON those planets? You think people—or, WHATEVER—really exist out there?
There's gotta be SOMEONE, right?
I wonder if they look up in the sky at OUR galaxy and wonder if anyone's over here?
What if we could send them a message?
Something like the Golden Record on Voyager, but on a craft that could reach them in our lifetime.
yeah...
Maybe just to let them know that they're not alone.

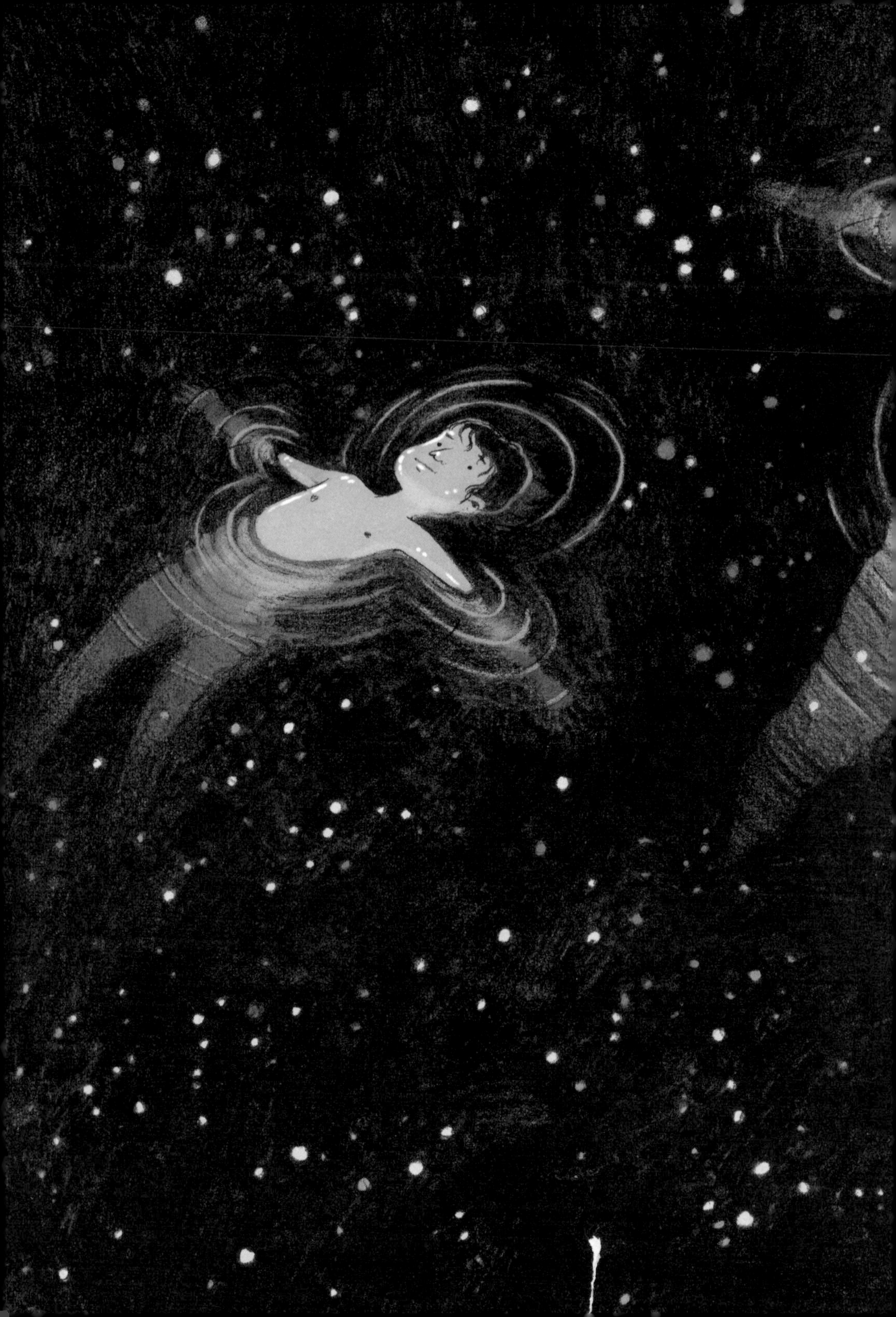

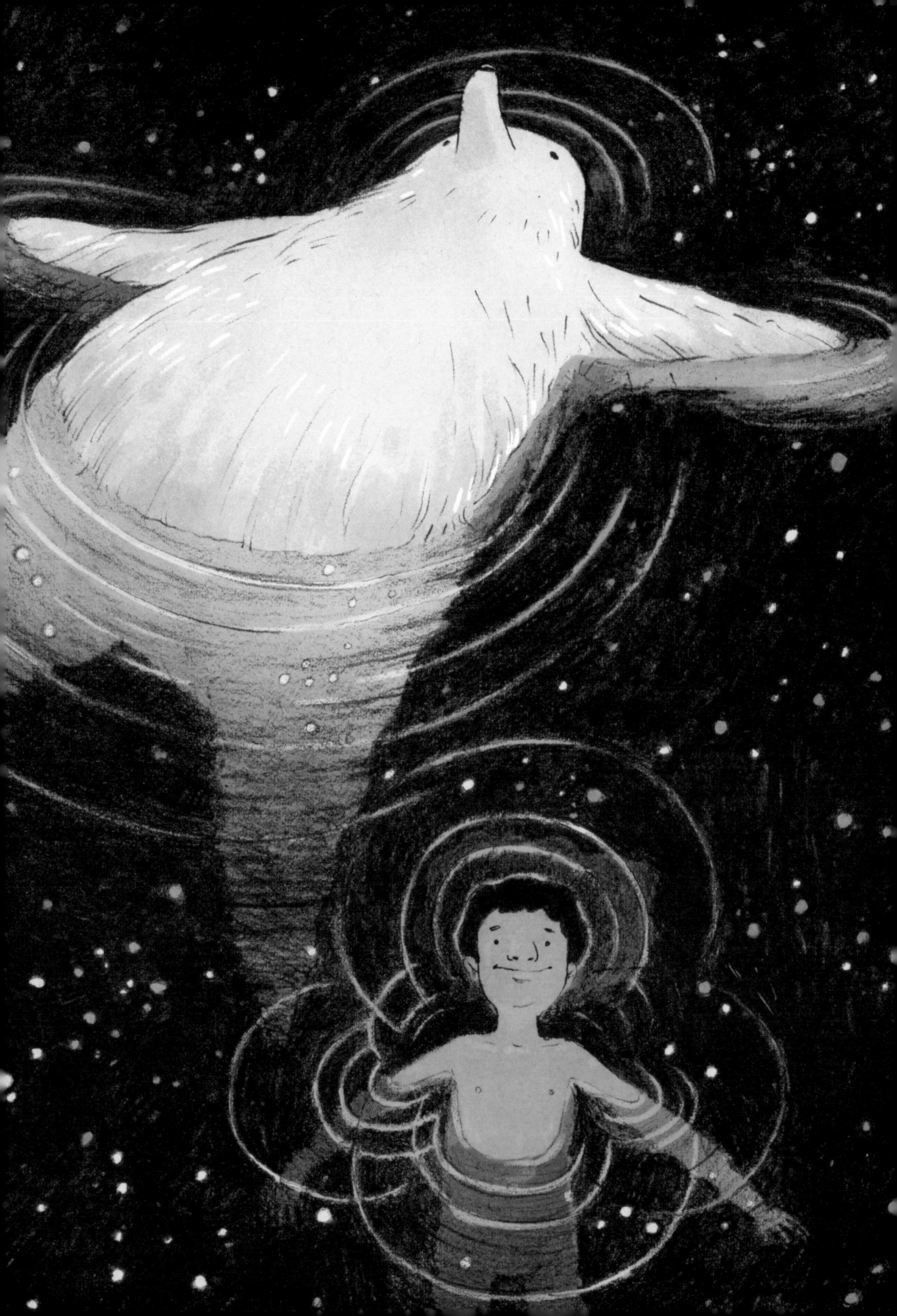

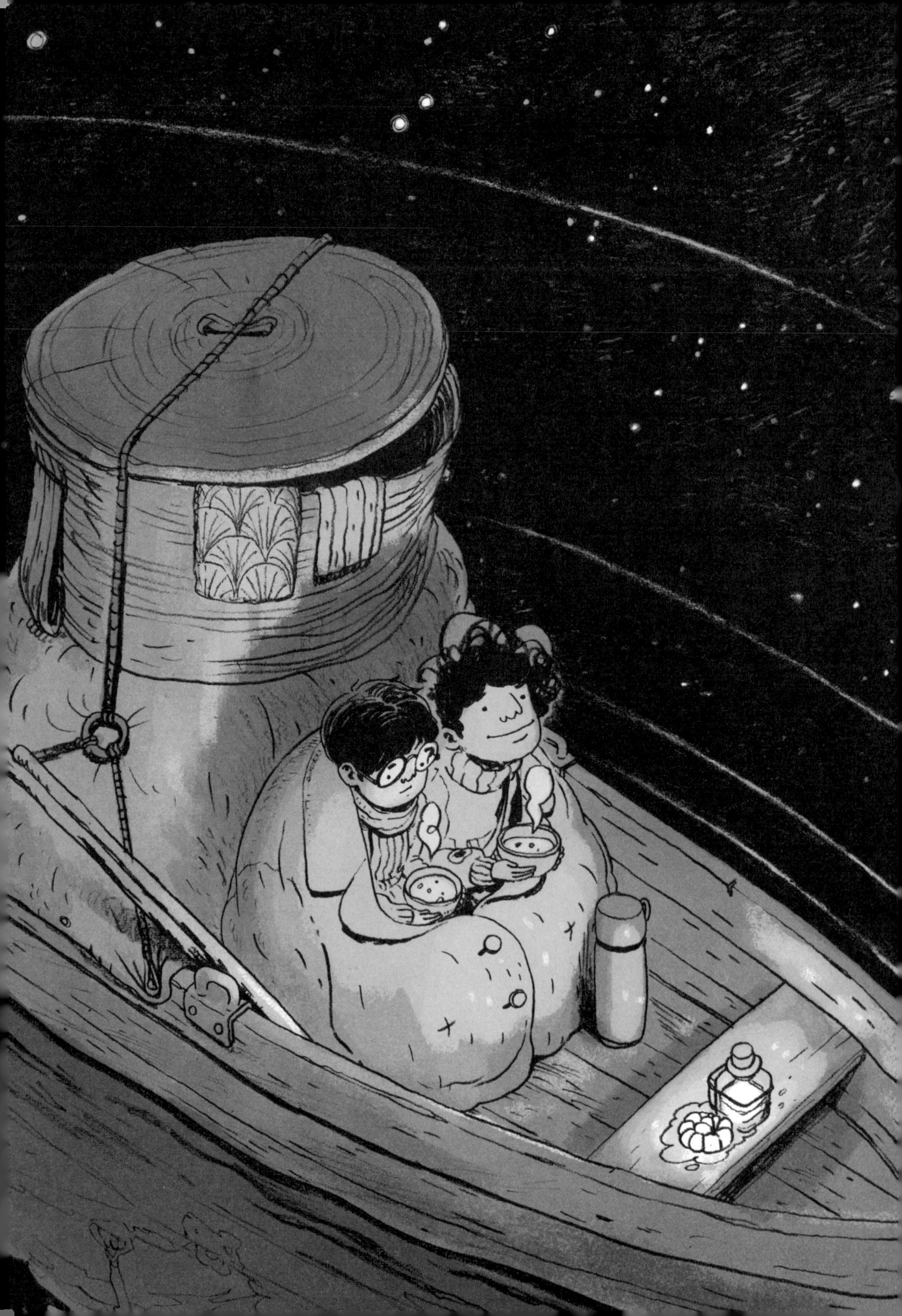

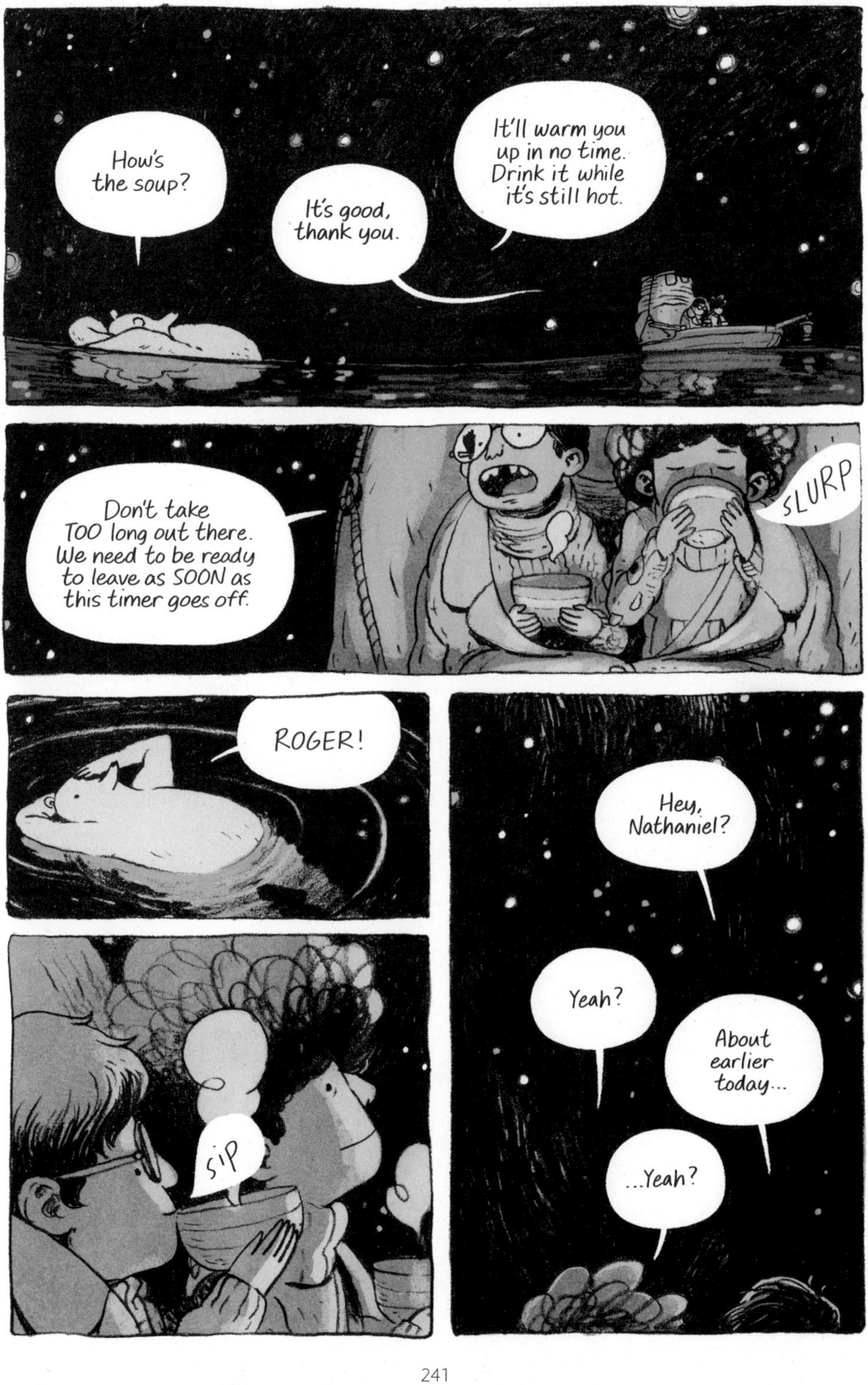
How's the soup?
It's good, thank you.
It'll warm you up in no time. Drink it while it's still hot.
Don't take TOO long out there. We need to be ready to leave as SOON as this timer goes off.
SLURP
ROGER!
sip
Hey, Nathaniel?
Yeah?
About earlier today...
...Yeah?

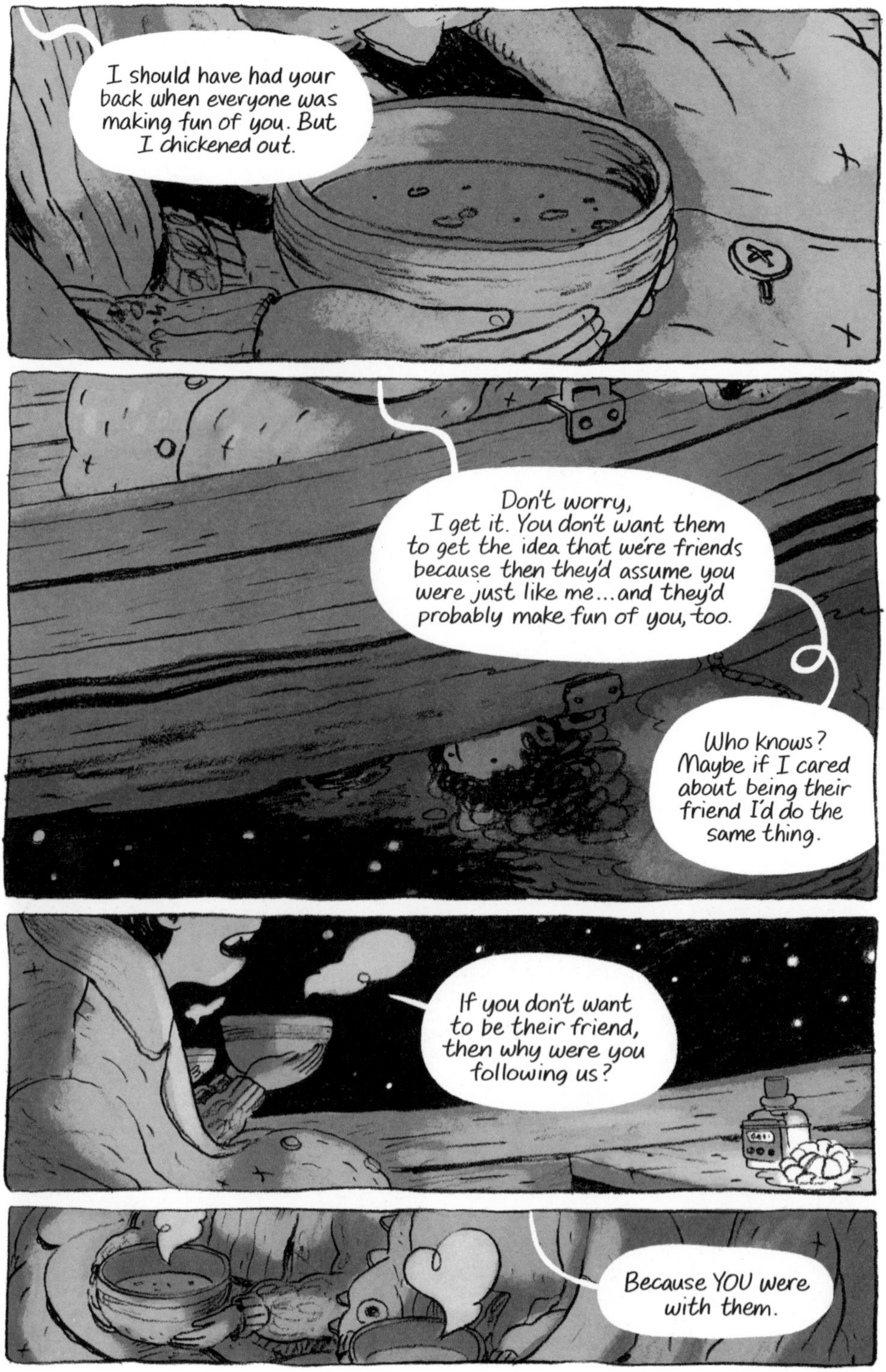
I should have had your back when everyone was making fun of you. But I chickened out.
Don't worry, I get it. You don't want them to get the idea that we're friends because then they'd assume you were just like me... and they'd probably make fun of you, too.
Who knows? Maybe if I cared about being their friend I'd do the same thing.
If you don't want to be their friend, then why were you following us?
Because YOU were with them.

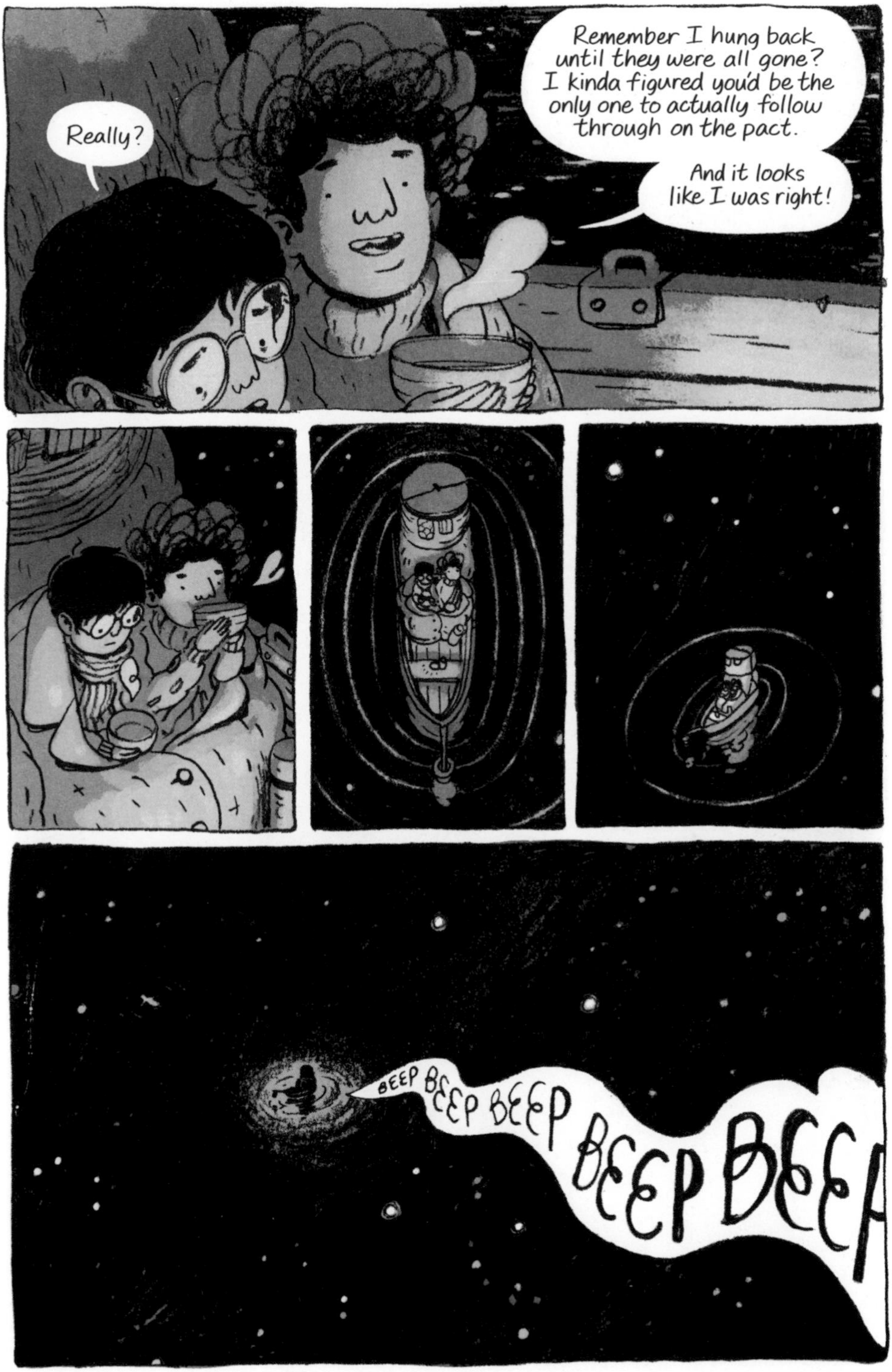
Remember I hung back until they were all gone? I kinda figured you'd be the only one to actually follow through on the pact.
Really?
And it looks like I was right!
BEEP BEEP BEEP BEEP BEEP

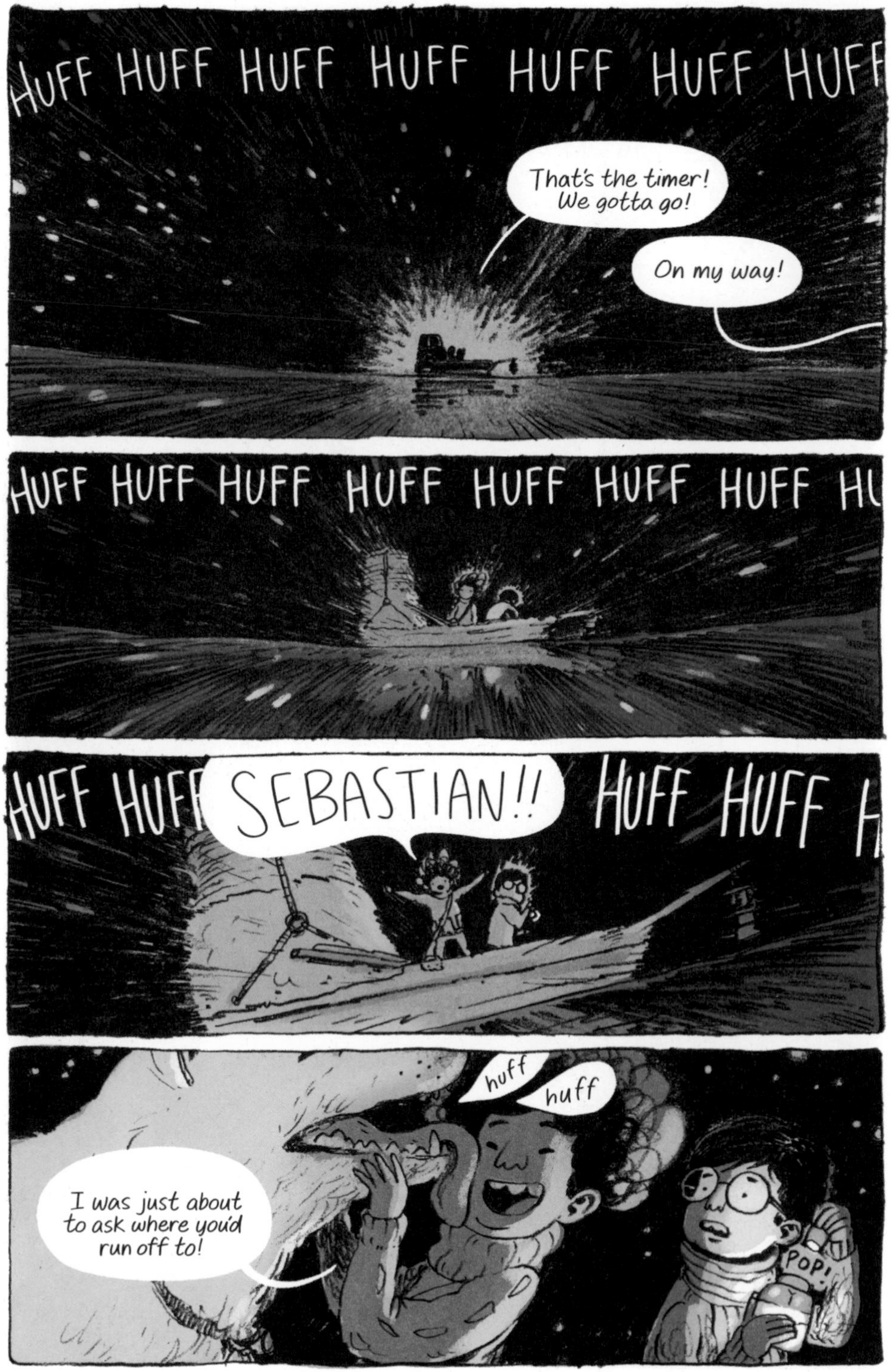
HUFF HUFF HUFF HUFF HUFF HUFF HUFF
That's the timer! We gotta go!
On my way!
HUFF HUFF HUFF HUFF HUFF HUFF HUFF
HUFF HUFF
SEBASTIAN!!
HUFF HUFF
huff
huff
I was just about to ask where you'd run off to!
POP!

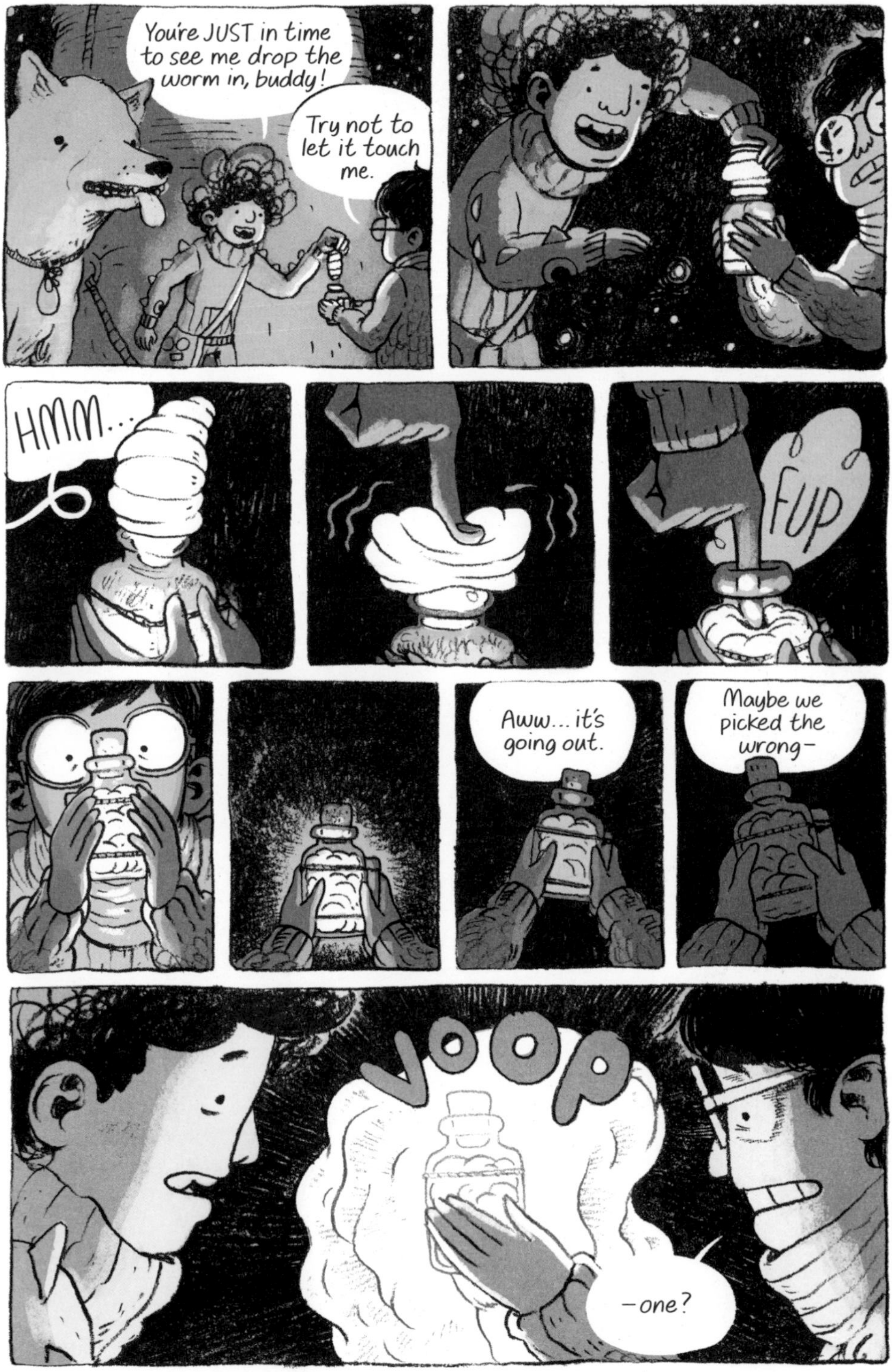
You're JUST in time to see me drop the worm in, buddy!
Try not to let it touch me.
HMM...
FUP
Aww... it's going out.
Maybe we picked the wrong-
VOOP
-one?

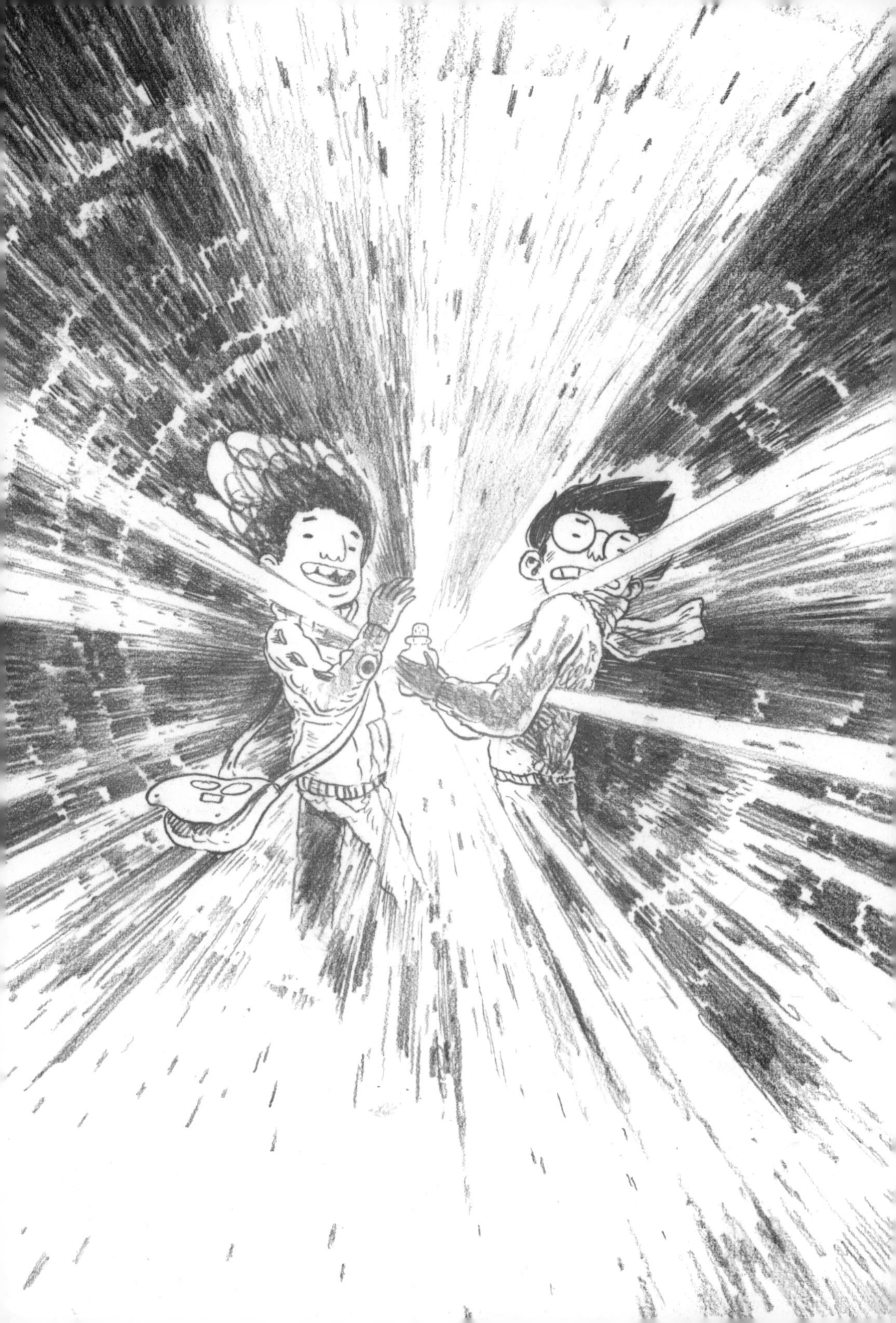

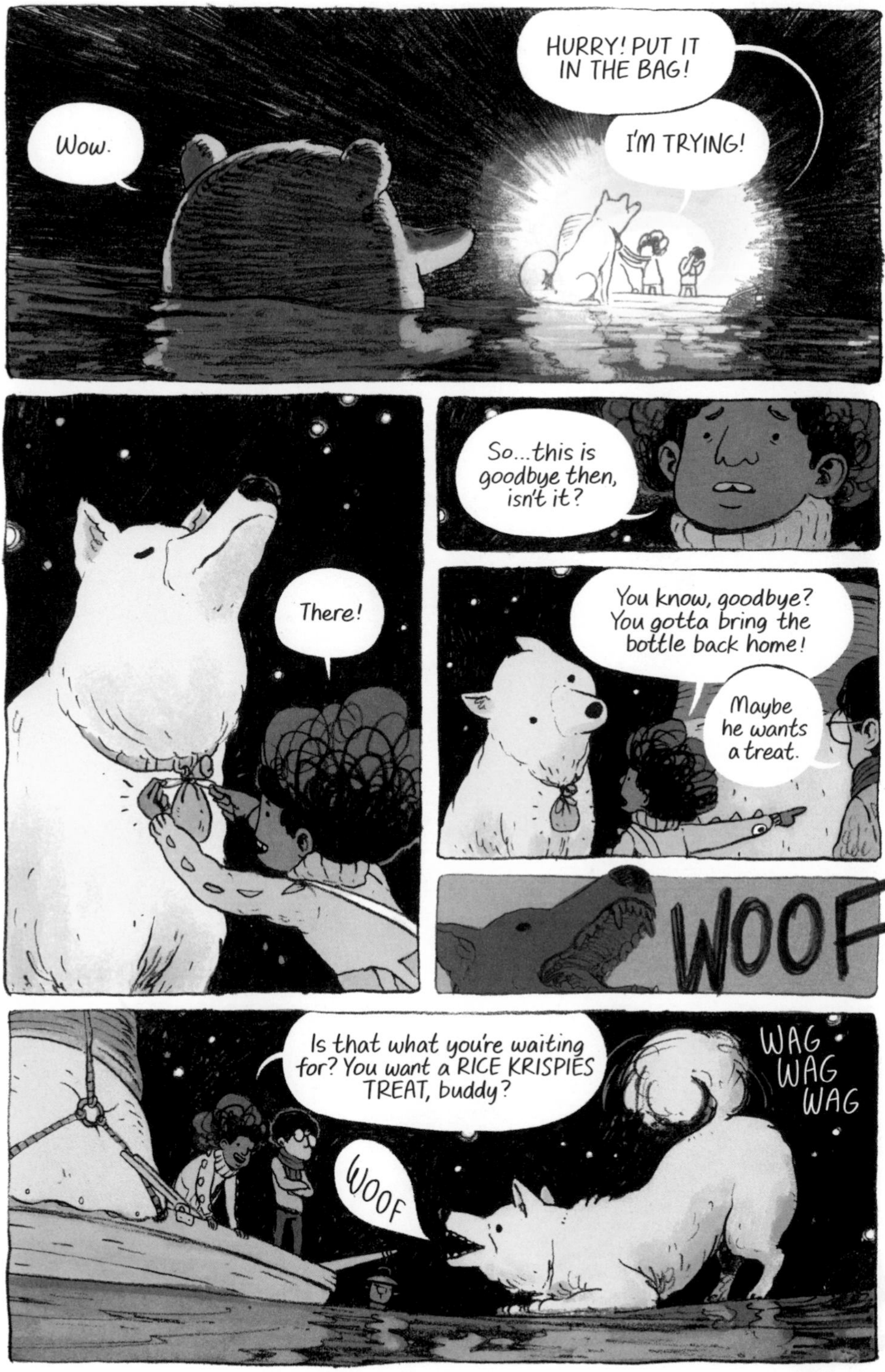
HURRY! PUT IT IN THE BAG!
Wow.
I'M TRYING!
There!
So...this is goodbye then, isn't it?
You know, goodbye? You gotta bring the bottle back home!
Maybe he wants a treat.
WOOF
Is that what you're waiting for? You want a RICE KRISPIES TREAT, buddy?
WAG WAG WAG
WOOF

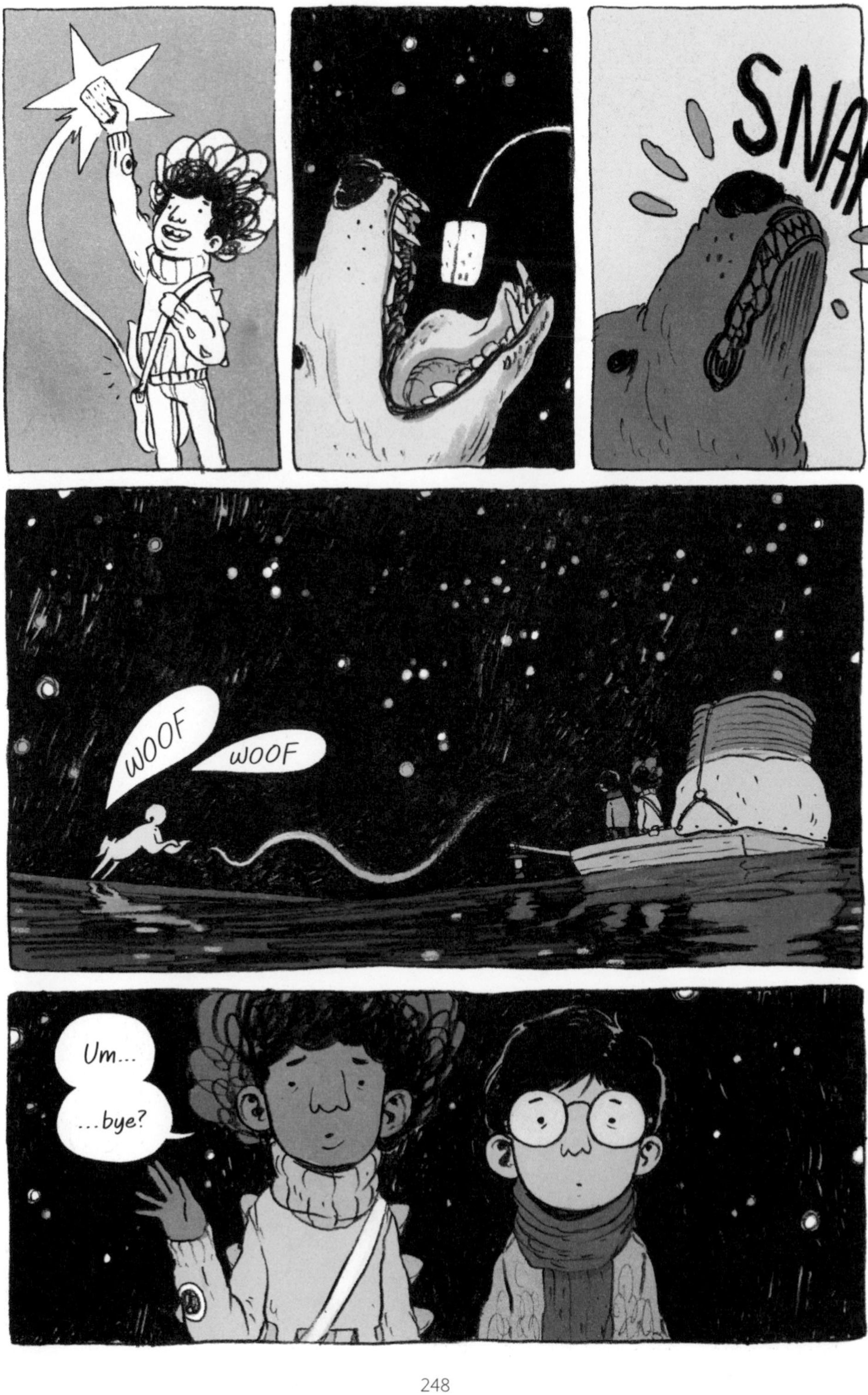
SNAP
WOOF
WOOF
Um...
...bye?

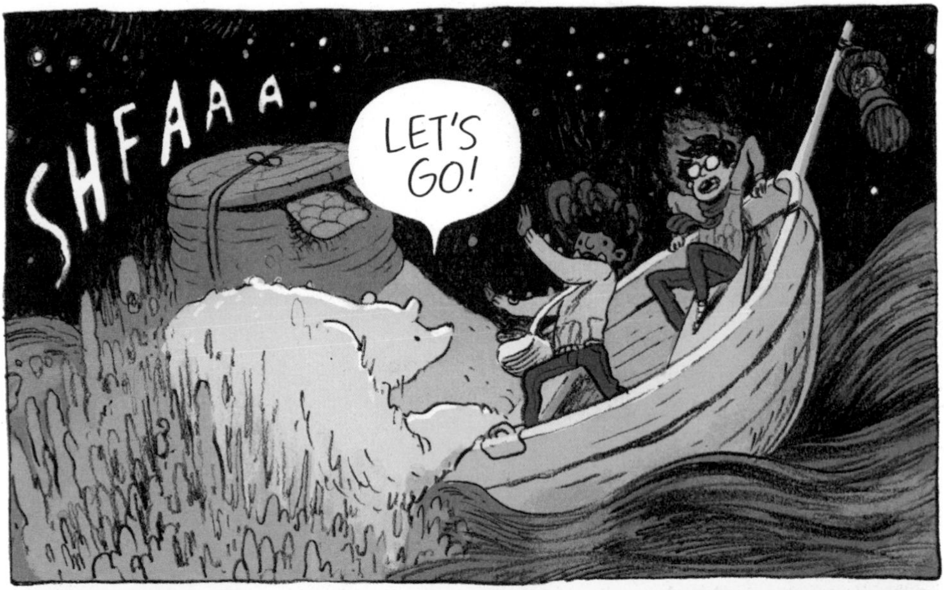
SHFAAA
LET'S GO!

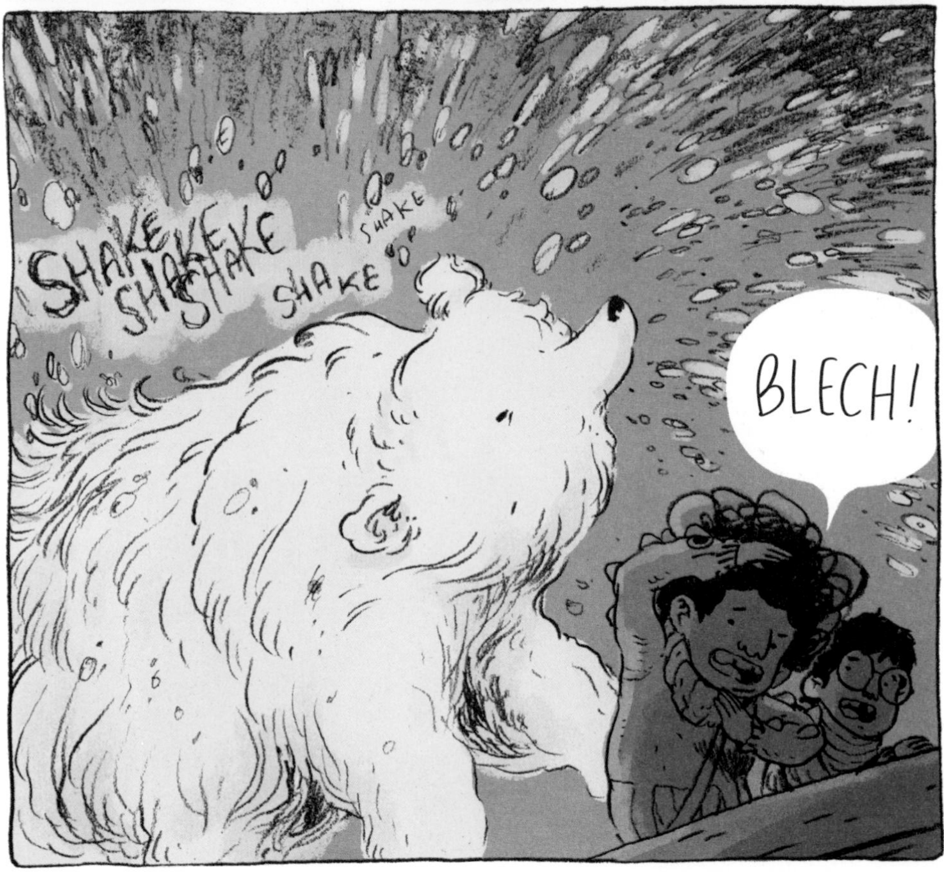
SHAKE SHAKE SHAKE SHAKE SHAKE
BLECH!

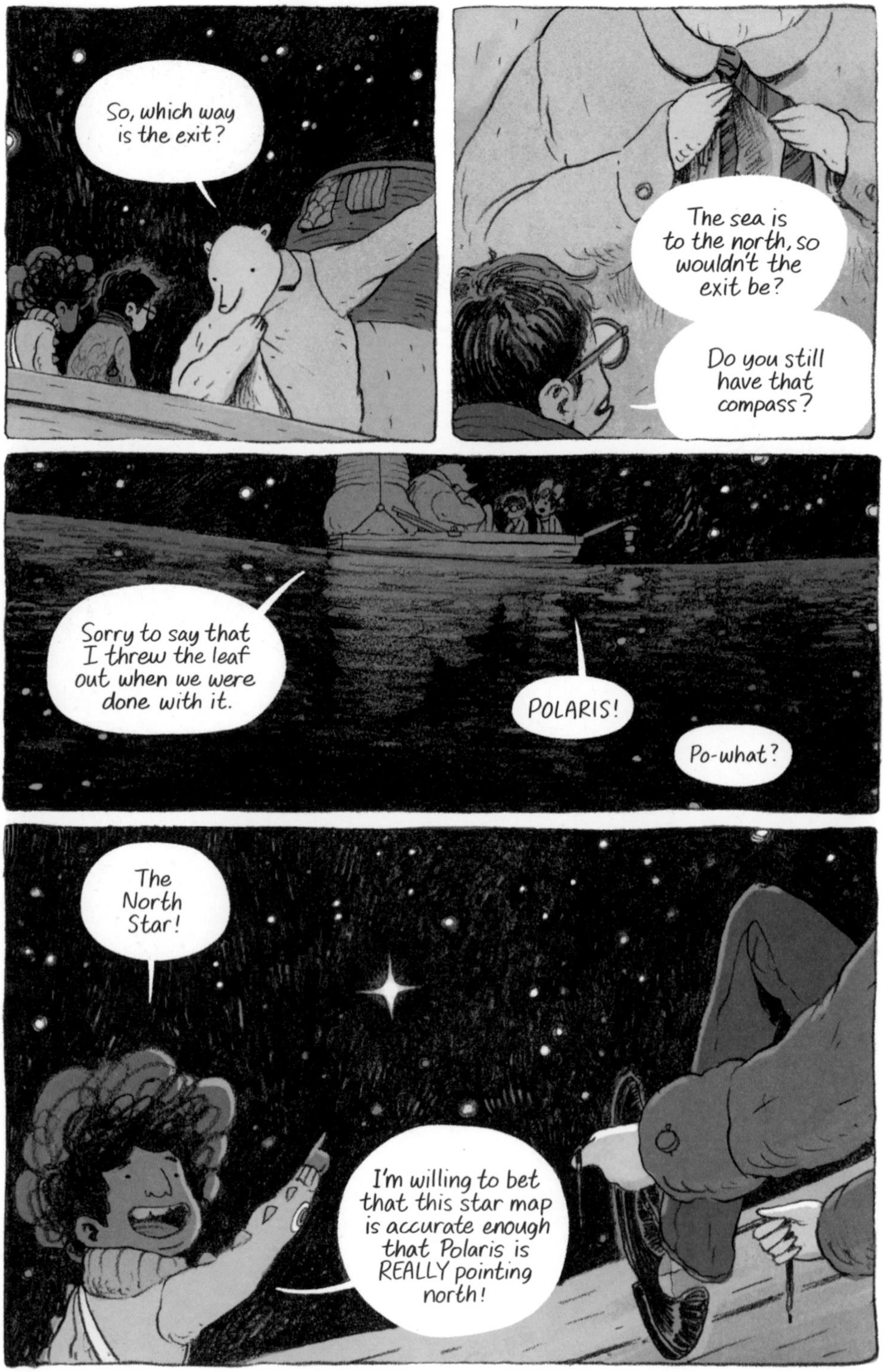
So, which way is the exit?
The sea is to the north, so wouldn't the exit be?
Do you still have that compass?
Sorry to say that I threw the leaf out when we were done with it.
POLARIS!
Po-what?
The North Star!
I'm willing to bet that this star map is accurate enough that Polaris is REALLY pointing north!

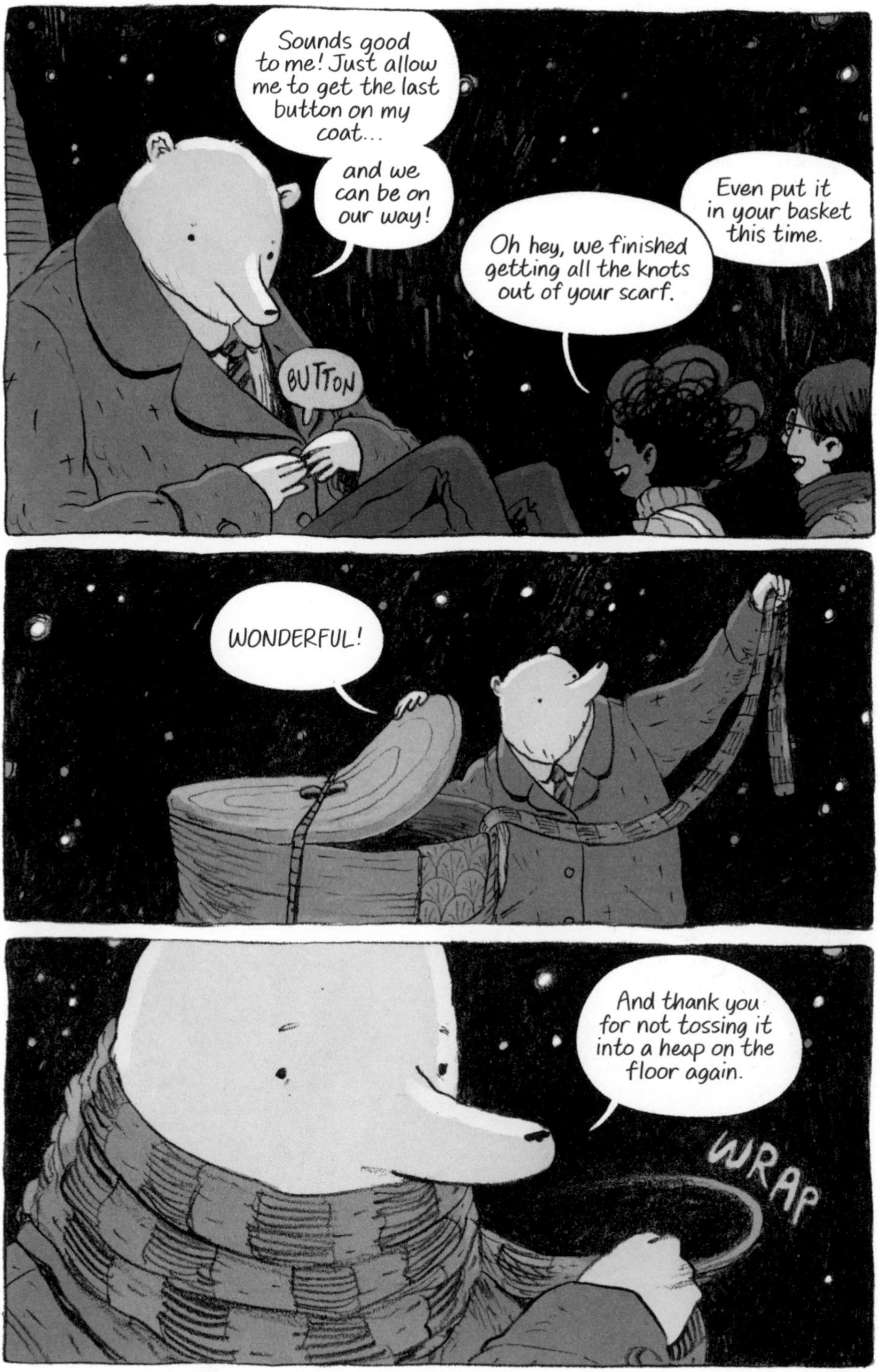
Sounds good to me! Just allow me to get the last button on my coat...
and we can be on our way!
BUTTON
Oh hey, we finished getting all the knots out of your scarf.
Even put it in your basket this time.
WONDERFUL!
And thank you for not tossing it into a heap on the floor again.
WRAP

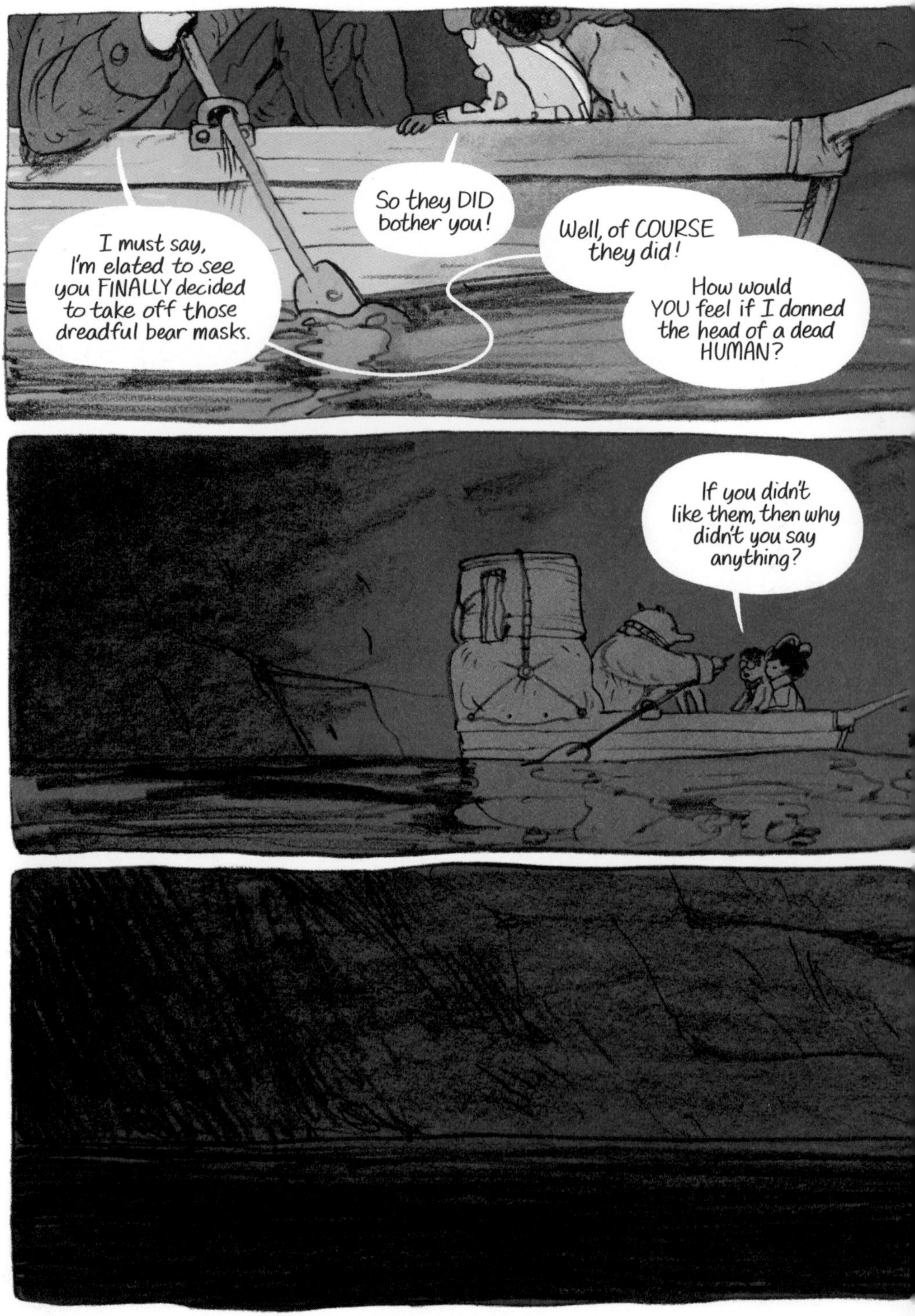
I must say, I'm elated to see you FINALLY decided to take off those dreadful bear masks.
So they DID bother you!
Well, of COURSE they did!
How would YOU feel if I donned the head of a dead HUMAN?
If you didn't like them, then why didn't you say anything?

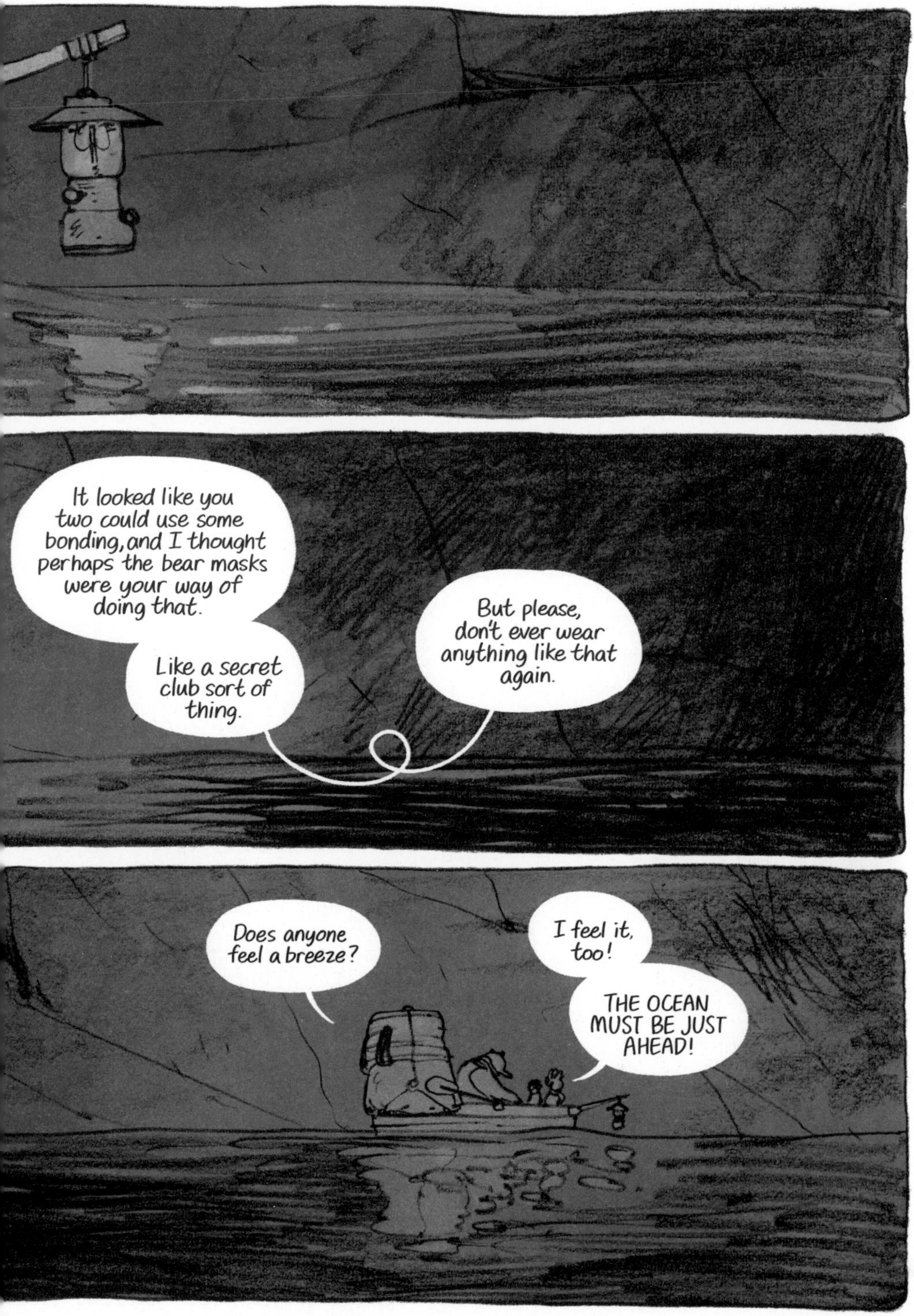
It looked like you two could use some bonding, and I thought perhaps the bear masks were your way of doing that.
Like a secret club sort of thing.
But please, don't ever wear anything like that again.
Does anyone feel a breeze?
I feel it, too!
THE OCEAN MUST BE JUST AHEAD!

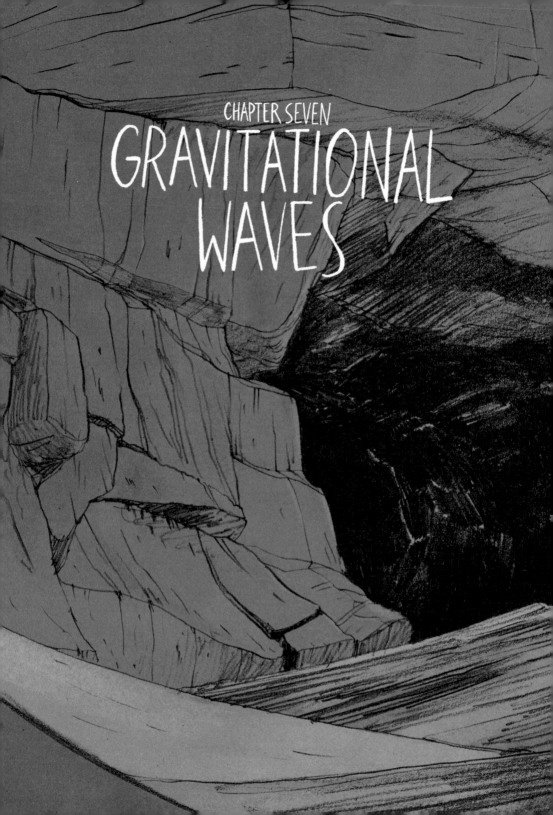

CHAPTER SEVEN

GRAVITATIONAL WAVES

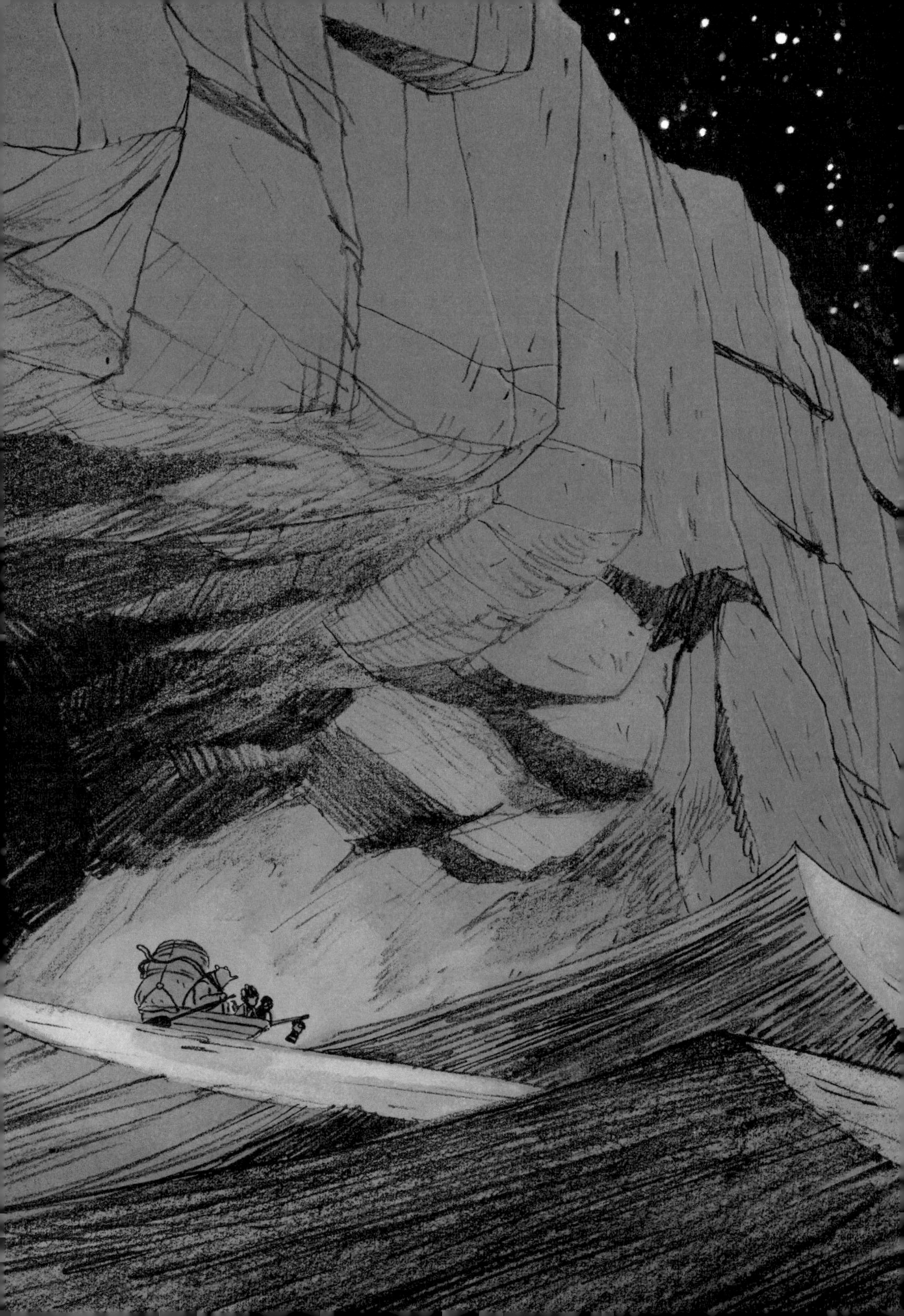

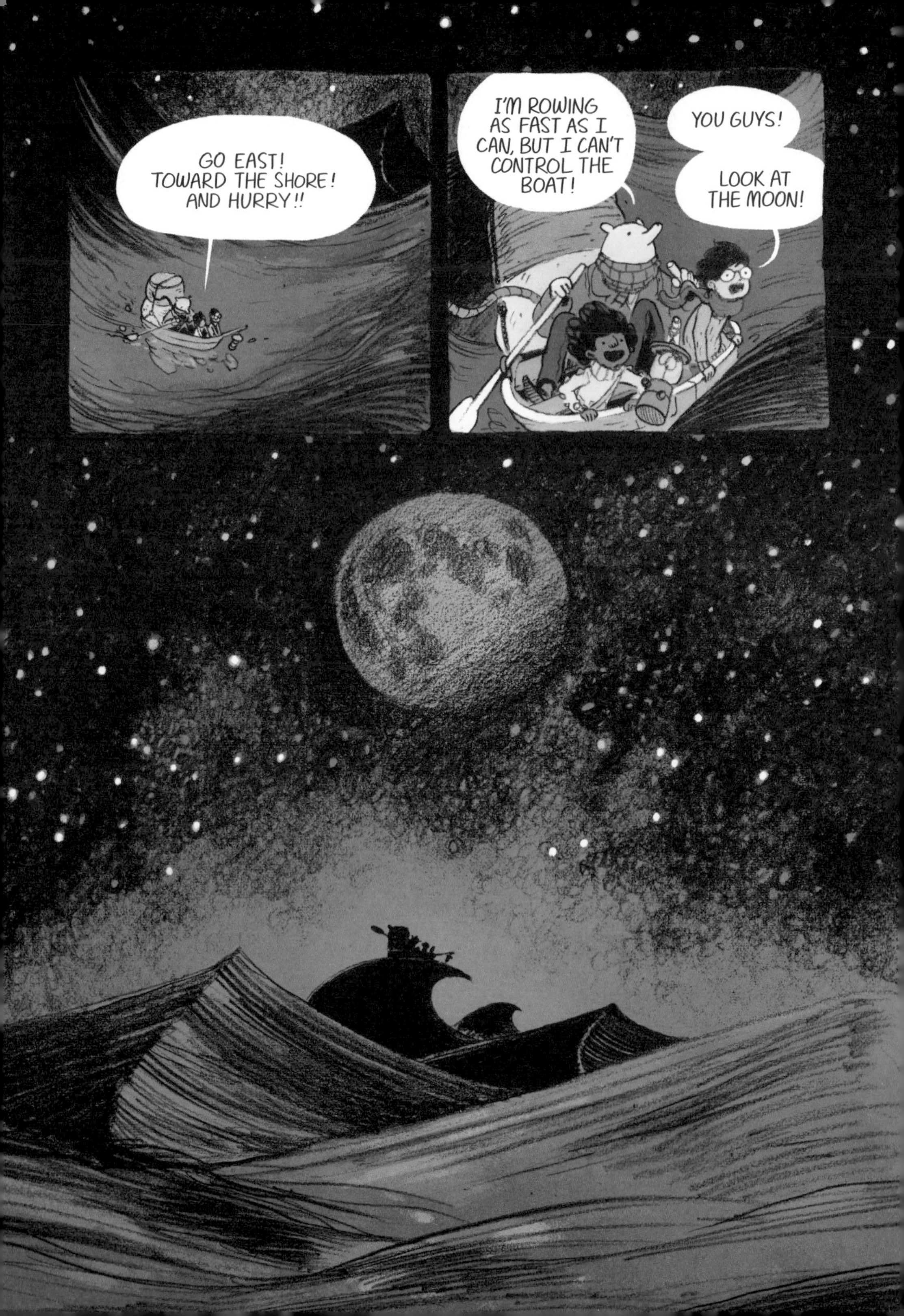
GO EAST! TOWARD THE SHORE! AND HURRY!!
I'M ROWING AS FAST AS I CAN, BUT I CAN'T CONTROL THE BOAT!
YOU GUYS!
LOOK AT THE MOON!

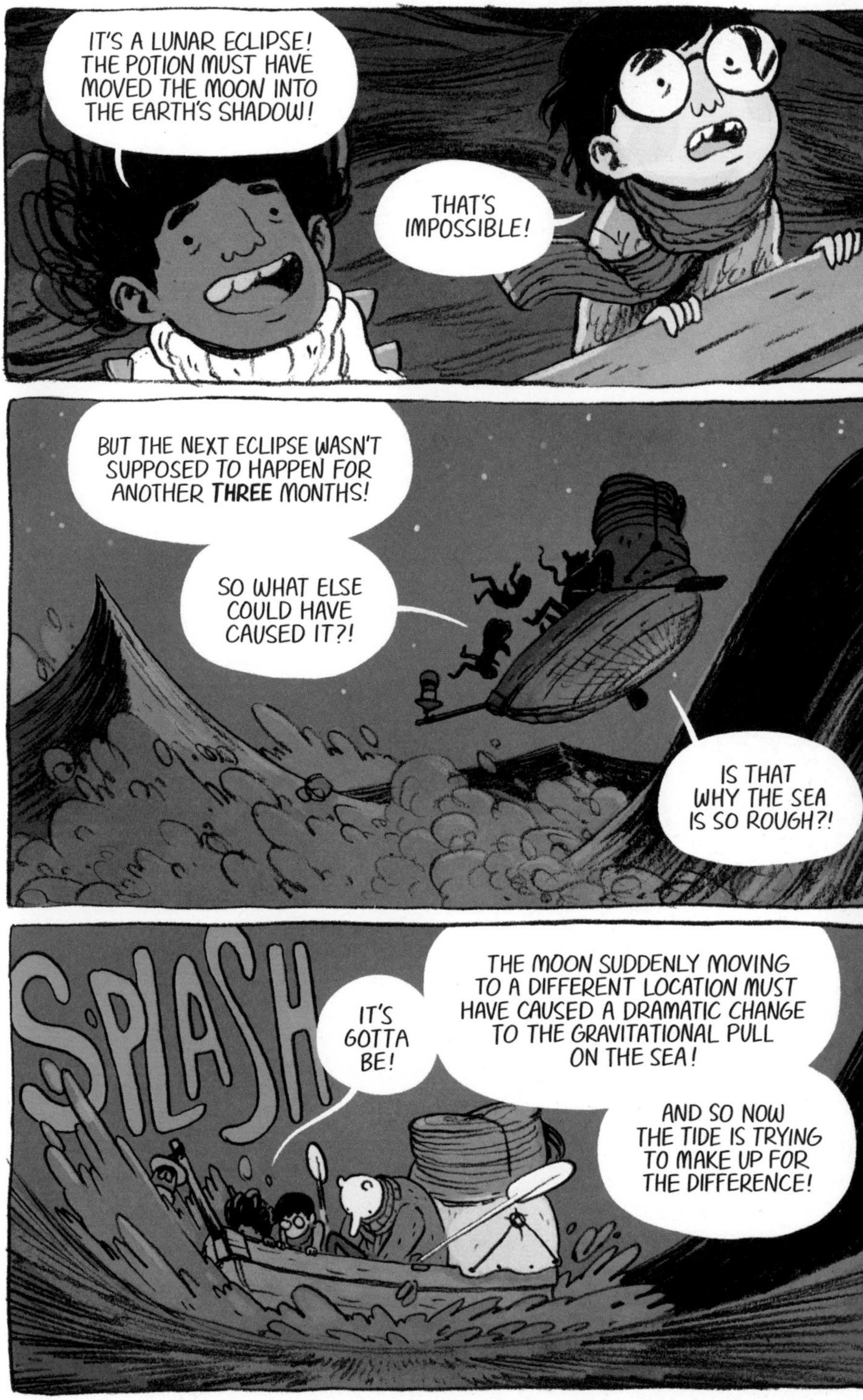
IT'S A LUNAR ECLIPSE! THE POTION MUST HAVE MOVED THE MOON INTO THE EARTH'S SHADOW!
THAT'S IMPOSSIBLE!
BUT THE NEXT ECLIPSE WASN'T SUPPOSED TO HAPPEN FOR ANOTHER **THREE** MONTHS!
SO WHAT ELSE COULD HAVE CAUSED IT?!
IS THAT WHY THE SEA IS SO ROUGH?!
SPLASH
IT'S GOTTA BE!
THE MOON SUDDENLY MOVING TO A DIFFERENT LOCATION MUST HAVE CAUSED A DRAMATIC CHANGE TO THE GRAVITATIONAL PULL ON THE SEA!
AND SO NOW THE TIDE IS TRYING TO MAKE UP FOR THE DIFFERENCE!

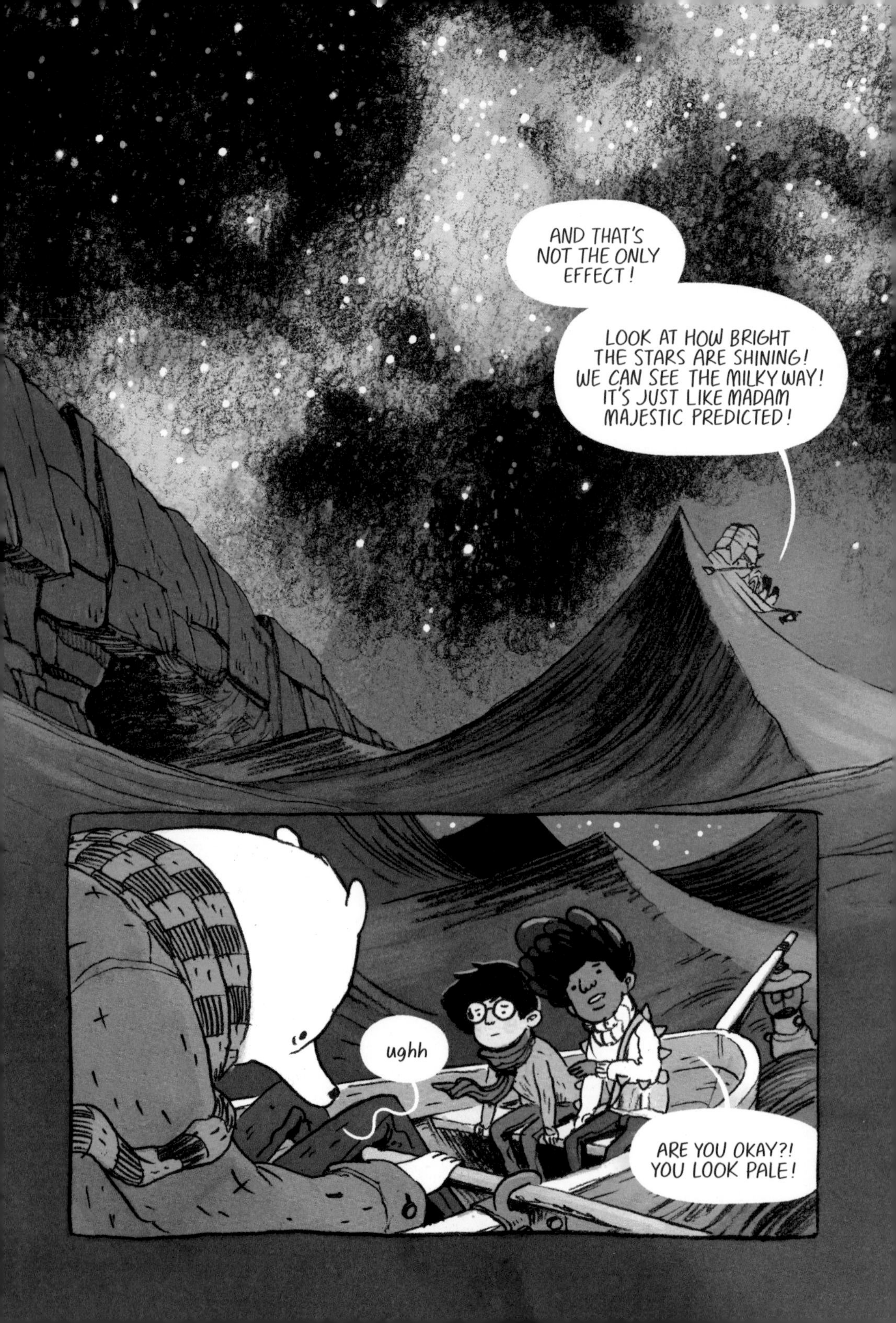

AND THAT'S NOT THE ONLY EFFECT!
LOOK AT HOW BRIGHT THE STARS ARE SHINING! WE CAN SEE THE MILKY WAY! IT'S JUST LIKE MADAM MAJESTIC PREDICTED!
ughh
ARE YOU OKAY?! YOU LOOK PALE!

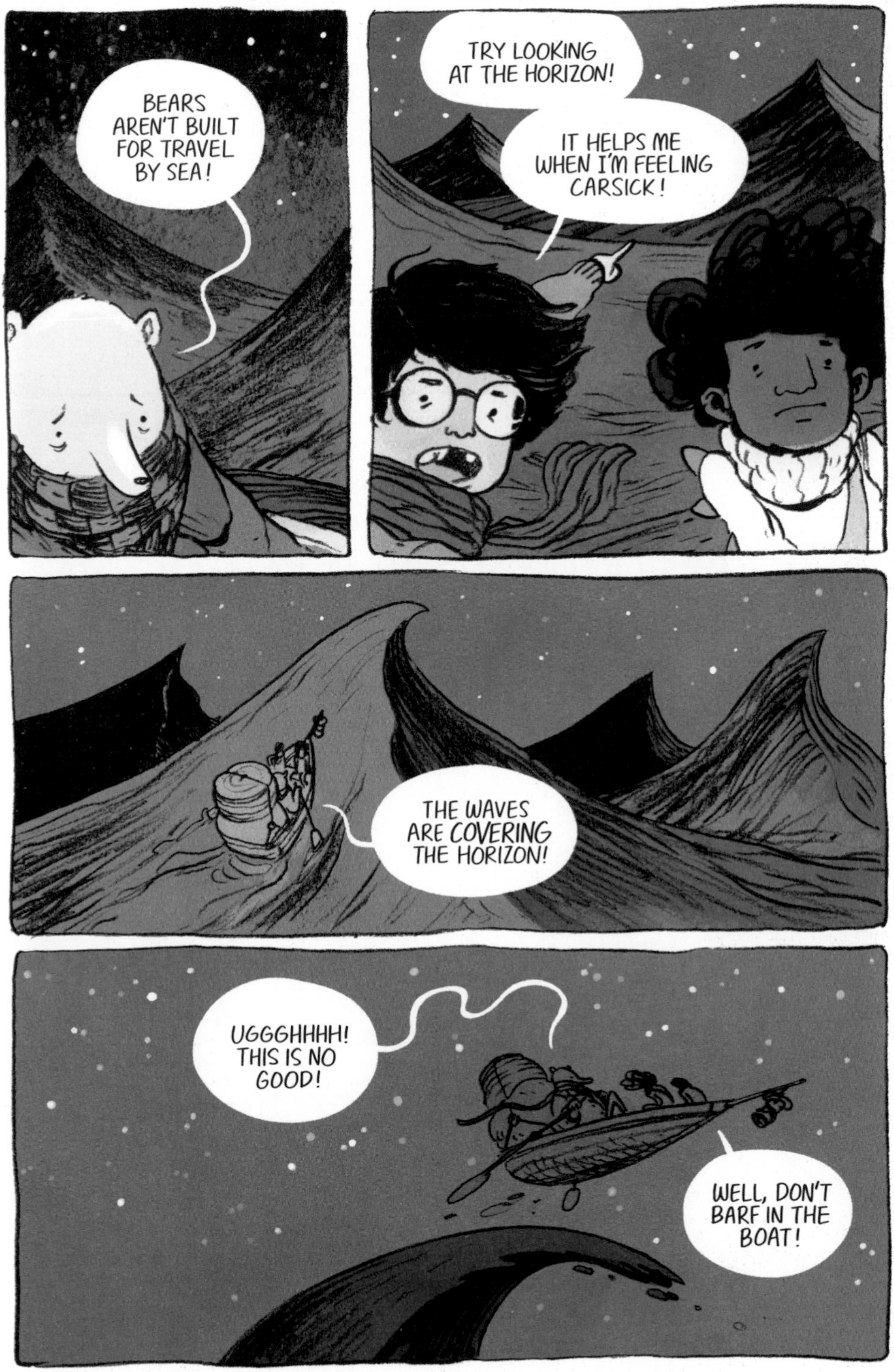
BEARS AREN'T BUILT FOR TRAVEL BY SEA!
TRY LOOKING AT THE HORIZON!
IT HELPS ME WHEN I'M FEELING CARSICK!
THE WAVES ARE COVERING THE HORIZON!
UGGGHHHH! THIS IS NO GOOD!
WELL, DON'T BARF IN THE BOAT!

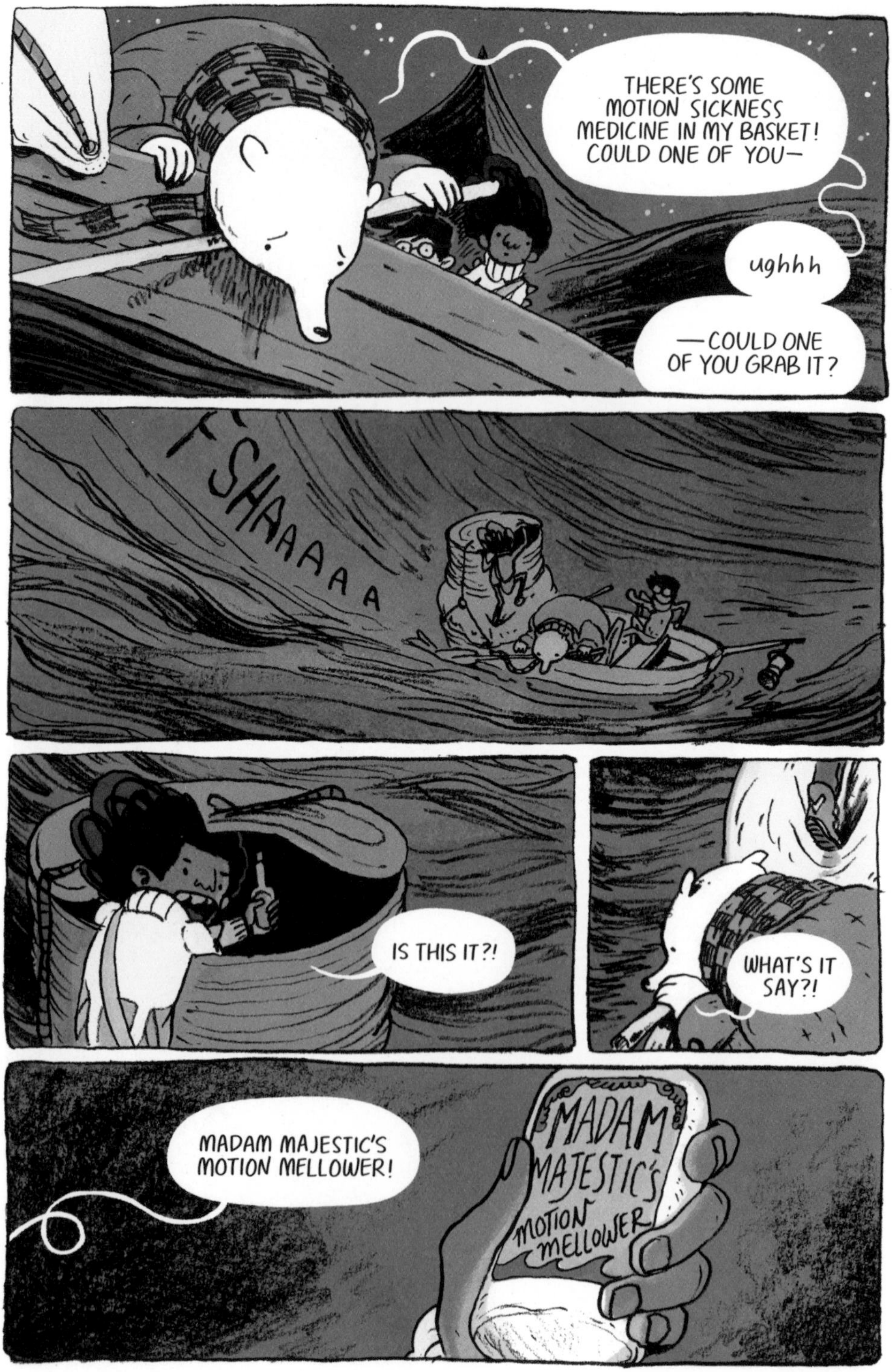
THERE'S SOME MOTION SICKNESS MEDICINE IN MY BASKET! COULD ONE OF YOU—
ughhh
—COULD ONE OF YOU GRAB IT?
FSHAAAAAA
IS THIS IT?!
WHAT'S IT SAY?!
MADAM MAJESTIC'S MOTION MELLOWER!
MADAM MAJESTIC'S MOTION MELLOWER

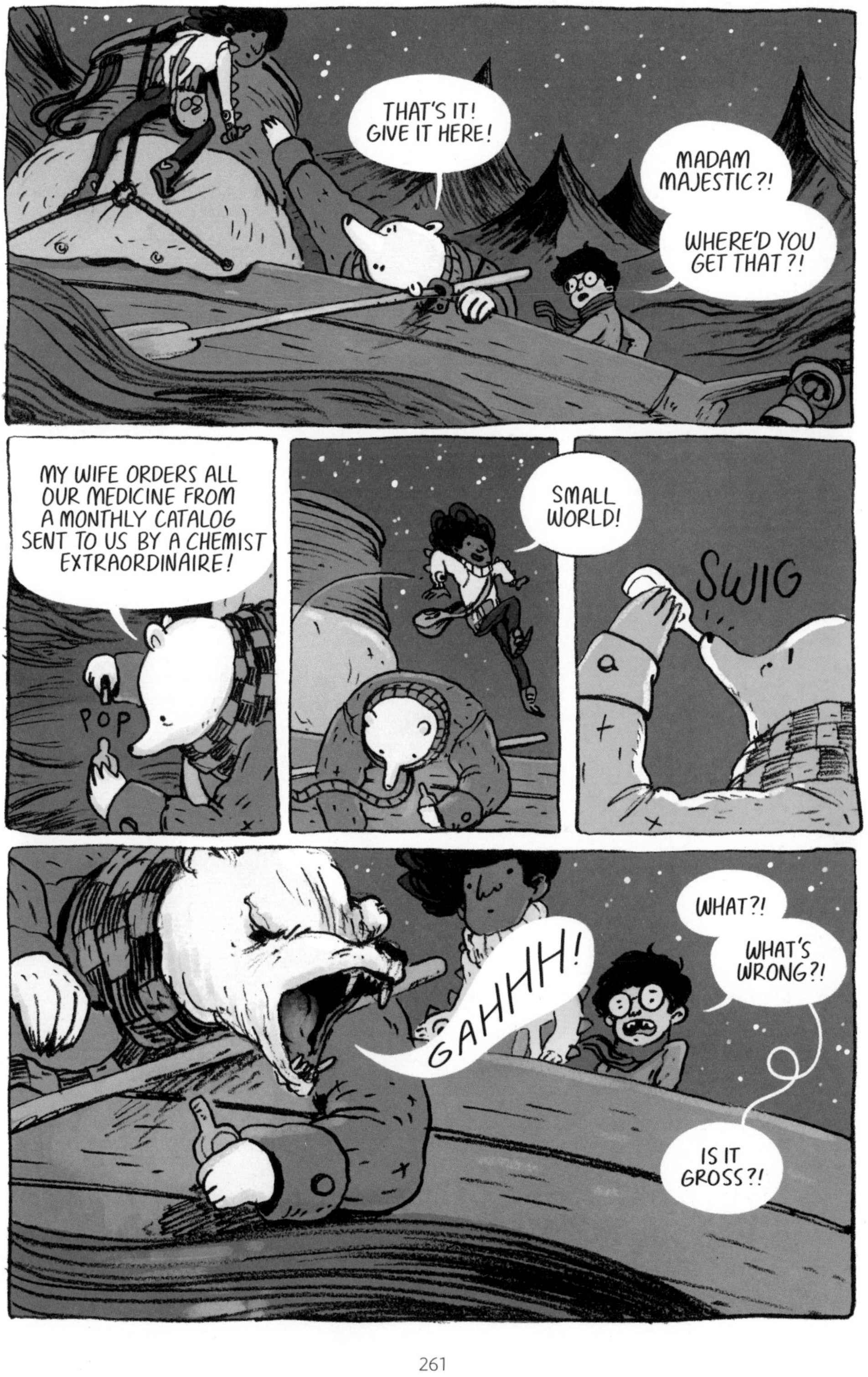
THAT'S IT! GIVE IT HERE!
MADAM MAJESTIC?!
WHERE'D YOU GET THAT?!
MY WIFE ORDERS ALL OUR MEDICINE FROM A MONTHLY CATALOG SENT TO US BY A CHEMIST EXTRAORDINAIRE!
POP
SMALL WORLD!
SWIG
GAHHH!
WHAT?!
WHAT'S WRONG?!
IS IT GROSS?!

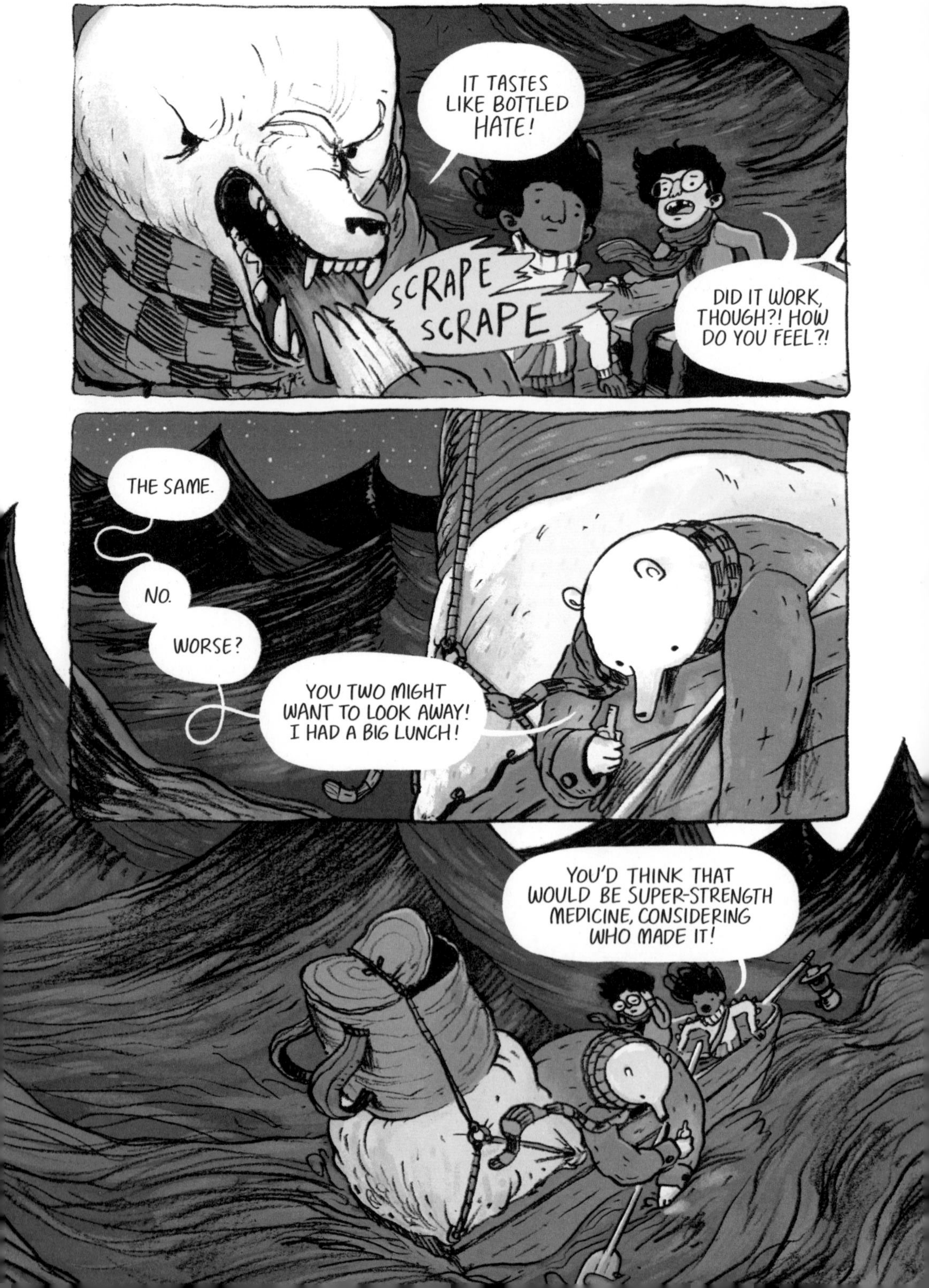
IT TASTES LIKE BOTTLED HATE!
SCRAPE SCRAPE
DID IT WORK, THOUGH?! HOW DO YOU FEEL?!
THE SAME.
NO.
WORSE?
YOU TWO MIGHT WANT TO LOOK AWAY! I HAD A BIG LUNCH!
YOU'D THINK THAT WOULD BE SUPER-STRENGTH MEDICINE, CONSIDERING WHO MADE IT!

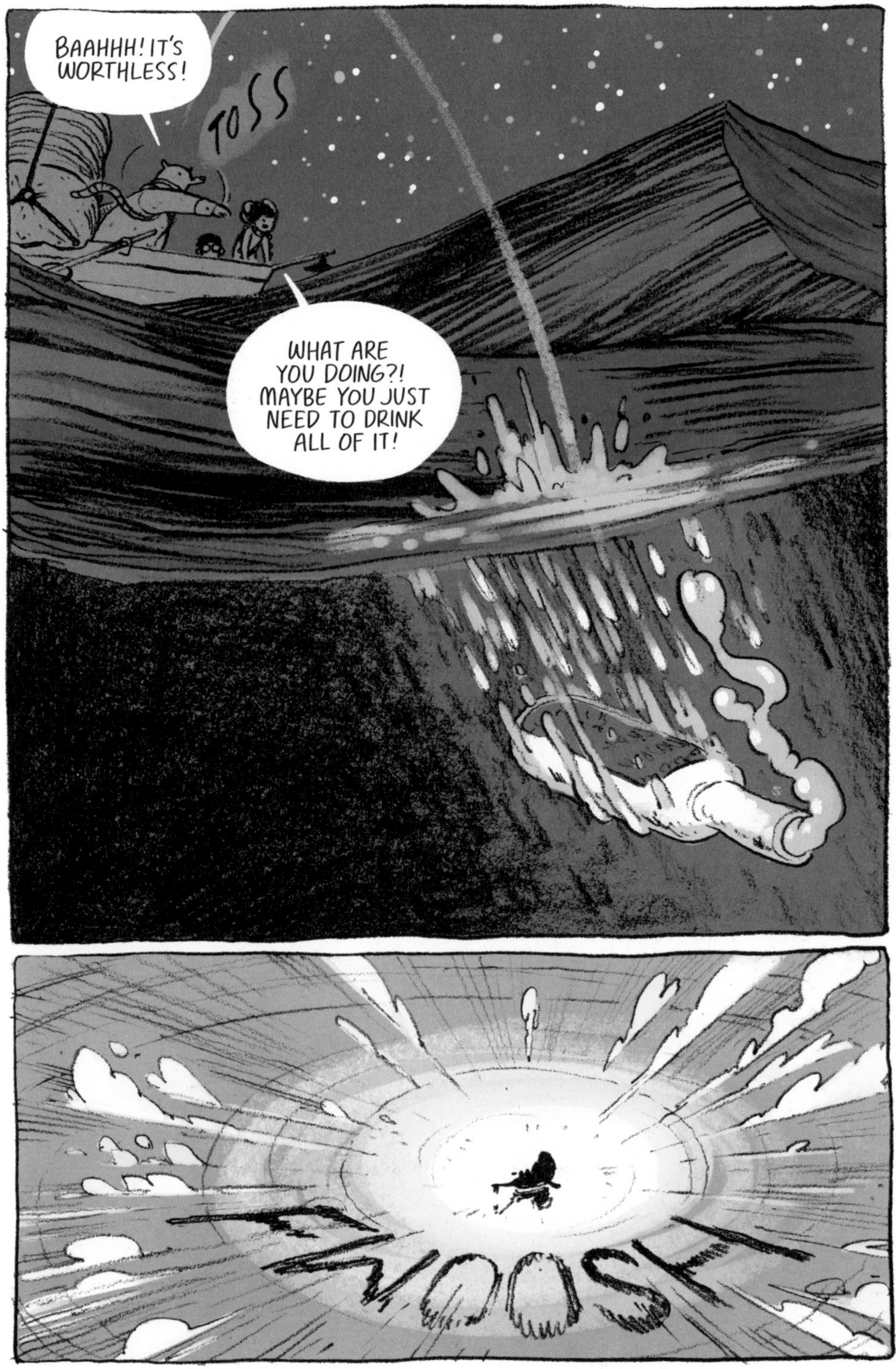
BAAHHH! IT'S WORTHLESS!
TOSS
WHAT ARE YOU DOING?! MAYBE YOU JUST NEED TO DRINK ALL OF IT!
WHOOSH

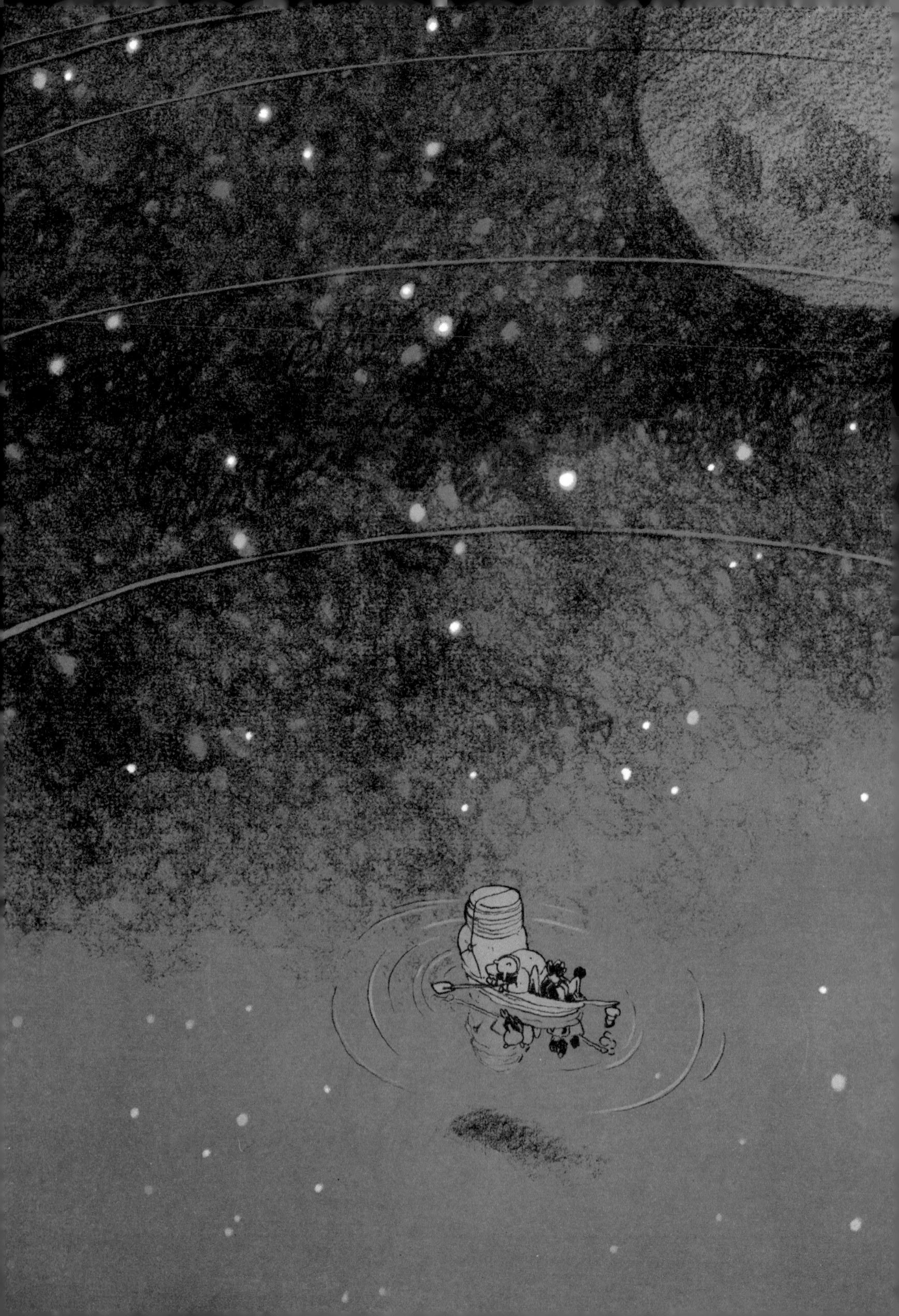

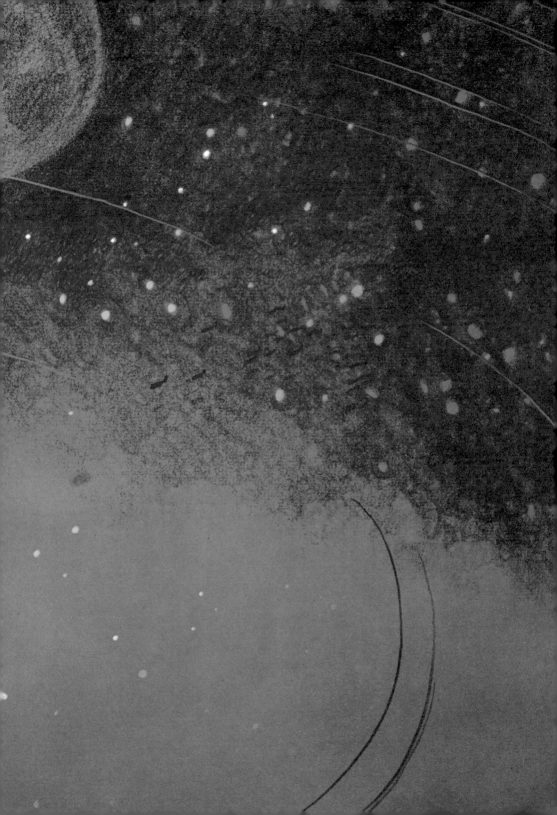

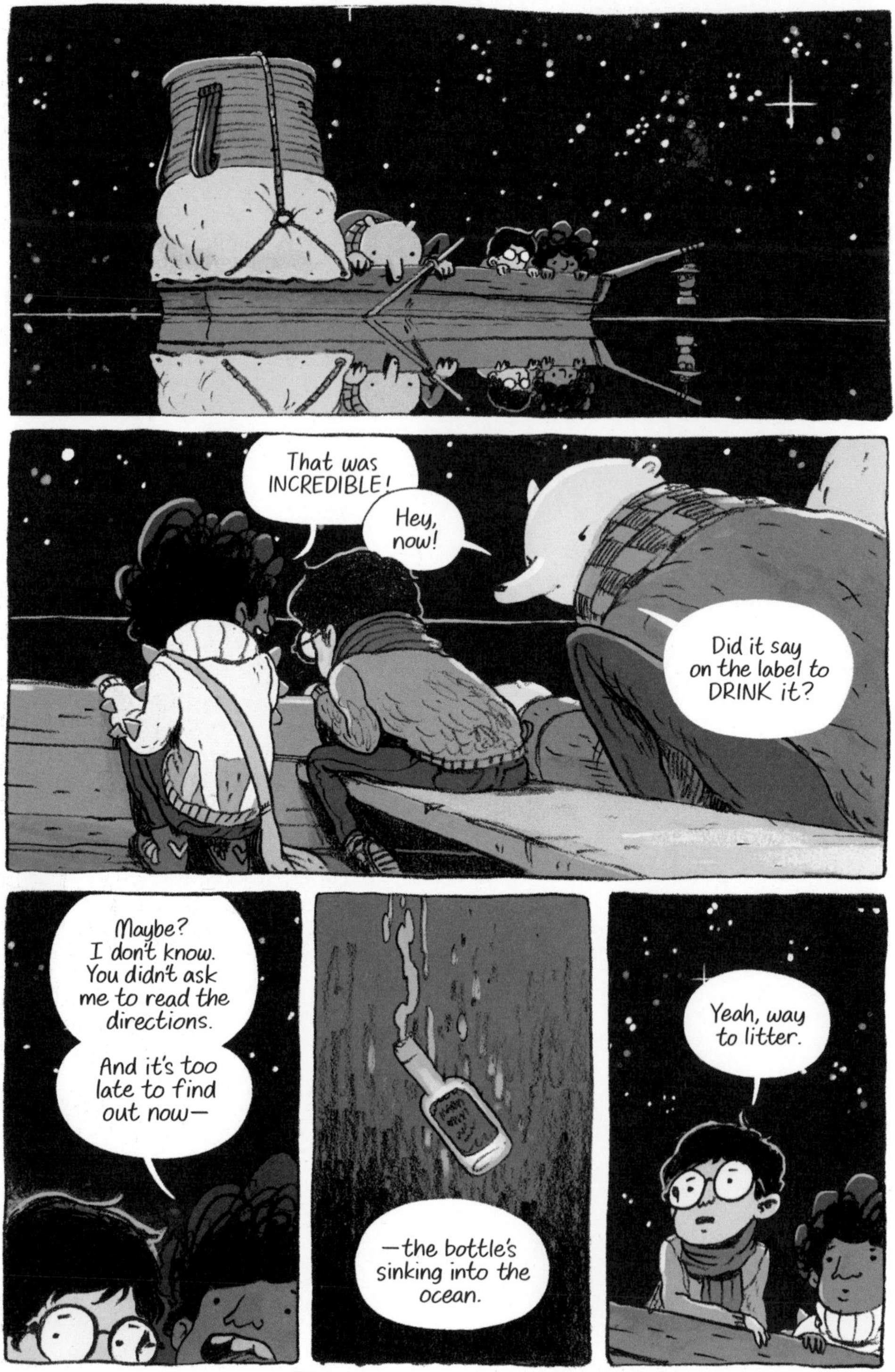
That was INCREDIBLE!
Hey, now!
Did it say on the label to DRINK it?
Maybe? I don't know. You didn't ask me to read the directions.
And it's too late to find out now—
—the bottle's sinking into the ocean.
Yeah, way to litter.

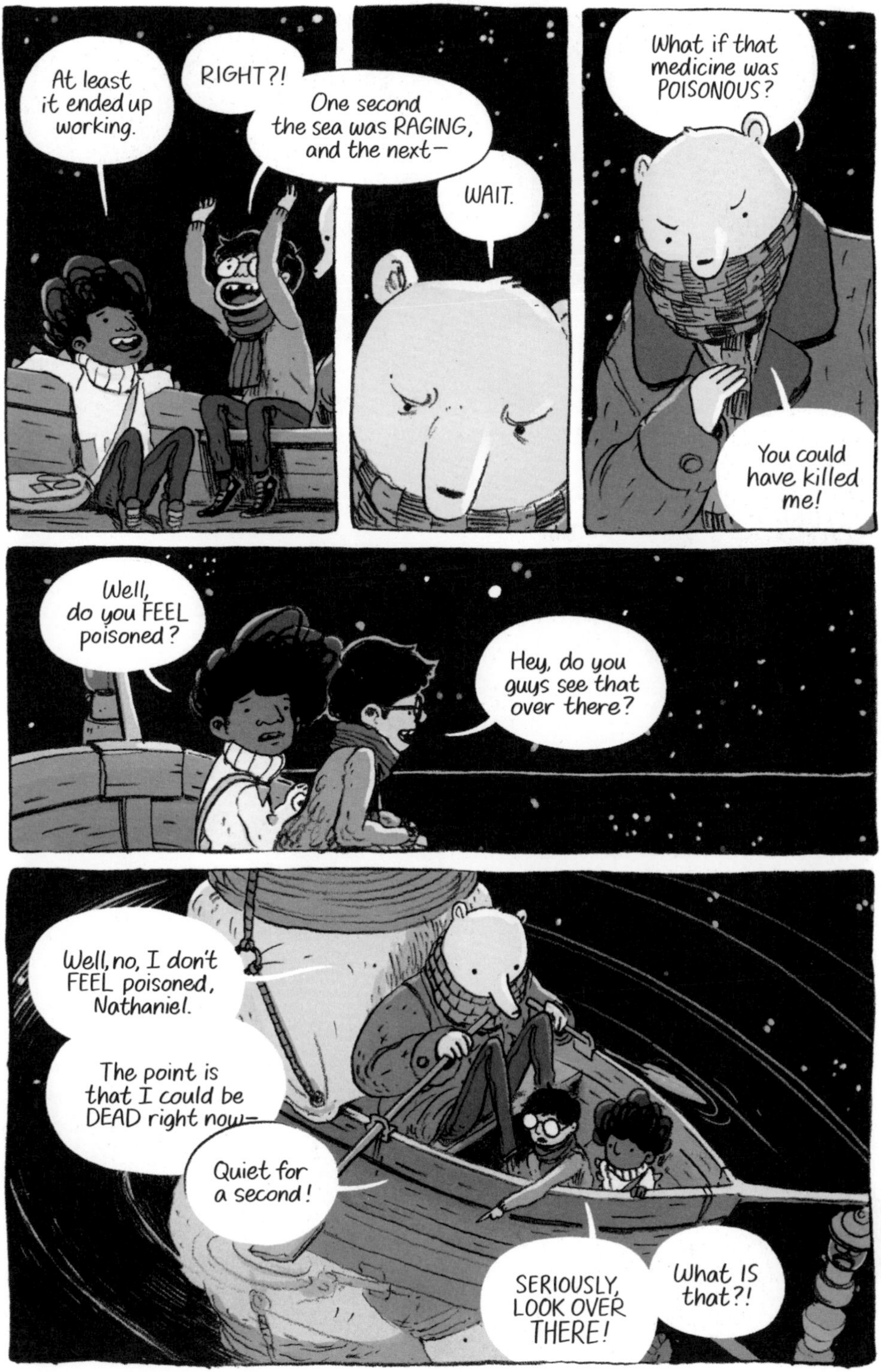
At least it ended up working.
RIGHT?!
One second the sea was RAGING, and the next—
WAIT.
What if that medicine was POISONOUS?
You could have killed me!
Well, do you FEEL poisoned?
Hey, do you guys see that over there?
Well, no, I don't FEEL poisoned, Nathaniel.
The point is that I could be DEAD right now—
Quiet for a second!
SERIOUSLY, LOOK OVER THERE!
What IS that?!

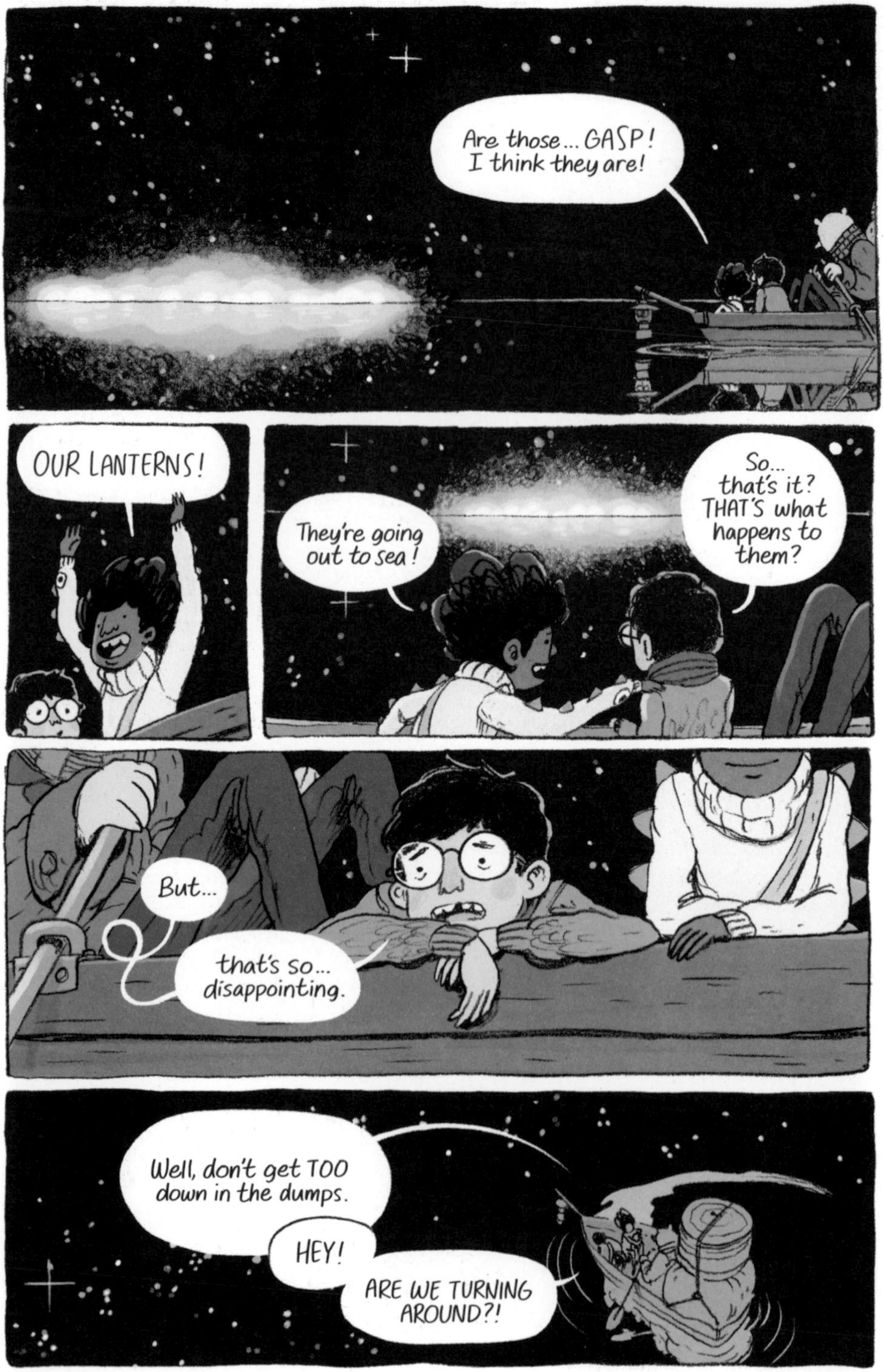
Are those... GASP! I think they are!
OUR LANTERNS!
They're going out to sea!
So... that's it? THAT'S what happens to them?
But...
that's so... disappointing.
Well, don't get TOO down in the dumps.
HEY!
ARE WE TURNING AROUND?!

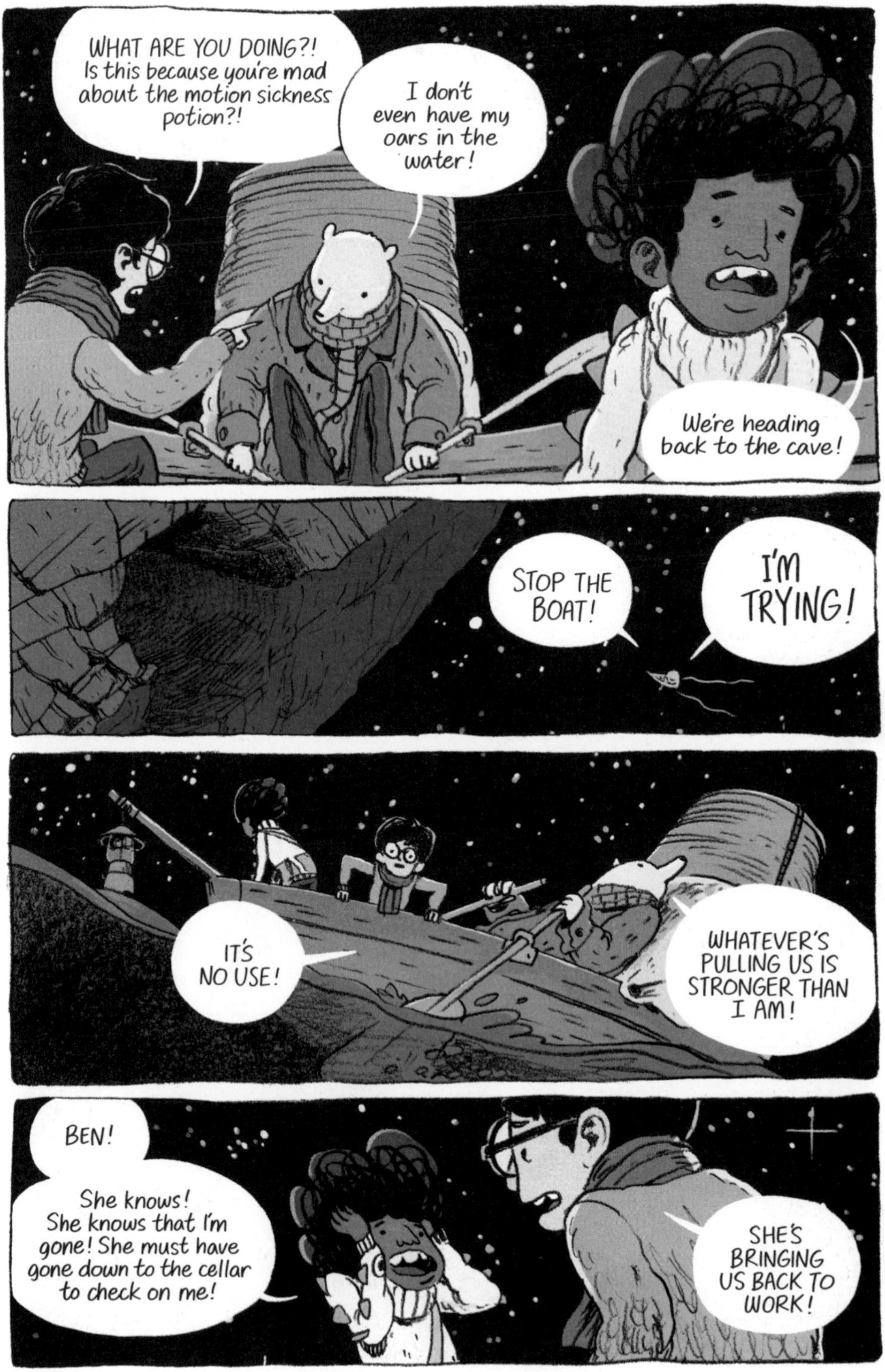
WHAT ARE YOU DOING?! Is this because you're mad about the motion sickness potion?!
I don't even have my oars in the water!
We're heading back to the cave!
STOP THE BOAT!
I'M TRYING!
IT'S NO USE!
WHATEVER'S PULLING US IS STRONGER THAN I AM!
BEN!
She knows! She knows that I'm gone! She must have gone down to the cellar to check on me!
SHE'S BRINGING US BACK TO WORK!

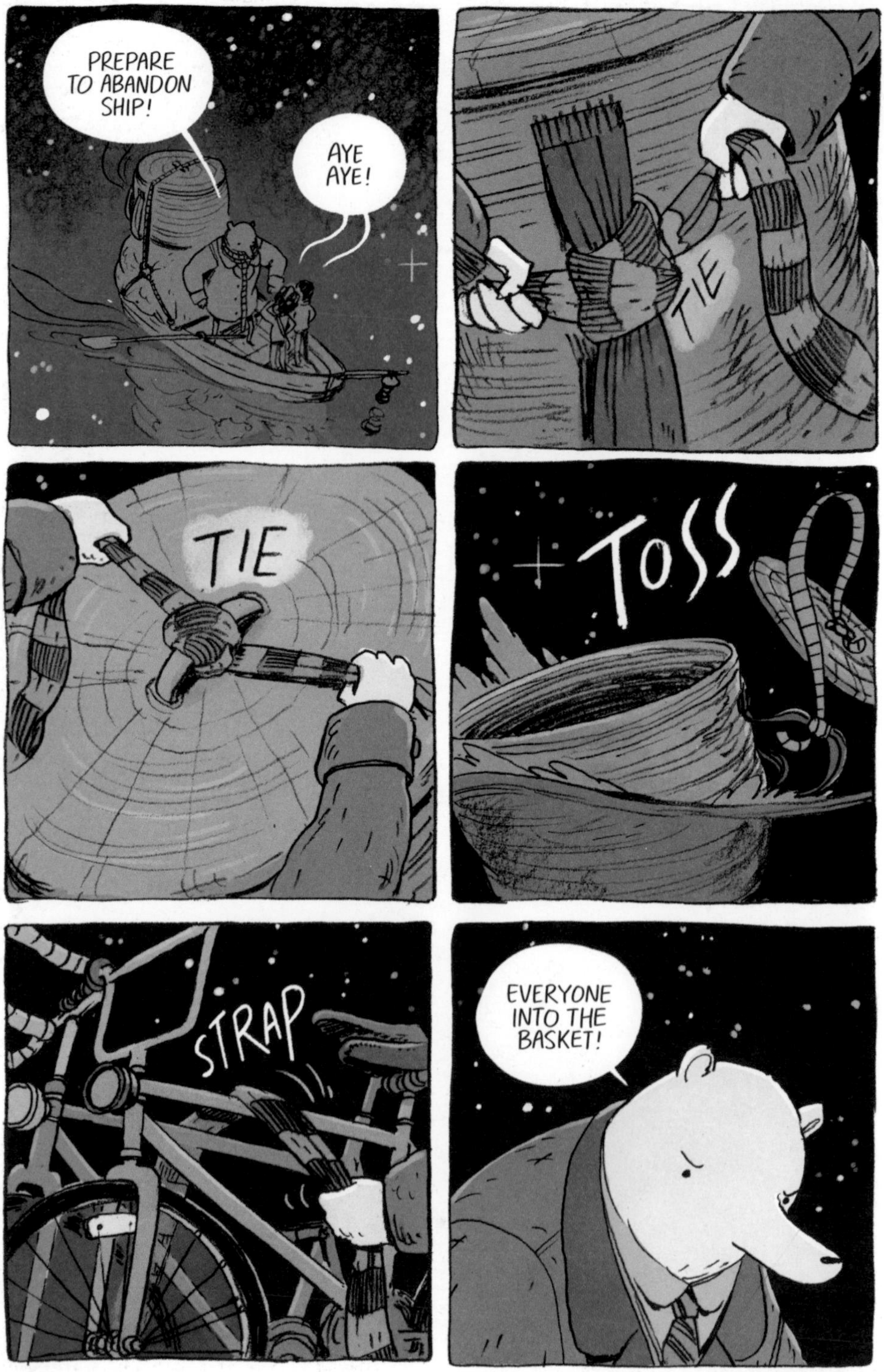
PREPARE TO ABANDON SHIP!
AYE AYE!
TIE
TIE
TOSS
STRAP
EVERYONE INTO THE BASKET!

We're stuck here, aren't we?

Yup.

AGGHH, WE WERE SO CLOSE!

Okay.

Stay calm.

Let's think for a minute. There MUST be a way out of this.

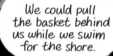
We could pull the basket behind us while we swim for the shore.

But that would take FOREVER.

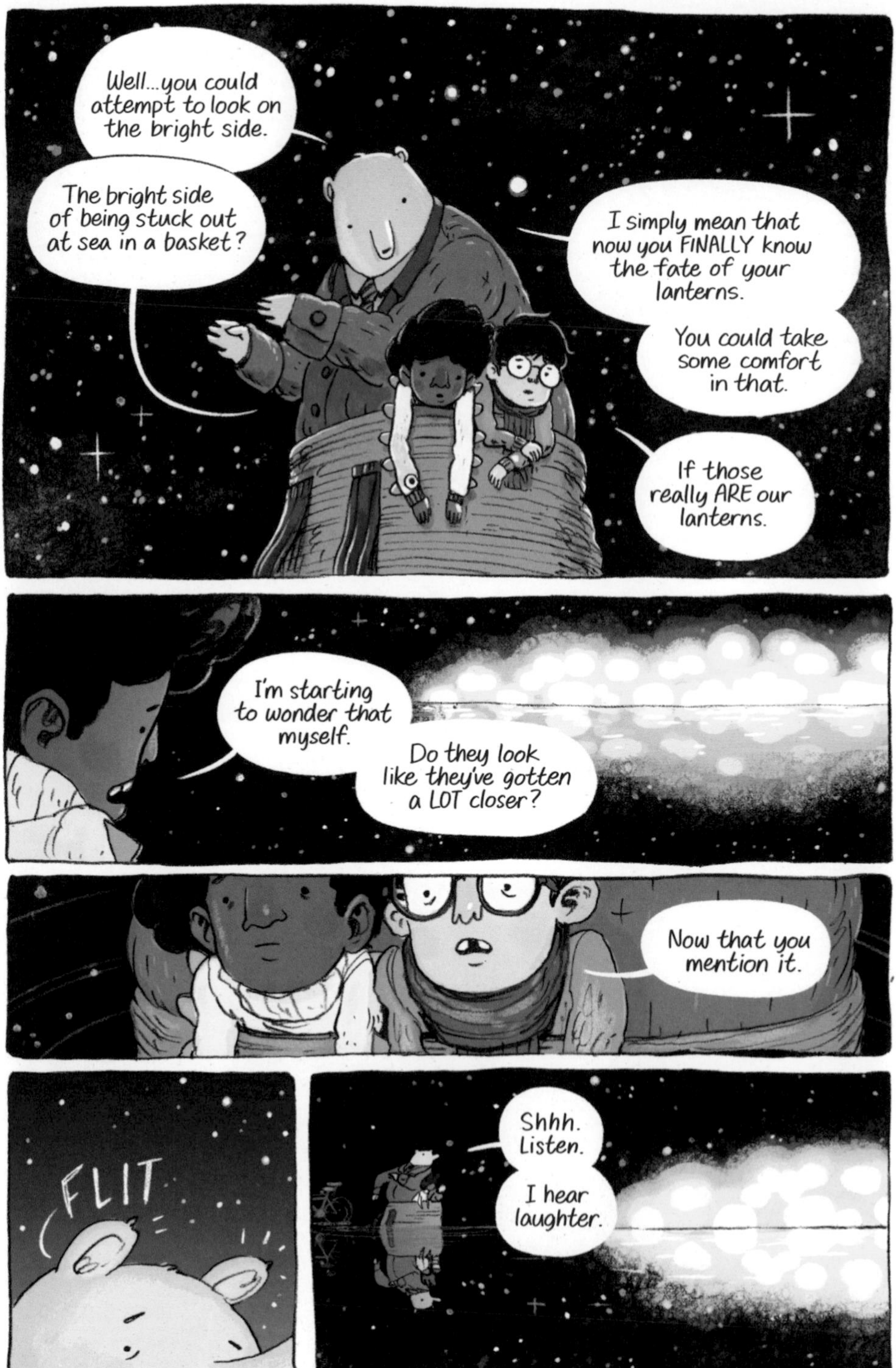

Well...you could attempt to look on the bright side.
The bright side of being stuck out at sea in a basket?
I simply mean that now you FINALLY know the fate of your lanterns.
You could take some comfort in that.
If those really ARE our lanterns.
I'm starting to wonder that myself.
Do they look like they've gotten a LOT closer?
Now that you mention it.
FLIT
Shhh. Listen.
I hear laughter.

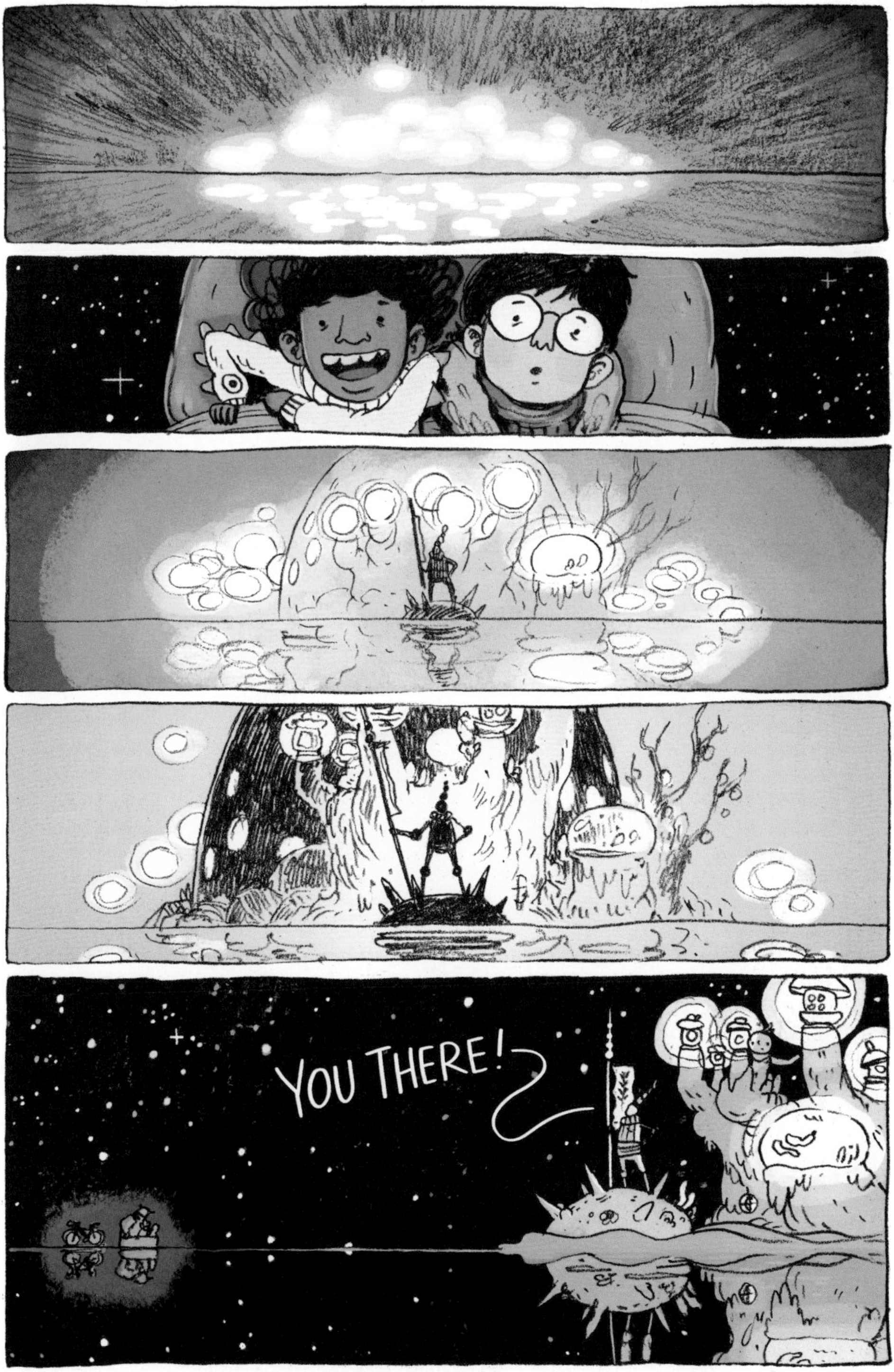
YOU THERE!

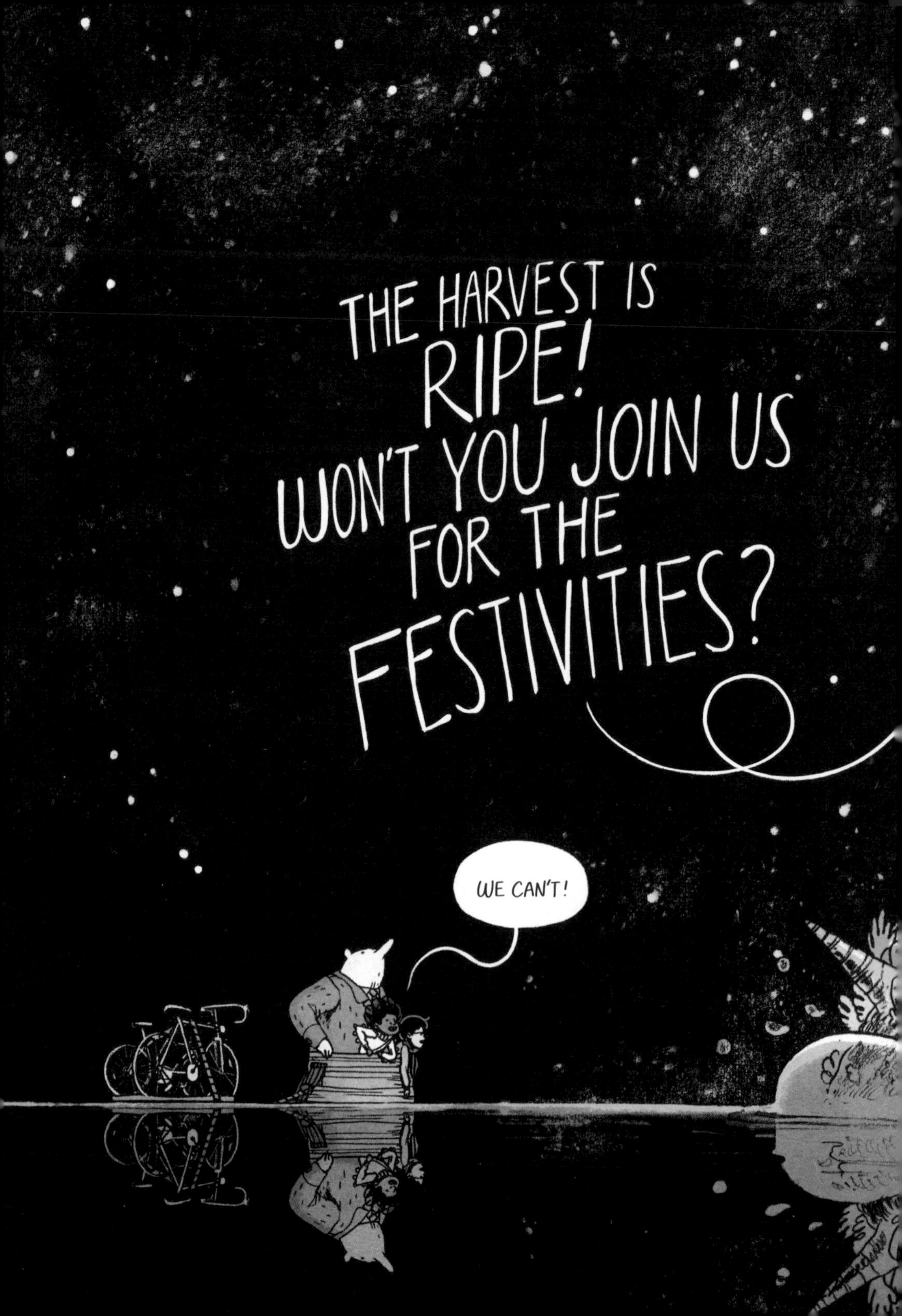
THE HARVEST IS RIPE! WON'T YOU JOIN US FOR THE FESTIVITIES?
WE CAN'T!

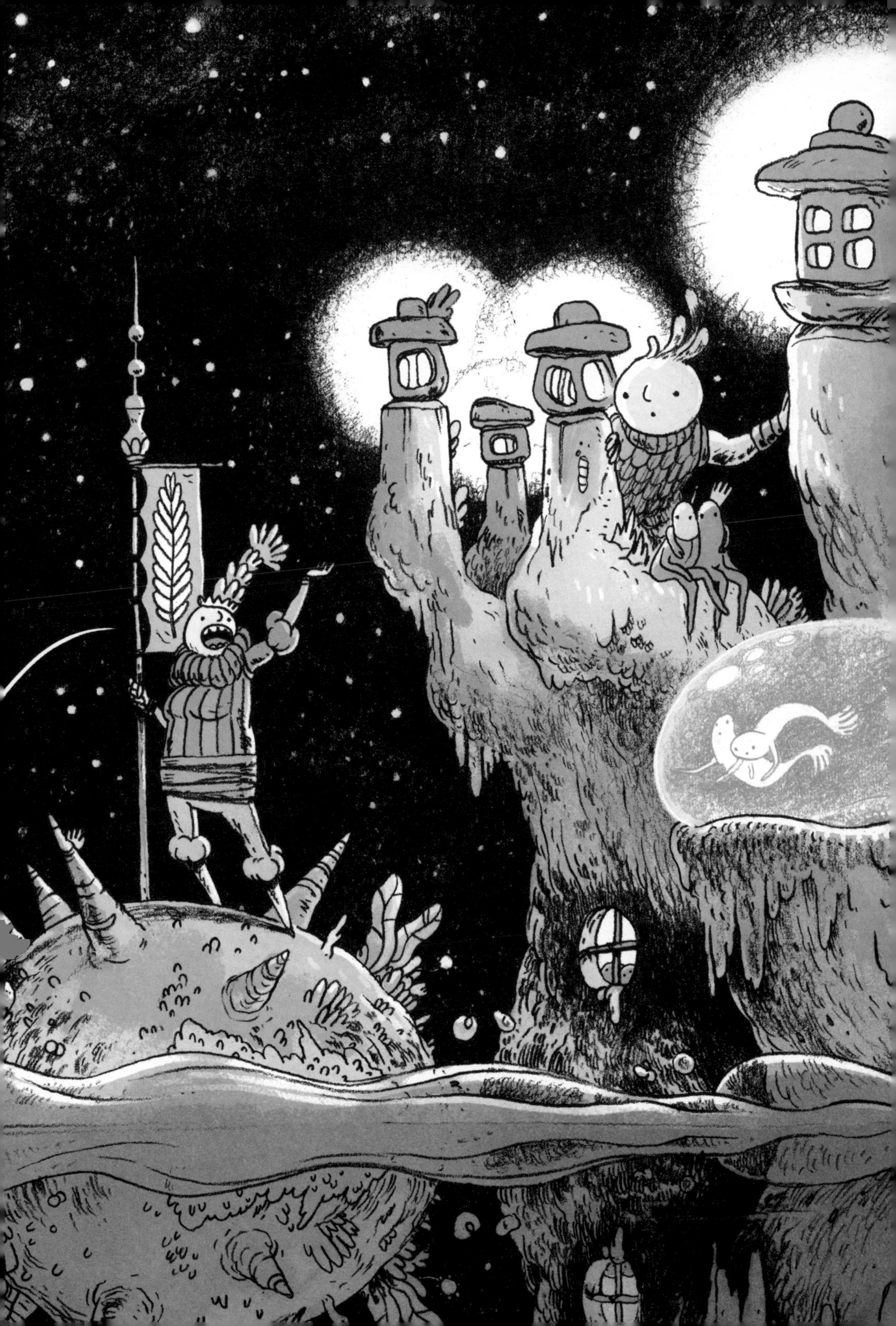

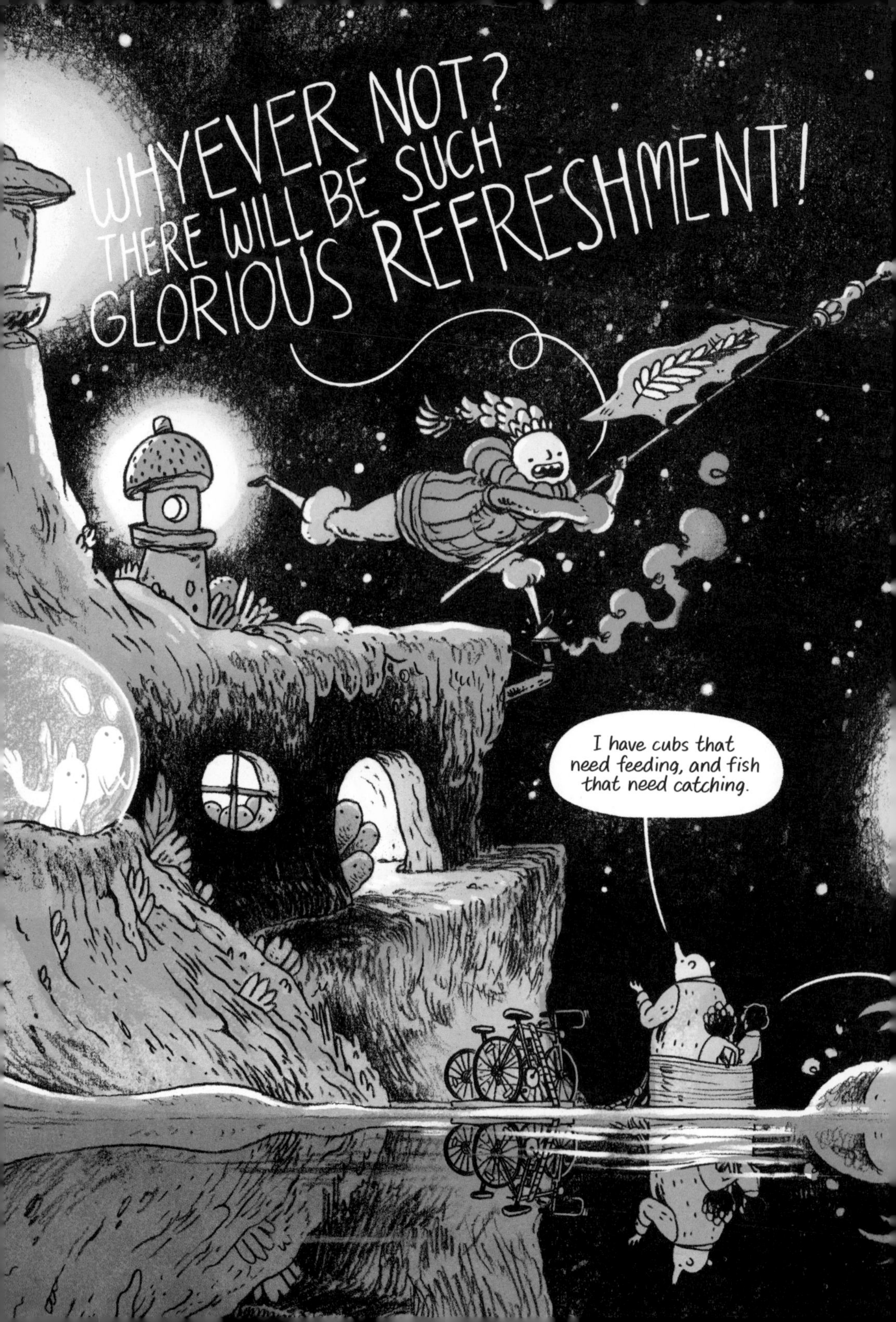
WHYEVER NOT? THERE WILL BE SUCH GLORIOUS REFRESHMENT!
I have cubs that need feeding, and fish that need catching.

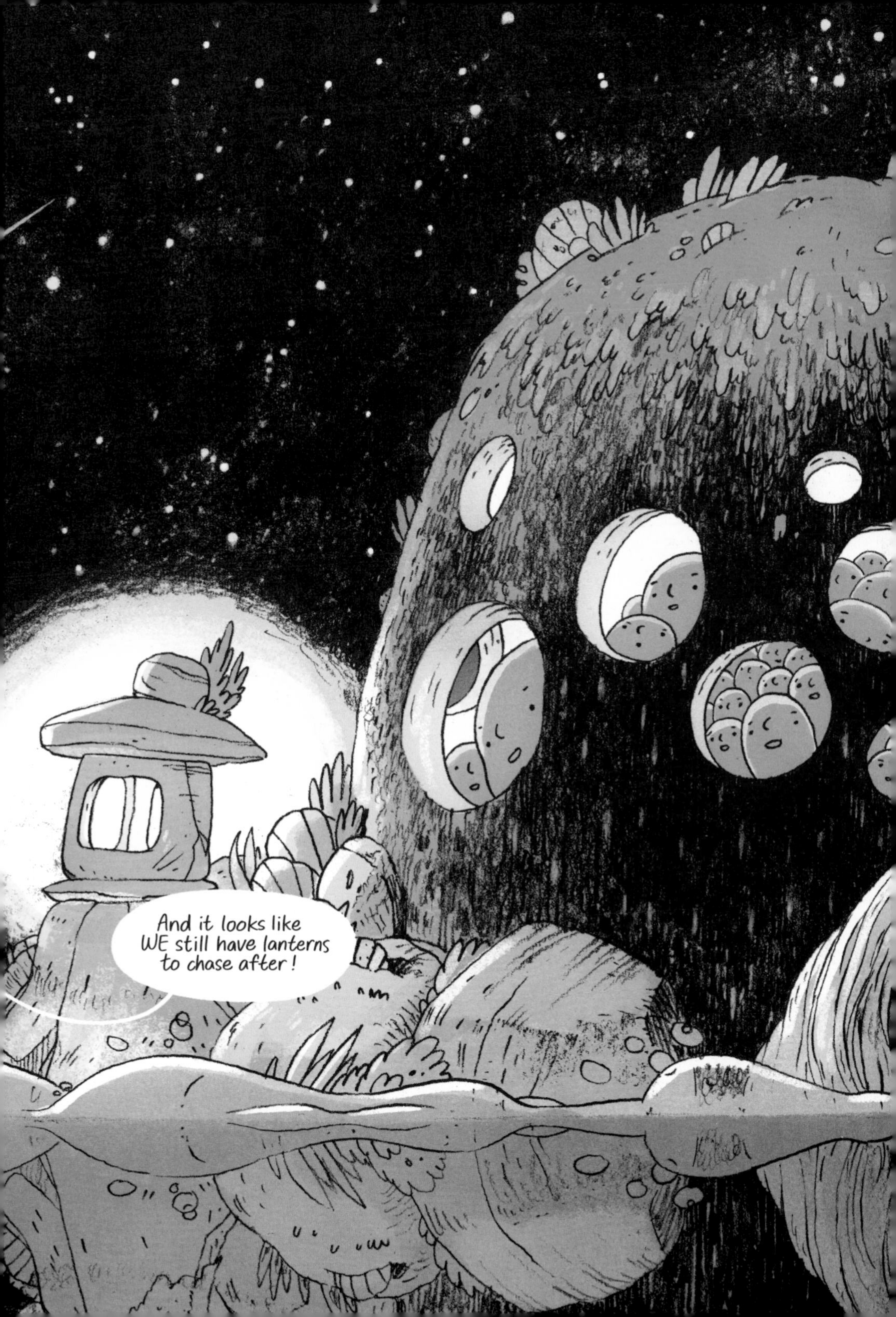
And it looks like WE still have lanterns to chase after!

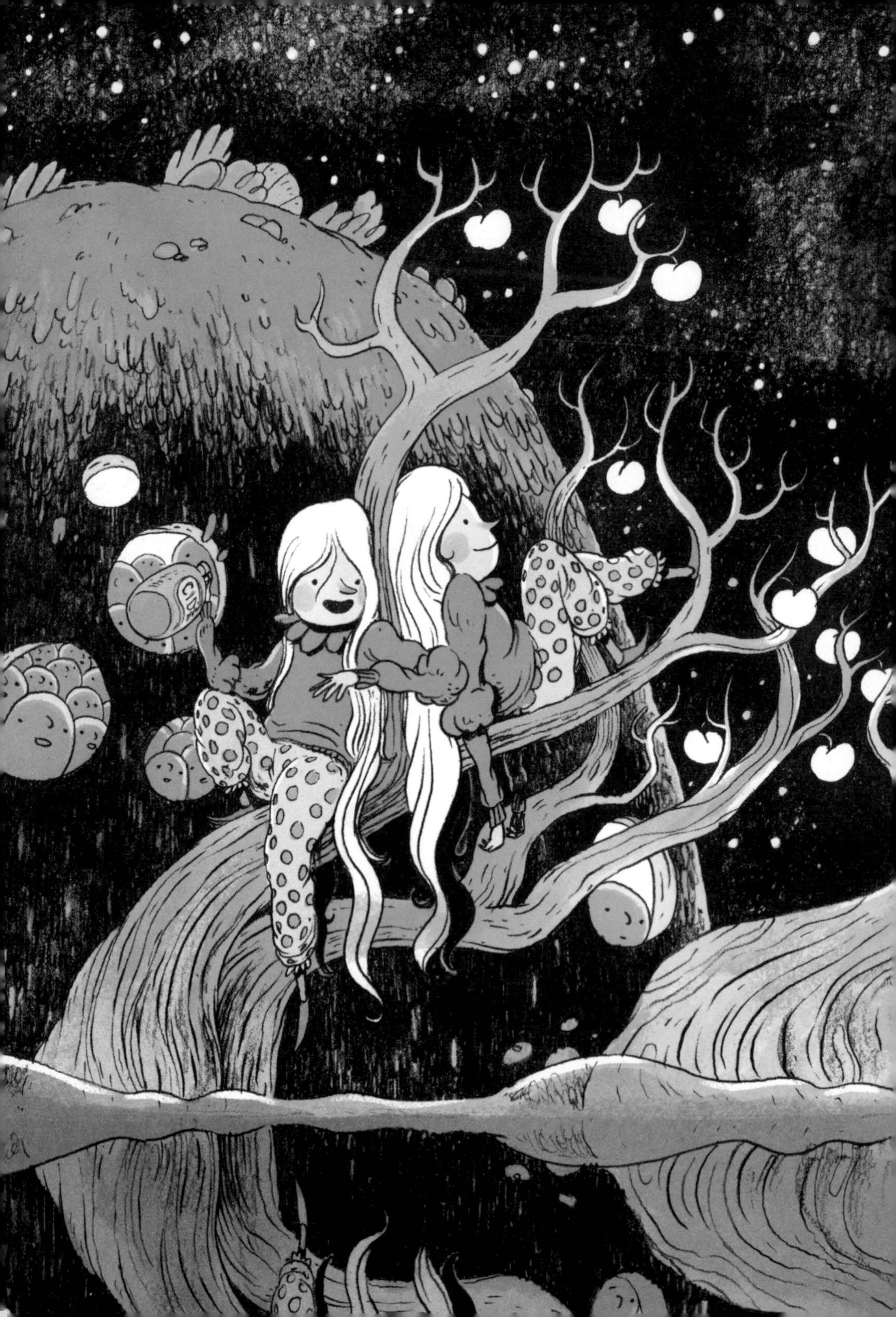

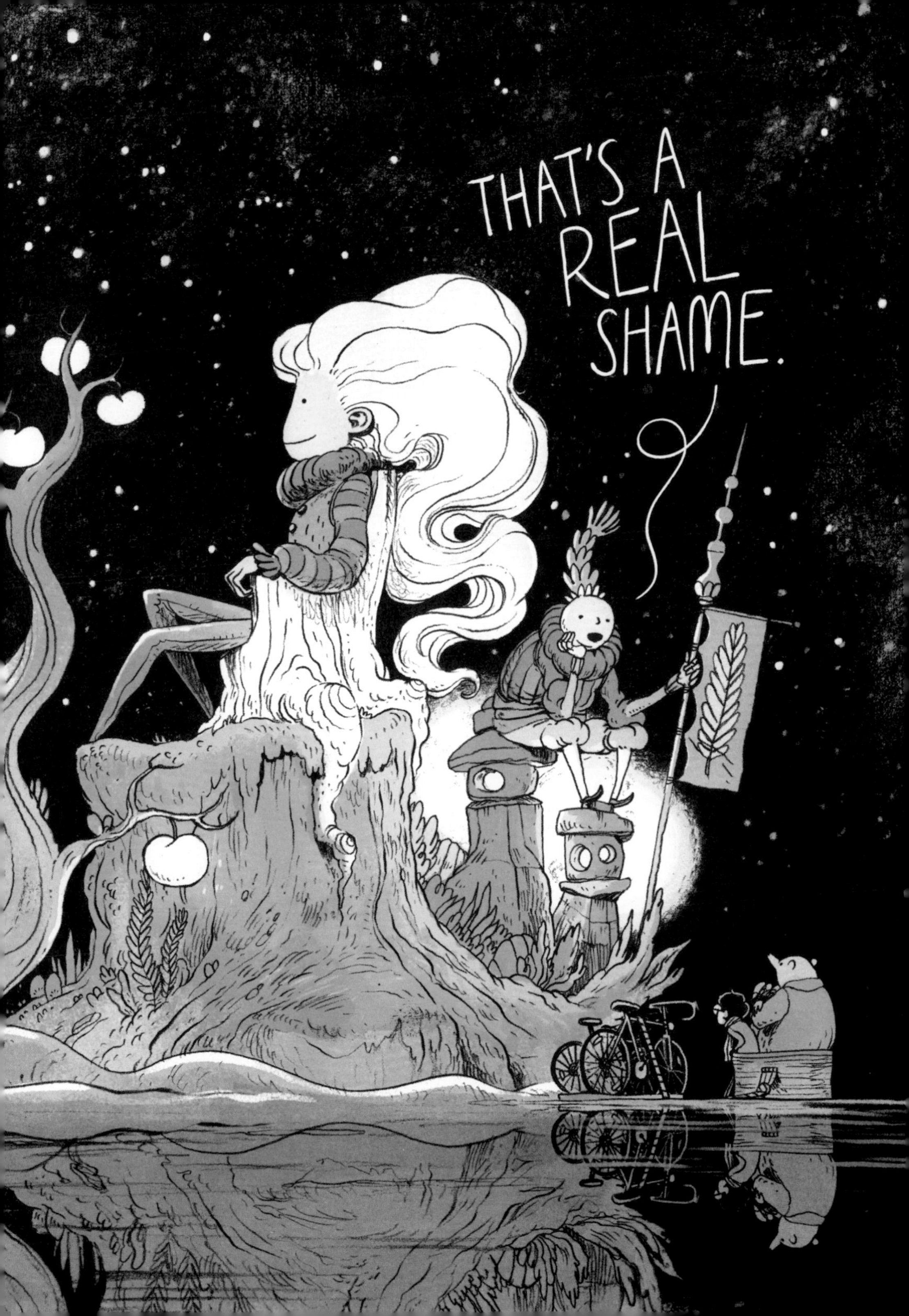
THAT'S A REAL SHAME.

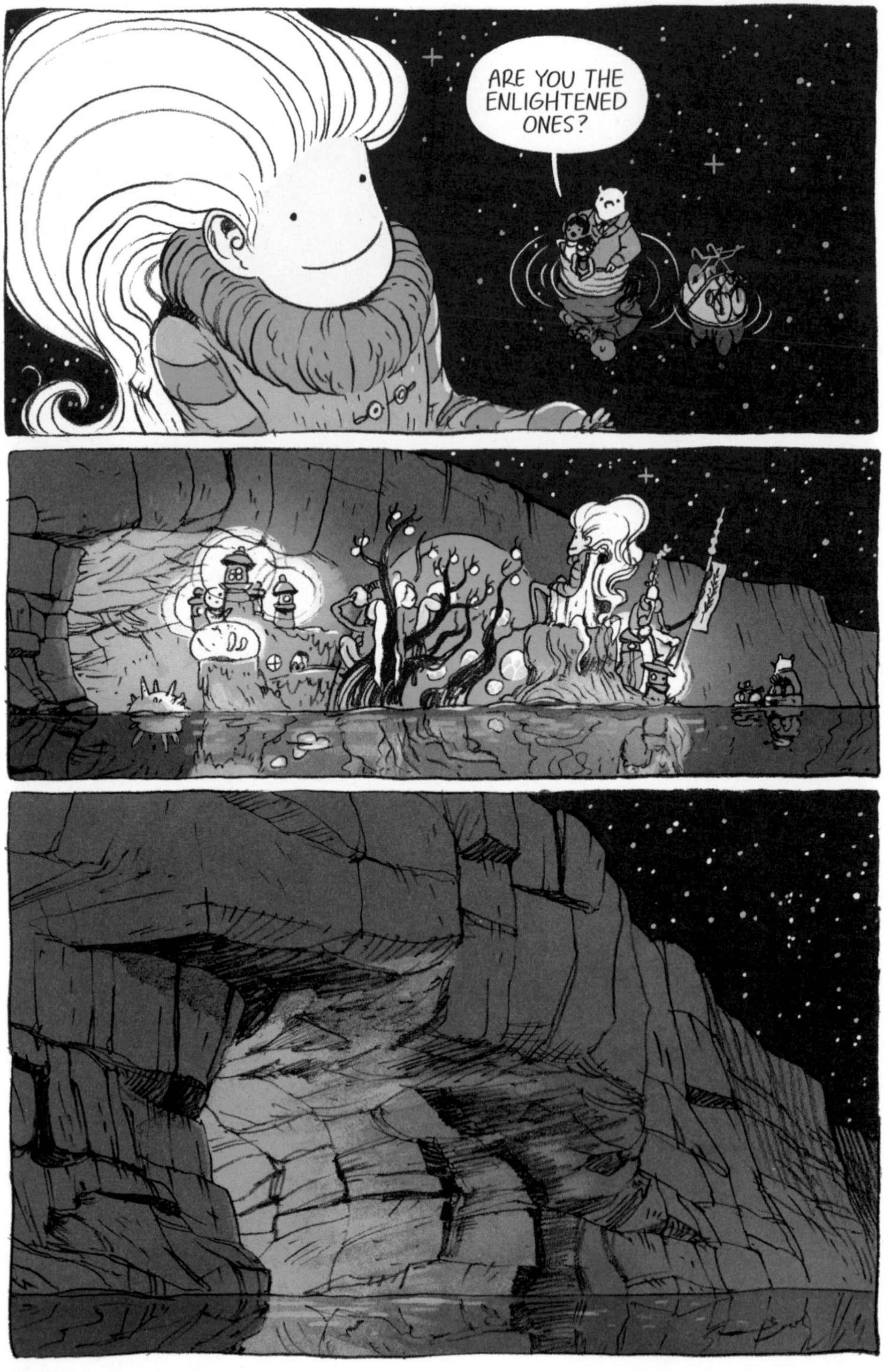
ARE YOU THE ENLIGHTENED ONES?

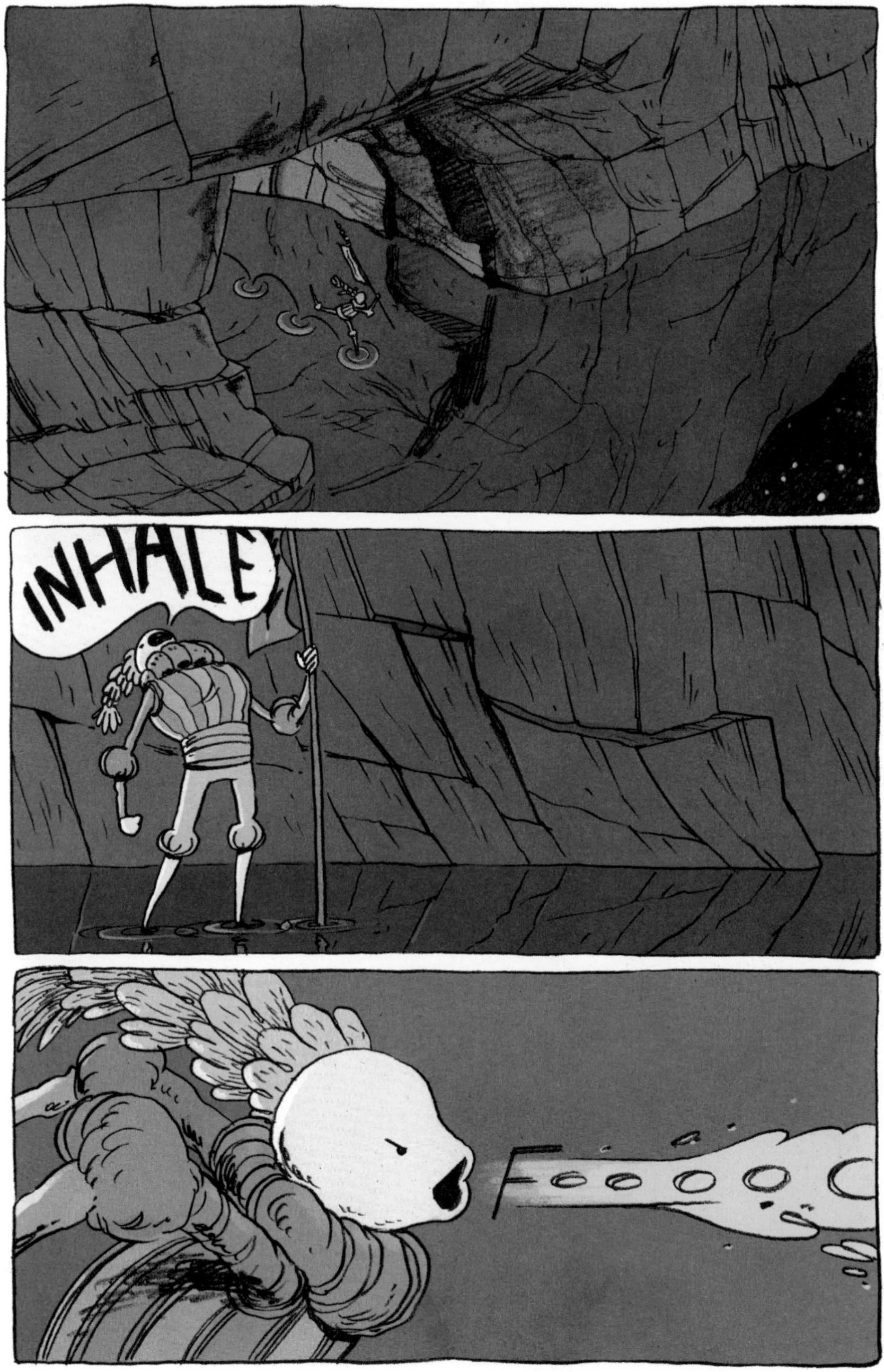
INHALE
FOOOO

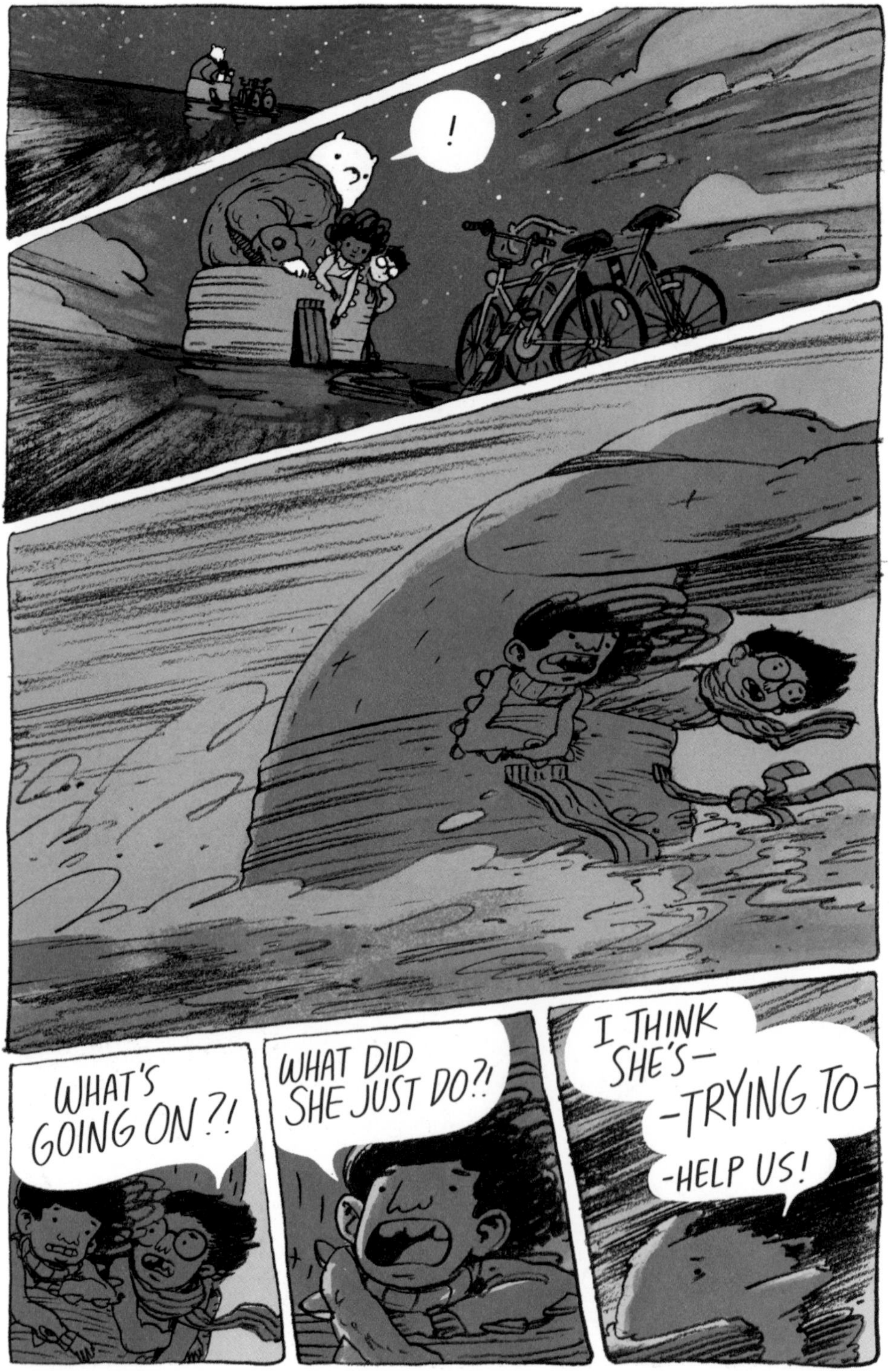
!
WHAT'S GOING ON?!
WHAT DID SHE JUST DO?!
I THINK SHE'S—
—TRYING TO—
—HELP US!

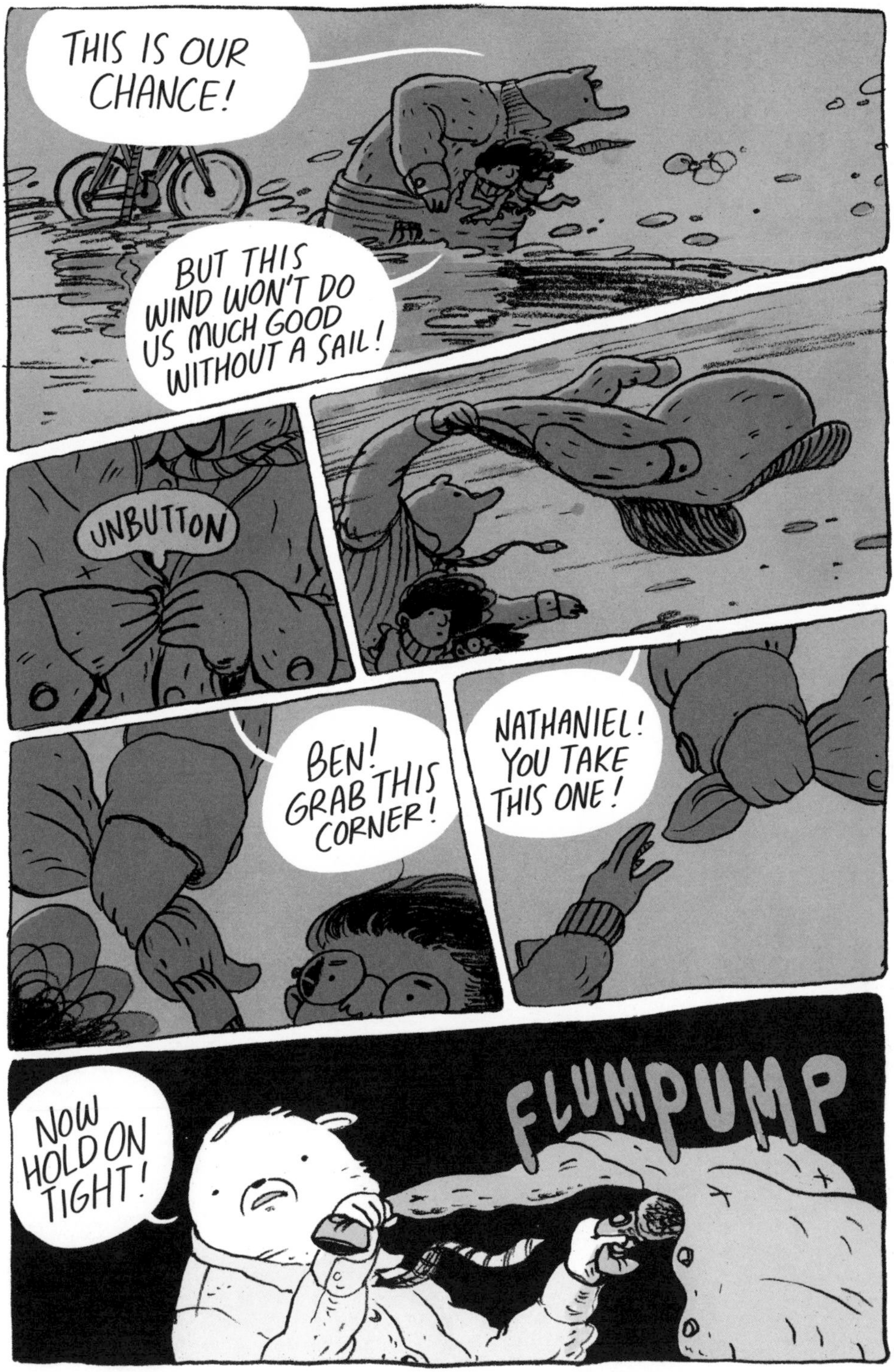
THIS IS OUR CHANCE!
BUT THIS WIND WON'T DO US MUCH GOOD WITHOUT A SAIL!
UNBUTTON
BEN! GRAB THIS CORNER!
NATHANIEL! YOU TAKE THIS ONE!
NOW HOLD ON TIGHT!
FLUMPUMP

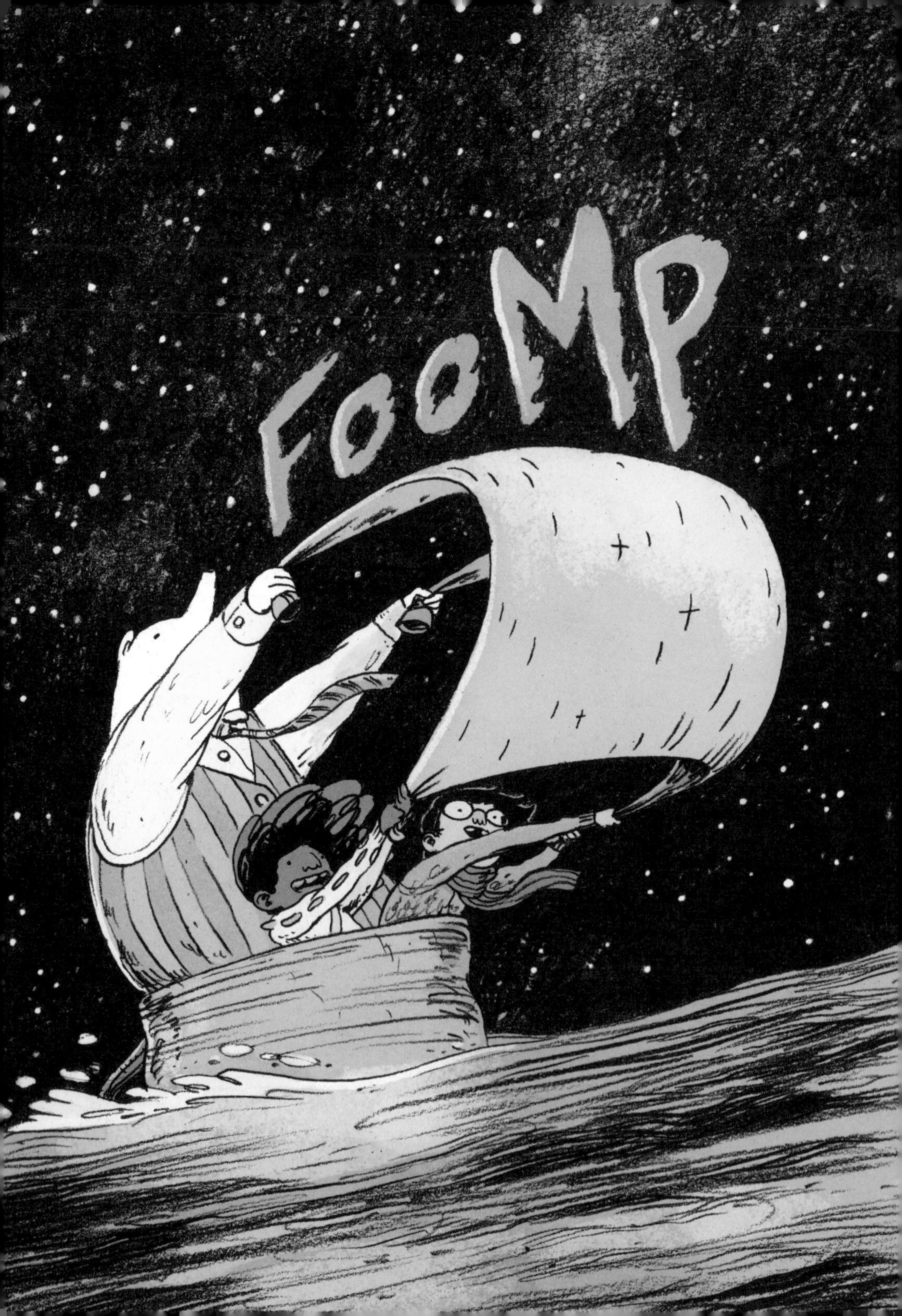
FOOMP

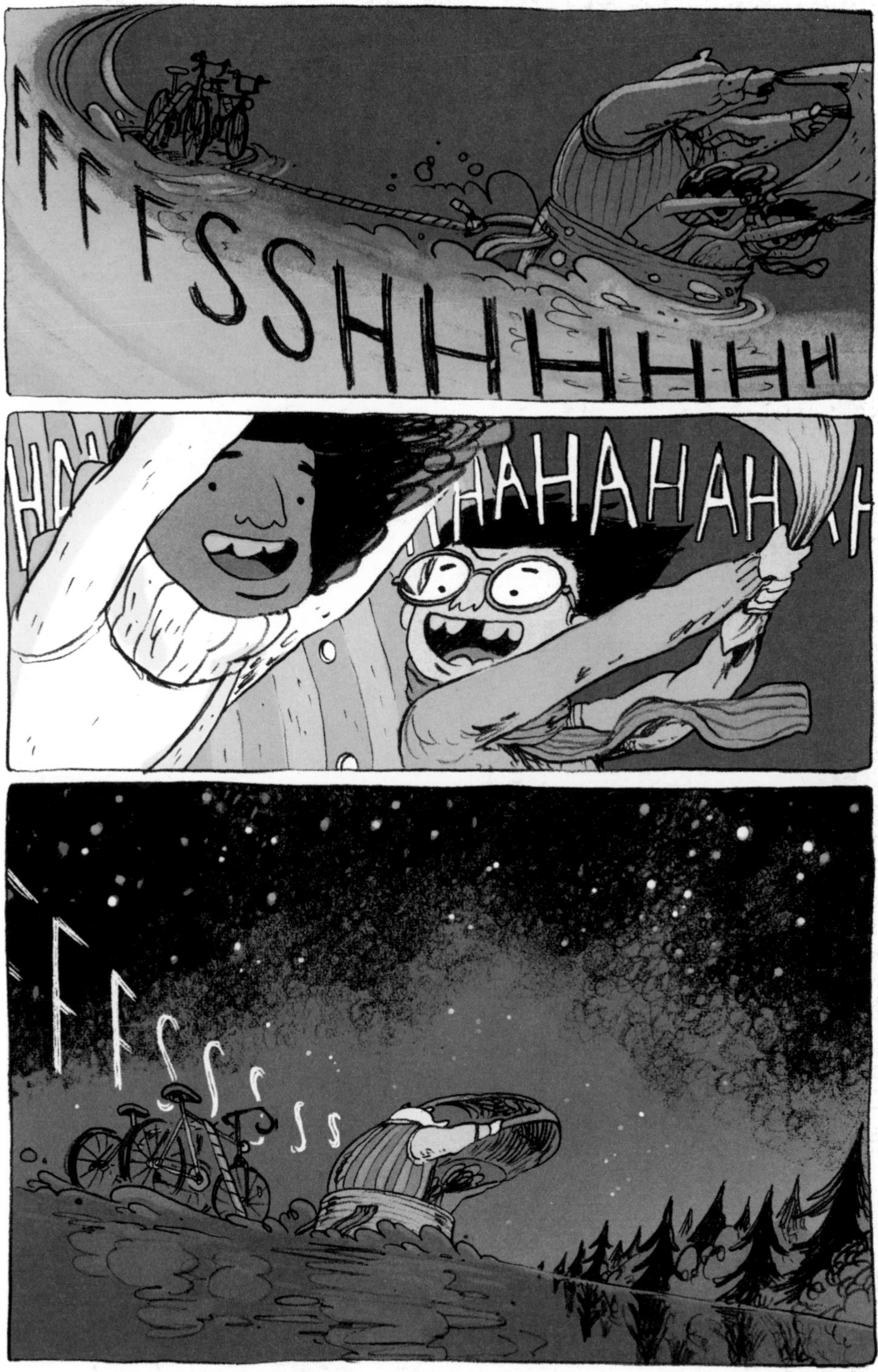
FFFFSSHHHHHHH
HAHAHAHAH
FFFSSSSSSS

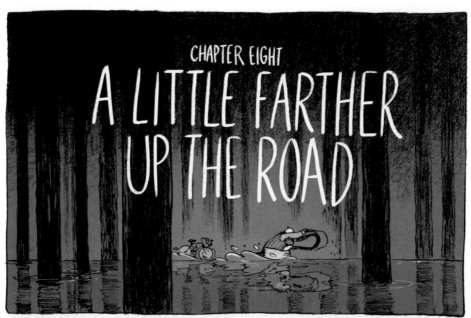

CHAPTER EIGHT
A LITTLE FARTHER UP THE ROAD

THE ROAD!

WE'RE PASSING RIGHT OVER IT!

TURN! TURN!

HMPH!

YANK

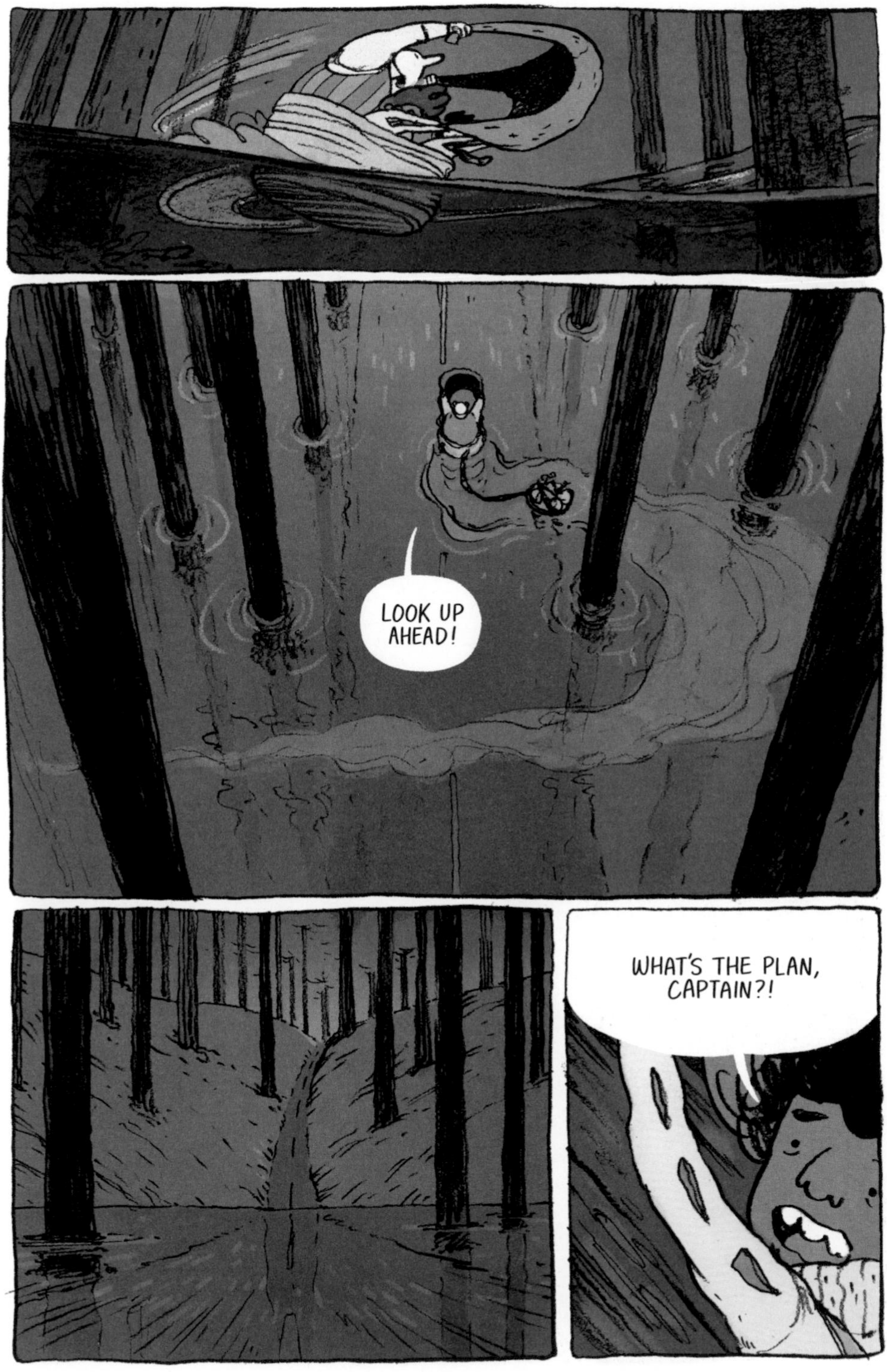
LOOK UP AHEAD!
WHAT'S THE PLAN, CAPTAIN?!

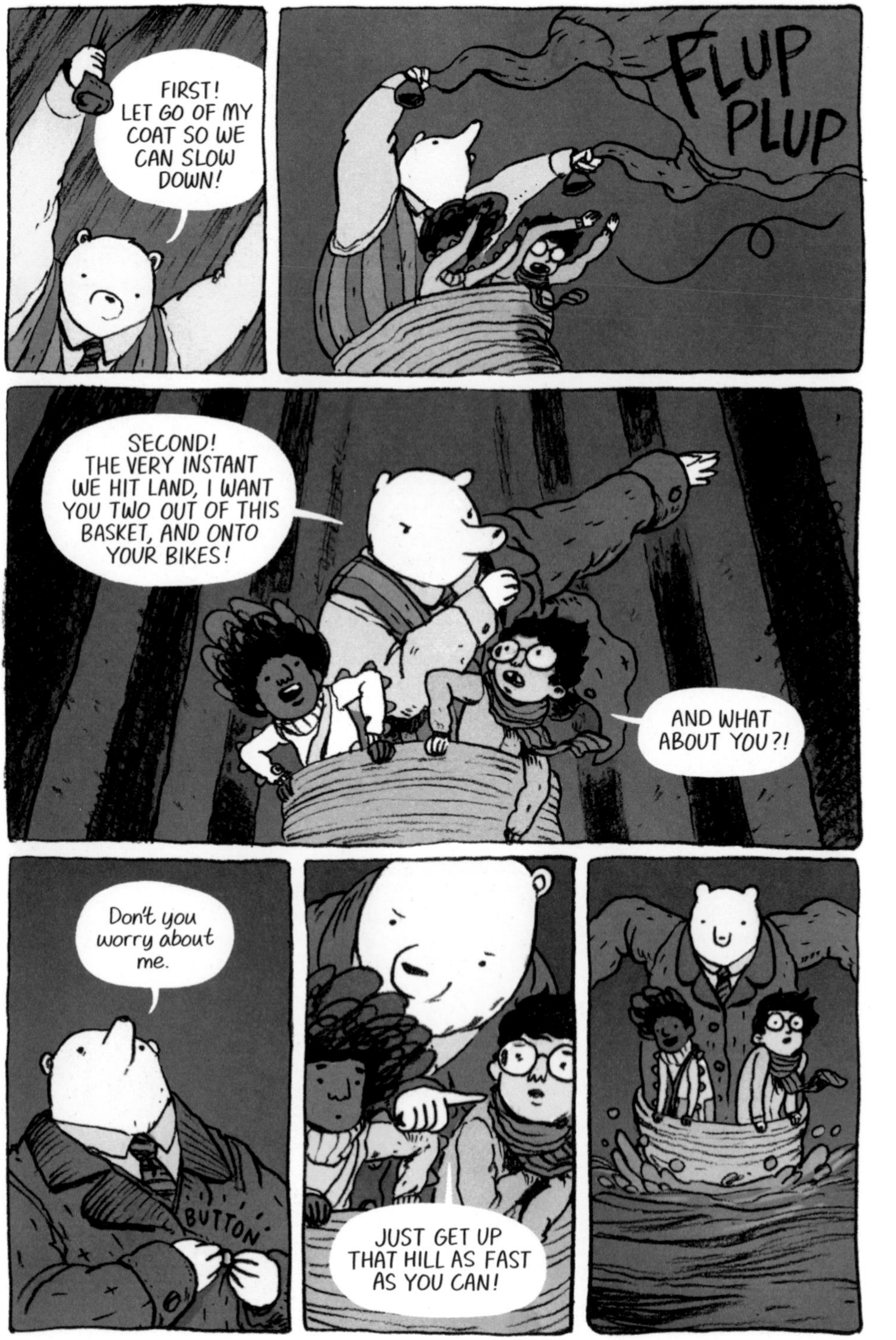
FIRST! LET GO OF MY COAT SO WE CAN SLOW DOWN!
FLUP PLUP
SECOND! THE VERY INSTANT WE HIT LAND, I WANT YOU TWO OUT OF THIS BASKET, AND ONTO YOUR BIKES!
AND WHAT ABOUT YOU?!
Don't you worry about me.
BUTTON
JUST GET UP THAT HILL AS FAST AS YOU CAN!

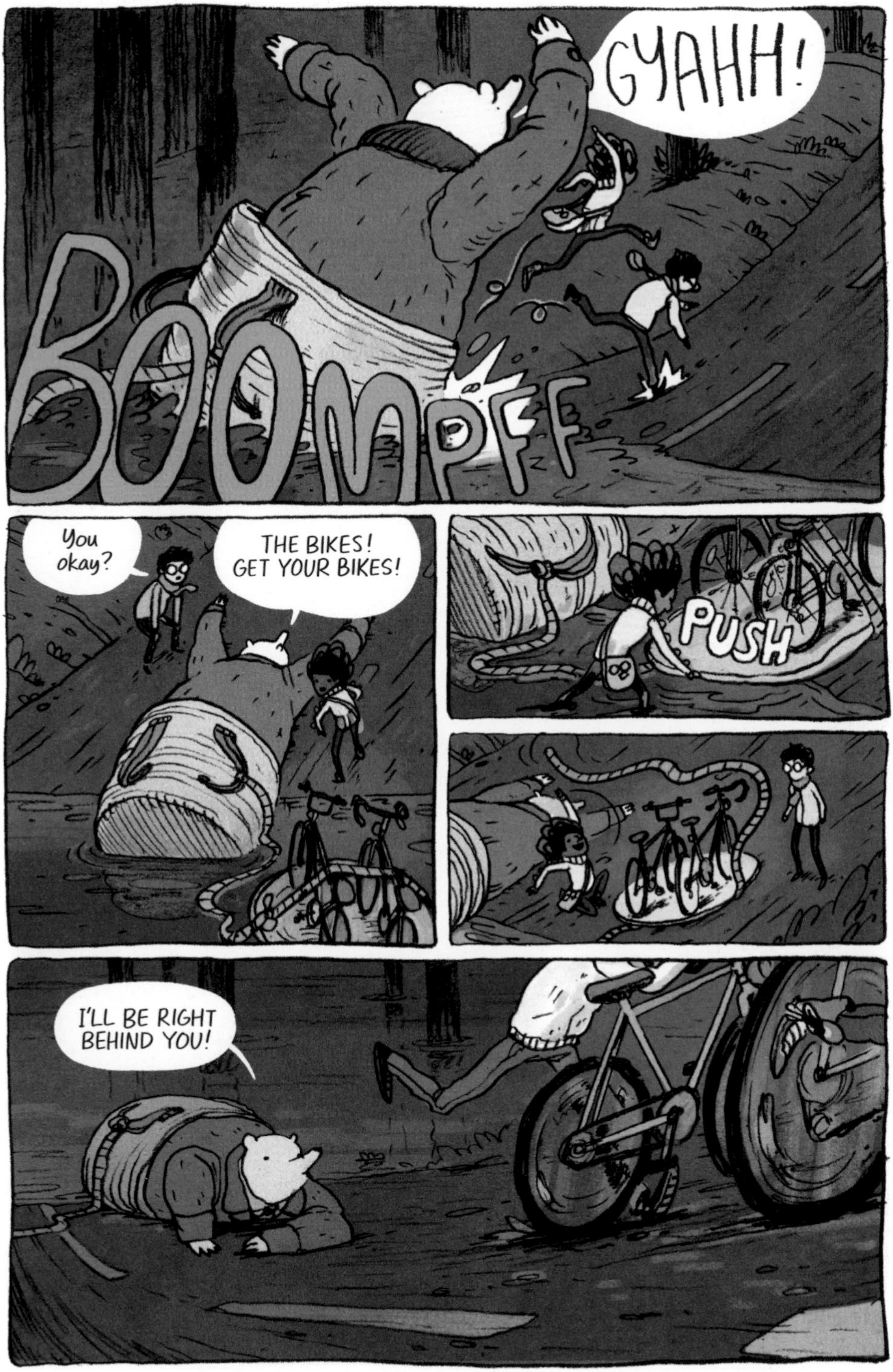
GYAHH!
BOOMPFF
You okay?
THE BIKES! GET YOUR BIKES!
PUSH
I'LL BE RIGHT BEHIND YOU!

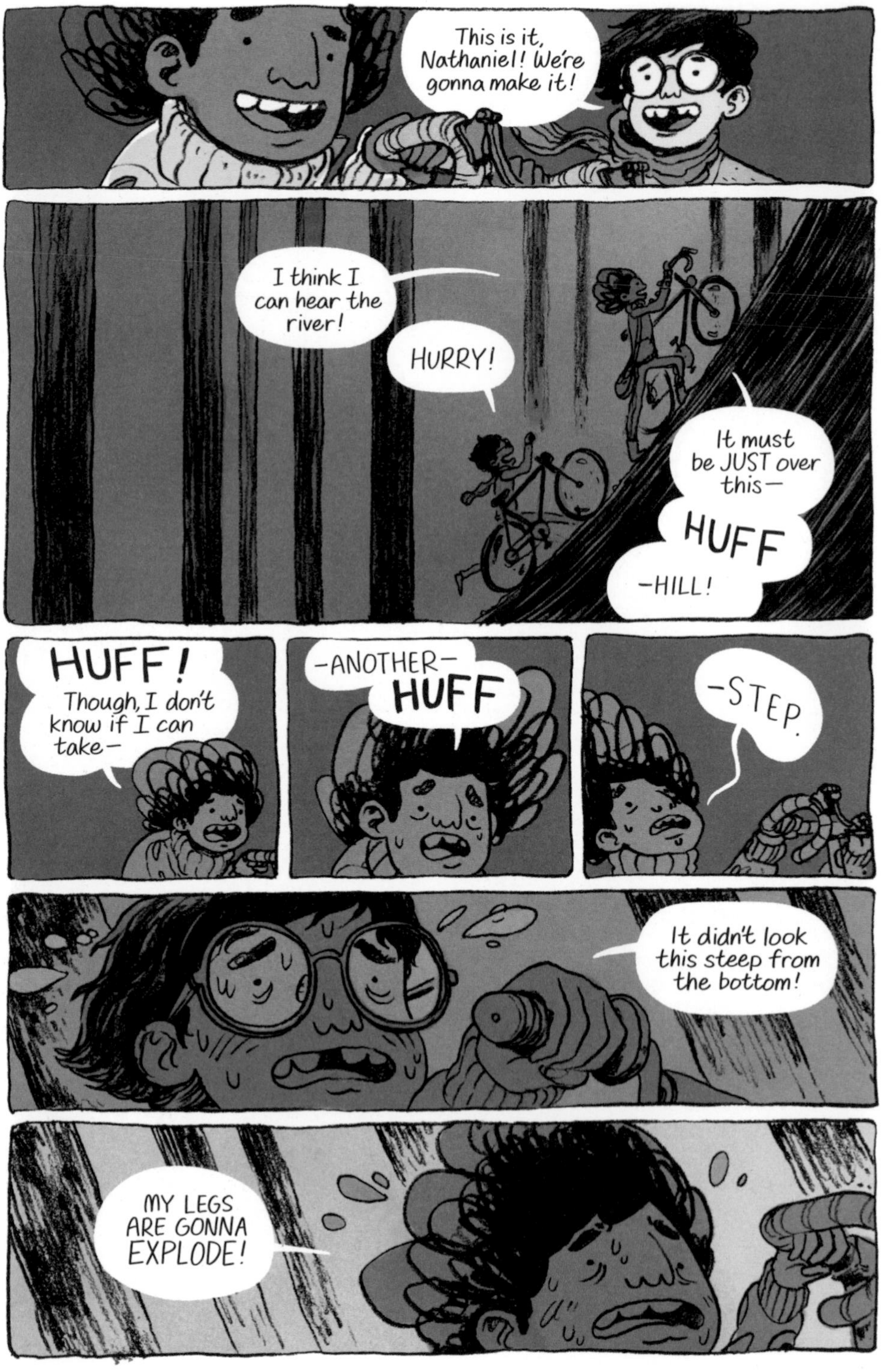
This is it, Nathaniel! We're gonna make it!
I think I can hear the river!
HURRY!
It must be JUST over this—
HUFF
—HILL!
HUFF!
Though, I don't know if I can take—
—ANOTHER—
HUFF
—STEP.
It didn't look this steep from the bottom!
MY LEGS ARE GONNA EXPLODE!

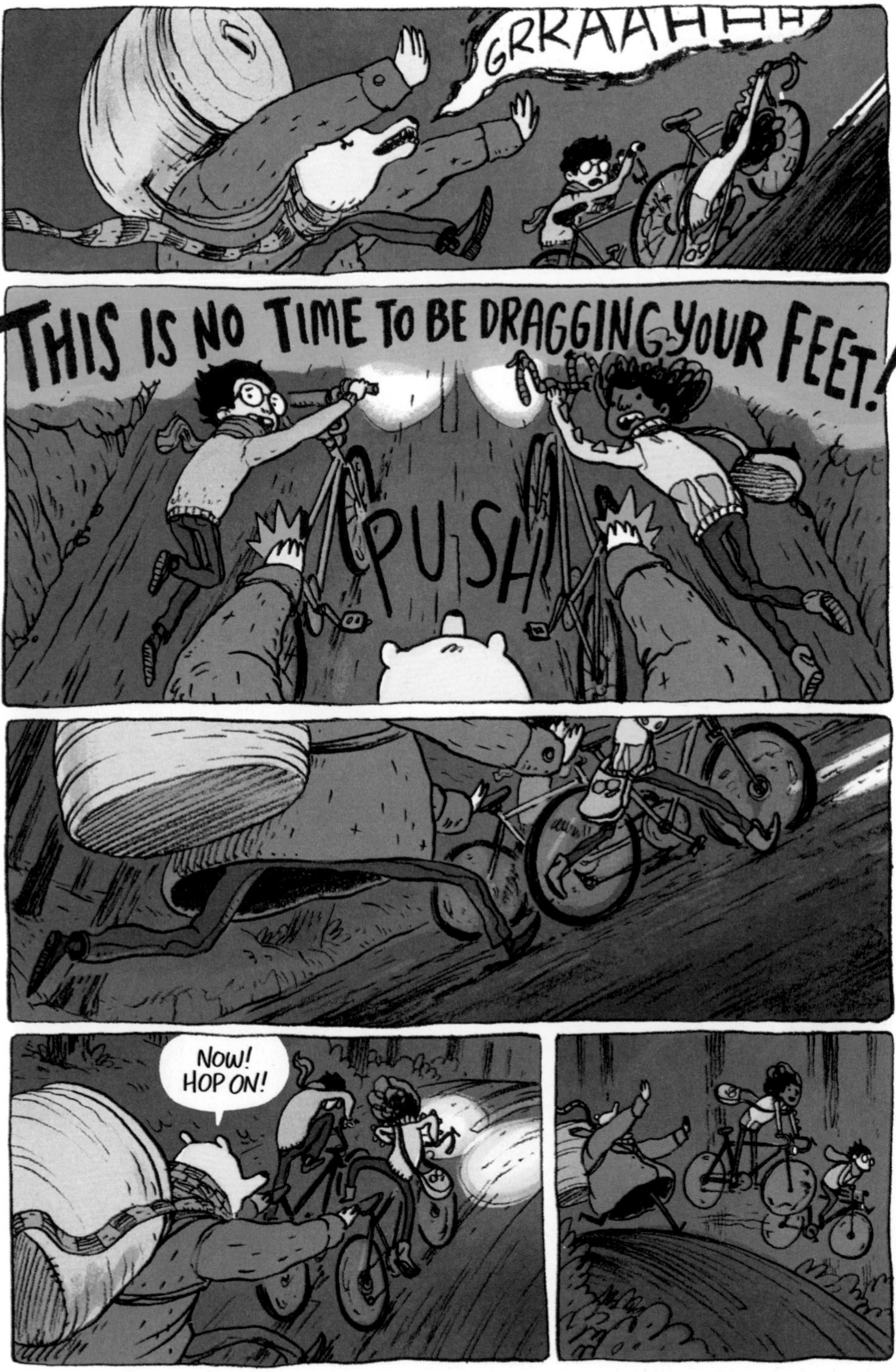
GRRAAHHH
THIS IS NO TIME TO BE DRAGGING YOUR FEET!
PUSH
NOW! HOP ON!

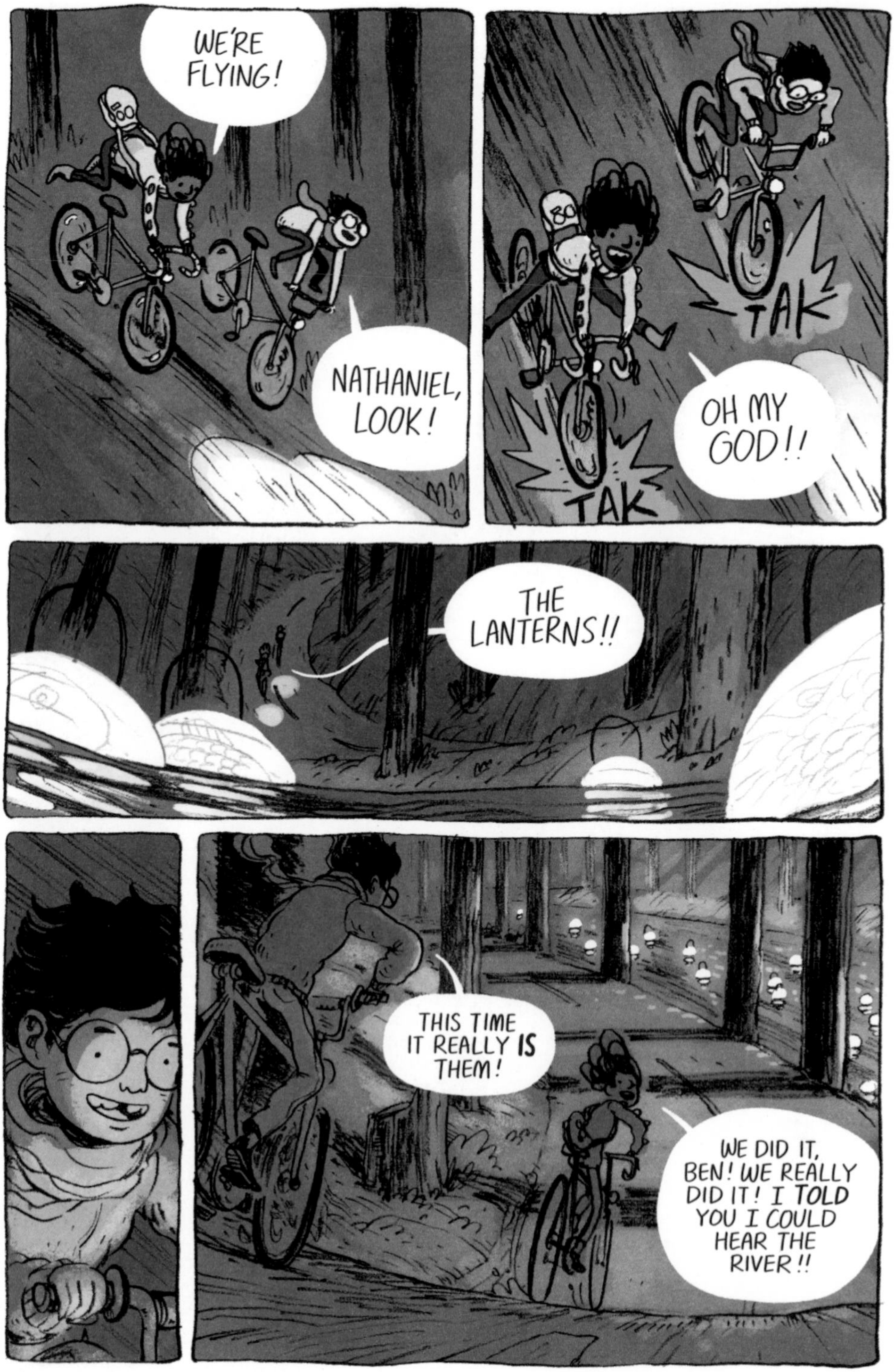

WE'RE FLYING!
NATHANIEL, LOOK!
TAK
TAK
OH MY GOD!!
THE LANTERNS!!
THIS TIME IT REALLY IS THEM!
WE DID IT, BEN! WE REALLY DID IT! I TOLD YOU I COULD HEAR THE RIVER!!

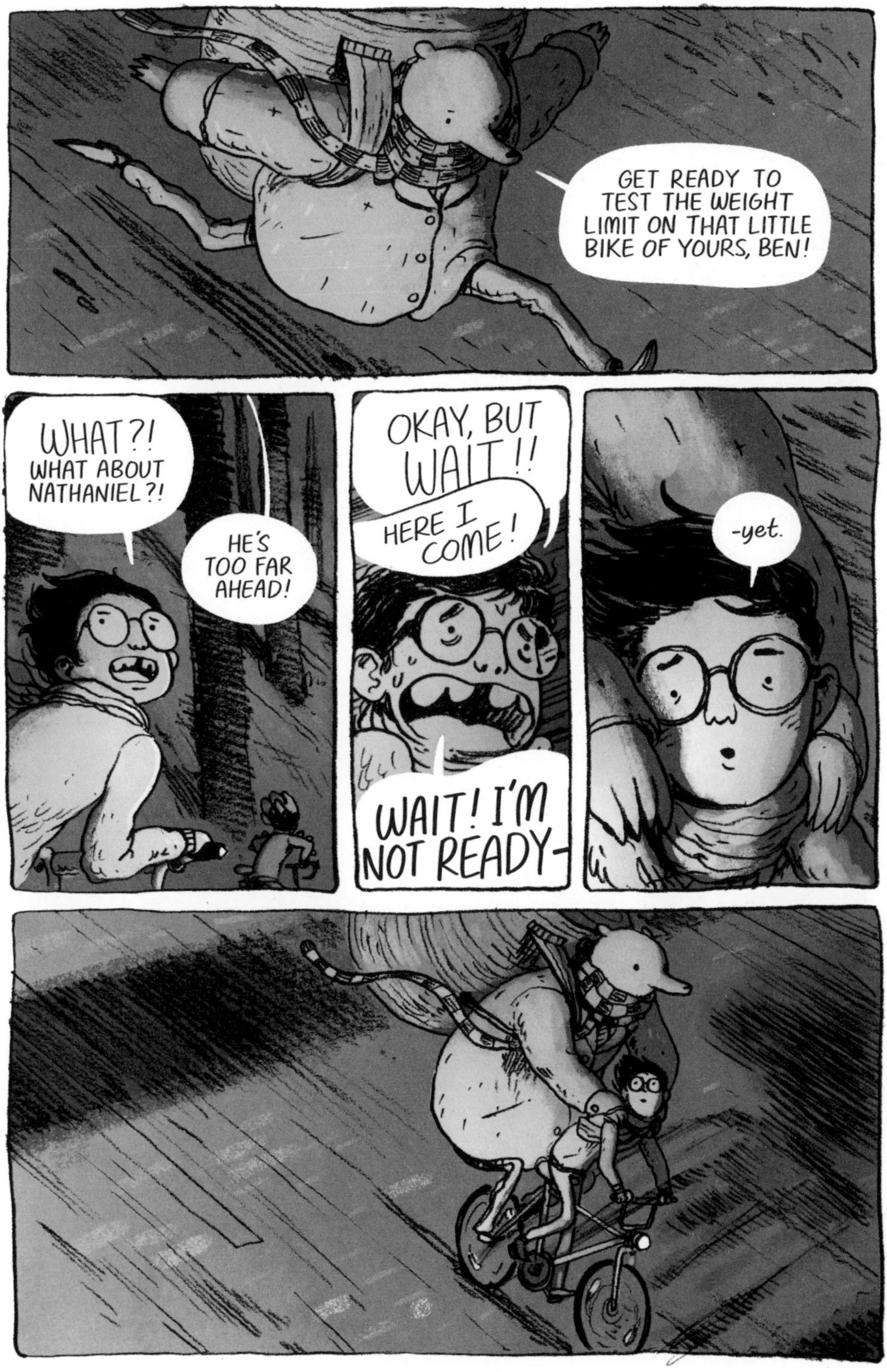
GET READY TO TEST THE WEIGHT LIMIT ON THAT LITTLE BIKE OF YOURS, BEN!
WHAT?! WHAT ABOUT NATHANIEL?!
HE'S TOO FAR AHEAD!
OKAY, BUT WAIT!!
HERE I COME!
WAIT! I'M NOT READY-
-yet.

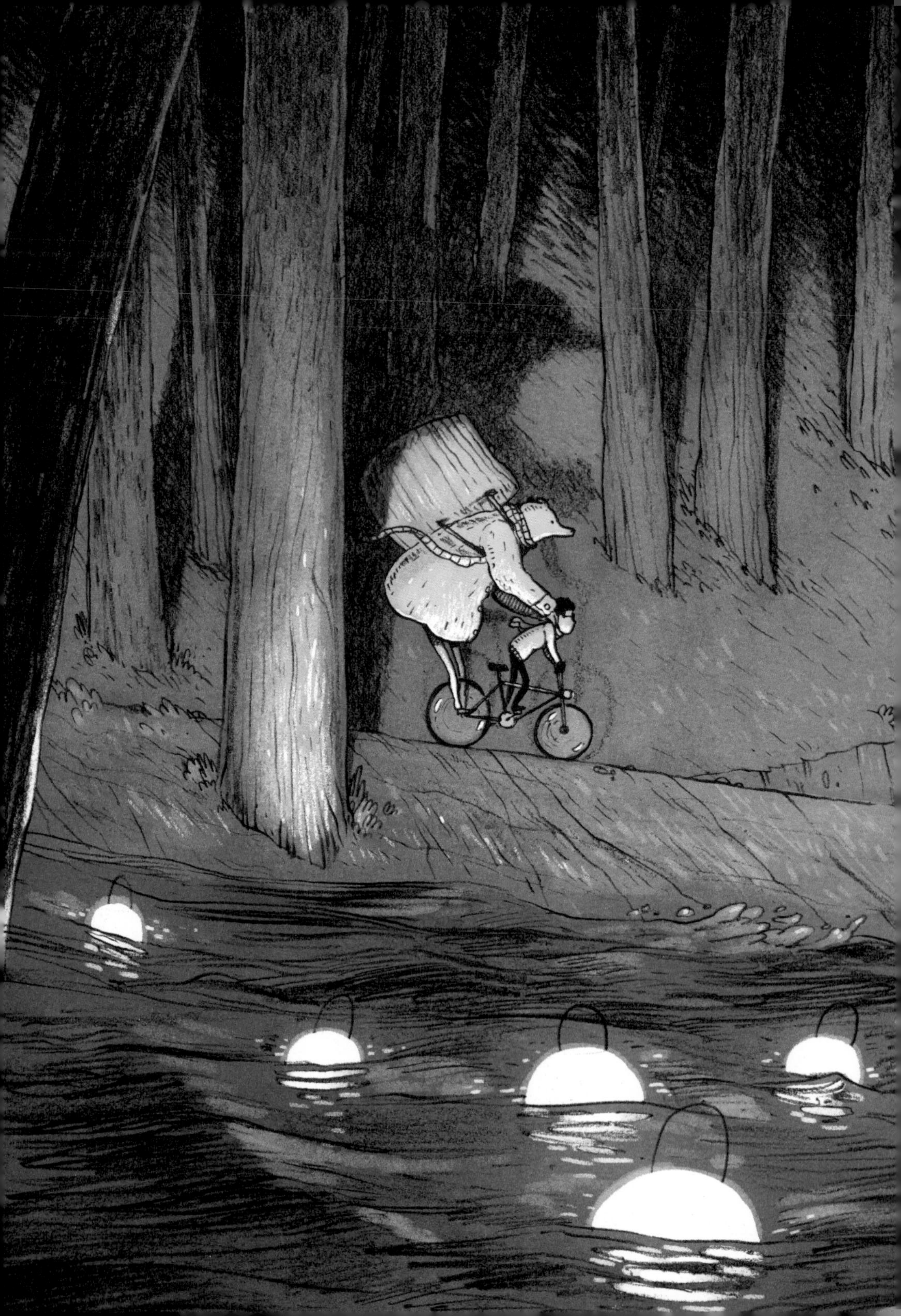

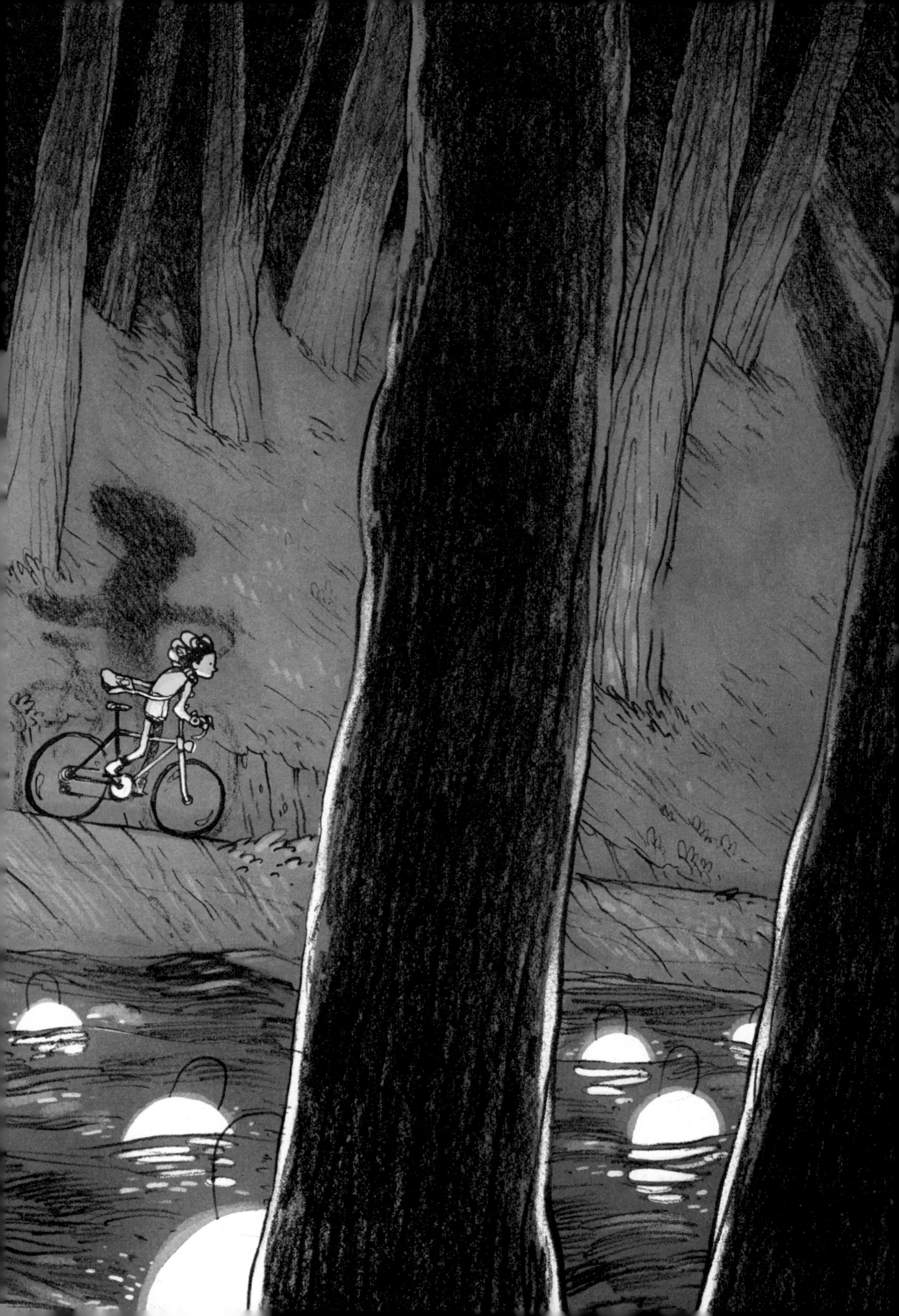

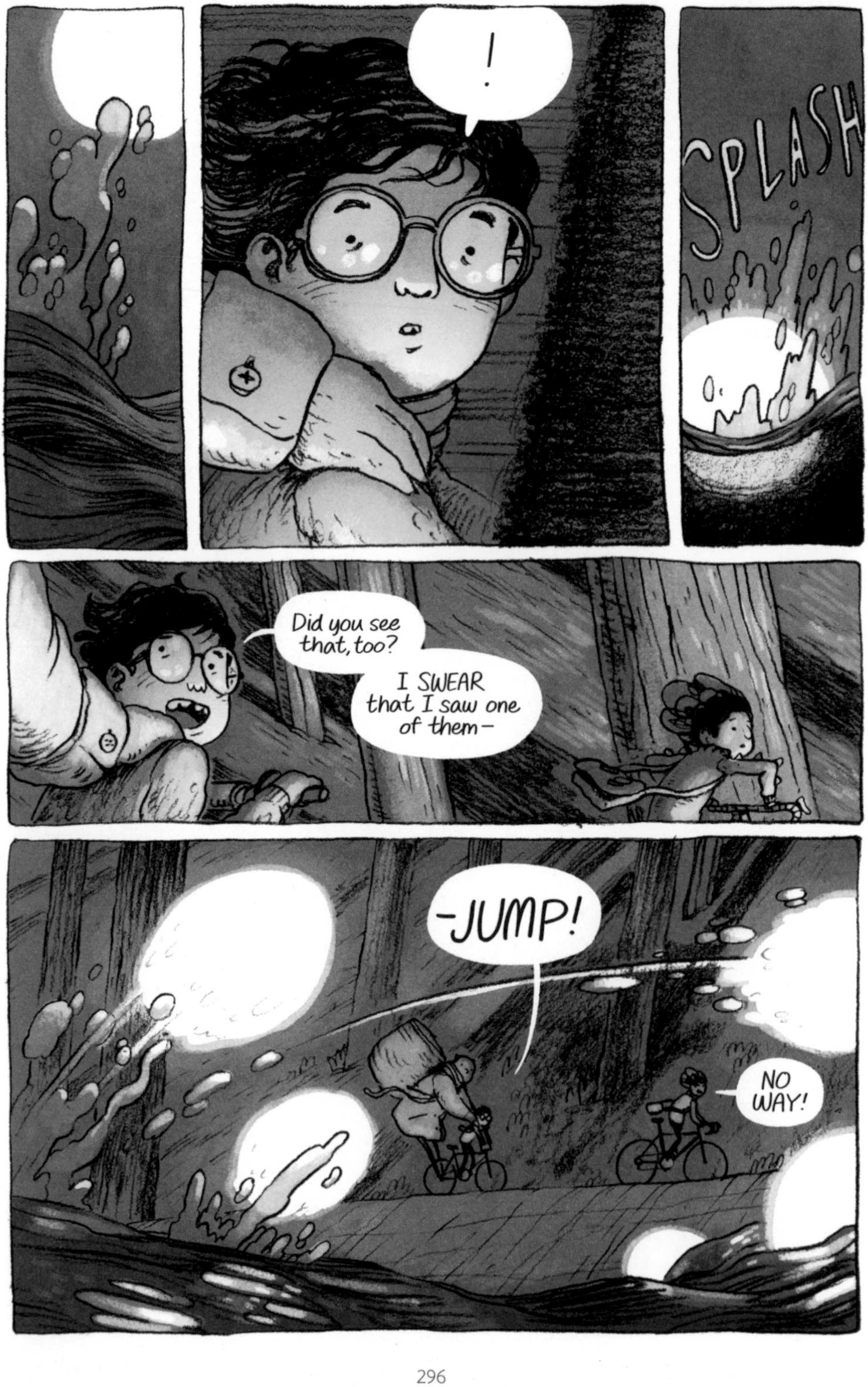
!
SPLASH
Did you see that, too?
I SWEAR that I saw one of them-
-JUMP!
NO WAY!

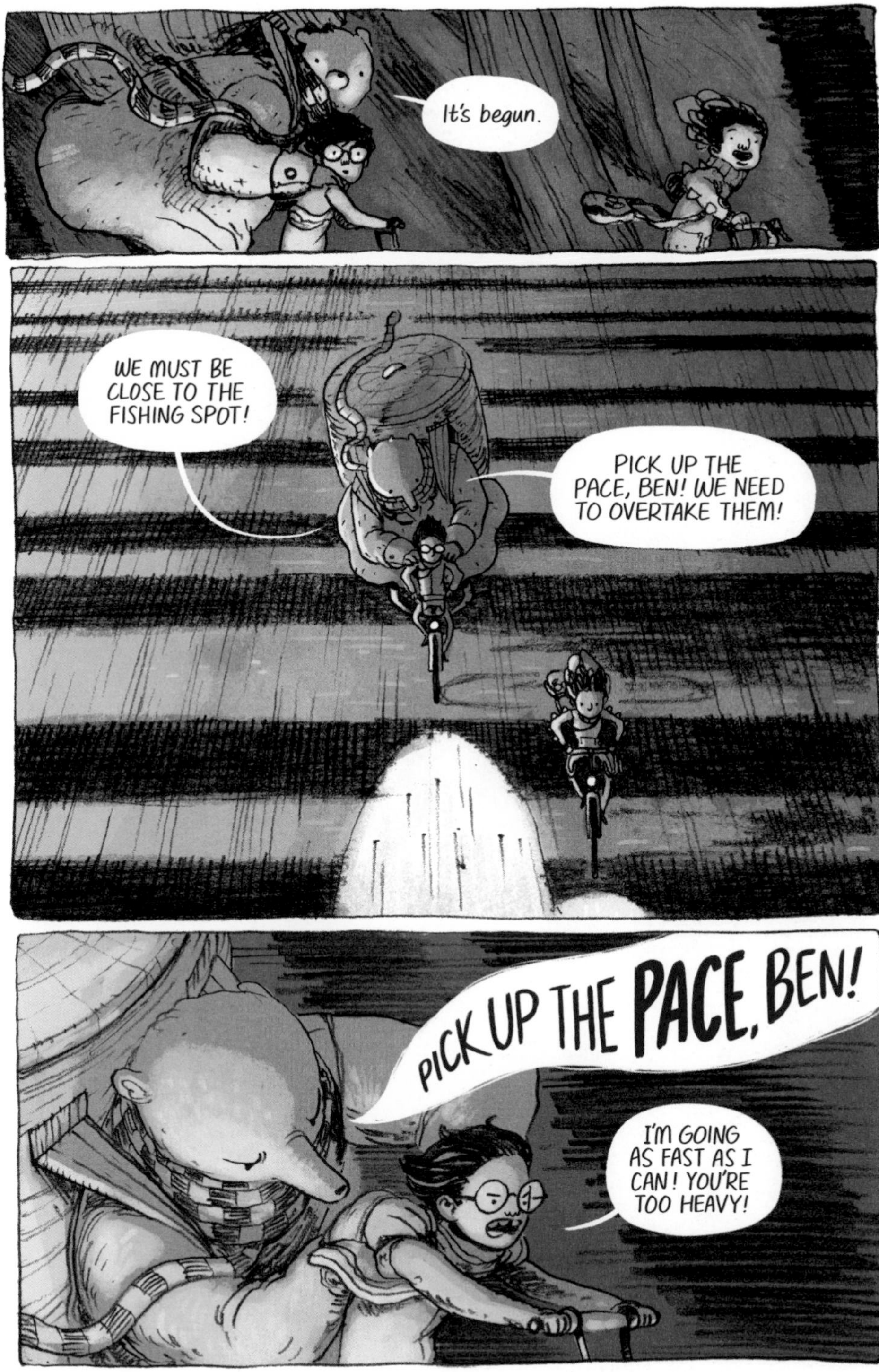
It's begun.
WE MUST BE CLOSE TO THE FISHING SPOT!
PICK UP THE PACE, BEN! WE NEED TO OVERTAKE THEM!
PICK UP THE PACE, BEN!
I'M GOING AS FAST AS I CAN! YOU'RE TOO HEAVY!

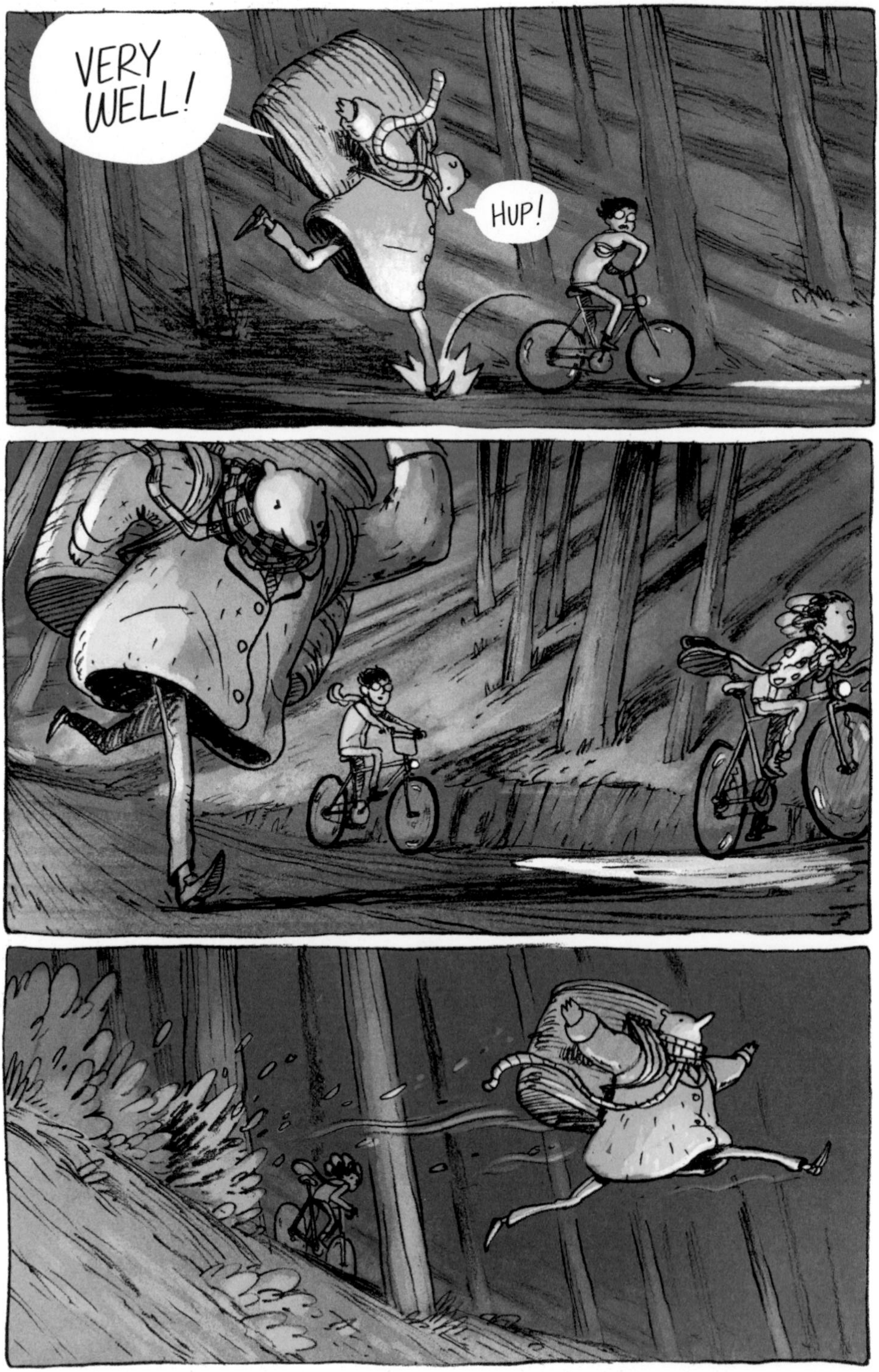
VERY WELL!
HUP!

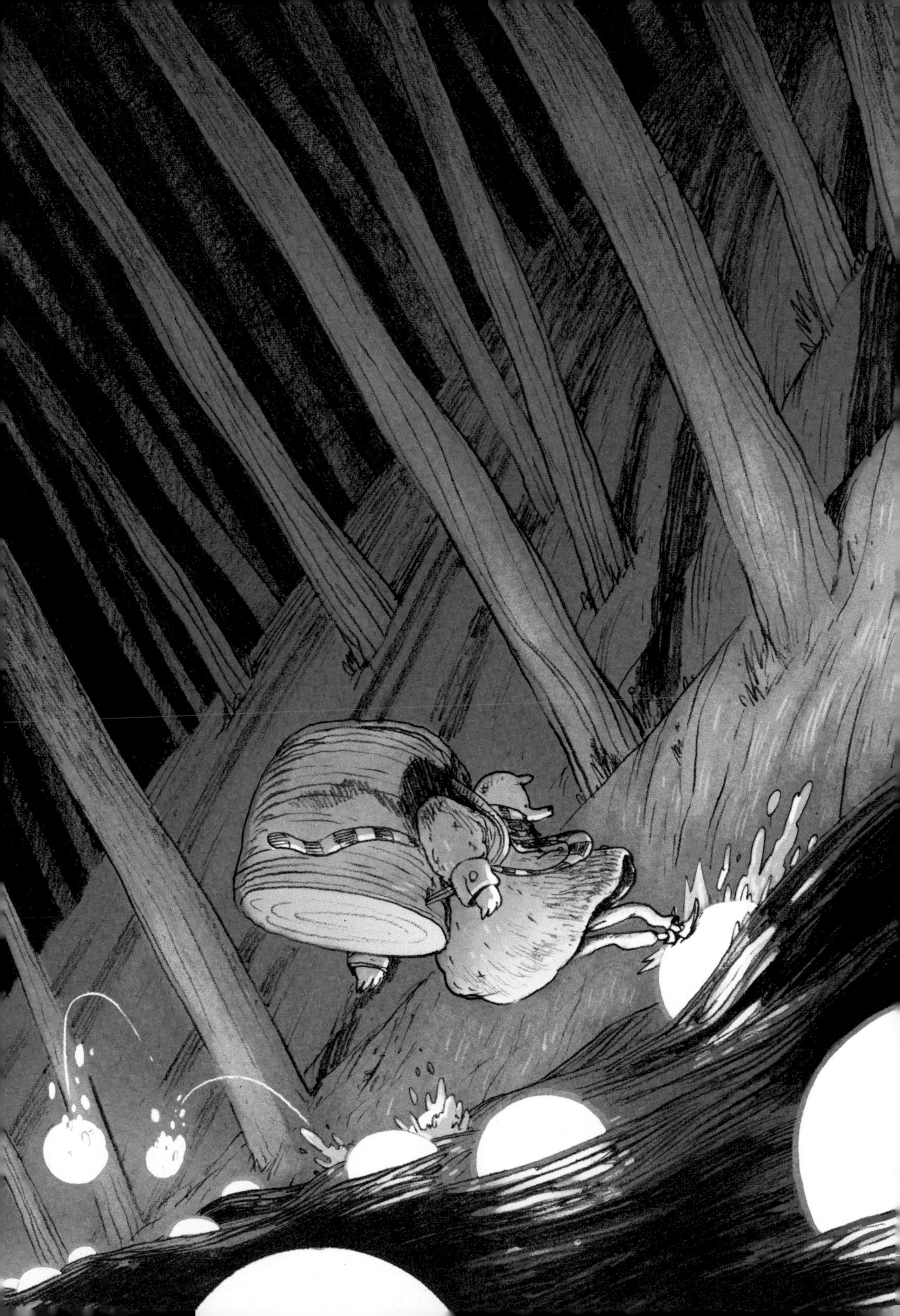

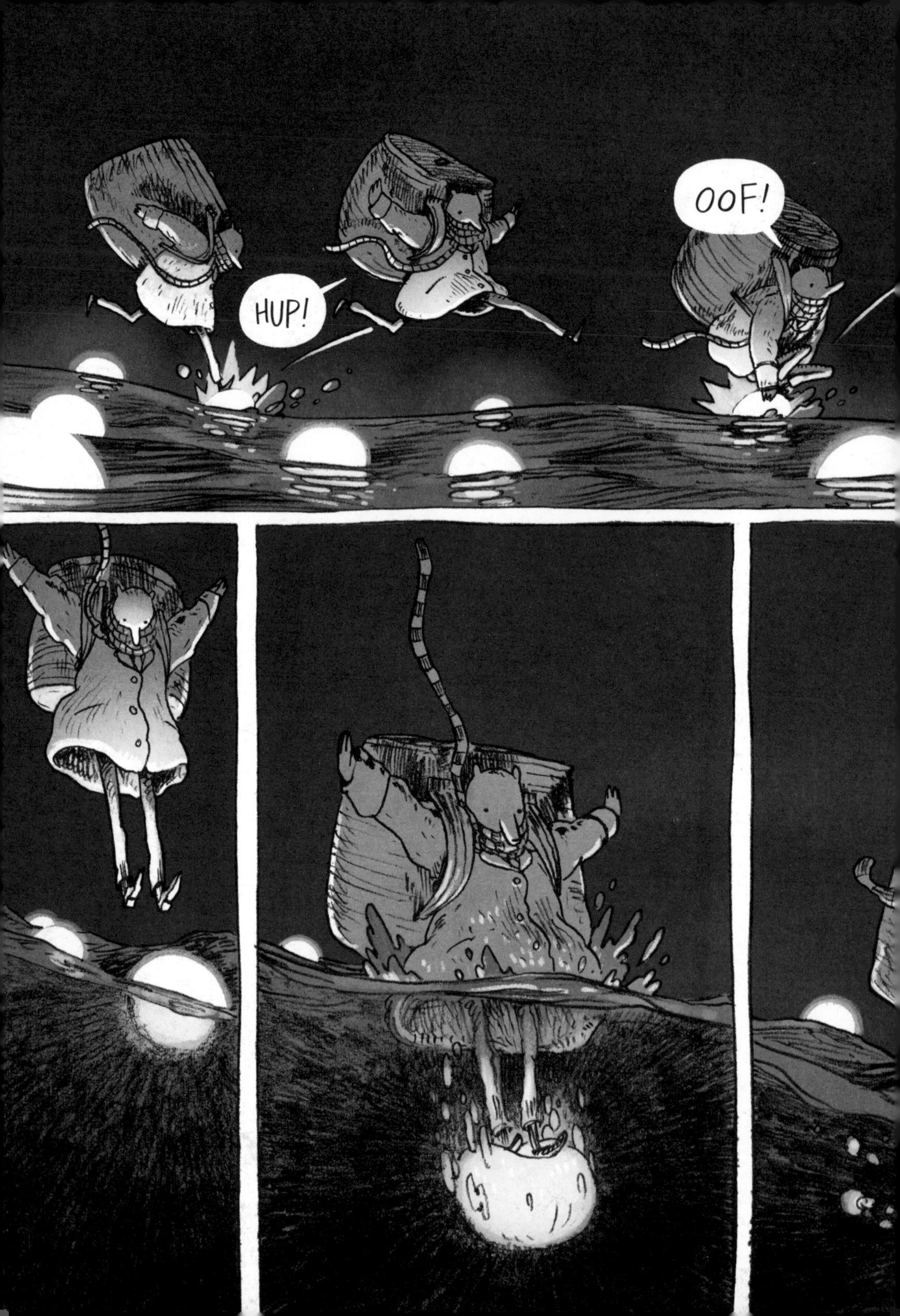
HUP!
OOF!

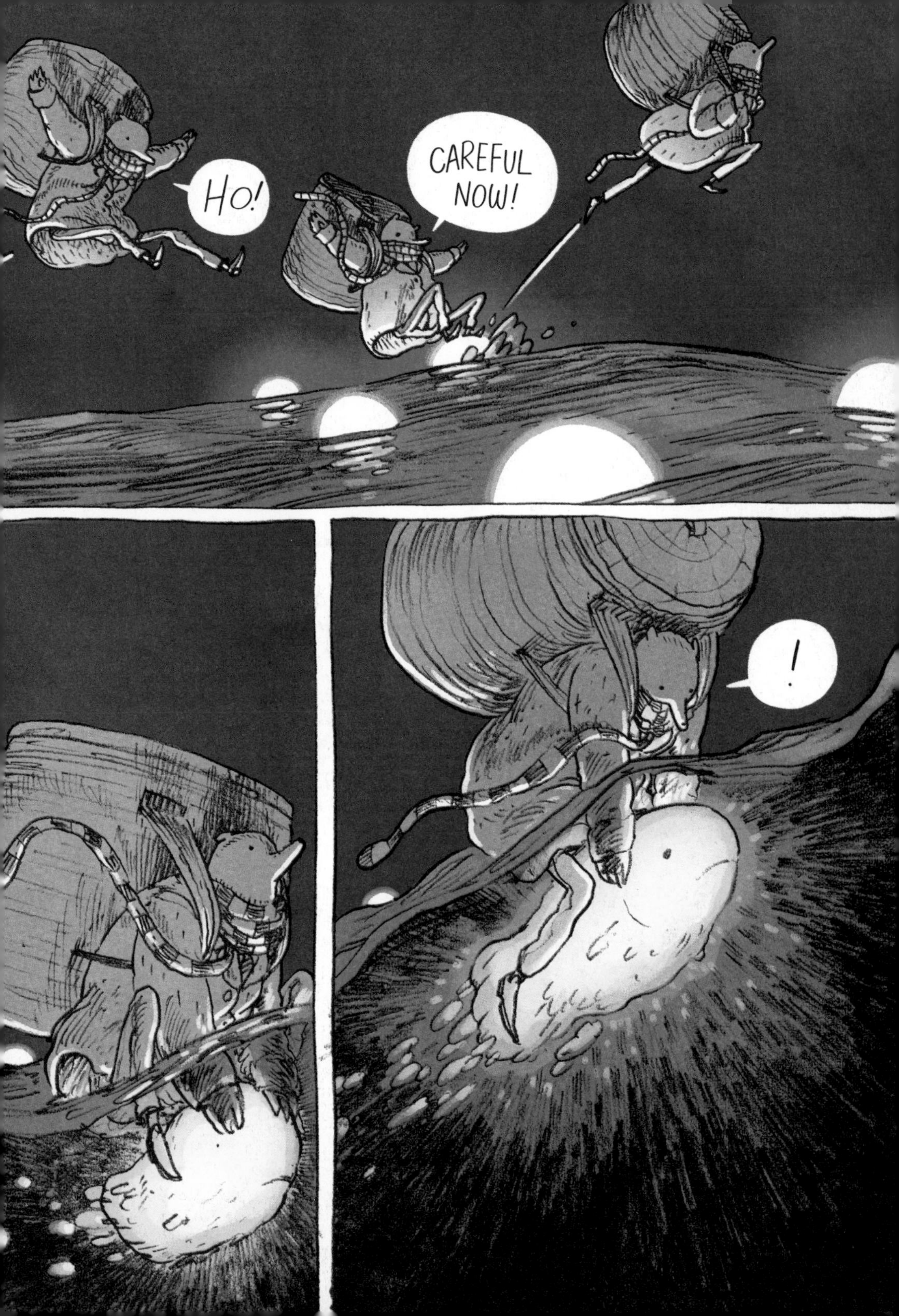
HO!
CAREFUL NOW!
!

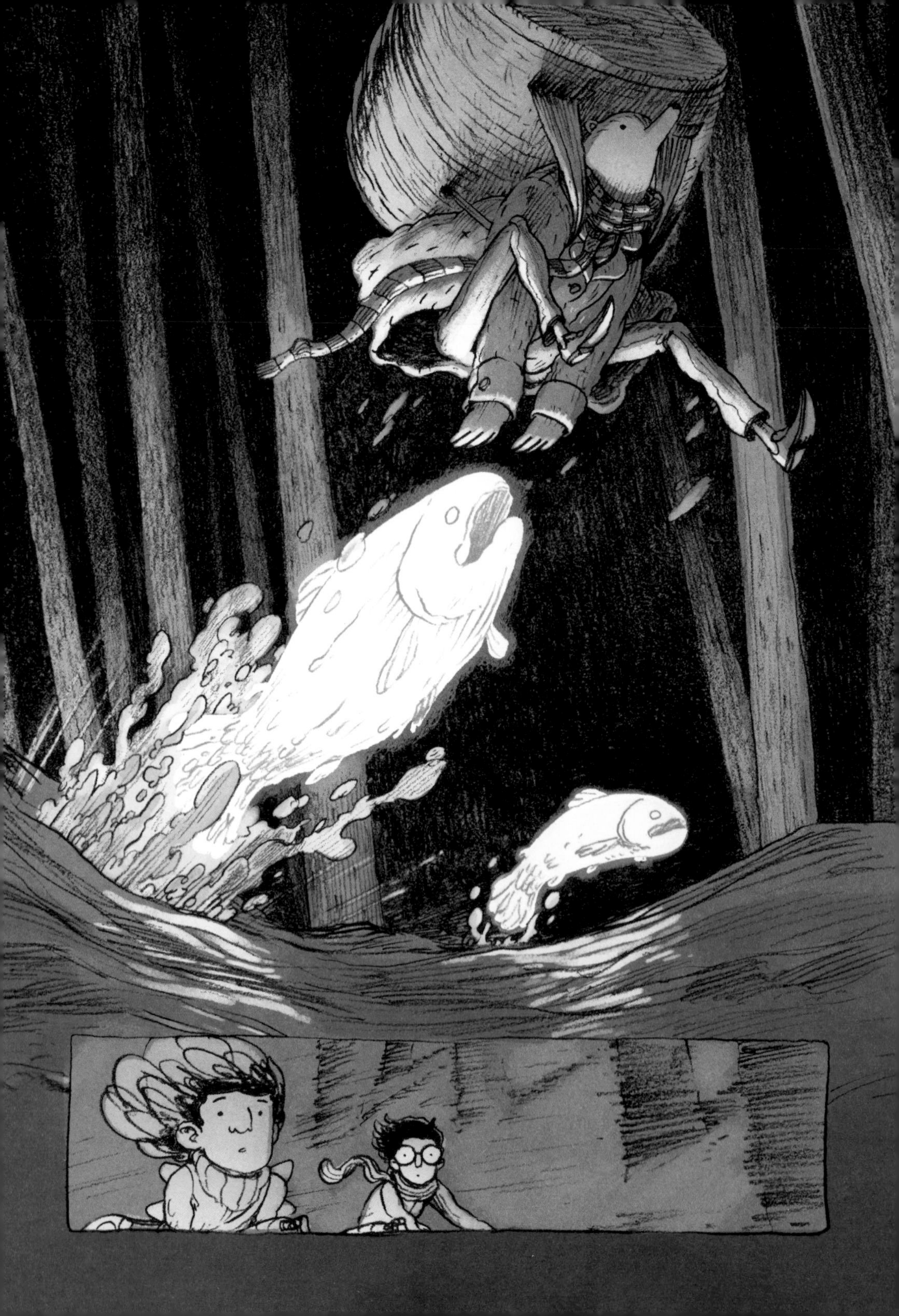

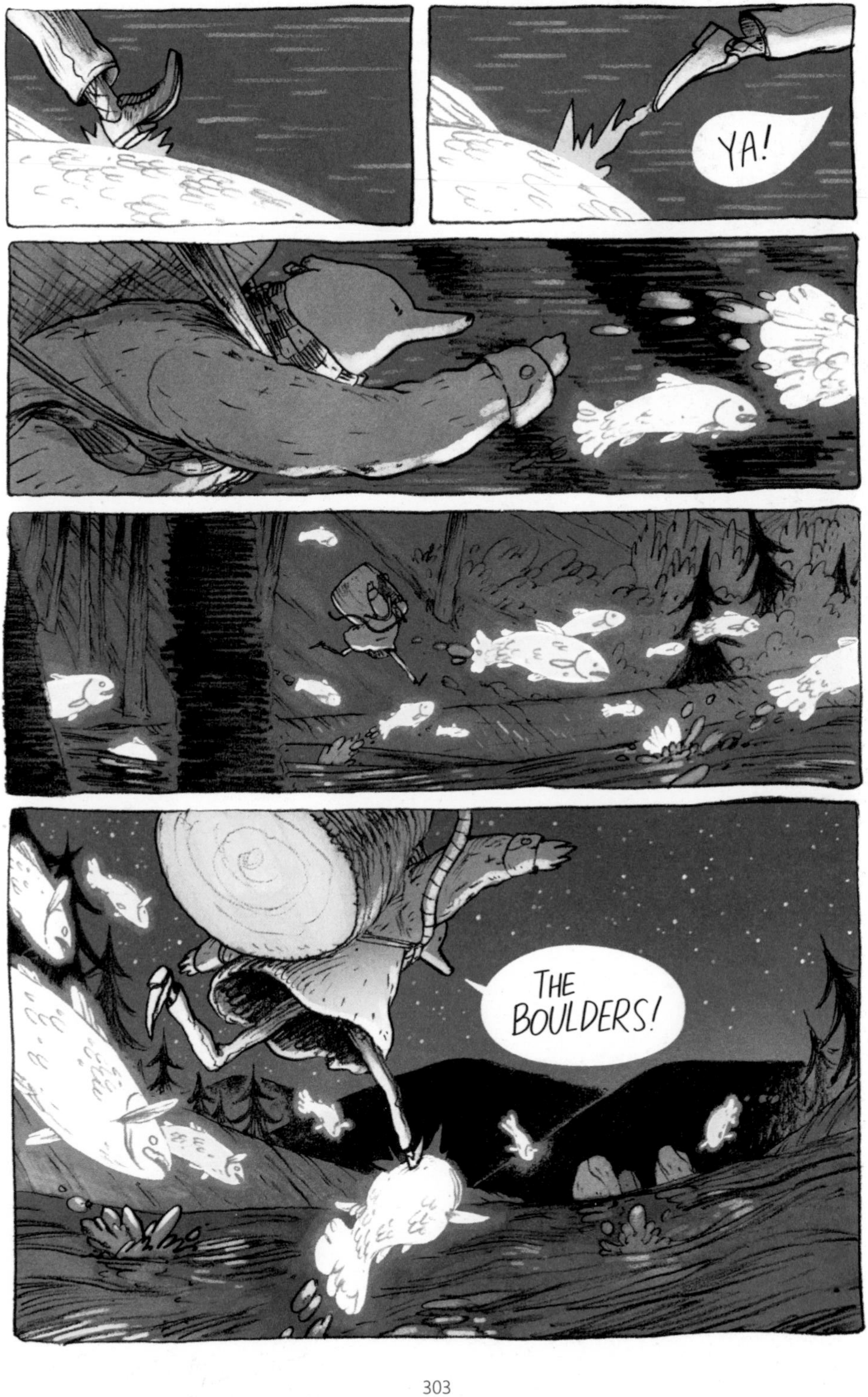
YA!
THE BOULDERS!

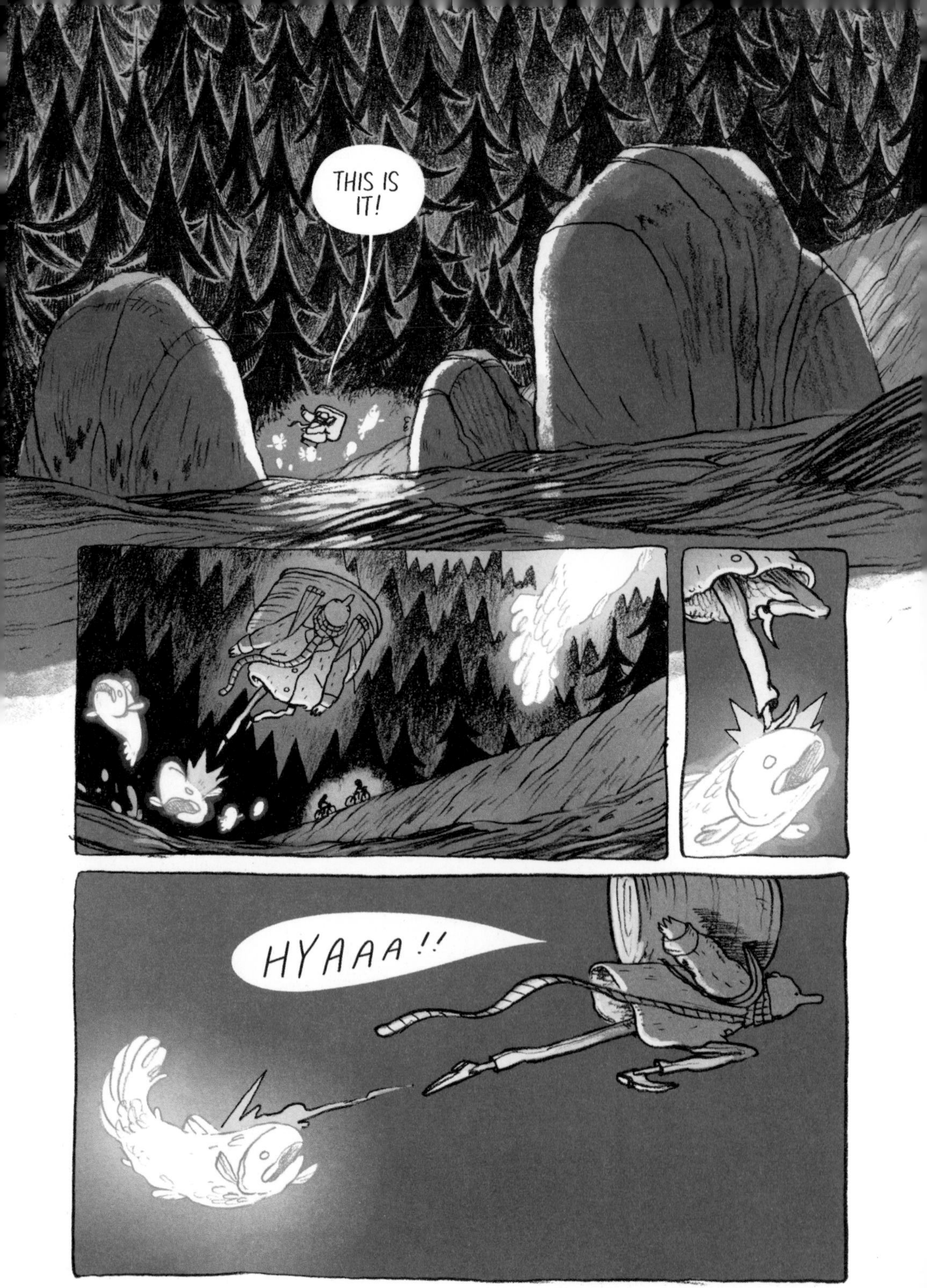
THIS IS IT!
HYAAA!!

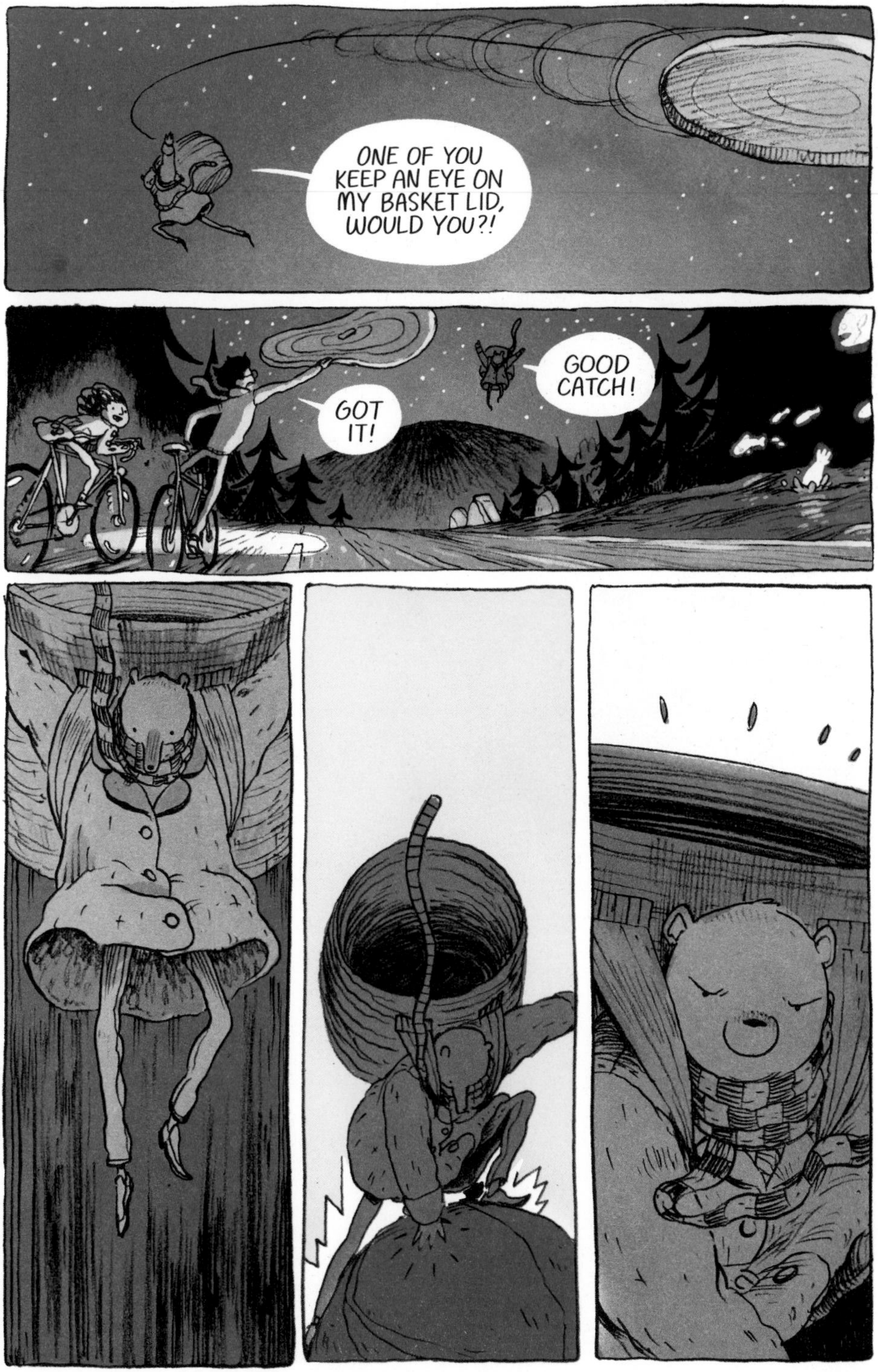
ONE OF YOU KEEP AN EYE ON MY BASKET LID, WOULD YOU?!
GOT IT!
GOOD CATCH!

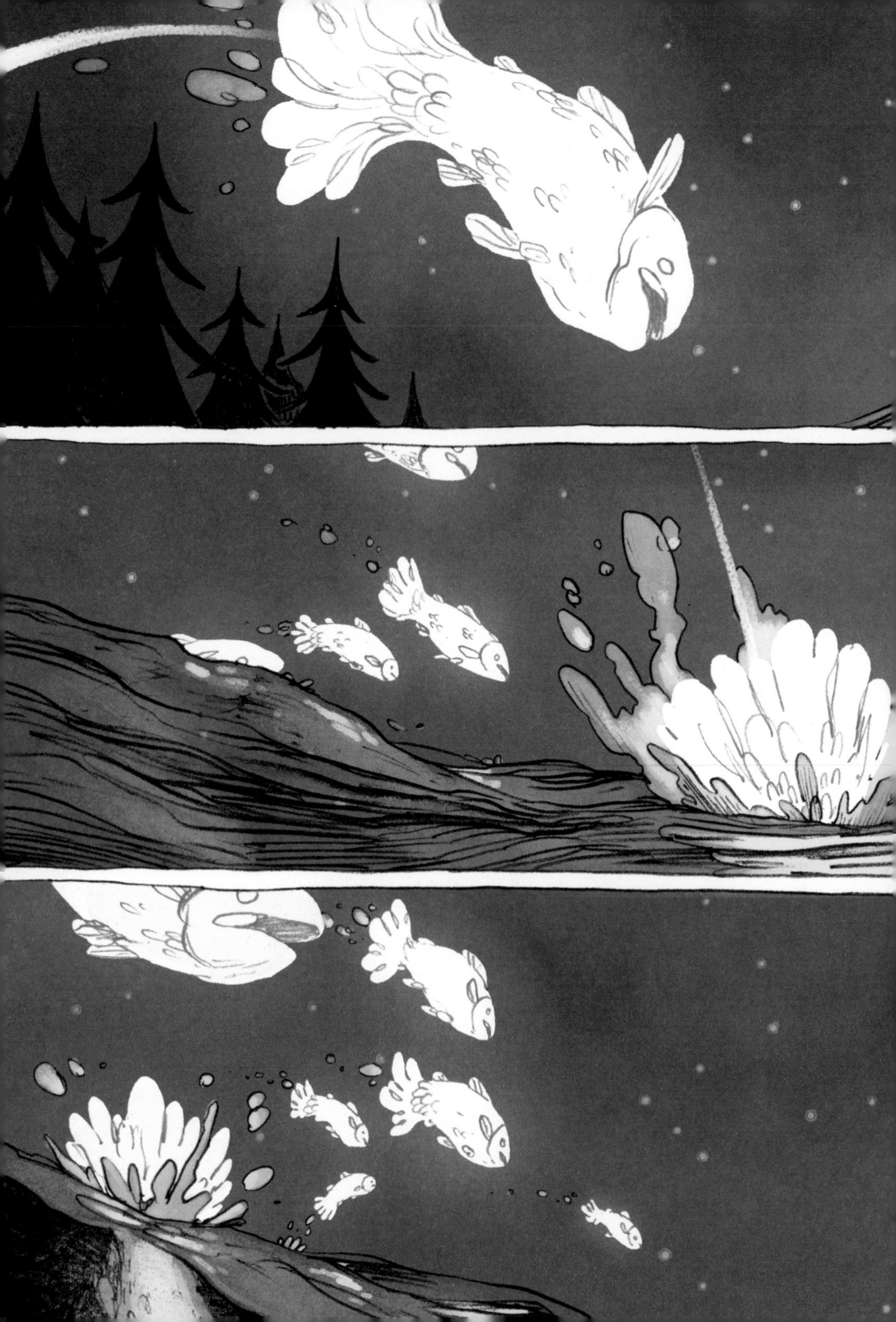

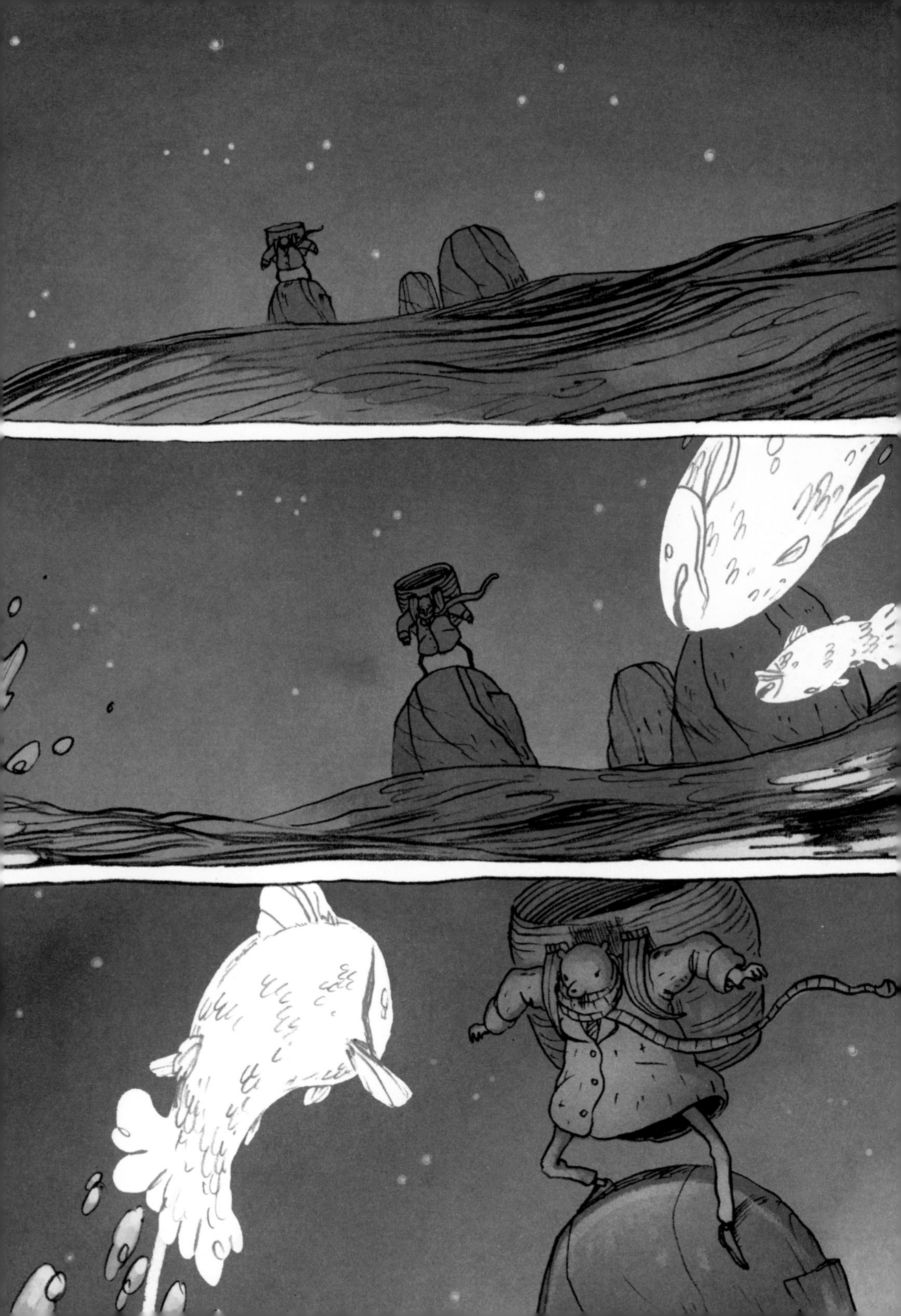

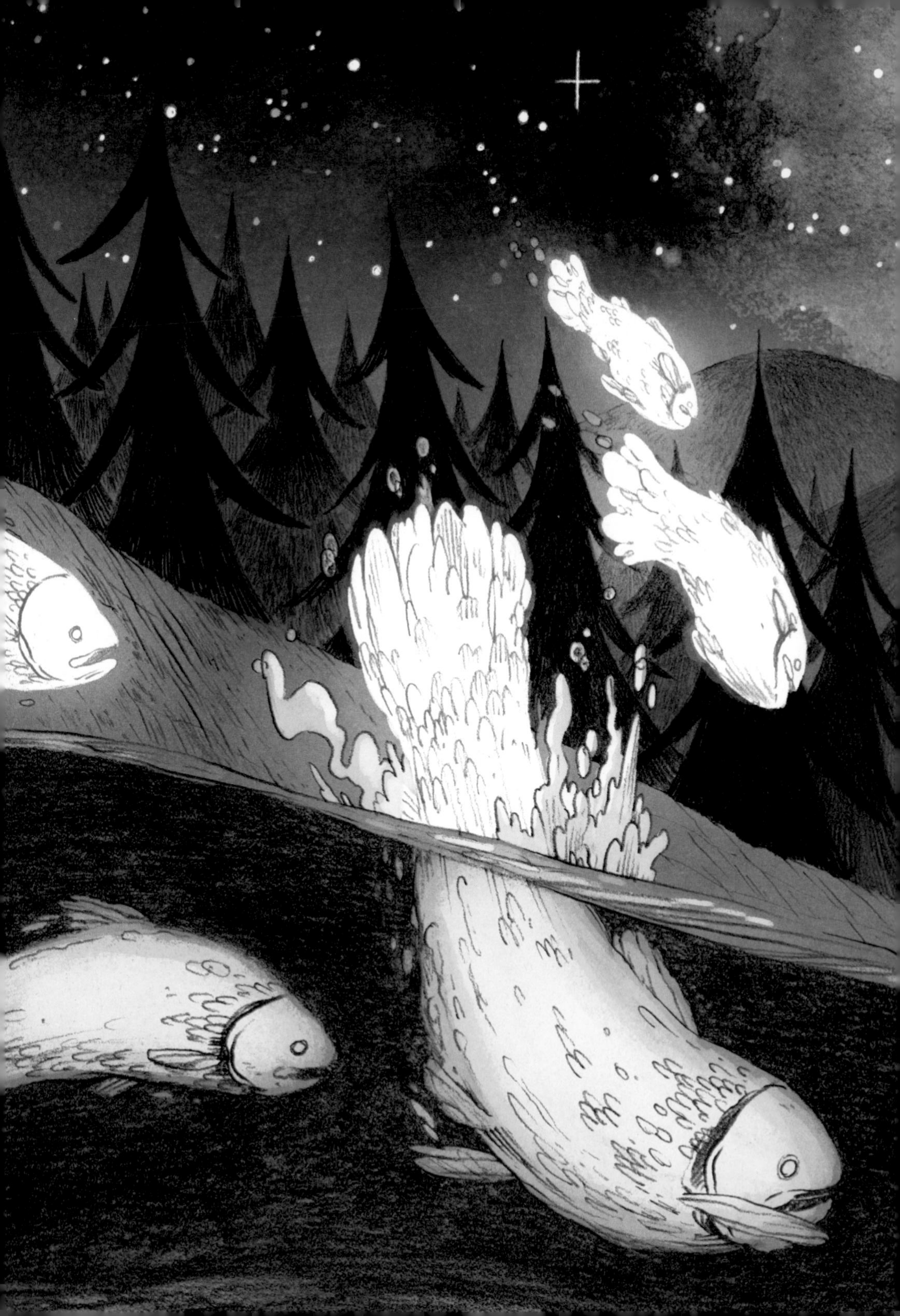

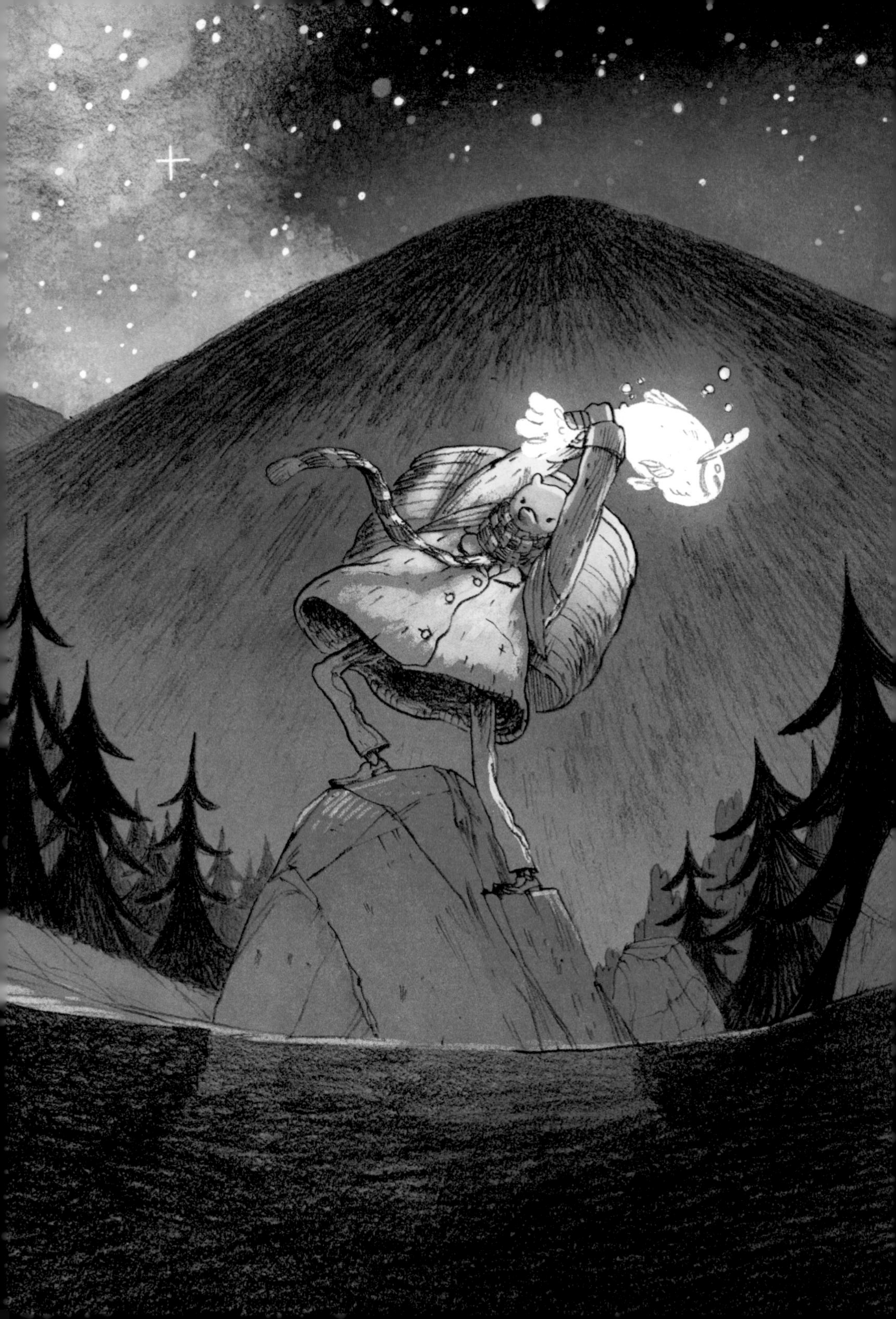

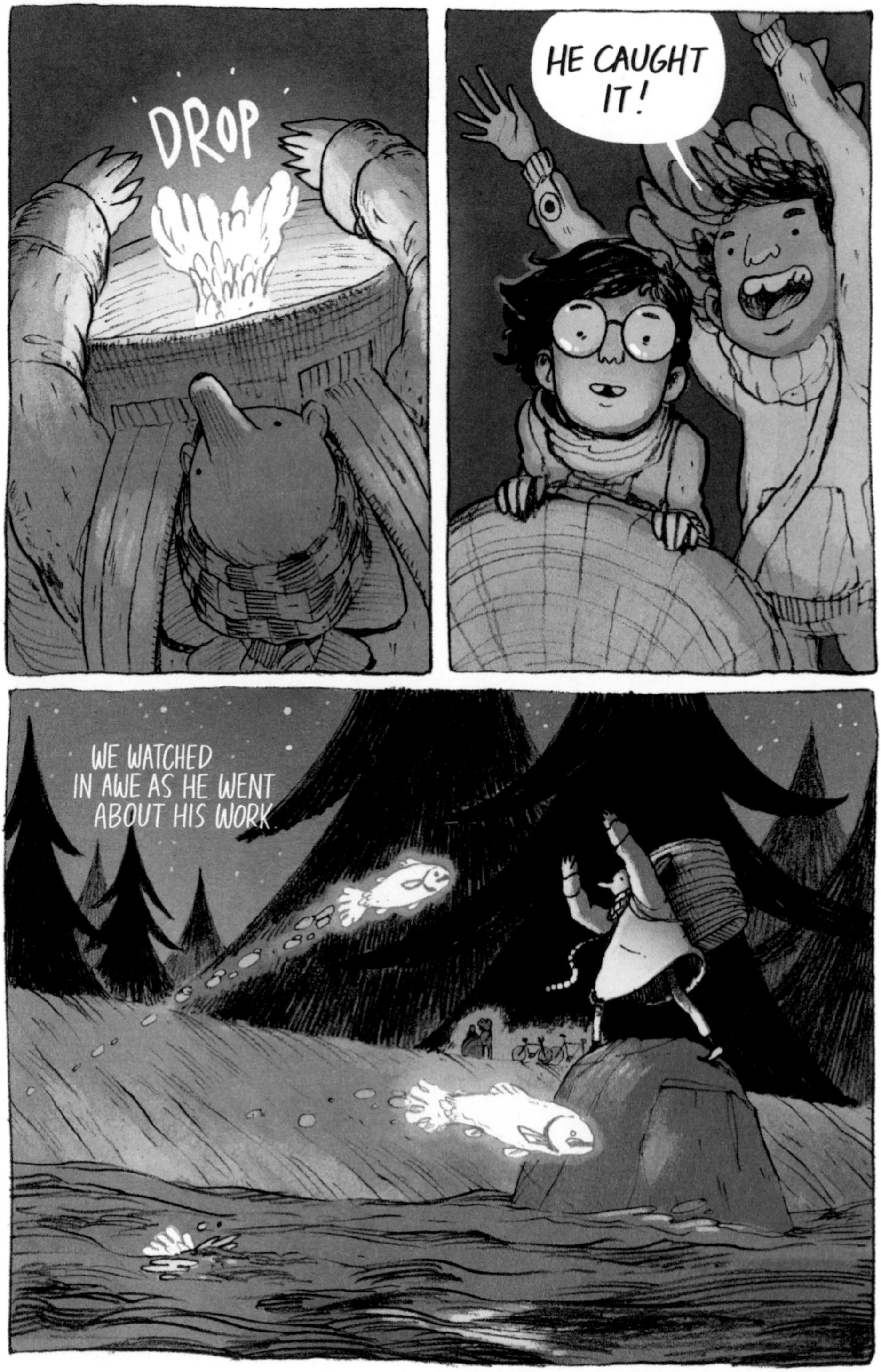
DROP
HE CAUGHT IT!
WE WATCHED IN AWE AS HE WENT ABOUT HIS WORK.

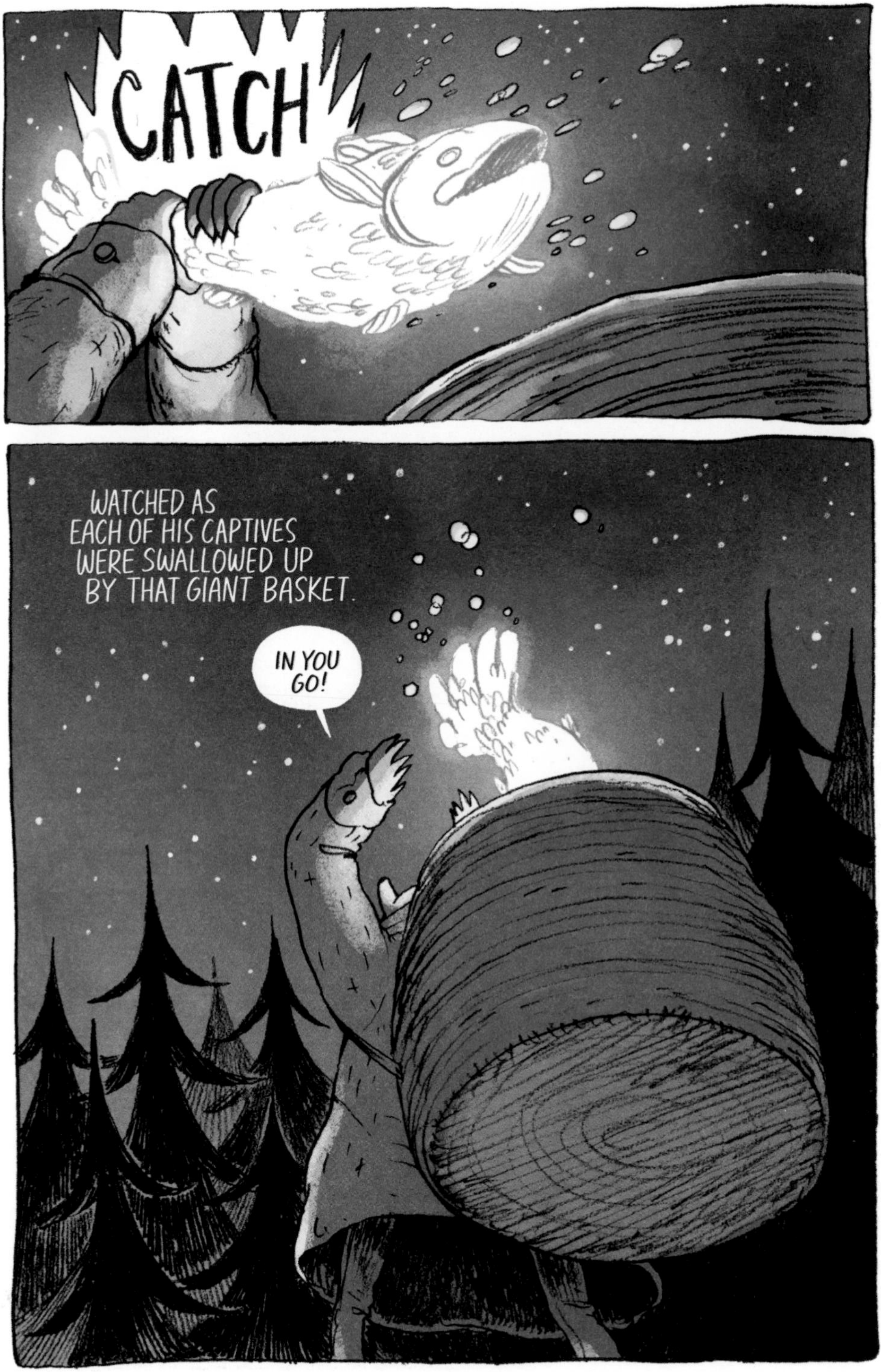
CATCH
WATCHED AS EACH OF HIS CAPTIVES WERE SWALLOWED UP BY THAT GIANT BASKET.
IN YOU GO!

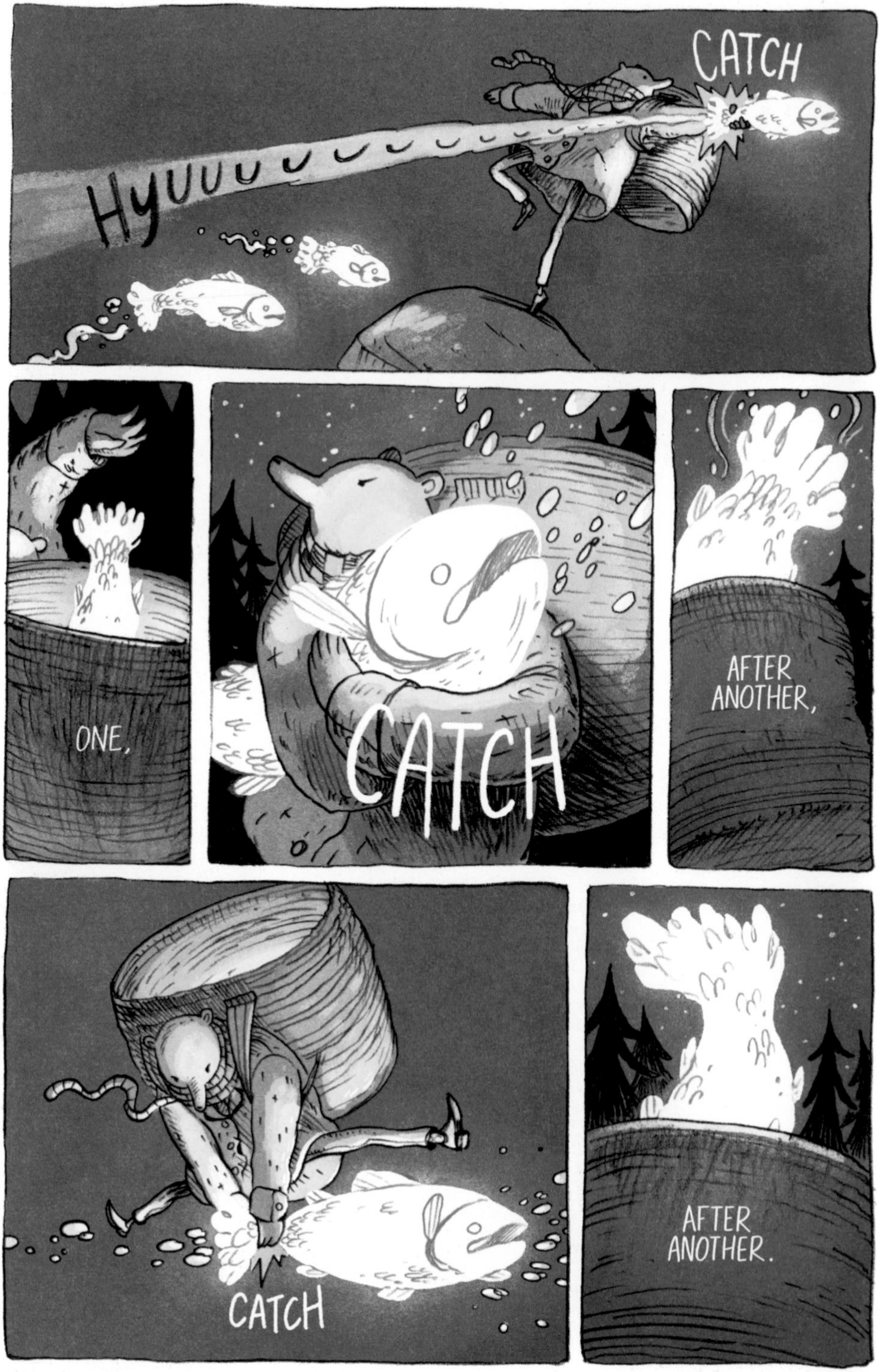

CATCH
Hyuuuuuuuuuuuuuuu
ONE,
CATCH
AFTER ANOTHER,
CATCH
AFTER ANOTHER.

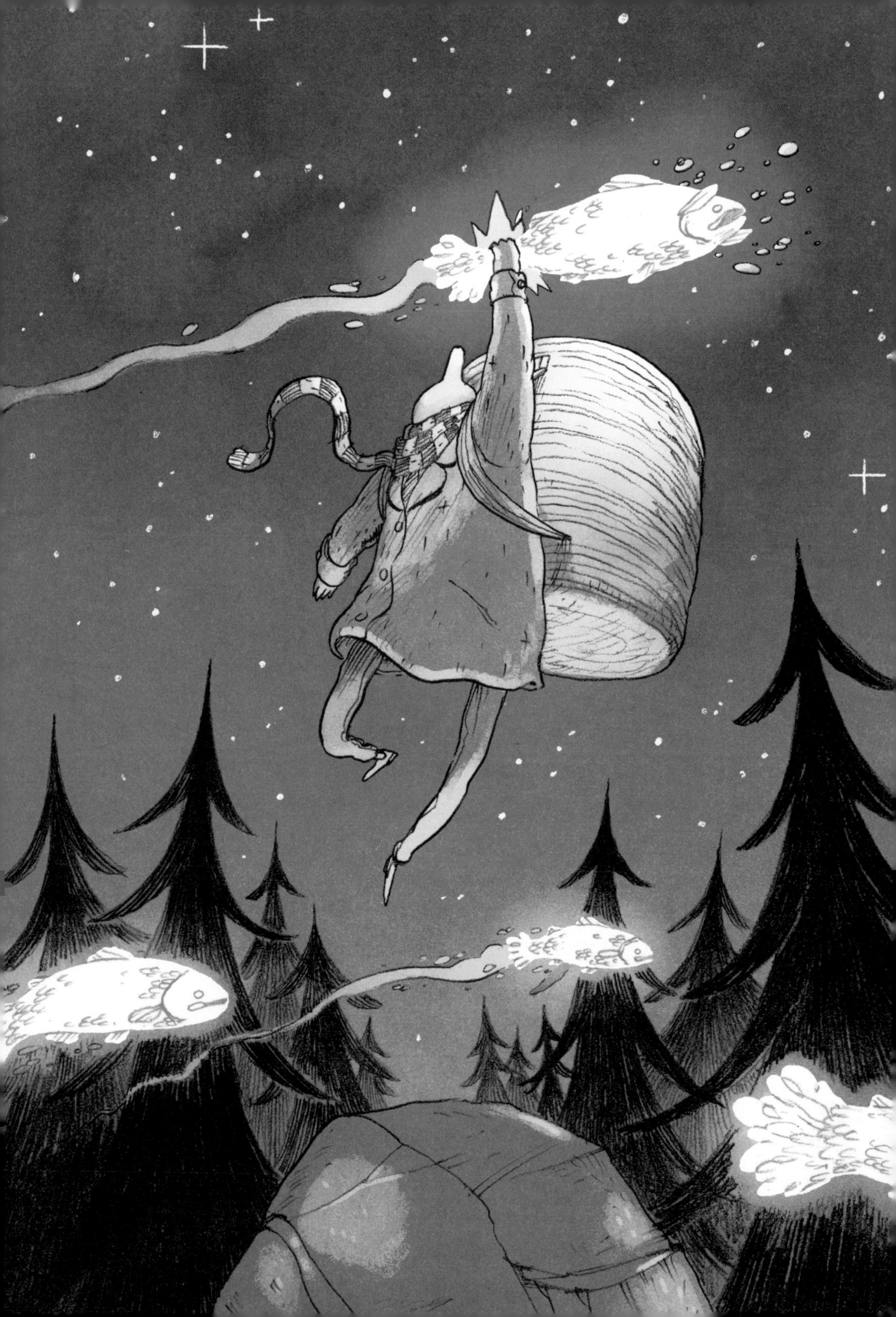

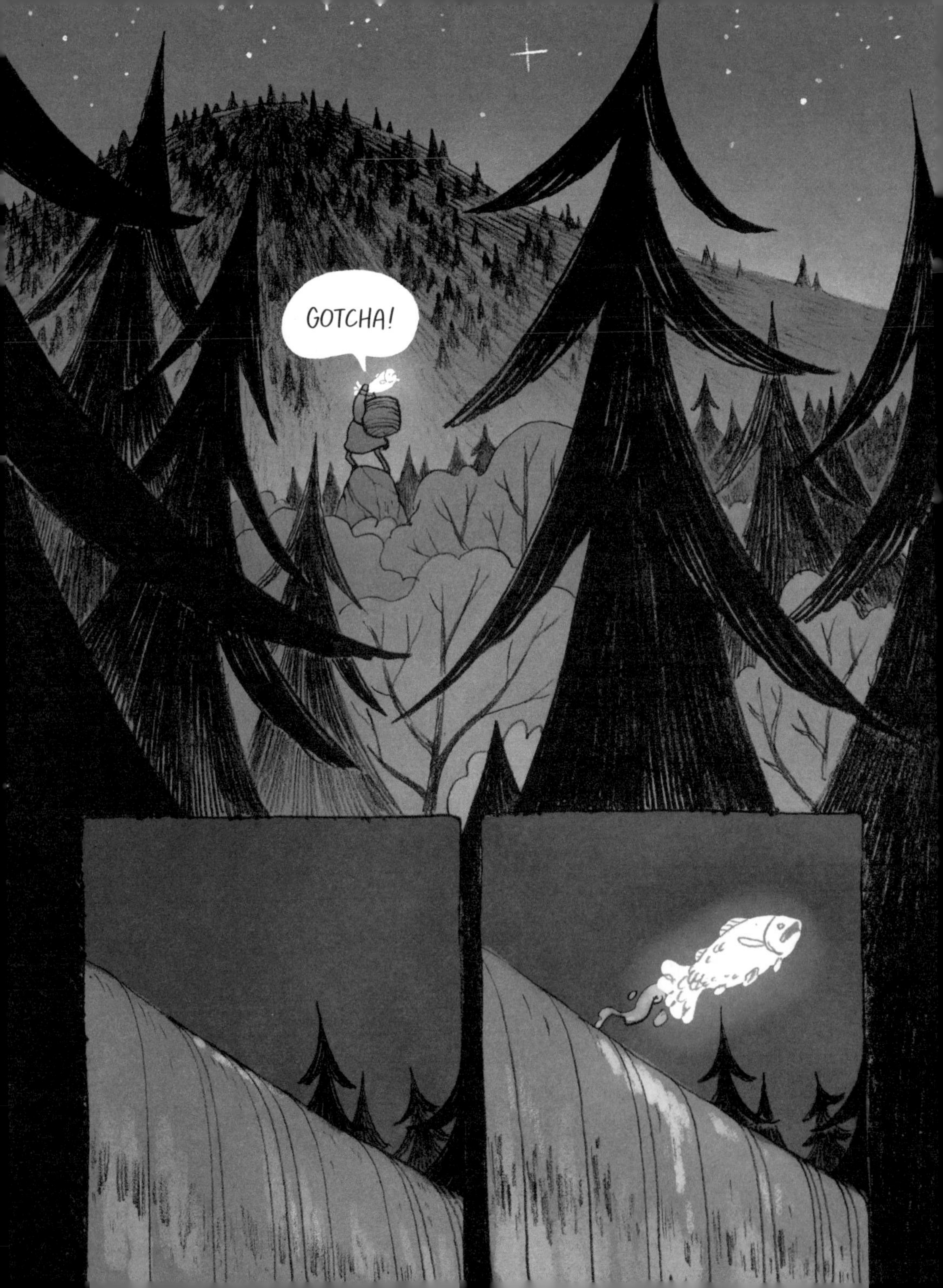
GOTCHA!

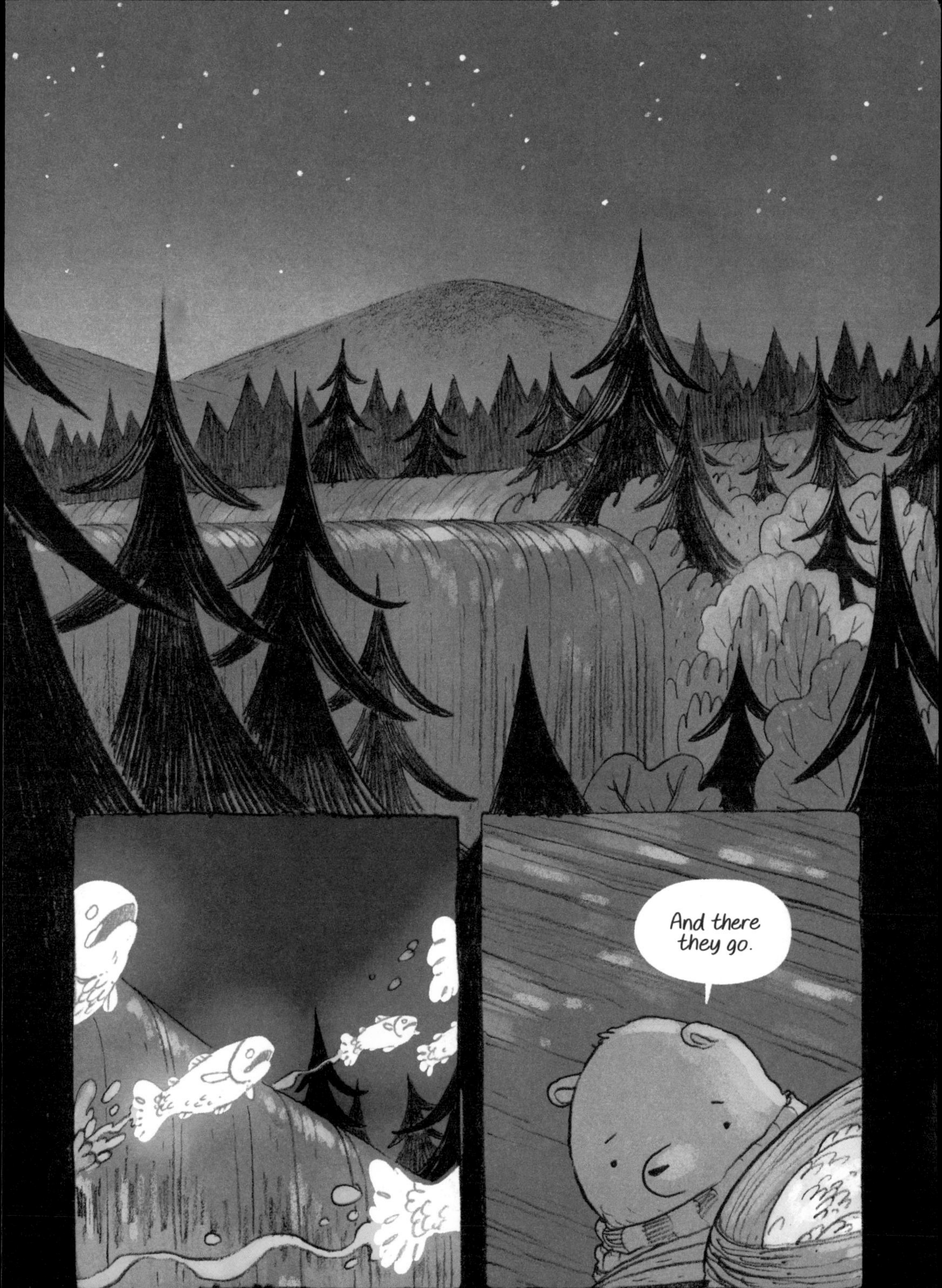
And there they go.

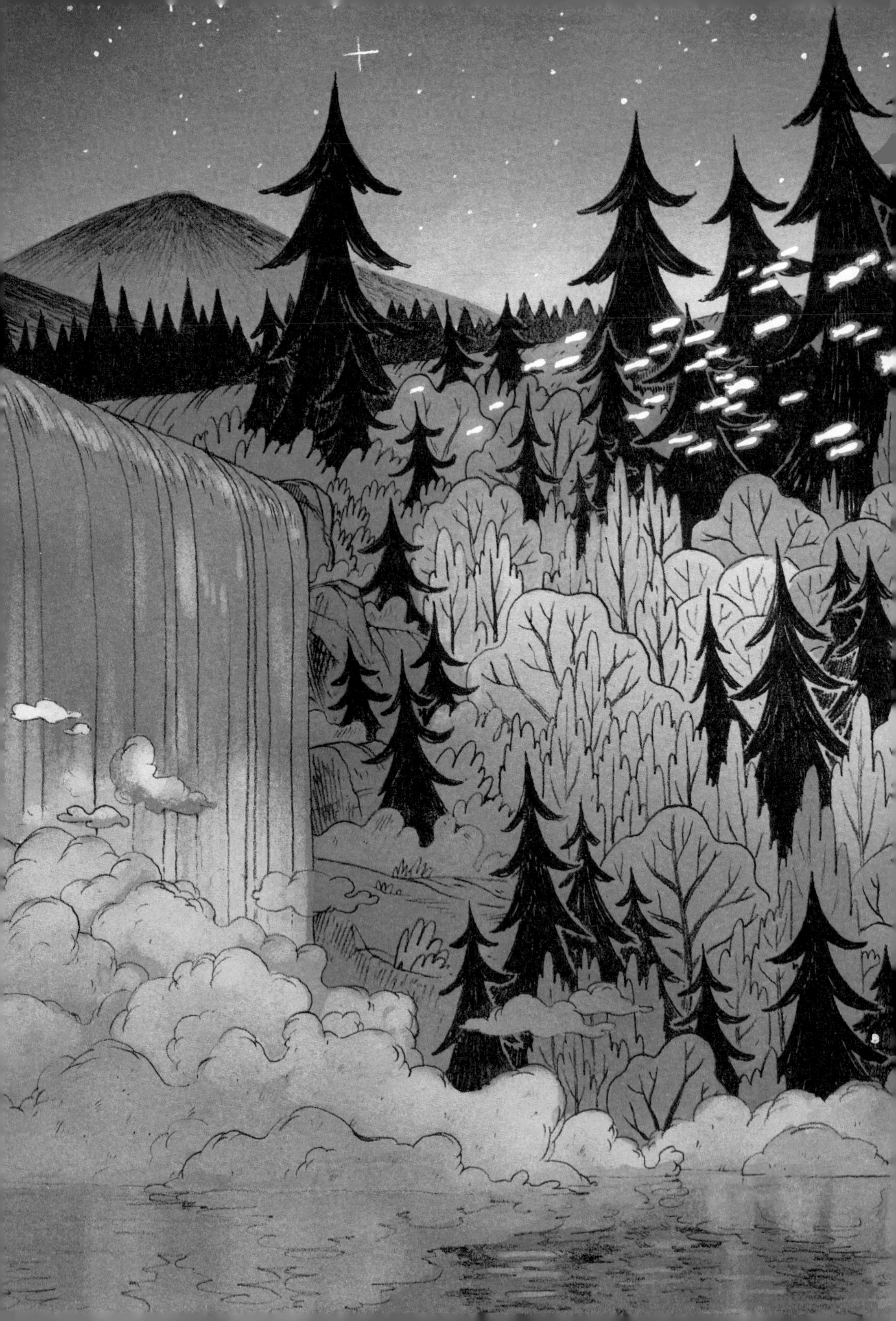

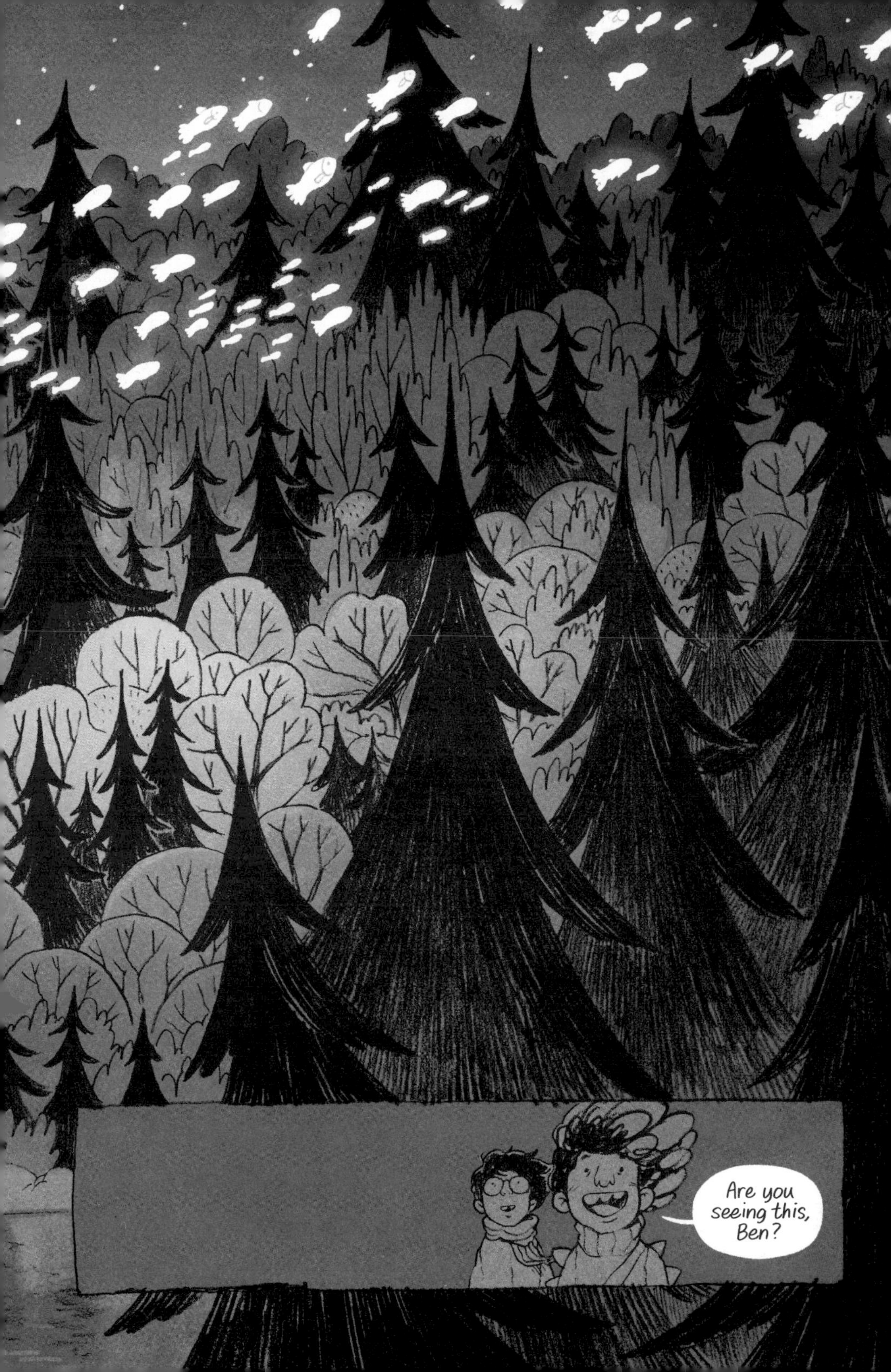
Are you seeing this, Ben?

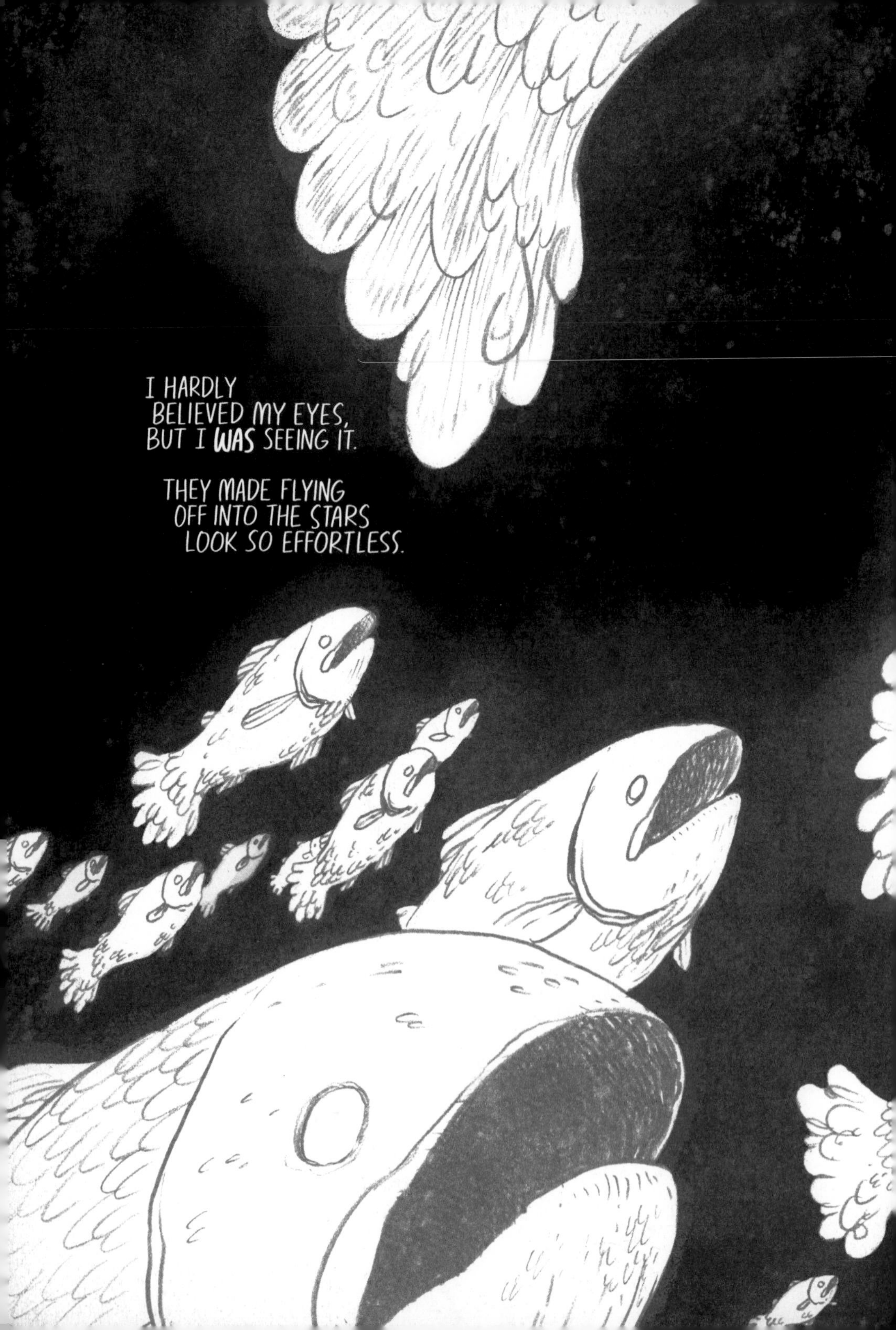
I HARDLY
BELIEVED MY EYES,
BUT I **WAS** SEEING IT.
THEY MADE FLYING
OFF INTO THE STARS
LOOK SO EFFORTLESS.

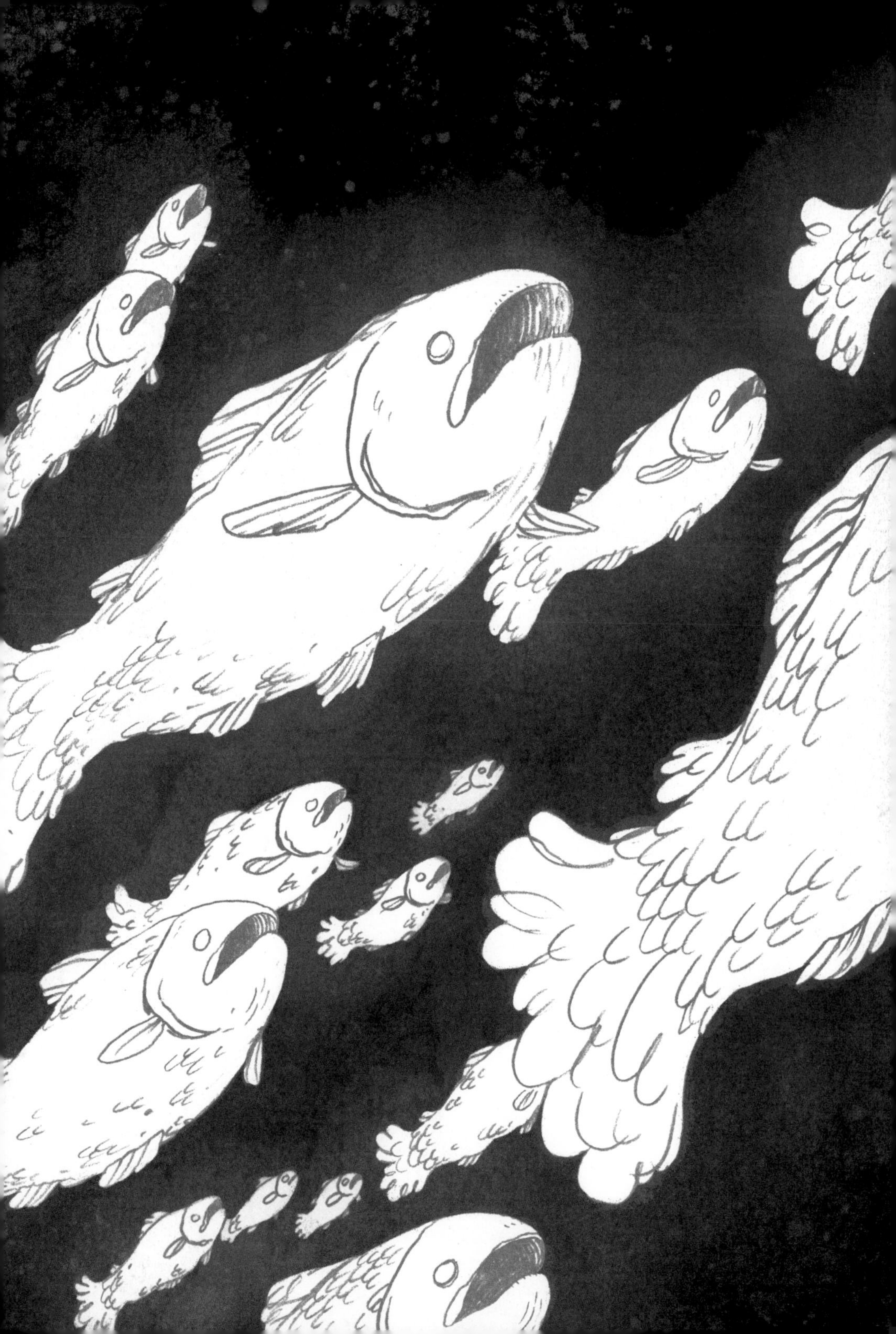

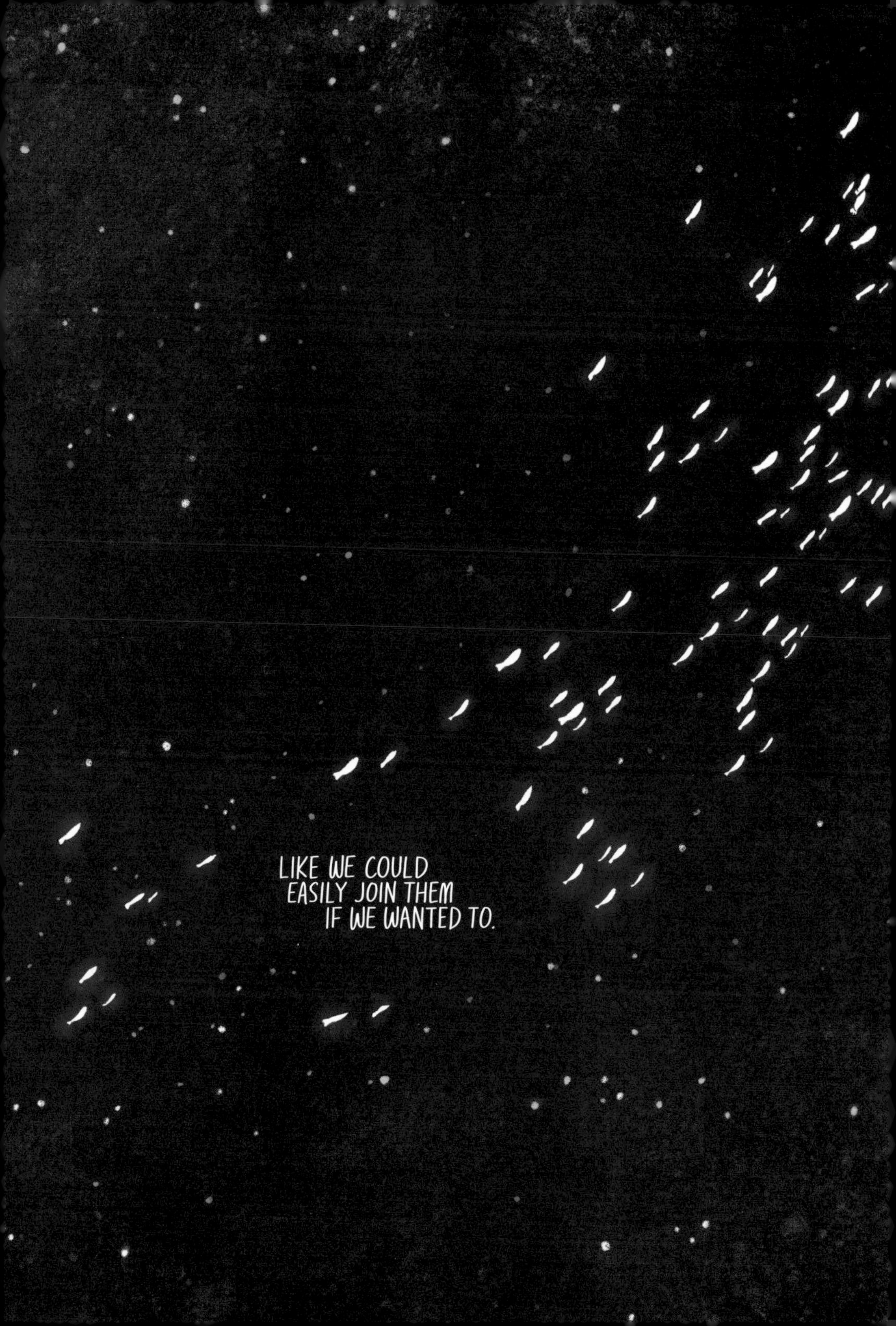
LIKE WE COULD
EASILY JOIN THEM
IF WE WANTED TO.

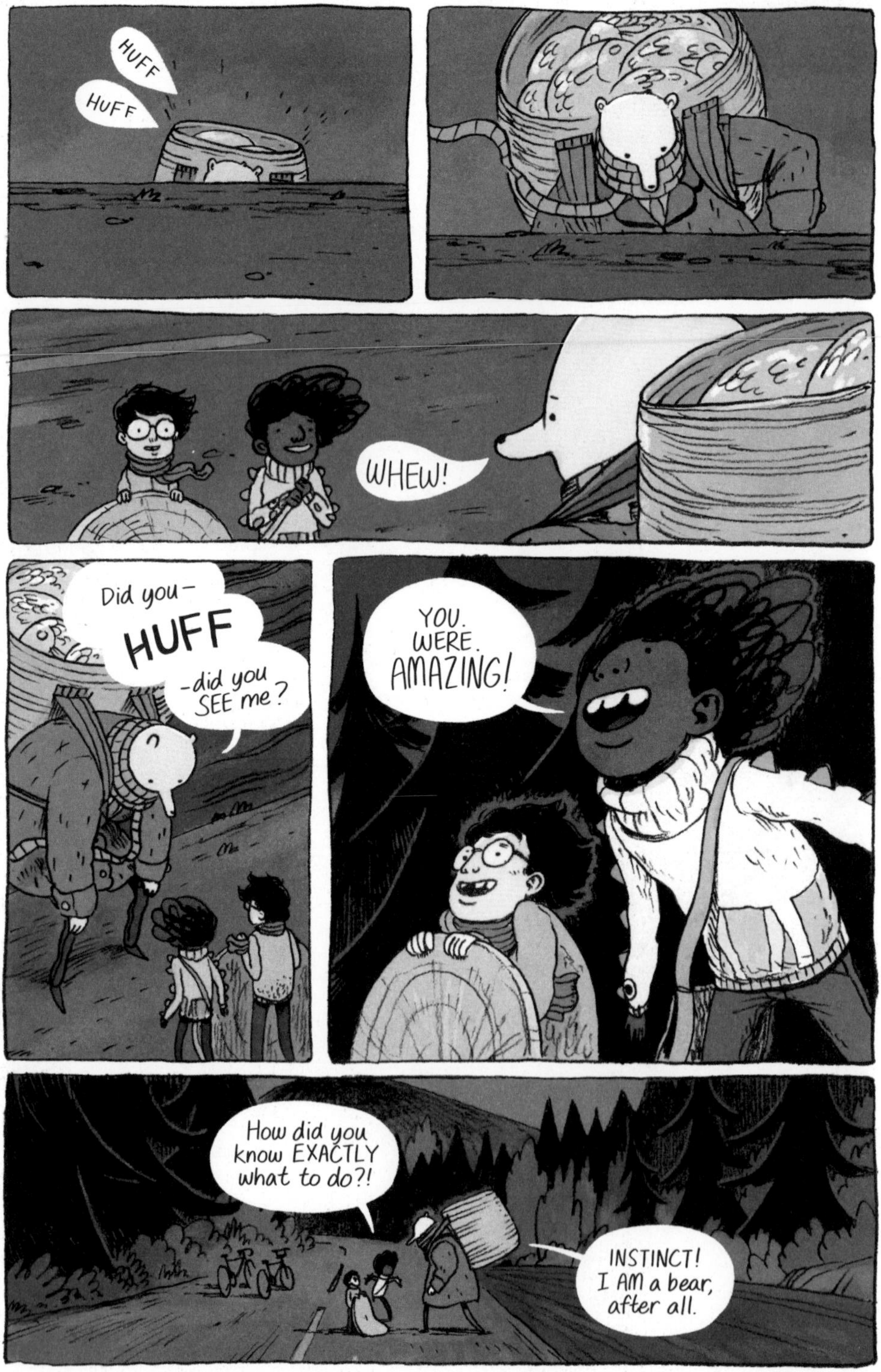
HUFF
HUFF
WHEW!
Did you—
HUFF
-did you SEE me?
YOU. WERE. AMAZING!
How did you know EXACTLY what to do?!
INSTINCT! I AM a bear, after all.

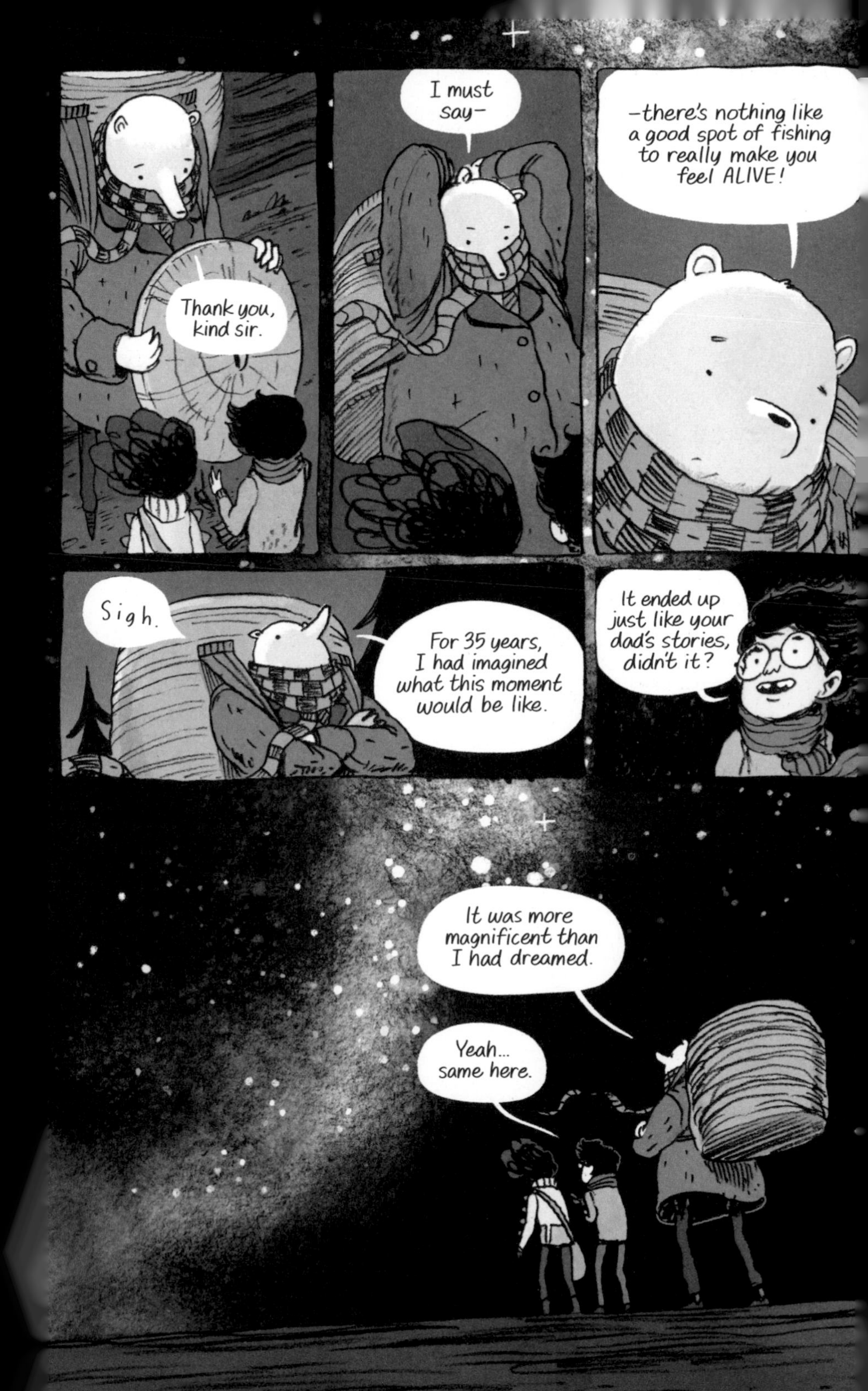
Thank you, kind sir.
I must say–
–there's nothing like a good spot of fishing to really make you feel ALIVE!
Sigh.
For 35 years, I had imagined what this moment would be like.
It ended up just like your dad's stories, didn't it?
It was more magnificent than I had dreamed.
Yeah... same here.

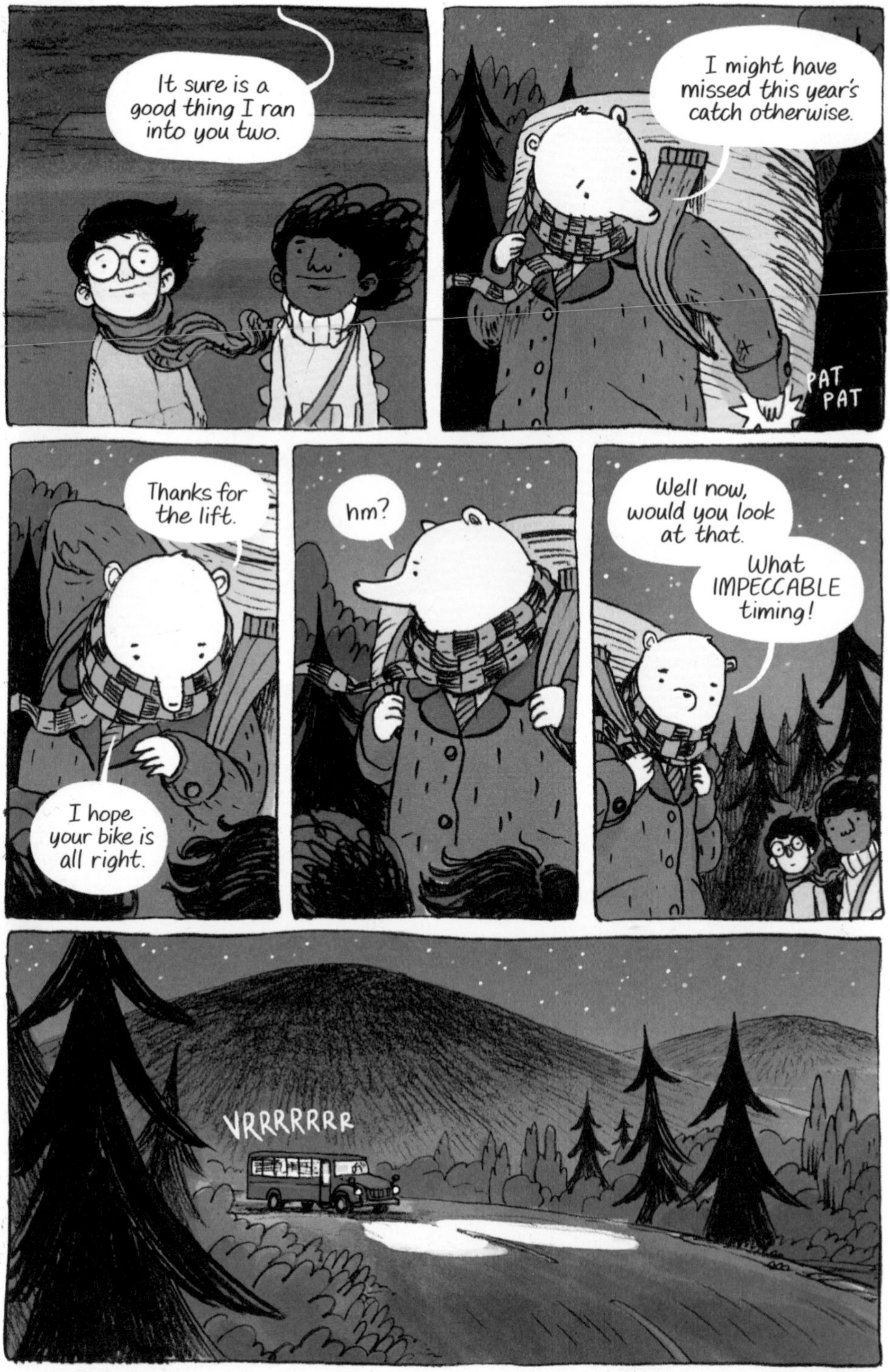
It sure is a good thing I ran into you two.
I might have missed this year's catch otherwise.
PAT PAT
Thanks for the lift.
I hope your bike is all right.
hm?
Well now, would you look at that.
What IMPECCABLE timing!
VRRRRRRR

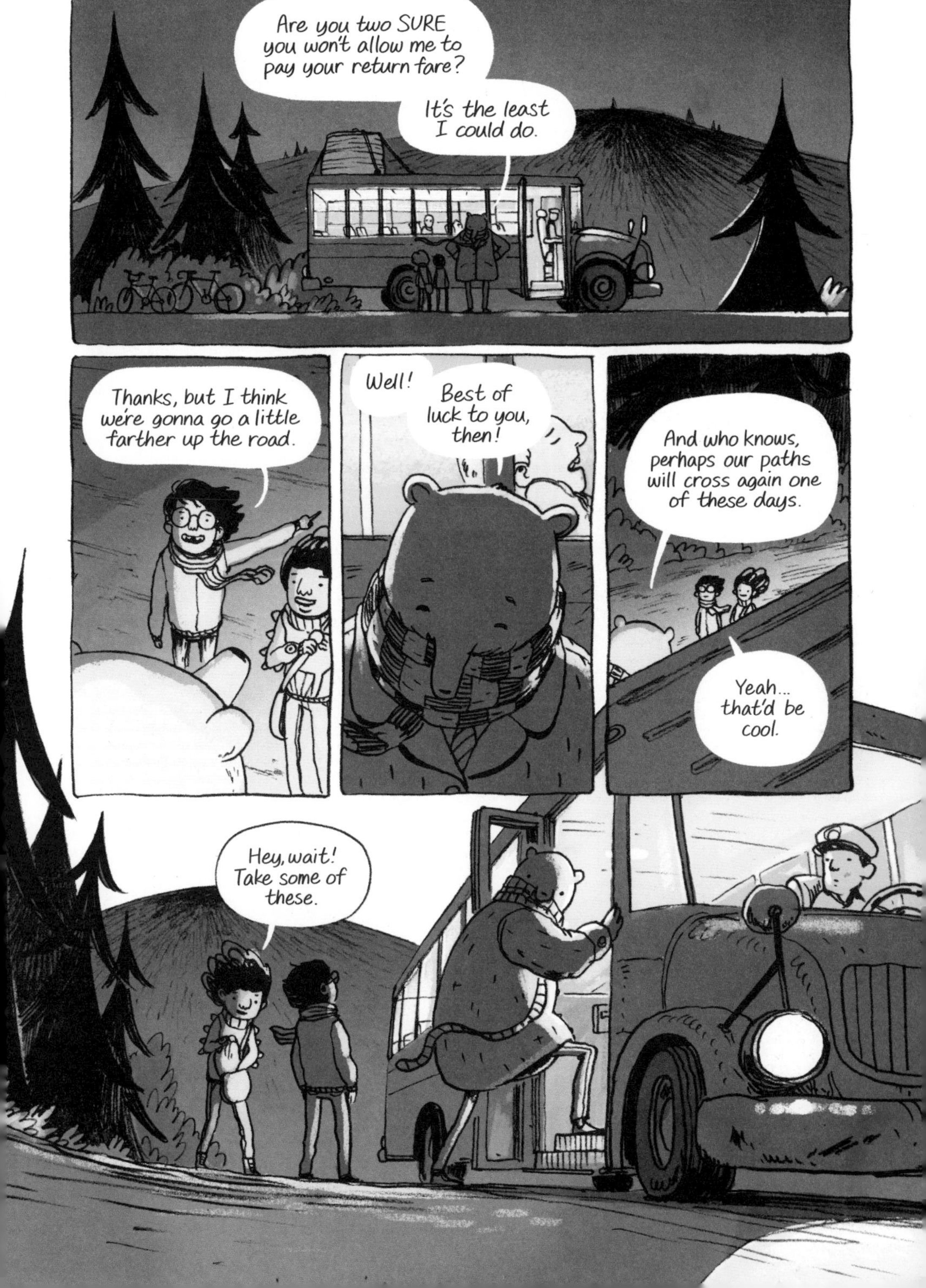
Are you two SURE you won't allow me to pay your return fare?
It's the least I could do.
Thanks, but I think we're gonna go a little farther up the road.
Well!
Best of luck to you, then!
And who knows, perhaps our paths will cross again one of these days.
Yeah... that'd be cool.
Hey, wait! Take some of these.

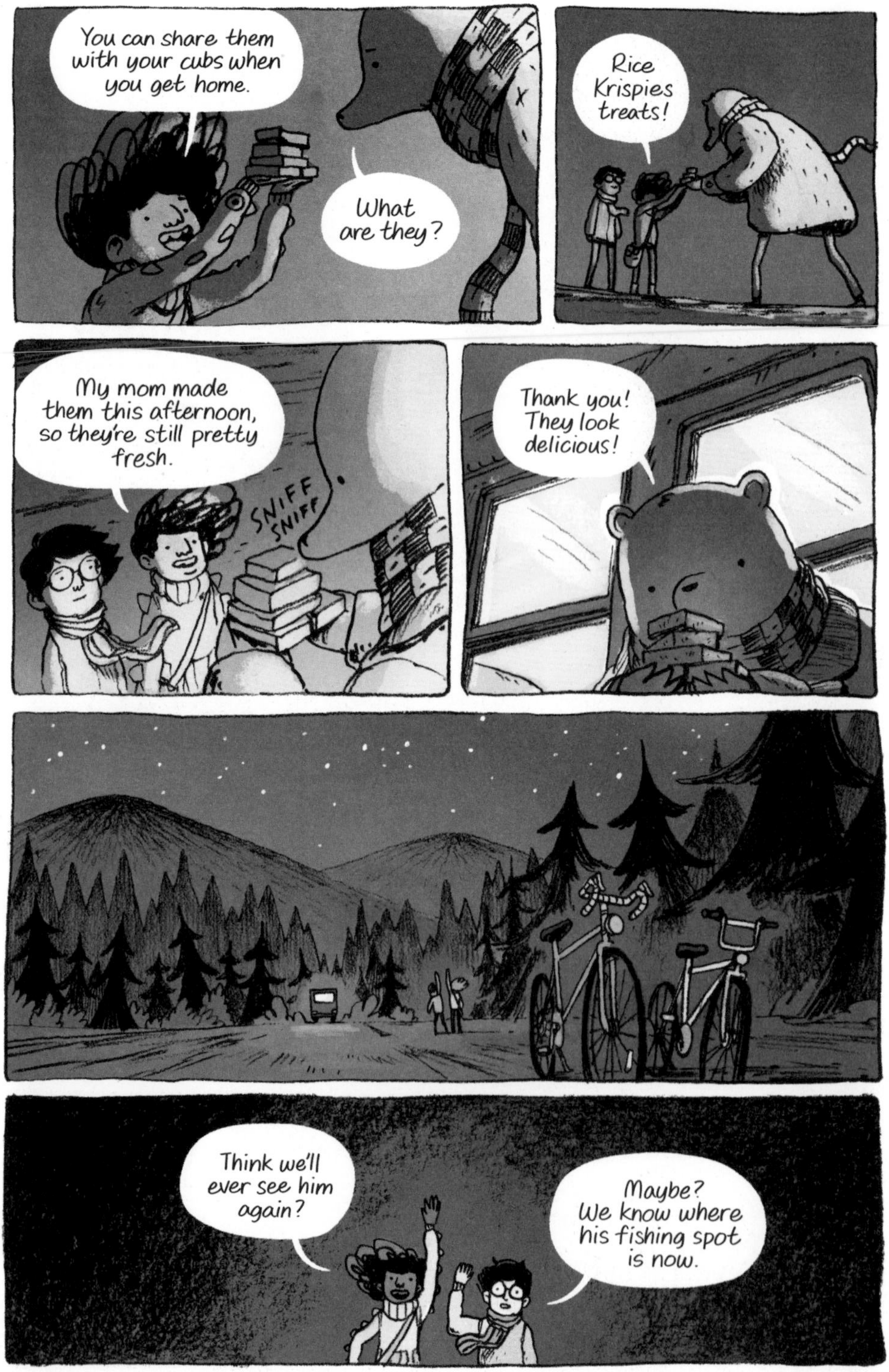
You can share them with your cubs when you get home.
What are they?
Rice Krispies treats!
My mom made them this afternoon, so they're still pretty fresh.
SNIFF SNIFF
Thank you! They look delicious!
Think we'll ever see him again?
Maybe? We know where his fishing spot is now.

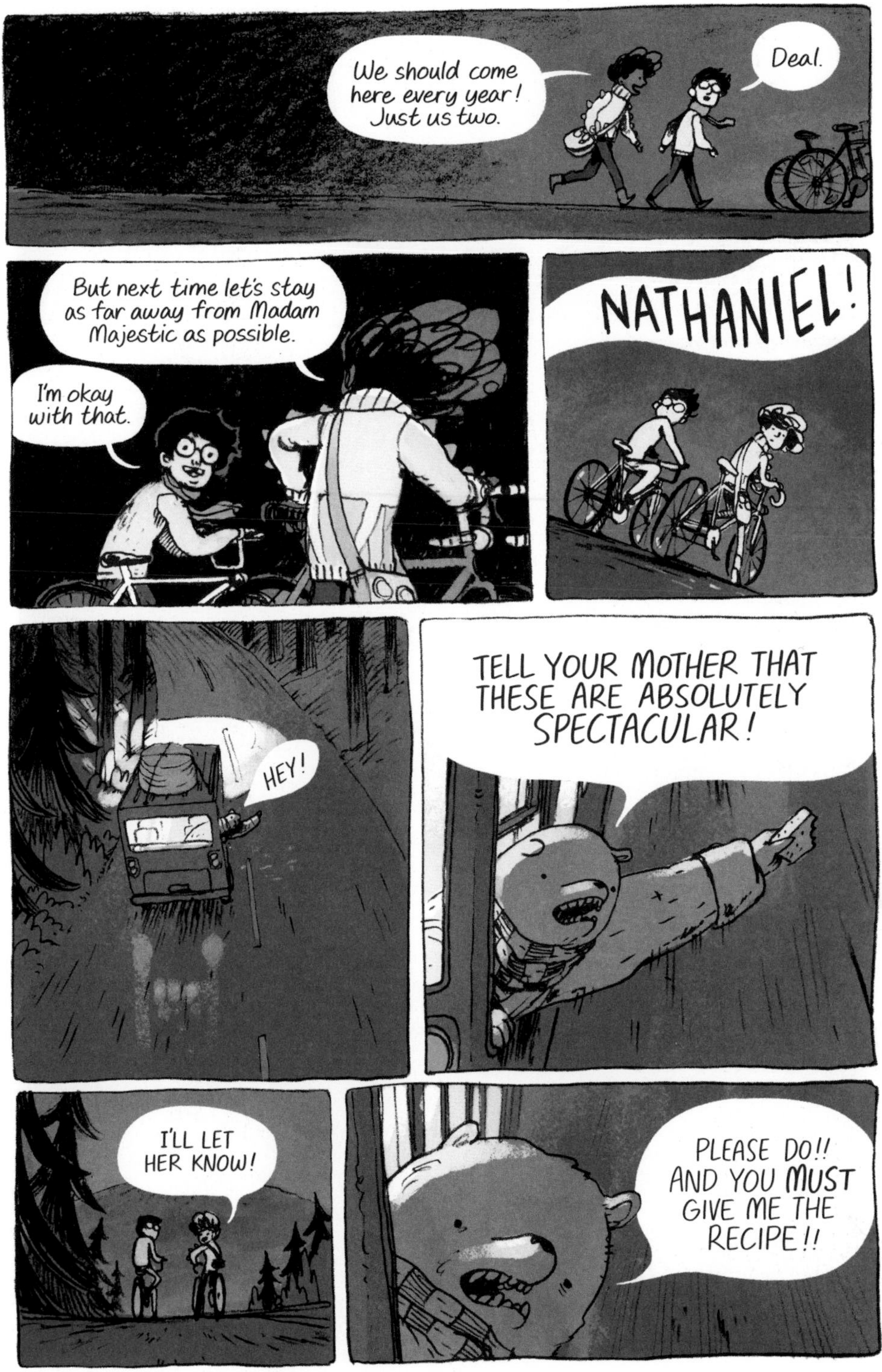
We should come here every year! Just us two.
Deal.
But next time let's stay as far away from Madam Majestic as possible.
I'm okay with that.
NATHANIEL!
HEY!
TELL YOUR MOTHER THAT THESE ARE ABSOLUTELY SPECTACULAR!
I'LL LET HER KNOW!
PLEASE DO!! AND YOU MUST GIVE ME THE RECIPE!!

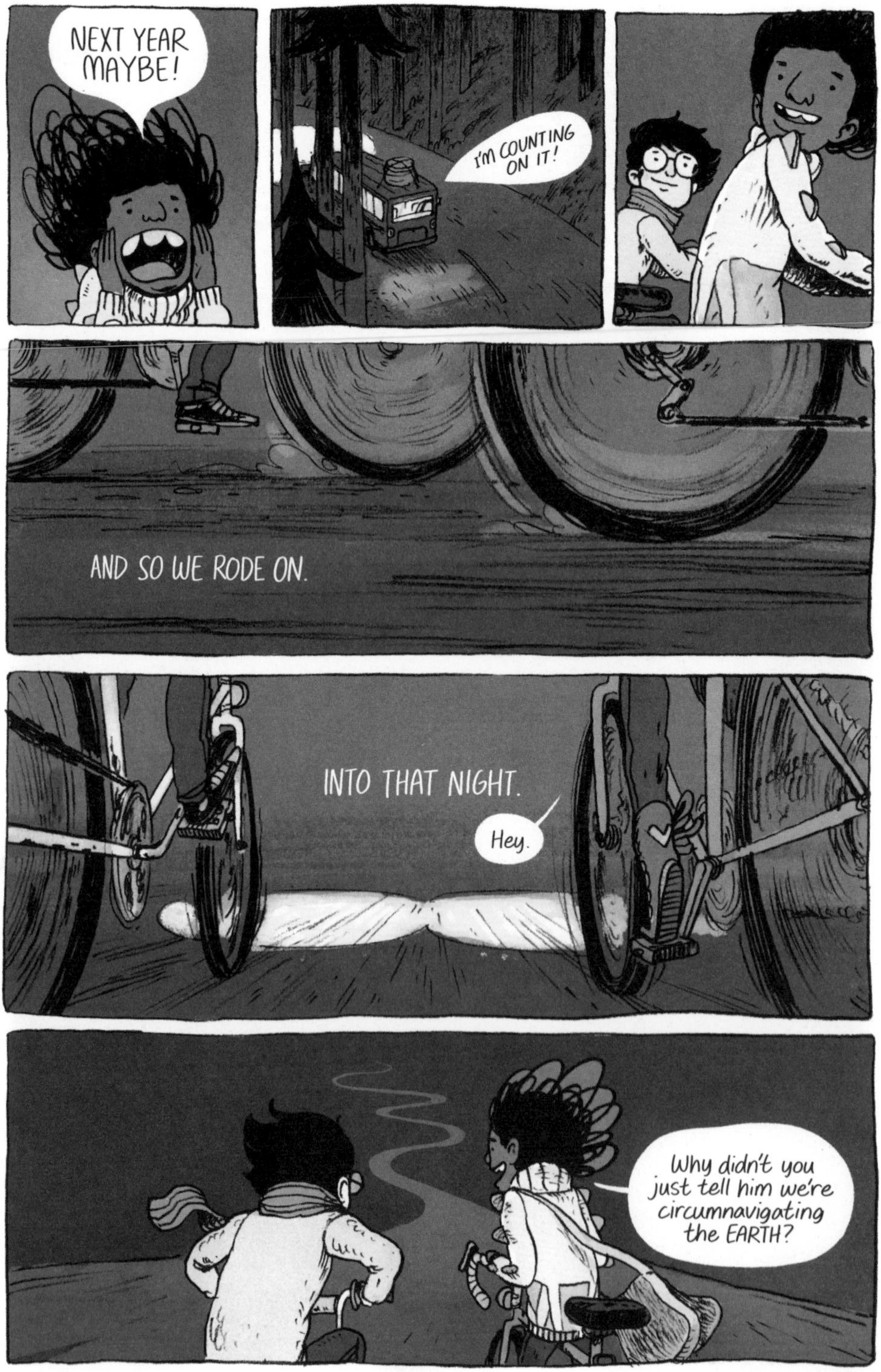
NEXT YEAR MAYBE!
I'M COUNTING ON IT!
AND SO WE RODE ON.
INTO THAT NIGHT.
Hey.
Why didn't you just tell him we're circumnavigating the EARTH?

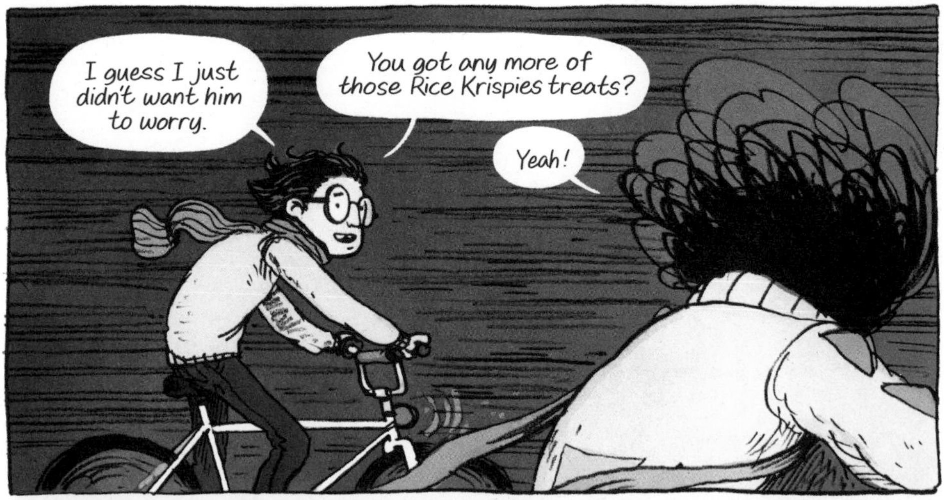
I guess I just didn't want him to worry.
You got any more of those Rice Krispies treats?
Yeah!

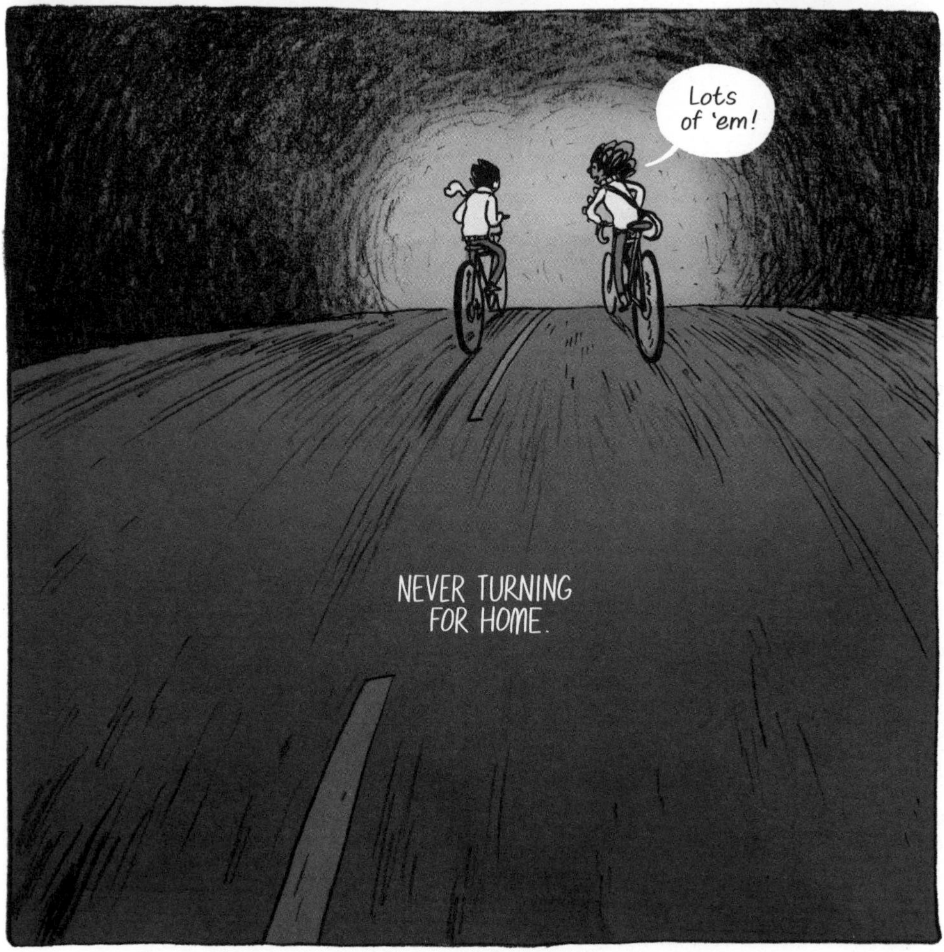
Lots of 'em!
NEVER TURNING FOR HOME.

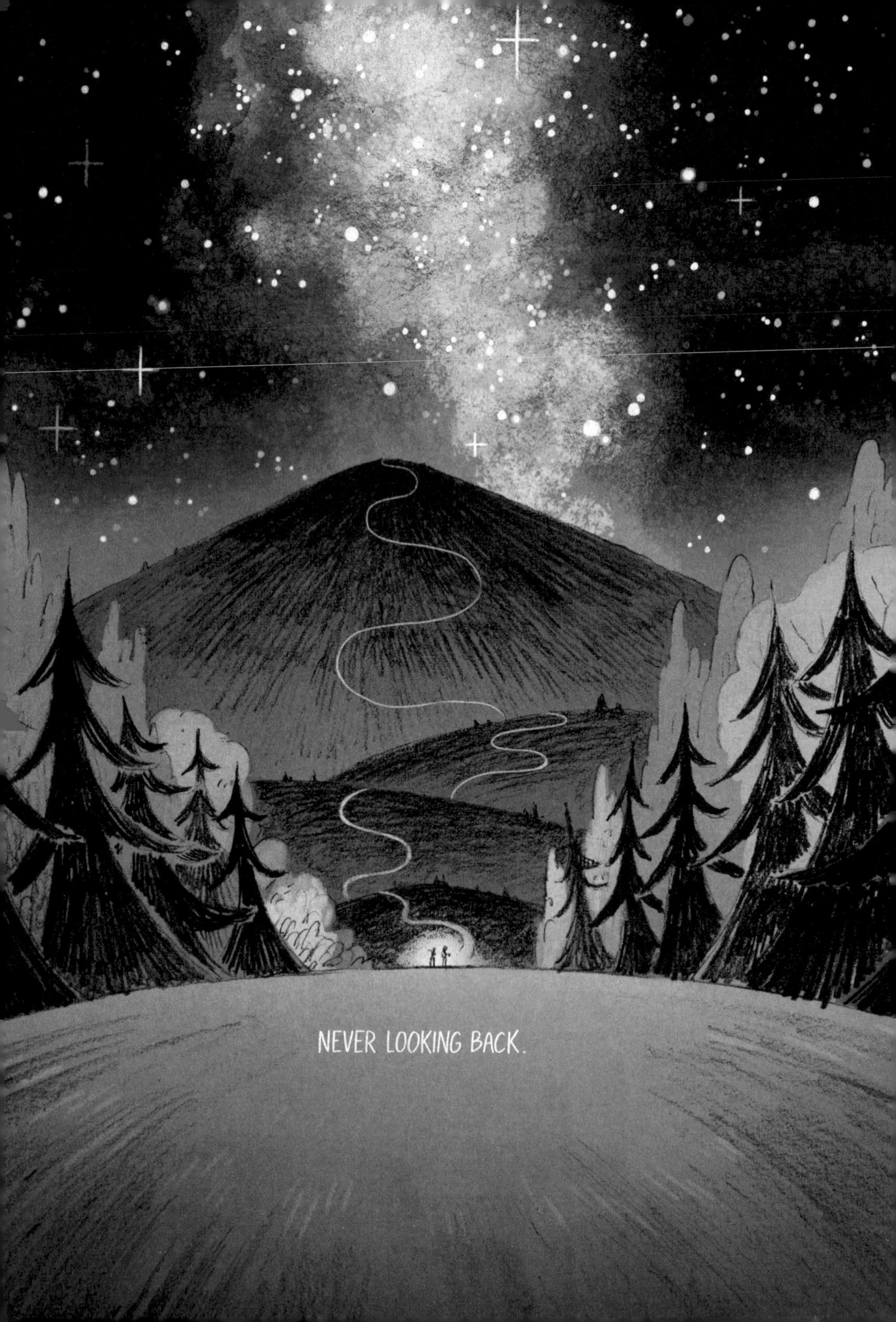
NEVER LOOKING BACK.